Bound Together
By
Marie Coulson

*To Natalie
Lovely to meet you.
With love
Marie Coulson xx*

Bound Together

Copyright © 2012 by Marie Coulson
All rights reserved. No part of this book may be used or reproduced in any manner without written permission from the author, except in the case of brief quotations embodied in critical articles and for review purposes.

This book is a work of fiction. Names, characters, places and events are products of the author's imagination or are used fictitiously and are not to be construed as real. Any resemblances to actual events, locales, organizations, or persons living or dead, are entirely coincidental.

The use of artist and song titles throughout this book are done so for storytelling purposes and should in no way been seen as advertisement. Trademark names are used in an editorial fashion, with no intention of infringement of the respective owner's trademark.

Cover Design by:
Sarah Hansen at Okay Creations
http://okaycreations.net/site/

Editing Provided by
Anastassia Parchment

Proof Editor
Jennifer Roberts Hall

Formatting
Amanda Heath at Little Dove Formatting

ISBN-13: 978-1480125711
ISBN-10: 1480125717

For the man who has held my hand and my heart for the past seven years.

Table Of Contents

Chapter 1: Empty Space
Chapter 2: Amy
Chapter 3: An Apron and an Adonis
Chapter 4: Playing The Game
Chapter 5: Money, Money, Money
Chapter 6: You Spin Me Right Round Baby
Chapter 7: Mel, Dinner and Daddy
Chapter 8: Toot, Toot, Beep, Beep
Chapter 9: Propositions
Chapter 10: You've Got A Friend
Chapter 11: Knowing Me, Knowing You
Chapter 12: The Boss
Chapter 13: Crazy
Chapter 14: All That Glitter Is White Gold
Chapter 15: Out Of My Dreams & Into The Car
Chapter 16: I Want To Be A Rock Star
Chapter 17: Tables and Chairs
Chapter 18: Getting It Straight
Chapter 19: The King and I
Chapter 20: A Mothers Love Can Be Painful
Chapter 21: Oh What A Wicked Web
Chapter 22: Four Days
Chapter 23: Gifts, Glamour and Girl Talk
Chapter 24: It Must Be Love
Chapter 25: Tying Me In Knots
Chapter 26: Ruby Tuesday
Chapter 27: Love Online
Chapter 28: Lean On Me
Chapter 29: In The Still Of The Night
Chapter 30: A Long Hot Talk
Chapter 31: One Tequila, Two Tequila, Three Tequila, Floor
Chapter 32: Handcuffs and Heels
Chapter 33: A Picture of Mass Destruction

Chapter 34: Party Like A Rock Star
Chapter 35: Unexpected Guests
Chapter 36: Numb
Chapter 37: Shall We Dance?
Chapter 38: Winter Wonderland
Chapter 39: Happy Holidays
Chapter 40: Steady As She Goes
Chapter 41: Playing Games
Chapter 42: Unfaithful
Chapter 43: Time
Chapter 44: Fired Up
Chapter 45: Moving On
Chapter 46: Heart To Heart
Chapter 47: Dangerous Territory
Chapter 48: Risky Business
Chapter 49: Listen To Your Heart
Chapter 50: Taking The Leap
Acknowledgements
What's Next

Chapter 1

Empty Space

    I looked around the empty room. Big, brown cardboard boxes now replaced my once bright and cluttered bedroom. I couldn't help but feel a little sad for the room. We'd been through a lot together over the past nineteen years, and now I was abandoning it for a cold and lifeless living space.
    College dorms weren't exactly renowned for being spacious or luxurious, and from the fractional amount of information I'd received, I was also not going to be living alone. Mom had urged me to opt for a shared room.
    "It's best to have someone else with you, Layla. If you don't come home one night because something awful has happened to you, then at least your roommate can alert the authorities. Safety in numbers, dear. Besides, won't it be nice to have someone to talk to and connect with on an intellectual level?"
    My mother was delusional. She was constantly worried for my safety to the extent that she bought me a 'stranger danger' kit. Equipped with pepper spray, a personal safety alarm that could burst an eardrum and a book on self-defense, I was definitely the most lethal teenager in my high school-probably the state.
    She obviously had no idea what college was like. I was fairly confident that if I didn't come home one night, my

roommate would just assume I'd either gotten lucky, passed out drunk somewhere, or decided to move out.

Having a roommate didn't automatically guarantee that you had someone else to look out for your well-being. People sharing a dorm didn't always become best friends, and in most cases you'd be lucky if you could even tolerate each other. I was healthily pessimistic about the entire situation, but I couldn't help wondering what my new roommate would be like. We'd be spending the best part of a year trespassing through each other's personal space, and I was a girl who needed her own little territorial bubble. I liked my privacy and peaceful existence.

The most unruly person in my life was my best friend Mel, and even she understood my need for distance. I hoped this wasn't going to be an issue with the girl I would soon be sharing my room and my privacy with. And if it was, realistically, what could I do? Could I get a new roommate?

"Ready to go, Lay?"

Dad was standing in the doorway. His silver hair was shining in the sunlight that poured through the hallway window. He never bothered to color it, saying that he was more than happy wearing his age as a badge of experience. He was dressed in his faded denim jeans and his usual flannel shirt which made him look like he was more suited to a career as a lumberjack, rather than a mechanic.

Holding his car keys in his hand, he scanned the bare walls of my room and let out a long sigh.

"Ready as I'll ever be. These are the last boxes. I think I've got everything I'll need." I gestured to a couple of large boxes stacked next to my desk. "Those two are the heaviest. If you can carry those, I think I can manage the others."

Dad smiled, but as he glanced around my empty room, I could see that this entire day was going to be difficult for him. He grabbed one of the boxes off the floor and took it out to the car. I took one last long look at my room. Yep, it was time to move on. Picking up one of the smaller boxes, I gripped it tightly in my hands and followed him out.

When I reached the car, he was leaning against the passenger door, gazing at me with a pained expression.

"You know, you can still change your mind. Go to school somewhere local and live at home."

I heaved the box that I had been holding into the trunk and went over to him. Standing on my tippy toes, I kissed him on the cheek. I didn't need to say anything. We'd had this conversation a million times, and by his admission, I was going to the best college in the state. California State University was exactly where I wanted to be. And in just a few hours that's exactly where I would be.

* * * *

The drive down was very quiet, and the radio was the only sound that filled the silence. He never said it, but I knew Dad was struggling not to let his emotions show. I tried to reassure him for weeks that I would be home as much as I could, but it seemed to just make him more upset. At one point, I thought he would cry; I was sure I'd seen him swallow a lump in his throat.

It had been just the two of us after the divorce. Mom had moved across state to San Francisco, and I wasn't willing to leave my school in Pasadena to follow her there. It had been bad enough that my parents were breaking up and that my mom was leaving; I wasn't ready to leave my friends behind as well.

When they'd sat me down to discuss the living arrangements, I'd plead my case, and Dad told me it was fine with him as long as it was fine with Mom. Considering she was the one who wanted the damned divorce in the first place, I would have been furious if she had said no and I think the guilt of tearing our family apart had convinced her to let me stay.

We talked on the phone a lot. She's a nurse, so it was easy for her to get a transfer to a new hospital. I visited her two weekends each month. It was an arrangement that worked for everyone, and it didn't interfere too much with mom's work schedule, but that was going to have to change now. With all the school work and going home to visit Dad as much as I could, it was going to be hard to make the trip to see her twice a month. I hadn't mentioned it to her yet, but it was only a matter of time before she would figure it out.

Dad wasn't good with letting people go. As his only child, he'd put all his paternal love and energy into raising me, and after the divorce I think he felt guilty that I didn't have Mom around full time anymore. He seemed to step his parenting up several notches, almost to the point of suffocation.

We spent every weekend doing something together, and we always made time to share a meal every evening. Discussing how our day had been over dinner was Dad's favorite time, he told me. Once I got older, my weekends were spent with my friends, but dinner was still always our time.

Now it was just going to be him and the empty house. I felt a sudden stab of guilt. Maybe I should have stayed near home, but this was my future. Plus, Dad had always been the one to tell me to never settle; he'd be ok. He still had his work buddies and our neighbors were great.

Pam, Eddie and their daughter Mel, had lived next door since we moved in. Mel and I grew up together, and we knew each other inside out. She was my guardian angel, supporting me through the divorce and defending me whenever I needed her. Her flame red hair complemented her fiery temperament perfectly. She had a lean figure and pale white skin with a few freckles spotting her cheeks, and I thought she was a real natural beauty, though she always struggled with her self-esteem and always ignored compliments with a roll of her big green eyes.

Mel was fiercely loyal to her friends and family and had a mean right hook to back it up. I could remember the first time I'd seen it, and it still amazed me how a girl of her build had packed such a punch.

When we were in high school, we'd become friends with a guy named Chris. He was fun, smart, super cute and my first kiss. We were close right up until tenth grade.

That's when he met Rebecca. She didn't like him hanging out with us and gave him an ultimatum. Naturally, he chose the bimbo. To this day, I still don't know how she knew, but she'd made my life hell when she found out he'd been my first kiss.

We were in the high school cafeteria one day when Rebecca came over to the table where Mel and I were sitting. She sat opposite to me, and without a word, spat in my face and called me a whore. Everyone was staring at me, whispering and pointing. My ex-friend, Chris just watched the whole thing unfold. I was about to stand up and walk away before I burst into tears, but Mel dived across the table and wrestled Rebecca to the ground. When she finally kicked Mel off of her she tried desperately to scramble away, but Mel grabbed her ankle and pulled her hard. Rebecca jolted backwards and her face landed hard against the tiled surface of the cafeteria floor, knocking out three of her front teeth.

Mel and I were both sent to the principal's office, and she had taken the blame for the whole thing. She was suspended for a week, but she simply stood up, brushed herself off, lifted her chin and calmly said, "I would do it again in a heartbeat. That girl is a bitch and deserves to have all her teeth knocked out."

I had never loved her more.

I was really going to miss Mel. She was going to one of the local colleges and had been a little mad at me for leaving to go to Long Beach State. After I'd reminded her that I would be meeting lots of cute college guys and that I would be getting invited to parties that I would absolutely be bringing her to, she was cool with it. She attracted men like bees to honey, but her lack of confidence in her looks always ended up pushing them away. She would always comment on how she wished she could look like me, and I still have no idea why.

I wasn't overweight, but I was on the curvy side. Luckily I had the bust to make it look good. Everything was proportionate, but I wished for a few less curves and a little more rock hard abs.

I knew that was never going to happen. Genetics had made sure I got my mom's figure and my dad's blond hair, which fell limp and lifeless as it rested on my shoulders. But my eyes were something else. They were a little of both my parents. A little blue from Mom and a touch of green from Dad gave them the hue of an ocean, and I was often complimented on them.

I was so busy scrutinizing my looks that I didn't notice we'd arrived till we pulled up outside the dorms. This was it. My new home for the next year…at least. Dad leaned forward, peering through the windshield.

"You chose this over our three bedroom house? You sure this is what you want?"

Ok, it wasn't the most attractive looking place I'd seen, but it seemed perfectly average considering it had been used by thousands of students in its time. What was he expecting? The White House? I let out an exasperated sigh, raising my eyes to the heavens as I got out of the car. I couldn't wait to see my new digs.

After exploring for several minutes, I found the main reception and collected my key. According to the letter that was attached to it, I was in Room 21 and sharing with an A. Brookes. She sounded just like the blonde cheerleader type that I had loathed back in high school. I cursed myself for judging my new roommate and for making assumptions based solely on her name. I hadn't even met her yet!

I made my way to the building indicated on the map and began searching for my room, passing new students like myself as I went by. The hallways emanated a musty and extremely unpleasant smell that reminded me of sweat and dirty laundry. There were students unloading boxes, suitcases, and large trash bags. Someone even had a huge TV, and I wondered if they were actually allowed to have it there, but I was more irritated that I hadn't thought of it myself.

Swerving out of the way so they could pass, I looked back over my shoulder and watched as two guys lifted a very heavy looking box through the hallway, before dropping it with a thud onto the floor. They began to open it, but I didn't get the opportunity to see the contents of the box because a second later, I was stumbling backwards and crashing onto my ass. My legs flew up in the air, and the paper I was carrying flew across the floor along with my key. I'd somehow managed to walk headfirst into the broad muscular back of a guy who was now looking down at me, on my back, spread eagle on the hallway floor. Thank god I was wearing jeans, or he would have gotten an eyeful. First impressions at this point, I imagined, were probably not very good. Maybe I should have worn a skirt. Panty flashing might have made this a little more bearable. Well, for him anyway.

He held his hand out to me and smiled.

"Need a hand down there?" he asked.

I held out my own hand, and he pulled me to my feet. Now that I was face to face with this guy, I could see how dazzlingly good looking he was. His hair was black and rested just above his chin. It was straight, but he wore it a bit tousled underneath his gray beanie. He had an eyebrow ring in his right brow and a ring piercing on the left side of his mouth.

I found myself staring at his lips. They were plump, and the lip ring pinched and pressed against the corner of his mouth when he smiled. I wondered what it would be like to kiss a guy with a lip ring.

"You looking for your dorm?" he asked, pulling me away from my inappropriate thoughts. I glanced up to discover the deepest brown eyes I had ever seen.

"Yeah. Sorry, I was miles away. I didn't see you there."

He shook his head and held up his hands. "No need to apologize. This place is a lot to take in. So, which room are you in?"

I surveyed the hallway only to discover that my dorm was opposite to his. "Um, this one actually."

Bending, he grabbed my key which was sitting on the floor next to his foot, and opened my door.

The room was a comfortable size, lit by a large window on the far wall. Pushed against the corner of the room was a single bed which separated the room almost completely in half. A small, modest, en suite bathroom with a shower was visible in the other corner. The whole space appeared so bare compared to my old bedroom, but I told myself that with a few pictures and some keepsakes it would feel just like home. I turned around with a satisfied smile on my face. He was leaning in my doorway with his hands in his pockets.

"It's not the Ritz, but it'll do, right?" he said, before I took my key from him and gave him my friendliest smile. He was right. It definitely was not the Ritz, but yes, it would do.

"So I guess we're going to be neighbors." I tried to sound like it was no big deal, but this guy was hot and I was desperately trying to control myself from letting my eyes and hands wander all over him. Knowing that he would be living just across the hall from me gave me sinful ideas. I mean, our beds would be literally a few yards apart. Yeah, I know there are walls and doors too, but it was still pretty close.

He shrugged impassively and smiled. "Guess so."

He walked across the hall to his room, and I followed, thinking that I must have seemed to be the biggest, clumsiest idiot in the place. I mentally chastised myself for my stupidity in the hallway and also for my lustful inspection of him.

I had just started heading down the hallway when he yelled after me, "Oliver Green, by the way!"

I turned and nodded. "Layla Jennings."

The corner of his mouth turned up, almost as if he were amused by this, then he walked into his room and shut the door.

Well, that went well. The first person I meet at college, and not only did I crash into him, I landed flat on my back with my legs in the air. Great start, Lay.

When I finally returned to the car, Dad was already unloading the boxes. Generally, unloading the trunk took him seconds, but today he seemed to take his time. I supposed he did this just to be with me a little bit longer, or maybe he was still trying to accept that I really wasn't going back home with him.

Even though I was tremendously excited about starting my new life at college, I had always known that this day was going to be challenging for both of us, But I never imagined I would feel so guilty about leaving him. Dad's pained expression reminded me that while I was making new friends, going out and having fun, he would be having meals for one in an empty house.

I strolled over and began to help him unload. Dad shook his head at me.

"I got this, honey. Did you find your room?" The smile he gave me was not his usual bright and cheery one. It was forced, and I could see that he was trying hard to conceal his emotions, but I decided to play along for both our sakes.

"Yeah, I found it. Think I made a great first impression on the guy living across from me, though." I rolled my eyes at myself. What a klutz.

Dad's eyebrows shot up, and his eyes narrowed as he stared down at me with a dubious look on his face. "Guy? There's a guy living across from you?"

I prepared myself for his overprotective and highly anti boy speech. I'd heard it hundreds of times before, but something told me that I was about to hear it again.

"Layla, you're a young woman now. I know you're intelligent enough to recognize who you should, and shouldn't, associate with, but I also realize that this is college. Hell, I remember college which is why I'm concerned. Don't get too caught up with the guys here. They're young, reckless and only looking for one thing. I don't have to give you the other talk, do I? You don't want to flunk out because you're knocked up by some frat boy."

I rolled my eyes and instantly regretted it as I caught a glimpse of the stern look he was directing at me. I shook my head and ran to him, flinging my arms around his neck. He squeezed me tightly, lifting me off the ground and burying his face in my hair. I could feel the sting of tears in my eyes, but I couldn't let Dad see me so upset. He kissed my forehead and set me back on my feet. I could see the tears beginning to form in his eyes.

Staring down at me with a serious expression, he held my hands firmly in his.

"If at any point you want to come home, just call. I'll come straight here to get you. Any time, night or day. You can always change your mind."

I placed my index finger over his lips to silence him.

"Dad, it's going to be fine. I'm going to be fine, and you're going to be ok without me. It's not forever. I'll be home this weekend, and we'll have dinner; it'll be good." I beamed at him, hoping that he wouldn't notice the tears which were trying to fall. The dam was sure to burst soon.

I hated long goodbyes. Needing the separation to be short and sweet, I picked up one of the large boxes and looked up at him.

"Well, I better go unpack. I'll see you this weekend. I love you, Daddy."

He nodded and focused his eyes at the ground. I turned on my heel and headed to the dorm building, glancing back to see him in the car with his forehead on the steering wheel. His hand came up, and I knew he was wiping away a tear. My own warm tears began to flow freely down my cheeks. It was going to be ok.

I kept repeating that to myself as I walked to my room. It was going to be fine, and all I had to do was believe it.

Chapter 2

Amy

I stood for a few minutes, scrutinizing my side of the room. Everything was unpacked, and I simply couldn't believe my whole life had been in just four large cardboard boxes. Everything had its place. Books were on the desk in alphabetical order, my clothes were color coded and hung neatly in my closet, and the bed was made with military precision.

Mom had always called my need for order and organization nit-picky. Dad called it quirky. I called it necessary. My grandmother had always told me, "A tidy home, a tidy mind!", so I could never get anything done if my living space was cluttered with junk; it was distracting and unproductive. My mind was almost instantly swamped with thoughts of my roommate. There was a good chance she would not be so quirky.

Just as I had begun to wonder what hell I was in for, the door flew open. Standing in the doorway, holding a Louis Vuitton purse, was the most striking girl I had ever seen. Her long dark hair flowed down to her shoulders and a few locks hung just around her face, highlighting her huge green eyes. She was slender and had an impressive athletic figure - the complete opposite to me.

She sauntered in and placed her purse on the empty bed across the room. As she turned around, the beaming smile on her face indicated that she had finally realized there was actually someone else in the room and her eyes lit up.

"You must be L. Jennings. I'm Amy Brookes. Oh this is wonderful. I've never had a sister, or even a best friend, and now I have a roommate. I just know we're going to be BFF's. I'm so excited!"

She was crazy, jumping up and down on the spot and giggling with delight. I arched my brow in response. Two more people entered the room; both male, appearing to be around my age and very well built. I assumed that they were also students at the college. They carried two large Louis Vuitton suitcases. Of course, she would have a matching set.

"Thanks guys. Just put them on the bed there."

She smiled, and they waved as they left. I was dumbstruck. This girl was waltzing straight into this room with her designer luggage, manic and energetic persona and two random guys in tow. What planet was she from? This was going to be difficult. I could tell.

Amy began unpacking while I sat on my bed reading the latest issue of Cosmo. I glanced up now and then to watch her. Everything she took from her suitcase was greeted with enthusiasm and awe. She was exhausting. The next thing to emerge was a pair of red and white pom-poms. I had clearly been right about the pom-pom waving cheerleader bit.

Amy caught me looking and shook them at me. I smiled, but in my mind I was imaging that she was probably one of those girls in high school. She walked over and sat next to me on the bed. Tilting her head to one side, she appeared to be studying me.

"So, L. Jennings, where are you from?"

I glanced up from my magazine. She was staring at me with that goofy grin on her face again.

"Pasadena. And it's Layla."

We sat in awkward silence for several seconds before I realized what she was waiting for.

"So where are you from, Amy? You from around here?"

Bingo.

Her eyes danced as she told me all about her life in Beverly Hills. Amy's dad was a judge and her stepmom an interior designer for the rich and famous. Her mom had died while giving birth to her. She'd chosen Long Beach State after her father told her that it had an impeccable record and reputation in the field of human science. He wanted her to be a doctor, but Amy had always wanted to be a fashion designer. They compromised, and she agreed to take some human science classes while he agreed that she should take some art classes. He was paying for it, after all.

After listening to Amy talk about her life at home, I began to think about my mom and dad. I missed Dad already. Mom sent a text that morning, telling me that she'd call later after work, but I wasn't going to hold my breath.

Amy let out a long sigh, bringing me out of my day dream. "I'm starving, and I could use some caffeine. There's a cute little coffee shop just off campus. They make a latte that's been brewed in heaven! Wanna get some?"

I shrugged and swung my feet off the bed, placing them into my black pumps. I nodded, and she beamed at me, then grabbed her purse before we headed out the door.

What did I have to lose?

* * * *

Amy was right, the coffee shop was cute. It was a small place with large windows and dim lighting, which gave it a warm glow. There were several sets of tables and chairs around the edges of the room and in the center were two couches and a coffee table. The walls were magnolia with bold colorful paintings of coffee cups hanging on them. They were retro, and I loved retro art. The whole place had a cozy and intimate feel to it. The atmosphere was relaxed and casual with an air of camaraderie. The aromatic scents of roasted coffee beans and vanilla filled the air, and I was suddenly hankering for something sweet and creamy.

Amy put her hands on my shoulders and steered me to the counter. She ordered two caramel lattes and refused to let me pay. We sat at a corner table next to one of the large windows. I gazed out the window at all the people going about their day; I liked people watching and could have spent hours doing it. Most of my classes mainly consisted of human behavior and psychology, but I got the feeling Amy would keep me engaged in conversation rather than let me sit in peace, watching the world go by.

"So, Layla, did you get a scholarship to come here or are you paying your way through school? Or your parents?"

She sat back and blew at the coffee in her cup. A little foam dripped down the side and she quickly scooped it up with her finger before snorting a laugh and licking it off. This girl was something else.

"Actually my parents are paying, but I guess I should really get a job to help out. I mean, books and food don't come cheap."

I sat back and stared out the window. I really was going to have to get out there soon and find some work. Amy jolted forward, nearly spilling her coffee. She bounced up and down animatedly on her chair.

"Oh, Layla, how lucky! They have a position here. I was passing through the other day with Daddy. We were looking at the campus and stopped for coffee. Anyway, while we were here, I overheard one of the waitresses talking about needing to hire someone to work a few hours a week. You should totally apply! It's right near the campus, and you'll never have to drink bad coffee again."

She was grinning and looking at me as if I were her new favorite doll. At that moment, I kind of felt like her new project. I winced a little and shrugged, creasing my eyebrows together.

"I don't know. Maybe. I don't even have my class schedule worked out yet."

Amy rolled her eyes at me and tutted. "Oh, Layla. It wouldn't hurt to ask. I'm sure they could work your hours around classes. Plus, once you're in you can pretty much make your own hours. You said you needed a job, well here's your chance. Stop rolling your eyes at me, get off your ass, and get up there."

She pointed at the counter and glared at me. I bit the corner of my lip and begrudgingly stood up, grabbing my coffee as I headed over to the counter.

An older woman was at the register looking at receipts. She seemed a little upset, and every now and then she would shake her head while studying the small pieces of paper in her hand. It was now or never. I approached the counter, and she peered over her glasses at me.

"Hi, can I get you another?" She pointed at my cup and I shook my head with a small smile.

"Um, no thanks. I'm good here. I was actually wondering if you had any open positions? I'm a student over at Long Beach State and I was looking for some part time work."

She angled her head to one side and looked me up and down, inspecting me. "Well, I do have a few shifts available. Have you ever worked in a shop before?" I shook my head, biting on my lip again.

"But I'm a really hard worker, I learn fast and I'm always willing to cover shifts. I'm dedicated, focused and I swear you wouldn't regret it." She sighed and rubbed her forehead with her hand.

"Well, considering you're the only applicant I've had who isn't covered in tattoos, piercings or black nail polish, I don't have many other options. Ok, we'll give you a trial and see how you do. It's simple enough to learn. Can you start tomorrow for training? Say 9a.m.?" I nodded and grinned at her.

"I'll be here. 9a.m. sharp. Thank you so much…" I leaned in to read her name badge, "Lorraine. Really. Thank you."

She sighed again, shaking her head as she rummaged under the counter for something. She handed me some forms to fill out for tax and emergency contacts. I filled them out on the spot and gave them back to her. She studied them and gave me a sympathetic smile.

"One of your parents an Eric Clapton fan? That's a great song, Layla." She said the last few words in a bit of a singsong and I knew exactly what she was talking about.

Dad loved that song. He used to sing it to me when I was little. He said I used to giggle and laugh so much, it just made him want to sing it more. I'd heard the song many times, but people rarely connected my name to it. I mean, not many people my age knew about it.

Mel had always known, but she had grown up with me. Dad had played it in the house so often that Mel would fall about laughing and playing air guitar. I missed her. I would have to call her later as promised. I couldn't wait to tell her about Amy.

I finished making arrangements for the next day with Lorraine and went back to the table. Amy had been watching me the whole time. I sat back down and she raised her eyebrows at me.

"So?" I gave her a brief smile and shrugged as I sat down.

"I start training tomorrow at 9a.m." She let out a small squeak and grinned.

"See, Layla Jennings, you're at college now. It's time to take chances! Maybe some risks, too. Who knows, it could open up a whole new world for you. And now you have me, I'll be making sure you take lots of chances *and* risks!"

Something told me that she was dead serious. But what could I say? She was right. I took a chance and now after only being here for a few hours I had a job. I'd been off campus, had coffee with my new roommate and got a job. Things were already looking up. I rested back on my chair and grinned inwardly as I listened to Amy talk about all the parties and socials we were going to this year.

I had to admit that this year could actually turn out to be a lot of fun.

Chapter 3

An Apron and an Adonis

    The sun was warm and it heated my skin to the perfect temperature. I could feel the breeze tickling and cooling the nape of my neck as it caressed my exposed flesh. I was laying on a red and white checkered cotton blanket, in the most beautiful meadow that I had ever seen. I lay there for a while, just thinking about how I had gotten there. I could see the outline of a man in the distance. Tall and broad, he was striding over fast. I could just make out his handsome face; the dark penetrating eyes, slight stubble from his morning shave and thick brown hair. He was delicious. My heart was pounding as he came closer to me, and my breathing was becoming harsher and quicker. Leaning over me he slowly moved his hand up my thigh, his fingertips caressing my skin as they slid upwards. Leaning into my face, his lips almost touching mine, he let out a soft sigh and breathed my name…
    "Layla!"
    That wasn't what I expected…
    "Layla wake up! You're late for work!"
    Shit!
    My eyes flew open and straight to the clock. 9:15 a.m. I was late. I'd only been working at Lorraine's coffee shop for a week, and I definitely did not want a reputation for being late, so I jumped out of bed and ran for the bathroom. I showered,

pulled on my clothes as fast as I could and pulled my damp hair back into a tight ponytail, quickly putting on some mascara and lip gloss. There was no time for the full works this morning. Looking in the mirror, I winced at my reflection. Not great, but it would do.

I rushed back out to find Amy holding the door open with one hand and a granola bar in the other. "You're an angel." I grabbed the granola bar, which would have to serve as my breakfast, and ran out the door.

"What would you do without me?" she yelled after me.

"Go hungry!" I shouted over my shoulder, before running as fast as my feet could carry me to work.

This was not good. I could see the shop, and it was clearly busy. Breakfast and lunch times were the most hectic for us. I was sure I was in trouble. I crossed the street and hurriedly walked the few yards to the shop. Searching my bag for my apron, I leaned back against the door and gave it a hard push with my behind so that it opened while I continued to look for my apron.

"Shit!"

I snapped my head up, turned around, and gasped in horror. Holding his coffee in one hand and his now dripping nose with the other, stood a tall, highly irritated man.

"Oh my god. I am so sorry. Here let me help you." I grabbed some napkins off the nearby table and began trying to stop the man's nose from bleeding.

He waved me off and pinched the bridge of his nose with his fingers.

"No, no. My mistake. How was I to know that someone would be ass walking their way into the shop? I mean, who watches the direction they're going these days?" His voice was oozing with sarcasm. I was a little pissed at his attitude. It wasn't like I'd done it on purpose.

"It was an accident. I didn't see you because I was looking for my apron. What's your excuse for not seeing me through a glass door?"

He gawked down at me, raised his eyebrows and shook his head. I stood my ground and stared right back at him. Opening his mouth to respond, he was interrupted by a frantic looking Lorraine who had left her spot at the counter and was now striding over to us. She scanned our faces and then held her hands to her mouth.

"Oh my goodness, Jared. Are you alright? Do you need to go to the hospital?"

Well, at least I knew the name of the man I had just assaulted with a coffee shop door. He took his fingers away from his nose and checked to see if it was still bleeding. It wasn't. Lorraine led him to the office, and I followed, feeling like I should apologize again, even if he had acted like a jerk. I stood in the doorway and watched Lorraine. There really wasn't that much blood. What a baby.

Jared was sitting on the chair at the large desk, facing Lorraine as she wiped him down with a damp cloth. Once she'd finished cleaning him up, she lifted his chin so she could inspect his nose.

"There. Good as new and as handsome as ever." She said smiling at Jared before giving me a warning look as she walked out of the office. Yep. I was in trouble.

I rolled my eyes and stared at a now clean and composed Jared. Lorraine was wrong, he wasn't handsome. He was gorgeous. He had piercing blue eyes that were peeking out from beneath his long dark lashes. He had a dimple in his chin and beautiful light brown hair mixed with a few wisps of blond, giving it a golden appearance as the light caught each strand. It was cut short and he obviously used some product to give it that 'I just crawled out of bed' look.

As he stood, I couldn't help but admire his amazing physique. He was tall with broad shoulders and his white shirt, which was now stained with hot coffee, clung to his body. I could see his impressive chest and rock hard abs underneath the now ruined shirt. My cheeks were feeling warm, and I hoped he didn't catch me blushing.

I watched as he began wiping himself down with a tissue, trying in vain to get rid of the stain. I gave a loud sigh and walked over to him. Staring at the floor I began to make my apologies.

"Look, I'm really sorry about the door. And your shirt. And your nose. But it really was an accident. I don't make it a habit to walk around backwards. I was late for work and-"

He stopped rubbing at his shirt for a moment and set his gaze on me. He held up his left hand to silence me.

"Wait. You work here? At Lorraine's?"

I nodded. His head fell back and he closed his eyes tightly. He ran his hands over his face and then stared down at me.

"Well I'll be sure to send you the bill for my now completely un-wearable Armani shirt. The nose that you damaged, I will have to live with."

What a jackass. I was apologizing, and he was giving me such a hard time. Jeez, was he always such a jerk? I fisted my hands on my hips and with a furrowed brow I glared up at him.

"Hey! I already apologized and I'll be happy to pay for your shirt to be cleaned. It was, after all, my fault. But if you think for one moment that I'm going to stand here and put up with your attitude, then you're very much mistaken. You'll find me in here most afternoons, so please do drop by when you have something useful for me. Like the bill for that shirt." Gorgeous or not, he was still a jackass.

I turned on my heel and stormed out of the room. He was clearly stunned into silence because he didn't respond. I wrapped my apron around my waist and began collecting coffee cups off of the empty tables. He breezed past me a few minutes later. Reaching out for the handle on the door he glanced back at me and shook his head before leaving.

What a rude, ignorant, jerk-wad!

Chapter 4

Playing the Game

    Amy rolled around on her bed, clutching her stomach. She'd been laughing so hard for the past five minutes I thought she might lose control of her bladder. Tears were running down her face as she tried to calm herself. Sitting on the edge of her bed she wiped her eyes.
    "So, let me get this straight. You've been here for one week, and you've met two smoking hot guys. And somehow you have managed to land flat on your back in front of one, then ruin a very expensive shirt and break the nose of the other."
    She brought her hands up to her mouth, trying to hide her laughter. I cringed and pinched my eyes tightly closed.
    "Yes. But in my defense we don't know for sure that I broke his nose. It just...bled...a bit." That was it. Amy was in hysterical fits of laughter again.
    She slid forward off the bed, her ass landed on the floor, and she began to roll on to her back, laughing hard. I was glad someone found this funny because I was mortified.
    Lorraine had been rather lenient with me. She'd given me a warning about being late, but had also said that if the job and school work were too much, she could work out a new schedule for me. I appreciated the thought, but I assured her that it would not happen again. As for the assault on Jared, she

had simply chuckled and told me to watch where I was going in the future. I had assured her the Jared incident was certainly never going to happen again.

I laid on my bed and stared at the ceiling. Amy had finished her hysterical floor show and was now a little more composed. She got up and sat by the edge of my bed.

"You going home for the weekend, Layla? I heard there's a great party going on over at one of the frat houses, first week freshman party. We should totally go!"

It sounded fun, but I had promised Dad I would go home for the weekend. Plus, I wanted to see how he was doing on his own. I sat up and shook my head at her.

"I can't go. I promised Dad I'd visit for the weekend. But you should totally go. Meet people. Meet guys. You'll fit right in." I smiled and patted her on the shoulder. "Besides, it will give you plenty to tell me about when I get back on Sunday. We could discuss it over some take out and junk food."

That seemed to work. She returned my smile and nodded. "Ok, but you don't know what you're missing."

It had been a long day. With the incident at the coffee shop and the whole week of meet and greets, I was exhausted. Lying on my bed, my arm shielding my eyes, I was just staring to allow myself to doze when someone knocked loudly on the door. Amy was immediately on her feet. I sat up and glanced over at the door.

"Who the hell is that?" She strode over and opened it.

Standing in our doorway was Oliver. He was wearing a pair of loose jeans and a hoodie. He smirked at me as Amy gave him a questioning look.

"Hey, Layla."

He walked into the room and right past a stunned Amy. She fisted her hands on her hips and stared at him.

"And you are?"

He turned to face her and let out a small laugh. "Oh yeah, sorry. Oliver. I live across the hall. I met Layla here on moving day. You must be the roommate."

"Amy." She glared at him and then turned her attention to me. I shrugged and gave her a half a smile.

"Flat on my back." I said. She snorted a laugh, suddenly knowing who Oliver was. He sat down by the edge of my bed.

"Anyway, I just came over to see what you were doing tonight. There's a bar a couple of blocks over and its open mic night. I was just about to head over with my roommate Nick and thought you might wanna get outta here for a while."

Amy looked at me with hope in her eyes. It was obvious she was desperate to go. Other than the coffee shop, I hadn't been off campus, and it was Friday night.

"Sure. What the hell. Give me five minutes and I'll be ready." I said.

Amy winked at me and turned to Oliver. Grinning at me he nodded, stood up and walked out the door. Amy closed it behind him and jumped up and down enthusiastically.

"Oh my god, this is going to be so much fun!"

* * * *

The bar was heaving with people, and the smell of sweat and bitter ales coming from the overflowing crowd was pungent, but not repulsive. One look around, and I could tell that the décor had clearly not been modernized in quite some time. The dark mahogany bar and large wooden pillars were thick with dust and had several gouges in them, probably caused by numerous fights and brawls. The walls were covered with old photographs of singers like Elvis and Johnny Cash. There was a sign lit up in florescent blue over the stage with the name Benny's across it. Instruments were set up, and a single microphone stood next to a black chalkboard which had the words, Open Mic Night, scrawled across it. Waitresses were darting between tables and the bar, frantically taking orders.

Every table was crammed, including our own. Oliver and Nick had invited a couple of the guys from our building to join us, but Amy and I were the only females in our little group. We sat at a table near the stage, and the guys immediately started talking about the need to find a girl and get laid. Oliver looked over at me and half smiled. I rolled my eyes at him. Men. Always looking for an easy piece of ass. It didn't bother me, but for some reason I found myself hoping that Oliver wasn't like that.

He leaned in and whispered in my ear, "Just ignore them. They're all talk and no action." He winked at me with a sexy grin on his face.

I felt my cheeks flush and hoped that he wouldn't notice. His hot breath on my neck made my hairs stand on end, and my body suddenly stood to attention at the sensation of it. I nodded in the direction of three scantily dressed girls who were now approaching. I let out a small chuckle.

"I hope not, or those girls are going to be very disappointed."

He laughed and shook his head. "Yeah, I guess you're right. So, how about you, Layla? You got a guy back home writing you sweet letters and calling you every day?" Tipping my head back, I let out a snort of laughter.

"Nope. I'm single and have been now for over a year." I wanted to add, "That's right, Oliver. I'm on the market", but decided to leave a little feminine mystery for him to toy with.

I had been with Josh, my high school sweetheart, for two years. He was my first everything. First real, heart stopping, full on French kiss, first love and the first, and only, guy I'd ever slept with. The summer before senior year he'd started working in his dad's shop. We saw each other less and less, and I knew we were growing apart. He would hardly call, and when I called him, he was always too busy or on his way out.

One day, Mel had suggested we go to the beach to "get me out of my stupid, mopey mood". I'd agreed and it had made me feel a little better until I saw Josh walking down the beach holding hands with a long legged, bikini wearing girl from the cheerleading squad. They stopped and I saw him kiss her deeply. I marched over, shoved him hard in the chest, and told him I never wanted to speak to him again.

And I never did.

Oliver leaned forward, putting his elbows on the table. "What happened?"

I glanced at him, then back down at the drink in my hand. "The usual thing. Young. First love. Guy turns out to be a cheating slime ball."

He put his hand over mine and smiled. "Well, I'd say he's an idiot and a real douche."

I knew he was trying to reassure me, but the touch of his hand on mine was giving me sinful ideas. I thought about his hand sliding up my arm to my neck, caressing it as he kissed me with those beautiful lips. I could feel myself blushing again. What was wrong with me? I nodded and smiled back at him as he removed his hand from mine. Oliver wasn't like the other guys, I could tell, but boy did I hope he wasn't all talk. I could use a little action in my life.

I was just starting to relax and enjoy myself when a large, balding man walked onto the stage, bellowing at the crowd for the first sacrifice to come and take the mic. People were talking amongst themselves without paying him much attention, and a few heads turned his way, but no one seemed to be brave enough to volunteer. Then, out of nowhere, Amy's hand shot up like a rocket. I stared at her with wide eyes. What was she doing?

"We are!"

I nearly choked on my drink. Who the hell were we? I glared at her and prayed that she was talking about herself in the third person or at least that she meant the royal we, and not me and her *we*. The guy at the mic smirked, clearly entertained by Amy's enthusiasm, and invited her up. She quickly got to her feet and grabbed my hand, which I tried frantically to release, but her deathlike grip kept me captive in her palm.

"No, Amy. No way. Not in a million years are you getting me on that stage. You're crazy! I can't play an instrument and I am not singing." I sang on stage in high school when I was the lead vocalist for a small band, but that was years ago and I was extremely out of practice.

Amy pulled my arm so hard I thought it might dislocate. Instead, I was flying out of my chair and onto my feet.

"Oh nonsense. I've heard you singing to your iPod and in the shower. You rock! And I play the piano and sing. Come on, we'll be like our very own girl band! This is college and we're supposed to be having fun, remember, so play the game, Layla."

I wasn't getting out of this.

Before I knew it, Amy was pulling me to the stage. I glared back at Oliver, pleading with my eyes for help, but he just shrugged at me, shaking his head and grinning from ear to ear.

"Thanks a lot," I mouthed, feeling a little pissed that my new friend was taking delight in my predicament, but that just made him laugh. Giving Nick a nod, he gestured for him to join us on stage. Rolling his eyes, Nick got to his feet and followed us up. He sat behind the huge, red drum kit that was on stage. A guy from our table had also joined us and was hooking up a gorgeous metallic blue guitar to an amp. Feeling like a proper band, I smiled to myself as the anticipation and adrenaline began to bubble beneath the surface of my skin. Nervous butterflies swarmed inside my stomach, and I fought the urge to bolt as Amy sat at the piano.

"Let's sing this one!" Amy shoved a sheet of paper at me that had the music to the song 'Fading Like A Flower' by Roxette. I did love the song, and I knew it well, but singing in the shower was one thing; singing it up on stage, in front of a herd of strangers, was another. But there was no time to chicken out. Amy was already playing the intro with Nick and the blond stranger not far behind.

Giving them a quick nervous smile I took a deep breath, walked up to the mic, closed my eyes and sang. It actually sounded good. Really good. I snuck a peek over my shoulder at Amy; she was beaming at me so brightly that I thought she might explode. This was fun. My lungs belted out notes that I didn't know I could reach.

I felt amazing!

I grabbed the mic stand and caressed it with my free hand as I sang. The bar was buzzing as people began to walk over to the stage area to watch. People were rocking and singing along to the chorus with me. The adrenaline rush I felt made my confidence soar, leaving me breathless as I sang every note pitch perfect and loud. My ears were ringing as the sound from the large speakers boomed through the bar. People were dancing and singing to the beat. I'd never felt so exhilarated.

When the song ended, the whole bar cheered, and Oliver was on his feet whistling at us. I grinned and bit my lip, suddenly feeling a little self-conscious.

As I came down from the stage, Amy wrapped her arms around me. "Oh my god, that was great! I told you that you'd rock."

Turning her attention to the guys, she hugged them both, equally as grateful. "You guys totally rock, too! Awesome!"

The blond guitarist blushed as she pressed her lips against his cheek, leaving her shocking pink lipstick on his pale flesh.

I could still feel the adrenaline pumping through my body when I got back to our table. Oliver was still applauding when I approached. I gave him a small smile, bowed gracefully in jest and sat back in my seat, exhaling loudly. I hadn't realized I was even holding my breath.

"Well, well, well. Who knew that the musically named Layla would also be a rocking pop star?"

Feeling a little shy, I gave him another quick smile and took a big gulp of my drink. I needed it. My heart was pounding so hard in my chest that I thought it was trying to escape my ribcage. I could feel his eyes on me as I tried desperately to concentrate on the glass in my hand, but they were penetrating my thoughts. I glanced sideways at him, and the corners of his mouth curled up as he bit his lip. Then almost simultaneously we were diverting our attention, me at my glass and he at a group of guys now setting up on stage.

A jolt of exhilaration ran through me. He was flirting with his eyes. Or had I imagined it? If I did, then Amy had too. Our exchange had not gone unnoticed. She was giving me a goofy grin as her eyebrows bounced up and down. I rolled my eyes at her as she gave me a knowing look. I was sure we'd be talking about this later.

The rest of the evening was spent talking about our performance on stage and discussing classes. They would be starting on Monday and everyone was taking something different. After explaining that I was majoring in psychology, Nick and the blond guitarist, who turned out to be named Eric, announced that they were taking sports and music. Their silent friend, Henry, was taking Media and Journalism. I turned to Oliver and arched an eyebrow.

"So, what are you taking?"

Sipping his drink, he smiled. "Psych and music. So I guess we'll be in some classes together this semester. And there I was, thinking it would be boring."

Ok, he was definitely flirting, and I was enjoying every last moment of it. This college thing was going to be more fun than I thought.

Chapter 5

Money, Money, Money

It was finally Saturday morning, and I was working. I'd promised Dad I'd be home for the weekend, so when I called to tell him I was doing the morning shift at the shop, he insisted on picking me up in the afternoon and driving me home himself. I got the feeling he was desperate for me to come home.

It was quieter in the shop today. I assumed that was because people weren't at work on weekends, so they wouldn't need to grab a coffee on their way in. The majority of customers were students from Long Beach State. I recognized a few from my dorm, but didn't know them well enough to make conversation.

No one had come in for nearly half an hour, so I pulled up a stool and sat by the counter. Grabbing a caramel latte, I opened up one of the magazines sitting in the rack next to the register. I rested my elbows on the countertop and blew on my hot coffee. I was just reading an article on how shoes can cure depression when I was distracted by someone clearing their throat.

The sound startled me, causing me to almost spill my coffee. I jumped off my stool, trying to look professional. I put the magazine aside, along with my coffee, and looked up from the counter.

Oh, what new hell was this?

Standing in front of me, with a wry grin on his face, was Jared. He was wearing jeans and a white t-shirt that showed off his impressive arms. I plastered my most genuine looking smile on my face and looked up at him.

"Hi. What can I get you?"

He regarded me for a moment -almost amused- before scanning the board behind me.

I drummed my fingers on the counter impatiently and stared at him, waiting for him to make a choice. I was sure I saw the corners of his mouth curl upwards. Not quite a smile, but he was certainly amused by my irritation.

"So many to choose from. What is one to do?" He had his head angled to the right and was biting his lip. My eyes were fixed to his mouth as I watched his teeth sink into his flesh, wishing I could be doing the same. He may be a douche, but my god he was hot. I was only human after all.

Continuing to um and ah over the menu, I realized he was now trying to provoke my irritation deliberately. Happy to oblige, I folded my arms across my chest and tapped my foot loudly. His eyes darted to me.

"I'm sorry, I didn't realize that your service came with a side of attitude."

I couldn't believe how rude he was. Just when I thought he couldn't become any more discourteous or irritating, he did. I'd had enough of this game. He was seriously pissing me off, and I was going to make damn sure he knew it.

I leaned across the counter with my hands tightly gripping the edge.

"Look, I don't know what your problem is. I apologized for the coffee. I offered to pay for the shirt, and I even apologized for your stupid nose even though the fact remains that if it had been pointing in the right direction you would have seen me through the glass. It's you strolling in here with your laid back, make her wait while I dick around attitude that really grinds my gears."

Oh. My. God. Did that just come out of my mouth?

He took a step back from the counter and stared back at me. His eyebrows were raised and his mouth was pulled into a tight line. I stood back and crossed my arms again, staring right back at him. He cleared his throat and smirked wickedly at me.

Urgh!

"I'm so sorry. I didn't realize you were busy. I'd hate to tear you away from your very important task of sitting on your ass and reading articles about how chocolate is better than sex." He glanced over at my magazine which was still sitting on the counter. Ah crap. "By the way, I can assure you that it's not."

I could feel my cheeks warming. This was getting tiresome. I had a job to do, and he was a customer. We couldn't go on like this. I decided to take the moral high ground, which itself was very difficult for me. I always had to have the last word.

"You're right. I apologize for my rude behavior. What do you say we start over?" I shook my head and tried to regain my serene and impassive disposition. I walked up to the counter and smiled at him.

"Good morning, sir. What can I get you?"

He eyed me cautiously and then tipped his head back and laughed so loudly, I thought he might shatter the windows. His heavy shoulders bounced up and down as a deep laugh rumbled through him. Wiping his eyes, he shook his head at me and grinned.

"First of all, call me Jared. Secondly, that was by far the best performance I have ever seen. Though, I recommend a dentist because you were gritting your teeth so hard the whole time I think you might need a root canal. You should probably work on your fake smile too, because that was hilarious." He stifled another laugh with his fist.

My mouth opened wide in irritation and pure shock.

How dare he?

Here I was trying to be nice, trying to be polite, and he had the sheer audacity to insult me! I was just about to let him have it when he held up his hand to silence me.

"That being said. I appreciate the effort. I'll have whatever it is you're drinking there." He pointed to my cup which was sitting on the counter.

I rolled my eyes and walked over to the coffee machine. It was only then that I had thought to look around the shop. I glanced up and my eyes took in the room. There were a handful of people sitting at their tables staring at me. A few had begun to speak softly to each other and were nodding in my direction. I felt the embarrassment creeping up my skin all the way to my cheeks. Just like that, I was back in the high school cafeteria. I cursed myself for allowing this man to get under my skin. Causing a scene at work was just one more thing to add to my list of horrible experiences this week. This one was certainly up there with lying spread eagle at Oliver's feet.

I put it to the back of my mind and served Jared his coffee to go. Placing it on the counter, I gave him my most genuine smile. Well, as much as I could force myself to give to this man. He gave me a cautious look as he grabbed the cup off the counter.

"That's $1.96 please," I reminded him. He gave me a quizzical look.

"I said that's $1.96. You know, cash? Around here people generally pay for coffee."

The corners of his mouth curled up, and he took a sip of his latte which he had yet to pay for. Who the hell did this guy think he was? Glowering at him, I placed my hands on my hips, gripping them firmly; mostly to stop myself from slapping him hard on the face.

"Well, I don't usually, but since it's you I'm only too happy to oblige."

He reached into his pocket and produced a $10 bill. I held out my hand, and he pressed the bill between our palms. I felt like a bolt of lightning hit me. What was that?

Gripping my hand, he leaned into the counter, and I could smell his aftershave. It was deep, sensual, musky, yet sweet at the same time. Or maybe that was just him, his natural scent. It inflamed my nostrils, and I felt my blood beginning to boil. What on earth was he doing to me? He was a rude, insensitive dick and yet his touch had left me stripped of my senses.

"And because it's you, I'll even let you keep the change. Call it a tip for your warm customer service." He gave me a wink and turned on his heel. He pulled the door open and then shot me the sexiest smile I had ever seen.

Wide eyed and shocked I walked to the window, $10 bill in hand, and watched him as he walked down the street. Once he was out of sight I turned around and leaned against the counter. I shook my head and massaged my temple. Get a grip girl. What the hell had just happened? I'd gone from absolutely outraged one moment to intensely aroused in a matter of seconds.

He was so infuriatingly frustrating. So then why the hell couldn't I stop thinking about his touch? My heart was pounding, and I could hear my breathing quickening as I thought about it all. I needed some air. I ran to the back of the shop and opened the door. The cool air washed over me as I tried to calm my racing pulse.

I darted my eyes over to the clock next to the doorframe. 11:30 a.m. Only thirty more minutes and I was going home. Thank god. I didn't think my heart or my nerves could take one more encounter like that one. And yet, deep down, I really hoped it would happen again.

Soon.

Chapter 6

You Spin Me Right Round Baby

    I couldn't get what happened that morning out of my mind. How could that one small connection of our fingers make me feel so alive? The electricity I'd felt was still pulsing through my veins as I walked back to the dorm. This was insane. I hardly knew him, and what I did know of him, I certainly didn't like. He was rude, cocky, arrogant and insensitive, and as if that wasn't enough, he was a total dickweed.
    So why couldn't I stop thinking about him?
    As soon as my dorm was in sight, I practically ran to my room. I needed some space. I had to forget the whole thing.
    Amy was sitting on her bed with her laptop in front of her. I closed the door behind me and leaned against it. My head fell back and I closed my eyes, letting out a long sigh. When I finally opened them to peek over at her, she was watching me with a questioning look on her face.
    Great, I was going to have to re-live it all over again.
    Leaning her head to one side she eyed me with concern.
    "You ok honey? You don't look so hot."
    I walked over to my bed and collapsed onto it. I flung my forearm over my eyes. This was exhausting.

"He came into the shop again today, and I tried to be polite, but he decided to be an ass." I exhaled loudly and sat up with my legs hanging over the edge of the bed.

"Anyway, we got into it in the middle of the shop, and I told him off. And not quietly either." I stared at my feet and then sheepishly raised my head to look at her.

Amy was staring at me wide eyed with her hand over her mouth.

"I tried to be professional, so I apologized for my behavior and tried to start again. The jerk laughed in my face! We did a little more to and fro and then he finally ordered his coffee. When I asked him to pay, he seemed confused. It was like he'd never been asked to use cash to purchase goods or something. When he finally handed me the money, our hands touched and…" I swallowed hard and took two deep calming breaths. "It was like electricity, Amy. My heart was pounding, and my pulse was racing. His scent was amazing, and it was lingering for what seemed like forever. I can still remember the smell, even now. I can't stop thinking about it. When he winked at me, I swear I felt my panties get looser!"

Just thinking about it again was making my blood warm. My cheeks were flushed, and I could feel the heat radiating from my skin.

Amy stood up and sat next to me on the bed. She put one arm around me and rested her head on my shoulder.

"Well, I'd say you've had one hell of a week. First you crash into Oliver, who is so into you by the way, but we'll get to that in a minute. Then, you almost break some guy's nose at work. And to top it off, you go and fight with him and he gets you all hot under the collar. Damn, girl. What the hell do you do to these guys? Oliver was practically undressing you with his eyes last night. The entire time we were on that stage he could not take them off you. It didn't change once we sat back down. And I saw the way you were smiling at him. His eyes, when he bit his lip, were practically begging you to sink your teeth into it for him! And now there's this guy at the coffee shop. Whatever it is you're doing…keep doing it! Have a little fun. Take a chance. If he comes into the shop again, just play it cool. You know, be aloof even if you are boiling on the inside!"

She winked at me and smiled so wide that I could see her perfect white teeth.

After we got back from the bar last night, we were both so tired we never had the chance to discuss the whole Oliver thing, but I'd had the feeling it was going to come up, and I was right. I shrugged and got to my feet. Dad would be here soon, and I needed to get my things.

"Thanks, Amy. I think I'll just play this one by ear." I gave her a half-hearted smile and hoped it would make her feel that I was alright. Inside I was so confused it made my head spin.

Amy was right about Oliver, though. That moment we shared at the bar was more than just flirting. It was almost suggestive. But could I really read into it as much as Amy had? Maybe he was just the flirtatious type. Maybe he had a little black book full of women he's shared "moments" with, though he really didn't seem the type to indulge in meaningless and casual encounters. At least I hoped he wasn't. Those lips did look delicious, though. And it had crossed my mind to just lean in and give that bottom lip the tiniest of nibbles but, unfortunately, I wasn't that kind of girl. After today's events, I wasn't even sure what kind of girl I was anymore. How could this guy that I hardly even knew make me feel so hot? I'd heard that people change at college, but this was ridiculous!

I shook my head and rolled my eyes at myself. Grabbing an overnight bag from the closet, I chucked in some cosmetics and a change of clothes. Grabbing my cell, I realized that Dad had sent me a text.

> On my way, sweetie. Can't wait to see you. I'll call when I'm outside.
> **Received: 13.38**
> **From: Daddy**

Typing a simple 'Ok' in reply, I hit send. I was just about to slide the phone into my front pocket, when it chimed in my hand.

It was another text, but I didn't recognize the number. I opened the message, curious to find out who had acquired my digits without my knowledge.

> Hello, Layla. Sorry to disturb you, but I thought I would let you know that the bill for my expensive Armani shirt is $275 exactly. I'll be by the shop on Monday. You can pay cash or give me a check. Have an enjoyable weekend. Jared :)
> **Received: 13.42**
> **From: Unknown**

"What!"

Amy jumped slightly and stared at me. I was gripping the phone so tightly in my hand that I thought it might shatter into a thousand pieces.

"That asshat! Just look at this!" I handed her the phone and began pacing the room.

"How the hell did he even get my number? Is he serious? $275 for a dry cleaning bill? He's got some nerve!"

Amy shook her head in disbelief. Her jaw had dropped and she appeared to be as shocked as I was. And what the hell was with that smiley face at the end? Like that made it all ok. I could almost imagine that stupid smirk on his smug face as he sent it. What a jackass!

I was furious. My whole body was shaking with the rage I felt building inside me. My fists were tight at my sides, and my teeth were clenched so hard that I may have cracked the enamel. He really was dicking with me now.

Asshole.

Granted, he was a gorgeous, sexy and oh so sweet smelling asshole, but an asshole none the less. I crashed onto my bed and tried to snap out of my bad mood before Dad arrived. Amy squealed as the phone rang in her hand. I jumped up and took it from her.

"Hey, sweetie. I'm downstairs."
Too late, he was already here.

Chapter 7

Mel, Dinner And Daddy

I climbed into the car, slinging my overnight bag onto the back seat. I gave Dad my sweetest smile and leaned over to kiss him on the cheek. His enormous grin was reaching all the way from ear to ear. He'd missed me. His eyes danced as he told me how he couldn't wait to take me out for dinner and hear all about my first week. He was so distracted by all the plans he was making for our weekend that he never noticed the bad mood I was still in. I leaned back in my seat, and we set off for home. I couldn't wait to be back home, where I was safe from all the drama that the week had brought.

The drive home felt like it took forever. I was still trying to get my head around everything that had happened that morning. I would have to talk to Mel about it all. She was my best friend and knew me better than anyone in the whole world. She was sure to have some insight regarding the week's events. We turned on our street, and I saw our house. Home. I felt my whole body relax as I let out a satisfied sigh.

It was good to be back.

We pulled into the driveway, and Dad turned to me. "It's good to have you home, kiddo." I beamed at him as a feeling of pure contentment ran through me.

"It's good to be home, Dad."

As I got out of the car, I scrutinized the exterior of the house. The porch swing had a new coat of paint and the once broken shutter on the window had been fixed. The lawn was cut and there were some flowers freshly planted around the edge. Dad had clearly been busy.

I was just about to follow him into the house when I was ambushed from behind. I fell to the ground with a hard thud and turned over to find Mel, her arms wrapped tightly around me and her head buried in my chest. I laughed breathlessly and tried to push her off, but she just gripped me tighter. Giving up, I lay back on the grass and rested my hands underneath my head.

"Hey, Mel. How've you been?"

I watched her in amusement as she crawled backwards off me and rose to her feet, brushing herself off. Giving me a shrug, she put on the best performance of indifference that she could manage.

"Oh, you know. Chilling, shopping, and perfecting my sneak attack. Same old shit."

I laughed and clambered to my feet. Brushing off my own clothes, I smiled at her. She was grinning at me like she hadn't seen me in a year. Gripping my shoulders she pulled me to her for a hug.

"I missed you so much, Layla. How dare you leave me to go be a big shot Long Beach State student? I hardly spoke to you all week. Where the hell have you been?" She finally released me, and it was my turn to shrug at her.

"It's a long story. Wanna come in for a snack? I'm starving." She nodded and followed me into the house.

Sitting in my room, I filled her in on the events of the past week. I told her everything. Meeting Oliver, Jared, Amy, getting a job at Lorraine's, fighting with Jared and finally the text he'd sent me. When I told her about my performance at Benny's Bar, she applauded me and laughed.

"Well one thing is for sure, Lay, you have two guys that want into your panties."

Was she serious? I could understand her assumptions about Oliver, but Jared? She must have seen the confusion on my face.

"Layla, don't be so naïve. He's pulling your pigtails! If we were in high school, he'd be calling you names and pretending he didn't like you. But we're not in high school, so he's acting like an ass to get that reaction out of you, and apparently you are more than willing to give it to him. I bet he likes his women with a little fire in them. It's obvious you like him, too."

My mouth fell open, and I almost choked on my own breath.

"I do not like him! I hate him. I told you what he said to me. How he treated me with utter contempt. I even showed you the text he sent me. How the hell can you think I like him? Yes, he's hot and yes, this morning at the coffee shop I felt something between us. But I'm a hot blooded woman. A guy gets that close to me and my body reacts. It's a primal instinct. I do not like him."

Mel shook her head and laughed.

"Oh, Layla. Thou doth protest too much. Plus, if you really didn't like him and he really irritated you so much, how would you explain your heated reaction to him whenever he's around? Ok, so he says things to grind your gears, but if you really didn't care then it really wouldn't bother you. Would it? But whatever you say sweetie, I believe you. So what did you say to him after he texted you?"

She sat back on the bed and stared at me, waiting for my answer. She knew damn well that I hadn't replied.

"Well, actually, I decided not to reply. I won't get drawn into his little game. I will simply discuss it with him on Monday." Mel leaned over and rolled her eyes at me.

"Oh come on, Layla. We both know you won't last that long." I pushed her aside, grabbed a pillow and hit her with it. Sniggering like children, we fell back onto the bed. I turned to her and stuck my tongue out, but she simply shrugged. "I give you till the end of the day. I'd even bet my best DKNY dress that you're already thinking about him now." She gave me a wicked grin.

Damn. She was right, I was thinking about him. I hadn't stopped thinking about him all morning. And I was certainly tempted to reply to that text, but I had to take the moral high ground here and be the better person…again. I would not let Jared do this to me.

I was still curious as to how he got my number in the first place. I thought maybe I could just ask him. It was one little text, right? No. I would confront him in person on Monday.

Probably.

* * * *

Dad took me to my favorite Italian restaurant. Mama's Little Pizzeria was a small family owned business. The owners, Marco and Marie, were an older couple who, along with their two sons, ran the whole restaurant. They were obviously a close family and were always happy to see us when we came for our usual Saturday night meal.

"Andrew! Layla! Is so nice to see you. You want your usual table? Come, I get you a menu."

Marco was as welcoming as ever. He showed us to a small table by the window and placed two menus in front of us.

 "So, Layla, when you gonna marry my boy, huh? He's just graduated at the top of his class you know."

I felt my cheeks warming and stared over at Dad, pleading with my eyes for help to get out of this.

"Ah, Marco, you know how it goes. She's a college girl now. She's got her head in the books, and I hope that's where it stays till she's twenty one." He reached over and held my hand in his, giving me a smile.

"Besides, no one will ever be good enough for my baby girl." Winking at me he turned to Marco who was smiling and shaking his head. "We'll have the usual please, Marco, and two glasses of lemonade."

Dad had come to my rescue, just as he always did. Marco's son Roberto was twenty one and had just graduated from Long

Beach State. He had studied biology and human science and was well on his way to medical school. He was a nice guy who had even asked me out once, but I'd had to let him down as gently as I could. He just wasn't my type.

Dad and I spent the evening talking about my new job. I told him about Amy and Oliver, but I decided to leave Jared out of the conversation. Dad was very protective, and I knew he wouldn't take kindly to anyone upsetting his baby girl. Plus, I could handle Jared all on my own.

I was thinking about him again. What was wrong with me? Here I was in my favorite restaurant, my dad animatedly talking about how he had fixed every appliance in the house that week, and I was thinking about that jackass. I tried to focus on what Dad was saying. I was finally caught up on his week of projects and meals for one when I felt my phone buzzing in my pocket.

Excusing myself, I made my way to the bathroom. Once safely inside, and away from Dad's prying eyes, I pulled out the mobile. There was a text, and I knew exactly who it was from. I had saved his number in my contacts as

The Asshole.

I exhaled a deep long breath and opened the message.

> Layla. I do hope you weren't offended by my previous message. I did not intend for it to anger or insult you in any way. However, I must admit I am a little disappointed to have not received a message back from you. I almost looked forward to seeing your name pop up on my screen followed by a sarcastic comment or infuriated response. I will assume from your silence that you have found the request of $275 agreeable. Looking forward to seeing you on Monday. Jared. ;)
> **Received: 20.21**
> **From: The Asshole**

What the hell? Was he serious? And what did he mean he was disappointed not to have heard from me? I couldn't stop reading the same sentence over and over.

"I almost looked forward to seeing your name pop up on my screen."

Almost? What did that even mean? Was he being sarcastic? Or was Mel right?

First there was that smiley face and now a wink. This was becoming too much to handle. I turned around and gripped the edge of the sink in an attempt to steady myself. Looking down into the basin, I shook my head, trying to regain my composure. Raising my head, I gawked at myself in the mirror. My eyes were red, and the lack of sleep I'd had that week was showing in the dark circles that surrounded them. I ran the cool water and splashed a little on my face. Feeling a little more refreshed I walked back to our table.

Dad had paid the bill and was standing by the door. "Ready to go, kiddo?"

I nodded and followed him back to the car. As soon as we got home I kissed him goodnight and went to bed. The moment my head hit the pillow I was out, but the week's drama invaded my sleep. I woke up and glanced over at the clock. 2:28 a.m. Gripping my pillow, I tossed and turned, trying desperately to go back to sleep, but it was no use. I wasn't getting any peace while thoughts of Jared and that text loomed over me. I picked up my phone and typed out a new message.

> When you assume, you make an ass out of you and me. But in your case, making an ass of yourself seems to come naturally. Layla
> **Sent: 2.36**
> **To: The Asshole**

I hit send and immediately wished I could take it back, but it was flying through the world of digital communication. Oh boy, was I in trouble. It was past two and there I was texting him and playing his stupid game. I clearly needed help. I switched the damned thing off and dropped it on the floor before temptation to send another could take hold.

I was in hell, and sleep was clearly not an option. Especially now.

Chapter 8

Toot, Toot. Beep, Beep

    My head was pounding as if someone had taken a hammer to my delicate and fragile skull. I opened my eyes and scanned the room. A small glimmer of light was beaming through the window, and I could hear the chirping of a bird's morning song. Slowly raising my head off of my pillow, I rubbed my sore and tired eyes. They felt heavy, and the sting of another night's restless sleep was beginning to burn into them. I hauled myself out of bed and swung my feet onto the floor. As it landed, my foot hit something, and I glanced down in curiosity. It was my phone.
    Oh. Dear. God. No!
    The events of the previous day suddenly came rushing back through my mind, playing out like a montage in a movie. It was my very own horror flick; the coffee shop, his texts and, oh good heavens, my text. I winced and held my head in my hands. What was wrong with me? He was plaguing my thoughts, and I was encouraging it. He hadn't replied, but I was sure I'd be hearing from him at some stage in the day. Based on what I knew so far, I was fairly sure he'd never let me have the last word.
    Trying to put it all to the back of my mind I showered, dressed, slipped my cell phone into my pocket and went downstairs for breakfast. The massaging beat of the shower

had gone a long way to relieve my headache, and as I entered the hallway I could smell the aromatic fragrance of cinnamon, causing me to hurry down the stairs.

Dad was in the kitchen making pancakes. He beamed at me as he tossed one into the air. It landed with a smack onto the counter top. I stifled a laugh and he smiled over at me with a shrug. I sat at the breakfast bar and poured myself a glass of orange juice. Handing me a plate of pancakes, Dad nudged my hand with his to get my attention.

"So kiddo, what time were you thinking of heading back? Not that I'm trying to get rid of you, I just have something planned for today and need a time scale."

I swallowed a mouthful of pancakes and shrugged. "I don't know. I guess around lunch time if that's alright?" He nodded and slid onto a stool next to me. I loved meal times with Dad. We could talk about anything.

I finished breakfast, kissed him on the cheek and headed across the lawn to Mel's house. I didn't even have a chance to knock on the door as she opened it and hugged me.

"Hey, Lay. So how was your night? Anything interesting happen?" I rolled my eyes at her. She caught me and laughed loudly. "I knew it! I knew you couldn't resist. So fess up. What happened?"

Sitting on her porch swing, I told her about the restaurant and showed her Jared's message. Smiling at me with a wicked grin, she handed the phone back to me.

"I told you, Layla. This guy is into you. Why else would he care if you replied to him? I'd even say he's got it bad. You're obviously in his thoughts as much as he is in yours. So did you send one back?"

I could see the hope in her eyes as she listened to my mini drama unfold. I felt like I was in a soap opera, and Mel was my biggest fan wanting to know every little detail of the storyline. Without a word, I handed her my cell and showed her the "sent" item. Her jaw dropped and she held her hand over her now gaping mouth. Handing me the phone, she shook her head.

"Oh, Layla. Looks like you got it bad, too." I was about to protest, but she held her hand up to silence me. "Deny it all you want. But he's gotten into your head. You said yourself he's gorgeous and, let's be honest, there's not been anyone rummaging through your panties since Josh. I say have some fun. Let him play his game and you play yours. Nothing has to get serious. He's seeing how far he can push you before you break, but you're still springing back at him. That guy wants to crawl all over you, and you'll be panting like a dog in heat when he does. I'd bet my life on it."

As much as I wanted to tell her she was wrong, part of me hoped she was right. He wasn't just hot. He was flaming hot and it had been a long time since I'd been warmed by that kind of fire. It had been months since Josh and I broke up and there had been no one since then. I was a hot blooded woman with needs and Jared seemed to ensnare my senses and invade my thoughts every waking moment. So maybe I could play his game. I sure as hell could use a little fun.

I eyed her playfully and smiled, biting my bottom lip. Her eyebrows bounced up and down suggestively. She knew exactly what I was thinking.

"Oh, Layla. You'll have him on his knees in no time." She winked at me and giggled. We sat for a while, talking about school. Mel's classes were starting on Monday like mine. She was taking arts mostly but had a few English classes thrown in for good measure.

My attention was diverted when I heard Dad call out to me. "Hey, baby girl. I got something to show you. You too, Mel."

We gave each other a puzzled look and strolled across the lawn. Dad was leaning against the garage door with the remote in his hand. He held it out to me as I approached and gave me an enormous grin.

"Go ahead. Open it."

The door whirred and clanked to life as it lifted slowly to reveal a brand new Ford Focus. My chin nearly hit the floor and my eyes darted to Dad. He smiled at me and tossed a set of keys my way. I just about caught them as they flew at me through the air.

It was a beautiful shade of sky blue; the kind of blue that you would see on a clear summer day. The interior was an immaculate black and Dad had already hung a novelty stiletto air freshener on the mirror. I jumped up and down in delight then ran to him, flinging my arms around his neck. He heaved me off the ground and laughed as he kissed my hair.

"I thought it would be best if you had your own car. That way you can come home whenever you like. You can also drive to visit your Mother. I know she's dying to see you."

I was grinning like a lunatic as he set me back onto my feet. "I'll call her later to arrange something. I don't know what to say, Dad. It's amazing. I absolutely love it!" I squealed with enthusiasm and kissed him hard on the cheek. I'd had my license for almost a year now, but the only car I'd driven was dad's and even that was only on weekends to the mall. This little baby was all mine!

I turned to face Mel who was positively glowing with happiness. "You realize, Layla, that now you have absolutely no excuse not to come and pick me up for all those parties you're going to be invited to."

She gave me a hug and we said our goodbyes. We both had to prepare for classes the next day, and Mel hated long goodbyes as much as I did.

I was on cloud nine as Dad and I headed back into the house, but with a sudden bump, I crashed back down to earth. He had made a valid point about Mom and a pang of guilt was creeping up my stomach. We'd spoken over the phone during the week, but our work schedules made it hard to have any kind of real conversation. Now that I had the car, I really had no excuse not to drive to San Francisco. I had decided already that I would go and visit her for a week during winter break, and she was over the moon about it. She started making all kinds of plans for us, like spa days, shopping, dinner and a movie. It sounded wonderful, and I couldn't wait to have some quality mother/daughter time.

By the time Dad had given me a "tour" of the car and I'd packed my overnight bag again, it was almost 3 p.m. I knew I'd need to leave soon or risk hitting the weekend traffic. He walked out to the car with me and I hugged him tightly.

"Thank you so much, Dad. You're the best and I love you."

He opened the driver's side door and indicated to me to slide in before he closed it behind me. I wound down the window and he leaned in to give me a kiss.

"I love you too, baby girl. Now, have a safe journey back. Call me when you're in your room."

I nodded and pulled out of the driveway. Giving him a final wave I began my journey back to college. Back to coffee shops, singing in bars and most certainly another round of verbal boxing with Jared. That last thought had left me with a dangerous smirk on my face. Oh, he really wasn't going to know what hit him.

Chapter 9

Propositions

I parked outside the dorm building and pulled out my cell, sending Dad a quick text to let him know I'd arrived safely. It usually took an hour to drive from home to Long Beach, but the roads had been fairly clear, so it hadn't taken me as long as I had anticipated.

I sat back in my seat and stared down at the phone. Jared still hadn't replied to my message, and now I was the one wondering if he was offended. Had I taken it too far? Cursing myself, I grabbed my overnight bag off the back seat and got out of the car. Letting out a satisfied sigh, I stood back to admire her one last time before turning and walking to my dorm.

I was just putting my key in the door when a strong pair of arms wrapped around my waist. I froze, and my body felt weak. I felt like I was going to faint. This was it. I was going to be attacked just a few feet from the safety of my room. When he lowered his mouth to my ear, and I felt the cool metal of a lip ring, my whole body relaxed in pure relief.

"Hi, superstar. How was your weekend?"

I turned around and shoved him hard. "Oliver, you scared the shit outta me! I thought you were some kind of attacker or something. What the hell?"

He frowned, and his eyebrows pinched together on his forehead.

"I'm sorry. I never meant to scare you. That's the last thing I wanted to do. I'd never hurt you, Layla."

The smell of his hair and the scent of peppermint on his breath swirled and intoxicated my senses as he spoke. Maintaining my ire, I rolled my eyes at him and took a deep calming breath.

"It's ok. I'm fine. Just don't ever sneak up on me like that again. Ok?"

He nodded and then gave a quick salute. "Yes, ma'am."

I smiled, raising an eyebrow as he pulled open the door to our building and held it for me to enter.

Ducking under his arm, I gave him a quick peck on the cheek. "Douche."

He shrugged and grinned at me. "Tease."

I swiveled my head around and poked my tongue out playfully.

"So, Amy told me you spent the weekend back home with your pops."

We were walking through the long hallway towards our rooms. I gave him a satisfied smile.

"It was great. I got to spend time with my best friend, Mel, and Dad took me out for dinner. He got me a car, you know. It's parked out front, the sky blue Ford Focus. I had no idea, so it was a total surprise."

I was practically bouncing up and down as I filled him in on what had happened that weekend. I was gushing, but he humored me, smiling and nodding as I spoke.

"Yeah, I was doing some work on my motorcycle when I saw you get out of the car so I ran over to say hi and I couldn't resist the urge to give you a hug."

He had a motorcycle? Ollie's hotness rating shot up like a rocket. There was something about a guy on a motorcycle that really revved my engine. Maybe it was the idea of having some huge powerful machinery between his legs. Either way, I could imagine Ollie looked smoking hot in his bike gear.

"I didn't know you had a bike. Where is it?" He pointed out of the window across the parking lot to a hot red motorcycle with a sparkling chrome finish. It was enormous and absolutely stunning.

"It's a Ducati Monster. When I got her she was junk, I bought her cheap and decided to fix her up. Took me two years to get her up to scratch, but she's a real hottie, don't you think?"

I nodded in agreement, my cheeks beginning to heat as I imagined his firm thighs straddling the monster. Easy girl, you're just getting to know each other.

"We missed you around here. That party over at the frat house was a total snooze. Amy got really drunk on Cosmos, so I ended up babysitting her all night. I didn't want some boozed up man whore taking advantage, so we left around eleven, and I had to practically carry her back here."

Oliver was a real gentleman. He was the type you heard of, but never actually met. I wondered how the hell he was still single. I mean, he was sweet, funny, caring and smoking hot. How could some girl not have snagged him by now?

Biting my lip I let out a small snicker. "So, Amy kept you busy then. Sorry I wasn't around to help, or laugh at you. I'll be there for the next one. I swear."

He draped his arm around my shoulder and pulled me into his side as we walked. "I hope so, because I am not doing that again. She was totally out of it. She puked on the sidewalk, just outside the frat house. If I hadn't jumped out of her way at just the right moment, my brand new converse would be covered with pink puke."

I couldn't help it. I rolled my head back and laughed so hard that my ribs hurt. He laughed right along with me and we were still giggling when we got to our rooms.

Stopping outside our doors, he gazed at me and ran his fingers through his thick dark hair. "So, I was thinking maybe we could catch a movie tomorrow after class before you head off for work? I'm getting real shit sick of sitting around here. I'll even buy the popcorn. What do you say, Layla? Come hang out with me."

I pondered it for a moment before smiling at him. "Yeah. Sounds great. But I get to pick the movie."

"As long as it's not some tear jerking chick flick then I'm cool with that."

He gave me a tight hug. I was sure he had inhaled my scent as he buried his face into my hair, but I decided not to draw attention to it. Giving me a flirty wink, he raised his hand to signal a goodbye and disappeared into his room.

He really was wonderful. So why didn't I feel the urge to go for it with him? He was my type in every way possible, but he just didn't get my blood boiling or excite me like...

I gasped, realizing exactly where that thought was going.

Oh no. Mel was right. He didn't make me feel like Jared did. That man was trouble for me with a capital T. And tomorrow trouble would be strolling straight through those coffee shop doors. I had to do something about this soon. This back and forth between us was making me feel things that I didn't want to, or at least I thought I didn't want to.

I leaned back against my door and let out an exasperated sigh. Suddenly it flew open and I found myself staggering backwards before landing with a bump on my ass. Laying on the hard wood floor, lost for words, I looked up at a now grinning Amy. A breathless laugh escaped my lungs.

"Well that's twice now that I've ended up on my back around here"

Amy let out a snort. "Nothing wrong with that honey, but next time, make sure there's a warm blooded male on top of you first."

With a wicked smile, she winked and held out her a hand to help me up. Grasping it tightly, I pulled myself to my feet and stood in front of her.

"I'll keep that in mind."

* * * *

Sitting on my bed, the two of us swapped stories about our weekends. Amy filled me in on the frat house party I'd missed and all the hot guys she'd flirted with.

"It would have been perfect, if not for my shadow. Ollie followed me around all night. I swear he thinks I'm a child or something. I don't need babysitting; I was just a little inebriated."

I chuckled and patted her on the shoulder. "I'm sure he was just worried about you being taken advantage of. Think of him more as a concerned friend, than your babysitter. And, come on Amy, be honest. How many Cosmos did you actually have?"

Her cheeks flushed and I realized that it was the first time I'd seen Amy blush. Covering her face with her hands she let out a long sigh.

"About ten or twelve. But in my defense, they were delicious and the pink vomit I'd had to endure later was a small price to pay for an amazing night out."

I fell back on the bed and roared with laughter. I could almost picture Oliver trying to stop her from puking a colorful new pattern onto his shoes.

Wiping the tears that had formed in my eyes, I sat up and shook my head at her.

"Oh, Amy. Don't worry. Next time I promise I'll be there and I'll be the perfect wing woman. Your new shadow can rest easy knowing I've got it covered. I'm pretty sure he and his shoes will be very relieved."

She nudged me with her shoulder and we both laughed. I had really missed her over the weekend. We'd only known each other a week, but it felt like much longer.

"Layla, you can tell me to mind my own business if you want, but how do you feel about Ollie? I mean, there's obviously something between you. I can see it every time you're near each other. You both look ready to jump the others bones."

I shifted awkwardly, not really knowing the answer to that question.

"I don't know, Amy. He's great. Sweet, funny, caring, unbelievably hot and definitely my type, but I don't know. He makes me hot, and when he's near me, Oh. My. God. He's got lips I want to gnaw on and a smile that makes me weak in the knees. Don't even get me started on his come to bed eyes. I bet he's dynamite in bed, but I guess apart from the physical and intense sexual attraction, he's just…Ollie. My friend and the guy I goofed around with at orientation day."

She smiled and shrugged at me. "So basically he pushes all your buttons and gets your motor running. But you don't think he could drive the car?"

Laughing hard at her analogy of my sexual attraction to Ollie I shook my head at her.

"Oh, Amy, that's exactly how I feel. He's a great guy, but I need excitement, fire and passion. Ollie's like the guy next door and in this case he actually is the guy next door. He's the guy you take home to your parents, but I want the guy who's so bad, he's great."

Images of Jared flashed before my eyes.

Fire? Check.

Hot? Scorching hot!

Passionate? He was certainly holding his own so far, and as for excitement, considering the way my body reacted every time he was near me, I'd say he was very exciting.

I glanced at Amy who was watching me with curiosity as I sat in silence drooling over my coffee shop antagonist. I hadn't told her about Jared's message at the restaurant, and I was too embarrassed to admit that I'd texted back. I was just contemplating telling her when, as if on cue, my cell buzzed in my front pocket. She eyed me curiously as she rose from the bed and walked into the bathroom. I shrugged at her and pulled the phone out. There was a message from Jared. I glanced over at the bathroom, but the sound of the shower could be heard even from the bedroom, so I gingerly read the text.

> Well, I must say I was a little shocked to receive your message last night. I was just getting home when I got it. What were you doing up so late? Partying, I suppose? I appreciated the thought anyway. However, pray tell, what have I said to deserve such comment? I was simply being honest. I never intended to upset you in any way. Forgive me?
> **Received: 17.11**
> **From: The Asshole**

Forgive him? A small smile had begun to form on my lips and a shiver of anticipation rushed through me as I frantically typed my reply.

> First of all, I was at home, in bed. Sorry to disappoint, but I'm not much of a party girl. My comments may have appeared harsh, but I was a little irritated at your previous message. $275 is a lot of money for a girl on a part time salary with college supplies to purchase. Food is a must, and I really cannot go without my copy of Cosmo every month. I am willing to forgive and start fresh if you are willing to admit you were an ass.
> **Sent: 17.13**
> **To: The Asshole**

I hugged myself in triumph. I'd played the game, and I felt confident that I was winning. Almost a second later he replied.

> Oh, Layla. I'm flattered and thrilled by the notion that you were in bed thinking of me last night. ;)
> I will admit that my behavior may have been less than gentlemanly, however, "ass" may be a little too strong. $275 is the going rate for a new shirt. Unfortunately, the dry cleaners couldn't remove the stain that is now permanently etched into my garment. As to the payment, I'm sure we can come to some sort of an arrangement. J
> **Received: 17.16**
> **From: The Asshole**

Arrangement? Like a payment plan? My heart was pounding and I could hear it beating in my ears. A shiver of anticipation ran like electricity through my veins. Shaking slightly from the adrenaline pulsing through my veins, I responded.

> Arrangement? What did you have in mind?
> **Sent: 17.20**
> **To: The Asshole**

My hands were sweating as they gripped the phone; I bit down on my lip waiting impatiently for his next message. This was crazy. I hardly knew him and he was turning me into a hot irrational mess without even being in the room. The phone buzzed and I stared at it. I was biting my lip so hard that I could taste the blood from the small incision my tooth had made in the flesh.

Licking it into my mouth, I opened the message:

> I thought we could start with you letting me take you to dinner.
> **Received: 17.24**
> **From: The Asshole**

I gasped, my mouth falling open as my eyes read his words over and over again. Did I really want to do this? He was asking me out. I'd been thinking about him all weekend. My mind suddenly wandered back to the office that morning in the shop: his dimpled chin, penetrating blue eyes, wet shirt clinging to his hard abs and his heart stopping smile.

The more I thought about it, the hotter I felt. My heart wasn't just pounding anymore, it was trying to escape from my chest, thumping hard beneath my ribcage, which was rising and falling rapidly as my breathing quickened.

Taking two long calming breaths, I sent him my reply.

> When?
> **Sent: 17.28**
> **To: The Asshole**

There was no turning back. It was typed, sent and delivered. I imagined the look on his face when he read it, that sexy satisfied smirk. Thinking about it made me utter a girlish squeal of excitement. I glanced over at the bathroom door.

Amy was still in the shower, and I could hear her singing as she always did while she was in there.

Waiting for what felt like an eternity, but was probably only moments, the phone finally buzzed in my hand. I took a deep breath and opened the message. Reading it I let out a loud squeal.

"Oh my god!"

Amy flew out of the bathroom with a towel wrapped around her chest and her hair still had the foam from her shampoo that she had obviously been rinsing from it when I'd yelled.

"What!? What's happened?"

She was looking at me up and down I imagined, checking me for any injury or ailment. My mouth was gaping open and I shook my head. Pulling my gaze away from the screen, I looked over at her and she gawked at me waiting for a response.

"I think I'm having dinner with Jared."

Amy held her hand to her mouth and gasped. "Oh my gosh, Layla. When?"

I suddenly found myself grinning as I re-read his message.

> How about right now?
> **Received: 17.32**
> **From: The Asshole**

I showed it to Amy and she threw her arms around my neck, getting residue shampoo bubbles on me in the process. Releasing me, she jumped up and down, clapping her hands.

"First you have to tell him to pick you up in one hour. Then get your ass in the shower. I have the perfect outfit for you to wear. We'll fix your hair into an up do and give you a little natural makeup. He won't know what's hit him. You're gonna knock his socks off girl! And I'm gonna help you do it."

This was going to be interesting, and I couldn't wait.

Chapter 10

You've Got A Friend

"There. Finished. You look amazing."

Amy lowered the makeup brush and spun me around to face the mirror. I gingerly opened my eyes and gazed in astonishment at my reflection. My once lifeless and frizzy hair was now set into loose curls. Amy had taken a few ringlets and pinned them at the back to give me a beautiful retro beehive. The rest flowed down to sit on my shoulders. It was glossy, and the hairspray made the blonde shade glisten as I moved. My eyes had a smoky effect and the lashes that framed them were long, thick and dark. Amy called them smoldering. My lips were shimmering from the light pink gloss she'd applied.

Bringing my hand up to my mouth, but not covering the gloss, I gasped.

"Amy. It's amazing. I look gorgeous. Thank you so much."

I stood up and hugged her tightly.

"Hey, careful. It took me forever to get your hair and makeup perfect. Don't go ruining it now."

Patting me on the back with both hands, she gave me a gentle shove. Taking my hand, she twirled me around to admire her work. She had been rummaging through her wardrobe for some time before she finally decided on my current outfit.

I was wearing a little black dress. It was strapless and had a sweetheart neckline. With a matching black clutch purse and some silver and diamond earrings, I looked like a model you'd see in a magazine. I'd never dressed that way for anyone or anything for that matter. Even at my prom I wore a simple long line dress that hid my curves well. Mel had called it frumpy, but I didn't care. I wasn't willing to advertise my body to anyone, but this felt different. A knock at the door drew her attention, and she shouted over her shoulder at it.

"Come on in. It's open."

It swung open, and Oliver stood in the doorway. Resting his arm on the frame he leaned into it. His eyes met mine and then made their way down my body slowly before returning to hold my gaze.

"Wow."

It was barely a murmur, but I'd heard him loud and clear. I was hot. Swallowing hard, Oliver gave me a seductive smile.

"You didn't have to get all dressed up for me, but boy do I appreciate it."

My cheeks flushed as I could feel him mentally undressing me with his eyes. Amy gave me a nudge and glared at him.

"Well, she didn't do it for you. She's got a date. I told you at the party, Ollie, you snooze you lose, emo boy. Coffee shop guy snapped her up. He's taking her to dinner."

I rolled my eyes and avoided looking at him. I wanted the ground to open up and swallow me whole. I know Oliver and I had never really got things going, but I couldn't help but remember Friday night at the bar. I had flirted, and only moments ago I'd made plans to go to the movies with him. But that was just to hang out, right? It wasn't a date. Tonight with Jared was most certainly an official date; he'd made his intentions clear simply with the tone of his text. I prayed Ollie didn't think less of me and that he also didn't begin to think that I had been leading him on. It was disturbing, to say the least. I was a great many things, but a tease I was not.

When I finally plucked up the courage to face him again, I could see that he wasn't pleased by the news. His mouth was set into a hard line, and he was standing rigidly with his hands in his pockets. He shrugged and lowered his head, studying the floor before raising his hand to rub the back of his head.

"Well I just came to see if you guys wanted to order a pizza and hang out, but since Layla has plans already, we can do it some other time maybe. And Amy, while we're on the subject since when is my romantic life any of your damn business?"

Amy stood straighter, obviously shocked by his demeanor and fisted her hands on her hips. She opened her mouth about to respond when he turned on his heel, held his hand in the air to signal a wave, walked back over to his room and slammed his door shut.

Shit. I had definitely upset him.

Amy turned her stare at me with her mouth still gaping open, closing it she pointed at the door. "What the fuck was his problem?"

I rolled my eyes and cocked my head to the side. She couldn't be that dim, surely.

"Oh come on, Amy. Have a little respect for his privacy. Whatever you two discussed at that party was probably not meant for me to hear. Plus, I don't think he was that thrilled about me having a date. I did flirt with him all evening at the bar. He must think I'm a total tease, or worse."

Amy was shaking her head at me, and now she was the one rolling her eyes. "Layla, he had his chance to make a move, and he didn't. He can't be sore now, just because he missed his opening."

I felt terrible. I couldn't enjoy my date feeling the way I did.

Grabbing my purse off of the bed and breezing past a stunned Amy, I walked out into the hallway, closing the door behind me. I could hear loud guitar music coming from his room. Swallowing the lump that had formed in my throat, I held my head up and knocked hard on his door. The music stopped, and Nick answered. Holding the door open just enough for him to be seen, he grinned widely at me.

"Well, what are we all dressed up for?"

A voice from behind him snapped a reply. "She's got a date."

Oliver was still pissed at me, that was for sure. Standing on my tiptoes, I yelled over Nick's head.

"Come on, Ollie. Come talk to me. I won't be able to enjoy myself at all tonight knowing you're upset with me. Please."

"You're not exactly giving me any good reason to change my mind now that I know that."

I heard him let out a long sigh and hoped he would reconsider so we could thrash this out and move on. Nick glanced back over his shoulder, obviously waiting for Oliver to give him the ok before moving aside to let me in.

Oliver was sitting on his bed, gripping a white electric guitar which was attached to a large amp. My eyes scanned the room and I realized I'd never been in there before that moment. Every available space was covered in posters of different rock groups. The Ramones, Greenday, All Time Low, Muse and Nirvana were just a few that I recognized. Nick's side was littered with junk food wrappers and he had a drum kit set up in the corner. The room was enormous, and I couldn't quite believe that no one had complained about the noise. Nick left the room, giving Oliver a quick nod as he shut the door.

Looking up from his guitar, Oliver glanced at me with a pained expression. I walked over to his bed and sat next to him.

"Oliver, please don't hate me. You and Amy are the only friends I have here. I mean, that's what we are, right? Friends? Can't you be happy for me? I mean, who else is going to pick me up when I'm spread eagle on a hallway floor?"

He put his guitar down and gave me a sideways look, his long black hair hung in front of his face restricting my view of his delicious brown eyes. Tilting my head so that our eyes met,

I gave him a hopeful smile. I nudged him and he draped his arm around my shoulders, pulling me into his side. I leaned my head on his shoulder and heard him let out a long sigh.

"Ok, Layla. I'm happy for you if that's what you wanna hear. So go enjoy your date, but if he tries anything or gets too heavy handed, you call me and I'll come get you. I mean it."

I nodded and gave him a tight hug, wrapping my arms around his back as I rested my head on his shoulder again.

"I promise I will call you, Ollie."

He stood up and outstretched his hand. Placing my hand into his, he pulled me to my feet. As he opened the door for me to leave, I gave him one last tight squeeze before planting a quick peck on his cheek. I saw him blushing as he raised his hand, in typical Ollie fashion and closed the door.

Relieved that we had now defined our relationship as friends, I could now focus on the knot of nerves beginning to form in my stomach. I cast an eye at my watch. It was almost seven. I checked myself over and straightened my dress before making my way down the hall to the exit. Taking my cell out of my purse I checked if I had any messages.

There was only one.

> I'm parked right outside. Waiting with bated breath for your arrival. J
> **Received: 19.00**
> **From: The Asshole**

* * * *

The butterflies in my stomach were in a frenzied swarm as I walked through the heavy exit doors. Jared was leaning against a beautiful, sleek black car. I didn't have to look twice to know it was a Jaguar XK. Dad had always talked about owning one. It was his dream car. The walls of his study were papered with pictures of the car, and a miniature model in silver sat on his desk. It was not a cheap machine. Jared clearly wasn't scraping by.

Seeing me at the top of the steps, Jared started grinning as his eyes made their way down my body, slowly; as if he were willing my clothes to disappear, leaving my bare flesh for his viewing pleasure. With his eyes fixed on me, I felt naked. He was wearing dark blue denim jeans that had a slight tear design on the right knee. A blue tee was visible underneath his crisp white shirt which was unbuttoned at the top and the sleeves rolled up to rest just above his elbows. I could see the impressive size of his arms, which were practically bursting to be released from the binds of his sleeves.

He strode over to the bottom of the steps and held out his hand.

"Your carriage awaits, my lady."

I smiled and bit my lower lip. It was something I always did when I was anxious or excited. Taking his hand, but being conscious of the five inch heels on my feet, I carefully walked down the three small steps and onto the side walk. Leaning in, he opened my door, and his body was so close I could smell his cologne. I inhaled the scent deeply as he pulled away. It was masculine and it suited him perfectly. Eau de Jared was a heady scent.

I was still swooning over his delicious fragrance when he helped me into my seat. I watched his every move as he ran around to the driver's side and jumped in. I couldn't take my eyes off him. He smiled over at me, turning on the ignition and as the engine roared to life, his smile grew wider.

"Ready?"

I nodded and smiled to myself. For whatever you can dish out, Jared. Bring it on.

As we drove along in silence, I began to wonder how we'd gotten to this moment. It was then that I remembered an important question that needed answering. Looking straight ahead I took a deep breath and asked, "Jared. How did you get my number?"

The corners of his mouth turned up, and he gave me a quick glance before turning his eyes to the road as we sped along.

"Does it matter? Or, better yet, do you actually mind that I have it?"

Cocky Jared had made an appearance once again and surprisingly, I was pleased to see him.

I turned in my seat so that my knees were facing him as I waited for an answer to my question. I wasn't responding to his until he had explained himself. His answer would certainly influence my own.

"I got it from Lorraine. I told her I needed to reach you and discuss financial matters with you in reference to that coffee incident the other day."

My mouth dropped open. I was angry at him again. Turning back to face the windshield, I crossed my arms over my chest and stared out of the window. How could he invade my privacy like that? And why had Lorraine so willingly given him my details? He could have been a stalker for all she knew.

I was suddenly aware that we were pulling over. Turning off the ignition, Jared opened his door and walked around to my side. What was he doing? I watched him curiously as he tapped on my window indicating that I should open the door. I motioned for him to stand back and did as he'd asked. Was he going to throw me out?

I was just about to unbuckle my seatbelt when he crouched down next to me. He held onto the door with one hand and took hold of mine with the other. I couldn't look at him. I knew if I did I would melt and my resolve would weaken. He'd done something that I was not ready to forgive so easily, and he had to know it.

"Layla, I'm truly sorry for invading your privacy like that. At the time, I wasn't thinking clearly. I knew-."

He broke off and stared at the ground below his feet. I found myself gazing at him, wondering what he was going to say. I didn't have to wait long. Exhaling loudly, he looked up and met my gaze. Taking a deep breath, he continued.

"I knew that after the way I'd behaved in the shop, there was no way you would give me your number if I'd asked for it, but I really wanted to talk to you. I wanted to apologize and ask you out right there and then, but you made arguing with you so much fun I just couldn't help myself. Especially when it made you blush the way you are now."

He was giving me that same sexy, smoldering smile I'd seen in the coffee shop. I hadn't even felt my cheeks get warm, but I was certain they were beet red by now. The touch of his hand had sent a jolt of electricity like a bolt of lightning through my chest, and my heart had responded immediately. It was drumming below my now rapidly heaving chest. His eyes were burning through me, almost begging for me to respond, and pleading with me to forgive him. His lips were slightly parted, and I had to fight my uncontrollable urge to kiss him, even though I was sure he wanted me to. His lips were simply tempting me to take them with my own and I wanted nothing more than to oblige him, but I was determined to play it cool.

As though he read my mind, he ran his tongue over his bottom lip and nipped it gently with his teeth. That did it. I couldn't fight it anymore. I hurriedly unbuckled my seatbelt and cupped his face with my hands, pulling him to me. A spark of lustful excitement ignited inside my body as I pressed my lips to his. He responded with the same urgency, running his hand up my arm and around the back of my neck as he pulled me to him with a passionate force. My hands skimmed across his face and ran freely through his golden hair. His tongue traced my bottom lip and my mouth opened, granting him access. He kissed me deeply with a hunger I'd never experienced before.

I pulled away from him, trying to catch my breath. Our eyes met and a smile spread across his face. Running his thumb over my lips, he grinned.

"Does that mean you forgive me?"

I bit my lip, hard. I could still taste him on my flesh. I nodded and released my lip into a smile of my own. "I think we can work something out."

His grin widened and almost reached his eyes. Standing up, he kissed my hand before closing the door. How the hell were we going to make it through dinner?

We drove for what felt like forever, and I wondered where we were going. Apart from the coffee shop and the college campus, I wasn't familiar with the social scene of Long Beach. I glanced over at Jared. He was concentrating intently on the road, and I couldn't help but smile when I noticed him singing along to a song on the radio. He was so quiet it was almost a whisper and he was fumbling over some of the lyrics. I couldn't help letting out a small snigger and I hastily covered my mouth. He shot me a quizzical look and raised one eyebrow.

"Something amuses you, my lady?"

Letting my hand fall back to my lap, I shook my head and cleared my throat. "No, sir. Not at all. I was just thinking that if one is going to sing, one should do so audibly and with correct lyrics."

Now he was laughing. His eyes glimmered with mischief as he gave a nod of acknowledgement before turning the volume up.

Beyoncé's 'All The Single Ladies' echoed through the speakers. Jared began bobbing his head to the music, and as the lyrics to the chorus began, he burst into song. He held up his left hand and began doing the dance, showing me his palm, then the back of his hand and repeating the movement quickly about ten times. I burst into laughter. Clutching my stomach, I continued to watch him as he belted out each word. His head was bobbing left to right along with the music, and his hand was now his microphone. His facial expression was that of a diva performing on stage to millions of fans. My ribs were aching, and my eyes were beginning to fill with tears.

Once the song was finished, he cleared his throat, turned down the radio and glanced at me with a playful smile. He was a blurry outline as I tried to focus through the tears trickling down my face. I tried to stop the rolling laughter that was heaving inside me, but every time I looked at him I fell into hysterics again. This time he laughed with me. I took a few deep breaths and massaged my ribs.

"Was that what you had in mind? I thought I performed rather well myself. However, the audience appears to be of a different persuasion."

I reached over and patted his knee. "Oh, I think you did wonderfully, sir. You were extremely entertaining. Bravo. Encore."

He moved his hand towards the volume control slowly as if he were daring me to stop him. My stomach couldn't take it if I were to laugh any more. Moving quickly, I grabbed his hand and shook my head.

"I was kidding!"

He brought my hand to his lips and placed a soft kiss on my knuckles before returning it to my lap. I reveled in the tender moment we had just shared. He really wasn't the man I had thought he was. The Jared sitting next to me right now was sweet, funny, charismatic and playful; a far cry from the sarcastic, arrogant and rude Jared I had met at the coffee shop.

But somehow, I found them both equally exciting.

A ringing echoed through the car speakers, and pressing his fingertip to the panel on the dash, Jared answered.

"Harrison. I'm not alone."

A deep voice boomed through the sound system, and I sat quietly as they conducted their conversation.

"Understood. I'm sorry to disturb you Jared, but unfortunately, that thing we were concerned about needs dealing with right away. Unexpected turn of events, I'm afraid. I've set wheels in motion, but I fear this may spiral faster than we'd hoped."

Jared's mouth pressed into a hard line, and he slammed his palms on the steering wheel in frustration.

"Damn it! Keep me posted."

After he hung up, we continued the rest of the drive in silence. I didn't want to pry into his business as I felt it was none of mine.

I was still in the dark as to where exactly we were going when we turned onto a road named Victoria Street. The houses were enormous. All lined up in a row, each house was protected by tall iron gates. Some had gravel driveways and others were paved. The houses themselves had a modern appearance and were surrounded by lawns that you'd expect to see at a garden show.

Pulling up to a pair of large black iron gates, Jared leaned over to a security system on the wall adjacent to his door. He quickly punched in a code, and the gates slowly opened, allowing us to enter. The house was the biggest on the street. It was white and had beautiful full length arched windows. The lawn was immaculate, and the edges were decorated with rose bushes. The roses were stunning; their several different shades of pink had me in awe and I found myself staring out my window trying to take it all in.

Parking the car in front of the house, he turned to me and smiled. I was confused. With my brow furrowed, I stared at him.

"Where are we? I thought we were having dinner?"

He gave me a wicked grin. "We are. I told you I was taking you to dinner. I just neglected to say where. Welcome to chez Jared."

He let out a small chuckle and got out of the car, jogging around to my door to open it for me, before taking my hand and assisting me to my feet. He interlocked our fingers and held my hand tightly as he led me into the house.

Once inside, I realized that what I'd seen outside was just the tip of the iceberg. I was standing in the most exquisite foyer I'd ever seen. Glistening crystal chandeliers hung from the high rise ceiling above me. The staircase in the center of the room was perfectly white with a black railing that twisted and wound into a beautiful vine pattern all the way to the top. The floor was white marble with a minimalistic design of small black diamonds evenly set into a pattern across the massive room.

Jared ran his fingers over my knuckles before pressing his lips on my hand. I could feel my cheeks turning crimson again. He had this amazing ability to make my blood boil in fury, but also to make it simmer inside me.

"Would you like a tour?"

I suddenly became aware that my mouth had been gaping open the entire time. I quickly closed it and cleared my throat. Turning my face to him, I nodded.

He led me upstairs and showed me the bedrooms. At one end of the house were three large rooms, each with an adjoining en suite bathroom. They were an impressive size and certainly big enough for two. Each bathroom had his and her basins and deep bath tubs with a chrome and glass shower. The bedrooms were decorated in neutral colors, and I got the feeling that they were intended to be guest rooms.

Jared's hand hadn't left mine since the car, and as he tightened his grasp, I could feel the heat radiating from his palm and pulsing upwards through my hand into my arm. We stopped outside a pair of very large white wooden doors. Taking my other hand in his, he faced me and smiled with a boyish grin.

"This, my lady, is the master suite. This is my room."

Sinfully tempting thoughts ran through my mind as he let go of my hands and opened the double doors.

The room was the size of a small apartment. My heels clanked and clapped as I walked across the stone colored marble flooring to admire the room.

The walls were painted a beautiful pure white and two opposing walls were papered in a cloudy gray. Long crisp golden threaded curtains hung over the full length windows and at the far end of the room, a stunning king size bed took center stage. The white metal head board was decorated with a thick golden edging, and between the bars a plump gold cushion was fixed into the center. Brilliantly white sheets covered the bed and a bright golden throw was draped over the end.

Turning around the room, I saw a luxurious vintage white couch and two chairs that were positioned strategically around a glass coffee table in the corner. Elegant pieces of artwork hung on the walls. One I recognized as a recreation of 'Water Lilies' by Monet. It was one of my favorite paintings, and I walked over to admire it closely.

Staring dreamily at the painting, I became aware of Jared's presence behind me. I could feel the warmth from his body on mine as he placed his hands on my arms and leaned in, speaking directly into my ear. His breath on my neck made me hot and my breath quickened.

"I bought this painting because of its tranquil colors and perfect brush strokes. It's a beautiful piece, don't you think?"

I was speechless. My heart was pounding in my chest so hard that I thought he might hear it. I swallowed hard and turned to face him. Looking into his beautiful tanzanite blue eyes, I responded weakly.

"It's stunning."

I wasn't sure if I was talking about the painting anymore. His eyes were captivating, and I felt lost as I gazed into them.

Never taking his eyes from mine, his hands moved from my arms around to my back, enveloping me in his strong embrace. My hands raised and rested on his shoulders. He leaned forward, his lips barely touching mine; his forehead pressed against my own and he let out a long staggered breath.

"Layla, you are exquisite. This painting in all its elegant wonder could not hold a candle to your beauty. You fascinate me."

I couldn't breathe.

My heart was now pounding so hard that I felt it in my throat. My lips were begging for him to take them and the fire deep inside my belly was growing into a raging inferno. His tongue grazed my bottom lip, and I gasped as he placed a small kiss on my jaw. He trailed more soft kisses down my neck to my collar bone. A soft moan escaped me and I closed my eyes, finding the sensation of his mouth on my skin immensely pleasurable. I raked my fingers through his thick, golden brown hair, gripping it as his lips made their way up my neck again. He traced my lips with his tongue and my mouth opened, welcoming it inside. My own tongue hungrily met his, tasting, feeling and demanding more.

Gently, he pulled his lips from mine and planted another soft peck on my mouth as he nuzzled my nose. Feeling slightly bereft, I exhaled a breath that I hadn't realized I'd been holding. With his forehead once again resting against mine, Jared smiled. It was infectious and I found myself grinning back at him.

"Oh, Layla. What you do to me..."

I rested my hands on his chest and smiled up at him seductively. "I have many things that I'd like you to do to me."

He pulled his face away and eyed me with a shocked expression. Slowly, a wicked grin spread across his face. I stood on my tiptoes and planted a chaste kiss on his lips.

Smiling, I whispered, "Like, right now... I want you to feed me."

Jared let out a breathless chuckle and took my hand, leading me out of the room. "I am happy to oblige, my lady, and dinner is certainly something I can do."

I followed him down the stairs, leaving the temptations and delights I'd experienced in his bedroom behind me. The kitchen was at the far end of the house and was as large as his bedroom had been. The surfaces were black marble and the furnishings were a gleaming white with a high gloss finish. The appliances were a glistening stainless steel, and the floor was a silver laminate. A breakfast bar was situated in the center of the room with three stools pushed in beneath it. It was stunning to behold.

He released my hand and motioned for me to sit at the breakfast bar while pulling out a stool. I couldn't stop smiling. I was really enjoying myself.

He walked around the counter and leaned on his elbows, gazing at me, mere inches from my face. His lips were beautiful and I couldn't stop staring at them as he spoke.

"Welcome to chez Jared. I can serve you anything you want. Italian, Chinese, Japanese, gourmet. Anything your heart desires."

Breaking our connection, he opened a drawer in front of him and took out some pieces of paper, laying them in front of me. I eyed them curiously before throwing my head back and laughing.

"As long as it comes from one of these take-outs."

He was obviously not a cook. I composed myself, smiled at him sympathetically and began browsing a Chinese menu. Out of the corner of my eye I could see him grinning at me. I handed him the menu and gave him a playful smile.

"Surprise me."

It was almost a dare. His grin widened, and I could see he was imagining doing just that.

"Oh, I think I can manage that, my lady. Most definitely. But first let's eat. I want to know everything about you."

Oh be still my beating heart. His voice was dripping with sexy suggestions and I was drooling at the thought of wrapping myself around this man.

Chapter 11

Knowing Me, Knowing You

The food arrived quickly, and Jared insisted that we eat it off of his expensive looking plates, even though I told him I was perfectly happy eating straight from the container. We sat side by side at the breakfast bar. Glancing sideways at me, he wiped his delicious mouth and turned to face me.

"So, Layla, I know you're at college so that makes you what, eighteen?"

I smiled and swallowed my mouthful of rice.

"Nineteen. Being born in October, I had to wait a year to start school. My mom decided she'd rather I go with Mel anyway, for safety in numbers, and I think my dad was just glad to get an extra year to save for my college tuition. He's paying it all, even though I told him I would help once I got a job, but he wouldn't let me. He's a proud man and always says that, as my father, he should be able to provide for me. But anyway, the important thing is I'll be twenty in a few weeks and only one year away from being able to be legally inebriated. What about you? When's your birthday?"

Pushing his plate away, he leaned his elbow on the counter next to him and tilted his head onto his fist.

"I turned twenty two last month. I know what you're thinking, though. How can he look so good for twenty two?"

Giggling I gave him a gentle nudge. Following what he'd done I pushed my plate away and faced him. Our knees were directly opposite each other's. I had to fight the urge to put my hands on them; not that I imagined he'd mind, but I wanted to get to know this man on an emotional level as well as the physical.

"You're only twenty-two? How did you end up living in a place like this? I mean, it's amazing. Did you win the state lottery or something?"

Jared winced a little and I wondered if I'd said something to upset him. "It belonged to my parents. This was their place."

I couldn't help but notice the way he said was their place. His demeanor changed and he visibly stiffened as though recalling a painful memory. I didn't want to press him, but my curiosity hoped he would elaborate. He took a deep breath and straightened up again, rubbing his eyes with his thumb and index finger.

"They died three years ago. Dad was a great businessman. He owned a lot of real estate. Houses, apartment complexes and before he died the company was beginning to construct a mall. When he and my mom passed, I inherited everything. I'm an only child, so there was a lot to inherit. Dad's business, the properties, the house, the car...everything."

I frowned as I saw a grieved expression appear on his beautiful face. Leaning forward on my stool, I took his hand in mine and wound my fingers through his. He gazed at me with an expression I couldn't quite understand. I gave him a sympathetic look.

"That's a lot for a nineteen year old guy to deal with. Especially with college, too. What happened to them? Your parents, I mean. You don't have to tell me, I just thought I'd ask in case you wanted to talk about it."

He took a deep breath and looked down at the floor.

"Mom had a shop in Long Beach. Dad had bought it for her, and it was the first piece of real estate he owned. Anyway, one evening they were at the shop closing up when they heard yelling coming from the place next door. When they checked it out, the clerk was being robbed by a guy in a ski mask. The guy shot the clerk before turning the gun on my parents. Someone across the street saw what happened and called the paramedics and the cops, but by the time they got there it was too late."

I could feel the sting of tears forming in my eyes. He'd been through so much and at such a young age. He looked up at me as a single tear began to roll down my cheek. Raising his free hand, he wiped it away with his thumb and smiled sweetly at me.

"Hey, no tears, ok? This world has enough to make you cry, my pain shouldn't be one of them. I dropped out of college and took over Dad's business, and I'm actually pretty good at it. The mall he was building was completed a year after he died and I have new projects coming up in Europe. I wouldn't say I'm filthy rich, but I can live well on what the properties and the mall rake in.

"Don't be sad for me. I miss them like you wouldn't believe, but I can't live my life while I'm dwelling on the past. It's not what they would have wanted. It took me a long time to realize it, but now I look to my future. All the crying, screaming and anger in the world won't bring them back, so there's no point wasting time and energy on it. Alright?"

I nodded weakly and gave him a half-hearted smile. The icy cold way he spoke about their tragic death left me feeling a great deal of pain for the nineteen year old Jared. Having his life turned upside down, and then inheriting a fortune and a business, must have been so overwhelming. I doubted very much that he'd ever even had time to grieve for them. My heart was aching for him and his loss. He looked so lost, sitting there across from me. At that point, he must have sensed my anguish because he removed his hand from my face and laced his fingers through mine.

I stared down at his strong masculine hand; it was wonderfully intimate. I felt a surge of electricity cracking in the air as he gazed at me with his stunning soulful eyes.

"So, you know about my family. Tell me about yours."

I shrugged.

"Not much to tell. I grew up in Pasadena. Dad's a mechanic and Mom's a nurse. They divorced when I was thirteen, Mom was the one who filed, then she moved to San Francisco. I'm an only child too, but Mel has been my best friend since we were kids, so she's more like a sister. I didn't wanna leave her or Dad when my parents divorced, so I stayed, but I visit my Mom a couple of times a month. Obviously with college I won't be doing that anymore, but I'm going to stay with her for a week during winter break.

"They're both great parents and Dad has always been easy to talk to. Mom's a little more difficult. She gives great advice, but she's not the best listener. She worries a lot. I think the distance between us makes it worse. She's constantly terrified about something awful happening to me. As if I'll be kidnapped, tortured or shot."

Realizing what I had just said, I covered my face with my free hand, screwing up my features in disgust at my insensitive comment. Murmuring through my hand, I apologized profusely.

Gently taking my hand from my face, Jared smiled at me then leaned in to plant a soft kiss on my lips. He took me completely by surprise, and the butterflies in my stomach were fluttering up a storm. His kisses were so warm and gentle; I decided then that I could really get used to him kissing me more often. The thought made me giddy with anticipation and excitement.

"It's ok, Layla. Don't beat yourself up. I can totally understand how your mother feels. When someone you love is hurt, and there is absolutely nothing you can do, it's soul destroying. Let's change the subject shall we? What are you studying at college? Made any friends yet?"

Releasing my hand, he took a sip of his wine. He'd poured us a beautifully sweet and fruity red to accompany our meal. It was a perfect match for the oriental spices and red meat. He certainly knew his wine.

I smiled at myself, wondering how this young sexy male had become so knowledgeable in the art of choosing wine. I cleared my throat, realizing I hadn't answered his question.

"I'm mostly taking psych classes, but I'm taking a couple of English classes too. I love literature. While my friends were out partying in high school, I was curled up on the sofa with my nose in a book. Boring, huh? But now I have a new roommate, and I'm almost positive that with her organizing my social life, I'll have little time for books, or sleep for that matter.

"Oliver is pretty cool, too. He lives across the hall from me and Amy. He plays the guitar, and he showed us a great bar a couple of blocks from campus. I have a feeling it's gonna become our new Friday night haunt. They're the only friends I have there so far."

Jared raised an eyebrow at me and ran his fingers up and down the stem of his glass.

"Layla…Is Oliver gay? Because I would hate to think I have competition, especially with him living just across the hall and all."

Was he jealous already? This was only our first date. I stared at him, puzzled. He must have seen the look of confusion on my face because he stood up and gazed down deep into my eyes. Lifting my chin up to look at him, I saw his serious expression.

"I just need to know if I've got a fight on my hands. I really like you, Layla. I like you a lot, and I want to see more of you, but I won't share your affections. It's all or nothing. If you have anyone else in your life, I'll walk away tonight and never bother you again. I won't fight for a woman who belongs to someone else."

Standing up I pressed my hands against his hard chest. Returning his gaze I shook my head. "There's no one else Jared. I don't share either. I'm a one man woman, and I expect the same from the men I date. If you can promise me that, then I can guarantee that while I'm dating you there will be no one else. Oliver is a friend and that is all he'll ever be."

I really hoped I could believe what I'd said. There was no denying the chemistry between Ollie and I, but what I felt for Jared was more than just physical.

It was intense.

"Good girl. That's exactly what I wanted to hear." Tilting my head up with his hand holding my chin, he lowered his lips over mine and kissed me deeply. He kissed me with a carnal hunger I'd never felt before. It was clear that he wanted me, and I wanted him just as much. I kissed him back with the same urgency. I needed him. I ran my hands up his chest and wrapped them around his neck, pulling him closer to me. Cupping my face with his hands, he let out a soft moan. My knees weakened and my breathing quickened.

Jared must have felt my sudden weakness because his hands wrapped around my waist, holding me tightly. Without removing his lips from mine, he lifted me up and sat me down on the counter top. I wrapped my legs around his waist, pulling him against me. His hands wandered from my middle to my knees, slowly sliding up my thighs and going underneath my dress before settling around on my behind. He pulled me to the edge of the counter and, removing his lips from my mine, trailed kisses down my neck. I moaned loudly with pleasure as he reached my collar bone. His lips travelled further south to my chest and down to my cleavage.

I leaned back slightly, granting him better access to my breasts. Arching my back, I steadied myself with my hands as I gripped the counter. His hands slid out from beneath my dress and were now wrapped around my back. Pulling me back up to him, his lips made their way up my neck then to my face. The two of us were breathing heavily as our eyes met. I was completely aroused. My skin was screaming to be touched, and my breasts were fully aware of his proximity to them. I could feel my nipples harden beneath my dress. I ached for him.

I knew I'd been having the same effect on him as I could feel his erection pressing against my thigh. I had to fight to control my urge to release it and beg him to take me there on the counter. He took a long calming breath and rested his forehead against mine. I could feel his hot breath on my face. I was sure it was flushed from the heat radiating inside my body.

"Oh, Layla. You have no idea how much I want to scoop you up in my arms, carry you upstairs and do bad things to your hot, curvy body. Very bad things. But what I want to do to you could linger on for hours into the night, and you have classes tomorrow."

He was right. Caught up in my desire for him, I'd completely forgotten about classes. Hell, I'd forgotten my own name! I let out a disappointed sigh. He opened his eyes and gave me serious look.

"Don't pout, Layla. Education and knowledge are valuable assets. Don't take them for granted."

It was almost a command and for some unknown reason I found it highly exciting.

"I'll take you home."

Licking my lips, I smiled at him seductively. He took a step back as I slid myself forward and off the counter. Reaching for my hand, which I gave him willingly, he led me outside to the car. Pausing for a moment, he faced me.

"I'd like to see you again tomorrow night, say seven?"

I nodded as he brought my hand to his lips and planted a gentle kiss on the back.

The drive home was quiet, and I often caught him glancing over at me as he drove. I couldn't help steal looks at him myself. He was delicious. He was chocolate ice-cream, strawberries and cream, caramel lattes and everything I found most tempting. He pulled up outside the dorms and ran around to my side to open the door.

Taking my hand, he helped me to my feet.

"I had a wonderful time tonight. I'll see you tomorrow. I'll pick you up right here. Wait for me to contact you."

He leaned in and kissed me deeply before letting me go. I wished him a goodnight, kissing him back. Walking in a daze to the doors, I looked back at him and playfully blew him a kiss. He grinned and held his hand to his chest, pretending my kiss had hit him in the heart like an arrow. I chuckled at him before turning away and heading inside.

When I got inside, I wandered down the hallway with my head in the clouds. Well, not quite in the clouds. My mind and my heart were still standing with him on the sidewalk outside. I almost missed my room, except a hand had reached out, grabbed me by the arm, and pulled me in. Amy was standing in front of me, wearing a pair of pink spotted pajamas and fluffy kitten heel slippers. With her hands fisted on her hips, she was glaring at me.

"What time do you call this? It's almost midnight. And did I just see what I thought I saw? Because honey that was capital H-O-T, hot! From that goofy look on your face, I assume it went well?"

I grinned at her and fell onto my bed. "Oh, Amy. He's wonderful. He's sexy, smart, funny, successful, and oh my god, he can kiss. I have never felt like this before. I'm seeing him again tomorrow night."

Her mouth flew open and she took a sharp breath. "Oh my god, Layla! You lucky little minx! Well I'd say that man is hooked on you and has been ever since you backed your ass into that door. Maybe that's why he never saw you coming. He was too busy staring at your ass through the glass."

I laughed and hurled my pillow at her. She chucked it right back, and we both fell into hysterics. Composing myself, I slid out of my dress and into a night shirt. My cell phone buzzed inside my bag making it move across the bed as if it were possessed. I took it out and opened the message.

> Counting down the hours till I shall see you again. Sweet dreams. J xx
> **Received: 23.34**
> **From: The Asshole**

A girlish squeal escaped my lips, and I hugged the phone to my chest. Amy eyed me quizzically.

"What did he say?"

I wasn't sharing this with her. This was mine, and I wanted to hold the moment captive forever.

"Oh nothing. Just wishing me a goodnight."

Quickly changing his name in my contact list, I placed the phone on my bed side cabinet and yawned loudly.

"I'm really tired, and I gotta get up for class in about seven hours. Goodnight, Amy."

Raising her eyebrows at me she shook her head. She wasn't buying my "Just wishing me goodnight" story one bit, but she obviously respected my privacy because she didn't press me for information. Wishing me a goodnight, she switched out the light. The sooner I slept, the sooner tomorrow would come, and I would be with him again.

The thought brought pleasant memories to my mind, and I welcomed them as I began to drift off to sleep. Sweet dreams indeed. Sweet dreams of Jared, the white and gold bedroom, the kitchen counter and whatever tomorrow night would bring.

Chapter 12

The Boss

I made my way through the crowded college halls to my first class. Coming to a halt outside Room 108, I checked my schedule. Doctor K. Harman, Psychology, Room 108. I was definitely in the right place. Nervously, I opened the door and scoured the room for Oliver's familiar face. Two rows from the back I spotted him. His hand was waving frantically at me to come over. Giving him a relieved smile, I waved back and made my way to the seat next to him.

"Hey, superstar. Ready for this?"

Slumping into my seat, I grinned. "Most definitely! I can't wait. What about you?"

He shrugged and gave me a bump with his shoulder. "I dunno, it's only a matter of time before we all learn too much and come to the conclusion that we're all total whack jobs, right? Men in white coats will be carting us off in no time. But I promise I'll still visit you when you're drugged up and drooling."

I laughed and nudged him back. "Good to know."

Before I knew it, the whole 3 hour class had flown by. Maybe it was because I'd spent at least half the time thinking about Jared and the other half laughing at our professor with Oliver. Doc. Harman had made the mistake of wearing a long white doctor's coat to class and Ollie and I simply couldn't control ourselves. We sniggered and joked throughout the entire class, getting irritated looks from some of the other students, but Oliver simply brushed them off with a shrug and a "what are you looking at?" glare.

He was quickly becoming one of my best friends. We had the same sense of humor, taste in music, and we'd even discovered that we shared the same taste in movies. I told him my favorite was Constantine, and he'd enthused how that was his too.

Sauntering out of the class and into the crowded halls once more, Ollie walked close beside me and draped his arm over my shoulder.

"So, how was your date? I hope he behaved like the perfect gentleman."

I smiled bashfully. Ollie spotted it and rolled his eyes.

"Oh I see. It went well then? Seeing him again?"

I leaned into him and sighed. "It was great. I had a really good time. He was a perfect gentleman. In fact, it went so well that I'm seeing him again later tonight. I just have to get through my afternoon shift at the coffee shop first."

Ollie pressed his lips to my hair and kissed me.

"I'm glad you had a good time, Layla. You deserve the best." I was lying, of course. What he was doing to me on top of that counter was not chivalrous, but Ollie didn't need to know all the intimate details of my evening. I got the feeling he still wasn't quite in the friend zone yet, but I hoped he'd get there soon and I hoped that I would join him.

* * * *

The movie theatre wasn't the usual hustle and bustle, but I was secretly relieved. I just wanted to hang out and enjoy some down time with Ollie before work, and speeding through lines was definitely going to help that. Ordering a large popcorn, Ollie grabbed my hand, entwining our fingers.

"Don't want us to get separated in this crowd."

I glanced around at the desolate foyer and shoved him playfully. "Any excuse to get your hands on me, Oliver Green."

He blushed, but played it down by mischievously dragging me through the hall to the theater. He was practically running, and I had to jog to keep up, giggling as I did so. I loved hanging out with him; we had so much fun together. Ollie loved the classic movies almost as much as I did. We also had a love for indie and alternative rock, though we did each confess to being classic rock fans in the privacy of our bedrooms.

The choices I had for our viewing pleasure were slim; especially since I couldn't bear to put Oliver through an entire ninety minutes of a girl dying of a broken heart and everyone crying. I went for the resident horror flick instead, knowing very well that I would be watching most of it through the gaps in my fingers as I pressed my palms over my eyes, shielding them from the gore and violent scenes. This, of course, entertained and amused Ollie endlessly as he sat there munching on popcorn.

At one particularly scary part of the movie, I had just lowered my hands when the murderer performed a very sick and gory act on his victim with a long blade. I let out a scream and gripped on to Ollie's hoodie, burying my head in his chest for comfort and safety. I felt his arms wrap around me as he pressed his lips against the top of my head.

"We can leave if you like; if it's too scary for you."

Being in his arms felt so natural, as though we'd been doing it for years. I felt completely at ease, brave enough to continue to watch what was happening on the screen. With my head on his chest, I could smell the fresh scent of soap and something else that I couldn't quite place. It was sweet and fruity and I assumed that it must have been his natural scent as I had never found cologne that smelled quite like that.

Peering up at him I smiled. "Just don't be surprised if I end up using your chest as a shield when the scary things happen."

He pressed his lips against my forehead and smiled. "My pecs are your pillow."

Begging Oliver to walk me to work was a low point even for me. The movie had left me a little shaken and cautious of everyone; just the way a good horror flick should leave you feeling. Joking, laughing and recalling my many jolts of fear during the movie, we walked the short distance to the coffee shop. Pausing outside, he wrapped me in a tight embrace, swaying from side to side as he did. Pulling away, he gripped his hands on my arms and smiled.

"I had fun today. We should totally do it again, make it a regular thing. You, me, popcorn and a movie. What do you think?"

Giving him a quick peck on the cheek, I nodded. "I think it's a great idea. I really loved hanging out just the two of us. It was fun."

Glancing behind me, I looked through the window of the shop and realized that my shift had started five minutes before. Giving Oliver another quick hug, we said our goodbyes and I walked through the glass doors.

* * * *

I made my way out to the back room to store my things away in one of the lockers. I heard a pair of heels clattering in the direction of the door, and Kate entered a moment later.

"Hey, Layla. Just a heads up, the boss is in today. He wants to look over the books and make sure everything's running in tip-top form. I'm guessing that means meeting the new girl, too."

Kate had worked at Lorraine's for a year now and was the most interesting girl I'd ever met. Friendly and helpful, she was a breath of fresh air during a hectic shift. Her dark hair and pale skin made her look like a china doll, but she was far from it. She had a wicked sense of humor, a filthy mind, and she cursed like a guy which didn't bother me. In fact, I found it rather amusing.

She patted me on the shoulder before propping herself up against the lockers to face me.

"Just so you know, he's a total hottie! But from what I've heard he doesn't do the whole dating thing, so try not to fall too hopelessly in love with him, ok?" She gave me a wink.

Laughing at her, I tilted my head and smiled. "Actually, I don't think that's going to be a problem. I had a date last night with an amazing guy and I'm seeing him again tonight."

Her mouth dropped open, and she shoved me on the shoulder playfully. "Good for you, girl! Only been here a few days and snagged yourself a man. Way to go."

The commotion of the afternoon rush of students filing into the coffee shop distracted us. Kate's head rolled back and she groaned. Glaring at the door, she pulled her long hair back into a ponytail before glancing over her shoulder at me.

"Well, better get out there before a riot breaks out."

Tying my apron around my waist I followed her out.

Two hours later, the student mob that had descended upon us had settled down, and the shop was beginning to empty when Lorraine came into the front of the shop.

"Layla, the boss man would like to see you in the office, please. He wants to meet you properly and talk about how you're doing. It was really ideal conditions to do it on your first day. Don't worry, he won't bite."

Shooting Kate a nervous and confused look, I made my way through to the back. He was here before? As I glanced back over my shoulder at her, she gave me a sympathetic smile. Butterflies were swarming inside my stomach. What if he didn't like me? What if he decided I wasn't someone he wanted working at Lorraine's coffee shop? A hundred worrying thoughts ran through my mind as I approached the office door.

Taking a deep breath, I knocked lightly. The door swung open, and I gawked in total shock and horror.

"You!"

Standing in front of me, wearing a gray suit with a black silk tie, was a smoldering Jared. He beamed at me, but the distress on my face must have been apparent to him because his smile disappeared instantly.

"You're Mr. Garrett? You're my boss? You own Lorraine's and you never thought to tell me? How could you not tell me? Do you get some kind of sick pleasure out of humiliating me?" I was rambling frantically and furiously.

Jared stretched out his hands to me, but raising my own in front of me in warning, I recoiled and backed away. I was furious with him. He'd had every opportunity to tell me the truth, but instead he'd kept it to himself just to humiliate and embarrass me at work. He stared at me, and I could see the regret painted all over his gorgeous, perfectly chiseled face.

"Layla, calm down. I was going to tell you last night, but it never felt like the right moment. I didn't do it to humiliate you in any way. Please let me explain."

I shook my head and glowered at him.

I turned to leave, but his hand seized my elbow, and he hauled me into the office. I grabbed at his hand and shoved it away from me. I was breathing heavily as my body quaked with fury. I was pissed at him and I was in no mood for his games.

"There is no explanation you could possibly give me to excuse the fact that you lied. And don't give me that crap about no opportunity. You could have told me the first day I met you, or you could have told me when you came in for coffee the following day. You could even have told me last night, but I guess you were too busy trying to get into my underpants to consider how I might feel once I found out you're my boss!

"No, Jared. I will not let you explain. Now, if you'll excuse me, Mr. Garrett, I have to go back to work. I may even stay for the late shift to allow Kate to leave early. It's not as if I have any plans this evening."

My goading had struck a nerve. His expression had darkened and it wasn't remorse anymore. Now he was irritated.

We stood there for a moment, just glaring at each other. I could feel the sting of tears pricking my eyes and I did not want him to see me cry. I stormed towards the door, but before

I reached it Jared was there, blocking my exit with his rock hard body. I tried to push him out of my way, but he was as solid as stone. Thumping my fists against his chest in frustration, I growled at him.

"Jared, get out of my way! We're done here. We're done period. Let me go, please." He gazed down at me without budging an inch.

I ran my fingers through my hair feeling totally exasperated. He reached out quickly and caught my wrists, gripping them tightly in his hands.

"Layla, stop being so damn melodramatic. It's not an attractive trait. I said I'm sorry for not telling you, and I mean it. I thought if you knew you'd never agree to go out with me, which is absurd because I'm not even really your boss. I'm more like the silent partner. This was my mom's shop. All I do is handle the finances. I was wrong not to tell you, but it really isn't a big deal. It doesn't change anything between us."

I shook my head and glared at him as my voice trembled with the anger and unshed tears building inside me. "It changes everything!"

Twisting my wrists free from his grasp, I pushed him out of my way and ran into the ladies room, locking myself in a stall before burying my face into my hands and sobbing. How could he have done this to me? I thought he was different. The Jared I'd been with the night before was now just a painful memory. How could he believe it didn't change anything? He was my employer, he issued my pay check. We could never be equals now.

The unmistakable squeak of the bathroom door opening caught my attention.

"Layla? You in here, sweetie? I saw you run out. Are you alright?"

It was Kate. I took a deep breath, grabbed some toilet paper and began dabbing my eyes as I sauntered out of the stall. Sniffing a little through my tears, I glanced over at her.

She gave me a concerned look before wrapping her arms around me for a hug.

"Oh, sweetie, what happened? Was he a jerk to you? He didn't fire you, did he?"

I shook my head and pulled away from her embrace. Wiping my nose I exhaled loudly.

"No. It's nothing like that. He's a head and heart fuck, not a jerk. You remember I told you about the amazing guy I went out with last night?"

She nodded and began to run some water in the basin.

"Well it's him. Jared is Mr. Garrett. I had no idea he was my boss. He lied to me."

Kate's jaw dropped, and she clasped her hand over her mouth, staring at me she shook her head. "You're kidding. Oh my gosh. What a tool! Although, technically, he didn't lie. He just neglected to tell you. I understand you're upset and hurt, but does it really matter that he owns this place? I mean, he owns the business, but its Lorraine's place. He only comes in here to get coffee and check the books once a month. If you like him that much it really shouldn't be an issue, honey. Did he give you a reason why he never told you?"

I told her the reasons Jared had given me for his deceitfulness, and she listened attentively, nodding and giving me understanding looks throughout. When I was finished, she pulled me in for a hug. I rested my head on her shoulder and heard her let out a small sigh.

"Oh, Layla. You really are crazy."

I pulled away and stared at her in total bewilderment. Had she not been listening? Taking a small rag from her apron, she soaked it in the basin of cold water before going to work on my makeup smeared, red and blotchy face. Shaking her head at me again, she tutted.

"Layla, Layla, Layla. He made a mistake. He's a guy. They do that shit all the time. Hell, we women are no better. Think of it this way. If you forgive him for this, when you mess up you'll have leverage. But bottom line here, sweetie, you like him, he likes you, just start fresh and give him a chance. What have you really got to lose?"

She had a valid point. I did like Jared. I liked him a lot, and the thought of not feeling his arms around me, never feeling his lips on mine, or the thrill of pleasure that ran through me when he was around, was frightening. But if there was even a slight chance that I would forgive him, he was going to have to work much harder than an apology in the back room of the coffee shop. Stepping back, she gave me a small smile.

"There, all cleaned up. Now get your ass back out there and show that prick that he's not getting the upper hand. Flaunt that sexy little ass of yours right in his face. Make him suffer for his stupid behavior."

Winking at me, she turned and walked out, leaving me alone with my thoughts. I looked at myself in the mirror. Kate had cleared me up so well you couldn't see a trace of the tears that were running down my cheeks just moments before. Inhaling deeply, I straightened my clothes and walked back out into the shop.

When I entered the shop floor, I spotted him sitting at a table opposite the counter with Lorraine. They appeared to be going through the receipts that she had collected at the end of every shift. I was acutely aware of his eyes on me as I made my way past his chair to the counter.

Kate was watching me as I approached and gave me a knowing smile. Standing behind the counter, I tried desperately not to look at him, but it was almost impossible. His suit jacket was hanging off the back of the chair and his shirt sleeves were rolled up to his elbows. He'd loosened his tie and was leaning back with his hands behind his head. There was something hypnotic about a man in a suit. It heated my blood and called to me deep inside.

He glanced over at me, and a shock of electricity hit me as our eyes met. Damn, he'd caught me. Turning to Lorraine he said something I couldn't quite hear. She waved me over.

"Layla, dear. Could you come here a moment?"

Shit, now he'd use Lorraine to win me over. Knowing I couldn't avoid him this time, I took a calming breath and made my way over to the table.

I stood there rigidly as Lorraine smiled sweetly at me and leaned forward across the table.

"Would you be so kind and bring us some coffee, dear? I'll have my usual and whatever Jared would like. Thank you, sweetie."

Rolling my eyes, I turned to face him. A playful grin was spreading across his face, and it irked me. I tapped my foot impatiently and glared at him. He was enjoying this far too much.

"I'm sure you can make the right choice for me, Layla. I have faith in your judgment, and knowing exactly what I want."

It was oozing with sexual suggestion. I was beginning to feel my cheeks warm, and he was certainly enjoying watching me squirm. Shooting him an evil glare, I turned on my heel and walked back to the counter, cursing him under my breath. Jackass.

Kate eyed me as I stepped around the partition. "What was that about?"

Grabbing two cups from beside her, I rolled my eyes. "Asshole thinks he can get around me. They want coffee and he is using it as an opportunity to manipulate my feelings and make sexual innuendos. Again."

Kate snickered and handed me a teaspoon. "Well, I'd say he's having some effect on you already. Your face is as red a stop sign. What the hell did he say?"

I told her about his "faith in your judgment and knowing what I want" comment. She stifled a laugh and seeing my irritated expression, used her hand to gesture zipping her lips.

I made Lorraine her usual cappuccino and something for Jared that I felt was appropriate. Taking them over, I smirked to myself. Two could play this game. Jared was watching me attentively as I approached the table.

"One cappuccino with extra foam for you Lorraine. And for you Jared, a chilled Frappuccino." Lorraine thanked me before taking her coffee and flicking through a file on the table. Jared was staring at me with a mischievous smirk lingering across his lips.

"And what made you choose the Frappuccino for me Layla?"

I smiled pleasantly and put on the best acting performance of my life. "Well, Mr. Garrett, I thought the refreshing iciness would help cool you off. Plus it's a favorite of mine. It's simple, uncomplicated, and most importantly, it's honest."

Bam! How do you like that, Mr. Garrett?

I mentally hugged myself for my sheer brilliance. Jared raised an eyebrow at me.

"Touché, Miss Jennings."

Walking away, I grinned with satisfaction. Round one to Layla Jennings.

Chapter 13

Crazy

Following through with my threat to Jared, I told Kate I would stay and do her late shift, allowing her to get an early night. She thanked me profusely and gave me a tight hug, whispering a warning in my ear. "Don't take any of his shit Layla."

She nodded at Jared and winked at me before grabbing her things and leaving.

The shop was quiet. The usual evening rush was over, and all that was left was to clean the machines and the shop floor. I glanced over at Lorraine and Jared. They'd spent the best part of the afternoon pouring over the accounts. Lifting her glasses off of her face, Lorraine rubbed her eyes and yawned. Jared rested his hand caringly over hers and smiled.

"You look beat, Rainy. We're pretty much done here, why don't you take off and I'll lock up?"

Oh shit. Oh shit. I was going to be alone with him in the shop. I prayed that she would decline, but hugging him tightly she thanked him and gathered her things. Jared's eyes darted over to me standing behind the counter. I looked away, pretending to busy myself with arranging the cups in size order. This was not good. Without anyone at the shop to act as a buffer, I would have to face him, and I wasn't sure how long I could hold my reserve.

* * * *

Somehow, I managed to avoid him like the plague for the rest of my shift. I'd spent so much time cleaning the coffee machine that it was now gleaming like a NASA space shuttle inside and out. He hadn't tried to speak with me or even approach me since Lorraine left. Maybe he'd decided I wasn't worth the effort? The thought irked me. After all, he was the one who had been dishonest.

The final customers were a couple of teenage girls who had been studying for the past three hours. Pulling down the blinds, Jared informed them that we were closing and after shooting him a dreamy smile, they left the shop.

He locked the doors behind them. We were alone. The air between us was thick with things that needed to be said, but neither of us breathed a word.

I busied myself with cleaning the counter top as he gathered up all his books and papers from the table he and Lorraine had been occupying. I could feel him watching me, and I desperately tried to avoid the temptation to look at him. His cell phone rang and with an exasperated sigh he answered. His face turned dark, and I could see that whatever the call was about, it was making him angry.

Breezing past me he walked into the office and slammed the door behind him. The loud bang made me flinch, but I breathed a sigh of relief. What was going on? The call in the car, his irate demeanor he adopted as he answered that call...I was baffled, but grateful for the distraction as it meant I could finally finish cleaning the shop and get the hell out.

Reaching underneath the counter, I turned up the stereo and the speakers began pumping music into the empty room. Kate's usual classic rock filled the shop with electric guitar and heavy bass lines. Grabbing my rag and some cleaning fluid, I made my way around the floor wiping tables and picking up empty cups. Swaying to the music, I lost myself in my task and tried to forget about the smoldering sex god who was currently barricading himself in the office.

I was just leaning over one of the corner tables when I became aware of his presence in the room. The air buzzed with the tension that was between us whenever we were together. It was electric. I tried to steady my breathing, not wanting him to know how his mere presence in the room affected me.

I continued cleaning, hoping and praying he would turn and go back into the office, but he didn't. Grabbing the empty cups from the table, I walked over and placed them on the counter. Jared was standing against the far wall behind it. His hands were gripping onto the edge and his legs were crossed at the ankles. I had to remind myself not to stare, but he was so tempting. His tie was gone, leaving his shirt unbuttoned a fraction so that I could see a little of his hard muscular chest. I could feel that familiar fire simmering inside my belly. If he tried to touch me, I feared I'd ignite into a blaze of lust and passion. But he didn't. He just stood there, watching me clean.

As I reached the last table, a familiar song played loud and clear through the speakers. 'Crazy' by Aerosmith. It was one of my favorites, and I'd usually be swaying my ass around to it by now, but I wasn't in the mood to dance.

I felt him before I heard him; he was right behind me. My body stood to attention and stiffened. My breathing quickened, my heart thundered inside my chest and my face began to heat. His breath was on my neck as he pressed his mouth to my ear. He was singing the lyrics in his deep and smooth voice, and it drove me wild. His hands slid down my waist to my hips, gripping them tightly as he began to sway them against his own.

My legs turned to jelly, and every nerve ending on my body was acutely aware of his touch. Letting my head fall back against his chest I closed my eyes, taking pleasure in the sensual sound of his voice. His scent engorged my senses. He smelled delicious; like soap and sex, sheet clenching, pillow biting sex, and Jared. His hands tightened around my waist as he trailed tender kisses down my neck. I ran my own hands through his thick hair as his soft warm lips caressing my skin.

The sexual tension was building rapidly between us like a train gaining momentum.

Spinning me around to face him, he cupped my face with his hands and pressed his lips to mine with an urgent hunger. I was losing control of my senses as lust and need took me over. My hands made light work of his shirt buttons as I quickly tugged and ripped them apart before pulling it down his strong arms. Momentarily releasing me, he dragged the sleeves from his wrists and tossed the shirt aside. His eyes were dark and hooded, his arousal obvious as his erection pressed against my hip.

Grabbing the waist of his slacks, I yanked him to me while his fingers hurriedly untied my apron. He kissed me hard, thrusting his tongue into my welcoming mouth. Overcome with carnal hunger for him, I bit down on his lip, and he let out a low and primitive groan.

"Oh, Layla. I swear I'm going to make it all up to you. I'm going to make it up to you right now."

Grasping my behind, he picked me up, and I wrapped my legs securely around his waist. Holding onto my aching body with his strong and powerful arms, he carried me to the leather sofa and sank onto the seat. I sat straddling him and began running my hands eagerly over his bare chest. It was perfectly sculpted as if it were carved by an exceptionally skilled artist. The lines and contours ran deep, and his caramel colored skin looked good enough to eat. The deep V that defined his torso made me lick my lips in anticipation of what was currently being confined beneath his zipper.

His hands tugged at the bottom of my work tee and he slipped it easily over my head, revealing my simple black lace bra. He stared at me for a moment, his eyes drinking me in as he reached his skillful fingers behind me and expertly unhooked my bra. Peeling it from my body, his hands moved teasingly over my breasts, cupping, massaging and caressing them; making me moan with pleasure.

An aching throbbed between my legs as I arched my back and his hand slid around to support me, gliding down the full length of my spine. Leaning forward, his mouth found my breast, and I gasped as he gently nibbled on my hard, sensitive nipple before rolling his tongue around and over to soothe the hurt his teeth had caused.

I drew myself up to face him and fumbled for his zipper. I could feel his hard length against my thigh, begging to be released. He thrust his hips upwards to allow me to pull down his pants and shorts. Springing free, I caught hold of him and moved my hand up and down the shaft of his solid, throbbing cock. Every inch of him was hard and delightfully rigid. He gasped and rolled my skirt up, creasing it as it gathered around my hips. Gliding his hands over my bare thighs, he deepened our kiss with a lascivious need.

"I want you so much. I ache for you."

The feeling was mutual.

Tugging my panties aside with one hand he reached into his pocket with the other and produced a foil packet. Taking it from him, I ripped it open impatiently with my teeth. Gripping him firmly, I continued to stroke my hand up and down his hard length before carefully sliding the condom over him. Gazing into his eyes, I held on tightly to the back of the sofa with both hands as I lowered myself onto him slowly. His head fell back as his lips parted to make a perfect O. With his hands grasping my hips tightly, I began to slide up and down, enjoying every last inch of him bit by bit as he filled me. I could feel his tip stroking a sensitive spot inside me, causing ripples of lip biting, orgasmic pleasure to flow through me.

Skimming his fingers teasingly from my hips to my breasts, his eyes fixed on mine; penetrating even deeper than where we were currently connected in erotic harmony. I moaned softly, reeling in the intensity of my orgasm as it drew tantalizingly closer. Gripping the sofa even tighter, I began to increase my speed. Jared slid his hands around to my back and pressed me to his chest so close I could feel his hot breath on my neck as he gasped and panted for breath.

"Come on, Layla. Give it to me. I want it badly. Come for me baby."

Pressing his mouth firmly to mine, he grazed my lips with his own and let out a loud moan. It was the push I needed. My breath quickened, and my heart pounded like a drum inside my chest as my orgasm surged through me like electricity through a wire. Panting, I was unraveling in his arms as the waves of pleasure continued to pulse and ripple inside me. I could feel my muscles tightening around him as I continued to move.

Moaning through clenched teeth and gasping, he gripped my thighs firmly as he found his release.

"Oh, Layla."

Stilling, I buried my face in his neck, inhaling his enchanting scent as he held me tightly to him. His hand caressed my hair gently as we both struggled to calm our ragged breathing.

"Oh, Layla. What on earth are you doing to me?"

Placing my mouth next to his ear, I breathed hard. "I imagine the exact same thing you do to me, Jared. You drive me crazy."

Turning his head to face me he gazed into my eyes. Raising his hand, he swept a strand of hair from my face and placed it behind my ear. Cupping my face in his hands, he pulled me in for a deep, lingering kiss. He was casting a spell over me and I was powerless to stop it. I wasn't sure I even wanted to. He was intoxicating, and I was drunk with desire for him.

Lying on the sofa with one hand behind his head, Jared stroked my hair as my head rested against his firm muscular chest. Teasing my fingers lightly over his perfectly sculpted abs, I sighed with pure satisfaction.

"Does this mean I'm forgiven?"

Raising my head I rested my chin on his chest.

"I wouldn't say I forgive you, but I'm willing to let it go. Just don't ever lie to me again, Jared. I won't allow a man to run around on me again. I learned my lesson the first time."

He gazed at me and ran his thumb over my cheek.

"I would never knowingly cause you emotional pain, Layla. If you never believe anything else I say, you must believe that."

I smiled at him before lifting my face to his and planting a chaste kiss on his luscious lips. Sighing, he looked around the room and chuckled.

"We'd better find our clothes and fix this place up for tomorrow. Otherwise, Lorraine's gonna have my balls, and I'm rather attached to them."

Smiling, I sat up and scanned the room. Our clothes were scattered across the shop floor, and the sofa was definitely going to need a good cleaning. Jared got to his feet and began gathering our discarded garments. Tossing me my bra and tee he grinned.

"Get dressed, my lady. I have something I want to show you before I take you back to my place and feed you."

With that grin, I would let him take me anywhere.

Chapter 14

All That Glitters Is White Gold

We dressed quickly and cleaned the shop, making sure to give the couch some extra attention. The two of us were grinning like idiots, and every opportunity he got, Jared pulled me to him for another heart stopping kiss. Once everything was sparkling and suitably hygienic again, he ushered me out of the shop, locking the door behind us.

The streets were busy with people making their way home. Shops were closing their shutters, and fast food vendors were packing up, too. I looked up at Jared as he pressed his hand against the small of my back, leading me across the street to a parking lot. I could have stared at him for hours. His eyes were truly hypnotic. The deep blue reminded me of the ocean at night as it glistened in the moonlight. A satisfied sigh escaped my lips and he raised an eyebrow at me before smiling and kissing the top of my head.

Opening the car door, he held my hand as I slid into my seat, before running around to his side and practically jumping into his own seat. His expression reminded me of a child on Christmas morning. I giggled at him as he started the engine. Glancing over at me, his eyebrows bounced up and down on his forehead.

"Ready, my lady?"

Biting on my bottom lip, I smiled seductively. Leaning forward, I let the tip of my nose just touch his so that our lips were mere inches apart. He was breathing hard as his eyes watched my lips with intense attention.

"When it comes to you, Jared, I'm always ready."

He grinned widely before grabbing the back of my neck and pulling me in for a passionate, deep, breathless kiss. When he came up for air, I licked my lips, still tasting his on them.

"Well, I won't keep you waiting then."

We drove through the streets, passing small boutiques and shops on the way. I hadn't had time to explore the shopping district surrounding the campus yet, but after spotting several stunning shoe stores I would certainly be doing so soon. The idea of shopping immediately made me think of Amy. Sliding my cell out of my pocket I typed a quick text to let her know what was happening. I didn't want her to worry. Turning on the phone I noticed that there was a message waiting for me.

> Hey, Superstar. Where are you? We thought we might get some food in tonight. Just wondered if you wanted to eat with us before your date. Gimmie a heads up. Ollie xx
> **Received 19.35**
> **From: Ollie**

Jared glanced over at me with a furrowed brow, a look of concern on his face.

"Something wrong?"

I shook my head and smiled. "No, just Ollie. He wanted to know if I wanted to eat with him and Amy before my date. We went to the movies earlier today, so I'll tell him I ate at work, so he doesn't worry."

Jared's expression changed. I studied his face, trying to figure out what it was. His lips were pressed into a hard line, and his hands were gripping the steering wheel tightly. Was he jealous? I decided not to broach the subject and replied to Ollie's message asking him to let Amy know I would be home late.

"When you say we went to the movies who do you mean? Oliver, Amy and yourself?"

"No, just me and him. We saw some awful horror movie, and I swear I only managed to see half of it because I had my face buried in Ollie's hoodie most of the time, trying not to look."

He slammed on the breaks and the car screeched and halted to a stop. Unbuckling his seatbelt, Jared got out and slammed the door behind him. I watched him, completely dumbstruck at what had just happened. He shouted obscenities and kicked the ground hard before raking his hands through his hair, clearly furious and frustrated. I wanted to leap out of the car and confront him about what was happening, but I was glued to my seat with fear at his reaction.

He stood still for a moment, facing the road behind us, and fisted his hands on his hips. Biting his bottom lip, he stared down at the ground and shook his head before returning to the driver's seat again. I sat, frozen and speechless, just staring at him, waiting for him to explain, but he didn't. He never uttered a single world. He was icy cold, and when he began to drive again, he didn't make eye contact, speak, or acknowledge my existence at all.

Looking out of the window, I tried to shake off the uneasy feeling I was getting from Jared's sudden cool demeanor towards me. Ollie was just a friend, and we had already had this conversation once. Turning to him, I placed my hand on his knee and he glanced down at it as if I'd just laid a gun in his lap. He looked fierce, his eyes blazing and his jaw clenched. I removed my hand quickly and sighed.

"Jared, Ollie is just a friend. We just hang out. I swear there is nothing between us. Don't you trust me?"

Snapping his head at me he glared. "It's not you I don't trust. You're a very attractive woman, Layla, and there are a lot of guys out there just itching and squirming to get into those panties and make you moan for them, but you belong to me. You're mine. And I am not willing to share you with some frat boy who thinks he has a chance, understood? You need to make it very fucking clear to him that you are spoken for. Or I will."

A shiver of thrill and excitement pulsed through me. I liked angry, possessive Jared. Why did alpha male demeanors get me so turned on? He was smoking hot, and it took every ounce of my self-restraint not to jump his bones there and then. Instead, I settled for a kiss on his cheek and a ghost of a smile crossed his lips as I made contact with his skin.

"You have absolutely nothing to worry about."

Entering an enormous parking lot, I looked up at a beautiful glass building. The colossal structure had been built with glass walls and lustrous golden doors. It was extraordinary in every way. I spotted the sign above the entrance, Garrett's. It was the mall his father had been building, the same one Jared had completed after his death. It was dark, and the parking lot was completely vacant. The whole place was obviously locked down. I stared at Jared, perplexed. Smiling he turned off the ignition, ran around to my door and extended his hand out to me.

"Welcome to my palace, my lady."

Unlocking the large golden doors, he strode fast across to a security office adjacent to the entrance. Punching in a code, the alarm ceased its deafening screech and lights began to illuminate the pitch black halls. I gawked in amazement at the rows and rows of little boutiques.

Taking my hand, Jared led me through the enormous entrance hall to a store at the far end of the building. Passing beautiful displays of clothes, accessories and appliances he stopped in front of a small boutique. Grinning at me, delight gleaming in his deep blue eyes, he opened the door and ushered me in. The lights flickered on, and I gaped in wonderment at the shining displays of jewelry which glistened underneath heavily lit glass counters.

I turned around, turning my gaping expression to him. Smiling widely back at me, he walked over to a counter in the corner of the room and unlocked it. Reaching in he pulled out a beautiful white gold and diamond encrusted bracelet. He raised his hand and gestured with his index finger for me to come over to him. Taking my chin from the floor, I tried to regain my equilibrium as I moved towards him anxiously and gave him my hand. He slid the bracelet over it and onto my wrist. His fingertips brushed my skin, sending electricity surging up my arm and throughout my body. I stared at the stunning piece in total disbelief as he raised my hand to his lips and caressed my knuckles, smiling sexily.

"There. A bracelet fit for a princess. You should always be dripping with diamonds, Layla, but this," he paused and lifted my hand up so that the bracelet gleamed and shimmered in the light, "is a start."

Draping my arms around his neck, I kissed him hard. He enveloped his arms around my waist and swept me off my feet, pulling me tight to him. I was overwhelmed with emotion and furrowed my brow as I stared at the jewels dangling on my wrist. Jared pulled his lips from mine and looked at me with concern.

"What's the matter? You don't like it?"

I shook my head as he returned me to my feet. "It's not that, Jared. It's all of this."

I gestured around the room vaguely, but his eyes were fixed on me. "It's too much. You hardly know me, and yet you're giving me a piece of jewelry worth thousands of dollars. It's crazy. Are you doing it because you feel guilty for the whole coffee shop thing? Because if you are, you really don't have to. I told you, I forgive you."

Lifting my hand, he ran his lips over my knuckles and placed a gentle kiss on the bracelet that adorned my small and dainty wrist. "No, Layla. I gave you the bracelet because I wanted to and because I can. This is my store. I just had this bracelet added to the collection yesterday, and when I saw you coming out of your dorm building last night, all I could think about was how perfect it would look on your exquisite and elegant wrist. If you really don't want it, I understand, but don't refuse it because you feel it's a gift that comes with an ulterior motive. It is certainly not."

I nodded and placed a chaste kiss on his oh-so-slightly parted lips. His expression softened as he lifted my chin and gazed into my eyes. "You have the most beautiful eyes I've ever seen. I could get lost in them for days. But for now, I'll settle for staring into them over a candle lit dinner. Come on. Let's go back to my place. I'll even cook this time."

I raised an eyebrow playfully. "You cook, sir? My, my. Is there no end to your talents?"

Giving me a mischievous grin, he whispered into my ear, sending shockwaves through my body to my belly, igniting a now familiar fire inside. "I have a great many talents, my lady, and I intend to show you all of them."

I was sure I was blushing scarlet, but I didn't care. Jared made me feel alive, desirable and sexy like a scorching hot temptress. It was exciting, and I was eager for more of anything he could dish out.

Sitting in the passenger seat of his luxurious car, I looked down at the bracelet on my wrist. It really was beautiful, but something inside me was uncomfortable with this token of his affection. Although he had given me his reasons for the gift, it just didn't sit well with me.

The bracelet itself was stunning. The purest of white gold and each diamond had been cut to complete perfection. It glistened and sparkled as the streetlight beamed through the window. It was heavy and according to the information I had read on the ticket back at the store, it was worth a staggering $11,050 and contained eight carats of diamonds.

The fact that he was totally at ease about giving me such an expensive piece of his collection made me wonder if this was something that he did often. Was I just one in a long line of women he'd given jewelry to? And if so, did he assume that a casual fuck every so often was all I was hoping for? I glanced over at him as hurtful and unwanted thoughts consumed me.

Why was I torturing myself? I should just ask him. Swallowing hard I tried to sound as impassive as possible.

"Jared, this bracelet-"

Putting his hand on my leg, he gripped me tightly and gave me a long hard stare, silencing me immediately.

"No. Whatever it is you're thinking about, the answer is no. I gave you that bracelet because it's a stunning and breathtaking piece of art. Just like you. When I purchased that piece, I thought it was very attractive, but could never really understand the enthusiasm my associates had given it. That was until you walked out of that door last night. You looked amazing, and the moment your hand was in mine, I knew that bracelet was made for your delicate, little wrist. And before you ask, no, I don't make a habit of giving women diamonds. In fact, apart from you, the only woman I ever gave a diamond to was my mother, and it was a pair of earrings on her birthday.

"Don't over think this, Layla. It's yours, and I don't want to hear another word about it. Understand?"

It was as if he had read my mind and in one swoop had completely dissolved all of my doubts about the wonderful gift he had given me. Mentally chastising myself for questioning his motives, I gave him a smile, leaned across to his side and kissed him on the cheek.

* * * *

Amy was practically giddy when I'd told her about our evening at the coffee shop. She wanted every last detail, which I happily gave her. Although she did agree that he should have been forthcoming about his ownership of the shop, she understood his reasons for not telling me. Naturally, she instantly forgave him after I showed her the diamond bracelet he'd given me.

Ollie hadn't been so thrilled about it all. "He was totally dishonest about who he was. How can you continue to date someone when you have no idea who he really is? Can you honestly say you trust him? A diamond bracelet doesn't make up for lying and pretending to be someone you're not. He's a fuck-nut if you ask me."

His comments had irked me a little, but I tried to understand where they were coming from. Ollie cared about me and probably not in a strictly friendly way.

"Ollie cut him some slack will you? Besides I'm a grown woman who is perfectly capable of deciding if someone is trustworthy or not." Kissing him on the cheek, I smiled sweetly. "But thank you for looking out for me."

He flushed a deep shade of pink which, not wanting to embarrass him, I decided was best to ignore.

Chapter 15

Out Of My Dreams & Into The Car

The next few weeks passed very quickly as I began to settle into my new routine. Now that I was in a relationship, I was aware of my need to be cautious. After making an early appointment with Dr. Roberts, I decided against the contraceptive pill. I knew myself well enough to be sure that, at one time or another, I would forget to take it or miss one, so I chose the safer option of a shot instead. My ass was still a little sore from it as I drove back to Long Beach, hopefully in time for class.

Classes were getting intense, but with Ollie there they felt more like hanging out with a friend. Assignments were rolling in thick and fast, and I worried how I would find time for everything in my life. I hadn't been home for a while as I found myself constantly busy with shifts at the shop and Jared. I had planned on going the last weekend that had passed, but after Dad called and told me he had to work, I decided to have a girly evening with Amy instead. We were now halfway through October, and the weather was turning, which made the walks to work a bit of a chore. Amy was a regular there by now and would often meet me at the end of my shift for girl talk.

Things with Jared were also beginning to fall into place, and I felt truly in awe of his world with all the beautiful places he was taking me. Stunning gardens, museums, fancy restaurants and tonight I was escorting him to a formal dinner and dance at the Hyatt Regency, one of Long Beach's finest hotels and home to an exquisite ballroom. He looked so distinguished in his black tux, and I could fully appreciate the powerful and influential businessman that he was during the week. But the way he grinned at me when I had stepped out of the door in my new designer dress he had insisted on buying me, he was every bit the sexy, smoldering twenty-two year old man I had grown to adore.

Grecian in style, the dress was a striking blue that he said matched my eyes perfectly. Floor length and held by a strap on only one shoulder, it had a long slit that ran from the hem to the top of my thigh, stopping just before my panty line. A glittering silver design weaved and sparkled around my waist and a matching pattern adorned my shoulder where the front attached to the back. A mischievous smile was spread across Jared's face, and he struggled to keep his hands to himself in the car on the ride over to the venue.

I'd been introduced to some of California's elite and although I felt extremely out of place, Jared hadn't left my side all evening, and I held his arm tightly as we circulated the room. I thanked god for my overbearing mother having sent me to dance classes as a teen because when the band started up, Jared eagerly led me to the dance floor where we danced effortlessly and easily to every tune that was played.

Ballroom dancing was something I had always excelled at, and I'd dropped all other styles just to focus on it. If it hadn't been for my sudden growth spurt I could have pursued it as a career but, unfortunately, no sixteen year old boy wants to dance with a girl who's almost a foot taller than he is. Gratefully I'd stopped increasing in height and stayed at a comfortable five foot six while the boys who had originally snubbed me as a partner shot up.

As we danced and mingled with California's finest, I became fully aware that I was a direct reflection on Jared and tried to carry myself with elegance and grace, trying to be a little less Layla.

Standing amongst a group of large men who were considerably older than he was, Jared leaned into my ear. "Stop worrying. You look stunning, and everyone here will agree. They'll think you're as amazing as I do. Relax."

Kissing me tenderly on the cheek he grinned. A gong sounded and an announcement was made that everyone should take their seats for dinner.

Sitting at the table I was surrounded by businessmen in designer tuxedos. Jared sat on my right and placed a possessive arm around my shoulder, letting everyone at the table know I was his and his alone. The gesture excited and thrilled me. Knowing that he felt strongly enough about us to be so openly attentive was endearing.

The food was truly spectacular. According to the menu, it was being prepared by Renee Dupree, a well-respected and highly praised chef. Jared had taken the liberty of ordering for me, and I dined on the finest chicken tagliatelle of my life. Mindful that people would be watching how I carried myself during dinner, I carefully ate my food - slowly and with as much elegance as I could. Jared was seemingly engrossed in conversation with several men at our table who were looking for investors in some of their new building projects. Leaning into the table, he rested one hand on his glass and the other on my leg, squeezing and rubbing it suggestively.

I continued to eat and tried desperately to hide the arousal that was building inside me as his hand caressed my thigh. I let out a small moan and his eyes immediately darted to me. My cheeks immediately colored as he leaned in to whisper in my ear. "Was that vocal praise for your meal or something a little more carnal? Because either way, I like it."

Placing my hand on his underneath the table I smiled wickedly. "I guess you'll never know."

"Is that a challenge, my lady? Because I am more than happy to rise to it in every sense of the word."

I bit my bottom lip as a thrill of anticipation ran through me. Leaning into the table, I decided to play his tempting game. Addressing one of the gentlemen Jared had been conversing with, I began asking about his project to build a new mini mall aimed purely at students and their interests.

"So, Mr. Kent, tell me, this new building project you're proposing, you say it's mostly aimed at the growing student population in Long Beach. I think that's a wonderful concept. However, I'm concerned that, with the current economic crisis and hardships faced by those studying these days, your new stores and restaurants will be left desolate due to the insufficient finances available to students such as myself. How do you plan on appealing to us on a consumer level?"

Jared's eyes widened, and he had a look of surprise as though he were amazed that I knew so much about such subjects. But a distinct smile of what I hoped was pride was now very visible, and he immediately moved his hand from my leg to my back in a supportive gesture.

Mr. Kent cleared his throat and smiled at me. "Well, that's a very good question, Miss Jennings, and something my development team and I have been poring over for a while. I would very much like to get your insight on the matter if you are willing, of course. I can arrange a dinner perhaps? Jared, old boy, we should arrange it. Have your assistant check your schedule and call me. This charming young lady is an absolute delight. How on earth did you manage to catch such a creature, Garrett?"

Tracing his fingertips up and down my bare spine, Jared grinned at him. "I didn't know what hit me, Arthur. She was truly a wonderful surprise. And I'd have to agree, she is spectacular." His hand returned to my thigh, and he gently slid his fingers through the split in the side of my dress.

I gasped as he softly caressed the lining of my lace panties which were hugging my hip snuggly. He hardly batted an eyelash as he listened intently to the conversations across the table, making comments where required. I squirmed in my seat as his hand travelled down and over the inside of my thigh. Hooking his foot over mine beneath the table, he firmly pulled it towards him and parted my legs. His hand darted between them, and my body began to react quickly to the feel of his touch against my sex.

His finger softly stroked back and forth over my cotton panties teasingly. Closing my eyes, I bit down on my lip and tried to maintain my composure, but the darkness I saw in his eyes revealed that he was extremely aroused. Seizing my opportunity I ran my fingers over his zipper and tugged at it. Removing his free hand from his glass he grabbed my wrist and lifted my hand to his lips, running them across my bare knuckles before kissing them gently. His eyes met mine, and he shook his head slightly in warning. He would deny me my fun, yet he continued to torture me under the cover of our table. Slightly irritated, I shifted in my seat in an attempt to stand, but his hand pressed firmly into my thigh, keeping me pinned to the chair.

Pulling my panties aside, he slid his finger up and down the slit of my sex teasingly. I stared at him in disbelief. Was he seriously going to do this here? Now? I got my answer as the next thing I felt were two of his fingers sliding inside me as he began to rub my throbbing clit with the pad of his thumb. I jolted in my seat, startled, which earned me a concerned look from the other members of our dinner party.

"Are you quite alright, my dear?" Mr. Kent was regarding me with curiosity.

Swallowing hard, I tried to sound as unflustered as possible. "Oh yes, sorry. I'm just a little cold. Had a slight chill, but I'm fine now."

Placing his mouth against my ear, Jared growled low and hungrily. "I'd say you're a little hot myself. You're positively scorching." He nipped gently on my earlobe with his teeth, and I moaned deep in my throat. His hand moved rhythmically over my sex, his wet fingers sliding in and out as I grew more and more aroused. I was practically drooling as his thumb brushed against my clit, driving me into a frenzy.

Cupping me in his hand, he pushed his fingers deeper, and I felt the tips brush against my g-spot. A shock of pleasure rippled through me as my orgasm built, growing closer and closer with every stroke of his tempting digits. My chest rose and fell sharply as I had to try frantically to mask my panting. Jared's demeanor was cool and calm, but his eyes were showing me just how excited he was. Hooded and dark, I could see the lust blazing inside them. He was just as hot, and I could imagine he was probably in agony as his solid hard cock pressed against his slacks, begging to be released.

My heart was hammering so hard beneath my ribcage that I could feel my body pulsate with every thundering beat. Adrenaline was coursing through my veins, knowing that we could be caught at any moment and, with my orgasm building, there was a very distinct possibility that I wouldn't be able to control myself enough to be quiet.

Feeling the urgency of my release growing, I leaned into Jared's shoulder and his head immediately turned to me. A wicked smile on his lips, he leaned over to my right ear, allowing me the chance to hide my face by nuzzling into his neck and out of sight of our present company. "Let go, baby. Come for me, right here, right now in my hands. Do it for me." With one last thrust of his fingers, I was tipped over the edge as my orgasm came crashing down inside me. My insides convulsed as pulsating waves of pleasure caused my back to arch which Jared masked by shielding me from view with his broad shoulders and back. I bit down on his shoulder groaning softly as I tried to calm my ragged breathing. Placing a gentle kiss behind my ear he smiled against my skin.

"Good girl."

Withdrawing his hand, he sat back in his chair, took a napkin from the table and began to wipe his hand beneath it. Giving me a satisfied grin, he folded it up neatly and placed it in his pocket. I shifted in my seat, uncomfortably aware that I was flustered and was no doubt a deep shade of crimson. Getting to my feet, I excused myself and headed to the ladies to clean up. I gazed at myself in the mirror and tried to calm myself as my cheeks continued to glow and flush a dazzling shade of pink. What the hell was that about?

When I returned to the table, Jared was standing against the far wall with his cell to his ear. I couldn't hear what he was saying, but his face was visibly twisted with rage. Hanging up, he walked over and took my hand.

Apologizing to our fellow diners for the interruption, he said his goodbyes and informed Mr. Kent that he would be in touch about the dinner date. His hand resting on my lower back, Jared guided me out of the building and back to the car.

"What was that call about? You seem distressed."

Shaking his head firmly, his mouth pressed into a hard line. "Nothing for you to concern yourself with. Just something I have to get sorted out. It's nothing for you to worry about."

Deciding not to press him for information while he was still so irritated, I remained silent as we approached his car. He had hired a chauffeur for the evening, and I was pleased to have him next to me in the back seat for a change where his attention could be on us rather than driving. Holding out his hand, he assisted me into the back before sliding in behind me.

His thumb brushed back and forth over my knuckles as we sat side by side with my hand resting on his knee. Leaning forward, I knocked on the glass that separated us from our driver. "Would you be so kind as to take us for a drive around the city? I do love Long Beach at night."

"Of course, madam. Just inform me when you are ready to return home." The dark glass glided back up, leaving us totally alone. Returning to my seat I glanced at Jared, who had a very puzzled look on his face.

"What was that about?"

"I could ask you the same thing, Mr. Garrett. That was a very risky game you played in there tonight. We could have been caught."

Leaning over to me, he brushed a lock of hair behind my ear and caressed my cheek with his thumb. "Oh, darling, if there were any chance of that, I wouldn't have done it, but I certainly enjoyed it. Dinner and a show. And what a performance you gave, Miss Jennings. I demand an encore."

Happy to oblige, I jumped onto his lap and straddled him firmly between my thighs. Unbuckling his belt, I leaned against his chest and placed a soft kiss on his lips. I could feel his erection press against my ass as it rested firmly against his perfectly tailored slacks. The fabric pulled taut against the zipper and in one swift movement I lifted up and released his hard, temptingly solid cock from its restraints. His hands slid around my back, and he pulled me determinedly against him. Kissing me deeply, his tongue darted into my mouth, seeking mine. He tasted of delicious mint and chocolate which was still lingering from the perfectly sculpted soufflé he had eaten for dessert.

The smell of the leather seats paired with the scent of Jared's sweet cologne was a heady combination and my arousal began to build once more. Uncontrollable lust was taking control of my body as I leaned back and ripped his shirt open impatiently. Buttons pinged and flew around the cabin, but I was too caught up in the moment to care. A small chuckle left his lips, but I silenced it quickly as I pressed my palms against his chest and kissed him passionately and urgently.

Lifting onto my knees, I gathered my dress up to my hips, pulled my panties aside and positioned myself over his rigid, delicious cock before lowering myself down onto it, savoring the sensation as every inch filled me. Breaking the connection of our lips, my head fell back in pure ecstasy. He hissed a breath and his jaw clenched as I began to move slowly up and down, still firmly pressing my hands on his perfectly sculpted and smooth chest.

My hips rhythmically grinding on his, I moaned with pleasure while he matched me, thrusting upwards, deepening the penetration. I gasped as a twinge of pain shot through me, the thick tip of his cock pressed into me, and I could feel it all the way inside my belly. It was a momentary stabbing as I quickly became overcome with raw animal hunger. I needed him harder and faster thrusting inside me.

As though he'd read my mind, Jared gripped my hips and hoisted me off of him, pushing me down onto the floor below us. My knees on the floor, he flipped me over, kneeling behind me. I heard the familiar sound of foil tearing. Entwining our fingers he held my hands firmly against the sleek leather seat and plunged into me.

Groaning, he moved in and out fast and hard, making my whole body shake and jolt forward as his hips slammed into my behind. His lips brushed my ear, and I could feel his warm breath on my skin, sending a shiver through me.

"Oh god, Layla, you're so fucking hot. This ass, these legs, this tight, wet little cunt - I can't get enough of you. I could spend hours just making your body quiver beneath me. You're my new addiction, my obsession, and I'm hooked on you."

I gripped our fingers tighter together as the carnality of his words echoed in my ear. My muscles tightened, and my legs stiffened as my orgasm hit me like a tidal wave. Thrashing and crashing inside me I cried out, unable to silence my pleasure as it blissfully ripped me apart. He plunged into me again before stilling, biting down on my neck passionately as his own orgasm gripped him. I could feel his heartbeat against my back, and the pounding of my own echoed in my ears as I basked in the afterglow of our post coital embrace.

 Releasing my hands, he snaked his arms around me and sat back on his heels pulling me to him. My back pressed against his strong and muscular chest, and my head rolled back onto his shoulder. Sliding his hands from my waist to my stomach, he held me tightly to him as I turned my face toward him. He pressed his lips to mine, kissing me gently, caressing my lips with his tongue before pushing it into my mouth. He kissed me tenderly, with loving gentleness. Leaving one hand around my waist, he lifted the other to my face and cupped my jaw.

He began to place tiny, sweet kisses all over my face, my cheeks, my nose, and my forehead before returning to my lips, grazing them with his own. I opened my eyes and found him gazing at me. His deep pools of blue sparkled in the moonlight, and I couldn't help but feel that our relationship had deepened in the past few hours. I felt a connection to him that was slowly consuming me, and the realization that I was falling in love was leaving me slightly nervous. I'd never felt that way before, and this new territory was unfamiliar and frightening. Holding me tighter, he brushed my cheek with his thumb.

"I don't know what it is you've done to me, Layla, but I love it. I'm caught up in your world, and I never want to escape. You're mine, Layla. I'll give you the world and everything in it if you'll just give me your promise."

Leaning my forehead against his, I sighed with happiness.

"I'm yours. For as long as you want me."

I had been his since the moment he'd first kissed me, and as he held me in his arms, I couldn't imagine ever being with anyone else.

Chapter 16

I Want To Be A Rock Star

Jared was busy working for most of the week. After having spent most of my time with him in the past few weeks, I felt slightly abandoned with his absence - especially after what had happened between us at dinner the previous night and then in the car. But with classes and my shifts at the coffee shop, I had more than enough to keep me busy.

He'd given me a schedule of his week when he'd dropped me off that night so that I knew exactly where he was when he wasn't with me. It made timing my calls easier. Though he had told me to call him whenever I wanted, I felt uncomfortable interrupting his work just because I was missing his voice. Work was keeping him so busy he'd had little time for anything else and I worried that he was overdoing it, but he reassured me that this was nothing unusual for him. He'd quipped that if he ever needed nursing in bed, I'd be the first to know.

I mentally hugged myself for being so lucky.

* * * *

When Friday night rolled around, Ollie invited Amy and me to Benny's bar with him and Nick. Amy was dying to get away from the pile of books that had gradually been growing on her desk since classes had started. I'd held onto some hope that Jared might have called and arranged to get together, but I hadn't heard from him all day. The thought made me feel a little dejected, but I reasoned with myself that he was probably busy with meetings and work commitments. Checking my phone one last time for any messages, I shrugged and smiled at Ollie.

"Sure, why not? But I am not singing this time!"

He laughed and rubbed the back of his neck with his hand, which he often did when he was nervous. "Actually I'm playing tonight. Nick's on drums and Eric plays bass. I play lead and vocals."

Amy shrieked. "Oh my god! You're like a real life rock band. This-is-going-to-be…so cool!"

I chuckled at her before returning my gaze to Ollie. He was laughing at her too, but he simply shrugged and shot me a smile. "Guess we'll find out, won't we?"

The bar was buzzing and was considerably more crowded than the previous week. I glanced at Ollie, who had also clearly noticed the swarm of people gathered at the bar. His face was pale, and he swallowed hard. He was tense. I reached out and gripped his hand firmly. He turned his head and looked at me as I leaned forward with my mouth to his ear. "Don't worry. You're gonna totally rock. It'll be awesome. Just imagine they're not even here. That it's just me and Amy."

He gave me a faint smile as I released his hand. Making his way through the crowd, he headed towards the stage where Nick and a guy with spiky blond hair and a 'Will Rock For Food' t-shirt were setting up. I assumed the other guy was the bass player, Eric. They greeted him with a slap on the back, and he said something that made Nick throw his head back and laugh.

Amy grabbed my hand and began pulling me through the hoard of people to an empty table she'd spotted. "This is so cool. Can you believe our Ollie is a rock star?"

I cocked my head to the side and rolled my eyes at her. "Amy, they're playing at an open mic night. But, yes, it's pretty cool."

The microphone made a high pitched screech, catching my attention instantly. Turning to face the stage, I saw Ollie standing in front of the mic with his guitar strapped around him. Leaning forward, he cleared his throat and addressed the crowd that was now falling silent to listen to the group. "Hi, we're D.O.A and we're gonna start with a song most of you will know. It's 'Iris' by the Goo Goo Dolls, and it goes out to my girls in Room 21."

Winking at Amy and me, he smiled and began to play. His voice was husky and low, and he sang every word with passionate emotion as if it were the air he breathed. Amy squealed with joy as he played, glancing over at us every so often. She'd suddenly become the guy's very own groupie. Ollie was hypnotic. His voice was deep, and his lip ring pinched between his lips as he sang.

I was staring at him in awe when he looked directly at me and our eyes met. He held my gaze and sang into the mic with intense emotion, every word hitting me like a bullet. My heart stopped as the words left his lips. His eyes were penetrating mine as his expression became pained, and his eyebrows pinched together. My chest tightened, and I was gasping for air. My pulse jumped, hearing the hardcore emotion in his raspy, husky tones. When he finally closed his eyes, losing himself in the music, I seized the opportunity to tell Amy that I needed some air. She gave me a concerned look, but nodded before returning her gaze to the stage.

I rushed toward the doors, not risking a glance at Ollie. I had just been given the answer to my question about his feelings towards me, and he definitely wasn't in the friend zone. I had felt it with every note that left his lips. The night air hit me like a wall as I pushed my way through the bar doors. The chill reached deep into my lungs as I tried to control my heavy breathing.

Putting my hands on my knees, I leaned forward trying to regain my composure. I felt sick as adrenaline surged through me. Ollie was my friend. I couldn't be who or what he wanted.

Why couldn't he just be satisfied with being my friend? Why did he have to complicate things? And why was I still thinking about his lips?

My head was pounding, and I began to feel increasingly light headed. Struggling to get my eyes to focus, the blur of headlights dazzled, and I began to stumble into the wall adjacent to me. The next thing I knew, I was scooped up off of the ground, one arm was hooked behind my knees and another around my back like I was a new bride.

"Christ, Layla! Are you ok?" I recognized his voice immediately and instantly felt more at ease. "Layla, open your eyes and answer me."

I looked up at Jared and wound my hands around his neck. "What happened? Did someone hurt you? Are you sick?" He was panicked as he scanned my face for answers.

Shaking my head weakly, I finally managed to respond. "No, I'm fine. I just got a little lightheaded. It's pretty crowded in there, and I'm kinda tired. I guess I just got overwhelmed. You can put me down now."

He held me tighter to him and stared at me with concern. "The hell I will. You're shaking, and you're as white as a sheet. I'm taking you home so I can keep an eye on you."

I tried to protest, but he ignored my efforts. Hugging myself to his chest, I glanced over his shoulder just in time to see Ollie storming out of the bar. His face was thunderous. "Hey! Dickwad! Let her go!"

Jared whirled around, his eyes immediately landing on Ollie who was sprinting towards us. Wrestling out of Jared's strong arms, I ran toward him. Pressing my hands firmly against Ollie's chest, I screamed at him.

"No, Ollie! It's Jared!"

His eyes darted between us before settling on me. Waving his hands in the air in a frantic panic he yelled at me. "Jesus Christ, Layla! I thought he was trying to abduct you! I got off stage, and you were gone. Amy said you'd stepped out, and the next thing I see is you being carried away by some heavy handed meathead."

Jared took a step towards Ollie, but I intercepted him and held up my hand in warning. He was glaring at him with a fury in his eyes that I'd never seen before. Pointing accusingly at Ollie, he shouted furiously.

"Who are you calling a meathead? I'm not the one who let her go outside into a dark street alone in the middle of the night, asswipe! Who the hell is this little fucker, Layla?"

Ollie's face grew dark, and I could feel his breathing becoming erratic under my palm. His fists clenched at his sides, and I feared this would soon turn into a full on brawl. Trying to push past me, Ollie yelled back at Jared, smirking.

"You wanna go? Come at me, bro!"

With my hand still pressed firmly on Ollie's chest, I gave him a warning look and turned to Jared.

"Jared, shut up! He didn't just let me go outside, he didn't know I'd even left. He was on stage when I ran out. And don't call my friend an asswipe. This whole thing is just a simple misunderstanding. Oliver is my friend from across the hall that I told you about. Both of you just calm down and act like grownups!"

Pointing accusingly at Oliver, Jared looked like he was about to lose all control as rage flared in his eyes

"*He's* Ollie? The friend you went to the movies with the other week and had your head in his fucking chest for two hours? And you're here with him! Fuck no! What the fuck, Layla?"

I glared at him, taking immediate dislike to the sarcastic tone he'd used when he'd called Ollie my friend. I prodded his chest with my finger making my point.

"I did not come here alone with him. He's playing with a band, and I was with Amy. He is my friend, Jared, and what we did at the movies was completely innocent. I thought we'd been over this already. Ollie lives across the hall, and we hang out. That's not going to change so just back off and stop accusing me of being unfaithful."

Jared opened his mouth to reply, but I shot him a cautionary glare and he closed it again before kicking at the ground and cursing under his breath. Amy finally joined us in the parking lot with a confused look on her face. I was almost relieved to see her. Her eyes darted between the three of us.

"What's going on?"

I rolled my eyes at her. "Nice of you to join us, Amy. I could have used your help about five minutes ago."

Turning my attention back to Oliver, I took his hand and unraveled his fist. He unclenched, but continued to glare at Jared. "Ollie, I'm fine. Jared saw me outside the bar. I was dizzy and lost my balance, but he grabbed me before I fell."

His eyes left Jared and were now gazing into mine. I gave him a quick hug. "But thanks for having my back."

He smiled back at me and kissed my cheek. "Always, baby girl, you know that. You sure you're ok now?"

I nodded firmly. "Positive. I'm fine now. Go back and finish your set, you guys deserve to have fun. Hell, I've had to hear you practice enough through the walls."

I glanced over his shoulder at Amy, and shooting me an understanding smile, she grabbed his arm and pulled him towards the bar with her. "Come on, rock star. I'll let you buy me a drink. No cosmos, I swear." Giving me a final nod, he turned and followed. I could have kissed her for that, but I had more pressing matters to attend to.

I turned to face Jared, who was glowering fiercely at Ollie as though he were willing him to burst into flames. I walked over and pressed my fingers to his face, turning his gaze to mine and away from Ollie.

"Layla, I never accused you of being unfaithful, but I see the way he looks at you. He's got it bad. I should know, I have it too. You're an addiction, and I'm afflicted. So is he."

I stood on my toes and pressed my lips to his, gently soothing his raw and ragged breathing. His expression softened, and he took my hands in his. Gazing into his eyes, I took a calming breath.

"Jared, you have to trust me. I only want you. He really is just a friend. We connect and we share interests. Besides, even if he did want me, that doesn't mean he gets me. I'm not discussing it anymore. Period. What were you doing here anyway?"

Running his thumb over my knuckles, he met my gaze. "I called your cell, but when you didn't answer I got worried. I went to your dorm and someone told me you would be here. I'd just pulled up when I saw you. Then that little shit starts throwing his weight around. And don't think I didn't see that kiss, Layla. I'm telling you, that fucker is trying to get into your panties, and he won't be satisfied till he has you. He is not your friend, and I don't trust him."

His tone was dark and angry, but luckily I knew just how to sedate him.

Wrapping my arms around his back I pressed my chest against his. He eyed me cautiously before exhaling loudly and enveloping me in his arms. Looking up at him, I took his chin between my thumb and index finger and tilted it down to face me.

"You might not trust him but you can, you must, trust me."

The fire in his eyes had reduced to a simmer as he stared down at me. He placed a chaste kiss on my lips and sighed deeply. "I will and I do. I'm taking you home now. I'm still not convinced you should be left alone after that dizzy spell. You can stay at my place. We'll swing by your dorm and you can collect some of your things. Not that you'll need your clothes."

I grinned to myself as he led me to the car and out of the cold. The thought of spending the whole night with Jared thrilled me in every way. I couldn't wait to spend an entire night wrapped in his strong warm arms.

Chapter 17

Tables And Chairs

Once we arrived back at the house, Jared prepared the most delicious pasta dish I'd ever eaten. The creamy mushroom sauce and succulent chicken was poured over a bed of penne pasta and was the best meal I'd eaten since arriving at Long Beach State. Although the dinner and dance was exquisite, there was something about the way Jared had prepared the food that made it seem that much more tempting. Maybe it was simply because it was his hands- which I adored so much -that had prepared it. Of course, it could have been all of the alcohol I had consumed at the bar. I was ravenous.

Taking the napkin from my lap, I dabbed it over my mouth to remove any residue from my lips. Jared was watching me from across the gleaming glass dining table. A smile teased over his lips as our eyes met.

"You know, I'd have happily licked your lips clean for you if only you'd asked. I'm now extremely jealous of your napkin."

His words lingered in the air like a sexy invitation. Leaning back in his chair he curved his index finger and motioned a "come here" gesture.

Pushing my chair back, I made my way slowly to him. He watched me move with dark hooded eyes, drinking me in as I sauntered over. Sliding between the table and his knees, I positioned myself onto the edge and let my legs dangle in front of him. Maintaining his gaze, he sat perfectly still with his hands together and his fingertips touching his lip. Leaning back, I supported myself on my hands and gave him a seductive smile. I ran my barefoot up his shin, over his knee and pressed it against his thigh. His eyes darkened from a beautiful tanzanite to a deep shade of cobalt. Swallowing hard, he broke our gaze to look down at my foot which was now comfortably resting on the seat between his legs. He looked up at me from beneath his long dark eyelashes with an arched brow. A wicked smile began to appear on his lips.

"Miss Jennings, are you trying to tempt me?"

Sloping forward, I slid my finger gently over his slightly parted lips. I ran my tongue softly over his bottom lip before nipping it with my teeth letting a small moan escape my lips.

"Always."

A fire ignited in his eyes and the blaze of lust I saw in them excited me beyond comprehension. I wanted to drive him wild to make him crazy and make him feel totally at my mercy, the way he had made me feel in the ballroom - the way I felt whenever he was near me. He was a chink in the carefully constructed armor I'd spent years perfecting. I'd never felt more invigorated, alive and out of control than when I was with him.

His eyes were aflame with unbridled passion and his hands gripped onto the arms of the chair that he was currently pinned to. My lips traced the line of his jaw, trailing kisses from his chin to the nape of his neck. His head rolled back, granting me better access as he unclenched the chair and ran his hands swiftly over my thighs to the hem of my dress. Pushing it up slowly to my hips, his thumb grazed the lining of my panties, and I gasped in surprise. Pulling back from him, I licked my lip suggestively. Without a word, he gripped my knees tightly and thrust my legs apart.

"Don't play games with me, Layla. I don't have the patience for them."

Grabbing the elastic of my panties, he tugged them over my thighs forcefully. Sliding them down my legs, he let them drop gently to the floor. My breathing grew faster as I became aroused.

Taking my foot in his hands, he pressed it to his lips and placed a soft kiss on my ankle. Smiling at me with a sultry grin, he trailed gentle kisses up and over my knee, before stopping at my thigh. He looked up at me with a hot, dark penetrating stare.

"Lie back flat on the table, hold your hands together, and stretch your arms over your head. Do not move your hands, Layla. If you move them, I will make you sorry. Do you understand?"

Biting my lip at the thought of the utterly erotic scene that was about to play out, with me in the starring role, I nodded and complied with his orders.

Staring at the ceiling, I was completely unable to see what he was doing, unable to predict the next explicitly sensual act he was going to perform on me. The notion of being completely at his mercy was both exciting and nerve wracking, but I trusted Jared completely. My body was his temple, and I wanted him to pray there for hours. His soft hands gripped my behind firmly as he yanked me down the table towards him, lining up my ass up to the edge perfectly.

"Remember what I said, Layla. Absolutely. Still. Understand?"

I nodded weakly.

"I can't hear you, Layla. I said do you understand?"

"Yes," I whispered. "I understand."

Leaning over me, his chest pressed against mine, our eyes met. Holding my chin between his finger and thumb he pressed his lips firmly against mine.

"Good girl."

Returning his attention to the throbbing that was now an ache between my legs, he continued trailing soft, infuriatingly teasing kisses up my thigh. His teeth gently nipped at a tender spot on the inside just inches away from my sex, which my body was acutely aware of as it immediately stood to attention and tensed. Casting my eyes downward at him, I knew from the wicked smile I saw on his face as he lifted his head to look at me that he was also aware of it. He slid his finger up and down my slit, gently parting the fleshy lips. He groaned softly.

"Mmmm, you're so ready for me, Layla. You're wonderfully wet and warm."

I gasped for air as he slid his teasing finger inside me and gently pressed the pad of his thumb against my clit.

"You are temptingly hot. I could play with your tight little cunt all day."

My back arched as I shamelessly wriggled my hips against his hand, looking for some release from the throbbing ache his fingers were causing. Withdrawing his finger from me, he pinched my clit hard, making me cry out at the sweet pleasure and pain that shuddered through me.

"I warned you to stay still. Now look what you've made me do. You're all flushed and pink down here. Don't worry, angel. I'll kiss it better."

His lips gently caressed the folds of my sex as his tongue ran slowly up from my opening to my clit. Using the tip of his tongue, he stroked it with exasperating slowness. A fire scorched in my belly as I begged for release.

"Please, Jared."

Blowing a cool breeze over the swollen and tender knot, he chuckled. "Shh. Don't worry, baby. I'm going to take good care of you, be patient. I want to savor you, Layla. Every last, sexy, scorching, hot inch of you. I want you to scream my name as you beg me to make you come."

I moaned loudly and gripped the edge of the table as his mouth closed over me completely. He worked frantically inside me, thrusting deeper with every roll of his tongue. Running it over my clit, he pushed two fingers inside me and began penetrating me over and over again, thrusting them hard into me before gently withdrawing them again.

I could feel the orgasm building inside me as he worked his magic on the most intimate part of my body, but every time I teetered to the edge of my climax, he would stop and slow his pace. It was infuriating.

"Jared. Please. Now. I need it now. Please. I'll beg."

"Will you?"

Lifting my head to see him, I watched as he stood at my feet. I gazed up at him, bedazzled by his gorgeous face. A mischievous smile spread across his lips, and he unbuttoned his shirt just enough for me to see the sculpted pecs, rock hard abs and perfect contours of his body. He was truly stunning to behold, and he wanted me. Me, Layla Jennings, a coffee shop girl from Pasadena.

Unzipping his pants, his erection sprung free and I heard the familiar sound of foil tearing. As he gripped my thigh with one hand and his cock with the other, he teased the tip provocatively over the opening of my sex.

"Beg, Layla."

I shifted my hips in the hopes I'd be able to slide it inside me even slightly, but he predicted my actions and held my thigh tighter in warning.

"I will make you beg. Stay still. Do as I say or this will be over much sooner than I'd like."

I groaned with the need aching deep inside me. I was standing on the edge of a cliff, ready to dive into the refreshing waters below, but he was holding me back.

He leaned over me and wrapped a hand around my neck lifting me from the table to meet his lips. Sealing his mouth over mine, he kissed me deeply and passionately with a violent hunger as he thrashed his tongue around in my mouth. I could taste the slick saltiness of my sex all over his lips. The scent of his skin paired with the tantalizing tastes in his mouth was a heady combination. He smelled of sweet vanilla, reminding me of ice cream and the beach. It was a powerful aphrodisiac.

"Beg, Layla."

I clenched my teeth together as his tip teased back and forth over the opening to my sex.

"Please, Jared. I'm desperate."

He took in a sharp breath as he thrust his long, hard cock inside me. My mouth opened, and my head tipped back as he filled me to the brim. He felt perfectly snug inside me as if he were made for me. His hand gripped my behind as he moved slowly in and out, stroking that sweet sensitive spot inside me. My orgasm was tantalizingly close.

"Oh, Jared. I'm close. I'm so close. Don't stop."

He slowed, and I growled in frustration. The corner of his mouth curled up, and he whispered low in my ear, "Beg me, Layla. Tell me what you need."

Panting, I writhed and squirmed beneath him. "Fuck me! Make me come hard. I need you. Please, Jared!"

Nipping on my ear lobe he moaned with satisfaction. "Good girl."

Surging into me, he rocked his hips in a sweet and blissful rhythm, making my orgasm grow closer and closer with every shove of his hips into me.

"Come for me, Layla. Let go. I need to feel you around me."

My body responded to his command immediately, my orgasm pulsing and jolting inside me. I moaned loudly as I called his name over and over as the pleasure surged through my body, forcing me to grip the edges of the table so hard I thought I might crack the glass. Jared thrust forcefully inside me. Staring intensely into my eyes, he panted before hissing out a long breath as he found his own release.

Collapsing on top of me, I could feel the sweat trickling from his forehead onto my cleavage. My dress was still in place, and the thought that neither of us had found time to remove our clothing was particularly arousing. Our need for each other was intense. It had to be right there, right then.

He was still panting with his head pressed into my chest as I ran my hand through his hair in a calming, caressing motion. Taking a deep breath, he shifted onto his elbows and gazed at me. His thumb grazed my cheek with a gentle tenderness. The Jared lying on top of me on that table was so different to the one who had been commanding me to behave just a few moments ago. He was so complex and entirely distracting.

"You're killing me, Layla. You drive me wild whenever I'm near you. The way your body moves when you walk, the way you bite your lip, the way your body responds to my touch and the smell of your perfume makes my blood simmer. You're intoxicating, and I'm dizzy from the fumes."

His words made me melt into a pool of happy and contented bliss. I smiled down at him before placing my hand over my mouth to stifle a yawn. I hadn't realized how tired I was. The events of the evening were catching up with me and I could feel my eyelids becoming increasingly heavy. Taking my hand, Jared got to his feet, pulled me into a sitting position and handed me my panties. He zipped up his pants, but left his shirt completely open. I wriggled off the end of the table, slid my underwear back on and straightened my dress.

Glancing over my shoulder, I scanned the table. It was smeared with sweat, evidence of the two hot bodies that had been writhing all over it just a few minutes ago. Taking my hand once more, he pressed it to his lips and placed a tender kiss on my knuckles.

"You're exhausted. Come on, time for bed, my lady."

Taking me into his arms he scooped me up as he had done at the bar, like a new bride being carried over the threshold. His strong arms held me closely as I wound my fingers together around his neck and buried my head in his chest.

He carried me up the stairs and across the hall to the three bedrooms at the far end of the house. I looked up at him a little confused as I'd assumed we would be sleeping in his room, together.

"We're not sleeping together?"

Placing me gently on my feet, we stood outside the door of one of the large guest rooms. Holding my hands in his, he shook his head and sighed ruefully.

"No. It's not that I don't want to sleep with you. It's that I can see how tired you are, and I know there's no way I can control myself lying next to you all night. You sleep in there tonight, and I'll be here when you wake up."

The plague of disappointment began to twist inside me. What we'd shared in the dining room was intense and I'd felt connected to him in a deep and meaningful way. Now he was casting me aside and I felt used.

Cheap and dirty.

The sadness and disappointment that I had been feeling a moment before suddenly turned into intense anger.

"You know what, Jared? It's fine. I get it. You want me to be yours, but on your terms. Dinner was delicious, and I very much enjoyed the fantastic fucking you gave me on the table. Thank you for your hospitality this evening, and for taking care of me at the bar. I appreciate it. I'll sleep for a few hours and be sure to leave before you wake. Don't worry about me. Goodnight."

His mouth pressed into a hard line, and his eyebrows furrowed giving me the distinct feeling he was not amused with my outburst.

"Layla, you're being melodramatic again and overreacting, as usual. I don't share that bed. I never have. You're being ridiculous."

Giving him an icy glare, I turned away and headed into the room, but he caught me by the elbow tightly and whirled me around to face him. Gripping my arms so I couldn't escape him, he pressed his lips to mine. I pushed him away from me and glowered at him.

"Layla, stop! This is absurd! I'm not throwing you out, and I don't want you to leave. If it means that much to you that we share a room tonight, fine! Now go to bed!"

I stood my ground and crossed my arms over my chest, maintaining the glower I was giving him.

Rushing toward me, he growled in frustration before hauling me off the floor and over his shoulder. He marched over to the large four poster bed and pushed me down onto the soft mattress. Staring down at me from the foot of the bed he let out a long sigh, closed his eyes tightly, and rubbed his forehead with his finger and thumb.

"Get undressed. I'll be back in a moment." I opened my mouth to shoot him a sarcastic comment, but he gave me a warning look. "Don't. Not a word. Just get undressed and I'll be back in a minute. I have to do something before I turn in."

I sat on the bed gasping, feeling as though the air had been ripped from my lungs. How could he be so hardhearted? Had what we shared meant nothing to him? Didn't he care about me at all? My mind was swarming with unanswered questions that my tongue was eager to fire at him. How could I have given him the power to make me feel this way after only a few weeks? His face had been so infuriated, and his tone so callous.

I could feel a lump in my throat that wouldn't budge, no matter how hard I swallowed. A barrage of tears began to flow down my scorching cheeks. Holding my face in my hands, my body rocked and shook as I sobbed.

"Christ, Layla, baby don't cry. I didn't mean to go off at you like that. Come here."

Crouching in front of me in nothing but a pair of sweat pants, he reached his arms out to pull me in. Shaking my head at him furiously, unable to speak through the sobbing, I stood up and stormed across the room and into the bathroom, slamming the door behind me. I leaned back against the hard cold wood and slid down to the floor, wrapping my arms around my knees.

I could feel him on the other side of the door as though the heat from his body were penetrating the wood. He tapped lightly.

"Layla, open the door. This is absurd. Come out here and let's talk about this like adults. Calm and rational."

"No! Just go back to your room and leave me alone! It's what you wanted anyway."

His fist hammered on the door with such a fury that it startled me. "If you don't open this door and come out this instant I'm going to open it and pull you out myself!"

I let out a snort and yelled through the door at him, "Go ahead!"

"I'm not kidding, Layla! Last chance." His voice was low, and I could tell he was getting angrier by the minute, but for some bizarre reason it turned me on.

"You don't scare me, boss." Ha! Take that mister insensitive. You don't scare me.

Silence ensued and it worried me. Curiosity plagued me, so I timidly opened the door just a crack to see if he had left. I couldn't see him anywhere in the room, so feeling rather triumphant, I walked out, closing the door quietly behind me. A floorboard creaked behind me, and I turned around to find Jared standing in the doorway with a very large power drill in his hand.

Staring at the enormous tool he had gripped in his palm, I crossed my arms and glared at him. "And what exactly did you plan on doing with that?"

His brow furrowed, marring his gorgeous features as he met my gaze and glared back at me. "Well, if the mountain won't come to me, then I must go to the mountain. You locked the door and refused to come out which, by the way, is extremely childish. So I was going to take the hinges off and remove the problem and also the door."

Dropping the tool on the floor, he slumped down on to the edge of the bed and rested his elbows on his knees. He rubbed his hands over his face and winced before looking up at me.

"I think we need to have a conversation. Some things need clearing up. And they need clearing up now, rather than later. Come on, we'll go to my room and talk."

He held his hand out for mine, but I turned away and skirted around him, storming down the hall to his room. Letting out an exasperated sigh, he followed me.

Chapter 18

Getting It Straight

The room was dimly lit by two tall, standing, glass lamps in opposite corners of the room. Making my way over to the lush white couch that I had seen the first night Jared had brought me to his home, I continued to ignore his presence. I sat down and put my feet up so that I was lounging comfortably while trying to retain my infuriated expression.

I really was exhausted, and after the performance in the dining room and the blow out in the bedroom, I was ready for some shut eye. But he was right. We did have things that we needed to talk about and one burning question I needed an answer to. Slouching into an arm chair directly across from me, he sat forward with his elbows resting on his knees.

"Layla, there are some things we need to get straight once and for all. First is for me to apologize for my behavior back there. I'm not used to this," he gestured between the two of us and immediately gave me an opening to ask him my question.

"Jared, someone told me you don't date. That you don't do the whole girlfriend thing. Is that true? Is this just a case of hot casual sex with no strings, no commitment and no feelings? Because if that's what you want then I'm sorry but I'm not the girl for you."

Raising an arched eyebrow at me, a small smile played across his lips. "I see. Been checking up on me, have you? Did you Google me as well? No matter. It's true I have never been one to date. I don't freely welcome people into my life, Layla. It's hectic, and I'm a very busy man. I have an entire enterprise to run and it's very important that I get it right. It's my kingdom, and I won't see it torn apart by power hungry politicians and developers who are just itching for me to screw it up. I like my life to be simple and uncomplicated. Getting close to people always ends up going the same way for me. I'm hot tempered and impatient. You saw that in the bedroom a moment ago and on the dining table before that."

This was it.

What it all came down to was that Jared couldn't commit to a relationship, and I could hope for nothing more than casual lovers. Feeling completely rejected, I swept my feet from the couch to the floor.

Standing up slowly, I gazed at him longingly. "I understand, and you know what? It's fine. Just let me get my things and I'll call a cab to take me home."

Immediately rising to his feet, Jared grabbed my hand and pulled me close to him. "You didn't let me finish. Just because I haven't dated, doesn't mean I don't want to. I care about you, Layla. I enjoy spending time with you and not just because of the raw, passionate sex. You're witty, sarcastic, intelligent, funny, and I love being around you. You brighten my day.

"When I was stuck in meetings all week, I hardly got anything done. I kept thinking about you. What is she doing? Who is she with? Is she thinking about me? My cell phone was practically super glued to my hand because I was worried I'd miss a call or message from you. I've never felt that way about a woman before. So, no, Layla. I don't usually date, but like I told you in the car the other night, I want you to be mine. Not just your body, not just sex, I want you. All of you for as long as you'll have me."

I was giddy with happiness. He wanted me, all of me, not just the sex and the frustratingly passionate arguing. He wanted it all. The feeling of elation flooded my veins and I couldn't control myself anymore; it was as if someone had hit a switch and all the lights had come on in a bright surge of power inside me. Snaking my arms around his neck, I clung to him, wrapping my legs around his waist. He staggered backwards a little, before gripping my behind to stop me from slipping.

"Does this mean you want me, too? I need you to be totally aware of what you're getting into. I'm bad tempered, impatient, possessive, and I need a certain degree of order and control in my life. I'm a business man, Layla. It's how we are. It's how I have to be. There are too many opportunities for me to fail, and if I do, I will lose everything. It's just the way things are.

I'll screw up more than once, and I only hope you'll forgive me when I do. But I'll always try and put you first when I can. I'll never deliberately try to hurt you, and I promise to treat you like the princess you are. You're very important to me, and I want to do this with you. If you think you can handle all of that, then I would be the happiest man in the state, maybe even the world, right now. What do you say, Layla?"

He returned me to my feet as he watched me, scouring my face for any hint of an answer. Taking a deep breath, I sighed and gazed up at him. I leaned my hip to one side and crossed my arms over my chest.

"Well, you're right. You are extremely impatient, bad tempered, hot headed, controlling, complicated, irrational and argumentative. Not to mention, from what I saw at the bar tonight, you certainly are possessive."

He rolled his eyes at me and held his hands in the air.

"Fuck, Layla. Kick a guy in the crotch, will you? It'd be less painful."

Raising my hand to his lips to silence him, he arched an eyebrow at me. "But you're also sweet, kind, funny, romantic, passionate, playful, and you make me feel like the most desirable woman in the world when you look at me. So for those reasons, Jared, I definitely think I can handle it."

Holding my fingers to his mouth, he gently nipped on the pads with his teeth before planting a soothing kiss on each one. I could feel fiery hot desire deep inside my belly, and the aching between my legs was returning with a vengeance. The lust in his eyes called to me like a siren luring sailors to their doom. He was my light and my destruction. His power over me was frightening, but invigorating all at once.

Grabbing me by the waist he pulled me to him, compressing our chests together. I could feel the rigid stiffness of his erection against my hip as he kissed me, driving his tongue into my mouth and seeking out my own. Letting out a moan he began sliding down the straps of my dress, letting it fall into a heap on the floor. Lifting me up, he used his foot to kick it aside. His hands worked quickly to remove my bra as his lips never left my own.

We staggered backwards toward the couch and, lifting me into his arms, Jared slowly lowered me onto it, forcing our lips to part from one another. He gazed down at me and stroked a strand of hair from my face with his thumb.

"Oh, Layla. You really are exquisite, and from this moment on, you are mine. Mine entirely. I want your body to crave my touch, to ache for me with a sensual and passionate need. I want to please you in every way possible, to give you everything your heart desires. But right now I'll settle for some mind blowing orgasms."

I arched my back as he trailed kisses over my breasts. Taking my nipple into his mouth, he swirled the very tip of his tongue over it, making it pucker and harden at his touch.

I wanted him desperately with an insatiable need. I needed him to wash away the hurt and angst I felt in the guest room, the feeling of deep, lingering disappointment and the fear that he was slipping through my fingers. As if hearing my thoughts, he pulled me close to him, holding me tightly against his body. His arms firmly across my back, he kept me enclosed in his embrace, his intense, ferocious kisses becoming tender and gentle with a sweet longing. Wrapping my arms around his torso, I ran my hands over his back as lust began to engulf my senses. I was done waiting. I wanted him inside me, bringing me my release from the tension of the evening's events.

I dug my nails into his back and dragged them gently downwards to the deep and sexy dimples on his lower back. I bit down carnivorously on his bottom lip, and he let out a primal groan, deep and husky. His eyes closed, and his head rolled back, forcing my teeth to release his deliciously plump lip.

"Fuck, Layla. You're an animal. It's driving me crazy."

With one swoop, he flipped me onto my front. Raising my hands above my head, he ran his hands down my arms, my shoulder blades, my spine and the curve of my hip, before sliding his thumbs into the elastic on my panties. He pulled me down to the edge of the couch so that my feet were now touching the floor.

Lying on top of me, his hot breath was warming my face as he spoke seductively into my ear. "Oh baby, these are so deliciously delicate I would hate to ruin them. Stay still."

His skin exuded his arousal and an intoxicating scent of soap, sweat and sex. It was an aromatic combination that left me feeling woozy and lightheaded, but also incredibly turned on.

His fingertips trailed gently down my neck followed by gentle and grazing kisses over my shoulder blades and all the way down my back. I held my breath as he nipped at the elastic waist of my panties before licking slowly over the curve of my hip. Clamping his teeth over the delicate lace, he gently slid one side down my hip and over my behind to my thigh. He was playful and sexy Jared once again, and I was eager to know what else he could possibly have in store for me.

Sex with Jared was beyond pleasurable - it was essential, crucial and vital to my health. He performed the same move on the other side of my panties, leaving them around my thighs, restricting the movement of my legs.

"You have a fine ass, my lady. A very fine ass indeed. Especially now that it belongs to me."

I stifled a laugh. "So you own my ass?"

He snickered and nodded. "Abso-fucking-lutely."

I blushed with embarrassment, but in all honesty I was his. I didn't want to be anyone else's.

His hands on my hips, he ran his fingers swiftly over my behind and slid my panties to my ankles. With a hard thrust, he pushed my feet apart, leaving me wide open.

He gently and attentively ran his fingers up my thigh and between my legs. My clit was throbbing, pulsing with a need for release. I was so turned on, a simple touch would have pushed me over the edge, but Jared was a sexpert and knew how to touch, stroke and tease me to the point of lunacy. I hated and loved that about him.

Sliding a finger inside me, he let out a soft moan, almost like the sound one would make when eating something particularly delicious. "Mmmm, baby, you are so ready for me. You're practically gushing with anticipation for my cock."

Panting, I wriggled my hips, urging him to move inside me, but with his other hand he grabbed me by the waist to still me. "No." His tone was strict and a definite warning.

He withdrew his finger and quickly reached into his pocket before pushing down his sweatpants, freeing his impressive erection. Closing my eyes in anticipation, I heard the sound of foil rip before, slowly and steadily, he entered me. I gasped for breath - he filled me so deep that I could feel him in the bottom of my stomach. Leaning forward, he cupped his hands over my breasts and massaged them firmly, but with perfect tenderness.

Pushing myself up on my hands, I straightened so that I was firmly pressed against him; my back against his rock hard abs and our hips fused in place. Holding his hand over my right breast, he moved his left hand down my body to my stomach and pressed it with his palm, forcing us together tightly into a standing position. His hips moved rhythmically as he thrust himself in and out. His mouth caressed my neck before moving to my earlobe and nipping it teasingly.

I ran my own hand up his neck to the back of his head and gripped a handful of his soft hair. It was wet with sweat, and I could smell the faint scent of a fruity shampoo as I rolled my head back onto his shoulder. His hand moved downwards from my stomach to my tender and swollen clit as he rubbed it in time to his thrusts.

My pulse spiked as a surge of pleasure rippled through my body like lightning. My heartbeat was pounding in my ears, and his panting breath on my neck pushed me over the edge. My legs weakened and shook as my orgasm came crashing through me like a wave. The muscles inside me convulsed and tightened around him. He gasped loudly, before hissing out a breath as he found his release, calling my name, "Layla! Fuck!"

My knees trembling, I collapsed onto the soft couch with Jared rolling onto his back next to me. Raising his hand to his forehead, he wiped his brow and exhaled loudly.

"Christ, Layla. You're going to kill me if you keep going at this rate. My heart feels like it's going to explode."

He was breathless, and I couldn't take my eyes off his stunning, beautiful face. Rolling onto his side, he propped himself onto his elbow and gazed down at me. My eyelids were getting heavy, and I began to feel myself drifting off to sleep. Wrapping me in his arms, Jared scooped me up and carried me out of the room and down the hall to the guest room. He laid me softly onto the bed before reaching for a blanket and draping it over me. I expected him to leave me and return to his room, but he didn't. Climbing in behind me he pulled me into him, spooning me in his arms. He pressed his lips against the back of my head in a kiss. "Goodnight, my lady."

I sighed with pure happiness and content. This was exactly where I wanted to be, completely sexed out and wrapped in his arms. I almost didn't want to sleep for fear I'd wake up and discover it was all a dream, but my exhaustion was growing, so I snuggled into the pillow and gently drifted into a deep sleep.

Chapter 19

The King And I

The sound of music woke me as the smell of cinnamon and maple syrup immediately stirred my senses. Opening my eyes I scanned the room, trying to fathom where I was. Lifting myself up on to my elbows, I looked around at the neutral magnolia walls. A large power drill was sitting on the floor in the middle of the room. Memories of the previous night came flooding back to me. The bar, the dining room, the fight and the mind blowing antics in the bedroom; it provoked an array of emotions inside me.

Hauling myself out of bed, I suddenly realized that I was stark naked. Wrapping a sheet around me, I made my way to his room at the end of the hall. I didn't pass him on my way and the music I could hear echoing through the large white foyer told me he was in the kitchen, and the scent of pancakes told me he was cooking breakfast. His room was empty, and his bed was exactly how we had left it the previous night: clean, crisp and perfectly straight. A condom wrapper was discarded on the floor beside the couch, so I picked it up and searched for the bathroom to dispose of it.

There was a white arched door in the far corner of the room which I assumed was the bathroom. I was right, and it was stunning! It was large and well lit by spotlights that were sunken into the ceiling. A big rectangular bathtub, equipped with Jacuzzi jets and a heat setting, was in the center of the room. It was on a platform and surrounded by tiny lights fixed into the tiles. The entire room was a shade of cream and the tiles were a brilliant and blinding gold. There were two sinks and the glass doored shower was big enough for two. Walking over to the sinks, I caught a glimpse of myself in the large golden framed mirror above them.

Oh, Layla. You are a mess, girl.

I needed a shower and a brush to hack at my hair, badly. Staring into the mirror, I eyed the reflection of the shower behind me. Grabbing a towel from the shelf on the wall, I stripped off the sheet that clung to my body and got in. It was heaven. I set the water as hot as I could stand it and groaned as the water pressure massaged my aching muscles. Sex with Jared was nothing short of a work out for my body and at the rate we were going, I'd be shedding my curves for an athletic figure in no time. I washed my hair and spent a few moments buffing and preening my body till I was satisfied I was clean and ready for the day.

Drying myself, I wrapped the towel around my chest before making my way back to the guest room where I dressed quickly. I brushed my hair and pulled it back into a tight ponytail. It was still wet, but I was starving and the smells that filled the house were delicious. The luxury of a blow-dry would simply have to wait.

A loud ringing echoed from Jared's room, and not wanting him to miss an important call, I hurried down the hall to answer it. It was sitting on the vintage couch vibrating, so I quickly picked it up. Looking at the screen, I noticed that the caller had withheld their number and curiously, I answered.

"Hello?"

"Hello? Jared?"

A woman's voice spoke down the phone which took me by surprise. Confused, I answered back.

"Who is this?"

The line went dead the moment my voice travelled through the receiver. Gripping it in my hand, I stared at it. What was that all about?

My mind swirling with unanswered questions, I made my way down stairs. The sound of the music became clearer, and the rock and roll rhythms of Elvis reverberated through the house. Passing the dining room, I smiled to myself as I caught a glimpse of the glass table that I had been laying on the night before. As I approached the kitchen, I quietly stood in the doorway. Leaning my hip on the frame, I watched him. Dressed in sweat pants and a simple white tee, Jared stood with his back to me, mixing some batter in a large glass bowl. The music stopped and another song began to play: 'Heartbreak Hotel'. He was clearly a fan.

I grinned as he began to sing loudly to the lyrics, gyrating his hips like the king himself. I'd almost forgotten that he was only twenty-two years old. He carried himself in a way that was so much older than he really was and I realized that had probably happened when his parents died. Jared had been forced to leave his adolescent days behind and take over his father's business, but the Jared in front of me now was young, carefree and very sexy. I stifled a laugh as he began to thrash his legs around in a move I'd seen the king perform during a music channel tribute to the man himself.

Spinning around, Jared stared at me in horror before running his fingers through his hair and blushing profusely. Realizing I'd embarrassed him, I grabbed a spoon from the counter top and held it to my mouth like a microphone. Singing loud and clear I sashayed over to him, spoon in hand. I laid on the diva nice and thick. He smiled at me so wide that it almost reached his eyes which were now gazing down at me in amusement. Thrusting my hips and curling my lip, pulling off an impressive Elvis pout, I shimmied and swayed around the kitchen, diffusing the tense atmosphere I had caused by disrupting his morning concert for one. When the song ended I placed my spoon on the counter top again and took a bow as he whistled and applauded.

"Bravo, my lady. A thoroughly good show all round, I'd say. And I'm not just talking about that performance. Last night was amazing."

Pulling me into an embrace, he kissed me tenderly before pulling away to gaze at me. His eyes were bright and almost danced as he smiled at me.

"In fact, I was wondering what you had planned for the weekend? I wondered if you might like to stay here, with me, for a whole two days. Mmm, just think what I could do to your delectably delicious body over forty-eight hours."

Raising my hand to his lips, he kissed each of my fingertips before trailing kisses over my palm to my wrist.

"Actually, I promised my dad I'd visit home this weekend."

"So tell him you're sick or that you have to study. I don't know, make something up."

Pulling my hand away, I regarded him coolly. "I'm not lying to my father, Jared. I never lie to him. I've only been home once since I got here and I made a promise. I never break a promise. So, as much as I would love to spend an entire weekend as your sex slave, I have to go home. And you have a business to run. Remember?"

Rolling his eyes, he let out an exasperated sigh. "Ok, ok, I get it. For the record, I don't usually work on weekends, but if you're going to be away then I'll have to busy my hands with something else. Figured that you'd be a daddy's girl. When I asked if you had any other men in your life I should be worried about, I forgot about your father being one of them. It's sweet that you are so close. You're very lucky."

"I know I am. Which is why I simply must drag myself away from you and go to Pasadena. By the way, you had a call. I answered, but they hung up. Number withheld, and it was a woman. Anything you need to tell me?"

Walking around the counter, I pulled out a stool. He shrugged. "Not that I'm aware of. It was probably just a business call. Nothing to worry about. Perhaps when you answered they thought they had the wrong number."

Kissing my forehead he smiled. I couldn't shake the feeling he was hiding something, but I had to give him the benefit of the doubt at least once. Didn't I?

Pouring a glass of milk for himself, he seemed a little on edge. "So how are you getting to Pasadena exactly?"

Resting my elbows on the counter top I answered, "By car, like everyone else. I'm driving. My dad bought me a car. It's a real hottie, too. Sky blue Ford Focus."

Arching his eyebrow at me he turned back to the stove and began heating a pan. "And you plan to drive there alone? And how long have you had this car? Is its engineering sound? In fact, how long have you had your license? Do you have much driving experience?"

Why was he asking me so many questions? Did he honestly think my father would give me a car if I wasn't perfectly capable of driving it? The thought that Jared doubted my driving ability was beginning to upset me.

"Whoa, calm down. First of all I wouldn't drive it if I didn't feel completely safe, my father is a mechanic, remember. I've been driving since I was sixteen and got my license over a year ago. I am perfectly capable of driving to Pasadena." His back still turned, I rolled my eyes at him. He was being so overprotective. I wasn't a child anymore.

"I know you just rolled your eyes at me, Layla. I also know you think I'm being over-protective, but I'm not. I'm realistic. It's not that I worry about your driving skills, it's the other assholes on the road. The last thing I want is for you to end up in the hospital because some coke snorting, joy riding dick on a dope high, runs you off the road. Will you at least take your roommate with you? The two of you are friends, right? You could introduce her to your best friend back home."

He did make a good point. It would be nice for Mel and Amy to meet. They were the only two girlfriends I had in my life and based on their personalities they were sure to get along really well. He poured some of the batter into a pan and with skillful grace and flipped the pancake into the air, catching it as it landed back into the scorching hot pan. He plated it up and brought it over, placing it in front of me.

"Bon appétit, my lady."

I melted a little inside. After all, he was just looking out for me. And wasn't that exactly what I wanted him to do? Picking up my fork I pointed it at him. "Fine. I'll take Amy. But not because you told me to or because I'm worried about driving alone to Pasadena. I'm doing it so she and Mel can get to know each other. Understood?"

Leaning across the counter he lowered my fork with his hand and placed a soft kiss on my lips. "Perfectly, my lady. You are your own boss as always."

Chuckling, I took a bite out of my pancake. "Technically, you're my boss."

He winked at me and grinned. "I'll keep that in mind. Now eat your breakfast so I can take you home before I end up sprawling you over that table again and giving you something to think about over the weekend."

Now that was an idea.

Pushing away the sinful thoughts he had provoked in me with that simple suggestion, I changed the subject. Nodding at the speakers mounted on the wall I smiled.

"So Elvis, huh?"

He realized what I was referring to and gave me a boyish grin. "Well, he's like me - a king. He was the king of rock and roll, and I'm a king of the business world and my enterprise, my kingdom. Besides, his music totally rocks. It's classic and never goes out of style. His lyrics are heartfelt and he sings them with real emotion. Not like that grunge and emo shit you get today."

I snickered at him. "You sound like my grandpa used to."

"Sounds like your gramps was a very wise man. Now, if you've quite satisfied your curiosity, I suggest you eat your breakfast so I can drive you back to campus. Lord knows I wish you wouldn't go, but the sooner I leave you, the sooner you can miss me."

I smiled and stuck my tongue out at him playfully. Arching an eyebrow, he leaned forward and stared at my mouth. "Don't stick your tongue out at me unless you know how to use it. And I can think of several better uses for that mouthwatering piece of equipment than to mock me."

Smirking at him, I stuck it out again very slowly before pulling it back quickly and pressing my lips together. Leaping across the counter he spun me around, his arms by my sides as he gripped the edge, caging me in. His mouth was inches from my own, and I could smell the minty freshness of his breath.

"Go ahead, Layla. Do that again. I dare you."

Holding my breath, I timidly parted my lips, but before I could even get my tongue towards them, Jared slid his into my mouth with a deep sensual hunger. An aching between my legs reminded me how quickly and easily this man could press my buttons. Knowing full well how fast things could develop I pulled away, breathless and panting. Placing my hand on his heaving, rock solid chest I breathed deeply, trying to regain my equilibrium.

"I have to go home, and if you keep kissing me like that, I will never leave. And no, before you say anything, that is not an option. I have to go see my father."

Sighing deeply, he pressed his lips into a hard line. Placing a chaste kiss on them I smiled suggestively.

"To quote the words of a very wise man I know, don't pout, Jared."

Chapter 20

A Mothers Love Can Be Painful

Jared had been very quiet on the drive back to the campus. I got the feeling that he was still brooding about the fact that I hadn't leaped at the chance to spend the weekend with him. It wasn't that I didn't want to. Lord knew I would have loved nothing more than to live in my underwear for two days and have Jared care for my every need. The thought was perfectly delicious, and I was practically salivating at the idea of it all, but the reality of the situation was that I had to go see my father. I missed him even though it had only been a few weeks since I'd left. He would have hit the roof if I'd called and told him that I was spending the weekend in Long Beach with this new guy I'd been seeing for little over a month now. He would have had a massive cardiac arrest right there on the phone.

Pulling up outside the dorm, I turned myself in my seat to face him. He was staring at his steering wheel with a sad look on his face. Hooking my finger and thumb on his chin, I drew his face away from the wheel to look at me.

"It's only for one night. I'll call you as soon as I get to Pasadena, and you can call, text, or email me whenever you want. We can have dinner on Sunday if you like. You'll be so busy with work, you won't even notice I'm gone. Trust me." I placed a soft kiss on his lips, and he sighed heavily.

"Layla, I most certainly will notice you're gone. In fact, it's going to plague me until Sunday. I'm going to worry and panic until you call to tell me you're safe and sound in Pasadena, and then I'm going to panic and worry, waiting for you to come back. But I will definitely be calling, texting and emailing you. In fact..." He reached into his pocket and pulled out a business card. Handing it to me he pointed at the listed numbers. "That's my cell, office, home and email. You can reach me anytime. Day or night. If you call my office, just tell them who you are and that I'm expecting your call. Don't worry, I'll be making Janine aware of you first thing Monday."

My head snapped up. Instantly tensing I gave him a curious expression. "Janine?"

"My secretary. You're not jealous, are you? You have no reason to be. Janine is a fifty-six year old grandmother with crow's feet and wrinkles even Max Factor can't cover up. Besides, I only have eyes for you."

Moving from my seat, I climbed onto his lap as he cupped my face in his hands and pulled me to him for a long, lingering kiss. Removing his hands from my face, he gently stroked up and down my spine and lightly ran his fingers over my thin blouse. Goosebumps began to appear on my skin as the feel of his gentle touch sent a prickling sensation through me.

Coming up for air, I rested my forehead on his. Our noses touched, and our lips were so close that I could still taste him. "I have to go. I'll call you, I promise. Don't work too hard. Behave yourself as you would expect me to behave and try not to miss me too much."

Sighing, he opened his car door and I shifted off his lap, setting my feet on the sidewalk. Pulling himself up, he stood in front of me and held my hands in his. "I will try and get some work done, though with you on my mind that's not very likely. I will miss you like crazy. Now get in there before I come to my senses, haul you over my shoulder, drag you back to my place and imprison you in my bedroom all weekend."

Giving him a chaste kiss, I nodded and walked towards the entrance of the dorm. Glancing back one last time, I waved as he yelled after me, "I hate that you have to go. But I sure do love to watch you leave!"

Playfully, I smacked my ass at him and watched gleefully as his eyes widened and a wicked grin spread across his lips. Winking at him, I turned away and walked through the heavy double doors. I stood inside for a moment with my back against the wall, trying to catch my breath. The sound of his engine distracted me, and I watched through the corner of my eye as his car pulled away and sped out of the parking lot.

As I walked down the corridor to my room, I could hear the sound of a guitar reverberating through the walls. I knew exactly where it was coming from and as I got nearer, I could see a tall blond guy standing at Ollie's door, hammering loudly with his fist.

"Turn that fuckin' racket down. Seriously, dude, some of us are trying to sleep. I mean, shit, its fuckin' 10 a.m. Pause for the cause!"

I winced. Oh dear. My thought about our neighbors being ok with the guys playing was obviously restricted to certain acceptable hours of the day. Approaching the guy who was still furiously banging on Ollie's door I tapped him on the shoulder.

"Excuse me. Mind if I give it a try?"

Moving aside he waved at the door. "Go ahead. I've been banging on it for over an hour. The guy's a complete dick."

I stifled a laugh and gently rapped on the door. "Ollie, it's me. Would you mind opening the door so I can give you a hug before I go back to Pasadena for the weekend?"

The music immediately came to a halt and silence filled the hallway. Opening the door, Ollie grinned at me. "Hey superstar! Come on in. Sorry about the noise. Did I wake you, or Amy?" Giving the guy behind me a sarcastic smile, he ushered me into his room and shut the door behind me.

Laughing, I shoved him on the arm. "Ollie! Don't be such a dick. You don't want people complaining about you to the Resident Advisor. You could end up out on your ass."

He shrugged. "Like I give a shit what guys like him think. He and his little girlfriend make a shit-load of noise every fucking night and I don't go banging his door down. I mean, I know her name and I haven't even met her yet. He screams like a bitch whenever they're going at it. At first it was funny, but now it's kinda pissin' me off."

I fell onto his bed and laughed so hard my jaw ached. Sitting down next to me he chuckled. "It's not funny Layla."

Tears were running down my face as I sat up and leaned my head on his shoulder. "Maybe you should bring a girl back and make some noise of your own."

Giving me a smirk he draped his arm around my shoulders. "Is that an offer?"

I shoved him, and he shrugged. "Hey, it was worth a try. So you heading back to Pasadena, huh? Thought you might have been tied up all weekend with the meathead."

I shot him a warning look. Raising his hands in front of him in defense, he recanted. "Sorry, but come on, Layla. What is it you see in the guy? He's your boss, he lied to you, and he picked you up last night and dragged you away from your friends. I mean, who does that kind of shit? Plus, he's like twenty-two. You're only nineteen."

Shooting to my feet, I turned and glowered at him. He was overstepping the mark, and I was beginning to lose my cool with him. "First of all, Ollie, he's not my boss, Lorraine is my boss. Jared just pays the bills and oversees the finance. Secondly, he didn't drag me away. I went willingly. His age makes absolutely no difference to me, or to the way I feel about him and not that it matters, but I'll be twenty in a few weeks! I really don't know why you hate him so much, Ollie. He's never done anything to you. Tell me what it is that makes you loathe him so much. What exactly is your fucking problem?" I was fuming at him.

He stood in front of me, grabbed my arms and stared into my eyes, his face so close to mine I could smell the sweet fragrance of his cologne mixed with the scent of his hair product. "Because I'm not him! And because for all the stupid fucking luck, he got you first!"

My mouth fell open, and my chest constricted. I couldn't breathe. Ollie's words swirled around in my head like a vortex. Letting go of my arms, he turned his back to me and ran his hands through his long black hair. The sleeves of his t-shirt rose up, and I noticed for the first time that he had a tattoo. A snake wound its way down his thick bicep. Sinking onto the edge of the bed, he sat with his elbows on his knees and dropped his head into his hands. "Fuck!"

Lifting his head up to look at me, he sighed deeply. "Layla, could you go now, please? I'm sorry I snapped, and I'm sorry for everything I said. Your love life is none of my business. In fact, let's forget the whole thing. I'll save you a seat in class on Monday."

Letting out the tight painful breath I'd been holding inside my chest, I walked over and put my hand on his shoulder. "Ollie I-"

Standing up he kissed my cheek and hugged me tightly. "Don't. I'd really rather we just forget it. I'm fine. We're good. I'm glad you've found someone who makes you happy, and I'd rather have you in my life as my geeky, funny, sarcastic friend, than not at all. Ok? We're cool?" I nodded weakly and hugged him back. I really hoped we were ok.

The thought of losing Ollie from my life filled me with dread. I cared about him deeply and hated myself for hurting him. "I'm so sorry for what I've done to you, Ollie. I never meant to lead you on."

Holding his finger to my lips, he silenced me. "Shhh. No, it's not your fault. You have never led me on, Layla. I was the one who thought maybe we could be more than friends, but I was misguided, that's all. It's cool. I mean it. Now go and pack your shit up and head home. I hope Amy doesn't expect me to be her wing woman again this weekend."

I smiled at him. "Actually, I've decided to take her with me. I want her to meet Mel." He raised his eyebrow at me and shook his head. "That's like hurling gas on a fire if you ask me. From what you've told me about Mel she's a real firework, and Amy is definitely a big ol' tank of gas. Toxic and lethal."

I laughed and pushed him away from me playfully. "Whatever you say, rock star. I'll catch you on Monday. Don't do anything I wouldn't do. Which these days gives you an awful lot of wiggle room."

The men in my life appeared to have developed an interesting habit of raising their eyebrows at me. Jared did it frequently, and now Ollie was doing it too. I wondered what it was about me that provoked such a reaction from them. Giving me a wave, Ollie closed the door after me, and I walked over to my own room.

My heart was hammering in my chest. What was happening to me? For Christ's sake, I was completely falling in love with Jared, and yet Ollie had the ability to get right under my skin. The simmering sexual tension between us was electric and practically scorching with heat. My mind began to wander back to his tattoo, his lip ring pinching into his pink flesh, and his delicious chocolate brown eyes. I felt a clenching inside me as I thought about sinking my teeth into those plump lips and running my tongue over his cool metal lip ring. What the fuck was I doing? I was with Jared, but here I was mentally making out with Ollie. I needed to get a grip on this, and soon.

Entering my room, I stopped abruptly as I took in the scene in front of me. Sitting on the floor, cross legged in what could best be described as the lotus position, was Amy. Her eyes closed, she hummed quietly.

"Uh, Amy, what are you doing?" Slinging my bag on my bed, I sat in front of her and tried to mimic her pose. It was useless. I was about as flexible as a pencil and as graceful as a bull. My legs barely crossed, I giggled.

Opening one eye, she smiled at me. "Ommmm…I'm meditating. Omm…you're home late. Ommmm."

Trying desperately not to laugh I responded in the same fashion.

"Omm...I stayed at Jared's. Omm…we had mind blowing sex on a dining table before fighting and having sex again. Omm."

Her eyes flew open and in one swift movement she was on her feet. Rolling onto my knees, I hauled myself up. My body was still pretty sore from the sexual adventures of the previous night. Her hands fisted on her hips and her jaw almost scraping the floor, Amy gawked at me. I smiled back at her. "What? We had sex. We had a little fight and then more sex. Why do you have that stupid look on your face?"

Closing her mouth very briefly she continued to stare at me in shock. "You had a fight? What about?"

I wasn't sure if I should disclose the details of our disagreement to her, but she was the only girlfriend I had in college and I needed to get things off my chest. "After we had sex on the table he carried me upstairs, and I assumed when he took me to bed we would be sleeping together, but he said he couldn't promise to keep his hands off me and that I was already exhausted. I knew it was such a pile of bullshit, so I got really pissed at him and locked myself in the bathroom."

"Serves him right! I mean, how he could be so cold to you is beyond me. How ridiculous! Can't keep his hands off you. Did you call him on it?"

I flushed and brushed a lock of hair behind my ear. "No. I just kind of went off at the deep end and slammed the door in his face. When I came out he had a drill in his hand, ready to take the hinges off the door."

She rolled her eyes at me. "So for all you know, it could have been the truth? You're doubting him and calling him a liar. Now that's cold, girlfriend." Peeved at her for taking his side, I crossed my arms over my chest and scowled.

"You're taking his side now? He fucked me on a dining table, then told me to sleep on my own! He was the one being frosty!" Shocked by my sudden outburst, she backed away and rolled her eyes at me. "Oh come on, Layla. You still fucked him again after that, didn't you? So it can't have been as bad as you're making it out to be. Did you end up sleeping alone?"

She was right, again, but I still would have liked her to have been fighting my corner rather than defending him. "No, he curled up next to me, but I don't know if he stayed there all night because when I woke up he was making breakfast."

She flung herself onto her bed and stared at the ceiling. "You know, Layla, you can be a little overdramatic sometimes. I mean, I love you, honey, but maybe next time you could ask questions before you start throwing your tantrums and exploding at him. Ok?"

I rolled my eyes and nodded weakly. "Yeah, yeah, I get it. He's so hot headed, though, which actually brings me to my next question. Would you come to Pasadena with me for the weekend? Jared doesn't want me driving alone on my first trip, and he kinda made a big deal about it, so I told him I'd take you."

Sitting up, she gave me a pouty look and frowned. "Oh, I wish you'd said something sooner. Daddy called last night. He's coming to Long Beach on business, so were having dinner. Sorry, Layla. Will you have to cancel?"

Scrunching up my nose, I shook my head. "Nah, I'll still go. I just won't tell him that I drove alone. He's working all weekend, so he won't even give it a second thought. But for the record, if he ever asks, I was with you the whole time."

Lying back on her bed Amy sighed, exasperated. "Oh Layla, you are playing with fire, girl. He's going to go supernova if he finds out you lied." I stared at her with a serious expression.

"Not if you don't tell him, he won't. And I definitely won't be saying anything."

* * * *

The drive to Pasadena had taken me a little longer than usual because I had to pull over twice when Jared called, checking if I was alright. It was sweet that he was concerned for my wellbeing, but it was also beginning to irritate me. I was a grown woman who was perfectly capable of taking care of herself.

Pulling into the driveway, I noticed that Dad's car was missing. He was aware I was coming home for the weekend since I had called him before I'd left campus, so I assumed he'd run to the store, or that he'd been called into the shop. I opened the front door and slung my keys onto the table adjacent to it. Grabbing a handful of mail that was stacked on the coffee table, I kicked off my shoes and sprawled myself out on the couch. My cell buzzed less than a minute later. Seeing the caller ID I rolled my eyes.

"Hi, Mom."

"Don't you 'hi, Mom' me, Layla Jennings. I have been out of my mind with worry. Not one call or text to let me know how you are or if you're ok. It's as if you have no care for your safety or my nerves, Layla. I'm guzzling bottles of Pepto-Bismol like its milk! And your father isn't much help, either. When I call him to see if he's heard from you, he just lectures me on how I should give you space and trust you to make good judgments."

I let out an exasperated sigh. This wasn't going to be a short call. "Sounds like good advice if you ask me, mother."

"Don't take that tone with me, Layla. I do trust you. I raised you well, and I know you can be a good judge of character as well as make sound and rational decisions, but it's the other people I don't trust. I see the college kids coming into the hospital, Layla, drugged to the eyeballs, drinking till they can't even see straight, or form a coherent sentence. Rapes, shootings, stabbings...the list is endless. Don't get me started on all the pregnancies I've had walk in. I don't want you getting hurt or knocked up. Would a courtesy call to your mother be too much to ask, Layla? I mean really?"

She was overreacting again, but knowing this wouldn't end until I caved in to her demands, I gave her what she wanted. "Ok, Mom. I'm sorry I didn't call. I've just been really busy with work and college and everything, but I promise from now on I'll text you a goodnight message every day to let you know I'm tucked in safe and sound. Alright?"

The line went quiet for a moment, and part of me hoped we'd been disconnected, but alas, no such luck.

"What's everything else, Layla? College and work I get, but what else could make you so busy you can't call your mother?" She gasped. "You've met a boy, haven't you? I knew it. I knew this would happen. I'm too young to be a grandma, young lady. First thing Monday I want you to go see Dr. Roberts and get on birth control, do you hear me? Who is he anyway? This prospective father of my grandchildren."

Rolling my eyes, I rested my head back against the couch and pinched the bridge of my nose. I could feel the beginning of a tension headache in my temple.

"First of all, I'm aware of how to practice safe sex, Mother. I've been on contraception for weeks! And second, he's not a boy, he's a man. He's twenty-two, very successful, runs his own company and treats me like a princess. So stop worrying."

"What's his name, Layla?" She clearly wasn't letting this go.

"Jared. Jared Garrett. Mother, I swear if you even think about Googling him I will never speak to you again."

"Jared Garrett. The property developer? Jared Garrett the sole heir to the Garrett estate and fortune? Jared Garrett the millionaire?" Too late.

I held the phone away from my ear to avoid the screeching on the other end as my mother gushed and squealed about how I was going to marry a millionaire.

"Mother, calm down. We're just dating right now. I don't know where it's going to go. I think we're a long way from marriage talks, but since we're on the subject of Jared, I have to go. I promised him I'd call to let him know when I arrived safe in Pasadena."

I could almost hear her smiling. "Ah, see, someone else who worries about your safety and wellbeing. I like him already."

"Goodbye, Mother. I'll text you tomorrow night. Tonight I'm home with Daddy. I love you, even if you are a little unhinged."

"Layla!"

"Goodbye, Mother." My tone was curt, and she knew my patience was running thin.

"Goodbye, darling. I love you. Stay safe."

Holding the cell in my hand, I dialed Jared's number. He picked up on the first ring. "Layla. You're safe? You're home?"

The sound of his voice brought a wave of warmth through my body. "Yes, I'm here. Safe and sound. You can stop worrying now."

"I will worry and panic until you are back here with me, in my arms, where I can keep you safe myself. Amy settled in alright?"

Shit. Fuck. For the first time in my adult life, I was going to have to lie. And to Jared.

"Yeah, she's fine. A little tired from traveling, so she's taking a nap, but later we're going out for dinner with Mel and my dad."

Liar, liar, panties on fire.

He chuckled. "I'm sure that will make for an interesting evening. I'd sure love to be a fly on the wall. Well, have fun, my lady, and try not to miss me too much. Lord knows I'm missing you like crazy right now. Especially that delectable little ass of yours."

I gasped in jest. "Jared!"

The husky tones of his laughter made me miss him deeply. I wanted to be wrapped up in his arms, cocooned in Jared. The line went silent for a moment as we both caught our breath. Maybe he was thinking the same thing I was.

"So, what are you wearing?"

I grinned. "A smile. Goodbye, Jared."

"Tease. I'll get you for that. Have a lovely evening. Goodbye, my lady."

Hanging up, I hugged myself. He was utterly perfect. Sweet, caring, his trust and faith in me was unfailing...and I had just fed him a lie. I had made him a promise, and if he ever found out how badly I had broken that promise he would be furious. How could I lie to him after I had lectured and chastised him about the need for honesty in a relationship? But surely my little white lie didn't compare even slightly to his? After all, a lie of omission is still a lie. I was going to have to live with this one on my conscience and the thought made me feel queasy.

Hearing a key rattle in the door, I glanced over the back of the couch to see Dad putting his keys on the table next to mine.

"Hey, baby girl. Sorry I wasn't here when you got in, I had to go to work. You been home long?" Leaping over the back of the couch, I ran to hug him. He staggered back at little as the force of my body hit him like a wall, but he smiled widely. "I'm pleased to see you, too. So, what's been happening with you?"

Collapsing back on to the couch, I sighed loudly. "Got a call from Mom earlier, being her nervous self, as usual. I promised I'd text her every night before bed so that she knows I'm safe."

"Thank god. Maybe now she'll stop calling and hassling me. I mean, I understand she worries, but-"

The chiming of the phone in the hallway stopped him from finishing his sentence. Eying the caller ID, he groaned.

"Of course. Speak of the devil, and she's sure to be calling your phone." Begrudgingly, he answered. "Hello, Diane. Yes, she told me you called. No, I don't think she was quite aware of how worried you were, but you can stop calling me every hour on the hour for an update."

Mom was obviously giving him a hard time, but Dad had always been particularly skilled at cutting her off during a rant.

"Diane, I really don't think it's any of my business who my daughter does, or doesn't date. Why do you torture yourself? Yes, of course, I knew she was seeing someone. She tells me everything."

Peering over the back of the sofa, he raised his eyebrows at me and gave me a look that told me we would be discussing this as soon as he could get rid of my mother. I sank down into the large soft cushions wishing the floor would open and I'd be sucked into oblivion.

"Alright, Diane, I'll talk to her. Ok. You too. Bye."

Hanging up, he made his way over to his usual chair, opposite the couch. It was an old brown leather recliner which he had positioned strategically so that not only did he have the best view of the TV, he could see the front door and the stairs without having to move an inch. It had been designed so that he would be able to see me leaving and coming home whenever I was out with friends.

"So, you have a boyfriend? Naturally your mother has Googled him and told me everything about his social, financial and political status, but I want to hear it from you. What is he like? Where did you meet? How long have you been dating and why didn't you tell me about him?"

Taking a deep breath I straightened up and faced him.

"He's really sweet, caring, generous and a little overprotective, but in a good way. We met at the coffee shop. I accidentally got coffee all over his shirt, and kinda, almost, broke his nose. We've only been dating for a few weeks, but I feel like I have known him all my life. We really connect. He treats me like a princess, daddy, and you have nothing to worry about. He's very responsible, and as a successful business man he is focused and driven with a lot of ambition, too. I didn't tell you because there was nothing to tell. I wouldn't even call him my boyfriend. He's just a guy I'm seeing. Now, enough about Jared. I'm going to get Mel, and then we can all go out for dinner."

Jumping to my feet, I pecked him on the cheek and hurried out of the door. Ok, so I'd played down the whole relationship thing, but I was doing it to protect Dad. Besides, I really wasn't sure where things were going yet. I hoped that would be the end of our discussion about Jared, but I had a feeling Mel would be bringing it up again at dinner. That girl had no filter between her brain and her mouth.

Telling Dad how wonderful he was made my deceit feel that much worse. This guilt was going to eat me alive, and I still had dinner and a whole night's sleep to get through. Unable to stand the nauseous tension in my stomach, I decided to tell him the truth. Tomorrow, I thought, when I was back on campus, safe and sound and thus proving what a perfectly capable driver I was. I just prayed he wouldn't be too mad.

Chapter 21

Oh What A Wicked Web

Dinner at Mamma's Little Pizzeria was delicious as usual. Thankfully, Mel's presence had distracted Roberto's attention from me. He'd always been a little sweet on her, and I was sure she had a soft spot for him too, but typically Mel's self-esteem issues had always stopped her from asking him out. She was infuriating. She was one of life's natural beauties, yet she convinced herself that she was some kind of ogre.

I was still exhausted from spending Friday night with Jared, and hadn't felt much like talking through dinner. Guilt was still turning my stomach and had dissolved my usually ravenous appetite. Dad hadn't noticed, but Mel had raised an eyebrow at me several times. When we excused ourselves to go to the bathroom, I filled her in on what had happened between Jared and I: the table, the fight, the bedroom, breakfast and his warning about my driving. Although she agreed that he was being a little overprotective, she also warned me about spinning a web of lies. I wished so hard that she was wrong, but I had a terrible sinking feeling that this was all going to come back to haunt me. Lies rarely just disappear, they linger like a stalker, hiding, waiting for the moment they can spring out of the dark and tackle you to the floor.

Sunday morning started off with Dad's famous blueberry pancakes and bacon. It was also an awesome hangover cure.

After dinner, Mel and I had made our way through her father's bourbon. We'd mixed it with some cola, but it still packed one hell of a punch. I felt like my head was no longer attached to my shoulders, but that it was actually rolling across the floor, and I was just kicking it along as I walked. Dad must have noticed the bloodshot eyes, the nauseous heaving, and the painkillers I had swallowed, but tactfully, he never mentioned it. He simply plated me up with breakfast and told me it would make the day feel a little better. He really was amazing.

We'd made plans to spend the day watching movies and eating junk food, but after breakfast he'd got a call from work asking him to go down and help with a particularly difficult job they had. Wrapping me in a tight hug, he apologized. I would be heading back to the dorm by the time he was finished, so we said our goodbyes and exchanged kisses. Now that plans had changed, I decided to invite Mel over to veg out in front of the TV with me. After all, it was our favorite past time.

Pulling on my sneakers, I limped over to the door and pulled it open, ready to march over and drag her back for a day of hermitting. I stood frozen in shock and amazement. A very familiar sleek and shiny black Jaguar XK was parked at the end of the driveway. I slammed the front door shut and leaned against it, trying to control my now frantic breathing. My pulse skipped as the doorbell chimed and a knock rattled on the door behind me. Shit. Shit. How the hell was I going to talk my way out of this?

"Layla, would you please open the door. I can hear your heavy breathing through the thick wood, and as much as that gives me ideas and thrills me, I need to speak with you."

The way he growled my name caused my blood to heat and I felt my insides clench. Gingerly, I turned around and opened the door, inhaling a quick breath. He looked better than I remembered. His thick, golden brown hair shimmered in the sun, and his crisp white t-shirt clung to his chest. His dark denim jeans and sneakers reminded me that he was still only a twenty-two year old. He didn't seem so scary, but the look on his face was something else. He was mad, furious even. His eyes were dark, and his mouth was pressed into a hard line. His eyebrows pinched above the bridge of his nose as he scowled at me.

"Jared. What are you doing here? How did you even know where to find me?" I tried to appear that I was the one who was irritated, but it clearly didn't work as his expression never softened.

"Layla, where's Amy?"

A tingle of fear crept up my spine as my mind frantically searched for a plausible answer. "She's still in bed. We hit it pretty hard last night, and she's totally wiped."

His hands came up in front of him, and he winced. "Don't lie to me, Layla. I know she's not here. I know you drove all the way here alone, and I know that you lied to me about it! How could you lie? Why would you lie? But most of all, why would you directly disregard a simple request I made and a promise that you made? You broke your promise, and you lied to me. And you have the nerve to lecture me on the need for honesty between us? Nice play!"

His face was turning red, and the vein in his thick, muscular neck was protruding as he yelled at me. Part of me was so ashamed by my actions that I wanted to hang my head in shame. However, the other part of me was livid. How dare he come to my home and unleash this tirade? I was a fully grown woman, and I had driven safely and competently, and here he was screaming at me for lying. Of course, I'd lied. I knew he'd go off the deep end if he knew Amy hadn't travelled with me.

"I lied to you because I knew you'd go all bat shit crazy at me if I told the truth. I'm perfectly capable of driving from one place to another! Do you honestly think my father would let me drive that car if he didn't have complete faith in my abilities? Of course not! You're treating me like a child, and I do not appreciate you coming to my home, screaming at me and making me feel like I'm the one who's in the wrong. You didn't trust me, and that's the long and short of it, Jared. You have no faith in me, and you clearly don't respect me. We could have discussed this when I got back, but no, here you come riding in on your big black shiny horse to do what? Drag me back? Seize my keys? What exactly was your plan?"

Walking into the hallway, he grabbed me by the arms and pulled me inside. Twisting out of his vice like grip, I slammed the door and glared at him.

He ran his hands through his hair and sighed, exasperated. His expression grew darker, and I could see the anger simmering just beneath the surface. He was desperately trying to restrain himself.

"Layla, you lied to me! There is no excuse you could possibly give me for your betrayal. You're nineteen years old, and that is your first car! You have limited experience on the road as it is, let alone driving halfway across the state! I asked you to do one thing in the interest of your safety, and you promised me you would do it! I believed you. Well at least I did until I found Amy sitting in a booth at my coffee shop this morning! Christ, Layla I nearly had a heart attack when I found out that you drove here alone and that you would be doing the same thing to get back! I must have broken every damn traffic law to get here! How could you be so reckless?"

He turned his back to me, and continued to grip fistfuls of hair as he tried to reign in his temper which was beginning to sizzle in the air between us. The way he had roared at me had further fuelled my fury at him and his actions. I wasn't the only one with secrets around here. There was an awful lot he wasn't telling me, but I had continuously told myself that it was nothing.

I stood directly behind him with my fists pressed firmly into my hips. There was no way I was going to allow him to intimidate me. "I am not a child, Jared, and you can't tell me what to do, where to go, or how to get there! Long Beach to Pasadena is not half-way across the state. It's an hour, tops! I'm done here. I'm done with this conversation, and right now I am done talking to you! Go home Jared."

His head snapped up as he turned around to face me. The look of rage on his face was frightening, and I stepped back, slightly trembling in fear of what he might do next. Seeing the obvious alarm on my face, his expression softened, and he looked utterly mortified. Striding over fast, he pulled me to him and wrapped me in his arms. Pressing his lips to the top of my head, he kissed me repeatedly, muttering that he was sorry over and over. I buried my head in his chest and grasped his shirt for comfort. I was still mad at him, but I was relieved to see his gentler side emerging even if it was only momentarily.

Releasing me, he hung his head, and his face was twisted with remorse. "Baby, I am so sorry I frightened you. That look on your face…" He swallowed a lump in his throat. "I am so sorry. I would never, ever hurt you. You have to believe me. But God, Layla, you scared the fucking shit out of me, princess. The thought of you being hurt, or in trouble, and me being totally helpless…it terrifies me. I care about you so deeply, and that scares the shit out of me. The way I feel about you after such a short time is crazy and I'm completely out of my depth here. Please forgive me. I swear I would never, for as long as there is air in my lungs and a beat to my heart, I would never raise my hand to you."

Pressing my left palm against his chest, I lifted his chin with my right hand so that his eyes met mine. "I know you wouldn't. You just startled me. I'm sorry I lied to you, Jared, but you have to understand I'm a woman, not a child, and you have to let me have my independence. I can't always do as I'm told; I like my freedom and my space. It's just who I am. Please, have some faith in me, ok?"

He nodded weakly and bent down to place a chaste kiss on my lips. I had missed his mouth on mine, the smell of his spicy yet sweet cologne, the warmth of his arms and the comfort of his hard, muscular chest.

I scanned his face, trying to gauge his mood. He gave me a rueful smile and exhaled loudly. "Layla, I can't help feeling over-protective when it comes to your safety. I'd really appreciate it if you would come back to Long Beach in my car, and I'll have yours brought down this afternoon."

I swayed my head in a silent, but definitive, no. His shoulders sagged and his head rolled back. I could see he was used to getting his own way, but he was going to have to learn that Layla Jennings does not take orders. Rubbing the back of his neck he stared at me, but I stood my ground without giving him an inch.

"Fine, you win. But I will be right behind you, all the way there in my own car. Understand?"

Rolling my eyes I regarded him with frustration before finally conceding. "Fine, fine, stalk me all the way back to Long Beach if that will make you happy. I have to go pack and say goodbye to Mel. We can leave right after. You can wait here, or wait in the car. I don't mind."

"I'll wait in the car and give you and Mel your privacy. Don't be long. I want to get you home and all to myself."

Swiveling around, he opened the door and glanced back at me. "I've missed you, Layla. Truly I have."

I melted into a pool of dripping hot mess right there on the spot. God he was infuriating, and oh so sexy at the same time. His ability to completely unravel me with a simple sentence was astounding and completely disarming. I was still mad at him for his erratic behavior and icy demeanor, but I couldn't deny that I had missed him and that seeing him on my door step, even with his face contorted with anger, I was pleased.

* * * *

Jared had followed no more than two vehicles behind me all the way home. At one stage, I ended up a little further ahead than he liked, so he had called my cell. When I answered, he lectured and yelled at me for not concentrating on the road and answering my cell while driving. I'd yelled back at him and explained that my father, who was also a cautious driver, had given me a hands free kit that was linked directly to the dash and my cell. I had growled in frustration at his controlling behavior towards me.

I applauded myself for not bowing down to his patronizing tone, and for completely ignoring him as he barked orders on how to correctly cross lanes. Calling him a condescending ass munch may have been taking it a little too far, and I probably wouldn't get away with it either, but I felt it was worth it just to let him know that I wasn't intimidated, nor was I willing to be bullied by him.

When we finally pulled up outside my dorm, my patience was frayed, to say the least. Slamming my door, I stormed across the parking lot towards the dorm entrance. I could hear Jared's tires screech to a halt and his door slamming shut as he sprinted after me, yelling at me to stop. He caught up with me just as I was about to reach for the steel handle of the entrance, my salvation away from him. Holding his hand firmly against the glass, he halted my attempts to escape him, pressing the door forcefully closed.

"Layla stop this. Why do you always go off the deep end? You act like a child throwing her toys out of her stroller! It's fucking infuriating, and I'm at my wits end with it. Grow up!"

I tugged hard at the door with both hands, and lifted my foot against it in a futile attempt to pry it open. But it was useless, he was too strong, and I was tired of fighting. His eyes blazed with an emotion I couldn't fathom. Anger? Lust? Either way, I was momentarily mesmerized, so let go of the door in front of me. But it was only momentarily as my anger was soon spilling over and out of my mouth.

"Fuck you! Get out of my way, douchebag. You think I act like a child? Fine! I'll act like one!"

I kicked the door, hard, and growled low in my throat. Grabbing my wrist in his free hand, he yanked me toward him. His face was inches from mine, and I could see the burning fury in his eyes.

"If you ever talk to me like that again, I am going to spank you so hard that you won't sit, stand or walk for a month! For someone so well read, your vocabulary is repulsive. You kiss your mother with that mouth?"

Did he say spank? Was he serious? I snorted at him, but he was not amused. Shit. It was hot and frightening all at once.

"Do not try my patience. Grow up and get some damn respect."

My own anger dissipated as I looked up at him with regret. Maybe I had gone a little too far. Exhausted, I pleaded with him.

"Jared, let go of the door. Don't you think we've argued enough for one day? Hell, we've argued enough this week to last me a lifetime. I'm tired, and I just want to go upstairs and lie down. Please, Jared. Just let me go."

The prickle of unshed tears was beginning to overpower my desperation to stand firm and be strong in front of him. The salty droplets were falling down my cheeks, and I was unable to control the quiver of my lip, furious with myself for being so weak.

His cell rang loudly in his pocket. Staring at him through my tears, I waited to see what he would do. Growling, he pulled it from his pocket and answered.

"What? I'm busy right now. You need to handle it. What are you talking about? When? I thought we'd fixed this shit already! Fine, I'll be there as soon as I can."

Furious, I shoved him hard, and with a contrite look on his face, he immediately let go of the door. Swiping my face, ridding myself of my tears, I glared at him.

"Clearly I'm not the only one with a secret around here, am I, Jared?"

Pulling the door open with one strong tug, I ran as fast as my shaking legs could carry me to my room without giving him a second glance. I was too angry and upset to be able to control my emotions, and I feared we'd say things we would regret later.

The room was eerily quiet, and Amy's absence left me feeling slightly relieved. I needed some time alone to collect my thoughts and calm my nerves. Falling onto the edge of the bed, I wiped my face with my palms, trying to eradicate the evidence of my tearful episode. Crying was not something I did often, but with Jared it seemed to be happening more and more.

Placing my hand on my chest, I could feel the thundering beat of my heart which was pounding like a drum inside my ribcage. Taking two deep long calming breaths, I slid myself to the edge of the bed, and gripped the mattress as I sat up. Glancing at the window, I wondered if he could feel what I was feeling. Did he hurt the way I did? Was our fight haunting him too?

I clambered unsteadily to my feet and sauntered over to the large glass window, scanning the parking lot. His Jag was still parked next to my Focus, but I couldn't see him at all. He wasn't in his car, and as I continued to scour the ground two stories below me, I couldn't see his broad and muscular frame anywhere.

The need to cry to my best friend was now devastatingly important. I needed Mel's clear, rational, and logical input on the situation. She had always been completely skittish and hyperactive, but in a time of crisis or panic, she was level headed and calm. I needed that right now.

My head was pounding as I recalled our harsh words. My stomach was queasy with the hurt and anger that was swirling inside me. I looked around the empty room, searching for my purse which contained my cell, when I realized I had left it in the car. Shit. I was going to have to go back out there.

Staring across the hall, I considered knocking at Ollie's door and begging him to go fetch it for me. But after what happened at the bar, and discovering Ollie's feelings for me, I decided against it. I was going to have to do this myself. Straightening my clothes, I made my way to the entrance where I thought I had left all the drama behind me. As I rounded the corner, I froze. Sitting on the ground, his back against the glass and his head in his hands, was Jared. I wanted desperately to run to him, throw my arms around him and let him know everything was alright. But I couldn't let him treat me this way. He had to know how upset I was and that things needed to change if our relationship would continue.

Holding my head high, I strode to the door and pushed it open. Without looking at him, I walked by and headed to my car. My breathing was erratic, and I could feel his gaze on the back of my head. Just go to the car, get your purse and go back in. Don't look at him, or acknowledge him. Just haul ass, Layla.

Grabbing my purse, I made a conscious decision not to look at him as I walked back, but my eyes and my body betrayed me, and I found myself not only staring right at him, but my feet were also aiming in his general direction. Damn you feet. Damn you eyes.

His knees were to his chest, and his elbows were resting on them. He was gazing at me, and the closer I got to him, the clearer I could see the pained expression on his face, and my insides twisted with remorse and regret. After all, it had been my lies and deceit that had led us to this point, and I had to take responsibility for that. Taking a deep breath, I threaded my fingers in my hair, combing it back from root to tip. I sighed and sat myself next to him against the glass door. He continued to stare straight ahead, and it made me feel uneasy. The silence was leaving an empty feeling inside me, and the air was thick with things we needed to say. Touching his arm, I decided to make my apology.

"Jared, I'm sorry I lied to you. You were right, it was childish of me to lie, and throwing my tantrum wasn't particularly ladylike either. But you weren't totally blameless. Calling me in the car and expecting me not to pick up, really? I'm a grown woman, and although I love that you care so much about me and my safety, I'm not used to it, and it's kind of…" I paused, wondering if my next word would break us, "…it's suffocating. You need to let me make mistakes and experience things for myself. You can't keep me in bubble wrap."

He let out a long sigh and rubbed his hand on the back of his neck. Turning his head to face me, our eyes met, and I was once again lost in the deep pools of blue that glistened as he spoke.

"I know, baby, and I'm so sorry for everything I said. I didn't mean it. I was just so angry and scared. There are some real idiots on these roads, and it's them I don't trust, not you." Exhaling deeply, he broke our gaze as his eyes pinched closed, tightly as if he were in physical pain. "Layla, when my parents died I was in Seattle. That's where I went to college. I was studying business and economics and was finishing my first year when they were killed. I always regretted not being here when it happened. When I got that call, I felt completely helpless, devastated and angry beyond comprehension. They hadn't died from an accident, there had been no evil disease to carry them off. It was the actions of a desperate man with a gun. Another human being took away the two most important people in my life, the two people I loved and cared about the most in the world, and the thought that it could happen to me again, that it could be you who gets hurt, kills me.

"I keep having visions of someone running you off the road, a drunk driver, a joy riding college kid, a mom talking on her cell...all kinds of possibilities ran through my mind. I know it's irrational, and I know it's a lot to put on you, but I just can't help it. I care about you very deeply. I've never felt this way about a woman before. I feel like I could wrestle an alligator for you, or cross the desert just to see you, Layla. The thought of you being hurt tears me apart, and the idea that it could be somewhere that I can't reach you, or be there for you, completely haunts me.

"I'm sorry for how I behaved, but I can never be sorry for my reasons. I need you to understand that and try to forgive me because I told you I was going to fuck up, more than once, and you said you could handle it. I just hope that's still true."

I had been so stupid. I had completely overlooked the fact that his parents had been senselessly murdered. The two most valuable people in his life were tragically torn away from him, and I was being totally insensitive to his feelings. I couldn't get his words out of my head about how much he cared for me, and it gave me a warm glow, dissolving the queasy tension I had felt in my room. I leaned my head on his shoulder and nuzzled into his arm. He looked down at me with a distressed expression, and I smiled at him, trying to reassure him that everything was alright.

Resting his forehead against mine, he smiled weakly back at me. "Jared, I'm sorry. I never even thought about how you must have been feeling, with your parents and everything. I'm in awe of you. But this honesty thing between us is a serious issue. What is going on? You keep getting calls that make you furious, and then a woman calls your cell and hangs up the moment she hears my voice. If didn't know better, I'd say you were seeing someone else."

Cupping my face in his hands, he pulled me to him and kissed me deeply, his tongue stroking and rolling over mine. "There is no one else. I swear, just you. It's just something I have to deal with on my own. You're going to have to be patient with me on this one, Layla, but I promise, you have nothing to worry about."

His eyes were looking into my soul, and a simmering heat began to spread through my body, igniting between my legs. I had almost forgotten the powerful sexual chemistry between us. But kissing me softly, the moment his lips were pressed against mine, my body immediately stood to attention as goosebumps began to tingle and prickle over my soft pale skin.

Biting down on his bottom lip, I ran my tongue over it, gently caressing the plump flesh between my teeth. He let out a moan and pulled away from me, gazing into my eyes. His own had darkened, and I could see the lust scorching through the deep cobalt hue. His pupils had dilated, a sure sign that he was as turned on as I was. Grabbing his hand, I got to my feet and pulled him with me through the doors. I had an empty dorm room and a bed that was screaming for us to roll around naked on top of it.

Chapter 22

Four Days

I was totally breathless, my head resting on Jared's strong muscular chest. Listening to the thumping of his heart beat in my ear, I smiled with satisfaction. He had been so attentive to my needs, and the aching I could feel between my legs was a throbbing reminder of the sensational multiple orgasms that had surged through me only moments ago. I gently twirled my fingers around on his bare chest. His skin was smooth and hairless with a warm caramel glow. Nuzzling into him, I took a deep breath and breathed in his scent. He smelled like sex, sweat, soap, and delicious strawberries. His own hands were resting on my back, holding me close to him as he placed gentle kisses in my hair.

I glanced over at the clock beside my bed before darting my eyes to the door. Amy would be back soon, and as much as I wanted to spend the rest of my life right there in his arms, I knew we both needed some space to collect ourselves. The sex had been wonderful, but I was all too aware that it didn't erase the hurt we had caused one another over the past two days. We had a lot of issues to iron out, but I was hopeful that given time, patience and some understanding on both parts, we would work through it all.

I gazed up at Jared and sighed. Raising his hand over his mouth, he yawned.

"Looks like I've worn you out, stud."

I giggled as he tickled me over the ribs, not roughly, but enough to make me squirm in his arms.

"Jared! Stop!"

I batted his hands away, and he halted his merciless attack on me. Giving me a boyish grin he chuckled. "It would take a lot more than an hour of acrobatic, sensational fucking to wear me out, my lady. In fact, why don't you come back to my place and I'll prove it to you."

His hands snaked around my waist, but I pressed down firmly on his arms to prevent them from pulling me with him.

"No, you have work tomorrow, and I have classes. Besides, I think we could use a little distance right now."

He looked at me wounded and shot upright on the bed.

"You're kicking me out? Are you still mad at me? Layla, I explained, and I told you I was sorry. Please don't keep punishing me for this. What more do I have to do? You want me to beg you to forgive me?"

I held a finger over his lips to silence him "Shush. I'm not kicking you out. I am not still mad at you. I just think that with emotions running high, we should take a little breather."

His mouth opened beneath my finger to object, but I gave him a warning look, and he sharply closed it again.

"But I will see you tomorrow night. I have a shift at the shop, and then you can take me out to dinner. I think it's about time we went on a real date, don't you?"

Holding my hand against his mouth, he nipped at the pads of my fingers playfully.

"Ouch!"

He kissed each one individually to soothe them, and placed my palm on his chest above his heart. Pressing his hand on top of mine, he rested his forehead against my own.

"Layla, I don't know how to deal with all of this. I've never felt this way before. I'm way out of my comfort zone, and I can't seem to think straight around you. I get all stupid and crazy, but I can't seem to stay away from you."

My body was awash with emotion at the sincerity of his heartfelt words. He truly had no idea the spell he'd put me under since the moment I had met him. I was falling for him like a cannonball. Hard and fast.

Falling in love is like leaping from a cliff. Your brain screams that it's a bad idea, but your heart believes you can soar, glide and fly. That's exactly how I felt about Jared. I was leaping off a cliff and plummeting to my doom, but my heart was taking flight and spreading its wings. The thought of pain when I finally hit the ground consumed and devastated me, but as I gazed into his beautiful blue eyes, I could see myself riding the air currents and the breathless wonder of the view.

"Jared, it's going to be ok. This is all new for me too, but we'll learn together. Just you and me." I laced my fingers with his and grazed his knuckles with my lips. His body visibly relaxed as the sensations of my kiss comforted him.

* * * *

As promised, Ollie saved me a seat in class in our usual spot. Neither of us mentioned what had happened in his room on Saturday, and I decided it was best to simply let it go and move on. After all, if Ollie didn't feel the need to dwell on it, then why should I?

He acted exactly the same as he always had, sharing jokes, talking about music, and asking my opinion on song selections for open mic night. He even tried to convince me to become the band's new lead singer. I simply laughed and asked if he was looking to get booed off stage every night. He scowled at me when I joked about having the vocal stylings of a dying animal.

"Layla, have you forgotten that I've actually heard you sing? You've got some set of lungs, girl. And if what I heard from across the hall yesterday is anything to go by, you're not afraid to use them either. No matter who hears you. 'Oh, Jared, again, Jared, yes, Jared there, don't stop'."

My jaw dropped open in horror, and I blushed a deep crimson. Covering my red, mortified face I whimpered, "Oh my god, Ollie, I'm so, so, sorry."

Chuckling, he nudged my shoulder. "Hey, one of us has to be getting some action around here. Speaking of which, have you noticed Amy and Nick getting awfully cozy lately? I know for a fact he took her out last night. He told me he was just going to hang out with Eric and practice, but there's no way you wear that much cologne to jam with a grunge playing, rock kid from Michigan. And I noticed Amy leaving your room about ten minutes after, all dolled up for something. She mention anything to you?"

My head swayed in a silent no.

"Nothing. But to be honest, I was asleep when she got in last night. It was late, though, and she was in the shower when I left this morning. We just kind of kept missing each other all morning, so we never really got a chance to talk properly. Does it bother you, though? Amy and Nick, I mean."

Ollie shrugged. "Not really. I just don't want Amy to get hurt. Nick's got an eye for the ladies, and he's got a bit of a reputation around here already. But whatever, she's a grown ass woman and can take care of herself. So, got plans for your birthday yet?"

My birthday was on Saturday, and as of yet I had no plans whatsoever. I'd never really liked making a fuss on my birthday. Mom was always trying to arrange parties and get togethers, but I wasn't interested. I preferred having dinner with my parents and Mel before curling up on the sofa to watch movies and eat junk food.

"Not yet. I don't really do birthdays. It's not my thing. I'd rather just let it pass by as quietly as possible with as little fuss as possible."

Ollie sniggered. "So naturally Amy's throwing you a party."

My head shot up, and I stared at him wide eyed. Biting his lip, he murmured an "oops" and I glared at him, waiting for an explanation.

"Do not tell her I told you, but she's got this big party organized for Saturday night down at the bar. I told her she should run it by you, but you know how difficult it is to talk sense to her. She's a fucking whack job at the best of times, so put a planner and some party balloons in her hand, and she's downright lethal! I swear she nearly decapitated me with her clip board when I told her that you hate streamers. Hurled the thing so damn hard I thought she'd slice a chunk out of me if I hadn't ducked in time. Girl's a psycho!"

Leaning back in my chair, I laughed loudly which got me a scornful look from Dr. Harman. Stifling my sniggering, I put my arm around his shoulders.

"Oh, Ollie, thank god you have my back, but I don't think we're getting out of this one. I hope she invited Jared, though."

"Oh yeah, that's right, I'm supposed to steal your phone, get his number, and give it to her, so…"

Rolling my eyes I handed him my phone.

"Thanks, Layla. How very accommodating of you. Now remember. Total surprise on Saturday, ok?"

Shaking my head I smiled. "Yeah, yeah. Ok. I'll practice my surprised expression in the mirror all week. She'll never know."

* * * *

Monday evening, Jared called me to let me know he'd be going out of town for a few days on business. My heart sank.

"So how long will you be gone?"

"Just till Friday, baby. I promise I'll be back for your birthday. I really wish I didn't have to go, but this project in Europe is getting more complicated every damn day. I have to go to New York and meet with some contractors and my legal team. I'll call you every day. You gonna be alright without me?"

Four whole days without him felt like a month. Since our first date, we hadn't spent that much time apart. I was already feeling my heart strings tugging hard with longing.

"I'll be fine. I'm really going to miss you, though. I miss you now."

"I know, baby. I miss you too."

"When do you leave?" I held my breath, waiting for his reply.

"My plane leaves LAX at eight in the morning. I should be in the city by lunch. It'll be alright, sweetheart. I promise. In fact…" There was a pause and I could hear him shuffling around for something. "I'm having something sent over to your dorm now. My assistant Jerry is going to drop it off. It'll make the distance a little easier. I gotta go pack now. I will miss you more than you even know, and I will think about you constantly."

I could feel my heart sinking deeper as I thought about how I would get through the next four days without him. His touch, the feel of his lips, his warm and comforting arms, his raw animal passion and hunger for me; I would miss it all intensely. Reminding myself that absence makes the heart grow fonder, I cleared my throat and tried to sound more upbeat for his sake.

"I know you'll miss me, that's what makes it a little bit easier; knowing I'll be in your thoughts and on your mind till you're back in my arms."

I could almost feel him smiling down the phone.

"Oh, Layla, you have no idea. You are always in my thoughts. I really have to go now. You need me at any time, for anything, you call me. And I mean that, Layla. Don't make me worry. Be safe, take care of yourself, and don't get into any trouble. Understand?"

I felt like a scolded child, and a small part of me wanted to bite back with a sarcastic response, but recalling our fight over the weekend, I remembered everything he'd gone through when his parents died and let it go.

"I'll be fine, Jared. I will call if anything happens. Please let me know when you land safe and sound."

"I will. I'll call you tomorrow. Goodnight, my lady."

"Goodnight, pumpkin." I heard a chuckle.

"Pumpkin?"

A snort of laughter escaped my own lips.

"Well, I thought maybe since you have a term of affection for me, I should find one for you."

He laughed harder, and I had to hold the phone away from my ear until he was finished.

"That's adorable, Layla, but if it's ok with you…could we keep looking?"

So, not pumpkin then.

"Yeah, I think we should…sex on legs?" I was pretty sure that one would appease him. "I can certainly live with that one. Ok, now I really do have to go. Goodnight, my lady."

"Goodnight, Jared."

I heard him sigh loudly as he hung up. It was comforting to know he felt just as awful about our separation as I did, but I couldn't shake the uneasy feeling knotted in my stomach. Every time his cell rang, or he disappeared into his office, I felt an uncomfortable nagging in my gut that told me something was going on. I wanted to trust him completely, but I just couldn't convince myself of his innocence while this thing, whatever it was, was wedged between us.

Falling back onto my bed, I flung my arm over my eyes exhausted. I was just beginning to doze when someone knocked on the door. Jumping off my bed, I bounded over and swung it open.

In front of me stood a young, dark haired man holding a large brown box. He was slim, and his gray suit jacket looked large as it hung rigidly on his tiny frame. He gave me a weary and nervous smile.

"Miss Jennings?"

I nodded.

"Ah, good. This is from Mr. Garrett. He also sent this note with it."

Placing the box on the floor, he handed me the note and without a word, turned and left. I lifted the box off the floor and dropped it on to my bed. It wasn't heavy as such, but something told me it may be fragile. Grabbing a pair of scissors from the desk, I was about to open it when Amy stormed in.

She hurtled her bag at her bed and stomped into the bathroom, slamming the door behind her. This wasn't good. Leaving the mysterious box unopened, I knocked on the door.

"Amy? What's wrong, honey? Come on out and tell me what happened."

"Men are dicks! Every last one! I'm never, ever, dating again! And I am not coming out of this bathroom until I have washed every last morsel of that man off of me!"

I had an inkling that this had something to do with Nick. Without a second thought, I headed for Ollie's door and banged on it with a furious hammering of my fist. Ollie opened the door, and rolled his eyes, raising his hands to silence me before I even uttered a word.

"I know. I know. He's a douche canoe, right? Broke her heart, yeah? You wanna kill him, maim him and cut off his junk with rusty scissors. I get that. But he's not here. Amy almost took the damn door off just now when she threw those at me to give to him." Ollie nodded at a pair of girl's panties lying on Nick's bed.

My stomach turned in anger and sympathy for my friend who was, at that moment, barricaded in my bathroom, and probably crying buckets by now.

"What the hell did he do to her? I've never seen her like that, Ollie. She looked like she was possessed! I swear, I was waiting for her head to spin around when she stormed in like that. I could see she was furious, and that was before she decided to lock herself in the bathroom. Says she's not coming out till she's washed him off of her, whatever that means. What are you gonna do about it?"

Ollie snorted and gave me a confused look. "Me? What does this have to do with me? I warned her he was trouble. I warned her he would break her heart, and if she was still stupid enough to go out with him, then I guess she learned the hard way, huh? I mean, come on, Layla. She probably thought what every girl around here thinks. That Nick's a bad boy who is going to be a good guy just for her because she's special. But all he wants is a pulse, tits, ass and somewhere to keep his dick warm. Hell, you know what those kinds of guys are like, right? You know, they lie, cheat, scheme, and manipulate to get into a girl's panties."

It was definitely a dig at me and Jared. And he was way out of line.

I glared at him. "How dare you! Jared is nothing like Nick! You're such an asshole sometimes, you know that? And Amy is supposed to be your friend, Ollie! How can you say those things about her? Don't you give a shit what happens to her? She's fucking devastated, and I can't even get her to come out of the damn bathroom to talk to me about it! Now are you gonna stand there and insult us, or are you going to be our friend and help me get her out!?"

He stood inches away from me, his face so close to mine I could smell the rich and bitter scent of his skin. His lip ring glistened as he ran his tongue over his lips. "Fine, I'll help."

I found myself feeling hot, flustered and surprisingly turned on. The fire in his eyes was arousing, and part of me wanted to grab him tightly and kiss him, hard. I couldn't understand what it was about fighting with a guy that got me so hot! Jared had an uncanny ability to provoke it in me, and now I was getting the same reaction around Ollie. It was not only wrong but dangerous too.

Shaking the sinful thoughts about Ollie out of my mind, I felt a pang of guilt for Jared. I'd just mentally cheated on him. This thing with Ollie was getting more complicated by the day, and I wondered how long we could go on like this; pretending and acting like we were fine and that our friendship was the only relationship that existed, and would ever exist, between us. It would have to wait because right now, Amy was more important.

Walking straight up to the bathroom door, Ollie pounded on the wood. "Amy, get your ass out here, will you? This is stupid, and no guy is worth locking yourself in a room with a toilet!"

"Fuck you, Ollie. You're a guy, just like him. You're all the same."

"Don't go tarring me with that brush! I'm nothing like him. I never cheat and I never lie. The woman I end up with would be my princess. I'd treat her like damn royalty and worship the ground she walks on. I'd tell her every day how much I love her and every night how much she means to me. So don't you ever tell me I'm like all the rest, Amy. I'm not!"

Resting his forearm on the door, Ollie gazed at me. I knew what he was telling me without hearing the words. The woman he was referring to in his speech was me. His soulful chestnut brown eyes looked pained and he winced before turning his attention back to the door.

My heart ached for him. I was hurting him, and it was killing me. It was, of course, totally unintentional, but I felt responsible none the less. He'd made his feelings for me clear on more than one occasion.

Jared was creeping back into my thoughts again, and that same sting of guilt was now becoming a sharp pain in my chest. I was crazy about him, but I also couldn't ignore the chemistry and sexual tension that had been simmering between Ollie and me since I landed on my back in front of him. I prayed that these feelings would dissolve as I grew closer to Jared.

Pushing Ollie aside, I begged Amy to come out. "Amy, come on, sweetie. Come out. We'll get some food, veg out, cry, scream and bitch about men all night. Besides, don't you wanna help me open this box Jared just sent over?"

The lock clicked beneath my fingers. Opening the door a crack, I could see her. Her face was smudged with streaks of mascara caused by her tears, her lipstick was smeared across her chin, and her eyes were red, puffy and wet. It was the worst I had ever seen her.

Pushing the door gently, I pulled her into my arms and hugged her tightly like a small child when they're hurt or upset. Her body shook with every sob that escaped her, and I gave Ollie the nod to leave as I felt it best he not stick around once Amy had regained her ability to speak. He nodded back in agreement, and I was honestly glad to see him go. I couldn't bear the awkwardness any longer.

Chapter 23

Gifts, Glamor And Girl Talk

Scanning the room, I suddenly felt exhausted. The heap of empty food containers was beginning to turn into a trash pile. Ice-cream tubs dripped onto the hard wood floor, and the Chinese takeout containers were starting to stink with their oily, spicy, aromatic scent. I'd eaten so much that I felt as though I might explode. Amy, however, was still making her way through an enormous bar of Hershey's chocolate. I didn't even know they made a bar that size, but Amy had zeroed in on it the moment we hit the candy aisle at the supermarket.

"See, this is what I love about chocolate. It's rich, sweet, delicious, and better than sex. And I don't have to wax to enjoy it." Her uncontrollable sobs had soon turned to anger, and we were now in our third hour of bitching about men.

"He's a dick, Layla. A true, honest to god, cock. Telling me I'm special, I'm the one. He was sweet, charming, you know he even took me to my favorite restaurant? He remembered I loved it after I told him at the bar that night. He asked me out the night we performed. Ollie warned me about him, but I thought maybe he would be different if he met the right girl. Clearly that cheating, scheming, jackass will never change. Urgh, I feel so dirty. I can't believe I ever let him touch me, let alone sleep with me."

Scrunching up the chocolate wrapper, she tossed it onto the pile and sighed. Hanging her head she began to cry softly.

"I can't believe he used me like that. There I was in a gorgeous bed in a five star hotel room, lying in his arms, thinking how wonderful it all is and the whole time he'd been sneaking around sleeping with someone else. Her underwear was in his car. He tried to deny it, of course. Said it was from months ago before he even moved here to college, but it's all total bullshit. He never cared about me. He just wanted someone to screw. I hate him. I hate all men. Maybe I should try girls."

I stifled a laugh. Amy was the queen of dramatics. I came only a mere second to her and the massive soap operas she could create from situations in her life. But the hurt she was feeling right now was real, and I could see the pain she was in. Scooting over, I flung my arms around her neck and hugged her close. Stroking her hair, I tried to comfort her.

"Amy, I know it hurts now, but don't give up. Out there somewhere is a guy, or girl, who will treat you like the princess you are. My mom always says that you have to kiss a few frogs before you find your handsome prince. Consider Nick as just another frog in your quest to find your prince. He's out there, I know it, waiting to come rescue you and sweep you off your feet."

She lifted her head off my shoulder and wiped her eyes. Sniffing, she gave me a smile, the first I'd seen since she stormed in and locked herself in the bathroom. "Nick's not a frog. He's an ugly, fat little toad, and I hope he gets a fungal disease from one of his many little lily pad hopping harlots."

A loud chuckle escaped me. "That's the spirit. Now come help me open this box; he sent a note too."

Grabbing an empty shopping bag, I disposed of the evidence from our evening of gorging, bitching and tears. Amy sat on my bed and shook the box lightly. "Sounds fragile. What do you think it is?"

"I have no freaking clue, but if I know Jared, which I think I do, it's probably expensive and way over the top. Well, don't just sit there! Open it up for me while I take this trash to the dumpster."

When I re-entered the room, Amy was hopping up and down like an excited child. She squealed with delight. "Oh my goodness, Layla! You have got to see all of this stuff!"

Cautiously, I approached the bed, and as my eyes took in the box, my jaw dropped to the floor. Amy began taking everything out as I watched her, completely stunned. A brand new shiny laptop was first, followed by a Victoria Secret bag, a small velvet box, and three envelopes. I stared at Amy, who was giggling at my expression.

"Layla, you are by far the luckiest girl I know. This guy is amazing. And he's totally in love with you."

Her words snapped me out of my daze. Love? Did she say love? Surely it was too soon for the L word. But his generous gift was a sure sign that he was feeling something for me. Right?

Amy sat and began setting up the laptop while I inspected the other items Jared had packed in his treasure box. The Victoria Secret bag contained a beautiful black lace bra and matching French panties. The delicate material was luxurious and felt as soft as silk. I checked the garments, briefly looking for a price tag, but he had, of course, removed them. The set certainly looked expensive.

Turning my attention to the small velvet box, I ran my fingers over the fabric. Slowly and carefully I opened it and gasped. Inside was a stunning diamond, tanzanite and emerald ring. The deep blue and glittering green shimmered in the light. The emeralds were lining one side of the white gold band while the tanzanite and diamonds were lining the other. In the center, two pieces of crystal had been swirled with the same colors. It was breathtaking.

A tiny note was folded and taped to the inside of the box. Pulling it away, I unfolded it and read the words aloud.

"Because it matches your bedazzling eyes. Because it was made for you. Because I want you to have this. Because I can give it to you."

I stood there, staring at it. Taking it from my hand, Amy whistled as she plucked the ring from its box. Holding it into the light, she was the one now gasping for air.

"Oh. My. God. Layla, this ring is a Marcus Deboute ring! He's like the biggest and most expensive jewelry designer in the world. He only makes unique pieces. This ring is the only one of its kind. Eighteen carat white gold and I would say at least three carats of diamonds. Wow. This had to be at least six thousand dollars, Layla. You don't spend money like that on a girl you're just having fun with."

She had a point, but I wasn't sure I was ready to think about how deep our feelings ran. After all, we were still getting to know each other. He was wonderful, and I was falling for him, there was no doubt about it. But I knew that this was something I had to handle delicately. If I professed my emotions to him too soon, I could scare him away. And the idea of unrequited love with Jared was a devastating thought. I wanted to be his world, the way he was mine.

Sighing, I slumped down onto the bed. A red envelope fell onto the floor, and I remembered the other items in the box. The three envelopes each had a different day of the week on them including the current one marked Monday. Getting comfortable, I tore it open and began to read.

My Lovely Layla,

Today I told you I am going away on business. And believe me when I say that if there were some way to get out of it, I would not be leaving you. The gifts I have put in this box are to help you get through the next four days without me. So item one, the laptop. You're a student now, and no student should be without their very own computer. But this gift is also for other purposes. I have had Skype installed, and I have set you up with your own personal email account so that you can keep in touch with me, wherever I am. Skype will allow us to speak via a video link while I'm away...amongst other things.

The lingerie. You are the sexiest creature that walks this earth, and this gift is not only for my enjoyment, but yours as well. Wear it when you want to feel sexy. Imagine my soft hands caressing your skin as the silky lace rubs against your delectable curves. Tantalizing.

The ring. Before you overreact and decide to never wear it, or return it...you can't. I had this ring designed especially for you. The colors are a reflection of the striking hues of your dazzling eyes. Eyes that have bewitched me. Eyes that speak to my very soul whenever I gaze into them. I wanted to give this to you. I can afford it, and I will not accept it back. I want you to wear it. Every day.

The envelopes. Open them on their respective days. Be open-minded, and this is very important Layla, but DO AS THEY TELL YOU. I know how hard it is for you to take instructions, but please trust me. It will be fine, and you will have fun.

Until the next envelope...

Goodbye, My Lady
Xxxxx

Do as they tell you? A flurry of anticipation fluttered through me as I fought the urge to tear open the other envelopes. The idea of Jared giving me instructions from miles away was exhilarating and arousing. I glanced over at Amy who was hunched in front of my laptop clicking frantically.

"How's it going over there?"

Whipping her head up, she grinned at me. "This is an awesome piece of equipment. It's got everything, Layla. All the latest software you could possibly need for college, plus some games, shopping sites preloaded into your browser and...wow. You should see this."

Crawling across the bed, I looked at the screen. Amy was on the site of Garrett's Mall. Every store in the place had its own webpage. I was confused as to what had amazed Amy until I saw the tiny box in the corner of the screen that read:

Layla Jennings. Credit limit: $5,000.

"Is he nuts? I never applied or asked for that! Bring up the details, Amy."

Navigating her way around the site with incredible ease and speed, she pulled up the page titled 'Payment Details'. A note on the screen informed me that all invoices were to be sent to J. Garrett, and any spending over the limit was to be charged to his personal account.

Grabbing my phone, I sent him a text. We really needed to discuss boundaries and his spending habit.

> I think we need to discuss this CREDIT LIMIT. CALL ME
> **Sent: 18.04**
> **To: Jared**

Satisfied that he would see from my message exactly how I felt about his gesture, I closed the laptop, much to Amy's annoyance. She opened her mouth to protest, but giving her a warning look, I shook my head. My cell began to buzz in my hand, and I swallowed hard when I saw his name on the screen. Holding my nerve, I answered.

"Jared, can you please explain why I have a five thousand dollar credit limit at your mall? One that I neither need, nor asked for."

"It's a gift. You can use it online, or in the stores. I know how it can be when you're at college. I was there, remember? That money is for anything you want. Books, electronics, clothes, whatever you need, I want to provide it for you. I enjoy spending money on you, Layla. I've never been able to share my wealth with anyone till you came along. Don't argue about it because I'm not changing it. Period."

His tone was clipped and distinctly heated, but I wasn't intimidated by Jared. I was angry, and he was treating me like a child. Again.

"Well, I'm not using it. I don't care how much money you have, I am not going to be accused of only being in this relationship for what material possessions I can gain. That's exactly what people will think. That's Layla, Jared's little gold digger."

I heard him snigger, and it irked me. There was nothing funny about this situation.

"You know what, Jared? I don't appreciate your laughing at me right now. I have never been so insulted. I feel like your cheap little whore. I'm packing all of this shit back up and sending it to your office. You can collect it when you get back. Goodbye."

Hanging up, I saw Amy's shocked reaction at my outburst. "What?"

Getting to her feet, she walked towards the bathroom mumbling incoherently under her breath. I was sure I heard the words ungrateful and bitch, but I decided I wasn't willing to pursue another argument that evening. I couldn't be bought, and all these gifts were making me feel like a paid hooker. Sex for diamonds.

When she emerged from the bathroom, Amy scowled at me before shaking her head and sighing exasperatedly. To hell with it, she had a bee in her bonnet and we were going to have to thrash it out.

"Out with it, Amy. You're mad at me for what I said to Jared, aren't you?"

She arched her eyebrow and rolled her eyes at me. "Layla, you really are so ungrateful. You question everything to death, and you never just accept things at face value. He gave you that money to help you, and to give you some financial cushioning whenever you might need it. But instead of saying thank you, or showing your gratitude for his very generous nature, you snipe at him and make it seem like he's buying you, or something. You're the only one who is cheapening the whole thing, Layla. No one thinks you're a whore, and I'm pretty sure he's never treated you like one. You need a serious attitude adjustment. Soon."

How could she side with him? A few dollars is a gift. Five thousand is over the top and no doubt came with expectations and conditions. I had every reason to be mad at both of them.

Grabbing my jacket, I barked at her, "Fuck you too, Amy. You're supposed to be my friend."

Without giving her time to respond, I stormed out of the room without so much as a glance at her. I needed some space and a walk to clear my head. Everything was so complicated with Jared, always so intense. It was everything, or nothing, and it was getting exhausting.

I shuffled along the pavement, my head swarming with the events that had unfolded in my dorm room. The lavish gifts, the credit limit, fighting with Jared and Amy; it was all too much. Everything about Jared and I was too much, and far too fast.

The weather was still pleasant even as the sun was going down. The chill in the air was refreshing and lacked the usual bite one would expect for the season. The warm weather was winding down now, and the cool autumn days would be creeping in all too soon. I continued to walk, silently thinking and pouring over Amy's words to me.

Was I really that ungrateful? Maybe I did need a slight attitude adjustment. Jared's gifts were very generous, and I was probably wrong in how I handled the situation, but it didn't change how I felt about what he had done. I was uncomfortable with him spending money on me, and if he'd taken to time to speak to me about it, he would have known that. Jared's lack of communication and general ignorance was beginning to irritate me.

I glanced at my watch to discover that I had been walking for nearly an hour. Looking around, I realized where my feet had taken me. I was standing outside Lorraine's.

Pushing the large glass door, I walked in, and the warm, familiar aroma of roasted beans and vanilla instantly soothed me. Kate was behind the counter eyeing the latest edition of "Coffee House", a magazine keeping us all up to date on the latest flavors and concoctions to add to the menu. Lifting her head, she spotted me and grinned. Breezing around the counter, she ran up to give me a hug.

"Hey, stranger! I haven't seen you all week since they switched me to the evening shift. How are you?" She stood back and scrutinized my face as I shrugged. Her own expression turned from joy to concern. "Oh, sweetie, what's wrong? You and the boss been fighting again?"

Letting out a long sigh, I nodded.

Sensing my need for privacy, and no doubt itching to hear the juicy details, Kate took my hand and pulled me to the office.

"Now, what happened?"

She handed me a box of tissues from the desk before sitting on the edge of it and watching me intently.

"We had a fight. He keeps lavishing me with gifts, money, and expensive trinkets. I can't handle it all, Kate. I'm not used to handouts. When I was growing up, we lived modestly. Dad was working in a small garage and making little money, and mom was only working a few shifts at the hospital to spend time at home with me. I didn't have expensive clothes, high tech gadgets, or even money to just go shopping. I liked my life the way it was. Uncomplicated. Simple. Then Jared comes bursting into my life with his millions, expensive jewelry, five thousand dollar credit limits, and high tech laptops. It's too much!

"I can't understand why he feels the need to do it. Does he think that's all I want from him? That his money and the things he can buy me keep me with him? It's not. And I feel like a cheap whore if I even consider accepting them. And now I've fallen out with my roommate too. She told me I was ungrateful, and that I need an attitude adjustment. I'm so confused. I feel completely out of my depth. What should I do, Kate? Seriously, am I wrong in all this?"

She regarded me with disbelief painted on her face. Blinking rapidly, her mouth fell open. "Let me get this straight. He gave you jewellery, a laptop, a five thousand dollar credit limit, and enjoys spending his cash on you. And you're mad at him?" Shaking her head she gave me a sympathetic smile. "Oh, sweetie. You really are a nightmare. I understand where you're coming from with your history, and that you're feeling overwhelmed, but have you actually ever told him that? Because I think if you did, he might rethink some of his actions. Besides, maybe it's his way of expressing how he feels. Did you consider that?"

I thought for a moment, and wondered if she was right. I definitely needed to talk to him about his over the top gestures but the idea that it was how he expressed his feelings about me had never crossed my mind. The way I had treated him during our phone call sent a chill through me, and my heart ached with regret. How would I ever be able to apologize for the way I acted? Would he even forgive me? I'd taken his sweet gesture and thrown it in his face.

God, I really was a royal bitch.

Chapter 24

It Must Be Love

Kate left me alone in the office, telling me I could stay as long as I wanted before she went back out into the shop. Sitting in the cold leather chair, I rested my forearms on the desk and dropped my head. The wood smelled of citrus pledge, and it filled my nostrils as I pressed my nose against the desk. I was so tired that I could have easily nodded off right there in the office, but the sound of keys rattling roused me from my doze. Lifting my head, I slowly opened my eyes. Leaning his shoulder into the door frame, and thumbing his keys in his hand, was a disheveled and weary Jared. I instantly felt more alert. My breath caught in my lungs, and my chest felt tight.

His hair and clothes were damp and they clung to him like cellophane. I could see every curve, line and contour of his rock hard body through his white shirt. The deep Apollo's belt, which led to a very large and appetizing piece of erotic equipment, was prominent against his slick wet shirt. His jeans were soaked, and the light denim was now a deep blue. Water dripped from his light brown hair down the side of his face, glistening as it rolled over his caramel skin. I could feel my heartbeat quickening as my eyes roamed freely over his masculine, firm and completely beguiling body.

Our eyes met and he stared me down. His expression was difficult to gauge. He didn't appear riled, but he was certainly displeased.

"I just came by to get the receipts for the week. Do you mind?" Signaling for me to shift away from the desk, he brushed past me, and I had to fight the urge to throw my arms around him.

He stood beside me, flicking through the small pieces of paper in his hands. His icy demeanor increased my guilt as I stared up at him.

Gulping down the lump in my throat, I stood and placed my hand on his shoulder. He regarded it coolly before returning his attention to the receipts, and I let out a long sigh.

"Jared, I'm sorry. I acted like a child, and I understand if you're too mad to speak to me. I shouldn't have gone off like that, and I know I must have seemed ungrateful, but I'm not. It's very generous of you. It's all just a little overwhelming. I'm not used to having things just given to me like that. I had a very modest upbringing and these gifts and gestures are going to take some adjusting to. I am grateful, and I do appreciate your help and the beautiful gifts. Anyway, that's all I wanted to say. I'll leave you to your work."

I went to leave, but he caught my hand as I breezed past him. Shaking his head, he stared at me.

"It's raining out. Did you know? You see, I do because I got soaked roaming the streets of Long Beach searching for you. You had me worried fucking sick, Layla. Again!"

Wincing, I ran my fingers through my hair. "I'm sorry. Maybe I should go."

He groaned in frustration as his grip tightened on my hand. "Oh come on, Layla, we both know I didn't come here for the receipts. I called and Kate said you were here. I need to talk about this, and you need to listen."

Swinging me around, he sat me in the chair by the desk. Gripping the arms, he leaned forward, caging me in.

The dampness of his hair caused cool droplets of water to drip onto my cleavage and run down my chest.

"I'm sorry I upset you, and that you felt unable to have a rational conversation with me about it. But I couldn't leave things like this and go to New York, so I went to your dorm to find you. Amy told me the two of you had a fight, and that you'd stormed out in typical Layla fashion.

"I searched for you all over, then figured you might have come here. I was worried sick, especially when it started to rain. The last thing I want is you sick with flu. I'm sorry you felt my gifts were too much, but I'm not willing to accept them back. And for the record, I do not now, nor have I ever considered you a gold-digger, or a whore. I am furious that you could think that of me, and frankly, it's taking me a lot of self-control not to throw you over that desk and teach you a lesson."

My insides clenched at the very idea. Would he really do that? Here, now? I tried to keep my cool and calm my now heavy breathing.

"I'm sorry I yelled at you, and I'm sorry I made you worry. But it worries me how much money you're willing to spend on someone you barely even know. Isn't this all kind of fast?"

Resting his forehead against mine, he closed his eyes and exhaled loudly.

"Layla, the first moment I laid eyes on you I knew I had to have you. I watched you walk across that street to the coffee house in a complete daze. You were breathtaking. Fumbling around in your purse, your hair blowing in the breeze around your face. I couldn't take my eyes off you. In fact, I was so stunned that I never even noticed how close I was standing to the door when you backed your way into it. So when you asked me how I didn't see you through that glass, I did see you. Then when you told me you worked here, oh Layla, I can't lie, I was thrilled and worried, all at the same time. It meant I would be able to see you whenever I wanted. That's why I came in the next day, and every day after that, just to see you here.

"When you agreed to go on a date with me, I thought my head and chest would explode from the sheer joy I felt. You were so easy to talk to, and wonderfully fiery, sarcastic, yet warm and caring at the same time. I feel like I've known you forever. I've never shared a connection with anyone like the one I have with you. So no, I don't think it's fast."

I found myself grinning as I remembered the events of the day we first met. So he had seen me, after all. Part of me wanted to tease him about it, but something told me he wasn't quite finished. Taking my hands in his, he opened his eyes and gazed deeply into mine. His scent filled my senses, and the sweet aroma of vanilla and coffee, mixed with the delicious cologne he was wearing, made me swoon.

"Layla. I don't know how you feel about me. I hope you feel as deeply as I do, but I knew the moment I saw you how I felt. It hit me like a bolt of lightning right here." He pressed my palm against his chest, just above his heart. I drew in a sharp breath. "Layla, I'm falling for you. I'm deeply, madly and completely head over heels for you. You're mine, and I want to take care of you. Please, let me give you things while I can, let me spoil you and treat you the way you deserve. Like a queen. *My* queen. I…"

He took a long breath while I held mine in anticipation of his next heart stopping words.

"…I love you Layla."

I gawked at him, completely speechless. I was lost for words, yet a thousand ran through my mind at warp speed. Concern became etched across his face as I continued to struggle to form a sentence, or even a coherent word. Swallowing hard, I tried frantically to regain my equilibrium. He loves me. And not just puppy love, oh no. Its fireworks, hearts, flowers, diamonds and sparkles. He's madly in love with me. Releasing a sigh, he ran his thumb over my knuckles.

"I know it's a lot to take in. And I don't expect you to reciprocate. I just wanted you to know how much you mean to me. You're my world, Layla. My universe wouldn't be complete without you in it."

A long breath left my lungs, and I was finally able to speak. Holding my fingertips against his soft lips, I smiled up at him, gazing into his eyes. I felt the connection between us getting stronger and more intense with every word spoke.

"I feel exactly the same. I was just too scared to tell you. I wasn't sure you could love me back. But now that I know, I feel like I'm walking on air. I love you too. It's probably why you have the ability to make me so angry. You're so intense, and your whole body just calls to me in a way I have never experienced. I hate not being with you, and I miss you so much when we're apart. The way you make me feel when you're near me is incredible. I feel desirable, sexy, sensual and totally delirious with happiness. I'm not sure how long I can go without feeling your body against mine."

A suggestive grin spread across his face. "Agreed. Come on, let's go. I'm leaving the state in less that twelve hours and I want you in my bed, naked and warm before I go. Call it a going away present."

Grabbing me on the ass, he hauled me over his shoulder. I squealed and giggled with delight while kicking my feet which were now in the air, above his head.

"Jared! What are you doing? Put me down this instant!"

Swatting me on the behind, he laughed. "Not a chance. I'm not risking you storming off again, my lady. These sneakers are going in the trash too. They make it far too easy for you to make your get away. In fact…"

He grabbed my ankle and slid his hand downwards, pulling off my sneaker in the process, then repeated his actions with my other foot. Both my shoes landed with a loud thud on the office floor. Hanging upside down, my head in line with his broad back, I noticed Kate coming towards us through the crook of Jared's arm. I seized my opportunity to plead with her for some assistance, but from her delighted expression, I knew I wasn't going to be getting much help from her.

"Ah, Miss Danes. Could you please see to it that Miss Jennings' sneakers are disposed of in the dumpster out back?"

"Kate, don't you dare!"

Swatting me on the behind again, and this time a little harder, Jared instantly silenced me. "Miss Danes, if you would be so kind I'll be sure to include a generous bonus in your pay check this month."

"Bribery, that's really professional and ethical. Kate, are you seriously going to do this?"

Crouching down so that our eyes could meet, Kate gave me an apologetic smile. "Sorry, sweetie. I could sure use the cash. Besides, with your sneakers in the trash, Mr. Garrett will be forced to buy you a whole new pair. Right, sir?"

"Absolutely, Ms. Danes. Now, if you'd excuse us."

Heading into the now desolate shop, I gave Kate one last pleading look as she gathered up my discarded shoes. Smiling back at me, she waved before walking out back to the dumpster. I swatted Jared on the ass, letting him know I was peeved.

"Hey! Behave and keep your roaming hands to yourself back there, or I'll give you something to complain about." And with that, he smacked me harder on my behind, making me gasp in shock. It wasn't painful. In fact, I rather enjoyed it which shocked me even more.

"You are *so* buying me new shoes, Mr. Garrett!"

"Indeed, maybe a pair of fuck me heels?" I chuckled as we exited the shop and walked into the quiet street. Well, he walked, and I was carried. It was dark now and it had stopped raining, but the weather wasn't cold, just cool.

The rain had left the scent of damp, muskiness in the air. As I hung there, upside down over his shoulder, Jared used his free hand to fumble in his jeans front pocket.

"Uh, baby, while you're back there, would you mind reaching into my back pocket and getting my keys?"

I happily obliged, taking the opportunity to grope and grab his firm round buttock in the process.

"Down, girl. You keep that up and we won't even make it back to the house."

"I wouldn't complain at all, sir."

A sharp pain made me gasp, and my breath caught in my throat when Jared's teeth sank into the delicate flesh of my behind as he growled deeply in his throat. He hadn't bitten me hard, but it was enough to leave a mark for certain. Much like the spanking had done earlier, the sudden clamping down of his jaws around my tush excited me. It was arousing, yet frightening how much I enjoyed the pain and pleasure of it all.

Upon reaching the car, he set me on my feet. I felt a little unsteady as my eyes and brain tried to adjust to being the correct way up again. Advancing on me slowly, I saw the fire beginning to simmer in his eyes and the light blue turning darker, into a deep shade of cobalt once more. He looked like a predator homing in on its prey, and I was delighted to be caught. My back pressed against the cold steel of the car door. Gripping his hands on the car by either side of my head, he caged me in. My breathing became heavy as I eagerly anticipated his touch on my skin, his lips on mine and his hot body against my flesh. I was suddenly aware of my naked feet. While the rest of my body sizzled with heat and scorching arousal, my feet were beginning to feel cold. The parking lot had been sheltered from the downpour outside leaving the concrete dry, and I was grateful that my feet were merely cold rather than wet also. Glancing down at my feet, Jared noticed the predicament he had caused by casting out my sneakers.

Grabbing me on the behind, he hoisted my hips against his and wrapped my legs around his waist, pressing me further and harder into the cool steel. My head fell back against the roof, and I prayed he would take his chance to unleash his lips on my wanting, waiting skin. He didn't disappoint. Seconds later, Jared's soft and tender kisses caressed my exposed neck, slowly working his way from the nape to my jaw.

"I wonder how many kisses it would take me to get from here…"

He flicked his tongue over my bottom lip and a soft whimper escaped me.

"…To here." His hand left my thigh as he slid it swiftly between my legs. I smiled, biting my lip as his fingers brushed against my thin cotton pants.

"Oh, I wish you'd worn a skirt today."

My eyes closed as he ran his fingertips over my stomach to my hip, gripping it and running his thumb over my curves as he moved. Gradually he made his way up my side to my breast, removing it from the cup of my bra with a firm tug. I opened my eyes and scanned the car park, hoping we were alone, but I was so caught up in the moment that someone could have easily been standing right next to me and I wouldn't have cared. I wanted him desperately, needed him inside me.

With his keys in hand, I ran my fingertips all over his chest before sliding them to his back as his mouth found my breast. Stroking it gently with his tongue, he massaged and groped with his hand. I arched my back, pushing my chest firmly into his hand. He nipped gently on the fleshy rounded part of my breasts before lifting his head and closing his lips over mine, kissing me deeply and with an urgent need. I moaned into his mouth, and he thrust his hips against me hard and meaningfully.

The car sprung to life.

The ear splitting siren of the alarm echoed through the parking lot as the lights flashed wildly. Startled, I clung to Jared as he fumbled frantically in his pockets for his keys before realizing I had them still clutched in my hand. Taking them from me, he hit the button and the car was instantly silenced once more. Our moment of passion had been well and truly interrupted, and I couldn't help but laugh at the whole thing.

Releasing my grip on him, I lowered my feet to the ground, readjusted my bra, and laughed heartily. Jared ran his fingers through his damp brown hair and grinned back at me.

"Well. That was eventful. Let's say you and I get out of here and go somewhere a little warmer and a little less public. Besides, I don't want you getting cold feet." Giving me a playful wink, he scooped me into his arms, opened the passenger door, and placed me gently on the seat.

His damp clothes clung to his body as he moved around to the driver's door, and a shiver ran down my spine. My feet were freezing, but my blood was still running scalding hot.

He was mine.

The thought was almost too good to be true, but it was true. Jared Garrett, millionaire, businessman, playboy and philanthropist was in love with me, Layla Jennings, a simple girl from Pasadena with divorced parents and a high school diploma. It was mind boggling and a little frightening.

Everything had moved so fast between us. I didn't believe in instant love, or love at first sight, but what I felt for him was deeper than anything I'd ever felt before. I had always thought Josh had been my first love, but what we had shared didn't even scratch the surface of what I was feeling for Jared.

Had he ever been in love before? Had anyone ever even come close? Surely he'd had a high school girlfriend, and at college there must have been dozens of young preppy girls just itching to get into the shorts of the young Garrett heir. I instantly found myself wondering about the others. How many women had there been for Jared? He certainly wasn't short of admirers, and from what I'd heard, he'd not just sown his wild oats, there were entire plantations of them!

I watched him, deep in my own self torturing thoughts, and bit my lip. The questions were poised on the tip of my tongue. How many women? Did he love them? Are they still around? I didn't want to be that girl; the jealous, clingy and needy type. But surely it wasn't completely irrational to want to know a little about the relationship history of the man I love?

I mean, they do say that you're not just sleeping with them; you're sleeping with everyone they ever slept with. I just needed a rough idea of what I was up against. Josh had been the only man I'd ever been with until Jared. Well, except for Gary Colbert; but a fumble in the back seat of his car, followed by a premature ejaculation, really didn't count in my book.

Catching me staring at him, Jared raised an eyebrow and glanced at me quizzically. "What is it? You have that 'I've got something to say' look on your face. Come on, honesty, remember? Out with it."

I remained silent, weighing up the pros and cons of asking my intrusive questions. But he was right. We needed to build trust and honesty in our relationship. Taking a deep breath, I exhaled slowly.

"Ok, here goes. I was just wondering how many women you've been with. I know, I have no right to ask, and you have no obligation to tell me, but I just wanted to know. So there you go. Do with it what you will."

Slumping back into my seat with relief, I waited with bated breath for a reply, any reply, but mostly I hoped it would be one I could both swallow and accept.

Smiling, he licked his lips while his eyes stared straight ahead at the road. "You want to know how many women I've slept with. That right?" I nodded weakly. "Well considering I don't keep count, I'm going to have to give you a ball park figure."

Oh god, oh god, a ball park figure? He couldn't count them on one hand, or even two? My mind began to conjure scenes of lust filled orgies and hundreds of women flitting in and out of his beautiful white bed. He must have seen my anxiety because he immediately shut me down.

"Stop it. Right now. Why torture yourself, Layla? It's not as many as you think. If I had to give you a number which, by the way, I find a little unsettling, it would be…sixty, approximately. I started having sex when I was sixteen, Layla. So when you think about it, that's ten women per year. Not that many, is it? And that's including you. But none of them even matter because I'm with you. You're the only woman I want in my bed, shower, tub, dining table, counter top, sofa, and anywhere else I can throw you over. You, Layla Jennings, are the only woman I will sleep with from now till the day I die.

"And I bet I know the next question, and the answer is no. I didn't love them. I never knew what love was. I cared about them, sure, and I wanted to make them happy, but I didn't love them. I love you. I've never met anyone that affects me the way you do. I feel like I could conquer the world, bench press a bus, and run a marathon when I'm with you. You make me feel alive and so happy that I can't even think straight."

Sixty women! Sixty perfect strangers that the man I love had pleasured in his bed. I felt sick to my stomach as the images began to flash through my mind like a bad movie. Taking my hand, he held it tightly while steering with the other.

"Hey, don't do this to yourself, Layla. I mean it. They were meaningless, one night stands, trysts and fleeting romances. They can't even hold a candle to you. You're the only girl for me. It's like every other woman in the world ceased to exist the moment I laid eyes on you. Please don't dwell over this, baby. Promise me you will just forget them because it's about you and me now. No one else."

He was right. They were his past and as far as I was concerned that's exactly where they should stay. Stretching across from my seat, I kissed him on the cheek. A boyish grin spread across his face, and I was sure I saw him blush a light shade of pink.

"So, now you know my magic number, what's yours?"

Now I was blushing, but mine was definitely more obvious as my cheeks flushed and I was sure they were cherry red by now. Fiddling with my hair I stared at the floor. Jared brushed his fingers over mine reassuringly.

"Two. My high school boyfriend, Josh, and you. That's my big number. Most girls my age have been with more than two guys." Nerves were buzzing inside me while I sat, worried what he thought of my revelation. Would he think I was inexperienced? Would he treat me differently now? I didn't want our relationship or our sex life to change just because I had spent two years screwing the same guy instead of several.

"And this Josh, did you love him?"

It wasn't the reaction I was expecting, and to be honest, I was relieved.

"I thought I did. But now, being with you, I know I probably didn't. I was young, and I thought it had to be love. But it was probably just hormones mixed with lust and urges. What I had with him doesn't even come close to how I feel about you."

His face was contorted into a scowl.

"And this high school sweetheart is where?"

He was jealous, and secretly and perhaps even wickedly, I was enjoying it. But I wouldn't torment him with it, knowing I would be livid if one of his exes was suddenly a fixture in our lives. Putting his mind at ease, I explained how Josh had cheated on me before graduating high school and moved away.

"What a moron. He had a succulent juicy steak at home, but decided to man handle some sloppy joe? What a stupid move. Well you have nothing to worry about, baby. I'm a straight up sirloin man."

Chapter 25

Tying Me In Knots

The house was warm, and as I stepped into the foyer, I glanced back at Jared. Our time together was going to be bittersweet. He was leaving in a few hours, then I would be alone for four days without the man I loved. The thought brought a lump to my throat. I wondered briefly if he had sensed my dejection as he swiftly cupped my face in his hands and kissed me passionately, deeply and longingly.

Gripping my hands to his back, I noticed his shirt was still slightly damp. I tugged at it, pulling it free from the waist of his pants. Never removing my lips from his, I hastily unbuttoned it and slid my hands inside onto his hot, taut body. Grazing my fingers across his rock hard abs, I felt him tense slightly beneath my fingers. He let out a low groan as his arousal began to press into my thigh. A loud ringing startled me, and I halted my hands. Opening my eyes, I pulled away from his kiss and looked around, wondering where the sound was coming from.

"It's in my office. They know I don't take business calls after hours, ignore it."

Grabbing me around the waist with his strong arm, he pulled me to him and leaned in to resume our make out session. I pressed my hands against his chest and held him back slightly.

"It might be about New York. You have to get it."

He tried to interject, but I cut him off with a simple sway of my head in a silent no. He growled with frustration and turned his back to me, running his fingers through his silky watery locks.

Seizing his hand, I pulled him towards me and stood on my tippy toes until our noses were touching just at the tip. I could smell the rain in his hair and the heady scent of sweat and soap. It was an aphrodisiac I was becoming very accustomed to and I welcomed it eagerly whenever he was near me. Gazing into my eyes, he ran his tongue over his bottom lip. He growled again, but this time it wasn't frustration; it was carnal, sexual hunger. My lips were so close to his and his hot breath skimmed across the soft, plump flesh.

"Go answer your call, then come find me. I'll be waiting for you. Call it hide and seek?"

"More like hunter and prey, baby, because when I find you, I'm going to completely devour you." He bit down gently on my lip, and I closed my mouth over his, stealing another quick kiss before he reluctantly made his way to the office.

I waited until I heard the door slam behind him before making my way up the stairs. Quickly undressing, I left my discarded clothes trailing behind me straight to the bedroom. I didn't want to make him look too hard for me; after all, I was perfectly happy to be found.

Pushing open the large double doors to his room, I sighed. The beauty of it still took my breath away. It was elegant and tasteful. The vintage couches and gold detail made the room feel like a five star hotel. I decided to take this time to have a better look around. Opposite the bathroom was another large door, I poked my head around the corner to check that Jared was still busy with his call before opening it. What I found was beyond amazing. Hundreds of crisp shirts hung neatly lined in rows. Pants below them, and shoes on a rack perfectly polished and paired on the floor. The walk in closet was more like a dressing room with two full length mirrors and a couch against the far wall. Two enormous dressers sat on either side of the mirrors.

I walked along the clothes rack, thumbing the shirts gently, so as not to crease or mark them, when I came to one that I instantly recognized.

Hanging alone at the end of the rail was a coffee stained, white Armani shirt. Pulling it down, I inspected it closely. It was definitely the same shirt. The coffee stain was over the right side of the chest, and tiny speckles of blood were dotted around the collar. Without a second thought, I brought it to my face and breathed in deeply. It smelled of Jared. He certainly hadn't had it dry cleaned as he claimed. And he'd had the nerve to try and give me a dry cleaning bill! I did feel a little better though, now that he had told me the truth about what happened that day.

Grinning like a school girl, I hatched a plan. Returning the ruined shirt to its hanger, I searched the closet for what I needed then headed to the bathroom to primp myself. Rummaging through the cabinets for any form of moisturizer, I stumbled upon something I realized I probably shouldn't have. I was standing in front of a cabinet full of lubricants, oils, condoms and gels. Oh my. Jared's sex cabinet.

Holding my hand to my mouth in shock, I should have closed it immediately, but something was stopping me. I was…curious. Taking a small red bottle from the shelf I read the worn out label. "Essential Oils. Cinnamon and orange." Taking off the lid, I instantly smelled the sweet aromas. My plan was now taking a new direction.

The sound of yelling caught my attention and I quickly returned everything but the red bottle to the cabinet and headed for the stairs. Approaching the office, I could hear how enraged he was by the tone of Jared's voice, and it both frightened and thrilled me. I really did love it when he was mad.

The door was slightly ajar, so I stood, hovering and listening to the one sided conversation. He was standing stiffly with his back to the door, and I could see he was tense by the way his shoulders hunched to his neck. "I don't care how much it costs, just do it! I made a promise, and I'm going to keep it. It's totally fucking unacceptable and I'm holding you responsible. If anything happens to her, I'll…"

Her? Who was her? The floor boards creaked below my foot, and the sound halted his conversation as he turned around and glared at the door. I winced and turned on my heels running back up the stairs. I'd been caught eavesdropping, and I could hear him yelling after me, but I was not going back there while he was pissed at me.

"Oh you can run, but that just makes me want to catch you." His tone was harsh, yet full of passionate, lustful promise.

I could hear his feet pounding against the floor as he sprinted after me. Adrenaline surged through my veins as I ran for the bedroom, closing the door behind me to stall him. My heart hammered inside my chest, and I could hear the low thuds in my ears. I stared at the door, waiting for him.

Bursting into the room, he stopped dead and his jaw hit the floor as he took in my attire. His eyes scanned every inch of me, from my toes all the way up my body until he met my gaze. I bit my lip seductively. I stood perfectly still in the middle of the room as he began to circle me, admiring the view that he was clearly enjoying. Taking the thin white fabric between his fingers, he gave me a wicked smile.

"Miss Jennings, is that one of my Armani shirts?"

Pursing my lips together, I remained silent.

"I have to say, it looks a thousand times better hanging off your voluptuous curves than on me. I wonder..."

Lifting the hem of the shirt, he ran his fingers over the delicate lace of my panties. A low groan left his lips as his hand continued up over my stomach to my chest. His hand massaged and groped my breast, my nipple peaking and puckering as he teased, rolling it between his thumb and finger. A whimper escaped me, and a satisfied grin spread across his face.

"Oh, baby, I heard that." He leaned in close, our chests pressed together. Grabbing his unbuttoned shirt, I slid it down his thick arms and tossed it aside. Gripping my hands on his shoulders, I could feel the tension he was holding. Whatever had happened in that office had made him worried and extremely irritated. I began to work his tired muscles as his head fell back, and he moaned.

"Mmmm, that's wonderful."

Remembering the little red bottle in the bathroom, I took his hand and led him to the bed.

He arched his eyebrow at me and gave me a questioning look. "Can't wait to get me on my back, huh?"

"Actually, I want you to take off your pants and lie on your front. I'll be right back."

Grabbing the bottle from the bathroom counter, I stopped for a moment to check my reflection. My long blonde hair was frizzy from my walk in the evening air, and my makeup had begun to slide from its natural position on my face. His phone call was haunting me. Whatever was going on involved a woman, and my heart was hammering as I thought about the possibilities and explanations for his secret. Trying desperately to hold on to my faith in him, I hurried back to the scorching hot man waiting for me in the bedroom.

Jared was lying on the bed face down and completely naked. I actually grunted in sheer delight at the sight of him. His hands were gripped together above his head making the muscles in his arms pull taut and flex. His broad back was perfectly defined, with tempting lines and curves leading to his buttocks. His ass was dreamily rounded, like a delicious peach you just want to sink your teeth into, and boy, did I want to sink my teeth into him. His gorgeous caramel skin glistened in the lamp light. He looked good enough to eat.

Climbing onto the bed, I straddled him. My behind resting on his, I took a small amount of oil and drizzled it over his bare shoulder blades. He hissed through his teeth as the cold oil made contact with his warm skin. Placing my palms firmly on his back, I went to work on his aching, knotted body, kneading and soothing the muscles deeply. My hands roamed freely, exploring all the contours and lines of his body, taking a playful detour as they slithered nearer to his buttocks. The oil on my hands warming as it dripped and slid gently over his skin. A low moan escaped his lips, and he began to shift around on the bed as if uncomfortable. Turning over onto his back, I slid off him, the reason for his discomfort suddenly becoming very clear.

The beautiful, pink, solid length of his erection sprung free, and I licked my lips at the sight of it. He was positively delicious, laying in front of me; naked and aroused, just waiting for my next move. I felt like a powerful and sexy seductress, and he was a willing participant in my love games.

Positioning myself between his legs, I ran my tongue up the inside of his thigh, caressing and teasing him, kissing the deep V in his torso and flicking the tip of my tongue back down to his thigh. I rolled it back and forth everywhere, but the one place he was aching for it to be. "Oh god, Layla, you're killing me, baby."

Gripping him firmly with one hand, I took him into my mouth. He inhaled sharply as the warm wetness of my welcoming mouth surrounded his throbbing cock. Covering my teeth with my lips as though sucking a popsicle, I slid my tongue down and around the full length of his shaft. His tip almost touching the back of my throat would normally have been something to make me stop, or trigger my gag reflex, but I was so caught up in the moment, it never seemed to happen, and if it did I never noticed it as the deep pleasurable sounds he was making spurred me on. His eyes were closed tightly, and he had the ever familiar look of enjoyment on his face.

Focusing my mouth back to the silky smooth tip, I gripped him with both hands, gently letting them follow my lips as I bobbed up and down, massaging my tongue over him while swirling and flicking the sensitive ridge. I began to hum deeply, turning him into my very own vibrator while sucking and rolling my mouth up and down.

"Holy fuck! Jesus, Layla! Fuck!"

It was definitely having the desired effect.

Gripping the sheets beneath him, Jared tensed, and I could sense his climax was moments away. Slowing my speed, I glanced up at him. His lips were pressed into a hard line, and his face held deep concentration as if he were trying desperately not to lose control. I wanted so much to push him over the edge, to take him into pure ecstasy with my sexpert oral skills.

"Stop, Layla, Fuck... Stop!"

He was panting and pleading, but I continued, completely ignoring his plea. His hand gripped my hair, and he tugged me away, bringing my delicious Jared popsicle to an end. Sitting up, he ran his fingers through my hair before gliding his thumb over my cheek to my bottom lip.

"You keep doing that and this is going to be over far too quickly, and there is so much more that I have planned for us tonight, well for you.

Holding both my hands, he stared into my eyes. He looked serious, and I found myself feeling slightly apprehensive wondering what was going through his mind.

"Layla, do you trust me? For what I have in mind for us, I need you to trust me completely. I adore you, I worship you, and I want to worship your body from head to toe, but you must have total faith in me. Can you do that?"

I stared back at him, confused and a little worried about what exactly he was planning on doing to me.

"What exactly did you have in mind?"

He cleared his throat, and his expression was noticeably nervous. "Do you know anything about bondage?"

My eyes widened as I sat there completely dumb struck. Bondage? Was that what he wanted to do? Scenes of leather, whips, and chains ran through my mind. Was he freaking serious? With my voice slightly quivering, I found the strength to speak. "You mean like whips and chains? I really don't think I can do that. I'm sorry, I just really don't think it's my thing."

Pressing his hand to his mouth, he stifled a laugh and it instantly irritated me. I didn't see anything funny about the subject at all.

"What exactly do you find amusing about this? Because I have to admit, I'm kind of freaked out right now."

Cupping my face in his hands, he ran his thumbs over my cheeks. "Shhh, baby, calm down. No, I don't mean whips and chains. I mean bondage. It's…wait here."

Sliding off the bed, he disappeared into the walk in closet. I could hear him rummaging around inside before he finally returned with a large velvet bag. Placing it in front of me, he resumed his position on the bed. "Take a look. Empty the whole thing onto the bed. I'll explain everything, and then you can decide what you think you might like to try and what you would definitely rule out. There's no pressure here, Layla. I just want to see where you stand with all this. Ok?"

I nodded weakly and emptied the contents of the mysterious bag onto the bed.

A heap of items landed on the sheets and I eyed them inquisitively. Handcuffs I recognized, and some red satin ribbon. But the rest were an absolute conundrum. Picking up an item that looked like an elongated ping pong racket, Jared swatted the air and smiled at my perplexed expression.

"Don't look so frightened, Layla. This is a paddle. It's used mostly for spanking which is something that a lot of couples do. There's a fine line between pleasure and pain, and some of these items are designed to heighten your senses while also giving you pleasure. When I had you over my shoulder earlier, I spanked you and I even bit you. How did it feel?"

My face wrinkled and my nose screwed up as embarrassment flushed through my body. Could I really admit that I had liked it? That it excited me, and certainly heightened my senses as he just said? Swallowing my prudish pride, I decided to come clean. "I guess I kind of liked it."

"Kind of liked it?"

"Fine. It was hot"

He grinned. "So spanking? Something you'd be willing to try?" I nodded but remained silent. "I need a verbal and definitive answer here, Layla. Yes, or no?"

"Yes."

Placing the paddle on a pillow, he picked up the handcuffs and dangled them from his finger. Without hesitation, I nodded enthusiastically. He laughed lightly and tossed them onto the pillow with the paddle. Next was a set of leather straps held together by a thin chain. Each strap had a hook attached, and they looked a little menacing with metal studs embroidered into the cuffs.

"These are door restraints. The hooks go over the top of the door, and these leather straps are the cuffs to hold your wrists together. These, the handcuffs, and a few other items I possess are all for restraining you. Keeping you still and in place. They're not painful. I would never use anything on you that would cause you pain. Well, not excessively anyway."

He winked at me as I contemplated the idea of totally giving myself over to this man. To be at his mercy, at his every command as he made the choice to deliver me both pleasure and pain so readily.

I really didn't feel comfortable with the whole Dom and sub idea, but I was happy to spend time playing with a few toys and straps. Besides, the spanking he'd given me in the parking lot was exciting beyond comprehension.

 "Jared, I think cuffs, restraints and toys could be fun, but I'm really not into the whole BDSM scene."

"Neither am I, but I do want to possess you. You belong to me, Layla, and I want you to submit your body to me, only your body. I want you to trust me completely and give over to intense pleasure at my hands. I want to tease, tempt and devour you in every way, and I want you to be totally at my mercy. I will never do anything you don't want to do, and I will never be cruel. The moment you say so, we stop. We can even have a safe word if you want one."

"A safe word?"

"When you're in the throes of ecstasy, sometimes we say no, or stop when we don't mean it. The safe word is a cease and desist button. The moment that word leaves your lips, I'll stop. I'll release you, and I won't continue till you say so. Alright?"

That, admittedly, made me feel better about the whole thing. Knowing that at any time, if I felt uneasy or uncomfortable, I could end it with one word was comforting. Oh, screw it. I needed some adventure and fun in my life, and with Jared I was undeniably going to get it.

Looking around at the pile of toys on the bed, I scooped them all up in my arms and dropped them on the pillow with the others. Grinning at me like a school boy, Jared laughed.

"What on earth are you doing?"

"I've decided I'm ok with it. All of it. There's just one thing I absolutely do not want to do. I'm definitely not into anal play. None, zip, zero, nada. I know some guys are into that, but I'm just not comfortable with it. But other than that, I trust you. Whatever you want to introduce into our lovemaking, I have complete faith in your judgment. As for this safe word, I was thinking…coffee?"

Planting a soft, slow kiss on my lips, he murmured into my mouth. "I love it, and I love you for thinking of it."

Pushing me down gently on the sheets, his mouth sealed over mine. Slipping his tongue in and seeking my own, he kissed me tenderly, lovingly and with a deep passion. His hands were in my hair massaging my scalp with his fingertips. I groaned as he lifted himself onto his forearms and hovered over me. Brushing a strand of hair from my face, he gave me a half-hearted smile.

"I love you so much, Layla. The next four days are going to be torture. Being apart from you and these lips…" He gave me a gentle peck before moving to my eyelids and kissing each one sweetly and lightly. "…and these beautiful, dazzling eyes, this smooth, wonderful skin."

His lips travelled southwards over my cheeks to my jaw.

While tracing his fingertips down my neck, he unbuttoned his expensive shirt which was hugging my curves beneath him. "And these full, ample, voluptuous breasts…I could fondle them all day and never get bored. I love how your body reacts and readies itself for me, for us, for pure ecstasy and pleasure."

My eyes closed as the feel of his warm breath on my skin made the hairs on my neck stand on end. He was right. My body was standing to attention from his touch, his words, and the sexy purring of his voice. He exuded sex appeal. His power over me was all consuming, and I loved it.

His hands left my breasts for a moment, and my eyes sprung open as warm oil slid over my body, dribbling onto the sheets below me as it rolled over my skin. The scents of cinnamon, orange, Jared, and sex made me light headed, and I was almost swooning. His slippery fingers pinched and rolled my nipples between them, I arched my back and thrust my breast into his palms. He gladly kneaded and groped them, varying the pressure between soft gentle strokes and hard squeezing grips.

My breasts weren't the only part of me that was slippery at this point. I was so turned on by this touch that I was as wet as a water slide. The throbbing between my legs was now an aching painful need.

"Oh, Jared, Oh my god," I whimpered.

Leaving my breasts, he continued to glide his hands down my stomach, swirling around my navel gently. I was ablaze with desire for him as his hands travelled further over the curves of my hips, gripping them before letting go and caressing my thighs. More oil poured onto my flesh, leaving my skin drenched in a slick delicious coating. His hands and fingers expertly teased over every inch of my body, my toes, the soles of my feet, my calves, behind my knees and my thighs; no single area went unnoticed. His attentive and tender rubbing drove me wild with lust.

As his soft lips grazed the inside of my thigh, I whimpered. I could feel him smiling against my skin as he licked and caressed the inside of my silky and sensitive thighs while his hot mouth travelled further and further up. I thrust my hips upwards, begging him to give me what I needed, what I craved. Lifting his head, he shook it at me.

"Tut, tut, tut. I think now would be a very good time to introduce some of these toys."

I'd never tried anything like this before, and my nerves were beginning to grip me. I bit my lip, trying not to let my apprehension show as Jared crawled across the enormous bed to the pillow. He rifled through the pile before settling on one of the long pieces of red satin ribbon. Turning his gaze to me, he smiled.

"I think we'll start off gently. Come here to me. Lie down with your head on the pillow and put your hands over your head, interlocking your fingers."

Threading the soft, silky material between his fingers, he gave me a mischievous smile. I crawled across the bed to him, and did exactly as he asked. Taking my hands, he pressed them against a bar on the headboard and twisted the satin around both my wrists, knotting it firmly into place. I wriggled my fingers, but it was not going to budge. Tight enough to hold me, but not to bite into my wrists, the smooth material felt soft and cool against my skin.

Supporting himself on his palms, he lowered his mouth onto mine and kissed me sweetly. I moaned into his mouth, and he responded with his own deep, throaty groan. Sitting back on his heels, he grinned at me as my eyes roamed all over his sizzling hot body, his perfectly formed pecs, and his smooth caramel skin which was glistening from the oil we had rubbed all over each other. My gaze traveled south to his deep and defined Apollo's belt. The urge to run my tongue over the grooves made me very aware that I was tied to the bed. I was completely at his mercy…and I liked it.

"Enjoying the view, my lady? I hope so because it's the last thing you're going to see for a while."

Taking a long piece of black silk from the pile, he laid beside me, propped on one elbow. Dangling the fabric over my breast, he let it gently brush against my skin before dragging it slowly over my nipple, down my stomach and over my sex. I exhaled slowly, trying to calm my racing pulse as the tickling sensations sent shivers up my body and goose bumps appeared on my pale, soft skin.

Seeing my obvious pleasure, he continued to trail the fabric over me while I bowed and writhed, pulling tightly on my restraint. Bringing the material up to my neck, he let it slide gently over my cheeks and across my eyelids before gripping it with his hands.

"I'm going to blindfold you, Layla. Remember, you can say coffee at any time, and I will stop. Understand?"

Words escaped me. I was so aroused that I'd have agreed to join the mob if he'd asked me to. I would have given him anything just to feel him inside me, giving me my release. But at the moment, I couldn't even form a coherent sentence. As a small whimper left my lips, I nodded.

"Good girl."

Darkness consumed me as the soft, silky material covered my eyes, leaving me blind. I could smell the sweet fragrance of the oil and the musky tones of his cologne. His warm breath on my face revealed his position, and I bit my lip so hard I thought I might puncture it as I waited impatiently for his next move.

"Oh baby, you have no idea how good you look right now. I could eat you up. In fact, I think I might."

My breath hitched as his mouth swiftly moved south to my sex. His palms pressed firmly on my knees, he pushed my legs apart forcefully as he placed a soft kiss on my pubic bone and ran his hands up and over my thighs, massaging and groping as he moved them to my behind.

Lifting me up slightly from the bed, he positioned his hands on my ass and held me tightly. My knees became elevated on what I could only assume were his shoulders as his hair tickled the inside of my thigh and his mouth covered me, sliding his tongue up and down my moist slit.

"You taste divine."

He was teasing me, tempting me with his expert tongue. Tenderly, he pushed it through the fleshy lips. As I gripped the restraint on my wrists tightly, his tongue found my swollen clit. Flicking and rolling his way over it at varying speeds, he drove me to the edge quickly before slowing his pace, leaving me frustrated. I growled at the insensitive way he was torturing me, and I heard him give a throaty chuckle.

"Oh baby, you are so wet, so hot, so warm and totally delicious, I'm not ready to let you go just yet."

"Please, Jared. I need it. I'm so close it's practically indecent, please?"

His tongue resumed its frenzied attack on my clit and I moved my hips, matching his rhythm, but he continued to deny me my orgasm. In a last attempt to get what I needed, I thrust my hips against his mouth, urging him to go deep inside me. It worked, and his tongue darted inside and frantically began rolling, thrusting and licking my g-spot. The orgasmic sensations grew stronger and unbelievably intense. My breathing became harsher and more ragged until all at once a euphoric pleasure surged through my body like an electric current. My muscles stiffened as the ripples of ecstasy coursed through me, making me cry out in pure satisfied bliss.

Deprived of the privileges of touch and sight, I had submitted my body to his will and the reward was intense beyond anything I'd ever felt. His lips closed around mine, and he kissed me fervently. I could feel my slick wetness on his chin, and taste my salty liquid on his tongue.

Lying on top of me, he wrapped his arms around me tightly, holding me in a warm embrace. I pulled hard on the restraints, wanting so badly to run my hands over his body. I wanted to look into his deep blue eyes and lose myself in them as he loved and caressed every inch of me. Almost as though he read my mind, Jared removed the blindfold and untied my wrists. Casting them aside he smiled down at me with an expression of pure content. He ran his thumb over my cheek again and sighed.

"I can't believe I have to leave you in six hours. I wish you could come with me. Promise me you'll be ok while I'm gone. The thought of anything happening to you when I can't be here is crippling me, Layla. I'm tempted to tie you up again just to make sure you don't go anywhere and put yourself in danger."

I smiled and kissed the tip of his nose, knowing perfectly well that he had probably considered doing just that. "I'll be fine. I swear, I'll be right here waiting for you when you get back. Try not to worry too much, please, you'll make yourself frantic."

He kissed me deeply, and with my hands now free, I stretched them around his back, pulling him into me. His erection pressed hard into my stomach and I found it not only encouraging, but full of further sensual promise. He wasn't quite done with me yet.

Pressing his lips against mine, he murmured. "I'm going to make love to you, Layla. Slowly, softly and completely lose myself in you."

Reaching above my head, he grabbed a foil packet from the nightstand and tore it open, continuing his passionate kiss. Sitting on his heels, he slid the condom over his hard cock and gazed into my eyes as he gently sank into me. My mouth opened, forming an O as he filled me. I could feel every inch as he gradually moved deeper inside. His hips rocked slowly on mine as his hands explored my body, teasing my skin as he grazed it with his fingertips.

His kisses were profound and meaningful. It was as though our bodies were expressing our feelings for one another in a way words just couldn't describe. Nuzzling my neck I could feel his heavy, warm breath on my throat. I wound my legs around him, my feet pushing into his buttocks urging him to move faster and deeper, but he continued at his steady pace, prolonging our lovemaking.

The aching in my stomach intensified as I felt my orgasm building, and I began to rock my hips in time with his. He moaned deeply into my neck as I gripped my hands firmly on his back. My head fell back, my fingernails dragging downwards to the bottom of his spine as I held him tightly. Ecstasy poured through my veins, filling me once more. The room disappeared, and my senses deserting me as a whooshing echoed in my ears.

The pulsing pleasure of my orgasm along with the loving embrace that Jared held me in was an emotional overload and the tears began to slide down my face. One must have dripped onto his own soft skin because he immediately stopped moving and lifted up, staring down at me. His eyes scanned my expression, and a look of concern was etched on his face.

"Baby, what is it? Did I hurt you?"

A half sob, half laugh left my lips as I wiped the tears from my eyes. Shaking my head, I cupped his face in my hands and smiled up at him. "You didn't hurt me. I just got caught in the moment, I'm fine. I love you, Jared Garrett. I hope you know that."

He planted a chaste kiss on my lips and grinned. "I love you too, Layla Jennings. More than you could possibly fathom."

Moving back and forth gently, he placed tiny soft kisses over my face, caressing, loving and adoring every freckle, line and curve of my body as he rocked his hips into mine.

"You...are...so...beautiful. God, Layla. You're a magnificent work of art."

Slowly I felt another orgasm building, and I let out a soft whimper. Again? Really? I'd heard of multiple orgasms, but having never experienced so many in such little time, I'd assumed it was merely a myth. My muscles were clenching and tightening around him inside me.

With a clenched jaw, he panted in my ear. "Oh, Layla, come with me, baby. I'm close, try to hold on."

His words were an intoxicating aphrodisiac, and I struggled to control my body as I writhed and wriggled beneath him. Thrusting into me deeply, he tensed, gripping the sheets on either side of my head as he found his release. As if on cue, my own orgasm swept over me in an explosion of hot, mind blowing pleasure. Tears began to stream down my face once more, but this time he never questioned them, merely wiping them away as kissed me, holding me tightly to him.

We made love over and over for what seemed like hours before collapsing into a dazed sleepy state. Pulling me to him, Jared spooned me, enveloping in his arms. His face nuzzled my hair as he lay behind me, silently drifting in and out of slumber. I stared into the dark, my mind trying to make sense of everything that had happened since I'd moved here.

Thoughts of Ollie invaded my serene daydreams. The situation between us was gradually reaching boiling point, and our friendship was in jeopardy the longer things went on. I knew how he felt about me, yet there I was flaunting my happy relationship in front of him. He'd made it very clear what he thought of Jared, and that was something I couldn't easily let go of. He could be mad at me for leading him on, he could be mad at himself for not making a move, but being mad at Jared for loving me...that was not going to fly.

It was going to get ugly if I didn't do something soon. With my party only a few days away, I had a feeling that soon may have been a little closer than I'd have liked. The boys were just going to have to learn to play nicely. They both played a major part in my life, and I wasn't willing to give either of them up.

I dozed dreamily in and out of consciousness until I suddenly became aware that I was moving. Scooped in Jared's arms, he was carrying me down the hall to the familiar guest room once again. Something inside me tightened and pulled with an aching hurt. Why wouldn't he let me sleep in his bed?

Was I not worth it to him? Was that a place he'd had so many women before that now it was tainted? Thoughts buzzed through my mind, each more uncomfortable than the last.

Placing me gently on the bed, he shifted in behind me and squeezed me tightly. I tensed in his arms as my unanswered questions turned over and over in my mind. With his mouth to my ear, I could feel his long, even breaths.

"I don't know why you insist on torturing yourself all the time. I told you, I never share that bed, but I am sleeping with you whenever you're here. Shouldn't that tell you something, at least? I love you, Layla. Now stop thinking everything to death and go to sleep. You have class in the morning."

How did he know? He was right, though. The past two nights that I'd spent with Jared, I had been curled up in his arms until morning, so why was I still so uneasy about where it was that we did so? I held my hands over his, clasped together around my stomach, and sighed.

"Goodnight, baby."

Chapter 26

Ruby Tuesday

Jared left for the airport at 6 a.m. as planned, but not before making me breakfast and ensuring his assistant Jerry would have a car to pick me up and take me back to the dorm.

I hadn't planned on spending the night when I had been carried out of the coffee shop the previous evening, so I didn't have any clean clothes, or shoes. That would mean a frantic shower and change before class.

I stood there in a pair of his oversized sneakers like a child wearing her father's shoes. Before climbing into the black stretch limo that had arrived to take him to LAX, he gave me a long lingering kiss, and told me that he loved me. He would be traveling on the company plane, so there was no need for an early arrival to check in.

A second after his car left the driveway, an extremely expensive looking Mercedes pulled up in front of me. A young blond haired man got out and ran around to the back passenger side door. He was tall, and it was obvious that he took care of himself. His broad shoulders and thick muscular chest made his uniform look as though it were trying desperately to contain his enormous arms. He opened it, and gestured for me to get in.

"Your car, Miss Jennings. I'm Daniel and I'll be your chauffeur this morning."

Giving him a friendly smile, I climbed in and gazed at the beautiful cream interior. It looked brand new and smelled like pine and lemon. I stared out the window at the house as we reversed off the drive and onto the street. It would be several days until I was back there again, and back in Jared's warm, loving embrace. The thought was distressing, and I was instantly in a bad mood; a mood that didn't dissipate on the ride back to campus.

I thanked Daniel as he held out his hand to assist me out of the car, and made my way to my room. The halls were quiet except for the noise of the creaky, and well trafficked, floorboards underneath my feet as I walked down the long corridor to my room. I was just about to slide my key into the lock, when I was gripped on my elbow and hauled backwards.

"What the fuck?"

I stumbled, dazed, into Oliver's room. Staggering back, and trying to regain my equilibrium, I scanned my assailant. Standing in front of me, hair tousled as if he just got out of bed, and wearing nothing but a pair of sweat pants, Oliver held his finger to his lips and shushed me.

"I wouldn't go in there if I were you. Nick was banging on your door last night and he never came home. And unless Amy found a rebound guy sometime during the evening, I'm pretty sure it was him she was calling 'god' all night."

I cringed and put my fingers in my mouth, pretending to gag. "Too much information, Ollie. How could she forgive him like that? He had some girl's panties in his car, for heaven's sake! Is she nuts, desperate, or totally stupid?"

I rolled my eyes and shook my head, thinking about the emotional roller coaster Amy was willingly riding, and how bad it would be when it was over. "Anyway, how did you know I wasn't there?"

He ran his fingers through his dark tangled hair, and a ghost of a smile touched his lips. "I heard your door slam last night, so I opened mine and saw you storming down the hall. I was worried about you being out late, and it getting dark soon, so…I kind of followed you, but I didn't want to crowd you, so I hung back. You looked like you needed some space. I just wanted to make sure you were safe. It wasn't some weird stalker thing. When you got to the coffee shop, I waited on a bench across the street, but left when I saw pretty boy turn up. I figured you'd called him, or something."

I stared at him in total disbelief. He'd followed me all that way without saying a word? It was a little creepy, and yet totally sweet and typical of Ollie. He was obviously oblivious that the reason for me storming out was over an argument I'd had with Jared, otherwise I was pretty sure he'd have blown his cover and launched himself at him to stop Jared from upsetting me any further.

Tilting my head at him, I pressed my hands on my hips. This had all gone on long enough, and it was time I set him straight no matter how hard it would be.

"Ollie, you don't need to babysit me. I can take care of myself. It's really not your place to be following me around. What do you think would have happened if Jared had seen you? He'd have gone completely bat shit crazy. He likes you almost as much as you like him. And stop calling him names. I shouldn't have to keep telling you that. Jared is my boyfriend, and if we're going to stay friends, you two are going to have to learn to get along.

"I'm getting really sick of this bullshit, Ollie. I know how you feel about me, and I'm sorry. I'm sorry that I don't feel the same and that I've hurt you, and yeah, maybe if things had been different we would have ended up together, but they're not different. I met Jared, he asked me out, and now we're a couple. I love him, and he loves me right back. But that doesn't mean I don't care very deeply about you. You're one of my best friends, and I really want things to be ok between us. So would you please just try and be happy for me and move forward from this? Please?"

He winced, and his face was contorted as if I had just punched him in the gut. Staring at the floor, he shook his head.

"You love him?" It was almost a whisper. His voice was husky and pained as though the words stuck like poison in his throat.

"I do. I'm sorry if that hurts you, Ollie, but I won't lie. I love him, and he loves me back."

His head snapped up, and his expression turned quickly from sadness to intense anger. His eyes were dark, and he glared at me.

"Seven weeks. We've been here seven fucking weeks, and this guy comes along with his shiny fucking car, high society lifestyle, and sweeps you right off your feet and out of my hands! And after only a few weeks you fucking love him? Are you shitting me, Layla? How can you not see this guy for what he is? He's a tool. A bonafide cock! A liar, playboy, and a chew you up and spit you out jackass. He doesn't love you. You're just the next in a long line of women he uses to dick around with between meetings. You're a number, honey, so don't go thinking you're something special to him. You're not."

A loud crack reverberated around the room and it took me a moment to register that it had come from me. My palm was stinging as I watched the pale flesh on Oliver's cheek turn a deep shade of pink. I'd slapped him hard, and with violent intent. His eyes bore into my skull as he glowered at me. I couldn't bear to look at him. How could he be so crue? I knew he was hurting, but I never thought he could say such venomous things to me.

Turning my back to him, I cried gently into my hands. This really was going to end our friendship. I just couldn't see a way for us to get back from this; it was all just so fucked up.

His hand reached out and touched my shoulder, and as furious and upset I was with him, I still couldn't bring myself to reject his physical contact. Pulling me sideways, he wrapped his arms around me tightly and squeezed me to his chest. Resting my head on his shoulder, I continued to cry when I felt a drip of warm liquid slide over my forehead and down my nose. Lifting my head, I was taken aback when I saw the tears in his eyes. He was crying.

Brushing them away with my thumbs, my hands cupped his face. He gazed down at me, and swallowed hard, closing his eyes as his eyebrows furrowed together. When they reopened, I could see the regret and torment in them. My heart broke a little as I saw the pain he was trying so desperately to hide. I let out a long soft breath.

Without warning, he closed the distance between us and kissed me. I felt the cool steel of his lip ring pressing against my warm, plump flesh. His hands swept around my back as he pressed me against his body, deepening the kiss, but most shocking was the fact that I didn't stop him. I stood frozen and completely stunned the entire time his lips were against mine. I was unable to move, speak, or even think straight. My eyes closed and for a moment the entire world just melted away as I became totally absorbed in the sensations. When my senses finally returned, my eyes flew open, and I pressed my hands against his strong chest and pushed him away.

The two of us stood, gasping for air, equally dazed by what had just happened. My heart was hammering in my chest as adrenaline began to surge through my veins. I gawked at him, totally confounded. Raising his hands, he stepped toward me, but I immediately took a step back towards the door.

I touched my lips with my fingers, trying to comprehend what was going on between us, when a wave of fury flooded into my body. Outraged, I stormed at him and shoved him hard. So hard, in fact, that he stumbled backwards before landing with a thud on his bed.

Standing over him, I raged. "What the hell do you think you were doing? I have a boyfriend! Why did you do that?"

Shaking his head in bewilderment, he seemed at a loss for words. If he was, it was short lived. Running his fingers through his thick, dark hair, he winced. "I don't know what came over me. You were in my arms, crying, and when I looked down at you I just couldn't stop myself. It was like some uncontrollable force, and I just had to kiss you, Layla. I know you're mad, and I'm sorry that you feel that way, but honestly, Layla? It was wonderful. And I'd do it again in a heartbeat.

"I'm crazy about you. I can't stop thinking about you. You're the first thing I think about when I wake up, the only thing I think about all day, and the last thing I think about at night. You're my muse. I must have written at least twenty new songs since I've met you, and they're all about you. Your eyes, your smile, the way you laugh, and the way you make my heart want to tear its way out of my chest when you're near me. I can't fight it any more, it's killing me. I've tried to forget it, to get over you, but no other girl even compares. I don't know what to do anymore."

I stared at him in astonishment as his words spiraled and whirled inside my head. Sinking to the floor, his knees on the ground, he sat back on his heels and gazed up at me, imploring me to forgive him.

"I know I can't have you, but I want you. I need you, even if it's only as my friend. I'll take you any way I can. I will never ever bring this up again, and it will never come between us. We'll forget it all, and start over brand new. Please, Layla. Please forgive me."

I stared at him, still in a dazzled state of mind. His eyes were red, still slightly teary, and I wanted to say yes. I wanted to tell him it would all be ok, but how could things ever be the same now? Could we really, realistically, be friends after this?

His need for us to remain friends wasn't totally one sided. I loved Ollie in so many ways; his humor, his intelligence, and the way he could make me feel better when I was having a particularly crappy day…the way he cared about me and his sense of fun in life. I loved him for all those things. I just couldn't love him the way he wanted me to, and I wondered if it could really ever be enough for him.

Dropping to my knees in front of him, I took his hand in mine. "I don't want to lose you from my life either, Ollie. You are already one of my best friends, and I'm not willing to let you go, but is it going to be enough for you? I can leave that little lip locking mistake behind me and put it to bed."

Liar, you were so into that.

"But everything you just told me, all those words and feelings, you can't take those back, Ollie. It's different now. Do you honestly think we can carry on like nothing happened? And what about Jared? Can you truthfully, and sincerely, tell me that you could handle seeing the two of us together? Because if you say yes, then great. We'll start anew and forget this whole thing. But you have to be sure."

Placing his own hand on mine, he sighed. "No, Layla, I couldn't. I won't ever think he deserves you. I will always think he's wrong for you, and I will forever wish it was me in his place. But if being civil to him and pretending that I'm not completely obsessed with you is what it takes to keep you in my life, I'll do it, and maybe someday I won't have to pretend anymore. But I wouldn't hold my breath."

Needing to make things normal between us again, I did the only thing I knew; I threw my arms around his neck and pulled him into a warm hug. It felt forced and uncomfortable as though we were trying to push all the emotional torment out of our bodies. Our once warm and friendly gesture now felt detached and impersonal.

He gave me a quick peck on the cheek before standing up and offering me his hand. I could feel the distance between us and it tugged hard on my heart strings. Things would never be the same again. This was going to hang over our heads for a long time, and that kiss was going to haunt me forever. A shiver ran up my spine as I thought of what had happened. I had enjoyed it. For a brief and fleeting moment I wanted him to kiss me. I'd felt the spark, the electricity between us, and I couldn't ignore the sexual tension that had been building since the very first time I saw him. Guilt began to flow through me, and my stomach churned with an overwhelming feeling of betrayal.

I took a deep breath and pushed the urge to vomit down my throat as I swallowed hard. Pulling myself upright, I stood and glanced at the clock behind Ollie. I nearly had a heart attack when I saw the time.

"Shit! Ollie, we're late for class! Psych started fifteen minutes ago!"

Grabbing his hoodie, he began struggling into it. It got caught around his shoulders as he used both hands to pull on his sneakers while hopping around the room. I giggled at him, but stopped abruptly as my eyes travelled over his finely chiseled body. I had never noticed how physically fit Ollie was before. His arms were thick and a snake tattoo ran from his shoulder to his bicep. His abs were deeply defined and led to the equally deep V of his torso.

I quickly darted my eyes away as he turned around and straightened his hoodie before grabbing my hand and dragging me out the door, down the hall, and out of the building. Breathlessly, we sprinted across campus to our class, only to find the door closed and a sign saying:

"Tardiness in my class is not tolerated. Once the door is closed, you are not coming in. Report to my office at the end of the day to explain. Dr. Harman."

Great. Just what I needed.

Running his hand through his now even messier hair, Ollie kicked the wall he was standing adjacent to. "Shit! Well I guess we've got three hours to spare. Want to see a movie? Get some coffee? Try to forget that awful and painfully horrific incident in my room?"

I smiled at him, feeling awkward. I needed some space, and I also needed a shower. "Actually, Ollie, I didn't get to shower and change at Jared's, so I think I'll go have a long soak and relax for a bit. I hope you don't mind."

"No, of course not. Come on, I'll walk back with you."

With his hands in his pockets he walked beside me, chatting about the most inane of subjects, and I knew he was trying hard to put what happened behind us. I prayed for both our sakes that, if we tried hard enough, maybe we could and that things could go back to the way they were,

I was tense, confused, and very uneasy. His hands never left his pockets the entire walk back, and it made me feel strangely forlorn. We'd always been so comfortable together, draping his arm around my shoulder and even holding hands at times. Now we acted like two embarrassed teenagers who got caught making out under the bleachers.

I wished I had powers like superman so I could fly around the world, turning back time, or maybe even climb into a Tardis like Dr. Who. But all that would probably not have stopped Ollie's feelings for me, or the way I found myself feeling whenever I was near him. They say you can't help who you fall in love with, but I sure wished Ollie hadn't picked me. And I certainly wished my libido hadn't selected him as an object of sexual desire. It was becoming a very large problem, and either it would have to be fixed, or I would have to be.

* * * *

Entering my room, I breathed a sigh of relief. Sweet sanctuary. Amy was already at class, and I would have at least three hours until my next one. Collapsing on my bed, I spotted the pile of envelopes Jared had sent me on the floor. Rolling over, I picked them up and found the one marked Tuesday. Biting my lip in anticipation, I opened it.

Layla,

It's already day one, and that means that in less than 96 hours I will be back home with you. I can categorically say that I am missing you incredibly, and that you are invading my thoughts even as you read this.

Now don't get mad, but I rearranged your work schedule to coincide with my plans for you. Yes, that's right. Plans. Lorraine has ensured everything is in place and I will let you know in each letter when it is you have to work.

Today you have the day off. But that doesn't mean I'll allow you to sit around moping over me being in New York.

At 3 p.m. a very nice young lady called Rose will be arriving at your dorm to do your hair and makeup. She will then be followed by a young man called Christophe. Christophe is my personal stylist and will be presenting you with a variety of elegant dresses. I have already checked them all and have given him an idea of those I find acceptable for you to wear in public. I don't want anyone else ogling your goodies while I'm away, Miss Jennings.

A car will arrive at six sharp and take you to your destination. I know you will love this evening, and you must promise me that you will keep an open mind.

I wish I could be there to share your night, but I am certain you will have an incredible time without me. Try to relax and don't miss me too much. Also, no asking questions. Everyone is under strict instructions to tell you nothing about this evening's event.

So don't try.

I know you hate surprises, but I simply couldn't help myself.

I am without words to end this letter, and goodbye feels too final, so I have borrowed some from a man very deeply in love.

Ever thine, ever mine, ever ours.

Ludwig Van Beethoven

Jared xx

I hugged the letter to my chest tightly. Could he be more perfect? After reading the words he had written with his own hand, my heart was truly aching to be near him. I felt so far away, and yet with the piece of paper currently clutched to my chest, so connected also. I sat up swiftly and grabbed the laptop from the edge of the bed, firing it up. The moment it was ready, I opened my emails. There was nothing; a glance at my cell also revealed nothing. I knew he must have still been in the air at that very moment, but I was desperate to hear his voice, read more of his words and feel closer to him. Everything seemed so plain, and I felt melancholy. I needed to snap out of my mood. Considering I had missed my class, all I had left to do all day was visit Dr. Harman later and explain my absence, but that was over four hours away. Jumping to my feet, I headed for the shower.

The long hot soak did me the world of good, and as I ran my hands over my smooth wet skin, I thought about the hot, sheet clenching, pillow biting sex I'd had the night before. I was instantly aroused as thoughts of Jared's fingers, hands and lips caressing my body filled my mind. My hand slid down over my pert, firm breasts. Gently massaging them, I rolled my nipples with my thumb, making them peak and stiffen at my touch. I gasped as the sensation sent a direct message shooting through my body, making my clit throb and causing an aching between my legs. I'd never really touched myself before, but being with Jared seemed to keep me in a constant state of arousal. Even the mere thought of him had worked me into a sexy, hot mess, my body writhing beneath the streaming water. A very naughty thought entered my mind and I stood there, pondering it for a few seconds. Biting my lip, I reached for the shower head, turning the dial to massage. Pressing my back against the cold tiled wall I spread my legs wide across the shower floor. I hesitated for a moment before slowly moving the nozzle between my legs. The pressure of the water hit my clit and I inhaled sharply. It felt like nothing I'd ever experienced before. The warm gentle stream of water caressed and kissed my skin as it pulsed against my beautifully sensitive clit.

I slid my hand south and massaged it gently as the water continued its torrent against my skin. I could feel my orgasm building inside me rapidly, and just as I reached my peak, images of Jared's hot naked body played like a movie in front of my eyes and I called out his name. My knees grew weak as I panted heavily through my orgasm. The intense pleasure coursing through me left me longing for his touch once more. Struggling to regain my equilibrium, I reached for my towel and wrapped myself tightly in it. The warmth reminded me of Jared and our post-coital embrace. He'd spooned me all night, never loosening his grip on my waist, and I'd felt completely safe, loved and cherished just lying in his arms.

I glanced back at the shower and smiled mischievously. Picking up the nozzle, I gave it a quick wipe over and placed it back in the holder, smiling to myself as I did so. It was certainly no Jared, but as far as artificially intelligent boyfriends went, it definitely served its purpose.

A wicked idea was beginning to form in my filthy mind. I hurriedly dried myself off, then slipped into the sexy underwear he'd bought me that was sitting in a tempting Victoria secret bag in my closet. The delicate lace hugged my curves perfectly and was flattering against my skin. The shower had left my skin glowing and glistening with droplets of water sliding over every crease and curve. Grabbing my camera, I snapped a picture of myself in a provocative pose and uploaded it the laptop. This was going to blow his mind. I opened the email application and began frantically typing, feeling like an erotic fiction writer as I filled him in on my naughty escapades in the shower. I painted a vivid picture for his enjoyment before attaching the photo. The opening line read,

"Courtesy of your giving and generous nature, I am sure to have a spectacular evening. It seems only right I send you a gift also. Thinking of you. Layla."

Hitting send, I grinned to myself with satisfaction. Oh to be a fly on the wall when he gets that later.

* * * *

Making my way to Dr. Harman's office, I imagined I'd bump into Ollie, but he was nowhere to be seen. Surely he couldn't still be hauled up in his room brooding? I soon got my answer.

Opening the door to his office, Dr. Harman eyed me questionably. "Ah, Miss Jennings. Mr. Green here was just explaining the reason for your absence. You'll be pleased to know he told me all about feeling unwell, and your care for him in his hour of need. Commendable as that is, Miss Jennings, please remember to also be as attentive to your study. I will let this one slide, but don't let it happen again."

Ollie exited the room just as Dr. Harman was handing me the assignment I needed to complete to catch up. I gave Ollie a cautious smile, still unsure of our current relationship footing.

"Thanks, Ollie. Really. I mean it. You really are a true friend."

He stood there, staring at the ground, and shrugged.

"That's what they tell me. Always a friend. Never a boyfriend."

He walked me back to the dorms, and we made idle chit-chat, but everything continued to feel so forced, so fake and unnatural. I longed for the closeness we had, and felt genuinely bereft without the feel of his arm round my shoulders, or his hand in mine as we walked. I missed him, and I wondered if we would ever get back to the way things were.

* * * *

Three on the dot, Rose was at my door as promised. She must have been in her early twenties, and her long wavy auburn hair was flowing over her shoulders. She flushed when I shook her hand as I asked her in. Sweet, yet shy, she got to work on my mass of unruly blonde locks.

"So how do you know Jared?" I asked, watching her in the mirror as she teased a comb through my hair. A small smile grazed her lips.

"We met in high school. I was a couple of years older than him, and on the debate team. He joined when I was in my senior year and we became good friends. He's a really sweet guy. When I had my son, he helped me get one of his dad's apartments for almost nothing. I was only nineteen, and working part time as a hair dresser didn't pay much. Now I'm a personal makeup artist and most of my clients are recommendations I got through him."

I pasted a smile across my face, but her words stuck in my mind like thorns. I could only imagine the clients Jared was sending to her. Probably my fifty nine predecessors. The thought made me feel sick, so I tried to push it away and focus on enjoying my evening.

Two grueling hours later, Rose had completed what she was calling her greatest masterpiece. I stared at myself in the mirror. I hardly recognized my own face. My blonde hair was pulled back into an elegant and stunningly shiny beehive. My makeup was so well done that it looked completely natural even though she must have used an entire pot of cover up to hide my freckles and blemished skin. I raised my hand and gently ran my fingers over a spectacularly beautiful band that finished off the beehive perfectly.

Bending down to my ear, Rose smiled. "A gift from Jared. White gold and diamond. He said I had to put it on you whether you liked it or not, and that I wasn't to allow you to argue with me. But you do love it, right? I'd hate to have to pluck out this hive."

Of course, he'd provided something sparkly. It was his go to move these days. "It's gorgeous. I look amazing, thank you so much. I really don't know what to say. I don't think I have ever looked this good. You're a real genius."

She gathered all her things and packed them into a large case she had lying on the bed before giving me a friendly hug. "Christophe should be here any minute, so I better run. He hates having any distractions when he's working. He's a lot to handle, but he's great at what he does. You're in good hands."

Giving me a wink, she walked down the long hallway and out of sight. I glanced over at the clock on my wall. It was five in the evening and Amy still hadn't come home. I began to worry that she was still mad at me after our fight, but it was more likely that she was with Nick. I didn't have much time to dwell on it as moments later there was a frantic knocking at my door.

I opened it to find a tall rail with several long black covers hanging from hooks. A very flamboyant and vibrant young man was suddenly spinning the thing around and backing his way into my room. Leaving the free standing rail in the middle of the room, he turned and scanned me from head to toe. His suit was striped pink, green and white, and his hair was bright blond, clearly out of a bottle. He wore sunglasses and a pink tie to match his suit. He was very thin, and when he smiled at me his teeth were almost blinding, like looking directly into the sun.

"Well now, darling, you must be Jared's little lady. He's told me all about you. Now, based on a photo he showed me of you and what he's told me, we have selected these eight dresses for you to pick from. They have all been pre-approved by the man himself, so I'm sure we will have something you'll love. Shall we get started? Come on, sweetie, slip out of your clothes and let's get you dressed to the nines."

I tried on each dress and performed like a cat walk model around my room for Christophe as he sat on my bed and gave me endless direction and criticism. As if there was some trick or knack to wearing a piece of fabric. The elegant evening gowns were truly gorgeous, but the one that I loved the most was the final dress. A lovely floor length scarlet dress. The bodice was a sweetheart neckline with a band around the waist to separate it from the skirt. Tiny diamantés were lined around the bust and they sparkled and glistened in the light as I walked. The skirt was made up of several layers of ruffled fabric which felt as soft as silk. Twirling in front of Christophe, I bit my lip and grinned.

"I take it, darling, that you like this one? I have to say, it looks absolutely incredible on you. Here, slip these on too."

Grabbing a pair of heels from the bottom of the rail, he placed them in front of my feet and held out his hand for support as I climbed into them. They matched the dress perfectly. Deep crimson with diamanté detail on the heel, they were hardly visible beneath the dress, but they made me feel like a Hollywood starlet.

I showed him to the door and thanked him profusely for his help.

"My absolute pleasure, sweetie. Oh, before I forget, since you chose the red one, I have to give you this." He handed me a small gift bag, but stopped me as I was just about to open it. "No, no, darling, open it when I'm gone. Have a fabulous night, honey. Ciao!"

Closing the door, I sat on my bed and opened the bag. Two velvet boxes sat at the bottom. Taking out the long one first, I cautiously opened it, knowing exactly what it was before I had even laid eyes on it. Sure enough, another astonishing piece of jewelry was sitting inside. Lines of glistening diamonds and rubies lined the shiny white gold bracelet inside. It was incredible.

Placing it to one side, I opened the smaller box which contained a pair of tear drop earrings that matched the bracelet perfectly. I shook my head and smiled to myself. He was clearly never going to learn, but I had to admit I felt like a princess that evening, and the jewels were the icing on my glittering cake. Putting on the new frosting I had just been given, I told myself they were simply on loan for this evening and that I wouldn't be keeping them. I hadn't even felt comfortable wearing the ring he'd bought me yet, or the bracelet from our date. I was going to have to give them all back…eventually.

Chapter 27

Love Online

Stepping outside, I was relieved to see a face I recognized waiting for me. Daniel stood, dressed impeccably in his uniform, and tipping his hat as he opened the car door and offered me his hand. As I bent down to climb in, I froze. Sitting opposite me was Amy. She looked stunning in a silver floor length gown, and her hair in an impressive up do. She smiled nervously at me and murmured "Hi". I smiled weakly, and slid in next to her without replying. I was shocked to find her there, and still unsure how our friendship stood after our fight.

Setting off, Daniel pressed a button on his dash and a black screen glided up between us, giving Amy and me some much needed privacy. Turning to each other simultaneously, we both began apologizing. Giggling a little, we stopped, and I sighed heavily.

"I'm sorry, Amy. I shouldn't have gone off like that. You were right. I was being totally ungrateful and overly dramatic. I just can't help it when it comes to Jared. He has the power to make me feel so furious, and yet so wonderful at the same time."

"No, Layla, it was none of my business, and as your friend I should have supported you. Can we forget it and start over? I've been in hell all day, worrying you might hate me."

Leaning in, I hugged her warmly. "I could never hate you."

Pulling away I grinned at her. "He told me that he loves me."

Her mouth opened wide, and her eyes blinked rapidly. "Oh my god, Layla! You are so lucky. He's amazing. Just look around us! I told you that people don't do this shit for someone they are only screwing with. Damn girl, he's got it bad, huh?"

We chatted for what seemed liked forever and she explained what had happened with Nick after I left the night before. "He came begging at the door, trying to tell me that those panties and their owner were both way before we even got together, but I still don't know if I believe him. Anyway, I let him in, and he was so sweet and charming, one thing led to another, and…"

I cringed and let out a slight chuckle. "I don't need details. I get it. But just please be careful, Amy. I don't want to see you get hurt. Now, can you tell me what the hell is going on?"

"Sorry, I'm under instruction to reveal nothing. When I opened the box last night, the top envelope was addressed to me. I've had a mani, pedi, makeover, makeup and hair do. He also sent me to the mall with a personal shopper to get this dress. That guy is an angel. Hold on to that one." I grinned at her as I took in how spectacular she looked. She looked like a model ready to step onto the catwalk.

"I'm gonna try."

* * * *

Pulling up outside a beautiful glass building, I scanned the surroundings for a clue as to my location. Daniel opened my door and held my hand, assisting me out of the car. Once outside, I became aware of where I was.

The enormous building was white with long glass windows around the front, allowing the spectacular lighting and elegant dining facilities to be seen from the outside. Cars lined the entrance as the social elite of California climbed out for an evening at Segerstrom Hall.

I turned around to face Amy with my mouth wide. "The opera? Is he serious? Look at this place. I can't go in there. I'll embarrass him. I don't belong in a place like this. How could he think this was a good idea?"

Fisting her hands on her hips, Amy arched an eyebrow at me. "He told me you'd do this in his letter, and he also told me that when you did I was to tell you to shut the hell up, and to get your ass in there and enjoy your night."

Letting out a heavy sigh I conceded. "Ok, ok, fine. Come on, let's go see an opera."

Informing me that he would be waiting for us after the performance, Daniel departed. Clanking our heels across the pavement, we made our way to the hall. I gazed in amazement at the awesome structure I was currently standing in front of. The gigantic archway was remarkable, decorated with an interesting and awe inspiring sculpture. Amy stood alongside me, admiring it. A young man with blond hair, wearing a black tux, joined us and leaned in to Amy's ear.

"It's called the Fire Bird. It was created and designed by Richard Lippold. Do you like it?"

Amy was blushing deep crimson as she turned and smiled at the handsome stranger to her right. "It's very beautiful."

Holding out his hand, he smiled at her with a bright twinkle in his eyes. "James. James Felix. And you two lovely ladies are?"

"Amy Brookes and this is Layla Jennings. Her boyfriend is the one who arranged for us to be here."

I noticed how quickly Amy ensured that this little hottie was aware I was taken. I got the distinct feeling she was into him.

"So you ladies are here alone? That seems an awful waste. You both look positively stunning and should not be left unattended on a night like this. These old men would give their right arm to have you hanging off of it. I'd be honored to be your escort this evening."

Her eyes lighting up, Amy nodded frantically. I stared at her in horror, before turning my attention to her admirer.

"Excuse us a moment, won't you, James." Grabbing her by the elbow, I yanked Amy aside. "Are you crazy? Jared would never allow me to spend an evening with some strange guy. He'd be livid, Amy. We cannot seriously stay with this man all evening."

Pulling her arm from my grasp, she gave me a mischievous grin. "Well it's a good thing he's with me then, and that Jared is in New York, isn't it? Don't be such a spoil sport. You got your rich, handsome lover, now let me have mine!"

"And what about Nick? Or have you forgotten about him since this morning?"

Lowering her voice, she snarled under her breath. "Screw him. He can fuck whoever he wants without feeling bad, well, so can I." Rolling my eyes, I watched her as she sashayed back over to her new friend. Jared was not going to like this.

With Amy on his arm, James led us through the elegant foyer to a private restaurant reserved for V.I.P's. I sat uncomfortably at the table as Amy and James made goo-goo eyes at one each other. Oh for heaven's sake.

Clearing my throat, I leaned forward on my elbows and regarded him. "So, James, what do you do?"

Begrudgingly pulling his gaze from my friend, he smiled at me. "I own a large chain of restaurants and function venues. We entertain celebrities and high society members mostly. We also throw some wonderful parties. You ladies should join us sometime, or come by one of our restaurants. I'm based mostly in Long Beach, so if you're in the area I can guarantee you the best table."

I eyed him warily. He had an air about him that reminded me of a refrigerator. All sleek and shiny on the outside, but with a bitterly, cold interior. We enjoyed a luxurious meal and drank very expensive wine all courtesy of Amy's escort. As we stood to leave, a young woman approached us and nervously addressed James.

"Um, sorry to bother you, Mr. Felix, but the photographers would like a picture before you leave."

Rolling his eyes he sighed.

"Oh, the things I do for my celebrity status. Shall we, ladies?"

I was about to protest, when he grabbed my hand and pulled me along with him as Amy clutched his elbow like a true socialite.

Standing in the foyer were at least a dozen journalists, all aiming their expensive cameras at us and shouting over each other.

"Who are your two lovely ladies, sir?"

Glancing at the two of us, James slid his hands behind our backs. "Miss Layla Jennings and Miss Amy Brookes."

As his fingers brushed the base of my spine, I jumped at the unwanted contact. But there was no time to move away as lights began flashing left, right and center. This was not going well. My night of wonder and spectacular excitement, given to me by the man I loved, was turning into a hellish parade of poses and fake smiles.

"Miss Jennings!" I stood on tiptoes and saw a familiar face across the room. Waving frantically at me was the delightful man I had conversed with at the dinner dance.

Pushing my way through the crowd, and leaving Amy happily behind me, I strode over to greet him. Smiling broadly, he took my hand and placed a kiss on the back as a true gentleman would.

"Miss Jennings, how lovely to see you. How are you?"

"I'm well, thank you, Mr. Kent."

Chuckling heartily, he held my hand between his finger and thumb. "Call me Arthur, my dear. Garrett not with you this evening?"

Giving him a regretful smile, I explained Jared's unexpected trip to New York.

"Ah, terrible shame that, especially as it leaves a beautiful woman such as yourself alone for the evening. In fact, I couldn't help noticing that was Mr. Felix you were standing with over there."

I glanced over my shoulder and watched as James continued to pose with my roommate hanging from his arm.

"Yes, that young woman he's with is a friend of mine."

He arched an eyebrow at me, and his mouth pressed into a hard line. "I see. Well, I wouldn't want you to feel I was interfering, but I thought I should give you a word of caution. Mr. Felix and Mr. Garrett don't really see eye to eye, Miss Jennings, and I'm quite certain that your young man will be quite infuriated should he discover you had been in Felix's company this evening. I suggest you avoid him and the cameras for the remainder of the night and not mention it to your young man. Anyway, must dash as I'm sure the curtain shall be going up shortly. Lovely to see you again, my dear, and please give my regards to your sweetheart."

Giving me another quick kiss on the hand, he released me and disappeared into the crowds. I turned and stared at Amy who was now gazing starry eyed at James Felix. Why would Jared dislike him so much, and why would he disapprove of my being in his company? He'd never mentioned him before, and I was sure I'd never read anything about a feud between the two in any gossip column.

Shaking the thoughts from my head, I searched for a member of staff who could direct me to my seat. I found myself stopped by the same young woman who approached us at dinner.

"Miss Jennings? Sorry, I overheard Mr. Felix. My name is Jenny. Mr. Garrett left me instructions to show you to your private viewing box with Miss Brookes. Will she be joining you, or sharing Mr. Felix's private area?"

I snorted at the double meaning in that sentence. Amy would definitely like to share his private area, and soon I imagined. "No, I think it'll just be me, but if she does come searching for me, please show her to her seat."

Entering my own private viewing box felt surreal and entirely alien to me. I leaned over the balcony and gazed at the scale of the enormous theater. I'd read on an information board that it could accommodate three thousand people. I turned to my seat and smiled as my eyes fell upon an envelope with my name on it. I recognized the handwriting immediately and scrambled to get it open. Sitting in the plush cushion I read his note.

My Darling,

I hope you enjoyed your makeover and have had a wonderful evening so far. I am sure you look positively radiant and I am simply sorry that I cannot be there to admire the view. If there is anything you require throughout the evening, please ask Jenny, and she will provide it for you. I'm a much respected member there, and also a supporter of the arts, so anything your heart desires, please do not hesitate to ask. It's just money, Layla.

I cannot express how much I am missing you, and how you have flooded my thoughts all day. I know this before I even leave you. I hope you aren't brooding and dwelling on my absence too much. Try to remember that it's only a few days. Goodnight, my lady.

If music be the food of love, play on.

The words of William Shakespeare from the heart of Jared Garrett

Xxxx

Tears began to slide gently down my face as I read his words. My heart ached. I was truly missing him at this moment. I sat alone in my seat and watched as people began to flood the theater and talk in a low hum. I scanned the other boxes, looking for Amy, but I couldn't see her anywhere. A moment later she appeared in the seat next to me.

"Couldn't abandon you on your big night. Hey, have you been crying?" She pulled a handkerchief from her purse and wiped at my mascara stained cheeks.

"Jared left me a note. I really miss him, Amy. I never thought it was possible to fall so hard, so fast, but I have. I feel completely desolate without him here."

Tilting her head, she gave me a sympathetic look and placed her hand in mine. "I know, sweetie, but it's not forever. Try to enjoy tonight. He would hate it if it were ruined because of him. Please try?" Giving her a weak smile, I nodded and dabbed my eyes with the handkerchief I had clutched in my palm.

The rest of the evening went wonderfully. The opera performed was La Traviata and was truly breath taking. James hadn't made an appearance again until we were on our way back to the car. He and Amy exchanged numbers, and she practically jumped for joy as she climbed into the Mercedes. I eyed her curiously, worried that this could get a little complicated back at the dorm with Nick, but Amy was a big girl and this was her mess. Besides, she seemed so happy she was positively glowing.

Texting Jared from the car, I thanked him for a wonderful evening and told him how much he had invaded my thoughts that day. His reply was short, but to the point. I grinned as I read it, remembering my antics that afternoon.

> I received a rather interesting email today. We shall discuss it later. I'm glad you had an enjoyable evening. I miss you terribly and look forward to hearing the sound of your voice. Love J. xxx
> **Received: 22.10**
> **From: Jared**

Thanking Daniel once again for his fantastic service, we headed into our dorm. I kicked off my shoes and gently slid out of my dress with Amy's assistance before helping her with her own. Hanging them in the closet, I smiled to myself again and thought about how lucky I really was. My cell buzzed on the bed and I dived for it, knowing there could only be one person who would be calling at this hour. My heart skipped a beat as I read his name on my screen. Amy caught my eye and gave me a knowing smile before disappearing into the bathroom.

"Hello."

"Layla, Layla, Layla. You are going to kill me. I nearly had a stroke when I read that email. My my, aren't you a naughty girl. I do hope you enjoyed that little adventure in the shower because you won't be doing it without me again."

I held my breath as I listened to the purr of his voice when he said my name. The carnal hunger in his deep tones was intoxicating, and I felt my muscles tighten and clench as my body reacted to the sound of his breathing through the phone. Breathless myself, I managed to speak.

"Oh really, sir? And why is that?"

"Because I want you so fucking hungry for my cock when I get back that you can't stand it. I want you salivating for me, and when I get you back in my arms I'm going to drive you as crazy as that email and photo drove me. I was in a fucking meeting when that delivered to my Blackberry. I had to sit there with a raging hard on for an hour. That's right, an hour. I was that fucking hot for you."

I snorted a laugh as I thought about his predicament.

God, he was so infuriatingly sexy. His voice, his words, and the way he growled was making the blood warm in my veins.

"Oh my poor, hot entrepreneur. If I'd been there, I would have done anything to relieve that tension. Maybe even right there under the table on my hands and knees."

I heard a low groan escape his throat and became instantly aroused.

"Oh, Layla, don't make me promises unless you intend to keep them. The idea of you on your hands and knees, sucking my cock while I grip your hair, makes me want to fly you here for my next meeting, and I know I can't have you. Don't tease me. I'm hard right now just thinking about it."

I wished Amy wasn't in the other room, or I would have leapt at the chance to tease him over the phone.

Pressing my ear to the bathroom door, I heard the shower start and Amy begin to sing. Knowing we had at least thirty minutes until she'd be done, I seized the opportunity and decided to provoke him.

"Well tell me, Mr. Garrett, what would you like to do to me right now?"

"Ah, you want to play, do you? Ok, I'll bite. Quite literally, Miss Jennings, I'd love to sink my teeth into that hot little ass of yours right now. I'd spank you into the next week for that naughty little picture you sent to tease and entice me. I think I can accommodate you, Miss Jennings, if you promise to do exactly what I say."

I glanced at the bathroom door, wondering if I should really do this, but the thrill of knowing we could be caught just intensified my arousal.

"I will," I whispered, my voice hoarse.

"Good girl. What are you wearing?"

I looked down at my body. My red lace panties and strapless matching bra hugged my curves snuggly.

"Red lace panties and a matching bra."

I heard him moan. "Mmmmm, I'd love to see that. Turn on your laptop and start Skype. I have an idea."

He hung up and I frantically turned on the machine and fired up the program.

A moment later, he was calling me. I answered, clicking the button, and there filling my screen was the most handsome creature I had ever laid my eyes on. Lying on a large double bed, staring at me in front of his own computer, Jared smiled wickedly into the camera and my heart surged with happiness at the sight of his gorgeous eyes.

"Well hello there, my lady. Turn the laptop around to face the room, and give me a twirl then." I did as he asked and watched his face light up with enthusiasm.

"Good, now put your laptop on the dresser and point the camera at your bed." Again, I was fully obedient. "Good girl. Now take off your underwear, slowly."

Sliding my hands behind my back, I unhooked my bra and dropped the garment on the floor. Gazing into the camera, I ran my hands down my bare breasts and then down to my panties, hooking my thumbs into the elastic that was hugging my hips. Gently biting my bottom lip, I pushed them slowly down over my curves to the floor before gracefully stepping out of them. I watched him as his eyes grew dark and hooded, and he became more and more aroused.

"Sit on the bed and don't move. You've done well, so I'm going to reward you."

With my eyes fixed to the screen, I watched as he stood and unbuttoned his crisp white shirt, before tearing it from his shoulders and over his wrists. His hot tight body glistened in the lamp light, and a whimper of hungry desire left my lips. I saw a ghost of a smile appear on his face and I knew he had heard me.

His hands grazed over the bulging zipper of his pants, and his erection was visible through the taught fabric. As he slid both his pants and shorts down, I gasped as his hard long cock sprang free, pointing at the camera. I licked my lips, wishing I could wrap my mouth around it and suck him into a frenzy. He grabbed it and ran his hand up and down the shaft slowly. I was so turned on, just watching him was making my sex ache and throb. I needed his cock thrusting inside me, teasing and enticing my orgasm.

Lying back on the bed, he leaned on one elbow, angling the camera just enough to give me the perfect view of his stunning caramel colored body. "Lay down, baby, and close your eyes. Just listen to my voice and do what I tell you."

I lay there, wet with anticipation as I hung on his every word.

"Touch your lips with your fingertips, run one finger along the bottom lip and lick it gently. You feel that, baby? That's my kiss, my lips on yours, caressing you. My tongue on that hot little bottom lip you love to bite so hungrily. Now, run your sexy little hands down and over your neck slowly. Gently graze and stroke your skin. Take your time to enjoy every touch."

I moaned softly as I thought about his hands on my body, caressing and groping me gently and attentively.

"Good girl, you're doing wonderfully. Now massage your breasts. Again, slowly and with varying pressure, roll those perky, pink nipples between your fingers. Tease and tempt yourself, Layla."

I could hear his breathing become labored. I lay there encased in darkness as my hands groped, gripped and glided over my breasts. Biting my bottom lip, knowing full well how it affected him, I began to slide my hands south.

"Layla. Did I tell you to do that?"

Gasping, I pleaded.

"Please, Jared, I need it. I ache for you."

"I know, baby, I'm right there with you. My cock is rock solid right now, and I would love nothing more than to be sliding it in and out of your hot, tight little slit, but we're going to have to compromise on this for now. Do as I say, I imagine we don't have much time."

He was right. Amy would be done soon, and I was desperate for my release.

Returning my hands to my breasts, I continued to touch and caress them waiting for his instruction, praying he would soon allow my hands to roam further south.

"Open your eyes and look at the camera. I want to see you, and I want you to see me while we do this. I want you to touch yourself. Slowly and gently, run your fingers all over, pinch, rub and thrust them inside of you. I want to hear you moan and watch you as you come for me."

Without hesitation, my eyes flew open and I began to rub my sensitive and swollen clit achingly slow. I watched him stroking his long hard cock from the base to the rounded pink, flushed tip while his eyes were fixated on me. I slid two fingers inside my sex and rubbed my clit with my thumb. He gasped and moaned as I arched my back and began to grind my hips against my fingers.

"Oh, baby, that is so good. You look so fucking hot. Tell me how it feels."

I smiled, hearing his voice so low and husky.

"So good. Oh, Jared, I need you inside me. I'm so wet and hot, it's indecent. I was made for your long hard cock, and I ache for it right now."

My fingers slid and slipped in and out of my salivating sex as I watched him slide his hand up and down his cock.

"Oh fuck, Layla. I can just imagine your tight little cunt all moist and warm, squeezing me as I thrust inside of you."

It was entirely erotic to watch as he firmly gripped his cock in his palm, and as I continued to gaze at the screen, I felt my insides clench deliciously.

"Faster, Layla, I need you faster, harder." I moaned in response, too caught up in my own pre-orgasmic bliss to form a coherent sentence or word. Clutching the sheet beside me, I closed my eyes and panted as I felt my insides roaring into a hot, fiery inferno. His soft moaning, deep growls, and labored breathing worked like instant Viagra. My body was responding, and I could feel my orgasm building fiercely inside me as I continued to watch him. His mouth made that wonderful O shape and his head thrust back as he clearly tried to contain his own release, waiting for me to find mine.

"Come with me, Layla, I want to hear you and see you unravel. My hands on your body, my lips on your skin, my touch driving you crazy."

His words were my undoing as I practically levitated on the bed, my body writhing as I panted his name. Ripples of pleasure convulsed through me and I could hardly breathe. Our eyes connected, and staring into the camera I lost control of my senses as I gazed into his deep blue eyes, watching him shudder and come hard, emptying himself into a crisp white handkerchief. "Oh, baby. Fuck!"

Breathing erratically, I laid there gazing at the screen. My chest was rising and falling in rhythm with his as I watched the screen with a deep longing. I wanted to be near him, to feel his arms around me. Running his fingers through his sweat drenched hair, he smiled at me.

"I know, princess. I miss you too. I want to be curled up tightly with you as well. Grab your robe and climb into bed. I'll wait for you."

I heard the sound of the shower stop and hurriedly bolted for my closet, pulling on my robe quickly I climbed into bed, laying my head on the pillow and gazing at the screen once more. Jared had slipped into some lounge pants, but his strong chest was still visible and I drank him in.

"Wrap yourself in the sheets tightly. Feel that? Those are my arms around your waist, my head against yours, and my heart beating in time with the thunder of your heart. I'm there, baby. Maybe not in body, but I am there with you constantly. You carry my heart on your sleeve, Layla, and it keeps me close to you. No matter where I am, however far apart we are, I carry you with me. You are never too far for my heart. We're bound together."

Tears began to trickle down my cheeks and I sniffled shamelessly as I wiped them away. "Shhh, sweetheart, please don't cry. I'll be home soon. It's not long now. Go to sleep and I'll call you tomorrow. The sooner you sleep, the sooner I'll be coming home to you. I love you, baby."

I tried to smile, but it was no use. I was missing him so much that my breath caught in my throat. I could see the pain in his eyes and I knew how helpless he must have been feeling seeing me so upset, and not being able to hold and comfort me. Pushing back my grief, I took a calming breath and gazed into the camera.

"I love you too, Jared. Goodnight."

As the connection ended, I couldn't hold back any longer as my body racked and convulsed with sobs. Amy came out of the bathroom and ran to my side, holding me tightly in her arms she rocked me soothingly. She stroked my hair and whispered comforting words in my ear.

"Hush, sweetie, its ok. He'll be back soon. I know, you have a good cry, honey, it'll help you sleep."

And it did.

After some time of sobbing into Amy's shoulder, I was exhausted. The moment I closed my eyes, images of Jared lying next to me automatically drifted through my mind, and it gave me some solace to know he was feeling just the way I was right now. Pulling a pillow from beneath my head, I hugged it tightly to my chest and drifted into a long and deep sleep.

Chapter 28

Lean On Me

Wednesday, by comparison, was pretty standard. The work I'd had to do for Dr. Harman kept me busy most of the time and to be honest I was glad for the distraction. Although his letters and calls were wonderfully intimate, I still couldn't stop moping over Jared. Wednesday's letter had been short and sweet and was mostly to encourage me to go out with my friends and have fun. So that night Ollie took me and Amy bowling at the local alley which was only a few blocks away from campus. Sitting next to me as Amy took her turn, Ollie had draped his arm around me and given me a reassuring smile followed by a wink. I had felt the tension in my body lift almost immediately just from the very small but significant gesture. I'd really missed him, missed us and the connection we shared. Maybe things would be alright and that the kiss had finally put to bed all that chemistry and strange magnetism between us. It was finally comfortable to be around him once more and during our evening we had all laughed so much my ribs ached when we finally made it home. We ordered pizza and spent the rest of the night talking about everything from school to fashion. When the conversation turned to our sex lives, Ollie made his excuses and left us to our "seedy and sinful girl talk" as he called it.

Thursday's letter took me completely by surprise and brought a lump to my throat. It was deeply emotional and I could feel the passion in his words as I read them.

My Princess, Layla,

I cannot express how much I am looking forward to returning to you tomorrow. My heart feels heavy as I write this letter, and I haven't even departed yet. You left my company only moments ago, and yet my body, heart and soul are yearning for your return.

I'm afraid you have to work today, but at least it will distract you from counting the hours, minutes and seconds as I will be doing until I am reunited with you.

I'm not sure how you will feel about what I say next, but I hope that by the time you get this letter our relationship will have moved forward as I so desperately want it to.

Layla Jennings, I'm in love with you. Deeply, truly, madly and endlessly in love with you. I want to devote my every breath to making you happy and giving you everything your heart desires.

You're my sunshine, my rain and my evening stars. I feel as though I was living in the shadows, but you have entered my life in a blaze of color and light which has illuminated my very existence.

As for me, to love you alone, to make you happy, to do nothing which would contradict your wishes, this is my destiny and the meaning of my life – Napoléon Bonaparte

Until tomorrow....

Jared xxxx

A deep pang of sadness jolted like electricity through my heart. He'd written these words only moments after I had been with him, and yet felt he couldn't tell me in person how he felt about me.

It had only been after I had argued with him, and stormed out on Amy, that he had finally revealed he was in love with me. I had acted like a child, and though I felt exactly the same about him, I found it painfully difficult to discover the right words to express how profoundly, intensely, and genuinely I loved him also. I made a conscious decision to tell him precisely how I felt about him when he returned. I needed him to know that I was in this relationship just as much as he was, and that my feelings ran equally as deep. I read the letter over and over, reveling in the sweet sentiment.

A loud crashing pulled me from my hazy daydream. Leaping to my feet, I ran out the door and over to Ollie's room. It was unlocked, so I let myself in cautiously. I stood there in total shock as I saw the remains of his precious white electric guitar scattered across the floor. Ollie was rock and roll, but he'd never smash his baby in the name of art. Something was seriously wrong.

The bathroom door swung open, and Ollie froze when his eyes met mine. His hand was wrapped in a scrap of material, and I could see the blood stains seeping through.

"Oh my god, Oliver. What the hell did you do to yourself?"

Hurrying to his aid, I took his hand and led him to the bed. Pulling him down beside me, I unraveled the cloth from his palm. He hissed and winced as I removed the make-do bandage. There was a long shallow cut across his palm and it was bleeding slowly. Leaving him for a moment, I ran to my room to fetch the first aid kit that my mother had insisted I carry at all times.

Taking out an antiseptic wipe, I went to work on his wound. He watched me in silence as I cleaned and dressed his hand. Packing up the first aid kit, I glanced at him.

"So, want to talk about it?"

His eyebrows pinched together and he let out an exasperated sigh. "It's a family thing."

Ollie had never talked about his home or family before and I'd always assumed it was because he found it painful. Looking at the expression on his face, I felt I was probably right. Taking his hand, I held it reassuringly. He raised his head and stared into my eyes.

"I didn't have a great childhood, Layla. My mom took off when I was a kid to live with her junkie boyfriend. The state handed me and my older brother over to my deadbeat father, and I spent the next ten years of my life cleaning up empty bourbon bottles. My brother left the moment he turned eighteen, leaving me alone with a man who was more than happy to dish out his frustration on me with his fists. When I was sixteen, I ran away when he was passed out on the couch. I went to find my mom, but she'd moved, leaving no address. I wasn't going back home, so I hitchhiked my way to California where my brother was. Anyway, he didn't want me either, but he did find me a place to stay and I ended up crashing with a friend of his for two years before I got into this place. I never heard from my mom or my dad, and honestly I really didn't care. Until this morning."

Leaning across me, he grabbed a letter from his bedside table and handed it to me. I gasped, pressing my hand to my mouth as I read it.

"Ollie, I...I don't know what to say."

"What's to say? My waste of fucking oxygen father decided to write to me and let me know he's in prison and that my mother is looking for me. What else is there?"

He got to his feet abruptly and snatched the piece of paper from my hand. I sat there and watched him as he paced up and down frantically, growing angrier by the minute.

"I mean, why the fuck would he think I care? I haven't seen that abandoning bitch since I was six years old and she didn't exactly qualify for mother of the fucking year! And now that asshole is in prison for armed robbery. Big fucking surprise there. He was always going to end up banged up for something. He's asking me to go see him and he actually expects me to go. Is he serious?"

I walked over and gently wrapped my arms around him.

My friend was in pain and it pained me to see it. He stood ridged in my arms and made no attempt to hug me back. Releasing him, I placed my hand on his shoulder and shook my head.

"I don't know, Ollie. Do you want to see him?"

Pulling away from me he snapped. "Fuck, no! I don't care what he wants! There is no way on earth I will ever be in the same room as that man ever again in my life!"

Tossing the letter on the floor, he rolled up the sleeve on his sweater, revealing his snake tattoo. "You see this ink here? I got that to cover up the scar he gave me with a broken bottle. Yeah, I'd come home without his fucking booze one evening, so he pinned me down and carved the words little prick into my skin. And you really think I want to see him? I hope he gets fucking shivved and dies in there."

Trailing my hand over his shoulder, I gently traced his tattoo with my fingertips. I thought about the poor child inside him. The child who had been abandoned by the woman who should have protected him, who'd been brutally scarred by the man who should have been taking care of him, then left to fend for himself by the brother he looked up to.

He gripped my wrist and moved it away from his arm, dropping it by my side. Seeing my sympathetic and hurt expression, Ollie shook his head. His bandaged hand cupped my face and he sighed, pressing his forehead against mine.

"I don't want pity. I'm the man I am today because of all the shit I went through. Don't ever feel sorry for what happened to me because I'm not. Please, forget about it all, ok?"

How could I forget? Everything I knew about him had changed. He wasn't just Ollie anymore. He was a hurt, damaged little boy who'd been forced to grow up unloved and frightened of his own father.

I felt deeply ashamed of my inability to be strong for him. This was his time of need, and there I was, falling apart in front of him. Wrapping me in his arms, he rocked me side to side gently. I pressed my face into his neck and held him tightly.

"I really am alright you know. This whole thing just dug up a past that I thought I buried three years ago. I hate that man with every bone in my body, and I will never forgive him for what he did to me, but I will not let it own me. This is my life, my future and my decision now. He can't control me, or tell me what to do. I'm not going to see him, and I am not interested in why my mother is looking for me. She didn't care about me enough when I was a kid, so why should I care about her now that I'm a man. I just want to forget this whole thing. Ok?"

Lifting my head, I nodded weakly.

"Ok Ollie. But you know if you ever change your mind or you want to talk, I'm here for you."

He gave me a halfhearted smile and let me go.

Scanning the room, Ollie ran his fingers through his long dark hair and sighed. Crouching down to the floor, he picked up a piece of his shattered guitar and rubbed his thumb over the jagged edge before casting it aside.

"Great, good going, Ollie. Where the hell am I going to get another guitar by tomorrow night?"

Bending down beside him, I took his hand and pulled him up with me.

"I don't know, but I don't think you're going to feel any better if you keep looking at all this. Why don't you take a walk, cool off, and I'll have this all cleared away when you get back. Go on."

Giving him a playful shove, I grabbed his shoulders and pushed him towards the door. Stopping in the doorway, he turned and placed a peck on my cheek.

"You really are the best person I know, Layla. You're amazing, everything a man could ever dream of. He's a really lucky guy. I just hope he knows that."

Giving me a rueful smile, he turned and left.

Clutching my hand to my chest, I push the door closed and press my palm against the hard wood, trying to catch my breath. My head hurt, and I tried to process everything I had just learned about my friend as I searched for a box or bag to dispose of the guitar pieces. Gathering them up, I glanced at Ollie's night stand and dropped the sack of broken plastic and metal. A white frame sat directly opposite his pillow. Picking it up my jaw dropped in astonishment. There, caressing a microphone, was me. He must have taken it that first night at the bar. My hair was swept around one side of my face and I was clearly caught in a moment when he'd snapped me mid note. A ghost of a smile was on my face and my eyes were tightly closed.

Clasping the frame in my hands, I stared at the photo. Ollie was clearly not moving on, and I had the distinct feeling that as time went on, things were going to get more and more complicated. Dropping the photo on the bed, I finished cleaning up and left in a hurry. I needed him to know I had found his memento, but I didn't want to be there when he returned.

Closing my door behind me, I leaned against it and massaged my temple, trying in vain to relieve the throbbing headache that was forming. The sound of my cell phone buzzing distracted me, so I searched my purse for it. Without checking the caller I.D, I answered.

"Hello?"

"Hey, sweetheart. Missing me?"

My veins flooded with electricity as my body reacted immediately to the gentle growl of Jared's voice on the line. A tingling ran up my spine as he spoke my name.

"Layla? Baby is everything alright?"

Taking a calming breath, I tried to seem unflustered.

"Yeah, sorry. Everything's fine. I was just busy cleaning when you called, that's all. Of course, I miss you. I've been missing you ever since you left for the airport, and I'll miss you more every second till you're home. I could really use a hug right now."

I could hear concern in his voice as he responded to my last statement.

"Why? Layla, what's going on? What's happened? I'll come back right now if you need me. I can be there in a few hours."

Cutting him off, I sighed.

"No, Jared, don't do that. You have business to see to and I'm fine, honest. It's just been a bad day, that's all. Class dragged, then Ollie had this crisis and I had to be there for him, it was really emotionally draining."

There was a moment of silence and my stomach lurched as I realized my mistake.

"Oliver who lives across the hall? The same Oliver who practically accused me of abducting you the other night? The Oliver who is desperately trying to get into your panties? That Oliver? Well, how fucking convenient. Oh, I really underestimated him, didn't I. Seizing his opportunity as soon as I'm out of the picture to have a sudden melt-down, and there you are, giving him a shoulder to cry on. Sounds very fucking cozy, Layla. Truly, I hope he feels better for it because when I get back I'm going to give him something to cry about!"

Irritated at his assumptions, I snarled at him furiously.

"How dare you accuse him of being deceitful! You have no idea what he's going through. I've seen for myself firsthand, and it's not something he could, or would have made up just to get to me. Besides it was me who urged him to talk about it. He was more than happy to go along living in his hell alone. He's my friend, Jared, and he needs people around him who care. I will not just abandon him like everyone else in his life has. You need to accept that, or this, me and you, is never going to work.

"I told you before, you don't have to like him, and you don't even have to trust him, but you have to trust me! I would never cheat on you, Jared, and I thought you knew me well enough to know how I feel about you, that I want you, and only you!"

"Oh come on, Layla, you really think he won't use this sudden crisis to his advantage? Take the opportunity to get closer to you? He's a guy, Layla, he doesn't think like you do. And how can you think I'd know how you feel when you never tell me how you feel. You say you love me, but those three words begin to feel really numb sometimes. It's like I never know what you're really thinking or feeling when you say them.

"I'm totally devoted to you, Layla. I think about you constantly and can't imagine my life without you. You're the air in my lungs, the blood in my veins and the constant beat of my heart. I love you so much, I can't think straight. As long as you walk this earth, no other woman even exists to me. That's how I feel, Layla, every minute of every damn day since I first laid eyes on you. But how you feel about me is a total fucking mystery, and I get the feeling you're holding back on me. If this, us, isn't what you want, then just cut the fucking cord already. Don't keep torturing me."

Fury was coursing through my body as I yelled into the cell phone I held in my now shaky hand.

"Just because I find it hard to express my feelings doesn't mean that I don't feel anything! I'm not some ice queen with a heart of stone. I feel exactly the same about you and I can't understand how you could ever doubt that. I love you with every breath in my body. I have never felt so totally out of control in my entire life and it scares the hell out of me. I'm terrified by this awesome power you have over me. With one look, one word, one spine tingling touch, you can bring me to my knees and at the same time lift me so high that I feel like I can fly.

"I've never felt this way before about anyone, and knowing that you actually question my feelings about you, about us, breaks my fucking heart. I don't want us to be over, and if you ever really knew me you'd know I love you, Jared. I didn't realize I had to say it every damn minute for you to know that. You say you love me, Jared, but you clearly don't trust me."

Breathless, and shaking with anger, I dropped the phone onto the floor and launched myself onto my bed in a fit of rage. Growling in frustration, I lay staring at the ceiling. I could hear his yelling coming from the phone which lay abandoned on the floor, but I didn't care. I wasn't willing to speak to him while I felt so utterly outraged. I wasn't going to cry over Jared Garrett and his stupid jealousy. It wasn't worth the energy.

A key turned in the door, and Amy came in. Seeing me on the bed, and my phone on the floor, she rushed over to pick it up and moved away from me. She spoke in hushed tones, and I knew Jared must have been frantic on the other end because she repeatedly asked him to calm down and let me have some space to cool off. Hanging up, she hurried to my side and slid behind me on the bed, draping a protective arm over me. The emotional exhaustion of the day was catching up with me, and I felt so tired I could hardly keep my eyes open, but I still had a shift at the coffee shop to get through, a thought that made me feel completely drained.

"Oh, honey, I don't know what happened between you two, but he sounded completely devastated when you wouldn't talk to him. Is it really that bad?"

Turning to face her, I nodded. "It's this whole Ollie thing and the fact that, apparently, I can't express how I feel properly. I never wanted to hurt him, but I'm scared of letting myself get so consumed by what we have. What happens if it all ends? I don't think I'd survive it, Amy. I spent a long time building a wall around myself when Josh broke my heart, and now Jared has taken a sledge hammer and brought it crumbling down around me. He doubts everything I say and is constantly accusing Ollie of being some kind of woman stealing asshole. Ollie was in a bad mood earlier, and I offered him a shoulder to cry on, some support. Is that so wrong?"

She shook her head, but remained silent, allowing me to continue.

"Jared hated it when I told him about it and accused Ollie of making it all up to get close to me. We had a fight, and he said he never knows what I'm thinking, or how I feel because I never tell him. But I show him all the time, Amy. How can he doubt me?"

Pulling me to her tightly, she stroked my hair.

"Oh sweetie, you two are so crazy about each other, and you're both such passionate people that you're bound to get this way sometimes. Maybe Jared is just scared of losing you and this is the only way he knows how to deal with it? He's a business man, Layla. They're used to people being underhanded and sneaky, trying to get what they want, and he probably thinks Ollie is the same. Try and cut him some slack, honey. He's miles away, missing you like crazy, and here you are in the arms of another man. Ok, so it's only Ollie, but still, how would you feel if it were reversed?"

My heart ached at the thought of him in the arms of another woman, stroking her face and their lips touching. Pushing it from my mind, I lifted my head and looked at her.

"You're right. I'd hate it. But I would never question how he feels about me."

"No, but you question everything else he does."

I raised my eyebrow at her and rolled my eyes. She was right, but it didn't excuse his jealous outburst.

"Look, sweetie, you know he loves you because he tells you constantly how he feels and showers you with his affection. Maybe you need to find a way to show him you adore him too? In fact, I think I have an idea, but you have to be totally open-minded. Alright?"

Intrigued, I nodded and listened intently to her plan.

Chapter 29

In The Still Of The Night

My shift at the coffee shop dragged on and felt endless. Although it was only for five hours, it felt like a lifetime because I couldn't get Jared off my mind. He called relentlessly, ringing every hour, but I ignored and diverted his calls. He texted, but I couldn't bring myself to read them as yet. I was still so heartbroken over his questioning of my emotions, and his assumptions about my relationship with Ollie.

When he resorted to calling the shop, Kate had taken every call, begging him to leave me alone and let me breathe. He wasn't giving up easily, and I felt a slight pang of guilt, knowing what he must have been going through every time I refused to speak to him.

Finishing up my shift, I cleaned the tables and glanced at the door. Waving at me as she crossed the street was Amy. I smiled at her and felt a rush of relief. Just seeing her face made me feel comforted and more at ease. She'd been my lifeline through the whole episode that day, and between her and Kate, I was well and truly covered on the girl support front.

I thought about calling Mel so many times but with her college work and making new friends, I didn't want her to feel bad for being so far from me when I needed help. We were more like sisters than friends, and no matter how long we went without speaking, I knew I could always count on her to be there for me. But I had made this mess and I was going to have to clean it up like the adult I continuously told myself that I was. Even if there were times when I wasn't sure I believed it.

After letting Amy in, Kate locked the doors and poured us all some coffee. Lounging on the sofa, I ripped off my apron and stared at the swirling foam of my cappuccino. Kate and Amy slouched on either side of me, each draping a supportive arm around my shoulders. Pulling my coffee towards me, Kate nudged it, encouraging me to take a drink.

"Layla, honey I'm sure things will work out," Kate said.

"He was really upset when you wouldn't talk to him, and every time I told him you wouldn't take his call, it was like I was kicking him in the crotch. I think he's scared that the two of you might be over."

Snapping me out of my melancholy, I stared at her in horror.

"No, it's not over. I wouldn't end it like that. Oh god, what a mess. Why do I constantly make everything so complicated? First Ollie, and now Jared. What am I supposed to do, though? He doesn't trust Ollie around me, and no matter how much I tell him we're just friends, he doesn't seem to understand that I would never cheat on him, even if Ollie did feel that way about me."

Ok, so I'd neglected to tell them that Jared was totally right on the money and that Ollie was definitely attracted to me. And I was certainly attracted to him, but it was just a physical and sexual allure, nothing more, so surely it wasn't important enough to mess up my relationship over?

"And then to doubt and question how I feel about him? How could he?" I continued. "I have given him everything. I'm in this relationship one hundred percent. Isn't it obvious how I feel? I told him I love him. I've told him how much he means to me. I thought that was enough. I really don't know if this is going to work anymore. If he can't get past this Ollie thing and we don't have trust, then honestly, what do we have?"

Simultaneously, the two girls practically shouted the word "love" at me. Amy gripped my hand with both of hers and smiled widely.

"Oh, Layla, he loves you, and you love him right back, and you're both insanely passionate about each other. The rest comes with time and patience. You need to sit down and talk to him without the whole world getting in the way. Away from his work, away from yours, away from college, and away from Ollie. How much time have you guys actually spent talking to each other?"

I sighed, knowing she was fully aware that Jared and I spent very little time conversing, and most of our time roaming our hands all over each other.

"That's what I thought. Stop doing this to yourself, sweetie. You always take things to heart and cause tragedies out of hiccups. This is a hiccup, and I bet he's frantic right now and sick with worry. I know you want to talk to him really, so why don't you call him? Or at least read his messages."

Giving me a reassuring pat on the back, Kate stood up and winked at Amy to follow her, giving me some privacy.

They disappeared into the back room, and I pulled my cell phone from my pocket. I stared at the screen and sighed. Thirty four missed calls and five text messages. Ignoring the list of calls, I scrolled through my messages and began to read them.

> Layla, please pick up. This is ridiculous. You can't ignore me forever. We need to talk about this.
> **Received: 15.35**
> **From: Jared**

> Layla, please, for the love of god, pick up your phone. I just want to talk and work this out. Please call me.
> **Received: 15.48**
> **From: Jared**

> Ok. I get it. You're mad, but ignoring my calls and messages won't make this better. I'm in hell here, baby, please talk to me.
> **Received: 16.08**
> **From: Jared**

> What can I do to get you to talk to me? Amy says to leave you alone, Kate says to give you space. The only one not telling me what you want is you. I need to talk to you, please, just answer my calls.
> **Received: 16.29**
> **From: Jared**

> I do trust you, Layla. I'm just terrified you'll wake up one day and be over me, over us. I love you and I just want to know you're alright. Pick up. Jared. xxxx
> **Received: 16.55**
> **From: Jared**

Holding my head in my hands, I sighed. His last message tore my heart and anger to pieces. Holding my breath, I dialed his number, but it diverted straight to voicemail. Hanging up, I dropped the cell onto the couch and groaned into my hands. Amy and Kate were at my side within moments, and I was enveloped in a comforting hug from both of them as I fought to hold back my frustrated and anguished tears.

"I tried to call, but he's switched off his cell. I think it's over. I should have called him, or answered his messages, but I was too fucking stubborn for my own good. It's like I wanted to actually punish him or something. I hate myself, and he has every reason to hate me too. He's right. I am a child."

Struggling out of their arms, I snatched my purse from the couch and hurried to the door. Unlocking it, Kate gave me a sympathetic look and let Amy and I out.

We walked back to the dorm in silence. I had nothing left in me. I was completely shattered physically, mentally, and emotionally. When we got back, I saw Amy glancing at the clock almost every five minutes. It hadn't occurred to me that she might have plans that she was putting off so that she could be my shoulder to cry on. Sitting on my bed, I questioned her jittery demeanor.

"Amy, do you have plans tonight? Because you either have plans, or you're developing some kind of weird clock fetish. Every time you see the time, you seem to get a little agitated. So what's it to be?" Biting her bottom lip, she smiled.

"Actually, I do have a date. Remember James from the opera? He's supposed to be taking me to his restaurant for dinner, but I can totally cancel and stay here with you."

Raising my hand to silence her, I shook my head. "No way. You are not putting off the chance to eat at one of the top restaurants in the city to sit here with me while I wallow in self-pity. You better get ready. I'm just going to close my eyes for a little while."

Nodding, she pecked me on the cheek and disappeared into the bathroom.

Laying my head on the pillow, I thought about how enthusiastic I had been on my first date with Jared, which felt like a distant and hazy memory as I lay there mulling over the upsetting events of the day. The pain of our fight was now a familiar and uncomfortable fixture in my chest which constricted and heaved as tears began to fall down my cheeks. God, I seemed to spend so much time either screaming or crying since I'd met him. Surely that wasn't healthy. My emotions were constantly in high gear being with him. Softly sobbing, I gripped my pillow and cried myself to sleep.

I woke with a start and breathed a sigh of relief, grateful to have been pulled from my nightmare. With tired eyes, I glanced at my clock and groaned, seeing that it was only three in the morning. An urgent need to pee meant I was going to have to get out of bed. I looked over at Amy's bed and found it still empty. I hadn't woken when she left, but I assumed by her absence that her date must be going well.

Swinging my legs out of my duvet, I jumped as my foot hit something hard and cold on the floor. Turning on the bed side lamp, I stared down at the object next to my foot. Picking it up, I smiled. It was a white coffee mug with the words "I Love NY" printed across the front, and a message had been scribbled in permanent marker on the back. Turning it around, I read it as happiness and relief flooded body.

"I love you, Layla Jennings, I always have and I always will. Don't give up on me yet, baby."

Hugging it to my chest, I realized he must have been here in my room and I had missed him. Springing to my feet, I rushed to the window and saw the bright tail lights of the Mercedes pulling out of the parking lot.

Snatching my cell from the nightstand, my fingers frantically typed a message to him. I needed to let him know I was still in this as much as he was, and that giving up wasn't an option. Hitting send, I grinned and ran my fingers over the porcelain mug. To most people it was just that, a mug. But to me it was much more.

It was love.

He'd cut his trip short and come to my room in the middle of the night just to leave me this token of his affection, to make sure I was ok and to let me know he loved me. I hugged myself, knowing how truly lucky I truly was.

* * * *

Clutching the mug in my hands, I'd managed to get another three hours of sleep, waking when I heard the sound of keys rattling in the door. Sitting up, I rested on my elbows and raised an eyebrow at Amy as she totted in. Her shoes dangled in one hand, her lipstick smeared, she caught me staring and grinned.

"I take it you had a good night then?"

Tossing her Manolo Blahnik's on the bed, she sighed contentedly.

"Oh, Layla, he's so perfect. He's a real honest to god gentleman. He held doors open for me, pulled my chair out, everything. He's amazing. And he's smart, funny, witty and an amazing dancer. He took me to this exclusive club and we danced till the sun came up. And boy, can he kiss. I thought I might stop breathing, it was that good!"

I laughed as she fell backwards onto my bed, gazing at the ceiling. Crawling out of my duvet, I laid down next to her.

"So, no more frogs, huh? Prince charming at last?"

She laughed and turned to face me.

"Oh, I hope so. Don't think I could cope with anymore spawn sucking toads after last night. It was just perfect, Layla. Oh my god, listen to me going on. How are you this morning? Did you reach him?"

Grabbing the mug from next to my pillow, I held it out to her and she took it from me with a wide smile.

"Oh my goodness, Layla! He came here? He came all the way from New York just to see you? I told you he wouldn't give up on you two! What happened? What did he say?"

Shrugging, I shook my head. "Nothing. I didn't see him. I woke up at three and found it on the floor. He must have snuck in and left it there while I was asleep. I have no idea how he got in, but he did. I just managed to see the Mercedes he has Daniel chauffeur pull out of the parking lot. He must have come here straight from the airport. I haven't even spoken to him yet! He left me a note, and I sent him a text, but that's it."

Taking the mug from my hands, she tipped it up and read the note. Squealing, she kicked her legs in the air like an excited child.

"Him getting in is my fault. I was in such a rush that I must have forgotten to lock the door. But, Layla, could he be more wonderful? We have to be the two luckiest girls I know! Well, don't just lay here grinning at me. You have work in an hour, remember? It's Friday."

Realizing the time, I sprung to my feet and rushed around, pulling on my jeans with one hand and brushing my teeth with the other. Grabbing a blue t-shirt from my closet that had the words "Blondes Do It Better" across the front, I pulled it over my head and pulled my hair back into a tight ponytail. Holding out my apron for me, Amy smiled and shook her head. Plucking it from her grasp, I shot her a quick smile and ran out the door.

Turning the corner, I saw Kate at the doors ready to open up and sprinted across the street to meet her. Opening the doors, she smiled at me sweetly. "Hey girl, you look better today. You talk to the boss?"

Slipping off my jacket I filled her in on the events that had unfolded during my slumber and she reacted with the same enthusiasm as Amy had. We moved around the shop, fluidly working in the well-oiled machine way we had developed over the past few weeks. Setting up tables and warming the coffee maker, I stood for a moment and smiled contentedly to myself. Life was good. I had good friends, great colleagues, and a man who was desperately in love with me. Everything was perfect. So why did I have the horrible feeling that something was waiting just around the corner to bring it all crashing down around me? I'd leapt off the cliff, and was still flying, but eventually I was destined to hit the ground.

Shaking the disturbing thoughts from my head, I walked to the office to collect the mail. Lorraine had become so comfortable leaving me and Kate in charge that she was now only coming in to collect receipts, and to make sure that shifts were covered. We hadn't seen her in days. I never had much opportunity to meet the other staff that worked there because I was always scheduled on Kate's shift. It suited me that way. We were a great team, and we had fun.

The stereo fired up and I chuckled, knowing that Kate would soon be wiggling her ass around the shop to some sort of classic rock album she'd put on. But no heavy bass kicked in. No electric guitar twanged and strummed. Instead, the soft and cool sounds of an acoustic guitar echoed through the speakers. I made my way back out to the shop floor and scanned the room. Kate had disappeared and the shop was completely desolate. The sound of the guitar filled my ears as I stood at the counter, completely baffled at her choice of music. The intro ended and the deep and sultry voice of Elvis boomed over the sound system.

The hairs on my neck began to stand up, and a warm breath was grazing my neck. A recognizable scent of soap, sweet cologne and hair gel filled my senses. Engorging my nostrils, the familiar aphrodisiac caused my pulse to spike as I instantly became aware of a throbbing between my legs. There was only one man in the world that had that effect on my body and it was a welcome sensation. Singing the sweet words of 'Love Me Tender' in my ear, his deep sensual voice sent shivers through my body and a tingle down my spine. My legs grew weak, and my head rolled back as I closed my eyes, savoring every sweet hushed word, every breath he breathed on my sensitive skin, and the gentle caress of his hands as they slid around my waist.

Turning me to face him, he gazed deeply into my eyes. It was as though he was staring right into my soul. I could feel tears pooling as I stared into his perfectly blue eyes. Cupping my face in his hands, he pressed a gentle, caressing kiss on my lips. Tears began to slide down my face and over his thumbs as he pressed them firmly to my cheeks. Breathless, I pulled away and met his gaze. Wiping away my tears, he smiled ruefully.

"Shhh, baby, don't cry. I hate to see you cry. I'm sorry, for everything. I do trust you entirely. I'm just so damn terrified of losing you, and it makes me crazy knowing you're here with someone else while I'm miles away wishing I was with you. I'm sorry I went off at you, and I understand if you can never forgive me. I said some horrible things, and I hurt you. But please don't give up on me, Layla. I'll do anything to make it right. I love you so much."

Pressing his forehead against mine, he held my hand over his heart and placed his on top. I could feel the beat pounding beneath my fingertips.

A long breath escaped my lungs that I hadn't even realized I'd been holding. Closing my eyes, I smiled.

"Jared, I was never going to give up on you, it was never an option. I love you too. I know I may not say it, or show it the way I should, but never ever doubt how I feel about you. You're my oxygen and I can't breathe without you."

Taking his free hand, I placed it on my chest and pressed it against my own thundering heart.

"And this will always belong to you. I could never give it to anyone else. Your name is carved on my heart, Jared, and it can't beat without you. I love you, completely, entirely and desperately."

Catching me by surprise, he kissed me deeply and passionately. His tongue pushed into my mouth and fervently rolled and stroked mine. His hand released mine from his chest as he gripped the back of my neck, pulling me to him. I followed suit and slid my own hand around his back, pressing us closer together, deepening the kiss.

"Ahem."

Kate coughed lightly, distracting us from our impassioned embrace. Pulling away from Jared, I shot her an apologetic smile, but she simply shook her head and laughed.

"I hate to break this little love in up, but we have to open in about ten minutes. So if you could find it in your will power to keep your hands off each other for a few hours, I'd be most grateful. I can't run this place by myself."

Chuckling, I shrugged at Jared. "Sorry boss, we'll have to cool it off for now. I'd hate to get fired for indecent displays of affection at work."

He grinned at me mischievously.

"I don't think that would be a problem at all, Miss Jennings. I happen to know the boss would absolutely adore it if you got a little indecent with your man."

Shoving him gently away from me, he took my hands tightly in his.

"How can I possibly leave now? I've spent the most agonizing three days away from you, and now you have to abandon me for this place. Seems highly unfair if you ask me."

"You don't have to tell me. I would love to blow this place off and come with you, but I have to work. I have needs, Mr. Garrett."

His grin widened and he snickered. Breathing heavily, he whispered in my ear, sending chills through my body and goose bumps on my pale skin.

"Blow, come. Oh, Layla, you say such wonderfully sweet things to me. I would love for you to blow and come with me too, amongst other things. You don't have to work, you know. Anything you need I can get for you. You could spend all your free time tied up with me."

I rolled my eyes at his double entendre and shook my head at him. Feigning outrage, I shoved him a little.

"Mr. Garrett! Now who's being indecent? I am perfectly capable of providing for myself. I love my job, and I love the people I work with, and for. You can keep me tied up in my free time. In fact, I insist on it."

His eyes grew dark and hooded and I knew exactly what images he was conjuring because I was doing the same. Standing on my tiptoes, I gave him a chaste kiss.

"Those thoughts you're thinking, hold on to those. I'll be out of here in five hours."

Wrapping his arms around me, he held me tightly to him.
"I can't wait."

Kate re-entered and rolled her eyes at us. Gripping Jared by the shoulders, she marched him out in front of her and to the door.

"Ok, lover boy, I warned you, out! We have work to do, and if you like keeping my girl dripping in diamonds and living the life she should become accustomed to, then you'll let us open up and earn you some cash."

Reaching the door, Jared turned his head, grinned, then blew me a kiss before turning his attention to Kate.

"God, you're bossy when you want to be. I think we need to talk about giving you a promotion."

Sighing exasperatedly, she shoved him out the door and closed it. I laughed as he waved at me before turning and walking across the street to the parking lot. Kate raised an eyebrow at me, and gave me an amused look.

"Looks like you two worked it out then. I nearly squealed when he showed up and asked for a few minutes alone with you. You're not mad, are you?"

"How could I be mad? Did you see how he kissed me? Oh, Kate, I'm so happy I could burst!"

"Well how about settling for bursting into song?"

She fired up the stereo and exchanged the Elvis CD for her classic rock. The heavy bass and loud beats of Bon Jovi filled the shop and we both belted out the lyrics as we danced around.

If one could die of happiness they could have called me a doctor, because I was definitely terminal.

Chapter 30

A Long Hot Talk

Jared was waiting patiently outside the coffee shop the moment I finished. His sleek, sexy Jag was parked curbside, and he was leaning against it as I stepped out the door.

I took a moment to drink in the stunning man in front of me. His dark denim jeans gripped and hugged his waist, and a tight white tee was pulled taut around his chest and thick arms. His hair had its usual 'just fucked' look, and he wore dark sunglasses that hid his scorching, sexy eyes from view.

Rushing over to him, I practically launched myself into his arms. Gripping me tightly, he lifted me off the ground and twirled me around before pressing my back against the car and kissing me deeply.

"God I missed you baby."

I chuckled at him as he pressed another kiss to my lips.

"It's only been five hours since you saw me, Jared."

"Feels like a lifetime."

The drive back to his place took minutes, but it felt like forever as his hand gripped and stroked my leg.

"Did you manage to get all your business sorted out in New York?"

He gave me a confused look before understanding what I'd said.

"Oh, yeah, I hope so. It's complicated. Let's not ruin things with talk of work, ok?"

I nodded weakly and the familiar uneasy feeling that he was hiding something prickled and tingled up my spine. His hand roamed freely up and down my thigh, and the sexual tension was tangible. It cracked and sizzled in the air between us.

Stepping inside the grand entrance of his house, I pulled my jacket off and placed it in Jared's extended hand.

"So, what do you want to do first? The bed? The table? The kitchen counter? I'm open to suggestions."

Grinning, I rolled my eyes at him.

"Actually I'd love a nice hot bath right now, get the smell of coffee off of me."

Taking my hand, he raised it to his lips and pressed a kiss onto my knuckles.

"Your wish is my command, my lady. Why don't you go and relax and I'll run you a bath." Giving me a quick smile, he sprinted upstairs two at a time and I made my way to the kitchen.

Pouring myself a tall glass of orange juice, I decided to give myself a tour of the house. Since I'd been there, I'd never really explored it at all. I mentally hugged myself as I passed the long glass dining table and a smile crept across my lips. The large lounge was painted magnolia and had been kept with a minimalistic décor. Two large cream colored couches sat in the center of the room around a stunning silver and green glass mosaic coffee table. Each couch could easily sit at least four people, and the enormous plush cushions were as soft as feathers.

Placing my glass on the table, I flopped onto the couch and giggled when I bounced slightly as I landed. A large frame was hanging on the wall opposite me, and it instantly caught my curiosity. Getting to my feet, I went over and inspected it closer. The entire space was filled with a collage of photographs. Some were slightly faded and were clearly a few years old, where others were bright and colorful. I stared at the picture in the very center. A small lightly brown haired boy was eating a popsicle as a beautiful golden blonde haired woman wrapped him in a tight hug. Her eyes were a perfect blue, and I recognized them immediately. They were the same eyes I gazed into my first night there, the eyes I had fallen in love with.

This was Jared's mother.

I stared at her in total awe. She was truly stunning and one of life's natural beauties. I jumped as a pair of warm, strong arms snaked around my waist. Resting his chin on my shoulder, he sighed.

"I see you've met my mother."

Smiling I leaned my head to the side against his. "She's beautiful. You look just like her. You have her eyes. How old were you when this was taken?"

"About six years old. We used to take vacations every summer to Hawaii and visit my grandma. My father was born there, so we'd pack up and go for weeks on end."

Jared obviously got his caramel skin from his father, and as I scanned the frame, I spotted a photo of tall dark haired man in a speedo. It looked old and worn and someone had written the year at the very bottom. 1979. Seeing where I was currently looking, Jared pointed at the photo.

"That's my father. He must have been about nineteen in that one. It was the year he met my mom. She was only sixteen, but she fell head over heels. They met while she was on vacation there and hit it off right away. They got married only a year later."

He sighed deeply and I could see the pain in his eyes. Turning around, I brushed his cheek with my thumb, and kissed him gently.

"You're a credit to them, Jared. They'd be so proud of you and everything you've done. You have your mother's striking looks, your father's skin tone and business mind as well as my heart. They loved you, Jared, and I will forever be in their debt for giving me the most wonderful man in the world."

A ghost of a smile traced his lips, and he shrugged. "I know. Let's not dwell on my past though, ok. Right now there's a hot relaxing bath with your name on it."

Scooping me into his arms, he carried me upstairs to his master bedroom. Turning into the bathroom, the warming fragrance of jasmine and lavender surrounded us. Candles were scattered across every surface, lighting the room dimly with a relaxing glow. Placing me on my feet, his hands glided over my t-shirt. Raising an eyebrow at the slogan across the front, he grinned wickedly.

"I have to say, I agree. I can't speak for all blondes, but you, Layla Jennings, certainly do everything better than anyone I've ever known."

Tugging at the hem, he lifted it over my head and tossed it aside. I hadn't had time to hunt for a bra that morning, so my only option was to go bare-chested, something Jared discovered with gleeful delight.

"Have you been like this all day? This morning at the shop you were pressed against me with absolutely no bra? I'm shocked, Layla. How could I have missed such a golden opportunity to cop a feel of these gorgeous firm handfuls? I should hang my head in shame."

I gasped as his smooth hands glided up my stomach and cupped my breasts. Massaging them gently, he playfully rubbed my nipples with his thumbs, making them pucker and stiffen beneath his skillful hands.

Seizing his wrists, I clasped them tightly and shook my head. Smiling, I backed away from him and leaned against the tub.

"If you continue the route you are currently on, you're going to make us both very hot and my bath will become very cold. If you could keep your hands to yourself for a moment, I think I can slip out of my own clothes, thank you."

His eyes grew darker and he watched me like a predator stalking its prey as I sashayed across the room and began pulling down the zipper on my jeans. Standing just a few feet away from him, I hooked my thumbs inside the waistband and slowly pushed them down over my thighs, letting them fall into a heap around my ankles. Gracefully and skillfully, I stepped out of the crumpled denim and returned to the enormous tub. Leaning forward, I inhaled deeply, and as the scent of the aromatic oils filled my senses, I moaned with pleasure. Glancing over at Jared, I could see his erection tightly pressing against his jeans which were barely containing the impressive bulge beneath. I bit my bottom lip as I thought about his deliciously long hard cock. Reading my mind, he let out a low growl.

"You keep going on that route of thinking, baby, and we'll have a hell of a lot of fun in or out of the water. Now get those panties off before I tear them off with my bare hands."

Backing away slightly, I fixed my gaze on him as I gently, provocatively, and slowly ran my hands over the curves of my hip to the elastic waist of my cotton panties. Pressing my fingers to my skin, I pushed them down slowly and watched as Jared's eyes lit up with delight. His tongue grazed suggestively over his bottom lip, and a hiss escaped his mouth as the delicate panties fell to the floor. He bit down hard on his lip, and I could see the carnal desire building inside him as he hurriedly ripped off his t-shirt and unzipped his jeans.

I gawked at his gorgeous body as his hands worked frantically to remove his clothes. His hard, perfectly chiseled abs glistened and glowed in the flickering candlelight. I whimpered weakly as my eyes travelled down to the deep V of his waist. I really did love that particular definition of his torso.

His broad muscular arms flexed and pulled as he slid his jeans to the floor and pulled them away from him, tossing them aside. His shorts were hardly containing his enormous, throbbing erection, and I fought the desperate impulse to march right over and unleash it from its restraints.

In one swift movement he was beside me, scooping me into his arms and gently placing me into the wonderfully hot bath he'd prepared. He grabbed two large towels from the shelf beside the door before placing them next to the tub and sliding out of his shorts. Leaning back, I moaned as the waters washed over my skin and warmed my aching body. Closing my eyes, I felt him sink in behind me, pulling me close and my back pressed against his chest. The smell of the bath oils mixed with Jared's sweet natural scent was intoxicating and I felt myself becoming lost in sensation.

Taking the soap from beside him, he lathered up his hands and began to slowly work my tense muscles, massaging and washing my body simultaneously. I could feel his erection pressing into my back, and my own body reacted immediately as his hands roamed freely over every inch me. His hands slithered across my wet, soap slicked skin, over my breasts to my stomach, and finally settling between my thighs. Parting my legs, his fingers slid over the opening of my sex teasingly before slipping inside me. Softly, he stroked and caressed my clit with his thumb as my head rolled back onto his chest, exposing my neck.

His lips tenderly grazed my skin as he trailed light kisses from my nape to my jaw. Snaking my hand behind me, I caught his long hard cock and ran my hand up and down, holding it firmly in my palm. He nipped harshly on my earlobe, and I gasped at the pain followed by pleasure as he sucked, licked and kissed the hurt away.

I pressed my feet against the edge of the tub and lifted my hips so that my pelvis was hovering above his. I needed him inside me, filling me and satisfying my carnal pleasures of the flesh, his flesh. Taking his hand from between my thighs, I held it firmly against the rim of the tub as I slowly lowered myself onto his throbbing stiff cock. I gulped a breath as he slid inside me. He wrapped one arm around my waist, holding me firmly to him as the other held the side of the tub in a deathlike grip. Pushing my feet against the tub, I moved up and down on him, finding a rhythm as the water sloshed and spilled around us onto the floor.

"Oh, baby, I have missed you so much." He thrust upwards, plunging deeper inside me. I gasped and panted as my breathing quickened and my heart thumped like a bass drum.

Rising and falling, I slid blissfully up and down on the entire rigid length of him. He shifted beneath me, angling himself perfectly inside as the tip of his cock stroked my g-spot. The heavenly sensations sent waves of rippling satisfaction through my body, igniting a fire in my stomach. His hot breath breezed over my neck, intensifying the wild lust and passionate desire that was scorching through my veins. His hand slithered from my waist to my sex unhurriedly, and with infuriating ease he gradually slid a finger through my slit and onto my achingly sensitive clit. I cried out as his light and gentle fingers brushed and rubbed against me. My legs stiffened and I found it hard to move as my whole body writhed and wriggled on top of him.

Releasing his grip on the tub, he held my hips tightly and hoisted me off his lap. He turned me around to face him, and my thighs pressed against his as I straddled him. Panting and sweating, he surged upwards into me once more, making me moan noisily and shamelessly.

"Oh yes, Jared, oh god."

My knees pressed into the bottom of the tub on either side of his hips as I rode him fiercely, the need for my orgasm becoming all consuming. He kissed me hard and with a carnal hunger groaning deep in his throat, he murmured into my mouth as I continued my frenetic riding; lifting up and then slamming back down onto him.

"I'm close. Come with me, baby. I need to hear you. Fall apart with me, Layla."

Sliding my hands around his back, I dug my nails into his hot, wet flesh, gripping him tightly as my orgasm built faster and harder. I leaned forward and sunk my teeth into his shoulder, making him hiss and moan.

"Fuck, Layla, you're an animal. Don't stop, baby."

Moaning and gasping with pleasure, I slammed into him two more times as my intensely gratifying, and insanely pleasurable orgasm rolled through my body like the water in the tub, spilling and flowing a river inside me. I could feel my insides tighten and pulsate around him as I reveled in the euphoria of my orgasmic bliss. Arching my back, I stilled, my legs stiff and motionless, I cried out his name over and over again. Burying his face in my neck, he growled as his own release flooded inside me.

Gasping for air, we clasped each other's bodies close and tightly. My heart was beating fast, and I could feel his own thundering beneath me as I pressed against his chest. Lifting my head slowly, I opened my eyes and stared longingly into his. His eyes were speaking words that his mouth couldn't say, but I knew exactly what they meant and I felt the same. Within seconds, his expression changed from pure post-coital bliss to worried and anxious. Lifting me off him, he almost propelled me across the large tub to the other side. I sat mortified as he frantically ran his fingers through his hair.

"Layla, Fuck! Condom?"

In the time we'd been together, we'd always practiced safe sex. He'd never asked about contraceptives, and I'd never brought it up. As I watched the horror on his face turn into sheer panic, I realized my mistake and held my head in my hands. Heaving himself out of the tub, he quickly dried himself off and pulled on a pair of sweatpants that were hanging on the door handle as I stared at the water, feeling riddled with guilt. He paced up and down, still threading his fingers through his hair like he always did when he was irate or worried.

Carefully stepping out, I grabbed a towel and wrapped myself in it snugly before making my way over to him. Holding his face in my hands I pulled him to me and held him in place, his eyes fixed on mine.

"Shhh. It's ok."

Pushing me away, he regarded me coolly. "How can you say that? You could get pregnant, Layla! How could I forget? Shit! I was just so happy to see you, so desperate to be with you, I got totally caught up. Christ, how could we be so stupid?"

"Jared, will you stop! I've been on contraception for weeks! So if the possibility of getting pregnant is the only reason you were using condoms in the first place, we're fine."

He froze and stared at me in disbelief.

"Weeks? You mean this whole time you've been safe and you never told me? Why?"

Pressing my palms against his bare chest, I shrugged.

"I don't know. You never asked, and I assumed you used condoms with all the girls you've been with. I know I'm clean, but I thought maybe you couldn't take that risk, so contraception for me was a moot point."

He gave me a confused look, and sighed deeply.

"Layla, that's absurd! You really thought I didn't talk about it because I thought you might have something? I would never think that about you. A woman's body is her own possession and she has the right to choose whether she uses contraception. It's never been my place to ask you. I have always used condoms with everyone I've ever been with, and I assumed you were safe too. I get checked regularly, so I know I'm clean. If you tell me you are, then I believe you. I just wish you'd told me before and we could have avoided the anxiety attack I just had."

Hanging my head, I stared at the marble tiled floor as the realization hit me that, once again, honesty was not my biggest strength. Why could we never get past the need to keep things from each other? Ok, so this was only a little secret, but what about the next time? If I was hiding something as trivial as my shot, then what secrets could he be hiding? Would we ever be able to just be truthful and forthcoming about things to one another?

I always rationalized that the things I kept from Jared were to keep him from worrying, but this time I'd had the opposite effect. My whole body felt weak as regret and sadness filled me. This was never going to work if we didn't trust each other, and right now I'd given Jared every reason to doubt me.

Holding my chin between his thumb and finger, he lifted my head and his mouth covered mine as he kissed me tenderly.

"Stop it, Layla. I can't stand it when you torture yourself like this. I've seen that look on your face more times than I'd like to count now, and it's killing me. I understand why you never mentioned it, and I respect your privacy, but don't keep things from me again. We're in this together, remember?

"Stop over thinking and second guessing me. It's getting really frustrating when you constantly doubt my motives over things. If you have a question, then ask me and I will always give you an answer. No more secrets, no more lies, and no more keeping things from each other. Understood?"

Nodding, I diverted my eyes to the floor again. I still couldn't shake the feeling that he was hiding something.

"Layla, I mean it. Stop. Right now. No more guilt trips. You have to stop doing this to us. Do you want us to fail? Because your constant doubt over our relationship and commitment to each other will tear us apart. I know how I feel about you. There is no force in heaven, or on earth that could keep me from you."

Removing myself from his grasp, I picked up my discarded clothes and walked away from him into the bedroom. I couldn't bear to see the hurt in his eyes any longer. He was right, I was always second guessing him and for no logical reason. He'd always given me a straight answer whenever I'd asked him anything. Like when I asked how many women he'd been with, and he'd freely given me information about his parents. Holding my breath I asked the question that had been plaguing me for weeks.

"Jared what are all the phone calls about? I know there's a woman involved, I heard you in the office. Just, tell me the truth. I need to know."

Walking towards me he placed his hands on my arms reassuringly. "Nothing is going on I swear. It's something-"

I cut him off.

"Something you have to deal with. Yeah, I know. You get to have your secrets, but I can't have mine. Got it. Guess we're not as committed to this honestly thing as we thought."

I moved silently around the room as I pulled my clothes on. Jared stood in the doorway, rubbing his temple as though trying to sooth a headache. A headache I was causing. He exhaled loudly, and I could hear the frustration in his voice as he pleaded with his eyes for an explanation.

"For the love of god, Layla, what do I have to do to show you that I'm serious about us? You want me to buy you a diamond and get down on one knee? What do I have to do?"

Taken aback, I stepped away from him, scrutinizing his expression, and trying to see if he was serious.

"Layla, I'm not about to propose marriage. You're twenty years old for Christ sake. I know I'm going to spend the rest of my life with you, and I don't need a ring or piece of paper to tell me that, but if that's what you need to believe in me, then I'll give it to you. Hell, Layla, I'd give you the moon, stars and oceans if you asked for them, but please, in the name of all that is holy, just stop dooming us to fail."

Slumping down onto the vintage cream and gold couch, I held my head in my hands. I knew all along the cause of our problems, but not wanting to admit it, I'd convinced myself that it didn't matter. But the truth was that we really didn't know each other. We never talked.

Removing my hands from my face, Jared crouched in front of me, resting his forehead against mine.

"Layla talk to me, please. You're terrifying me with your silence."

"That's just our problem, Jared. We *don't* talk. We hardly know anything about each other beyond the physical. It's the reason I get mad when you give me lavish gifts because you have no idea why I find it difficult to accept them. It's the reason you get mad and scared when you think about me and Ollie. We jumped in to this too fast and we just don't know each other enough."

Grabbing me by the hand, he hauled me up and dragged me down the hall to the other side of the house. I stumbled along, trying to keep up with him, and felt a little frightened as his demeanor changed from worry to determination.

"Jared, what are you doing? Let me go!"

Turning the corner, we stopped outside a door at the far end of a long hallway that I hadn't been down before. Gripping the handle in one hand, and me in the other, he tightened his grip.

"You say we don't know about each other, right? Well let's rectify that right now."

The door swung open and he led me inside, still holding my hand firmly.

"Welcome to my world."

My jaw dropped as I gazed around the enormous room I was currently standing in. The walls were cluttered with news articles, photos, awards and posters. Endless rows of medals and plaques shone as they sat in mahogany display cabinets. A dark four poster bed was against the far wall, and a door which led to another equally stunning bathroom was opposite. Releasing me, he gestured for me to explore. In the corner was a walk in closet similar to the one in his bedroom except there were no clothes inside. Instead, there were dozens of brown cardboard boxes, and I could smell the dirty scent of dust as I entered the doorway. The entire room smelled old and musty as though no one had been there in years.

When I turned around, Jared was sitting on the edge of the bed with his hand extended out to me. Walking over, I placed my hand in his and sat next to him. His shoulders sagged and he stared blankly into the distance.

"This was my room. My whole life up until I was eighteen unfolded in this room. I can't say it was exciting, or extraordinary, but as you can see, I did ok. Right here, right now, we're going to talk. Anything you want to know I'll tell you, and vice versa. So, tell me, Layla Jennings, what do you want to know?"

"I want to know everything. Tell me about the six year old in that photograph downstairs. Who was he? What was he like? What were his hopes and dreams?"

He chuckled and his eyes danced.

"You want to go that far back, huh? Ok. He was funny, well, I think he was. He was demanding and some would say maybe a little spoiled, but he was usually quite tame in his wants. He wanted to be an explorer like Indiana Jones. He loved spaghetti and jumping in puddles. He hated baths, and boy, did he hate girls. They had germs, you know. I'd say he's come a long way since then."

I smiled as I thought about the golden haired little boy slurping Italian food and pulling pigtails.

"He sounds great. So what happened to him later? How did you end up at college studying business and economics?"

Lying back on the bed, Jared folded his arm behind his head and pulled me down to him with a sharp tug.

"Well, I stopped hating girls at about fourteen when I started seeing them more as objects of sexual arousal, rather than irritating cootie carriers. I met a girl in high school named Hannah, and at sixteen I lost my virginity in the back seat of her minivan. She dumped me that summer and moved to Oregon with her mom. I never saw her again.

"The next two years were pretty much girls, parties, and goofing off with my friends. Then at seventeen, my dad started talking about what I should do with my life, but what he meant was that he wanted me to take over the business. I didn't really have a direction. I was planning on traveling for a year, then going to college, but dad said he'd stop paying my bills unless I was taking a serious career choice. So I ended up at college until they died. That's pretty much it."

Leaning on my elbow, I gazed at him as he stared at the ceiling.

"So what about the rest of your family? You're grandma in Hawaii? Aunts? Uncles?"

He let out a long sigh, and shrugged.

"I don't have any. Grandma died when I was fifteen and my father was an only child. My grandfather had died when he was young and Grandma never remarried. I never understood when I was younger, but she always said he'd been the love of her life, and that for as long as she lived no man would ever hold her heart like he did. I thought it was crazy, but then I'd never been that deeply in love before. I was just a kid. But now…" He stroked my face with his fingertip and smiled sweetly at me. "Now I know exactly what she meant."

I held his hand to my face and pressed a kiss to palm.

"As for my mother, her family disowned her after she married my father. They were part of California's social elite, and when she fell for a small time shop owner's son, they gave her an ultimatum. She chose my dad, and they cut her off the day she said I do. I've never even met them, but I'm sure she had a sister here in Long Beach."

"You never looked for them?"

Sitting up, he pointed to the display cabinets on the far side of the room.

"You see all those awards? Well every time I got one, my mom would write back home to her folks telling them what a wonderful grandson they had. When I was born, she even tried to take me there to see them, but they wouldn't even open the driveway gates. They never wrote, called, or made any attempt to get to know me. When she died I left hundreds of messages begging them to call me, but they never even tried. I have no idea if they were even at the funeral, hell, I wouldn't be able to pick them out of a line up. So why should I bother trying to connect with people who would never even acknowledge my existence?"

Sitting up beside him I leaned my head against his shoulder. He'd had so much sadness in his life, and the thought that he had a whole family that had completely abandoned him when he needed them most made me sick to my stomach with grief.

Planting a kiss on the top of my head, he leaned his cheek into me.

"It's not all bad, Layla. I had a good childhood. My parents loved me and gave me the best start in life anyone could ever hope for. Besides, my story has a happy ending. Wanna hear it?"

Lifting my head from his shoulder, I nodded as he gazed down into my eyes. Hooking his hand beneath my chin, he lifted my face until his lips were so close I could feel his warm breath on my mouth.

"I took over the business and kept my mother's shop, turning it into a cozy little coffee house under a new name. I went in one day to get my usual cup of coffee and my life changed forever. A gorgeous, turquoise eyed blonde came crashing into my life and knocked me off my feet. She was fiery, strong, and infuriatingly stubborn. I was hooked. She stained my shirt and stole my heart right there in that shop, and I haven't been able to get her out of my mind since. She's amazing, and I've fallen head over heels in love with her. She's my happily ever after."

Launching myself into his arms, we crashed backwards onto the bed with a bounce. I kissed him passionately, murmuring between each press of my lips.

"You're mine too. I've never been so happy in my life. I love you so much."

He chuckled into my mouth and pressed his hands on either side of my head over my ears, slowing me. Taking control, he snaked his arms around my back and pulled me close, deepening our kiss. Coming up for air, I grinned down at him as a boyish smile spread across his delicious lips.

"Ok, your turn. I want to know everything. Who is Layla Jennings? Where did she come from? What does she like, hate, and everything in between. Go."

I giggled, then rolled off of his chest to lie beside him.

"Well I'd like to think I'm independent, strong-willed, and lots of fun. I grew up in Pasadena, in the same house my father now lives, and I loved it there. I was lucky enough to have the greatest friend in the world live right next door, and although my parents never had any other children, Mel is the sister I always wanted.

"My mom's a nurse and when I was growing up she spent most of her time at home with me. My dad worked in a small garage, so it meant we had to live modestly. I didn't mind that all the other kids had gadgets and gizmos and designer clothes because they hardly ever saw their parents. I got to see mine every day. We always had dinner together, and in the evenings we'd just veg out with popcorn and watch old movies. It was great.

"You already know about my love life and apart from wanting to be like Marilyn Monroe while growing up, I'd say I had a pretty standard life. Well, that was until I moved to college and started singing in bars, working in a cozy little coffee shop, and met this guy. I accidentally made him spill coffee on this shirt he was wearing, and he got all moody about it. Oh, and I may or may not have broken his nose, but boy did he act like a baby."

Rolling on top of me, Jared pinned me to the bed and ticked me relentlessly. I squirmed and shrieked as his fingers unleashed their assault on my body.

"He was a baby, huh? You sure you don't mean a total babe?"

I giggled harder as he continued to tickle me, digging into my ribs with his fingers. Wriggling out of his grasp, I kicked and rolled till I was out of his grip. Standing in front of the bed panting, I watched as his eyes took on that familiar predatory gaze. I was a gazelle caught in the sights of a lion with only one option. A mischievous smile spread across his lips.

"Oh, that's a dangerous game, Layla. If you run, I'll be forced to give chase, and you know how much I love to catch you. One way or another I'm going to get you, and when I do, oh baby."

I quickly glanced at the door before fixing my eyes on him once more. He ran his tongue over his lip and his mouth opened slightly. I could see the desire burning in his dark hooded eyes and it made me heat under his gaze. In a snap decision, I squealed and laughed breathlessly as I sprinted through the hallways and down the staircase. His feet padded heavily behind me, and as I glanced back I could see him gaining on me.

Darting through the doorways, I made it to the dining room before he cornered me. Standing on either end of the glass dining table we panted, trying to catch our breath.

"Cornered, Miss Jennings. Now, come here."

His long finger curved, beckoning me to go to him. Approaching the table, I lifted my knee high and climbed on top. His eyebrow shot up as he watched me crawl sexily and seductively across the glass towards him.

A low growl rumbled in his throat as I rose up placing myself less than an inch from him. My lips parted slightly, and I breathed gently on his lips.

"Oh you really are a tempting little siren. How the hell did I get so lucky?"

Gripping his hands on my ass, he swept my feet from beneath me and gently laid me on the cool glass. Lying on top of me, his hand slid up my thigh as the other continued its vice like grip on my behind. A vibrating in my pocket startled us.

"Is that a vibrator in your pocket, or are you just happy to see me?"

I laughed and pushed him off of me as I sat upright, digging my cell from my pocket.

Lifting a finger to him indicating that he give me a minute, I answered the cell, earning me a roll of his eyes.

"Hey, Amy."

"Layla, did you know it's Ollie's birthday?"

Confused, I glanced at Jared who was now sitting in one of the sleek black dining room chairs, watching me with a finger pressed to his lips.

"Are you sure? I had no idea. How did you find out?"

"Some guy came by looking for him and asked me to give him a message. He said he was Ollie's brother, and that he needed to talk to him about their parents and that I should wish him a happy birthday. Why wouldn't he tell us it's his birthday?"

I paused for a moment as I turned over the feeling of uneasiness I felt about Ollie's brother seeking him out over their father. He must have heard about him being in prison and their mother searching for Ollie.

"I can't believe his birthday is the day before mine. I have no idea why he'd keep it a secret."

"Maybe he didn't want to steal your thunder. We're going to do something though, right?"

"Of course we are! Ok, so we're at the bar tonight as usual, so we'll turn it into a birthday party. Here's what we'll do. You go get Nick, Eric, and whoever else you can muster from the dorm to the bar. I'll pick up a cake and we'll go halves on a gift? I have just the thing in mind."

Amy squeaked with excitement, and I had to hold the phone away from my ear to stop her perforating my ear drum. "This is so much fun! A surprise party for Ollie! I'll see you at the bar in three hours?"

I risked a chance look at Jared before answering. "Yeah, see you in three hours."

Placing my cell on the table, I scooted off the edge and over to the hot piece of ass brooding in the corner. Straddling his lap, I took his hands and wrapped them around my waist.

303

"Jared, I know how you feel about Ollie, but I really think you would feel differently if you got to know him. It's his birthday, so we're all going to Benny's bar to celebrate. I would really, really love it if you would come meet everyone."

"Layla, I really don't think…"

Frowning, he ran his hand through his hair, but I caught his wrist and threaded our fingers together. It was his anxiety tick and he needed to break the habit. "Please? I really can't stand the way you two hate each other like this. He's my friend, and you're the man I love. Please, for me?"

Leaning forward, I placed a soft chaste kiss on his lips. He groaned in defeat, and I knew I had won.

"Alright. For you I'll come. But I am only doing this to make you happy. You know I'd do anything to see you smile. Just don't expect us to be best friends because it won't happen."

Pleased with my victory, I grinned, jumped off his lap, and did a little dance in celebration. Chuckling, he stood and slapped me on the behind playfully.

"Behave yourself. You keep wiggling that sexy little ass in front of my face like that and we'll never make it there. Come on, I'll drive you to the mall so you can pick up a cake and a gift. You know what you're getting him, right? We're not gonna have to traipse around for an hour?"

I smiled.

"I know exactly what to get him. There's a music store in your mall, right?"

Chapter 31

One Tequila, Two Tequila, Three Tequila, Floor

Entering the bar, I grinned as I saw dozens of students from the dorm drinking, laughing and talking together. Amy had managed to get almost every member of our building to come, just to celebrate Ollie's birthday. Jared clutched my hand tightly and carried Ollie's gift wrapped present in the other. Leaning into my ear, he groaned.

"Are you serious? This is where you hang out?" Rolling my eyes, I had to balance the cake box steadily in one hand as Jared had insisted he was not letting go of the other one all night. Scanning the area where our usual table stood, I spotted Amy as she waved at me enthusiastically.

We made our way over, and after greeting us with a hug and peck on my cheek, she took the box from me and carried it off to the bar. I looked around for the guest of honor and noticed Ollie near the stage, talking to a couple of guys I recognized from our psych class. He hadn't noticed me come in yet which I was silently grateful for. I wanted to introduce him to Jared properly which meant at least giving him a heads up that he was even in the building. Amy returned to the table with a pitcher and three glasses.

"I didn't know what you drank Jared, so I thought beer would be perfect."

Raising his voice so that he would be heard over the crowd he smiled.

"I'm pretty sure you ladies aren't old enough to be drinking."

Giggling, she shrugged. "My father still thinks I'm a virgin. Some things are more fun when done in secret, I guess."

I stifled a laugh as he arched an eyebrow at her amused. Pecking him on the cheek, I took the gift from him and indicated I'd be back in a moment.

As I walked away, I watched as Amy pulled him down to sit beside her, and began introducing him to Nick and Eric. Ollie had finished talking and was now striding towards me quickly. Scooping me into a tight hug, he twirled me around and kissed my cheek.

"You are the best fucking friend in the world. I can't believe you did all of this for me!"

I grinned and glanced at Jared who was watching Ollie with a clenched jaw.

"Why didn't you tell us it was your birthday? We only found out after Amy saw your brother. Did you get a chance to speak with him?"

Shrugging, he brushed off my question. "No and I'm not going to." Gripping his injured palm into a fist, he frowned at it. "Let's not get into all of that tonight, ok? It's my birthday."

Nodding, I handed him the bright red package and smiled. "Happy Birthday, Oliver."

Tearing off the paper, he gasped and stared at me in shock. Stroking his bandaged hand up and down the long tight strings of his new guitar, he grinned. White with a black panel in the center, it had been marked with his name on the bottom curve.

"Oh my god, Layla. It's beautiful. It must have cost a fortune. How did you pay for this?"

"I didn't. Well, not alone. It's from me and Amy. Do you like it?"

"Like it? I fucking love it!" Holding it in one hand, he threw his arms around me again and whispered in my ear. "Layla, about the photo-"

I shook my head and gave him a gentle shove.

"It's fine. Another time alright?" He nodded and pressed his lips into a firm line. "Ollie, I brought Jared here tonight. I'd really love it if you two could meet properly. I don't expect you to be best buddies, but I would like if you would at least be civil for my sake. Will you come meet him, please?"

Taking a deep breath, he frowned at me before rolling his eyes. "Alright. You know I'd do anything for you. Where is he so that we can get this over with, and I can go back to getting hammered?"

The air was tense as we approached the table. Jared was on his feet before we even got near and immediately snaked a possessive arm around my waist. Ignoring his attempt to mark his territory, I introduced the two guys and held my breath as they stood sizing each other up. Holding out his hand, Jared made the first move and after glancing at my hopeful face, Ollie accepted. Letting out the breath I was holding, I sighed in relief.

"So, Layla tells me you play?"

Lifting his guitar slightly, he gave Jared a look that suggested "well, duh", but thankfully kept the sarcasm to himself and never actually said it. Glaring at him, I mouthed a warning.

"Be nice."

"Uh, yeah, since I was a kid. But Layla's the superstar. She made her debut right there on that stage."

He nodded at the empty stage across the bar and I smiled to myself, remembering the performance I'd made the first time we'd come to Benny's.

Grinning, Jared gazed down at me. "Really? I would love to see that."

Ollie took my hand and smiled enthusiastically. "We should do it, Layla! I'll get to fire up this little baby, Amy can play piano, and the guys can play drums and bass. Come on. Call it a birthday concert for me. Besides, Jared wants to see your awesome talent firsthand."

Jared's eyes travelled to where Ollie's thumb was currently brushing back and forth across my knuckles. Pulling my hand away quickly, I smiled nervously.

"I don't know, Ollie. I mean, I think it was a once in a lifetime performance. Besides, Amy doesn't want to do all that again."

"Amy doesn't want to do what?" That girl has hearing like a sonar system, I swear.

"Layla won't sing with us and says you're not up to playing piano tonight."

Almost hitting us as her drink sprayed out of her mouth, Amy jumped up and down enthusiastically.

"Are you freaking kidding me? Of course, I'll play and Layla will sing! Won't you Layla?" She stared me down as a silent understanding passed between the two of us.

Comprehending immediately what she was saying, I nodded and rolled my eyes. "Ok, I'll sing. But I get to choose the song. Agreed?"

Both she and Ollie accepted my terms, and before I knew it they were hustling Nick and Eric onto the stage to set up.

I looked up at Jared as he wound his arms around my back. "See, I can play nicely. I didn't spring over the booth to strangle him when he hugged you, I didn't shatter his jaw when he kissed your cheek, and I didn't break his fingers when he held your hand. You must appreciate how hard that was for me, Layla."

Sliding my hands around his neck, I pulled him to me and covered his mouth with my own for a kiss. "I do appreciate it, and later I'll make sure to show you my appreciation. Now if you don't mind, I have to go be a superstar now. Come be my groupie?"

Grinning like a Cheshire cat, he followed me to the stage and stood amongst the crowd. Turning to my new band, I told them what we were playing, and since the song didn't require a piano, I asked Amy to be my back up singer. Turns out the girls lungs weren't just there to support her endless talking.

Tapping the mic, I stood anxiously and stared into the sea of faces currently fixed on me. Finally, I saw Jared and my whole body relaxed. Smiling, I introduced us.

"Hi everyone, I'm Layla and these guys are D.O.A. Now usually Ollie would be the one standing where I am, but since it's his birthday I promised one performance, so this song is one of my favorites and tonight it goes out to a very special man in my life."

Gazing down at Jared I smiled as Nick began drumming the intro to "This Kiss" by Faith Hill.

Grasping the mic, stand I sang my heart out. I wasn't singing for Ollie. I wasn't singing for the crowd. I was singing for Jared, and as our eyes locked on each other the whole room seemed to fade away until all that was left was him and me.

His smile was bigger than I'd ever seen it, and his eyes glistened and sparkled as he watched me. I thought my heart would explode with the happiness that was flowing like a tsunami inside me. Butterflies swirled like a tornado, and the adrenaline that pumped through my veins made me feel like I could conquer the world.

Amy's voice alongside mine sounded as though we were made to sing together, and the cheers from the crowd as we finished were deafening. Wrapping me in a tight hug, Amy whispered in my ear, "I'd say operation serenade was a success. He definitely knows how you feel now."

I hugged her back as Ollie wrapped his arms around us both in a group hug. Kissing each of us on the head, he grinned. "You guys were awesome, you totally rock!"

Holding his hand up, we each gave him a high five. Turning my attention back to the dispersing crowd, I spotted Jared at the edge of the stage. Holding his arms out to me, he lifted me down and twirled me around, kissing me deeply and with loving tenderness. "

You were amazing. I loved it. I love you." I blushed shamelessly, still grinning from my performance. Through his eyes, I felt like a real star.

And the Grammy goes to...

* * * *

As the drinks flowed, the tension between Jared and Ollie softened a little, but I was more than aware that this was a temporary truce for my benefit. Once the night was over, things would return to the way they were, and I would once again be stuck between a rock star and a hard, hot sex god. Jared was my constant companion all night, and I could hardly breathe without him scrutinizing my actions. Even going to the bathroom became a group activity, with Amy and me using the ladies room while he stood vigilant outside the door. Though, in her current inebriated state, I was glad to have someone there to hold her up for me if needed.

"What ish hisss problem? Does he think you're going to be abducted from the stall or something? Jeesh, Layla. And have you seen the way he and Ollie keep giving each other daggers across the table when they think no one is looking. Gives me the creeps. You're living dangerously tonight, girl."

Shaking my head at her slurring, and washing my hands, I gave her a puzzled look. I'd thought things were going well, at least for now anyway.

Emerging from the bathroom, I gave Jared an exasperated look and swiftly breezed past him back to the booth. I felt like a child with a babysitter who was making sure I didn't stay up too late, or eat too much junk food.

Giving Ollie a gentle nudge, and encouraging him to make some space, I slid in next to him. Jared glared at me as he took the seat directly opposite. Gripping his glass of bourbon tightly, he downed it and slammed it back onto the table. Ollie gazed down at me and gave me a quizzical look. I shook my head and aimed a half-hearted smile at him.

"Not now."

Draping his arm around my shoulder, and giving me a peck on the cheek, he grinned and whispered into my ear, "Bit uptight, isn't he? Feel threatened, does he?"

Glancing at Jared, I could see the fire flickering in his eyes. He was livid. Standing quickly, he shook his head at me slowly in warning and stalked over to the bar.

I glowered at Ollie. Removing his arm from my shoulder, I shoved him, pissed at his stunt.

"Why do you have to push his buttons, Ollie? This was meant to be a nice evening where the two of you could be civil and at least pretend to get along. What happened to doing this for me?"

"He doesn't deserve you, Layla. You deserve better. I mean, Christ, the guy follows you to the fucking bathroom like he's your mother or something."

Scooting out of my seat, I picked up my glass and emptied it into his lap.

He hissed and growled at me. "What the fuck, Layla?"

Fisting my hands on my hips, I gave him a furious stare.

"No, Ollie. You think I deserve you. Well I'm sorry, but I've made my choice and you're going to have to accept it. Now I have to go do damage control."

Turning on my heel, I walked over to Jared who was leaning his elbows on the bar and swirling a drink in his hand. Placing a hand on his shoulder, I stood at his side and gently took the drink from his grasp, placing it back on the bar. He stared ahead, avoiding my gaze.

"He's trying my patience, Layla. I don't know how much more I can take. I'm this fucking close to ramming my fist into his mouth and tearing out his vocal chords. I'd like to see him whisper in your ear then."

Rubbing my hands over my face, I took a deep breath. "You know what? I can't excuse what he did, and I've dealt with it. He knows he was out of line, and I've made it clear that I will not let him do that a second time because I'll break his damn fingers myself. I'm yours. He can put his arm around me, whisper in my ear, and even kiss my cheek, but in the end it's you I climb into bed with. You have my heart, Jared, completely and totally. Don't punish me for this. It's not fair."

Turning to face me, his eyebrows furrowed together, marring his handsome face. Closing his eyes tightly as though in pain, his shoulders sagged and he sighed loudly. Opening them again, he stood up straight and gazed down at me. The piercing blue in his eyes was hypnotic and I could have easily lost myself in them for days. Taking my hand from his shoulder, he held it in his own, dragging his thumb back and forth over my knuckles.

"I'm not punishing you, baby. I'm just struggling with this. He loves you, Layla. It's in his eyes when he looks at you. Every time I turn around he's gazing at you and I can see it. I should know. It's exactly how I feel every minute of every day. He wants you, and I'm terrified that one day you're going to choose him. I couldn't take it, Layla. I'm close to the breaking point, and that fucker pushing every button I have. He needs to get it into his thick head that you're mine and that I won't let you go without a fight."

Stepping closer to him, I cupped his face in my hands. "I will say this one last time, Jared, and then I never want to talk about this ever again. I love you. I don't care if every man in this room is in love with me because I love you. I don't want anyone else. Ever. You're my future now, and there is no force on earth that could change how I feel about us, or keep me from you. I will only ever want you for the rest of my life."

Breathing hard, he pressed his forehead against mine while still clasping my hands in his. "I can't help feeling possessive over you, Layla. You're the most valuable thing in my life and I won't share you with anyone, ever. You're everything to me. I'd kill for you. I'd give up everything I own just to keep you. You're my whole universe and I couldn't exist without you."

"You won't ever have to. I'm not going anywhere."

His arms enveloped me in a warm embrace as he kissed me. Pulling me to him tightly, our kiss deepened and lingered. The gentleness of his lips paired with the ferocious lashings of his tongue in my mouth stirred my senses, and a soft moan escaped my lips.

A tap on my shoulder pulled me from my ecstasy. Turning around, I saw a very drunk Amy.

"Oh, you two are soooo cute! Layla, I'm starving! Can we go eat somewhere?" She stumbled in her heels, and Jared caught her in his arms just before she crashed into a bar stool.

"Whoa there girl. I think maybe you should eat something, soak up that alcohol. I'll walk you both back to the dorm, and we'll find somewhere for Amy to get something deep fried and greasy to eat on the way."

I nodded in agreement as I hoisted her arm over my shoulder to hold her up. "Oh, Layla, I love you sooooo much. You're my best friend. I've never had one before."

Pressing her palm to my face, she turned me towards her and planted a big wet smacker on my lips. Jared immediately fell into hysterics as I wiped my mouth with the back of my hand.

"Not so fast, pretty boy. You need to hold onto the other side, or she's going to fall over in these heels." That stopped him laughing.

"You're kidding, right? What if she hurls?"

I grinned back at him. "Well it's that, or haul her over your shoulder and carry her." He groaned, but grabbed Amy's other arm, and we slowly made our way to the exit.

Pushing our way outside, we'd only gotten about two feet away from the door when Ollie yelled behind us.

"Hey, where you going?"

He ran to catch up, then walked beside us as we practically dragged Amy along the sidewalk. I caught sight of his wet pants and smiled to myself. The liquid had seeped into his light denim jeans, making them darken around his crotch. Catching my line of sight, Jared sniggered at him.

"Huh, got a little over excited in there, did we?"

Glancing at Jared, Ollie shrugged. "No, some bitches just can't hold their drinks. Literally."

I gave him a disapproving look in response to his sarcasm.

"Amy's really drunk, and she needs to soak up some of this alcohol. We're going to get some food, then head back to the dorm."

Grabbing Amy's arm from around my neck, and hoisting it over his own, he eyed Jared coolly. "Seems pointless all of us going. Why don't you let me help, then he can head home. I can take care of them, dude."

Jared's feet came to an abrupt halt, and he glared at Ollie.

"Two things. One, I am not your dude, and two, there is no chance in hell I am leaving Layla alone with you and her drunk friend."

Ollie stifled a laugh. "Well, she's going to be alone with me eventually, bro. We're in the same class, she lives across the hall, and we're also friends. These girls are perfectly safe with me. I'd never let anything happen to them."

He winked at me playfully, and I took in a sharp breath as Jared's free hand clenched into a fist tightly beside him. He was trying devastatingly hard to restrain his anger. I was all too aware how ugly things could get if Ollie didn't back off soon. Jared's jaw tightened and he practically snarled at him.

"It's what you want to do to Layla that grinds my gears, *bro*."

The way he said the word 'bro' gave me the distinct impression that his feelings towards Ollie were as far from brotherly as humanly possible. The look on his face was murderous, and if he could have willed it, Ollie would have suffered a fatal heart attack right on the spot.

"Let's not pretend, huh? You want her, and you hate me for getting her. Well hard fucking luck because I am never giving her up, prick."

Ollie almost dropped Amy as he made a step in Jared's direction.

Frustrated, cold, hungry and pissed off I couldn't take it anymore. "Will you both just shut up? I really don't have the patience for your bitching right now. Either you both help me get her sober and into bed, or you can both go and Amy will be the only one alone with me!"

Directing my anger at Jared, I could see I'd made my point. With a wounded look on his face, he looked like a child who'd just been told Santa wasn't real, and my anger was suddenly disintegrating as I looked into his big, blue eyes. Letting go of my irritated mood, and putting him out of his misery, I gave him a reassuring smile. He smiled back before returning his attention to my beer stained crotched friend. Glaring at one another, and through gritted teeth they conceded, answering simultaneously, "Fine."

We walked in silence along the street, searching for anywhere that was still serving food. Since Ollie had taken Amy from me, he and Jared were now holding her so well that her feet barely touched the ground. Listening to her singing a song only she seemed to know the lyrics to, I laughed to myself at the scene I was currently taking part in. My boyfriend on one side, the man who wants to steal me from him on the other, and my intoxicated roommate between them. It sounded like a sketch from a sitcom, but this was my reality.

Spotting a Mexican fast food shop across the street, Ollie yelled at me, "I think we should find something there to feed her. To be honest, I don't think she'll make it anywhere else before she's asleep."

He was right. Amy was well on her way to a booze induced ten hour coma. Nodding in agreement, I crossed the street to the shop and got her three of the greasiest burrito's they served. Jared and Ollie had sat Amy on a bench just outside and were propping her up when I approached them.

Squatting in front of her, I placed the food in her lap and watched as she devoured it quickly. The guys' expressions ranged from shock to pride as she ate her way through all three in less than ten minutes. I could smell the spicy chili peppers on her breath as she belched loudly. Ollie and Jared found it highly hilarious, but I'd simply rolled my eyes and waited for them to heave her up again. I spent the rest of the journey, just praying that she wouldn't throw up on herself because that was something I did not want to be clearing up.

"What the hell was she drinking tonight, Ollie? The only thing I saw her drink was beer. She can't have gotten this bad with just a few glasses of beer."

"Well, there was the beer, and Eric gave her some of his bourbon. Oh, and Nick helped her polish off an entire bottle of Tequila."

My head snapped round at him, and I stalked over and prodded him in the chest. "You let her drink all that? Are you crazy? Jesus Christ, Ollie! She's a tiny little woman! She could have got alcohol poisoning! How could you be so irresponsible?"

Amy groaned, and I hurriedly checked her over, making sure she hadn't passed out. A slight smile grazed her lips, and I exhaled loudly with relief. "You really are a totally stupid dick sometimes, Ollie. You're supposed to be her friend."

"I did try and stop her! Have you ever tried to stop Amy once she's on a roll? It'd be easier getting a junkie to let go of his crack pipe. She's fucking impossible. Besides, Nick was taking care of her. They disappeared into the bathroom for, like, thirty minutes. I'm not her fucking keeper, Layla."

Jared chuckled and I glared at him in warning. He was enjoying my argument with Ollie a little too much, and I wasn't in the mood for his snide jokes or comments. "Just get her home, fast, so I can take care of her properly like a friend is supposed to."

Jared shook his head. "I don't understand how she was even able to get served all that alcohol."

I knew how.

"Amy has two weapons in her arsenal. One, get Nick who is twenty-one years old to buy it for her, or two, flash enough cleavage and skin at Greg, the twenty-three year old bartender, so that he gets all flushed and serves her."

He gave me a disapproving look.

"No, I don't drink. So stop giving me that look. I do not go flashing at bartenders to get served."

The corner of his mouth curved up. "Good girl."

Oh sweet mercy. Those two words had the distinct ability to make me clench on demand.

Heaving Amy through our bedroom door, Ollie and Jared groaned as she drooped and slid from their arms and onto her bed. I sighed with exhaustion, knowing that I was in for a restless night while taking care of her. I was still pissed at Ollie for allowing her to get into that state, but I had to agree, when Amy set her mind to something, she was hell bent on doing it.

Kneeling beside her bed, I brushed the hair from her face and rubbed my thumb over her cheek, removing a dried up piece of burrito in the process. Ollie snorted behind me, and I shot him an irritated look. Jared had taken it upon himself to get comfortable and was lying on my bed, staring at him.

"You two should go, I need to get her undressed, and I don't think she'd appreciate an audience."

Glancing first at me, then back to Ollie, Jared shook his head. "I'm not going anywhere. I'll step outside while you see to her, but I'm staying right here all night in case you need help."

I'd heard his words, but I could also hear everything he wasn't saying. Still aiming his daggers at Ollie, Jared wasn't giving him the privilege, or the opportunity to be alone with me tonight. Fed up with the tension between them, and mentally and emotionally exhausted, I snapped. Marching over to Ollie who was leaning against the open door and watching Jared with an icy stare, I turned him around and pushed him all the way to his own door.

"Layla what are you doing? I'm not leaving you and Amy alone with him. He looks like he might murder someone. You see the look in his eyes?"

"Yes, Ollie, you put it there. The person he will kill is you! You've been purposely overstepping the boundaries all night just to wind him up, and you've finally succeeded. Thanks a billion for that! Just go to bed and I'll talk to you in the morning."

Turning to face me, he raised his hands defensively. "Alright, alright I can take a hint. God, lover boy sure looks pissed, huh?" He stifled a laugh, but I wasn't in the mood for his bullshit.

"Ollie, shut up. God, you're determined to make this hard for me, aren't you?"

"That's what I should be saying to you, isn't it?"

Groaning with frustration, I opened his door and shoved him into his room. He stumbled backwards and gave me a playful grin, wiggling his eyebrows up and down suggestively. Rolling my eyes, I exhaled loudly.

"Goodnight, Oliver. Oh, and happy birthday." Closing the door before he could say anything else, I chewed on my bottom lip anxiously as I headed back into my room.

Jared's expression was fierce. Striding over, he slammed the door behind me.

"I mean it, Layla, one more fucking stunt like that and I'm going to kill him. The only reason he's still breathing is because I promised you that tonight I would be civil and control my temper. The moment this night is over, all bets are off and his ass is mine if he so much as breathes on you. I'm serious, Layla. I will not have that fucking little monkey trying to climb my tree! You're mine and he needs to get used to it."

I giggled.

"Your tree? The only wood around here usually comes from you. Seriously, Jared, you need to stop worrying about Ollie. He's just pushing your buttons, and the more you rise to it, the more he'll do it. Relax. I'm all yours."

Pressing my body against his, I grazed my hands over his broad chest and over his shoulders. My mouth partially open, I breathed heavily, my chest rising and falling, pushing my breasts into his muscular pecs. He swallowed hard as my favorite pleasure toy sprung to attention against my thigh. I liked teasing him; it made me feel powerful, sexy and tempting. My hands slid around to his back and I gently dragged my nails over his thin cotton shirt, down either side of his spine. He gasped as I gripped his buttocks tightly in my hands.

Amy snorted and I cast my eye back to discover that she was snoring loudly. There was no way I was going to get her undressed, now that she was officially passed out cold. I turned my attention back to the hot piece of ass I had currently grasped in my hands. His eyes darkened and I knew he wanted me, right there, urgently and passionately. I felt exactly the same, and as a low growl escaped his lips, my insides clenched deliciously.

Lifting me up, he wrapped my legs around his waist and kissed me fervently, pulling off my shoes and supporting my back with the other hand. Kicking open the bathroom door, he carried me in and backed into the door, closing it behind us. My mouth covered his as I rocked and writhed in his arms, rubbing myself against him. His tongue thrashed and rolled around my mouth and I could taste the bitter remainder of bourbon in his kiss.

Returning me to my feet, he made light work of my clothes, tearing them from my body and leaving me in only my Victoria's Secret lace bra and panties as I hurriedly unbuckled his jeans and pulled down his zipper. They hung loosely on his hips as I fumbled with his shirt buttons, desperate to run my hands over his hot caramel flesh. Backing away, I leaned against the cold porcelain basin and devoured him with my eyes. Pulling the cuffs of his shirt over his hands, he tossed it on the floor as his eyes travelled from my face all the way to my toes, lingering a while on the hefty curves of my breasts. I gazed at the deep V at his hips that led temptingly into his shorts. They really were becoming one of my favorite parts of his body.

The tables turned and now I was the predator and he was my prey. Gracefully, I stalked around him, licking my lips as my eyes roamed over his exquisite physique. Dipping my fingers into the back of his jeans, I slowly slipped my fingertips into the waist line of his shorts while hooking my thumbs through the loops in his pants. In one quick move, I sank to my feet behind him and pulled them down in one swoop. I gasped as my eyes came face to face with my name.

Mouth wide open, I rose to my feet and walked around to face him.

"I see you found my little surprise."

How could I miss it? How did I miss it in the tub earlier today? He'd been sitting behind me, and when he'd climbed out so quickly he'd faced me, shielding it from view, so this was a total shock.

"Do you like it?"

Words failed me as I continued to stand there, gawking at him. "I got it in New York. An old college buddy of mine has a shop there and I had him do it." I shook my head in amazement and quickly turned him around to look at it again, almost unable to believe what I was seeing. Right there, carved into the flesh of his left buttock, was my name. The elegant and stylish lettering was deeply black against his perfect skin, and part of me was mortified that he had permanently etched my name into his body while the other was thrilled. It was like a public declaration of his love for me, except a little less public and a little more under-cover.

"Why?" The question left my lips before I'd even thought about what the answer might be. Facing me, he chuckled. "It was something you said, actually. Something about me owning your ass. So now you literally own mine, too."

I pressed my hand over my mouth, still unable to absorb the shock of my discovery. A muffled laugh escaped my mouth, stifled by my hand.

"Do you like it?"

Grinning I gazed up at him, seeing the happiness, hope and humor in his eyes as he stared back at me.

"Like it? I freaking love it! In fact I think I need a better look. Turn around." Stepping out of his pants and shorts, he turned his back to me and leaned into his hip. Dropping to my knees I ran my fingertips over the beautiful lettering and smiled as goose bumps appeared over his smooth skin. Teasingly, I dragged my nails over the ink before sinking my teeth into the flesh around it. My persistent urge to bite into Jared's flesh was so disturbing; it was bordering on odaxelagnia, my own biting fetish.

"Hey, behave yourself back there! I'm still a little sore. You carry on like that and I'll make your own ass so sore you won't sit for a week."

Rising to my feet, I turned him to face me and grinned wickedly. "Promise?"

Catching my hands in his, he held them tightly in his palm as he ripped the belt from his jeans that were lying on the floor. Holding my wrists together firmly, he began to secure the leather around them. Once satisfied that I was adequately restrained, he drove me back against the door, and lifted my bound hands over my head.

"Don't. Move."

His voice was forceful and the anticipation of what he was about to do to me was overwhelming. Surrendering control to Jared was thrilling and surprisingly easy for me to do. Having never lost control in my life, this was a new experience for me. Just as it had been with the red satin ribbon in the bedroom, my body became a hot, lust filled and chaotic mess. His hands trailed down my arms slowly, tickling my skin as they glided downwards to my breasts. His fingertips traced the lines of my cleavage before snaking around my back and releasing the clasp. With my hands bound together, it would be impossible for him to remove my bra, or so I thought.

 Gripping the straps tightly, he ripped the delicate material from my skin. I feigned incense. "Mr. Garrett, did you know that was my favorite bra? It was a sexy gift from my lover. I'm appalled that you have now destroyed it."

Grasping my breasts, he massaged tenderly as he pressed me harder against the door. "I'm a man of little patience, Layla. I'll buy you a hundred of the little things plus lots, lots more. Now keep still."

Still holding my hands stretched high above my head I wriggled as his hands left my breasts and moved achingly slowly across my stomach, before skimming over the curve of my hips to my panties. Pinning me against the door, he slid his thumbs into the waistline of the garment and pushed them down so that they glided silkily over my thighs to the floor. Pulling me to him, he wrapped one strong muscular arm around my waist and lifted me slightly off the floor, brushing my lace panties away with his foot. I giggled as my back slid up the door and my bound hands almost touched the low ceiling. Grinning at me, Jared kissed me, instantly silencing my laughter. His lips were so soft that they reminded me of silk as they pressed lovingly against mine.

A rush of emotion washed over me and without thinking I lowered my arms around his head. Pulling away and releasing me, he licked his lips and lowered his head, shaking it slowly.

"I told you to stay still. Come here to me, Layla."

Cautiously, I walked over to him. His eyes were full of sensual promise and it left me wonderfully exhilarated. My body was scorching hot with arousal. An aching throb had settled between my legs and I was desperate for him to relieve me of the pleasurable clenching inside. My clit was hyper sensitive, and as I walked the friction between my legs was blissful.

I stood perfectly still in front of him. We'd both confessed to not being into S&M, but somehow I'd submitted to him entirely, without even noticing. My hands were tied, and I obeyed his every command, eager for the kinky and erotic pleasures he had in store for me. He'd introduced me into a whole new world of sexual satisfaction, and I was hungry for more.

His lips and tip of his tongue grazed my jaw, barely touching my wanting and warm skin. I whimpered in frustration. I needed his hands, lips and body on mine. I wanted him deep inside me, filling me to the brim with his milky white love potion.

"Put your hands on the edge of the sink and bend over."

My heart skipped a beat at the promise in his words. I wanted to please him, entice and arouse him, and as I leaned over the porcelain, I could feel his erection pressing hard into my behind. He was as solid as a rock and I wanted nothing more than to turn around, grab him, and suck on my favorite Jared flavored popsicle. But the look in his eyes kept me motionless as they gazed at me in the mirror. Bending over me, he whispered in my ear. His hot breath made me hitch a breath of my own and my heartbeat raced.

"Remember, baby. Coffee, anytime."

The safe word! What was he going to do? Why would I need it? I suddenly felt a little apprehensive, but reminding myself that I was with a man that loved me right through to my bones, I tried to calm myself by taking a deep breath.

"It'll be ok. You trust me?"

I nodded weakly. Inside, I was scalding hot with fiery excitement and expectancy.

Our eyes met in the mirror as his hand glided and rubbed against the pale skin on my behind. It was sensual and my body instantly relaxed as he palmed my cheek in his warm strong hand. A loud crack stunned me as a tingling and stinging bit into my soft flesh. I struggled for air as I attempted to comprehend what I was feeling. The warm sting on my skin was both painful and pleasant simultaneously.

"Again?"

He was giving me the chance to stop this and a sane person might have begged for him to release them, but I was a huge bundle of sizzling lust and the need for more overruled my need for sanity. Barely able to form a coherent sentence, I whispered. "Yes. Again, please."

His hand rubbed the sore and hurt area of my skin before striking it once more. The palm of his hand held firmly on my buttock, I panted, my sex dripping, salivating as my arousal grew stronger and fiercer.

"Again, Jared. Do it again."

Watching him in the mirror, I saw the fire in his eyes as a delicious grin appeared on his plump, pink lips.

I could feel the tip of his cock brushing against the opening of my sex and I couldn't help myself as I pushed my ass back, forcing him to slide inside me. I heard him hitch a breath as my hips rocked against him, pressing him further and further, deeper into me. He moaned loudly and his breathing was now as erratic as my own. Slowly pushing himself in and out of me, his hand left my buttock and I held my breath, waiting for the next blow. Never one to disappoint, he slammed his palm onto my behind as he surged inside me hard and forceful. I cried out as my insides clenched and convulsed around his long hard cock.

"Ah! Fuck."

The sensations I was experiencing all at once were entirely new, and completely orgasmic. My body tingled and shivered as sweat poured from my skin. Frantically pounding into me before gently pulling out, Jared moaned, groaned and gasped in my ear as he leaned forward and slid his hand between my thighs. His skilled fingers caressed and massaged my tender clit. My hands gripped tightly to the rim of the sink as my legs began to give way beneath me. Holding me tightly, Jared kept me up against him as his hips grinded against mine. My head lowered, I gasped for air as my orgasm built rapidly and temptingly closer.

His fingertips moved faster at varying pressures and I moaned and writhed in his hand. I was gripping the sink so hard I could have snapped a piece clean as he rammed into me harder, hissing through his teeth and groaning loudly against my ear. I could smell his cologne and the heavenly scent of jasmine and lavender oil that had seeped into his skin during our bath. His hand slid from my waist to my breast, kneading and fondling it gently while rolling my pert and sensitive nipple between his fingers and sending shock waves through my body to my sex.

"Oh, baby, you are so tight. You drive me crazy. Your scent, your delicate skin and the wonderful way your body responds to my every touch. I'd go insane without it." I could feel the muscles inside spasm and pulse.

"I need to see you. I need to be looking into your gorgeous eyes when you come for me. You're so fucking hot!"

I barely heard him through the hammering of my heart beating in my ears. Swiftly and effortlessly he released me and spun me around to face him. Hoisting me up, he sat me on the edge of the counter, lifting my bound hands over his head, and hooking them around his neck.

"Beg me, Layla."

I could hardly breathe let alone form words.

His hand pressed hard against my sex as he palmed my clit.

"Do you want to come?"

I nodded.

"Then beg me for it. You drove me fucking crazy tonight with that prick, and now you're going to make it up to me. Beg me to give this to you."

I whimpered as he continued to rub and stroke me. "Please, Jared. I'm sorry. Please."

"You're sorry? What are you sorry for?"

I jolted as he pressed harder with his hand. "For tonight. For Ollie. For making you jealous. Please, Jared."

Please what? What do you want, Layla? What do you need?"

"Fuck me. I need you to fuck me. Now!"

Grinning, he pressed his lips to mine. "Good girl."

Wrapping my legs around his waist, he pushed into me again and resumed his endless and harried thrusts into my wanting sex.

"Don't come, Layla. That's an order."

I stared at him in disbelief as my body shook with tension. My orgasm was building rapidly, and I was powerless to stop it.

"I can't. I'm so close."

He instantly withdrew, and I groaned with frustration.

"Don't come until I say you can. Understand?"

I nodded. I was desperate. I'd have agreed to anything just to get him back inside me.

"Answer me. If you come before I say so there will be consequences. Do you understand?"

My voice was hoarse and breathless.

"Yes. I understand."

Slipping back inside me, he thrashed and slammed against me. My body jolted, and my head fell back as pleasure vibrated through me. The tightness of the belt was pinching and jabbing into my wrist, but I didn't care. I was hot for him, and he was driving me over the edge into a sea of deep sexual gratification.

Panting, his hand held the back of my head and he lifted it so that our eyes met. "Look at me, baby. I want to see you and feel you let go."

I was so close it was painful. "Please, Jared, I can't hold on."

Grinning, he nipped gently on my earlobe. "Come with me. Now."

Those few uttered words were enough to push me off the edge and into a blissful oblivion. I cried out, clinging to his body as tightly as I could with my arms still hooked around his neck. My orgasm surged and pulsed through me, making me moan as he slammed into me, hissing, gasping and growling through his own intense orgasm.

My body weakened, and I sat there limp as I tried to calm my ragged and uncontrollable breathing. Resting his forehead against mine, he panted and trailed soft kisses all over my face.

"Good girl."

I smiled with satisfaction, closing my eyes and surrendering to the loving and sensual touch of his soft lips.

"God, you're beautiful. How did I ever get so lucky? I feel like my heart's going to explode from pure happiness. I've never loved anyone so much in my entire life. I can never lose you Layla. I wouldn't survive it, my heart would never recover." Brushing his nose with mine, I smiled. "You'll never lose me, Jared. I'm yours for as long as you want me. I love you too." His mouth closed over mine, kissing me sweetly as though it were our last.

An awful heaving sound diverted me from our post-coital cocoon and I realized Amy was vomiting. Cringing at the thought of cleaning it up, I looked regretfully at Jared.

"I'd better go clean her up. Would you mind?"

Unhooking my arms from his neck, I held my leather bound wrists in front of him. Grinning, he untied me and rubbed my red and sore wrists gently with his thumbs. He stared at the red marks on my pale wrists and frowned deeply.

"Does it hurt?"

Shaking my head I smiled. "No. But my ass is a little sore."

"Sorry. I got carried away."

Pressing my finger to his lip, I silenced him. "Shhh. Don't ever apologize for giving me what I asked for. I never asked you to stop, Jared. I enjoyed it, in fact, I freaking loved it. You can certainly do that to me again sometime."

Lifting me from the sink, he wrapped his arms around me, holding me in a warm hug. Happiness radiated from my body as he kissed the top of my head and sighed. I heard Amy heave again, and Jared immediately released me and began to gather up my clothes. Grabbing my robe from the closet, I pulled it on and left the bathroom for Amy's bedside.

Laying on her front, her head hanging over the side of the bed, Amy projectile vomited again, barely missing me. "Eeeew! Amy, you need to sit up, honey."

Appearing at my side in just his jeans, Jared scooped her into his arms and carried her to the bathroom. Turning his head back to me, he smiled. "It's ok, I got this. You clean that up and I'll make sure she gets it in the toilet next time."

Nodding, I began the disgusting task of cleaning up my roommate's tequila scented puke. This wasn't how I wanted my night to end, but as I glanced at the clock I realized it was after midnight which meant it was my birthday. Scooping the vile pile into a bag with a pair of gloves I found in my first aid kit, I had to try as hard as I could not to be sick myself. I could hear Jared giving Amy words of comfort as she continued to empty her stomach into the toilet. Every now and then I would hear him groan, and each time it made me giggle. It wasn't how I had imagined my birthday starting, but at least he was here with me.

All night.

Chapter 32

Handcuffs And Heels

The feeling of a soft hand stroking up and down my spine woke me in the most wonderful way. Opening my eyes, I grinned as Jared's warm, piercing pools of blue stared back at me.

"Happy Birthday, baby."

Enveloping me in his arms, he pulled me to him tightly. He'd stayed beside me all night, spooning, and if he'd had his way, forking too. Amy groaned, and I rolled over to see her bolt from her bed and dash for the bathroom. Laughing to myself, I turned my attention back to my lover. Sealing my lips over his, I kissed him, noting how bitter his morning breath was after a night of drinking.

I murmured into his mouth, "Mmmm, last night's alcohol. Delicious. And morning stubble too, smooth."

Chuckling he rolled me onto my back and laid on top of me. Reaching up to the bedside table, he grabbed a small gift bag and dangled it over my face. "Open it." Sitting up, he took my hand and pulled me to sit next to him. He'd slept in his shorts and after cleaning up after Amy, I'd finally slipped into some comfortable pyjamas. Biting my bottom lip, I smiled as I inspected the vibrant red bag.

"Don't sit there staring at it. Open it."

Draping his arm around my waist, he leaned into me as I pulled the tab and opened the gift bag. Inside was a small box containing two black pendants. Rectangular and about an inch and a half in length, each had a slit at the edge where an engraved piece of white gold sat. Noticing the small diamond at the tip, I ran my finger over the engraving as Jared read it aloud.

"Only Love."

Pulling one from the box, he placed it around my neck. "You are my only love, Layla, always and forever. And I will always be yours."

He took the other necklace and handed it to me to put around him. Hooking the clasp, I thumbed the pendant between my fingers as it sat against his caramel colored skin. The tiny diamond glistened in the early morning light and a warm glow filled my heart.

"I love them. They're perfect."

Cupping my face in his hands, he gave me a chaste kiss. "No, you're perfect." He kissed me again and sighed deeply. "I have to work today, baby. But I have arranged a little birthday surprise for you, and before you start protesting or asking questions, don't. All will be revealed."

Rolling my eyes, I gave him a suspicious look.

"Don't give me that look, Layla Jennings. It's your birthday. You don't want me to spoil you any other time, but at least let me lavish you today. I'm going to, whether you like it or not."

I smiled and shifted onto his lap. Straddling him, I slipped my hands around his neck and kissed him deeply, nibbling his bottom lip playfully. His palms moved down and around my behind, and I jumped as he stroked the sore and tender area where he had unleashed his spanking upon me.

"Oh, baby, I'm so sorry. I don't think I can do that again. I know you like it, but I can't stand watching your face screw up like that when I touch you."

"It's fine, Jared, honestly. It was just surprising, that's all. Please stop worrying over this. I liked it. A lot. I don't want you to stop. If I did I would say so, ok?"

Nodding weakly, he gave me a rueful smile.

"To throw your own words back at you, Mr. Garrett, don't torture yourself. Just torture me the way you did last night." I winked at him, and the light in his eyes ignited as he lowered me back onto the bed.

"Oh, Layla. You really are amazing, and I would love to spend all day teasing that hot little body of yours, but like I told you, I have plans for you." He gave me a quick kiss, before getting out of bed and pulling on his clothes.

I could hear Amy groaning and moaning in the bathroom and giggled to myself as I thought about the similar noises Jared and I had been making in there only a few hours before. Fastening the buckle on his belt, he grinned at me. I knew exactly what he was thinking because the same sexy replay was rolling through my mind too. A loud rattle on the door pulled me from my sinful reminiscing.

"Open up, birthday girl. I got breakfast and coffee."

Ollie's voice boomed through the door, and Jared's expression automatically turned from happy excitement to furious irritation in seconds. He glanced at me before making a move for the door. Sprinting across the room, and almost tripping on my bed covers, I beat him to it and opened the door. Ollie looked as bright as a button and fresh as a daisy. You would never have imagined he'd been drinking all evening. Pleased that I hadn't drunk more than a glass of beer all night, I smiled at him cautiously as Jared stood directly behind me.

Holding a tray containing two coffees from Lorraine's, and a brown paper bag from the deli two shops over, Ollie grinned at me and shot Jared a questioning look. I could feel Jared's hands tighten into fists as he wrapped a possessive arm around my waist.

"Oliver Green, you're a life saver. I'm starving."

Taking the bag from him, I moved aside to let him in as Jared shifted unwillingly beside me. Sitting cross legged on the floor, Ollie began sorting our coffees, completely ignoring Jared's icy glare. Pressing my hand against his cheek, I turned his head toward me, and away from Ollie.

"Thank you for last night, all of it. The bar, Amy..." glancing at Ollie, I lowered my voice, "the bathroom. But you need to go shower, shave and go to work, and I have to prepare for this surprise you have planned. Thank you in advance for whatever it is."

Standing on my tiptoes, I kissed the tip of his nose before I closed my mouth over his and kissed him passionately. I heard Ollie snort but decided to ignore him, giving my full attention to the man in my arms. Enveloping me in his embrace, Jared took the brown deli bag from me and tossed it in Ollie's direction. His arms pulled me tightly to him, and our chests compressed, making it hard to breathe, but I didn't care. I was totally caught up in the romance of our morning together.

Releasing me, he smiled down at me and chuckled. "I could get used to that kiss every morning. I'll call you later, before the party." He pecked my cheek and shot Ollie a warning look before heading out the door.

Leaning my back against the hard wooden door, I folded my arms and glared at Ollie.

"What? I just thought you might want breakfast."

Joining him on the floor, I shook my head. "You knew he was here, Ollie. You have to stop this. I love him, and nothing is going to change that. Now stop being such a dick and hand me a bagel."

Chuckling to himself, he passed me a delicious salmon and cream cheese whole wheat bagel. It was lightly toasted, just how I liked it, with a scattering of poppy seeds on top. A loud groan echoed in the bathroom, and Ollie almost spilled his coffee as he jumped.

"What in god's name was that?"

Pointing to the door, I laughed. "That would be Amy. Too much Tequila and spicy burritos. She's been in there for almost an hour."

Sputtering his coffee in a spray all over the floor, he laughed hysterically. Raising his voice, he yelled to her. "Ring of fire, huh Amy?"

"Fuck you, emo dick!"

Her reply made me almost choke on my breakfast as both Ollie and I fell into fits of laughter.

"It's not funny, guys. I think I'm dying."

Fuelling our laughter further, she groaned in pain. Giving Ollie a shove, I clambered to my feet and over to the door.

"There's some Imodium in the bathroom cabinet. Try that."

"Thanks, Layla. Uh...hey, Layla? Why are your panties under the sink?"

I blushed ferociously, and my eyes darted to Ollie who was staring at the bathroom door.

"Um, Jared, erm…"

"Never mind. I think I get it. I'll be out of here soon. I hope."

Flushed and embarrassed, I went and sat back next to Ollie who was frowning as he stared blankly at his bagel.

"Sorry."

Raising his hand, he shook his head. "None of my business. Layla, I wanted to talk to you about that photo."

Looking away, I winced. Ah crap.

"What about it?"

"I took it that night at the bar because I knew you were going to be someone special in my life and I wanted a memento from your big night, your debut. That's all it is. I swear. I just wanted a photo of my friend having a great time, but if it makes you uncomfortable, I'll tear it up."

Pressing my lips to his cheek, I shook my head. "Nope, keep it. Nothing wrong with having pictures of your friends, right?"

Grabbing my cell, I switched it to camera and held it in front of us. I leaned my head on his shoulder and snapped our moment on the screen forever. He smiled at me sweetly, then began devouring his bagel. I wasn't sure I believed Ollie's reasons for having my picture by his bed, but with the way things had gone between us, I didn't want to pursue it.

* * * *

After an hour and a half in the bathroom, Amy was finally feeling better. She was now dressed, groomed, and insistent that we go out for the day. She still had no idea that I knew about the party, and I didn't want to spoil all her hard work, so I decided to keep my mouth shut and go along with whatever she wanted to do.

Dropping my cell in my purse, I followed her out of the door. Ollie had left after breakfast as Amy had put him in charge of the entertainment at the party, so he was meeting with Nick and Eric to practice.

As we approached the exit to the building, Amy pressed her hands over my eyes. "Ok, no peeking. Put out your hands and push the door open. Watch the step."

Stumbling about in my sneakers a little, I pushed the glass doors open and stepped out into the cool air.

"Ok, ready. Open."

Removing her hands, I squealed as Mel came hurtling towards me. Jumping up and down with excitement, I ran over to meet her. Her arms wrapped tightly around me as we collided halfway across the lawn.

"Oh my god! I can't believe you're here! How did you get her? When?"

Holding me in a warm hug, she grinned. "Jared. He got my number from your cell and called me from New York. I got here yesterday. Amy met me for lunch, and we went over the plans for today. She's a real firecracker, huh? I can see why you like her. Anyway, we're under strict instructions to make you shop till you drop. He said that anything your heart desires you must have, no matter the cost. I think I love him."

"Sorry he's taken," I whispered into her ear.

Giving me another quick squeeze, she released me and waved her hand at Amy to join us. A horn beeped, and as I looked into the parking lot I spotted Daniel and the Mercedes. Amy grinned.

"Well, let's go shopping!"

The ride over to the mall had been full of girl talk and laughing. I had to feel sorry for Daniel as Mel bombarded him with questions, asking everything from his age to his marital status, I got the feeling she was kind of into him, and by the goofy grin on his face, he felt the same. Her smile almost touched her eyes when she found out he was only twenty-three and single.

The golden arch of the entrance glistened in the sunlight, and I remembered the first time I'd seen it. The night Jared and I first had sex, he'd brought me there and given me a diamond bracelet. I smiled as I glanced at my empty wrist. I really should wear it more often. As the heavy pendant around my neck swished and bounced against my skin I smiled, knowing that the most important jewellery he'd ever given me was also looped around his own neck at that moment.

The girls were grinning widely as we entered the mall. Amy's eyes lit up like a child at Christmas as we wandered from store to store. We shopped for everything from shoes to makeup. Pulling me into the jewellery store Jared owned, Mel gave me a nervous smile.

"Ok, so he told us to bring you here and that he's already picked something out for you. He said that you're not allowed to groan, bitch or moan. And you're not allowed to ask the price."

An older woman stepped out from the behind the counter and smiled at me. "You must be Layla. I'm Carmel. If you'll just wait here, I'll be right back with your item."

My eyes darted between Amy and Mel as I waited anxiously for her to return. They were both grinning like maniacs, and as Carmel laid a tiny velvet box on the counter, my heart skipped. Sliding her fingers over the clasp, she opened the box to reveal a stunning white gold ring. Amy and Mel both gasped as I held my hand firmly over my mouth in shock. It was truly magnificent. The perfectly smooth band was topped with a sapphire, surrounded by a cluster of diamonds. Inspecting it more closely, I saw the shimmer of light inside the sapphire and looked at the assistant confused.

"It's a black star sapphire. It's very rare and very beautiful. You're a very lucky lady. It's also engraved."

Taking it from the box, she showed me the message inside the rim and I smiled.

Forever and Always.

Taking my right hand, she slid the ring onto my finger. "A perfect fit."

Grabbing my palm, Amy held it to the light and sighed with satisfaction. "Oh, he really does have the best taste in jewellery. I wish someone would spoil me like that."

Biting my bottom lip, I smiled.

"If he continues to buy me jewellery, I'll be able to open my own store soon," Amy laughed.

"They make the best gifts. After all, diamonds are forever."

The assistant grinned at me. "There was also a note, Miss Jennings." Handing me a folded yellow paper, she smiled and left us alone, returning to the back room.

Moving to the side, and away from prying eyes, I read his little message.

This is a black star sapphire. Wear it always and remember that you are my world, and with this ring you hold my universe in your hand. Happy Birthday, my darling Layla.

With all of my love from here to eternity,
Jared xxxx

A single tear slid down my face.

Noticing my sudden emotional state, Mel and Amy both wrapped me in a tight hug while oohing and awing at the note in my hand. His sweet and sentimental generosity was overwhelming. I couldn't believe how much he'd given me already, and now that ring was just more than anything I could have ever expected. I wanted to do something for him; something special. A gift he could really enjoy. I gave the girls a mischievous grin. "I think I need some lingerie."

Hunting through the endless rows of shops, I finally found what I was looking for. An elegant boutique called 'Princess Alicia's Lingerie' was exactly what I needed.

Stepping inside, I noticed the sweet smells of vanilla and strawberry in the air. The luxury décor was beautiful with perfectly white walls and a hot pink carpet. There were two vintage white chairs in the corner with velvet cushioning, and rows and rows of the most gorgeous lingerie were hanging on rails on the walls. Approaching us with a wide and extremely white smile was a young and strikingly attractive brunette. Her lips were cherry red and her eye shadow gave her a smoky effect, highlighting her green eyes and beautiful long lashes.

"Hello ladies, welcome to Princess Alicia's. I'm Alicia. What can I help you with today?"

Her huge smile felt a little fake, but humoring her, Mel stepped forward and answered. Pressing her hands on my shoulders she stood behind me and plastered on a grin. "This young lady needs something scorchingly sexy that will make her man's blood simmer and sizzle in his veins just by looking at her."

Flashing me her pearly whites, and fluttering her eyelashes, Alicia showed me over to a changing booth.

Handing me several garments through the curtain, she smiled as I eyed them curiously and handed several back out to her. There was no way I was wearing anything made of leather or PVC. The final item she had handed me was a silk corset. Putting it on, I gasped as I saw myself in the mirror. The pink silk accented my pale skin tone perfectly while the black lace trim made my breasts seem bigger and more voluptuous as the bones held me in and pushed everything up.

Twirling around, I yelled out to the girls, "This is perfect. I'll take this."

Quickly taking it off and handing it to the assistant, I dressed and headed out to pay. Standing at the counter, Mel smiled at me as her eyebrows bounced up and down on her forehead. "He is going to love it! I think it's a perfect gift to give the man who has everything. Especially after he gave you that ring."

Glancing at the mass of jewels on my hand the assistant smiled. "That'll be three hundred dollars, please."

Leaning across the counter, Amy held out a small black card that looked like a credit card. "Put it on this account, please. Her boyfriend is paying."

Dropping the card like it was on fire, the assistant growled at me. "Jared Garrett? You are the girlfriend of Jared Garret?"

I froze in shock, not understanding why she was so irritated based on the man I was involved with.

"He doesn't date! He never has relationships. You're lying! There's no way he'd fall for a fat little harlot like you!"

Pushing me aside, Mel squared up to her. "Hey, who the hell do you think you are?"

Snapping her head to face me, she snarled, "Alicia Paige, and until about five months ago I was Jared's little bedtime buddy. That's right, every single night. On the bed, tables, chairs, kitchen counters, backseat of his car. Anywhere he wanted. If it's Jared you're looking to please, I would have gone with the leather. We both know how he likes his straps and buckles. But you look like someone he would hire to clean his laundry rather than clench his sheets. Maybe that's why he keeps you around. A good maid is so hard to find. Thanks for keeping the bed warm for me. Once he gets bored of you, he'll come running back."

Something inside me snapped.

I launched myself at her. "You bitch!" Falling to the floor, she landed on her back as I straddled her, punching and slapping her face.

"Get off of me, you dirty little tramp!" She pulled hard on my hair, making me fall to the side as she kicked my shins and scratched her perfectly manicured nails down my face. Mel grabbed her wrist, and Amy frantically tried to pull me away, but I was fierce. Gripping a fistful of her hair, I yanked at it pulling out a few strands.

Without warning, I found myself on my feet and being hauled away from her. My hands behind my back, a cold pair of steel handcuffs restrained me as I wriggled and pulled to get away and continue my attack. Another officer handcuffed Alicia while two mall cops restrained my friends. Kicking and shouting, I was carried off along with the other three to a squad car parked outside. I tried to spot Daniel, desperate for some help, but he was nowhere to be seen. Ducking my head, the officer helped me into the car with Amy and Mel. Alicia was taken to the car behind us, and I glared wildly at her as she grinned at me. Licking my lip, I could taste blood as it trickled into my mouth. She'd split my lip. Fuck, this was all I needed when I had a party to go to.

The police station was bustling with people. Sitting at his desk, my arresting officer told me that I was being charged with assault. Furious, I shouted at him, trying to protest my innocence and explain that I had been provoked. Giving me a caution, he told me I would be held until a judge could see me which could range from an hour to four hours.

I was taken back to the freezing cold holding cell. Outraged and upset, I sank onto the hard concrete bench where Amy, Mel and Alicia were glaring at each other.

"This is your fault, you fucking Barbie bitch," Mel sniped at Alicia who simply gave her a snort and a sarcastic grin.

"Just leave it alone, Mel. It's not worth it."

My jaw ached from the blow. My lip was split, and as I rubbed my sore and aching cheek, I noticed two long scratches that marked the pale skin next to my eye.

A large police officer approached the cell and unlocked the door. "Jennings. Someone here to see you."

Rising from my seat, I walked over where I was once again placed in handcuffs. Who the hell could possibly be here to see me? I hadn't used my phone call as I didn't want Dad to find out I'd been arrested, and I knew for sure that Mel hadn't called her folks. It really only left one person…

Oh no. Shit.

Now I really was in trouble.

"You too, ma'am." Nodding at Alicia, he gestured for her to come over where she too was cuffed. Gripped and pulled by our elbows, the pair of us glowered at each other as we were led into a small dark interview room. This was about to get a hundred times more painful than my aching ribs and throbbing lip.

Sitting comfortably at a desk in the center of the room, dressed in a black suit and deep purple tie, was Jared. Holy sexy, fuckable hotness. I felt my insides clench blissfully as I took in his unbelievably strict yet concerned expression.

Arms folded, he scanned me from head to toe. His eyes widened as he saw my face, and I could see the worry etched into his expression as his brow furrowed. My lip was split, and the marks on my face were prominently visible. He was clearly livid at finding me in my current state.

Darting his eyes at Alicia, he glared at her with a fiery hatred. Tapping his lips with one finger, he waited as we were escorted in and sat in two chairs opposite him. Giving the officer a thankful nod, he turned his attention to us. Getting to his feet, he paced back and forth before resting his hands palm down on the desk. "So, Thelma and Louise, who is going to tell me what happened today?"

Shouting over each other, and making snide remarks, we both simultaneously protested our innocence. Slamming his palms on the desk to silence us, Jared shook his head.

"I don't want to hear it. I've spoken to the arresting officer who tells me you were both charged with assault. Now since this incident happened in your store, Alicia, it appears that it is your choice entirely if you wish to press charges against Miss Jennings."

I opened my mouth to object, but he shot me a cautionary look and I immediately closed it again.

"However, I would strongly urge you to think carefully about filing charges against the woman I love because if you pursue this, I will come at you with everything I have. Counter charges will be made, and with the marks on her face I would have a strong case against you."

Getting to her feet, her hands bound in front of her, Alicia screamed tearfully in his face, "She was in my store, Jared! How could you do that to me? Like I meant nothing to you! Isn't it bad enough you broke my heart without flaunting your relationship in my face? I gave you everything! I fell hopelessly in love with you, but it was never enough! Why her? What makes her so different?"

Slamming his fist on the table, and making me jump in fright, he glared at her. "Don't bullshit me, Alicia. You were in it for all you could get, and we both got what we needed. You got a brand new shiny shop, and I got laid."

I flinched as unwelcome thoughts of them together swam through my mind. It was nauseating.

"Don't pretend that it was anything more than a good casual fuck every now and then. I don't have to tell you anything, but if you must know, I love Layla for everything she is and everything she's not. But most of all, I love her for not being anything like you!"

I gasped as the venomous words struck Alicia. I could see the pain in her eyes as she gasped for air. She sat down and sobbed into her cuffed hands. I stared at her, surprisingly feeling sympathy for the woman who had insulted, attacked and assaulted me. No woman deserved to hear those things, no matter what they'd done. Ok, I hated her for the things she said, but heartache can make people crazy and she didn't deserve that.

Glaring at him, I scooted my chair across and placed my restrained hands over her knee. "How can you be so callous? You have no idea, do you? It's impossible not to love you, Jared. No matter what you think, women don't have a heart of stone, and you don't cry like this if you never cared."

Rubbing his eyes, he sighed loudly. "Fine, I'm sorry, but I didn't love you. I didn't love anyone. Don't think that I didn't care just because couldn't give myself over to a relationship. I did care. I didn't know Layla would walk into your store today, but whatever issue you have with us is not her fault. I ended our companionship, so if you need to hate someone, hate me. Not her.

"Those marks you left on her face are making me fucking furious, and I'm so angry right now that I can't even see straight. Just look at her! Drop the charges and walk away with your head high, or I will make this get very ugly!"

His tone was callous and deathly serious. Raising her head, she looked at me and snatched her leg from my hands. "I don't need your sympathy, bitch! I hope you're happy while it lasts. He's a serial womanizer, and he can't help himself. He's dishonest, secretive, and he'll stray sooner or later. Then you'll be just like me, a notch in his bedpost! Ask him about all the others, go on! There are dozens of us! Broken, chewed up and spit out. You're doomed to join us."

A stabbing pain shot through my chest. She couldn't possibly be talking about the same man that stood in front of me, could she? Was that who he really was? Was the man I loved merely a diluted version of the philandering man whore she accused him of being?

Jared fumed, and I swore I could see smoke coming out of his ears. He was livid. Rounding the table, he grabbed her handcuffs and dragged her to the door. "Drop the charges, Alicia, or I will destroy you."

I'd never seen him so enraged. It frightened and aroused me to see him so worked up.

"Is that a threat?"

He spun her around, halting their steps as he grasped the door handle. "It's a promise."

She took a long breath, and stood inches from his face before firing a large mouthful of spit at him.

Classy.

"I'll drop the charges, and you can drop dead, asshole."

His shoulders hunched and he growled, then pulled a handkerchief from his pocket and wiped his face. I stood abruptly, and strode over fast, ready to go a second round with the woman I had only moments ago felt sorry for. Extending his arm, Jared stopped me and shook his head. I stood glaring at her, wishing she would suddenly become the first recorded case of spontaneous human combustion.

Jared sneered at her as he opened the door. "It's no wonder your husband got sick of you. You're a dirty little whore, and I was only too happy to let you fuck him by fucking me. But that's all you ever were, and that's all you'll ever be. Easy, cheap, and disposable."

Shooting him a murderous look, she stormed out.

Closing the door, he turned his attention to me. Walking towards me, he reached his hand out to touch my face and I recoiled. Alicia's poisonous words were replaying through my mind over and over. He stared at me, wounded.

"Layla, you don't seriously believe any of that shit she said do you? It's not true. You are not a notch on my bedpost. You never were. She's just bitter and spiteful. You mean more to me than any of them ever did. I love you, Layla. I would never, ever hurt you."

I scrutinized his face for weakness as I blurted out the burning question I was holding. "What does make me so different, Jared?"

He stared at me confused. "What?"

"I want to know. What makes me so different to the other sixty women?"

Threading his fingers through his hair, he stuttered and stumbled over his words.

"I...I don't know. You just are. They were so vain...high maintenance and out for what they could get from me. Some liked the lifestyle. Some, like Alicia, wanted my business connections. But you..." He paused and took my hands in his. "You were so fiery, argumentative, and downright rude. You excited, confused and astounded me right from the start. No one had ever spoken to me that way before. But even when you found out who I was and what I have, you didn't care. I've never been with a woman who just wants to be with me before. It totally knocked me on my ass. You're different because of everything you are and everything you're not. Most importantly, you're different because you're mine. My girl. My queen. That makes you more special to me than any of them. I love you. I never loved them. Does that answer your question?"

Looking into his bright blue eyes, I melted. He loved me and no amount of hurtful words from a jilted ex-lover were going to convince me otherwise.

"Yes. Completely. I'm sorry, Jared. About all of this. I just lost it. The things she said, about me...about you...about us...I couldn't stand there and take another word of it. I just snapped."

Gripping his hands on my arms, he rubbed them up and down gently. "It's alright. I get it. I don't think she's going to press charges. She has too much to lose."

Lifting my chin, he brushed my hair from my eyes and ran his thumb gently over the marks on my face. "Jesus, baby. That girl is a fucking animal. This is entirely my fault. She attacked you because of me and everything I did to her, and now look at you. I feel fucking sick. Did anyone see to these cuts?"

My split lip pinched and pulled painfully as I spoke, and the taste of dried blood was bitter and metallic. I shook my head weakly as his lips gently kissed my broken skin.

"Come on. As much as I love seeing you bound in handcuffs, I'd rather it was at my hands for your pleasure. I need to get you home and fix those cuts and bruises. That one on your chin is going to be a real shiner. From the way she was hunched over walking, you must have got a few good body hits in yourself."

I smiled, proud of my efforts to give as good as I got. "I got a few blows into her ribs and stomach."

Smiling, he kissed me gently, careful of my injuries. "Way to go, champ. We'd better go get Amy and Mel out, too. I owe Amy a thank you. She used her phone call to reach me. A shopper in the mall called the cops, and when Daniel saw them pull up and you guys being led out, he jumped in the car and came straight to my office to get me."

I smiled at the realization of all the people who had my back that day. Mel in the store, Amy calling Jared, Daniel going to get him, and Jared himself, who came straight down to get me out.

"What would you have done if she'd pressed charges? Could I have gone down for assault?"

He shook his head quickly. "No, nothing was ever going to happen to you. I wouldn't have let it. The judge here owes me a favor, and if all else failed I would have hired the best lawyer in the country to get you out of this. At most, you'd have got a fine, and I would have paid it. But it's done now. She won't be filing charges. I told you, Layla, I will do anything for you, and I will do anything to keep you safe. Come on, before those two end up getting into more trouble."

Waiting in the station reception area, I let out a sigh of relief. I could put the whole horrible episode behind me. Jared had an officer remove my handcuffs as he questioned him harshly on my treatment during my time there. He was still furious that no one had tended to my injuries, but after I begged him to forget about it and take me home, he dropped it.

Finally freed, Amy and Mel came running over, embracing me in a warm hug. Kissing me on the cheek, Mel growled. "I can't believe that bitch. Talk about ruining your birthday. I'm so sorry this all happened."

"It's not your fault. And besides, it's not ruined. I just have an awesome story to tell."

Amy snorted. "Yeah. Hey everyone, guess what I got for my birthday? Arrested!"

I laughed with her and Mel as Jared re-entered the station. "Car's waiting. Let's go, jailbait."

Feigning annoyance, Amy gawked at him. "Who are you calling jailbait?"

"You three angry birds. Really can't trust you to go anywhere, can I?" Taking my hand, he smiled at me and kissed the top of my head as he led us to the car. Threading our fingers together, he held me tightly all the way to the college dorms.

Climbing out of the car, he rushed to the other side to speak to Amy. I couldn't hear what they were saying, but she was nodding and smiling. Glancing inside, she ushered Mel out.

"Mel's going to hang here a while so that you and Jared can have some alone time. We'll catch you later, ok?"

I knew I would see her at my party and wondered if that had anything to do with Jared whispering in her ear. Smiling, I said good bye and watched as my two girlfriends walked away, chatting and laughing. I was pleased that they got on so well. I'd worried that some jealousy might have developed between them concerning me, but it never seemed to be an issue. They both knew they held a special place in my life, and I loved them both dearly.

Sliding in next to me, Jared instructed Daniel to take us back to his place. Brushing his thumb over my knuckles, he stopped as it hit against my new ring. Bringing it to his lips, he kissed the back of my hand softly. "Do you like it?"

Smiling broadly, I nodded. "I love it. It's wonderful, just like you."

My smile caused the split in my lip to pull, and I hissed in pain as it pinched and throbbed.

"I can't believe that she did that to you. I could have killed her when I saw you walk in like that. It took every ounce of my self-control to stop myself from strangling her."

He ran his thumb across my bottom lip, and I held my breath as he touched the tender and painful cut. Shaking his head, he scooted closer to me and pulled me onto his lap. Holding me tightly to his chest, he exhaled exasperatedly. He looked exhausted, and I couldn't help but feel guilty for his worn out state. The night with Ollie, and then our episode in the bathroom, was enough to wear out the best of men. Add to that your girlfriend and her two friends being arrested, and the pressure was enough to drive a man to murder. Throw in a venomous ex-lover, and you've got the worst twenty four hours of your life.

Nuzzling my face into his neck, I sighed deeply and winced. Lifting my head from his shoulder, he gazed at me confused.

"Baby, what's wrong? Are you in pain?" I shook my head weakly, then hung my head in my hands. Pulling my hands away, he lifted my chin, making me look at him. "Layla, you're avoiding me, what's wrong?"

"It's everything. Last night. Ollie. Being arrested. I'm too much trouble, and I don't know why you put up with me. I've put you through so much in the last few weeks, and it pains me knowing how much damage I've done. You're exhausted. I can see it, and it's my fault."

Holding my head to his chest, he hushed me as he thread his fingers through my hair. "Shh. No, baby. You are a lot of things, but trouble is not one of them. I can never get too much of anything you are, or anything you do. Last night was a necessary evil, and now it's done. We've met, exchanged words, and he knows exactly how I feel, and I have weighed and measured him also.

"I won't lie. Knowing he's around you makes me manic, worried, and insecure, but I trust you with all my heart. I know you'd never do anything, and if anything *did* ever happen between you, you'd tell me. As for you being arrested...granted, it was something I could have done without today, but it happened and I fixed it. It wasn't your fault. I have no doubt that Alicia instigated it and provoked you to attack her, so I want you to stop thinking about it and enjoy what's left of your day. No more talk of you being too much for me to handle. I am not exhausted by you. I just have a lot going on right now, but I wouldn't give you up for all the tea in China, baby."

Guilt was consuming me as I thought about what he had said. Would I tell him if anything happened between me and Ollie? I never told him about the kiss, or the way I'd felt about Ollie before he came along. Ollie was hot, and there was no denying there was a physical attraction between us, but I didn't love him. I loved Jared, and telling him about a kiss that I hadn't wanted, nor instigated, was pointless and could only do more damage than good. Honesty was clearly always going to be a deal breaker for us. How could I constantly berate and punish him for hiding things and keeping secrets when I was walking around with some of my own? Now I felt exhausted, and I still had my party to get through.

"Jared, what were you and Amy talking about?"

He shrugged. "Oh, just thanking her for calling me, and I told her I'd be bringing you to the party tonight. I have your clothes and everything you need, so don't worry. I just wish you didn't have to show up with those marks on your beautiful face."

Now I was the one shrugging. "It's fine. We'll call them my battle scars, but I can cover them with makeup anyhow."

Chuckling, he kissed my nose and gave me a very sweet butterfly kiss. "My very own warrior princess. I like it."

Chapter 33

A Picture Of Mass Destruction

After thanking Daniel for everything he'd done for me that day, I hurried into the house. I was eager to eat, shower and get ready for my party. Fishing my cell from my bag, I dialled my dad. Disappointment ached inside me as, for the third time that day, I couldn't get an answer. The same happened when I called Mom, and I was beginning to feel abandoned. Neither had called to wish me a happy birthday yet.

Trying to hide my hurt feelings, I made my way to the living room and flopped onto the huge soft cushions of the couch. Jared entered a moment later with a bottle of witch hazel and a cotton pad. Sitting beside me, he held my chin between his finger and thumb, and gently dabbed the ointment over my cut lip. I hissed as the sting bit into my sore flesh.

"Sorry, baby, but it has to be done."

The medicinal smell made me heave as my empty stomach lurched and rolled. Chuckling, he finished tending the scratches next to my eye and took my hand. He led me to the kitchen and sat me on a stool in front of the counter.

Opening the fridge, he scanned its contents. "Ok, so I have eggs, butter and a whole load of stuff I can't pronounce. Omelette sound good?"

"An omelette sounds great."

I watched as he worked his way around the kitchen like a pro. He was an excellent cook, and I was in awe of his many talents. After he'd glided me effortlessly around a ballroom, I knew he was a talented dancer, I'd heard him singing to Elvis on my first morning there, and his business empire was constantly expanding. He really was extraordinary.

Taking the glass of water he'd poured me, I smiled. "So, who taught you to cook?"

Turning his head briefly from the frying pan, he smiled at me. "My mother. She was an amazing cook. She could take the most unlikely ingredients and make a meal from them. As soon as I was tall enough to reach this counter, I was cooking."

I continued to smile, beaming at him as he spoke so warmly about his mother and how they'd spent hours baking and cooking together right in that room where I was sitting.

I glanced around the room and noticed a newspaper on the counter. I enjoyed the gossip and celebrity sections, so as Jared continued cooking, I slid from my stool and walked to the kitchen counter. Turning to the gossip pages, I gasped in horror. Jared immediately snapped his head up.

"What? What's wrong?"

Pointing at the article, I shook my head while my hand pressed against my wide open mouth. Taking up half a page was a picture of me and James Felix. Amy had been completely cropped out, so it looked as though the two of us were on a date. Striding over, Jared gripped the counter top on either side, caging me in as he peered over my shoulder and read the caption aloud.

"James Felix and date, Layla Jennings."

His grip on the counter tightened, and I could feel his breathing become heavier behind me as the warm breath blew against my neck. Still staring in total shock and confusion, I shook my head.

"I swear, Jared, I was not on a date with that man. That's the night Amy and I went to the opera. He was all over her, and if you could see the whole picture you'd know she was standing at the other side of him. I swear I had nothing to do with this. Ask Arthur Kent, he was there, he warned me about it and-"

Turning me to face him, he growled. "He has his hand on your skin, Layla! His grubby, disgusting hands on your flesh. How could you let another man touch you? And least of all, him!"

"I didn't let him touch me. The moment he laid a finger on me, I made my escape. This was right before I left to speak to Arthur. He told me that you and Felix don't get along and that I should stay away from him, so I did."

Letting go of the counter, he pushed away from me and paced up and down, running his fingers through his hair.

Great.

Anxious and irritated Jared was back.

"So, even though you were made perfectly aware that I wouldn't like that you were in his company, you neglected to tell me about it. Why? Why didn't you tell me you met him, Layla? That he posed for press photographs with you?"

"Because I didn't exactly expect them to turn up in a newspaper, Jared. He was flirting and romancing my roommate, not me. It was just dinner and a drink for goodness sakes! Calm down. It's not a big deal."

Pointing at me accusingly, he snarled. "Bullshit, Layla! You didn't tell me because you knew I'd get mad. Well I'm not mad, I'm fucking livid! If I had known, I could have at least ran damage control. God, now at every dinner, formal and social event, people will see you and think you and he were together! Do you know how that makes me feel? How that makes me look? Knowing people will look at you as another of his dirty little past times. Your name and face are a direct connection to me, Layla, and people expect me to date a certain kind of woman. How can I possibly fix this now? It's printed, read and seen by everyone. I can't believe you keep pulling this shit on me. You're such a fucking hypocrite!"

What did he call me? Was he freaking serious?

Infuriated and insulted, I picked up my glass of water and tossed it in his face, glowering at him as I did so. He stood frozen, scowling at me through his soaked hair.

"What the fuck?"

Storming out of the kitchen and into the sitting room, I searched for my purse so that I could leave, but he was soon on my heels. Grabbing me by the wrist, he twirled me around to face him.

"Where are you going? Did I say we were done here?"

Water droplets dripped from his golden brown hair as his shirt clung to his body, soaked right through to the skin. Twisting and pulling my wrist, I tried desperately to escape his clasp.

"Fuck you, Jared. I don't need your permission to leave. Let me go!"

I was through with his accusations, insults and icy tone. Fear crept up my spine as I realized that maybe this was it; maybe he'd had enough of all the drama too and was finishing our relationship.

Preparing myself for the end, I turned to walk away but Jared caught my other wrist and held them both in one hand as he pushed me down onto the sofa. Flat on my back, he laid on top of me, pressing me into the plush cushions. He held my wrists tightly at either side of my head, and although I was furious, I was also a little turned on. Water trickled from his hair onto my face and down my cheeks. His eyes flared and blazed with anger as he stared down at me, his mouth mere inches away from mine.

"You are going to hear me out and then we will discuss it. Understand?"

I kicked and squirmed beneath him, trying to get free, but it was no good; he had me pinned like a wrestler.

"If you don't stop wriggling and trying to cause me injury, I'm going to tie you to the table. Got it?"

I groaned in frustration.

"You called me a hypocrite, Jared, and what the fuck did you mean by people expect you to date a certain type of woman? What type am I exactly?"

He grimaced, and I could see I'd hit a nerve as his words fired back at him.

"I meant that people have a preconceived idea of the women I would be associated with, and someone Felix would date would not be one of them. And you are a hypocrite, Layla. You lecture and question me about having honesty in our relationship, and yet here you are, keeping things from me again. You promised that you wouldn't lie to me anymore. If you want trust between us, you have to start being more truthful with me. It's getting really fucking tedious, and I'm sick of being the last to know everything. James Felix is a slug. He chews women up and spits them out, and you and Amy should stay as far away from him as possible. It never ends well. He gets what he needs and bails. And if I ever see him so much as glance at you again, I'm going to throttle him with my bare hands. Stay away from him. Do you understand?"

I rolled my eyes at him and sighed, irritated.

"I'm serious, Layla. Don't fight me on this. Tell Amy she has to call it all off. It's better she end it now, then later when he has dragged her through the dirt and grime with him."

My scalp prickled as guilt flooded me. I'd decided not to tell him because I was worried he'd be furious, and after Arthur had warned me to keep quiet I felt I'd done the right thing. But now there was photographic evidence of my evening, and it had been poorly managed. I was finding myself second guessing and doubting him again, and I wondered if I was truly being fair. But I wasn't the only one with secrets, and there was one I had been dying for him to reveal to me for a long time.

Seizing my opportunity, I bit the bullet and fired my own anger at him. "You honestly want to talk about being more forthcoming? How about not telling me you owned the coffee shop? Or lying to me about sending the shirt for dry cleaning?

Yeah, I found it in your closet. And what about the fact that even though you tell me you love me, adore me and worship me, I still can't share your bed! Trust and honesty goes both ways, Jared, so before you start getting on your high horse about mine, take a look at yourself!"

His eyes scanned my face and he suddenly seemed anxious, rather than mad. Leaping to his feet, he stood a few feet away and frowned deeply.

"I told you about the coffee shop, and I gave you my reasons. As for the shirt, I didn't care about the fucking stain. I wanted to see you again. I just used it as an excuse to talk to you and I'm not sorry. I kept it because it means something to me. It's how I met you, and because of that shirt I got to spend time around you, getting to know you and falling in love with you.

"And I do love you, Layla. I worship the ground you walk on, and I can't stand when you lie and keep things from me. It makes me feel like you're afraid of me. Like you're scared of me losing it or something. It's not that I don't want to share that bed with you, Layla. I told you, I've never shared that bed with anyone and that's the truth, I haven't. And the reason I haven't is because…I don't sleep in it either."

I gazed at him, bewildered. It was his room, his bed, and he'd never slept in it? Or did he mean he just never slept in it because he was busy doing other things on it.

"I don't understand. What exactly do you mean? The first night I stayed here, you said you wouldn't sleep with me and that was in the guest room."

He let out an exasperated sigh, and I recognized the grieved look in his eyes as he sat down next to me.

"It's not my bed. It's not my room. It was my parent's bed and their room. I've tried to sleep in there, really I have, but it just doesn't work. Every time I wake up in that bed, my heart breaks a little. It's the bed I climbed into every Sunday morning as a kid. Mom would read the paper, and Dad had the business section, but he'd always read me the funnies. I brought my mom breakfast in bed on Mother's Day there. On Christmas morning, I'd run in and snuggle down for a festive movie and hot cocoa before opening gifts. I can't forget it all, Layla, and every time I wake up in that bed it just reminds me that they're not here anymore."

My heart broke for him as I watched him re-live some of the happiest memories from his childhood. Everything he'd ever known, trusted and loved had been so cruelly snatched away from him. It felt so unjust, so unfair, and so unbelievably cruel. The thought of losing a parent is devastating, but to lose both in such tragic circumstances, and at the hands of another human being, was brutal. Sliding myself onto his lap, I wrapped my arms around his neck and held him tightly as his head fell onto my shoulder.

"I couldn't put you in a guest room, then go sleep in the one next door, could I? You'd have known something was up and I wasn't ready to talk about it. I'm still not that comfortable, even now."

It was all so much clearer now. The bed, his anger at my questioning that night; it was all because he was nervous or ashamed. My chest was damp where he'd been lying on top of me but my emotions were running so high that I felt warm and a little flustered. Stroking his soaked hair, and threading my fingers through it gently, I pressed my cheek against his head.

"I'm sorry, Jared, I had no idea. I thought it was something to do with boundaries and personal space…I never considered…I'm sorry. I was wrong not to tell you about Felix, but I really thought I was doing the right thing. I never considered the consequences of being snapped by a photographer, but seeing your face when you saw that article tells me everything I need to know about him. I'll keep my distance, and I'll caution Amy, but I can't guarantee she'll listen.

"I don't know why you didn't tell me about the bed though, Jared. I love you. I want us to share everything. I know that sounds very hypocritical considering what I did, but we have to get past this honesty thing we have between us."

My pendant was pressing against his chest, and taking it into his hand, he ran his thumb back and forth across the engraved inscription. He raised his head and gazed deep into my eyes as he kissed me gently.

"Layla, tell me the truth, are you afraid of me?"

I bit my lip anxiously, but quickly released it as my tooth grazed my cut. "It's not that I'm afraid of you, Jared. It's that I never seem to know how you'll react. One minute you're calm and sweet, then the next you're flaming hot. I can't gauge your mood and that frightens me. How far can I push you before you break? I thought you were going to end our relationship after you saw that picture. You were so mad at me and I was terrified that we were through."

I hung my head and stared at my lap. Lifting my chin to face him, our eyes met and he shook his head at me. His eyes were glistening through the wet strands of gold and brown hair that hung in front of his face.

"I will never be through with you, ever. I don't know what I have to do to get you to realize that you're my everything. I exist to love you. You're my meaning of life, my reason to be. You were made for me, and I was made to make you mine. What we have is too important to me to just throw away because of a picture and an incorrect quote. But you have got to have some faith in me, Layla. I would never hurt you, you have to know that. I may get angry, lose my temper and storm away, but I will always calm down, and I will always come back. I could never leave you behind. I'd be lost without you."

Relief overwhelmed me as he wrapped his arms around me, enveloping me in a warm embrace. Slightly misty eyed, I smiled into his neck as I nuzzled against him. "I love you so much. I'm sorry, for everything. I swear, from now on honesty. Always."

Placing a chaste kiss on my lips, he smiled and rested his forehead against mine. The smell of something burning caught my attention and I suddenly remembered the omelette he'd been cooking when I'd found the picture.

"Jared! The stove!"

Lifting me off his lap, he sprinted toward the kitchen as I ran close behind him. Pushing the door open, thick black smoke came billowing from the room. Raising his hand to indicate that I stay exactly where I was, he disappeared into the gray and blinding smoke. I heard the sound of a fire extinguisher and my pulse quickened as I worried for his safety. Seconds later he re-emerged, and I was finally able to breathe again knowing that he was alright. Holding a cloth with the black and chargrilled pan in his hand, he grinned playfully at me.

"I hope you like your eggs over easy."

I laughed hard as the emotions of the past hour flowed and rumbled around in my body. All the hurt, anger and sadness instantly washed away with his humor and boyish grin. He chuckled and walked back into the kitchen to dispose the pan. The fire had mercifully been well contained, so there was minimal damage to the stove. Turning to face me, Jared held out his hand, and I rushed to accept it. Leading me into the foyer, he grabbed my shopping bags and ushered me upstairs.

"Time to get ready for your party, my lady."

* * * *

Showered, buffed, and feeling incredibly more relaxed, I made my way through to the master suite. Jared had brought up all of my things and organized them neatly on the dresser. I smiled at his sweet and caring gesture, and began sliding into my underwear. I'd decided on a black lace thong and matching strapless bra so that my dress would appear seamless as I danced and wiggled my ass around all night.

I'd just slipped into my thong when I spotted Jared leaning against the door frame, watching me. He'd removed his wet shirt and was now bare-chested in his black slacks. His eyes were dark and hooded as they followed me around the room.

Pretending to be totally unaffected by him, I sat on the vintage couch and slid into my brand new pair of five inch, black velvet, Gucci heels. They fit perfectly, and the cost definitely reflected the comfort. I stood up and walked to the full length mirror to check them out. My legs looked slimmer and longer, sleek even.

"You don't need that mirror to tell you how good you look. I can categorically tell you that you look tantalizingly fuckable, Miss Jennings."

I shot him a seductive smile and slowly sashayed over to the door. Dragging my nails over his chest gently, I breathed against his mouth, "That sounds deliciously erotic, Mr. Garrett. Care to elaborate? Maybe give me a demonstration?"

His eyes grew wild with lust, and a low primitive growl rumbled in his throat. "With pleasure. Hot, smoldering pleasure, my lady."

Breezing past me, he headed for the closet. I watched him, a little confused until I saw him re-emerge with the velvet bag.

Oh. My. God.

It was the first time we'd used it since the night he'd introduced me to the idea of bondage. Pulling it open, he smiled mischievously. He looked like he'd just won the lottery as he rummaged in the bag for his toys. Dropping it to the floor, he stood and gazed at me as he dangled the pair of door restraints from his fingers. I was biting my lip, but I always did that when I was anxious, and he knew it.

"Layla, you look worried. These are for restraining you, that's all. The cuffs are for your wrists, and the hooks go over the top of the door to hold you in place. Now, hold out your hands and put your wrists together for me, baby."

With only a slight trepidation, I did as he asked, eager to try this new and exciting lifestyle he wanted us to indulge in. I'd enjoyed being tied to the bed, blindfolded, and even secured by a belt in my bathroom while being spanked. I held my breath as he gently slid the cuffs into place on my delicate wrists. The leather was stiff and felt cool against my warm skin.

The band that held them together was elastic, but as he pulled my hands apart, I realized that they didn't have much give. Not that it mattered as I'd soon be suspended from the top of the door anyhow.

Taking hold of the cuffs, he led me to the door. Placing a gentle kiss into each of my palms, he turned me so that my eyes were now staring at the white blank wood in front of me as he pushed it closed. My heels dug into the carpet, leaving me to lean forward with my arms extended towards the ceiling.

Leaning against my ear, he whispered, "You look fantastic. Tantalizingly fuckable. Just like I said." His hands snaked around my waist as he stood behind me and pressed me against the door. Sliding them up to my breasts, he cupped, massaged, and groped them tenderly with wonderful care and attention. He pinched my nipples, and I gasped in shock. The pain was sharp, but the after effect was a warm and tingling sensation.

"I told you, Layla, there's a fine line between pleasure and pain. You really pissed me off today. You got into a fight and marked your beautiful face. How very careless of you. You got arrested, and I was forced to watch you sit in the same room as a woman I despise. And then I discovered you withheld information again. It really won't do. You've been a very bad girl, downright naughty, and now I'm going to have to spank you like the disobedient girl you are."

Holy fuck.

Instantly aroused simply at the suggestion of a spanking, my breath hitched and my pulse quickened. Swooping it through the air at high speed, his hand made contact with my behind and I squirmed. The feel of his hand caressing and rubbing my cheek before the bite of a hard and powerful slap crashed into my skin was blissful, and I simply adored it. I cried out as he palmed, groped, and grasped at my sore flesh. I could feel his erection pressing into my behind through his slacks. The moment of tender care soon passed as he struck another swift blow against my cheek. I pulled hard on the restraints as I writhed back and forth against him.

I heard the sound of his zipper and crossing my wrists, I turned myself around to face him, not wanting to miss the strip show happening behind me.

He didn't disappoint.

I watched with lustful hunger as his pants slid temptingly down and over his muscular, firm thighs. Stepping out of them, he hooked his thumbs into his shorts teasingly. I stared, willing them to disintegrate in his hands, but alas, no such joy. Slowly, he pushed them down and kicked them off. I licked my lips as I took in the sight of his gorgeous, eight inch, deliciously delectable cock. Rigid and still, I longed to hold it in my hands, to lick and caress it with my tongue, and to drive him to the brink of lunacy with my mouth. But with my hands bound tightly together, and my arms held high above my head, I was having little chance of that dream coming true.

He pushed me against the door and my back hit the wood, pressing onto it firmly as his hips pinned me against it. Tilting my head to the side with one hand, he trailed kisses from my nape to my jaw. I moaned as his lips touched my sensitive and wanting skin. He knew all of my erogenous zones and was an expert in torturing me into an orgasmic frenzy. His tongue glided and stroked across my collar bone and down to my cleavage. Smiling, he licked his lips.

"You taste like heaven, Layla. I've never dined on anything quite as delicious or exquisite as your body."

I whimpered as his tongue continued south to my nipples, nipping and nibbling on one then the other. The rolling and sucking made me groan as it sent a direct message to my sex. My clit throbbed, and I was soaking wet as my body reacted to his every breath, word, touch, and flick of his tongue. I whispered his name, my voice raspy and breathless.

"Oh, baby, when you say my name like that, it makes me want to do things to you, things that will drive you wild and make you scream it even louder. It's like needles and pins all over my body hearing that one little word."

His hand gripped behind my knee as he lifted my thigh against his own. I could feel the tip of his cock teasing at the opening of my sex.

"Now be a good girl and turn around. I wasn't quite finished with your ass. It is my very own hot property, after all."

I smiled as I thought about my own ownership of his ass. I still couldn't believe he'd had my name permanently carved into his flesh; it was by far the sexiest aphrodisiac. I owned his ass. Literally.

Dropping my leg, he stared at me and made a twirling gesture with his finger. Begrudgingly I turned around, aware that his arousing spanking session was not yet finished. Teasing his fingertips over my bare flesh, he dragged them down the length of my spine, making me bow beneath the gentle touch against my skin. A loud crack echoed through the room as his palm made contact with my behind. I jumped a little as my mind recalled the familiar pain, and yet my body was begging for more. Thrashing his hand against my now smarting flesh, I could feel his erection growing firmer and as solid as stone against the opening of my sex. I was panting and gasping as he unleashed his unremitting attacks on my ass.

Lifting his hand away, he tugged my panties aside as his cock drove into me deeply and quickly, making me cry out in shock. The entire length of him filled me as his hand came crashing down once more on my raw and stinging cheek, causing my insides to clench and pulsate. Bending over me, his chest resting against my back and I felt him smile against my ear.

"Good girl."

His words were all the encouragement I needed. My behind felt enflamed but my arousal was far hotter and it was certainly worth the sharp beating I'd received.

His fingers grazed back and forth over my lips as he held my face turned to his. Withdrawing slowly, he surged inside me again as he kissed me deeply, pushing his tongue forcefully into my obliging mouth. He withdrew again and I watched him as he disappeared back into the closet. What the hell was he doing? Here I was cuffed, restrained, horny, hot and desperate for him and he had just deserted me. When he exited the closet a moment later he was wearing that mischievous grin on his face. Grasped in his palm was the piece of black silk that I remembered from my time I'd spent tied to his bed. He approached me and placed a chaste kiss on my lips.

"Trust me?"

I nodded.

"Say it."

Swallowing the lump in my throat I breathed heavily. "I trust you."

His grin spread, reaching his eyes. "You won't be able to use the safe word with what I have in mind, so I need you to use a hand signal. If you want to stop just snap your fingers, and I will instantly release you. Understand?"

I won't be able to speak? Oh sweet god of all that is hot and erotic. With no hesitation, I smiled. "Yes. I understand."

His teeth sunk into my bottom lip, gently nipping, careful of my cut as his tongue slid soothingly over it. "Good girl."

Taking the silk, he lifted it to my mouth. "Open wide for me baby." I smiled playfully and moved my legs further apart. Shaking his head he chuckled. "Mouth, Layla." I did as he asked and he gently put the material in my mouth.

"Now bite down on it."

My teeth clamped down into the silk and made a squeaking sound as they ground into the soft, smooth fabric. Caressing my cheek with his fingertips, he smiled.

"Breathe, Layla. This is going to be good for both of us. Trust me."

My eyes widened. Good for both of us? I could see how much he was enjoying it already as his erection pressed against my thigh. Seeing my expression, he explained and tried to reassure me.

"It will be good for both of us. You really pissed me off with this Felix thing, Layla. You're clearly not listening to what I tell you, so I have to find other ways to get it into you. When I tell you to stay away from someone, I have a reason. You ignored me, and now I have to live with the damage. It won't hurt, but it will be intense. Take a deep breath and trust me. Relax."

Holy fuck.

Holding the ends of the silk in his hand, he resumed his position behind me. I gulped hard, and waited in anticipation for his next move. Slowly and gradually, he slipped inside me again, gripping onto the silk that was now keeping me silenced, and pulled on it. My body instantly moved back, slamming my behind into his thrusting hips. The silk acted as a harness in my mouth as he pulled hard and sharply with every shove, plunge, and surging thrust. Bound and gagged, I had given myself over to his control, and the payoff was immense. My insides tightened and clenched with every vigorous and relentless push his cock made against my G-spot. One hand was on the silk, and the other groped and caressed my thigh. I moaned and groaned through my muzzle, biting so hard into it that I thought my teeth would tear the delicate strands that held it together. His breathing accelerated and became ragged as he grew more and more aroused. I could feel his cock pulsating and throbbing inside me, building my orgasm rapidly. He hissed in my ear, causing my breath to hitch.

"Oh fuck, Layla, you're so fucking hot. I could break you in half. I want you so bad."

With the position I was in, and the ferocious and merciless way he was pounding into me, my body breaking into two was a distinct possibility. His hand slid swiftly from my thigh over the curve of my hip and between my legs. His fingers roamed over my cleft and to my throbbing, swollen clit. Stroking, rubbing and massaging it expertly, he groaned loudly in pleasure.

"You're so wet, it's delicious. Come for me, baby."

My behind crashed against his hips, my clit pulsated and throbbed at his fingertips, and my insides clenched, convulsed and contracted as my orgasm exploded like a bomb. My body shook and trembled as the complex cocktail of sensation and emotion overwhelmed me. The urge to cry, laugh, and scream was a confusing and mind boggling experience and my body reacted by crying out, muffled through the silk as tears of pure joy and satisfaction ran freely down my face. Panting and groaning, a primal and fierce growl echoed from his lips as Jared emptied inside me, thrashing and banging his hips against mine.

My arms sagged and my body grew limp, exhausted from our session of intense and exhilarating bondage play. Jared's forehead rested against my back, and I could feel the sweat and heat from him on my skin. His breathing was staggered, making me acutely aware of my own rapid breathing. Taking two calming and deep breaths, I tried to regain my equilibrium and find the strength to stand.

Releasing his grip on the silk, it now hung loosely between my teeth. With my hands bound, I used my tongue to force it from my mouth. My muscles ached and my behind was sore. I had no doubt that it was the color of a ripe strawberry at that point. I pulled on my restraints which were still tightly wrapped around my delicate wrists. He was completely lost in the moment as he kissed and caressed my scorching skin.

"Coffee."

My use of our safe word pulled him from his post-coital coma. Snapping his head up, he looked at me, confused. I nodded at my hands and he gasped, realizing he'd left me hanging, literally.

Freeing me, he apologized profusely. "God, I'm so sorry, baby. Are you alright?"

I nodded, but the moment I was free I instantly lost control of my limbs and fell to the floor. Jared caught me mid tumble and scooped me in his arms, holding me close to his chest. My arms wrapped around his neck and I nuzzled into him as the sweet smell of sweat, sex, soap and Jared filled my nostrils, bringing me comfort.

I felt truly content.

Laying me on the bed, he climbed in beside me and stroked my hair gently and attentively. "You constantly amaze and beguile me, Layla. I'm in awe of you. That was...incredible. You were incredible."

Lifting my wrist, I rubbed the light pink rings that had formed from rubbing against the thick leather cuffs. Taking my hand, he pressed his lips to each wrist and kissed my palms. His piercing blue eyes were bright and glittered like the sea on a bright summer's day. I smiled as I gazed into them. I could have lost myself in his eyes for days, months, even years.

Brushing a strand of hair from his handsome face, I sighed happily. Emotions were coursing through me, and I felt an overwhelming need to be closer to him. I wrapped my hands behind his neck and pulled him to me, kissing him deeply and lovingly. I couldn't possibly describe in words how I felt at that moment, but euphoric and unbelievably happy would be close.

I felt truly loved; I was truly in love. I pictured my entire life with this man beside me. Making a home together, marriage, beautiful, golden-brown haired, blue eyed children and vacations spent in Hawaii.

I had a ridiculously goofy smile on my face but I didn't care. I'd never been so entirely at peace. I was on cloud nine, and I wasn't willing to come down.

"What are you thinking about? Whatever has put that delighted smile on your face, I want some."

I snickered and pressed my lips to his. "I was just thinking about us. That's all."

He raised a quizzical eyebrow, and smiled. "Oh? All good things, I hope. Well, pray tell, Miss Jennings."

I continued to grin at him. "I was just thinking about how happy I am, how happy you make me, and that I've never felt this way before. I feel like I'm flying. I can't wait to start my future with you, Jared. You're my happily ever after too."

Gazing deep into my eyes, he beamed at me. My black star sapphire ring was still sparkling on my right hand. Sliding it off my finger, he held it in his palm.

"With this ring, I promise you a strong shoulder to cry on. I promise to hold and care for you whenever you need me. I promise to bring you comfort when you're sad and to defend you to the last. I give you faith, trust, and commitment unfailing. I promise to love you with every breath in my lungs and every beat of my heart until the end of time. I promise that the only heart I own will always belong to you and that it will never beat for another as long I live. I promise picnics in the summer, and cozy nights by the fire in winter. I promise to always cherish, and appreciate, you and everything you do, and to show you every day just how much you mean to me. I will always be yours, and you will always be mine. This I promise you."

Tears filled my eyes as I watched Jared slide the ring onto my finger once more and pressed a firm kiss onto it.

"Oh Jared."

I couldn't find the words, my heart was soaring, and my eyes were filling with the tears of happiness I felt inside, and yet I couldn't compose a single sentence to tell him how much everything he'd just said had meant to me. Smiling down at me, he placed a soft kiss on my lips.

"I know, baby. You don't have to say a word. I know."

Enveloping him in my arms, I kissed him deeply as he rolled on top of me. I wrapped my legs around his waist as my hands roamed over his broad, strong back. His lips lovingly and gently caressed my skin, and as the sun began to go down, the dreamy glow of sunset filled the room, making it warm and romantic.

Gazing deep into each other's eyes, and without a single word, we made love. It was intense and emotionally draining as I fell deeper into oblivion with him. The connection between us was profound, and my heart raced with every touch, kiss and embrace. Tears trickled down my cheeks as joy filled my body.

I was in heaven, and I had no desire to leave.

Chapter 34

Party Like A Rock Star

Checking myself in the mirror one last time, I cringed. My hair was completely straightened and my makeup was severely over the top. The industrial strength concealer had gone a long way to cover up my scratches; the bruise on my chin, and the bright red, non-smear lipstick, would hide my split lip perfectly all night.

I pressed my hands against my dress and brushed it downwards, removing any stray bits of lint or dust. It was black and strapless with a sweetheart neckline that showed off my ample breasts and cleavage. Short in length, the hem sat about four inches above my knee. The shimmering sequins on the bodice meant that every time I moved, they glittered and sparkled in the light.

Looking down at my shoes, I smiled to myself. The tantalizingly fuckable Gucci heels were blissfully comfortable, meaning I was free to dance the night away without the crippling after effects that an excruciating pair of low quality shoes would have brought. My pendant hung heavily around my neck, but I didn't mind. It was a sign; a symbol and public statement of my commitment and love to Jared. Swearing to never remove that, or my ring, I held my hand to the light and watched the diamonds and sapphire glisten. It was more than just a birthday present; it was a promise and a vow, and I would never take it off. They would have to pry it from my cold dead hands before I'd ever part with it.

Jared called up from the bottom of the stairs. Taking a deep breath, I grabbed my purse, walked out, and stood at the very top of the staircase, looking down at him. He was wearing dark denim jeans, a crisp white shirt and a black jacket. He looked smoking hot. He stood frozen and his jaw hit the floor.

Bam.

Layla Jennings once more renders her man speechless. Round two to me…not that I was keeping count.

Carefully I made my way down to him, smiling as his eyes followed me as I walked. I felt like a model, and the expression on his face told me I looked like one too. Gazing at me, his eyes scanned my body from head to toe.

"Oh. Hell. No."

I stared at him, confused.

"Where are your clothes? Tell me that's your underwear."

I stifled a laugh and did a little twirl. "You don't like it?"

He shook his head in amazement. "I love it! As far as handkerchiefs go, it's stunning! But honestly, Layla, I have the money and I would have happily bought you the whole dress! Now, if you could please find something to wear with that belt, I'd be very grateful. Because there is no way you are going to that party like that, young lady. That skirt is so indecently high. One sneeze and every guy in the place will get a great view of your behind, followed by a fantastic view of my knuckles."

I leaned forward and pecked him on the cheek. Straightening the collar of his jacket, I smiled at him sweetly. "Well, I guess I should probably give the whole going commando thing a second thought, huh?"

Walking past him with a satisfied grin on my face, I headed for the door. Holding his hand to his chest he gawked at me.

"That's just not funny. You're kidding right? Layla? Tell me you're joking. Oh god, help me."

Turning the handle of the door, I glanced back at him and smiled playfully. "I guess you'll never know."

His eyes widened and I could see the mischief painted all over his expression. "The hell I won't!"

Sprinting across the foyer, he grabbed me around the waist and swept me off my feet. Kicking and giggling, I batted his hands away, but he had me firmly in his grasp. Carrying me into the dining room, he sat me on the glass table. I yelped as my ass touched the cool glass. Grinning, he raised an eyebrow at me.

"Sit there and stay still."

Lowering himself onto the floor, he lay down and shuffled up so that he was now underneath the glass, staring straight up.

"Layla Jennings, you dirty little tease!"

I laughed hard, swinging my legs over the edge of the table. Ok, so I was bluffing, but it was worth it just to see that look on his face. Sliding out from beneath me, he stood abruptly and gave me a mischievous smile.

"That was not funny. I nearly had a stroke thinking you were going out without panties on. Jeez. You'll pay for that, you know."

I pulled on his shirt, forcing him to step forward towards me. His hands grasped my behind as he lifted me to my feet once more. My heels meant I now stood almost face to face with his six foot one frame.

"I'm counting on it."

Kissing me passionately, he smiled against my lips. "God, I really am the luckiest man alive."

I smiled back at him. Although I agreed with him, I was very aware that I was the luckiest woman alive as well.

* * * *

Walking up to the bar, I grinned. The lights were up, but the whole place was silent. If Amy thought I wouldn't guess there was a surprise party in there, then she should have made some sort of sound because the bar was never quiet on a Saturday night.

Glancing at Jared, I held his hand tightly, lacing our fingers together. Pushing the door open in front of me, he gave me a nod. I put on my best surprised face as I stepped inside and the room erupted in applause and cheers. Rushing in my direction were Mel and Amy. Jared darted out of the way as the two of them draped their arms around my shoulders and squeezed me tightly.

"Happy birthday!"

"Oh my god, guys! This is amazing! Did you do all of this?" The entire bar was covered in balloons, streamers and banners. Amy nodded, her eyes dancing.

"Wow, I'm speechless. You're both amazing. I love you!"

"We couldn't very well let you have a quiet one. Now come and mingle. Everyone is here!"

Taking my hands, they led me through the crowd. I turned back to look at Jared, who shrugged, and pointed at the bar, signaling he was going to get a drink. I nodded and turned my attention back to my friends who were gushing about how much fun we were going to have and everything they were planning for the evening. I'd been arrested, fought with Jared, and then spent two hours having mind blowing, kinky sex that had left me weak in the knees. I was already exhausted, and no doubt would be comatose by the end of the night.

Approaching our usual booth, I gasped, then grinned as my eyes fell on my father and my mother sitting together at my table. Getting to her feet, my mother rushed me with a warm hug.

"Oh, my baby girl. I have missed you so much. Happy birthday, my darling. Let me look at you." Holding my hands, she stood back and scanned me.

Raising from his seat and coming to my side, my father pressed a kiss to my temple. "She's beautiful, Diane, just like her mother."

Clearly agreeing with him, my mother nodded as her hand caressed my cheek. "She is beautiful, but she has your smile, Andrew. Perfect and completely disarming."

I looked at my mother, noting how positively radiant she looked as she and my father complimented each other for making a stunning child.

Pulling them both into a tight hug, I struggled to hold back tears. "I thought you'd forgotten me. I didn't hear from either of you all day, and when I called there was no answer."

Looking at me with regret, my mother gave me a half smile.

"Oh sweetie, I was working all morning, then jumped on a plane to get here. Your very sweet young man had me flown from San Francisco in his company plane. He offered to have a chauffeur pick me up, but your father insisted on doing it himself. By the time we got back to the house, we didn't have much time to get ready before we had to be here. But I would certainly never forget the day you entered the world. It was the best day of my life."

Looking up at him, she gave my father a genuine Diane Jennings' smile. He beamed back at her before turning his attention to me. "Seven gruelling hours of labor waiting for you to get here, I could never forget."

I beamed and hugged them again.

Reaching underneath the table beside him, my father produced an envelope. "This is from your mother and me."

Giving them a curious look, I opened it and shrieked as in my hand I held a gift certificate for an entire day of pampering at my favorite San Francisco spa. "Oh my goodness! You guys! I love it!" Hugging them both tightly, I grinned.

My mother chuckled in my ear. "I figure that when you come for winter break, we'll go and spend the whole day being massaged, polished and preened."

I grinned at them both. "Oh, I love you so much. I'm so happy you're here."

Sliding into the booth, we talked about everything. Mom told me all about her new position at work, and dad was working on a new project at the garage where he and the guys were building a hot rod from the bottom up. He spoke with such enthusiasm, and it made me happy that he'd found something to occupy his time, now that I was no longer living there.

Approaching the table, Jared cleared his throat. Sliding out of the booth, I took his hand and introduced him to my parents. Shaking their hands, Jared gave them the full on Garrett charm and instantly won them over. My mother blushed and batted her eyelashes as he complimented her, saying how he could see where I got my striking good looks, and he and my father shared the same love of cars. My father nearly spilled the beer Jared had bought him when he heard about Jared's Jag.

"You'll have to take her for a spin sometime, Mr. Jennings."

My mother placed her hand gently over Jared's and smiled. "Please, call us Andrew and Diane. We'd like that."

Smiling back at them, he nodded and draped his arm around me.

Amy and Mel soon joined us and the drinks were flowing as people talked and laughed amongst themselves. Leaving them, I worked the room, stopping to talk with people from my classes. Kate had gotten the evening off to come to the party, so I made my way over, grinning like a maniac. Beaming, she hugged me.

"Hey, girl. Happy birthday. Wow, nice frosting." Holding my hand, she whistled at my ring. I grinned.

"Thanks, Jared bought it for me. He also got me this pendant. He wears a matching one too."

She nodded in approval. "How do you do it, Layla? He's completely besotted. I envy you. How do I find a guy like that?" Pretending to frown, she winked at me before nodding at something behind me and walking away.

A strong pair of arms wrapped around my waist. The fruity smell of guitar wax, and the scent of his sweet cologne, made me fully aware of the owner of the arms which currently adorned my midriff.

"Happy birthday, superstar." His lip ring grazed my ear, and I smiled as he breathed against my skin.

Turning around, I gave him a warm hug. "Thanks, Ollie. So you're the entertainment tonight, huh?"

"Yep, me and guys are playing a set I designed just for you. But anyways, here." Handing me a small bag, he smiled and a slight pink tint appeared on his cheeks. As I opened the bag, I smiled and giggled at him.

"Wow, a blindfold. Should I even ask?"

Taking it from me, he placed it around my head and over my eyes. "I figured you could use it next time we went to the movies. I know how you enjoy horror flicks."

Laughing, I took it off and shoved it in his hand. "Very funny. I wasn't scared. I'm just easily startled, that's all."

Laughing hard, he draped an arm around my shoulders. "So, I hear you got yourself arrested today. That's one way to celebrate, I guess."

I shoved him a little and laughed. "It was not funny at the time, but now, I guess it's a little amusing. It would have to be me, though, who ended up cat fighting and getting handcuffed."

He ran his hand through his hair and smiled wickedly. "Wow, girl on girl and handcuffs. Why couldn't you have got me that for my birthday?"

I gave him a gentle swat on the arm and shook my head laughing. What a douche.

"I have got you something else, not just the mask, but you'll have to wait for it."

I eyed him curiously, but tapping his nose lightly with his finger, he indicated that it was clearly a secret, and winked before making his way to the stage to set up.

As I slid back into my seat, Jared raised an eyebrow at me. Leaning to his ear, I reassured him, "He was just wishing me a happy birthday before they play my birthday set. Ollie said he designed it specifically for me."

Taking a sip of his drink, he murmured just loud enough for me to hear. "I bet he did."

Here we go again.

Spotting Amy and Mel at the bar, I made my excuses and joined them. Mel smiled warmly at me.

"Hey, baby girl. Having fun?" I rolled my eyes and explained Ollie's greeting and Jared's reaction. Amy shrugged.

"Oh, let them just get on with it. It's your night and no one is going to ruin it."

Raising her glass, Mel agreed. "Here, here. Now get this down your throat." She handed me a cocktail glass full of something pink with a wedge of lemon on the rim. I shrugged and lifted it to my lips.

"Bottoms up!"

A hand quickly snatched the sweet smelling liquid from me.

"Yeah, I don't think so, miss overenthusiastic and underage." Giving me a stern look, Jared held my glass hostage in his hand.

"Oh, Jared, don't be such a spoilsport. It is her birthday, after all." Amy was never going to win this argument.

"I could always tell the bartender how old you ladies are and really spoil everyone's fun, if you'd like."

Pouting, Amy quickly shut her mouth. It was the first time I'd seen her speechless, and it made me laugh. Jared joined us and began talking to my friends about everything from college, to music and bands.

The talk of music made me wonder where Ollie had gotten to. I scanned the bar and spotted him animatedly talking to Kate. She was beaming at him while running her fingers through her hair. Was he seriously flirting with her? I liked

Kate, but I'd never imagined she was Ollie's type. I watched them, scrutinizing every laugh and facial expression.

Kate reached out to touch his tattoo and I gasped. "No." The word flew out of my mouth and I held my hand to my lips as three sets of eyes stared at me. Jared, Amy and Mel instantly turned to see what I'd been looking at, but in a quick and swift movement I recovered. "Oh, no wait, its ok. I thought I'd forgotten my purse, but I realized it's at the booth."

Mel gave me a nudge. "Scatterbrain."

Continuing their conversation, the girls turned away from me, but Jared was clearly not so convinced. Spotting Ollie, his fists clenched at his sides and he glared at me. Why was I staring at them? Why did I care? I couldn't understand it at all. Ollie wasn't my property. He could flirt, touch, or talk to whoever he wanted. So then why did I have a sudden urge to walk over and step between my two friends?

Jared's hand gripped my arm, and he pulled me over to the other side of the bar. Staring me down, his mouth pressed into a hard line. "What was that about? I saw you looking at them, Layla."

I swallowed hard, and tried to think on my feet. "I was just curious. I didn't think they were each other's, type that's all. I was surprised."

He closed his eyes tightly, and pinched the bridge of his nose. "And you expect me to swallow that?"

I pulled his hand from his face and gazed up at him. I had to rectify this, and quickly. "It's the truth. I was just shocked to see them together. I swear. You have to believe me."

And there it was again. My mouth was spewing lies once more. Lifting my hand, he pressed his thumb against my ring, making it shift and glimmer in the lights.

"See this? I wasn't lying when I said those things, Layla. My word is my bond, and this ring binds us together. You tell me that's your reason for watching them, I believe you. I trust you, remember, but I'm not an idiot. There's something you're not telling me, and when I find out what it is, I hope to god it's something I can handle. So here's your chance, Layla. Either you tell me, or I'll find out on my own."

Breathing hard, I gave him the only plausible excuse I could. "Ollie has a scar. When he was a kid, his father abused him. His tattoo is hiding a painful memory and Kate was about to discover that if she touched it. I was worried about Ollie's secret getting out."

He stared at me, questioning my words with his icy glare. "Is that true?"

In fact it was. It was the only truth I could think of that could possibly explain my behavior.

"Yes, I swear. Ollie told me about it himself the other day. That's why I was staring."

"So you don't want her to know, but you're ok telling me about it?"

"Of course. I trust you."

His expression softened as he pulled me into a warm hug, wrapping his arms around me tightly. "I'm sorry I doubted you. It won't happen again."

I nodded weakly as he held me to his chest. That had to be the reason. There was no other way to explain why it had affected me that way, was there? Pushing the disturbing thoughts from my head, I took Jared's hand and re-joined my friends.

The loud screech of a microphone being turned on caught my attention and the entire bar fell silent as Ollie stepped up to the mic. Dressed in his torn black t-shirt and jeans, he looked every bit like a rock star. His lip ring sparkled as the spotlight fell on him.

"Hey, everyone. We're D.O.A and we're gonna be playing a set list just for Layla. I'm lucky enough to call her one of my best friends, so without getting all mushy and shit, raise your glass to the birthday girl, Layla Jennings!"

A chorus of people shouting my name erupted and I blushed, pressing my face into Jared's chest to hide my awkwardness.

Ollie's guitar fired up and 'Sweet Child Of Mine' by Guns N Roses echoed through the speakers. Grabbing my hand, Mel dragged me away from the bar to the dance floor. People had already begun swaying and moving to the music and as her feet stepped onto the wooden area, Mel was the carefree rock chick I knew and loved. Kate appeared by our side, and grinned as she busted some moves of her own. Three die hard classic rock fans, we stayed on the floor as Ollie played more of my favorite songs. His husky tones and expressive eyes made every song into a masterpiece. I was having the time of my life.

Twirling around, I saw my parents laughing together at our booth. It was the first time in years they'd been in the same place for so long, and a small part of me wondered and hoped that the spark between them was still simmering somewhere. Turning back to the stage, I gazed up at Ollie in awe. He was an amazing performer. His passion for the music meant that every song he played, he played perfectly.

Amy and Jared were watching from the bar. With a raise of my hand, I waved at them to join us. Jared shook his head, grinning at me, but Amy was already bounding over. I knew for a fact that Jared could dance, in fact he danced very well so I couldn't understand why he wasn't going to dance with me on my big night. Leaving the girls to continue owning the dance floor, I walked over to him.

"Hey, don't you want to dance with me?"

He smiled and spoke into my ear so that I could hear him, "It's not that. I have to make a quick call to my office. Besides, if you start grinding and swaying that perfect little ass around at me, I can't be held responsible for my actions, and your parents are here."

I bit my bottom lip and smiled. "Ok, stud. But I'll save you the last dance, ok? Promise me you'll take it?"

Holding his hand to his chest, he winked. "You have my word as a gentleman."

Giving him a lingering kiss I made my way back to my friends.

Ollie's set had been going strong for hours and people were clearly enjoying themselves. Drink was well and truly playing its part as the majority of the crowd was now swaying with and without music. Laughing, I watched as Amy and Mel began playing air guitar to the music. Head banging, and acting like maniacs, they were kindred spirits.

My father caught my eye at the edge of the floor and ushered me over. "Baby girl, we're leaving. I have to get your mother back to the airport tomorrow morning."

I pouted. "You really have to go?"

Kissing me on the cheek, my mother nodded. "It's been wonderful seeing you, sweetheart, and your friends are amazing. You're very lucky." She leaned in, and whispered in my ear. "And Jared is gorgeous in every sense of the word. Hold on to that one."

I smiled as she kissed me again and rubbed her hand up and down my arm. Appearing from nowhere, Jared thanked them for coming and insisted that my mother use the chauffeur to get to the airport the next day. Thanking him, they said their goodbyes and I walked with them to the door. They gave me a last quick kiss and hug goodbye before they left. I felt a little bereft as I watched the car pull out of the parking lot. Seeing them together brought back memories I'd thought I'd long forgotten.

Holding me to his chest, Jared placed a kiss on the top of my head. "I think the band's finishing up. Last dance?"

Turning to face him I smiled and nodded as he took my hand and led me to the dance floor. Ollie's eyes fell on me the moment my feet touched the floor in front of him. Smiling, he winked at me.

"This is the last song because I'm tired as fuck, so everyone head to the floor."

Jared's arms snakes around me I rested my head on his chest. Amy and Mel had managed to secure themselves a partner each and had joined us. The band started up and the beautiful melody of 'Wonderful Tonight' by Eric Clapton played through the loud speakers.

Clutching Jared tightly, I moved and swayed to the music. As we turned about the floor, I looked up at Ollie. His eyes were fixated on me, and he looked pained as each word left his lips. I couldn't take my eyes from him. My heart ached as I stared into his soulful brown eyes. I could feel my body heating as I watched him strum his guitar and slide his hand up and down the strings. As he sang the next line he gazed deeply into my eyes, aiming every word directly at me. Tears threatened as I felt them hit my heart like an arrow, piercing and stabbing through to the very core.

As the song ended, Jared lifted my chin and placed a soft kiss on my lips. "I love you Layla. Happy birthday, baby."

Smiling back at him, I looked deeply into his eyes. "I love you too."

Breezing past me, Ollie stormed across the dance floor to the bar. My heart sank and ached as I watched Greg hand him a bottle of rum and a glass full of the bitter liquid which Ollie quickly swallowed. Excusing himself, Jared headed for the bathroom, and I took the opportunity to go see Ollie.

"Ollie, I…"

He shook his head and stared at his glass. "Don't, Layla. Please, for the sake of my fragile fucking heart, don't. I don't think I can take it. Do you have any idea how much you mean to me, Layla? Any at all? Because I sometimes think that if you did, you wouldn't keep torturing me like this. I can't keep watching you with him. The way you gaze into his eyes, the way he kisses you…and when you tell him you love him, I hate you. I hate you for loving him. I hate you for choosing him. I hate you for wanting him so badly. But mostly, I hate myself for not being him!

"I can't hide it anymore. I've tried so fucking hard that I swear I'm going crazy sometimes. It's eating at me. I can't sleep, can't think, I can't even function because I'm thinking about you so much. But I get it, I do. It's him you want, and from now on I'm hands off, but I have to let you know how I feel before I go nuts."

Striding across the bar, he took to the stage alone, and pulling out an acoustic guitar from the side of the stage, he began to play. I'd never heard the song before and the lyrics were clearly original. Ollie had written this song himself and I had a feeling I was his muse. Walking slowly to the stage, my eyes were fixed on him. His words were deep and full of emotion and I stood in front of him; my feet were glued to the floor as every word cut me like a knife.

> I never thought that I could feel this way
> Never thought I'd be falling in love
> Like an arrow right through my heart
> You bewitched me from the start
> How did you cast your spell on me
> Why would you be so cruel
> When you knew I couldn't have you
> You played me like a fool
> I can still see your lipstick on my skin
> Still feel your tender kiss against my mouth
> I can taste your sweet lips on mine
> And I don't think I will ever get it out
> Oh baby won't you please see me here
> I'm on my knees with my heart on my sleeve
> Wishing you'd be mine
> I loved you the moment I met you
> I loved you then and I love you still
> Baby you're breaking my heart with every step you take
> Please put me out of my misery
> I'm the choice that you should make

Dropping his guitar, he walked off the stage and right by me. I stood, frozen in shock, tears streaming down my face. Everything around me was a blur, and suddenly I felt sick. Turning on my heel, I bolted for the bathroom, but was halted in my tracks by a very tall, muscular, brick wall. Gazing up, I saw the thunderous look on Jared's face. The need to throw up grew stronger, and pushing past him I slammed the door open and leaned over the toilet, emptying the contents of my stomach. Amy and Mel came in behind me. "Layla, are you alright? What the hell was that?"

"I don't want to talk about it, Mel. Please, just leave me alone." It was the first time in our entire friendship I'd asked her to abandon me. Predictably, she was having none of it.

"Not gonna happen. Get your butt out here."

Stepping out, I looked at them both and broke into sobs.

"Oh, honey. What is it?" Amy's hand rubbed up and down my back as I racked and heaved, crying my heart out.

"It's Ollie. He's in love with me, and I hurt him. He kissed me, Amy. While Jared was in New York, Ollie kissed me, and for a split second I didn't pull away. I don't know why, but I just didn't. I've known how he feels for weeks, but I just kept pretending nothing was happening. I don't know what to do. I love Jared, but this attraction I have with Ollie is insane!"

They wrapped me in a comforting hug, and although I knew they meant well, there were really not enough hugs in the world to stop how I was feeling.

The sound of shouting and a loud crash pulled me from my depression, and my pulse spiked as I hurried to the door. Swinging it open, I watched in horror as Jared squared up to Ollie. Sitting at the booth with a glass in his hand, Ollie sniggered at him, fuelling Jared's rage. In a split second, he launched himself across the table at Ollie, knocking it and its contents onto the floor. The table landed with a crash as Jared clasped a fistful of Ollie's ripped t-shirt and hauled him to his feet. Slamming a right hook into Ollie's jaw, and then his stomach, Jared growled furiously at him.

"Keep your fucking hands off my girl, asshole!"

Ollie landed with a thud into the booth, and with determination on his face, kicked at Jared, sending him hurtling backwards. Springing to his feet, Ollie ran at him, tackling him around the waist and driving him back into the bar before unleashing harried and frenetic blows with his fist into Jared's abdomen.

"You don't fucking deserve her. I've loved her since the moment I met her, and all you've done is make her cry and lie to her. The only asshole around here is you, asswipe!"

Amy screamed beside me, "Layla, do something!" but I was frozen; my feet and my body completely fastened into place.

Shaking me, Mel spoke quickly and frantically, "Layla if you don't do something, they're going to end up killing each other. Snap out of it!"

Finally able to move, I ran to where the two men were wrestling and gripped each on the arm, pulling them with every ounce of my strength off of each other. They continued to throw blow after devastating blow into one another. Ollie shoved me hard away from them, and I landed with a thud on my ass.

Mel screamed, yelling at them hysterically. "You fucking jerks! Look what you're doing to her!"

Turning his head in my direction, Jared stared at me in horror before releasing his grip on Ollie's collar. I sat on the dirty bar floor and rubbed my elbow which had knocked into the fallen table as I landed. Great, I'd already acquired a busted lip, scratched face, bruised jaw, and now this.

Happy fucking birthday.

Rushing to my side, Ollie crouched beside me. "God, Layla. I'm so sorry! I wasn't even thinking. Baby, are you ok?"

Grabbing him by the scruff of the neck, Jared pulled Ollie to his feet and shoved him hard away from me. "Don't you dare call her that! You don't have the right!"

Mel and Amy pulled me to my feet, and I brushed myself down quickly, glaring at both men as they panted and glowered at each other. I stormed away from them and out of the bar door into the cool night air. It was sobering, and the light rain that was falling mirrored my mood perfectly. Jared had been so busy warring with Ollie that I wondered if he'd even noticed I'd gone.

Walking down the sidewalk cold, damp, and alone, I hugged myself as tears spilled from my eyes. I heard the pad of running footsteps behind me as Jared caught up. He moved in front me and gripped my arms, forcing me to stop.

"You kissed him? You fucking kissed him? I can't believe this. After everything we've said, everything we've been through, you gave your heart to someone else?"

I shook my head rapidly. "No! He kissed me. I didn't kiss him back, I swear. I pushed him away, and I screamed at him for being so stupid. It was totally one sided. You have to believe me. It happened weeks ago and I-"

"Believe you? You want me to believe you? How can I ever trust you again, Layla? If you had nothing to hide, why didn't you tell me? I would never keep something like this from you, no matter how much it might hurt. Because right now, it hurts like a dagger through my fucking heart. Did you like it?"

I stared at him, bewildered and taken aback by his direct question. I couldn't find an answer because the truth was too painful. I had liked it.

"No, of course not."

He glared at me as his face leaned in, fractionally close to mine. "Took a very long time to think about that, Layla. I can't believe this is happening to me. When did it happen?"

I swallowed the lump in my throat and stared into his pained blue eyes. The rain was getting heavier, and I could feel the water soaking through my dress, seeping into my skin.

"While you were in New York."

His face turned ferociously dark. "I see. It's not cheating if were in different states, huh? Was that how you thought of it? Is that why you didn't tell me? I bet the two of you had a good laugh about it, didn't you? Boyfriend goes out of town on business, so I think I'll have a little make out session with the guy across the hall. That sound about right?"

A sob escaped me as his callous and icy tone swamped me. "No! It was nothing like that. I swear, Jared. He kissed me, and I pushed him away. It lasted about two seconds and I screamed at him for what he'd done. Please, you have to believe me. I didn't want to hurt you over something that meant nothing to me. You want to talk about honesty, Jared? How about this secret you're keeping about some woman who calls your cell and hangs up. How about telling me the truth about those hushed and secret phone calls?"

Looking at me as though I had just torn his heart out, he shook his head. "I can't tell you."

"Can't, or won't?"

Staring me down, his tone was icy and clipped. "Can't. God, I can't do this right now. I have to go before one of us says or does something they'll regret."

He walked away from me, striding fast across the parking lot. I tried to run after him yelling, begging him to stop and talk to me, but he ignored my plea, getting into his car and speeding away without giving me a second glance.

I couldn't breathe. My heart hammered in my chest, and my stomach lurched and rolled again as nausea threatened. Amy and Mel hurried down the street to me.

"I can't believe it's over. He's gone. I don't believe it." I'd lost him, and I had no one to blame but myself.

Mel leaned her head against mine. "You don't know that. Let him cool off. Come on, you're soaked through. Let's get you home. It'll be better in the morning, you'll see."

Mel and Amy stayed up with me for hours. Mascara flowed down my nose as it rained a monsoon from my eyes, and my body ached from the heaving I was doing. How was I ever going to fix this? I'd lied again. He was never going to forgive me.

Curling into bed, I stared at the wall. My eyes drooped, and my body was exhausted. I was in desperate need of peace and sleep, but I couldn't stop thinking about Jared.

I was in for a rough night.

Chapter 35

Unexpected Guests

Mel's words echoed in my mind as I woke from my restless sleep. It will be better in the morning, she'd said.

It wasn't.

I called, but he wouldn't answer. I texted, but he never replied. It was official; we were done. I glanced over at Amy's side of the room. She was sleeping fully clothed as she and Mel had crashed out around three, when I had pretended to be sleeping. I looked at the clock and groaned. Seven in the morning.

Turning over, I tried desperately to go back to sleep, but it was no use. I couldn't leave things this way; I had to see him. If we were really finished, I had to hear it from his lips. Creeping around the room, I pulled on some jeans and a hoodie before slipping on my sneakers and grabbing my car keys.

The drive to Jared's house felt like hours as I went over and over everything that had happened, and mentally chastised myself for my part in it all. What would I say when I got there? How could I possibly justify my actions? A thousand questions ran through my mind at lightning speed and I didn't have an answer for any of them. Pulling up outside the gates, I punched in the security code that I had seen him enter a thousand times and drove down the long driveway. I sat outside his house just staring at the door. Fear and anxiety were keeping me strapped to my seat. What if he kicked me out and we really were finished? Going inside would make everything so final, while outside in my car there was still hope. But I had to know either way.

Taking a deep breath, I climbed out of my vehicle and walked up to the door. Nausea and a swarm of butterflies were turning my stomach inside out. I grasped the handle and opened the door. It was never locked. With his security system and the gates, he didn't need to worry about the front door. I could hear the sound of Elvis booming from the kitchen. The song 'Are You Lonesome Tonight' echoed through the vast foyer. I walked slowly and sullenly towards the kitchen, my breathing labored as I tried to control my nerves. Rounding the corner, I stood in the doorway and froze, gasping for air.

Long brown hair and a man's shirt barely covering a long pair of legs were all I could see as a woman stood with her back to me at the stove. The room disappeared around her as I stared, unable to breathe. My heart shattered, and my body trembled as I stood staring at the back of this woman's head. The door that led to the dining room opened and Jared strolled in, wearing a pair of sweat pants and no shirt. Without seeing me he stood next to her and smiled, inhaling deeply whatever she was preparing.

"Smells great. I'm starving."

She smiled back at him and stroked his arm. "I've seen you eat, remember? I thought there was no way you were going to finish those pancakes. New York breakfasts are something else, though, aren't they?"

My fists clenched beside me as fury boiled in my veins. New York? Did she just say New York? My chest constricted and my insides twisted with grief.

"I hope you don't mind, but I found this shirt in your closet and figured it's already stained so it was probably alright to cook in it." She turned around and I gasped in horror. She was wearing that shirt. Catching me standing there, she screamed. Jared immediately turned around and his eyes widened.

"No! Wait, shit, it's not what you think. Layla!"

Nausea crept further and further up my throat, forcing me to gulp hard as I sprinted for the door. He ran after me, pleading with me to stop.

"Layla, please. Wait! I swear it's not what you think! I didn't do it. Fuck! Coffee!"

Reaching the driveway, I halted. Did he just safe word me? Furious, I turned to face him. "You have got to be fucking kidding me. A safe word is for bondage play, Jared. It won't stop me walking out on you!"

"I didn't know what else to say to make you stop. Please, Layla, you have to believe me. I didn't do it."

"Didn't do what, Jared? Didn't get so pissed at me last night that you decided to get back at me? Is that what she is? Revenge?" He tried to reach for me, but I recoiled and gave him a warning glare. "Don't you dare fucking touch me. I never want your disgusting, lying, cheating hands on me again! New York? Is she what you went there for?"

Suddenly, the realization hit me. All the calls, hushed tones, secret conversations in his office, and his sudden trip to New York...it was all for her. The entire time we'd been together, he'd been involved with her. I was the other woman. My chest tightened further.

"I can't believe you had the nerve to say everything you did last night, when all this time you've had some skank in another state! How many are there, Jared? One in each place you visit? God, all this time I believed you when you said it was business. I knew there was something you were hiding, but this? How completely stupid am I?"

He walked towards me, but I wanted none of him. The thought of him touching me after having his hands on her made my skin crawl.

"I do not have women in every state, Layla. There's just you, I swear. Yes, she's the reason I was in New York, but I promise it's not what you think. You have to believe me."

I stormed over and shoved him hard on the chest. "Believe you? You've been lying to me since the moment we met! If she's not what I think, then who the fuck is she, Jared? Your maid? Do they all wear your shirts?"

I stood rigid as I waited for an explanation. Shaking his head, he gave me a rueful look. "I can't tell you."

Raising my hand to his face, I slapped him hard across the cheek. My palm stung and prickled as I remained silent, glowering at him. Staring back at me, his face was contorted with a deep sadness and tears pooled in his eyes. Squaring up to him, I clenched my fists as rage filled my body.

"I wish you could feel an ounce of how much it hurts to have something you value so much just fall apart right in front of your eyes because the way I feel right now is a fate worse than death."

Without thinking, I stormed to my car and yanked the trunk open, grabbing the tire wrench that my father always insisted I carry. I was livid, fuming, enraged, and my broken heart was making me crazy. Standing next to his sleek and sparkling car, I held the wrench firmly in my hands. "Who is she, Jared?"

He shook his head and stared at the ground.

"Wrong answer!"

My arms swung back, and in a heavy swoop I crashed the wrench hard into his side mirror, knocking it clean off and flying through the air. He stared at me with the same wounded and devastated expression on his face as before, like I hadn't just fractured his expensive and beautiful Jag. His silence fuelled my anger.

"Last chance, Jared. Who is she?"

He shook his head again and stared at me. "I can't tell you."

My blood boiled, and all my hurt, pain and grief was now flooding through my body as tears streamed down my face. Uncontrollably, I smashed the wrench into his car, sending the other side mirror hurtling across the driveway and landing at his feet. The windshield shattered as I struck a devastating blow right into the center. Dragging and slamming the wrench over the car, scratching and denting the body work, I growled and sobbed as the aching in my heart consumed me. Dropping the weapon, I dropped to my knees and cried shamelessly. My head in my hands, my body shook with every deep and agonizing sob.

Jared fell to the ground in front of me and took my hands from my face, holding them in his. "Please, Layla, you have to believe me. I can't explain, but you have to trust me. Please don't do this to us."

Snatching my hands away, I ripped the ring from my finger and hurled it at him. "I didn't do this to us. You did! You can take back all your promises because they don't mean a thing to me anymore, and they obviously never meant anything to you. You tell me she's not what I think, but won't tell me who she is or give me an explanation. I'm done!"

Pulling the pendant from around my neck, I held it in my palm and dumped it harshly onto the concrete. His own was hanging heavily around his neck, and as he looked deep into my eyes I could see the tears pooling.

"Please, Layla. I love you. I'd give up everything to hold on to your heart. Please don't do this."

Resting my forehead against his, I let out a heart wrenching sob. "You had my heart, Jared. I gave it to you willingly. And you just ripped it out and threw it against the wall."

Scrambling to my feet, I strode to my car and climbed in. With tears falling down my face, I looked back one last time. Broken and on the ground, he held my pendant in his hand as his own salty, self-pitying tears slid down his cheeks.

I started the car and pulled out of the driveway without looking back. Driving home to my friends, my grief, my shattered heart, and my lonely bedroom, I cried and cursed myself for falling in love. I'd jumped off the cliff, soared through the air, and now I had finally slammed straight into the ground. The pain was debilitating, paralyzing and my heart felt crippled from the devastating blow.

* * * *

The drive went in a blur, and I couldn't even remember how I got back. Sitting in the car, I couldn't move. My body felt weak from the crying, and I could hardly find the strength to breathe. My cell had continued to buzz in my purse all the way from his house to the dorm, but I couldn't even bear to look at it as his name flashed on the screen. My heart shattering into a thousand pieces, I stared out of the window at the dorm entrance. Taking a deep breath, I found the strength to stand and got out of the car. The cool morning air hit my face, stinging my cheeks which were sore from the river of tears I'd cried.

Standing outside my room, I could hear Amy and Mel talking through the door. I couldn't face their endless questions as yet; I just wasn't ready to relive the pain. Stepping back, I pressed my back against Ollie's door and slid all the way to the floor, wrapping my arms around my knees. Just when I thought I was all cried out, tears fell like a waterfall over my swollen, red cheeks.

I heard footsteps approaching and as they grew nearer, they broke into a run. Skidding down onto his knees beside me, Ollie's strong warm arms wrapped around me protectively. "What the fuck, Layla? What happened? Are you hurt?" Panic plagued his voice, and lifting my head to look at him, I nodded.

"Where? Are you in pain?"

Sobbing, I took his hand and placed it over my heart.

"Oh, baby girl."

"You were right, Ollie. He was just using me as a pastime between trips to New York. I went to his house to try and work things out and..." a gulping sob escaped me, "and there was a woman there. He tried to deny it, but I saw her, Ollie. She's the reason he was in New York. The secret phone calls. Everything. I'm so stupid."

Holding me tightly to him, he rocked me gently, pressing his lips to my head. "No, you're not stupid, Layla. He's an asswipe. You're worth a thousand of him. He's a fucking idiot."

Pulling me up with him, he opened his door and took me inside. We were alone, and I was glad for the silence. I couldn't think straight. Sitting on Ollie's bed, I held my head in my hands as he crouched in front of me.

"Layla, I know you don't want to hear this, but it's better this way. At least now you have the truth and you can cut him out of your life. He's a tumor, and you need to completely remove him."

I shook my head. "How will I ever get over him, Ollie? I love him. Even after all of this. I just can't stop loving him. I hate myself for ever falling for that man."

Holding me tight, he stroked my hair. "You'll get through this. You still have me, Amy, and Mel. We love you so much. We're right here with you. It'll be ok. Just give it some time. Here, why don't you lie down and try to get some sleep." Gently pressing me down on the bed, he brushed a strand of hair from my face.

The sound of knocking made my head pound. The moment Ollie opened it, Amy and Mel rushed past him to my side.

Jared had called Amy in a desperate plea to reach me, but telling him to drop dead, she and Mel refused to help him. Lying on either side of me on the small bed, they hugged me as I cried and sobbed myself to sleep.

Mentally, emotionally, and physically exhausted, I must have slept for at least six hours. Waking up, blurry eyed and alone, I scanned my surroundings. Posters, a guitar and a drum set reminded me that I was in Ollie's room.

And then, the stomach churning realization that it hadn't all been a horrible dream.

Running to the bathroom, I heaved and vomited violently. Hugging the toilet, I rubbed my sore and pounding head. The sound of yelling echoed outside the door, and I could hear Mel's high pitched screaming, then the low growling of Jared's voice followed by Ollie's. Gripping the sink, I hauled myself to my feet, staggered to the door, and pressed my ear to it firmly.

"Drop dead, shit streak! She doesn't want to see you ever again, so why don't you just turn around and go back to the sewer you crawled out of."

Ouch, Mel sure had a poisonous tongue when she needed it.

"Please, Mel. I just need to see her. I'm in pieces here. I swear I never cheated on her. I couldn't, I wouldn't. I just want to see her."

Opening the door, I stood staring at the group of people in the hallway. All eyes darted to me. Jared's face was pale and etched with worry as he gazed at me.

"Layla, please, I swear I just want to talk. Just give me ten minutes, then I swear I'll leave, but you have to hear me out."

Ollie squared up to him, practically spitting in his face. "What don't you understand about get fucked, jizz stain!"

Jared ignored him as his eyes pleaded with me for a chance, for hope. Holding the door open, I stepped aside and gestured for him to come in. Ollie stared at me in disbelief.

"Are you fucking serious?"

Closing the door in his face, unwilling to discuss my reasons, I walked to the bed and sat down staring at the floor, window, door...anywhere but at Jared.

Slumping down next to me, he exhaled loudly. "Layla I swear I didn't sleep with her. I-"

"Who is she?"

He shook his head ruefully.

"I can't tell you. But please, Layla, you have to believe me that I could never be unfaithful to you. I love you. Please come back. I can't be without you. You promised I'd never have to."

"No, Jared. I never thought you would ever hurt me the way you have, but every time you open your damn mouth I just get another painful reminder that you don't trust me, and I definitely don't trust you anymore."

He grimaced, and I could see the pain in his eyes as he gazed at me. Tears fell slowly from my red puffy eyes. Scanning my face for any glimmer of hope he shook his head. "What are you saying?" Gulping a sob, I gazed back at him. "It's over Jared. I just can't do it anymore." Nodding gently, he exhaled loudly.

Tears were stinging my eyes as I rose to my feet and opened the door. Ollie, Amy, and Mel were still standing in the hall with concern on their faces. They watched as Jared stood and walked out. Giving me a final heart-breaking look, he turned and walked away. I watched him go, away from me, away from us and out of my life.

And it hurt.

My legs gave way, and if not for Ollie holding me up, I would have been lying in a heap on the floor. My body trembled, and my blood ran cold as the three of them carried me into my room and laid me on my bed. There was nothing left. I had nothing left but to grieve and mourn for the love I'd lost. Closing my eyes, I let my misery consume me.

Chapter 36

Numb

The next few weeks passed in a hazy blur. Shutting everyone out, I went into auto pilot. It had always been my way of coping, and when my parents divorced I'd spent six months just wandering the school halls, going from class to class like a zombie.

When Mel told them what had happened, my parents called almost every hour making sure I wasn't about to hurl myself under a bus. Mel had begged me to come back to Pasadena and transfer to be nearer to her, but my life was here with Amy and Ollie now. It consisted of waking up, going to classes and sleeping; albeit not very well. I stayed away from social events, and I hadn't been to the bar in over a month.

Respecting my need for space, Amy and Ollie hadn't pressed me about it. I'd tried to continue working in the coffee shop, but the painful memories of Jared were a constant reminder of my broken heart. Lorraine was visibly upset when I gave her my notice, but understood why I felt I couldn't stay. She'd pulled me into the office and begged me to reconsider, but my mind was made up.

"He's a good man, Layla, but I've never seen him so broken. I can't help but wonder what it was that came between you. You seemed so happy together."

Resting my hand on her arm, I gave her a weak smile. "Our problems started from the word go, and we only have ourselves to blame. We just couldn't be honest with each other, and now we have to live with the consequences. I really loved working here, Lorraine."

Taking my hand, she smiled. "Then stay. Please."

I shook my head regretfully. "I can't. I'm sorry. Thanks for everything. I won't forget what you've done for me."

Promising Kate we'd keep in touch, I left the place I had once loved like a second home behind me, feeling it was now a painful reminder of everything I'd lost. Without work to distract me, I focused on my studies and spent most of my time hauled up in my room. It was quiet, empty and lonely; just how I felt inside.

Desolate.

Days were just melting into one long depressing month. For weeks, Jared had bombarded me with calls, texts and sent me dozens and dozens of bouquets. The last one had been considerably impressive. As I sat in psych class, a courier had wandered in with a very large bunch of long stem white roses. The note that accompanied them was a typical ploy from him to provoke warm and loving memories of our time together. This one was a doozy. Reading it aloud to Ollie, who was practically foaming at the mouth over the gesture, I winced.

"Baby since you left me I've found a new place to dwell. It's at the end of Victoria Street, the heartbreak hotel."

Ollie snorted and shook his head. I knew that Jared was referring to our morning together the first time I stayed with him. The morning I'd caught him singing Elvis, making him blush with embarrassment. I remembered how I'd picked up a spoon and belted out the song myself, just to ease his embarrassment. Annoyed that I'd allowed myself to dwell on such a painful memory, I took a pen, wrote on the back of his note and handed it to the courier. "Could you be sure he gets that along with his flowers. Thank you."

Ollie eyed me curiously. "What did you write?"

Smiling a little, for the first time in weeks, I was pleased with myself. "Return to sender. The truth unknown. Gifts unwanted. Leave me alone."

Staring at my notebook, I suddenly felt the familiar feeling that I always felt when Jared creeped swiftly and silently back into my life and my thoughts; nauseous. It didn't matter how hard I tried to forget him, I couldn't. I was in love, and he still grasped my heart in his hand. The pain was raw, and I gulped as a sob threatened.

Ollie draped a supportive arm around my shoulder and pulled me into him. Resting my head on his chest, I swiped at my eyes as tears slid silently over my cheeks. After weeks of being apart, I still couldn't forget. Would I ever stop fucking crying?

Friday came around quickly. I sat melancholy on my bed and watched as Amy dashed about the room getting ready for a night out at the bar. Turning to face me, she leaned into her hip and tilted her head at me.

"You sure you won't come? You can't sit in this room for the rest of your life. You need to get out there, Layla. You're a delicate flower who needs food, fluids and TLC. That's where Ollie and I come in. I promise you can just sit there all night and not say a word if you want, but you have to get out of this hell hole! You're going to end up rotting in that bed soon."

I shrugged nonchalantly. I didn't care anymore. Life had no meaning for me. Days were long, and nights were longer.

"That's it, you leave me no choice." Picking up her cell she hit speed dial. "It's me. Plan B." I watched her curiously as she stalked over to the door and pulled it open.

Standing in the hallway shaking her head at me was Mel. I hadn't seen her since Jared and I had broken up, and she was a welcome sight. Leaping from the bed, I ran to her and threw my arms around her neck, crying softly on her shoulder.

"Shhh, I know, baby girl, but you have to snap out of this. How long are you going to torture yourself, Layla? You have to get on with your life. Come on, you're coming out with us tonight. It's open mic night, and you are coming to that bar even if I have to drag you by your hair, and you know I will."

A slight smile grazed my lips as she fisted her hands on her hips and stared me down. Rolling my eyes, I nodded weakly.

"That's my girl. Now go shower. You look like a hermit in those sweats. I swear you need a babysitter."

I began walking towards the bathroom listening to her go on about me needing supervision. "That's why I've decided to transfer here."

I turned around quickly and gawked at her.

Grinning, she nodded. "As of Monday I'll be a Long Beach State student!"

I couldn't believe it. My eyes darted to Amy, who was giving me a knowing smile. "You knew about this?"

Nodding, she giggled. "We were talking the other day. Mel called to check how you were, and when I told her how bad you were handling everything she said she couldn't stand being so far away anymore. So first thing Monday, I went to admissions and picked up the necessary paperwork. Mel came down on Tuesday and filed it. And hey, presto college chango!"

Taking their hands, I pulled them into a warm hug. "You guys are the best. I don't know what I'd do without you."

Mel chuckled in my ear. "Right now, I'd be happy if you would just shower."

Laughing lightly, I left them in my room and headed for the bathroom. For the first time in weeks I was feeling ok again; a little more normal, a little more Layla. And I really had missed her; the feisty, independent and take no prisoners girl I was when I first came to college.

Would I ever get her back permanently?

* * * *

Sitting at our booth, I scanned the bar. The usual aroma of sweat and bitter ales was rancid, but in my current mood it seemed so comfortably familiar. Ollie, Amy and Mel had executed operation 'Don't leave Layla on her own' expertly for the past two hours. I was constantly in the company of at least one of my friends. Finding myself alone with Ollie, I suddenly felt awkward. He gazed at me from across the table and bit his bottom lip, making his piercing pinch as it caught on his teeth.

"How are you feeling?"

I shrugged as I took another sip of my drink. "Same old. You playing tonight?"

He nodded, and slid his fingers up and down the glass he'd been nursing for the past twenty minutes. "I spoke to my brother today. He wants me to go stay with him over winter break, but I'd rather not. He'll just use it as an excuse to try and talk about our parents, and I am not willing to open that fucking can of worms."

My stomach twisted as I realized that through all my own hurt and heartache, I'd forgotten about his. Giving him an apologetic look, I placed my hand over his on the table. "I'm so sorry, Ollie. I've been so caught up with my own crap, I completely neglected you and everything you're going through. If you're not going to be with your brother, where will you go?"

Winter break was only a week away. I was spending the first two weeks at home in Pasadena with Daddy and Mel before driving to San Francisco to spend a week with Mom after Christmas. Staring at the table, Ollie shrugged. "I don't know. Stay here on campus I guess."

My eyebrows furrowed as I thought about him being alone over the holidays. Amy was heading home too, so there would be no one to keep him company. Without thinking, I blurted word vomit right at him.

"Come with me."

His head snapped up and he looked at me, confused. "What did you say?"

Leaning forward, I repeated my statement. "Come with me. Come to Pasadena. You can stay with us for Christmas, then come back here after when I go to San Francisco. Say yes, Ollie. Please, I don't want you to be alone."

He gawked at me, clearly taken aback. After everything that had happened between us, I'd thought that Ollie and I were through. But on the floor outside his dorm room that fateful day, he scooped me into his arms and picked up the shattered pieces of my heart. I was in his debt. I'd put him through hell, yet he continued to take care of me, support me and be a constant pillar of strength. He truly was an amazing person with a heart of gold, and I owed him.

"You're sure about this?"

I nodded in a definitive and resounding yes.

"Then, sure. OK, I'd love to."

It was settled. Taking my drink, I held it in the air. "To having something to look forward to at last."

Raising his glass, he clinked it against mine. "I'll drink to that."

Amy slid into the booth, and beamed at me. Chuckling, I gave her quizzical look. "What's gotten in to you?"

Biting her lip, she squealed. "He's asked me out again!"

"Who did?"

"James Felix! He wants to take me to this big social dinner dance on Thursday!"

I remembered Jared's warning in my ear, but seeing the happiness on Amy's face, I decided not to mention it. Besides, the Felix that Amy knew, and the Felix that Jared knew, were two very different people. I smiled at her. "Congratulations."

Glancing at Ollie and Mel, she turned her attention back to me.

Oh dear.

"There's a catch. He has a friend in town who needs a date for the dance. Please, Layla. I know it's a lot to ask right now, but you've been to these things. You know the formality, and I could really use the support. Please, please, please. You don't have to like the guy. Just dance, smile and be your charming self. Please."

Did I say, oh dear? I meant, holy fuck.

I gaped at her, unable to truly believe what she was asking of me. My relationship wasn't even decomposing yet, and she wanted me to go on a date? Surely she wasn't serious.

Gazing at me with hope in her eyes, Amy waited patiently for my response. I stared at Mel, desperate for her to rescue me.

"I think you should go. It'd be a welcome distraction. Get dolled up and go out on the town. You still have that cocktail dress you bought on your birthday, the white one. Wear that, I'll do your hair, and I'm sure Amy can manage makeup. It's been over a month now, Layla. You need to try and move on, sweetie."

I glared at her. Thanks, friend.

Ollie was typically silent. He had learned it was best not to get involved when it came to Amy wanting something. The best course of action was to hide quietly in a corner and pray she didn't sucker you in.

Turning my eyes to Amy, I exhaled exasperatedly. "Fine, fine. But don't expect me to be the life and soul of the party, Amy. I'll eat, drink, smile, and make polite conversation. That's it. No hugs, no kiss goodnight, and no second date. Understood?"

Nodding, she flung her arms around my neck and kissed me. "Thank you!"

Getting to his feet, Ollie chugged the rest of his drink and gave us a quick smile. "Well, we're up to play next. Hey, you ladies wanna join us? Could be fun. Just like old times, huh, Layla?"

Slumping back in my seat, I shook my head. "I don't know, Ollie. I don't feel much like singing these days. I feel like someone stole my oxygen when Jared ripped my heart out past my lungs, through my mouth, then stomped on it."

Amy winced. "Graphic, Layla. Nice."

I shrugged. I couldn't help that she was squeamish, and besides, it's exactly how I felt.

"Well, maybe it's time you let some of that emotion out in a more productive way?" Mel was giving me her 'do as you are told' look, and I knew I wasn't going to wriggle my way out of this one.

Getting to my feet, I brushed myself down and took a deep breath. "Ok, I've got a song for you. You want emotion? I've got bottomless pits of the stuff." Striding past them, I walked right up to the stage and waited for them to join me.

Turning to Ollie and the boys, I told them the song I needed them to play. Eric, the bass player, rolled his eyes at me.

"Seriously?"

I glared as Amy and Mel shouted abuse at him for asking questions in the first place. Raising his hands defensively, he backed away from them.

"Alright, alright. Jeez. Woman scorned and all that."

Ollie laughed, and glanced at Nick who simply shrugged and began to drum the intro to 'I Hate Myself For Loving You' by Joan Jett. The lyrics, beat and hard hitting notes expressed exactly how I felt. As I belted out every powerful, emotion fuelled word, I could feel some of the tension in my body lifting and easing. Maybe people were wrong; laughter wasn't the best medicine, music was.

I glanced back at my friends. Amy and Mel harmonized as my backup singers and the band were as hot as always. Ollie grinned, his hand stroking up and down his instrument as the song hit the guitar rocking instrumental.

I watched as he bit on his lip and blew the hair that had fallen in front of his face out of his eyes. I couldn't stop gazing at him. His eyes sparkled in the spotlight, and his dazzling smile was intoxicating as I found myself grinning goofily back at him. His black ripped shirt was hot, very hot, and my mind suddenly began wandering to what was hidden beneath. I'd seen Ollie topless before, and he was a serious piece of hunk with a perfectly chiseled package. My heart beat faster, and I licked my lips as I continued to stare at him as he made love to the guitar. I was so caught up in my daze that I almost missed my cue.

What was that about?

When the song finally ended, I was exhausted. I'd poured every last drop of myself into every note and now I was spent. Ollie appeared beside me and kissed my cheek.

"Awesome as usual, superstar."

His breath in my ear sent a shiver up my spine. My hair stood on end and I felt my insides clench. Watching him walk away, I shook my head, rubbing my eyes with my thumb and index finger.

What the hell was wrong with me?

My heart was broken into tiny pieces, yet my body was firing up the furnace and heating up my libido again. I rationalized that it was just a phase. I hadn't had sex in over a month, and I was just going through withdrawal. Yeah, that's it. Sex with Jared was mind blowing and obsessively addictive, so the come down was always going to be grueling. I was just hankering for my fix, and my body had momentarily selected Ollie as a suitable dealer.

Deciding that the following day I would definitely have to invest in a B.O.B to get me through my sexual rehab, I pushed the thoughts of Ollie's rocking hot bod out of my mind.

Standing beside me, Mel leaned into my ear. "Horny for the rock star, huh?" I could feel her smiling against my cheek.

Shrugging, I chuckled. "Just horny generally, I think. It has been over a month, remember?"

Wrapping her arms around me, she pecked my cheek affectionately. "It's good to hear you laugh again. How do you feel now? I mean, aside from lusting after your dorm mate."

"I still love him, Mel, and I hate it. And if you asked me if I'd do it all over again, I would. It wasn't perfect, but most of the time I was happy. I miss him. Nights are the worst. I turn over, and reach out, but he's not there. I wake up, and sometimes for a split second I forget and it's all ok again. But then I remember, and the same raw pain cuts through me, and I have to face the day knowing it's that little bit harder because he won't be in it. I just wish I could forget and move on like everyone tells me to. I wish I could hate him, but I can't because for all the god awful, cruel and twisted punishment, I can't stop loving him."

Hugging me tightly, she stroked my hair as I buried my head into her shoulder. "Oh, girlfriend, I know. If I could take it all away and make it better again, I would. But you're going to be ok. You're a strong and beautiful woman, Layla Jennings. I should know. I learned everything I did through watching you. It's going to get easier. I promise."

Lifting my head, I wiped a stray tear. Her words were typical of her glass half full personality, but I couldn't share her optimism. I felt like someone had taken my glass and thrown its contents into my face. Would I ever stop being bitter? The heartache was bad enough, but the wrathful and scornful bitterness was by far the worst part of the whole situation.

Taking my hand, Mel led me back to our booth where Ollie had a drink waiting for me. Giving him a smile, I mouthed a thank you and sighed as I listened to my friends talk, laugh, and bicker about everything from the weather to the color of the sky. It was so normal, so every day, and I felt extremely out of place. My world had come to a standstill. It had stopped turning and was now just hovering motionless in my universe. It had halted the moment I left Jared's drive way, and I hadn't been able to get the damn thing to spin ever since. Maybe it never would again.

I stared down at my drink and felt my heart descend to the bottom of my ribcage. Getting up from his seat, Ollie slid in next to me and draped his arm around my shoulders. He pressed a kiss to my cheek. "I got you. It'll be ok, you'll see."

Gazing at his beautiful, heart stopping smile, I felt a thud inside my chest. Pressing my palm to my heart, I smiled.

The earth was finally moving again.

Chapter 37

Shall We Dance?

Dressed in a sparkling white cocktail dress, I stared at myself in the mirror. The ruffled bust line made the rounded curves of my cleavage prominent, and the black satin bow around my middle gave me a particularly curvaceous hourglass shape. Mel had styled my hair into an elegant up do; pinned, lacquered and curled neatly on top of my head. Amy's amazing makeup skills knew no bounds, and had been able to completely eradicate any trace of the dark circles that had appeared around my eyes these past few weeks. Sighing, I couldn't help but think of the last dance I had attended. Jared had bought me a beautiful gown, and dinner itself was anything but boring. A tingle of remembered pleasure shot through me, but lasted only a moment as it was soon replaced with a deep hurt and longing.

Amy squealed as her cell buzzed, letting her know our dates were here. Exiting the dorm, I rolled my eyes as a black limousine pulled up to the curbside. Stepping out in all his finery, James Felix shot Amy a devastating smile. There was no denying he was handsome. With his slender but fit frame, blond hair and boyish good looks, he was the regular boy next door.

Exiting the other side, I saw my date. Muscular in build, his dark hair was slicked back from his face, reminding me of

Superman and allowing a perfect view of his chiseled good looks. Was it a law that all these high society men had to be so overwhelmingly good looking?

The two men exchanged a look and Felix nodded with a wide grin on his face. What was that about? Kissing Amy on the cheek politely, he showered her with compliments before turning his attention to me. "Ah, the equally beautiful Layla. This is my dear friend, Sebastian."

Taking my hand, Sebastian placed a soft kiss on my knuckles. My mind played a dirty trick on me as an image of Jared doing the same thing on our first date flashed before my eyes. Shaking it from my head, I smiled and studied his face. Dimples appeared as he smiled, and he had the most dazzling green eye's I'd ever seen.

"Layla, it's an absolute pleasure to meet you. May I say, you look truly stunning."

I smiled and thanked him for his compliment as he took my hand and led me to the car, following Felix and Amy closely.

The drive was painfully uncomfortable. Amy and Felix were fawning all over each other as Sebastian and I made small talk. It turned out that he had known Felix since college, and while Felix went into restaurant ownership, he had decided to continue as a chef. He was very sweet, quite the gentleman, and any girl would have been swooning and giggling in his company. But there was only one businessman who would ever get me giggling, and Sebastian wasn't him. I tried to push Jared from my thoughts, but it was no good. There were reminders of him and our time together everywhere, and as we pulled up outside the Hyatt Regency, I knew it wasn't about to get any easier.

Taking my hand, Sebastian assisted me from the car and linked my arm in his own, escorting me in. The ballroom was just as magnificent as I remembered it. Decorated in white and deep reds, the tables and chairs were draped with the finest dining arrangements as glistening crystal and silver gleamed on top. Walking across the room, we passed the table where I had sat, dined, laughed, and reached orgasmic euphoria. A slight smile spread across my lips as I remembered the experience, but the smile didn't last as it was soon followed by a sharp stab through my heart.

I recalled the phone call that had followed. His call from her.

Amy caught my eyes and shot me a concerned look. Shaking my head, I let her know that I was not alright. I was still grieving for my relationship, the love I couldn't let go of, and for Jared. Understanding, she gave me an apologetic smile. Finding our table, Sebastian pulled my chair out for me and gestured for me to sit. I tried to put on a brave face, but I was hurting. Deeply.

Seeing the obvious discomfort on my face, he sat beside me and placed his hand over mine. "Are you alright? I can't help but notice you seem unhappy."

Letting out a long breath, I looked at him and shook my head. "I just got out of a serious relationship. This place has a lot of memories, and I'm just finding it a little difficult. I'm sorry."

His eyes lit up and he laughed. I stared at him in shock. What exactly had I said that was funny?

"Oh, Layla, thank god. I just broke up with my girlfriend two months ago, and this is the first date I've been on. James insisted I come this evening, that I needed a distraction. I hate to admit it, but I came here under duress. I'm really not looking for another relationship. I was terrified you were going to end up severely disappointed this evening."

I breathed a sigh of relief. "Oh that's wonderful news. I mean, it's not wonderful you got your heart broken, but I am glad were on the same page. I'm only here because Amy begged me."

Glancing across the table, we watched our friends canoodling and whispering to each other and laughed. "Well, since we're here, there's a free bar and music, so we might as well enjoy ourselves." Standing, he held out his hand for mine. "Want to dance and drink your troubles away with me, Layla?"

I took his hand and got to my feet. "Misery loves company."

Standing at the bar, Sebastian told me all about his ex-girlfriend and how he'd discovered she was seeing someone else behind his back. "I never did find out who it was, but to be honest, what does it matter? She told me she would end it, but I would never have been able to trust her again. I did get the feeling he was a nasty piece of work, though. She'd come home sometimes with strange marks and bruises, telling me she'd fallen or knocked against things. But if he was what she chose, then she got whatever she deserved. What about you?"

Swirling my drink in my glass, I stared at him. "We could never be honest with each other. That was the bottom line. Then I found a woman at his house and he couldn't give me an explanation. Game over. Cheaters and liars seem to be the running theme tonight."

The band began to play a beautiful waltz. Placing his glass on the bar, Sebastian bowed playfully. "My lady, may I have this dance?" My heart stopped as the words left his lips.

My lady.

Breathing rapidly, I chastised myself for allowing that man to haunt my thoughts again. Taking his outstretched hand, I smiled as he led me to the dance floor.

Amy and Felix joined us as Sebastian twirled me about the floor. My heels clanked and clipped against the wood as we danced swiftly and elegantly to the music. We talked, and he made jokes as we tried to forget our worries and enjoy the evening we had been forced into attending.

The music ended, so I took the opportunity to step out for some air. I was flushed and warm from all the dancing. Sebastian offered to escort me, but Amy interrupted him, insisting that she too needed some air. After the way she and

Felix had been carrying on, it was no wonder she was hot and bothered. They were like horny teenagers.

Walking through the lobby, Amy was grinning like a moron. "Things are going well between you two then?"

She skipped a little as she spoke. "Oh, Layla he's wonderful. He's such a gentleman, and he's so unbelievably charming, but he's naughty and rude at the same time. I'm in love!"

I smiled at her as we approached the exit. Pushing our way out of the hotel entrance doors, I froze. Standing next to a sleek silver Mercedes was Daniel.

He hurried over to greet me. Smiling profusely he gave me a warm hug, taking me completely by surprise. "Miss Jennings, it's so good to see you! How are you? Are you well?"

I glanced at Amy as she excused herself and headed back inside, leaving me alone with Jared's driver. "I'm well enough, thank you." I swallowed hard and nodded at the Mercedes. "Is he here, Daniel?"

He didn't answer. Staring over my shoulder, he nodded and walked back to the car. A scent filled my senses, and my heart constricted tightly in my chest. Sweet cologne, vanilla, and soap. My body betrayed me, heating my blood as my insides clenched.

Traitor.

Breathing hard, I kept my back to him, staring across the street. His breath warmed the skin on my neck, and a shiver crept up my spine as my stomach churned and somersaulted inside me. "My car is undergoing repairs." His fingertips grazed my bare shoulder, and I had to remind myself to stay calm. My breathing was already becoming erratic simply from the proximity of his body to mine. "You look breathtaking, Layla."

Turning to face him, I stared at him. His eyes were the piercing blue I found so hypnotic, but there was no light in them. His face was slender, and he seemed paler than I remembered, but his black tuxedo made him look every part the elite playboy.

"My god, I've missed those eyes." Reaching to my face, he brushed a lock of hair from my eyes. As his hand grazed my cheek, I closed my eyes, savoring the memory of his touch against my skin. I felt as though I could breathe again, but it was short lived. My eyes flew open, and I recoiled.

"What are you doing here, Jared? You're not in the culinary business."

His hands at his side, he looked at me, clearly wounded by my sudden frosty demeanor. "I own shares in a restaurant."

Snorting a laugh, I arched an eyebrow at him. "Have your fingers in a lot of pies, don't you?"

Stepping towards me, he leaned to my ear, "I believe the delicious temptation I had my fingers in the last time we were here was yours."

I flushed, and my insides clenched again, hard. Glaring at him, I sniped, "Well you can rest assured that's a delicacy you won't be indulging in again."

Skirting around him, I headed for the door. His hand caught my wrist and halted me. I stood broken and breathless, my eyes to the ground. "Please, Layla. I miss you. I can't stop thinking about you, about us, about everything we had. I've tried to leave you alone, telling myself it's the right thing to do and to let you move on, but I can't let you go. I can't stop loving you."

Tears pooling in my eyes, I couldn't look at him. "You had me, Jared. I gave you all of me, and I gave it willingly. But from the first time we met, you lied, hid, and kept things from me. We didn't have honesty, and without it our foundations crumbled, taking us down with it. I have cried a river of tears over you, and I can't do it anymore. I don't think I will ever stop loving you, no matter how heartbreakingly hard I try to, but it's not enough. Let me go."

I meant it in every sense of the word. I glanced back over my shoulder as he released my wrist. He stood on the sidewalk staring at me as I turned away and walked as fast as my feet could carry me back to the ballroom.

My heart was pounding, and tears were running down my face when Amy caught me in the lobby and ushered me to the ladies room. "Layla, oh my god, what happened?"

Shaking and sobbing, I sniffled and sputtered through my tears. "Jared is here. He saw me outside. I can't think straight. He's hurt me so much, and yet I can't stop wanting him."

Wrapping her arms around me, she held me in a tight hug before grabbing a handkerchief from her purse and getting to work on my mascara smeared face. "You're only human, Layla. You can't be expected to just get over someone in a few weeks. You were in love for goodness sakes. Stop hating yourself for having feelings. It's not wrong to feel this way. You will get over him. Not tomorrow, maybe not even this year, but you will, I promise. Now let's get back in there and try to enjoy ourselves. Sebastian seems nice, and he told Felix he's having a really good time."

I smiled at her, knowing that Sebastian was as heartbroken as I was and that the reason we were having fun together was because there was no pressure to perform. We both knew where we stood, and it was a welcome relief for us both.

Walking to our table, the two men stood and pulled our chairs out for us to sit. Taking my hand, Sebastian smiled. "Are you alright? You seem a little flustered."

I nodded weakly. "I just saw someone I wasn't expecting, that's all." An understanding passed between us, and he tightened his grip on my hand knowingly.

Sitting for dinner, the four of us talked about the restaurant business and I was fascinated by the many different cuisines Sebastian was expert in. I had been placed between Felix and Sebastian, and I was entertained, as they poked fun and ribbed each other about their time in college.

"He was a complete ass. The great James Felix. Every girl wanted to get in his pants, and all their boyfriends wanted to smash his face in."

Felix laughed, tipping his head back in the process. "Good thing I had the sports star here to back me up. He was so huge, like a brick wall."

I laughed as Sebastian shrugged. Amy was speaking to an older woman who was sat at our table. Felix explained that she was the chief buyer for one of California's top designer stores. Amy was desperate to get into fashion. Her excellent taste and keen eye for trends made her a perfect candidate for any possible internship. Excusing himself, Sebastian left the table to speak to a colleague who was standing at the bar.

Taking a sip of my drink I sputtered and choked as a hand slipped up my thigh underneath the table. Snapping my head at him, Felix gave me a wicked grin. What was he doing? Not wanting to make a scene at the table, I quickly brushed his hand away and glanced at Amy.

Leaning into my ear, he growled, "Oh she's sweet and all, but there's something about you, Layla, that brings out the animal in me. This food is delicious, but I'd much rather be devouring you."

I flinched and nausea flooded me. Turning her attention to us, Amy touched his arm and he immediately regained his charming and gentlemanly disposition as if nothing had happened.

The band began to play and Felix stood, offering me his hand. "Miss Jennings, would you do me the honor of giving me the next dance?"

"Over my cold, lifeless, dead body she will!"

I turned in my seat and stared in shock as Jared swiped Felix's hand away from me.

Straightening up, Felix gave him a smirk. "Garrett. Nice to see you too. Come to make sure I'm keeping your money in good company?"

Jared stepped closer, his eyes filled with fury and his voice spitting with venom. "Get your filthy paws away from my girl."

"I do believe you forfeited that title. She's a free agent now. And besides, it's only a dance."

The sound of shouting pulled our attention toward the bar where I saw Sebastian exchanging words with a very familiar brunette. I stared mortified at Jared. He brought her to the dinner? And after everything he'd said outside, he was still seeing her?

Storming away from Felix, and giving me an anxious glance, he headed for the two of them. I could see the woman crying as Jared tried desperately to calm everyone down. People were beginning to stare. Just as I got to my feet, Sebastian came hurtling towards Felix and hit him square in the jaw.

"You fucking asshole! You're supposed to be my best friend!"

Amy shrieked, and I quickly darted to her side as the two men fought against the table.

"I didn't mean for it to happen, I swear! It was a mistake. She's not worth this, Bastian." Hammering blow after blow into Felix's face, Sebastian spat and hissed at him. "She was the love of my life! I was going to marry her, and you took it all away from me!"

Jared and the woman appeared behind them, and with a forceful tug Jared dragged Sebastian away from Felix. The brunette was sobbing beside them, and I couldn't help but feel slightly pleased, as if justice were being served.

"I'm so sorry, Bastian. I never meant for this to happen. Please, you have to believe me."

He glared at her and snatched his arm from Jared's grasp. Pointing at her face, he snarled, "You're a dirty little whore, and you deserve all you get. You should have stayed in New York. Is there nowhere I can get away from you, you soul sucking bitch?"

"Hey!"

Jared jumped to her defense, and it instantly got my back up. Amy stood at the table wide eyed and tearful. Staring at them all, I yelled over the shouting back and forth that was going on, "Hey! Will someone please explain what the hell is going on here?"

Sebastian faced me with fury in his eyes.

"That whore over there is my ex-girlfriend. And this dick, who I thought was my friend, is the one that's been screwing her!"

Grinning, Felix laughed. "Yep, and what a good little lay she was too. Never had better." He reached out a hand and stroked my arm which I instantly pulled away. "Well, yet anyway."

A crash reverberated through the room as Jared dove at him, completely destroying the table as they landed on top of it. His fist pummelled relentlessly into Felix's stomach, chest, face and ribs. "Don't you ever fucking touch her again!"

The brunette screamed at him, "Jared, stop! He's not worth it!"

Releasing Felix, Jared stood back and surveyed the damage as well as the faces of all the people currently staring in his direction. Squaring up to him, I scowled. "What do you care anyway? You've clearly moved on. What is it, Jared? You can't have me, so no one can?"

Grabbing me by the wrist, he dragged me away from the table and through the hallway to the elevator. "What the hell are you doing? Where are we going?"

The brunette followed closely behind us, and as the elevator door opened, he swung me inside. "We need to talk. Right now." Standing in the corner as far away from him as possible, I glared as his guest stepped inside to join us. She was still crying, and her body shook as she sobbed into her hands. "You have no one to blame for this mess but yourself, Lucy. I warned you." She nodded and cried a little harder if that were at all possible. Turning his gaze to me, I could see he was furious. "And I told you to stay away from him. I begged you to listen, but once again you just can't do as you're fucking told!"

I glowered, snapping back at him, "You don't have the right to tell me who I can or can't see anymore, Jared. Like he said, you forfeited that right when I caught you with her!" I pointed at the sobbing woman in front of me, and she quickly shot Jared a pleading look, but he completely ignored her.

The elevator came to a halt, and taking my wrist once again, he pulled me along beside him down the hallway to a room. I glanced behind me to see the woman I now knew to be Lucy following behind. If he thought for one minute all his naughty little fantasies were about to come true, he was wrong! Why the hell was she following us?

Opening the door to a large suite, he pulled me inside as Lucy shut the door behind us. The walls were magnolia, and a corner couch was sitting on the far side of the room. A light wooden coffee table that sat in front of it, and a large dining table set for six were the only other pieces of furniture.

Gesturing at the couch, he asked me to sit. Begrudgingly I did. He turned to the blotchy, red faced woman in the corner.

"You lied to me. All this time you've lied. You swore you ended it, that it wasn't Felix. But it was, wasn't it? Every cut, bruise and scratch. It wasn't Sebastian at all. All this time the man I should have been going after was in the same state as me!"

Hurrying to him, she gripped the collar of his jacket. "I'm sorry, I'm so sorry. I knew once you found out you'd go crazy, and we both know Felix isn't the type to let things go. I know I lied, that I told you it was over, but I couldn't end it. Without Bastian, I had nothing."

"You had me! You had your mother!"

Standing, I dropped my purse on the table. "Will someone kindly explain what the hell I am doing here?"

Looking at me, and then Lucy, he sighed. "Tell her. Tell her, Lucy. Tell her the truth, all of it. There's not much sense in keeping it a secret now, is there?" My heart stopped, and I felt sick to my stomach as she turned towards me.

"I'm not Jared's girlfriend. I'm his sister."

What?

Slumping onto the couch, she gazed up at me. "I'm his sister. And this whole mess is because of me. Because I was stupid enough to get involved with Felix."

Grabbing a handkerchief, she sobbed and ran out of the room. Jared tried to stop her, but she shook her head and breezed past him to the solace of the bedroom. Walking over to me, he rubbed his eyes with his thumb and index finger. I was speechless. He had a sister?

"But….you said you were an only child."

"I lied. According to you it's what I do best." He took a long, deep breath. "Lucy is my father's daughter."

Taking a seat on the couch, he joined me as I slowly lowered myself on to the cushion beside him. "When my parents died, I took over their finances which included all the accounts and my father's office. When I finally sat down to look at it all, I noticed some discrepancies. Every month, thousands of dollars were just disappearing into an unknown account, so I started digging. I looked in every possible business, personal and savings account but I came up with nothing. I was going crazy trying to figure it out, so one evening I tore my father's office apart, looking for anything that could tell me where all this money had gone, and that's when I found them."

Getting to his feet, he stood staring out of the window. "Letters, hundreds of them all from the same woman. I discovered that when I was a very small child, my father had an affair with his secretary. It didn't last long, but long enough to get her pregnant. When he found out, my father made sure that the child would have everything she needed, and in return her mother sent letters and photos. I don't know if my mother knew, but finding out I had a sister turned my world upside down. So I went to find her, and that's when I met her mother."

He had a family? Another heir to the Garrett fortune.

"I told her I wasn't there to cause trouble, but felt she ought to know my father had died, and that meant the money would be stopping. Lucy had moved to college in New York, but her mother was so sweet she insisted I stay and talk, ask questions, anything I needed really. She was so nice and understanding, and for the first time in a long time I felt like I had someone who actually understood what it was like to be alone with such a huge responsibility.

"We kept in touch, and she introduced me to Lucy, who was surprisingly accepting of the fact she had a brother. She was practically giddy. We got along great, and I saw her every month for dinner in the city when I was there on business. Lucy has her inheritance, but it's secured until she's twenty five. My father's very own insurance that she went to college.

"When her mother fell into financial trouble, Lucy asked for my help. She didn't want a handout, so I gave her mom a job instead. I gave her the coffee shop."

My mouth fell open in shock. "You mean, Lorraine? Lorraine was your father's mistress? This is a lot of information, Jared."

Coming back over, he crouched in front of me. "I know, but I had to tell you. The only reason I didn't is because Lucy's got herself into trouble and the less people who knew, the safer I could make her."

I stared at him.

"What kind of trouble?"

Exhaling loudly he shook his head. "She was in an abusive relationship with a man in New York which, until about five minutes ago, I thought was Sebastian. But finding out it's Felix changes everything."

He winced, and I could see he was stressed. This was taking its toll on him. "What did he do to her?"

"He doesn't like the word no, so whenever she used it he'd give her a good beating and make sure she knew her place. He's a very well respected member of the California social elite, and now she's pregnant with his child. When people discover she's my sister, she's going to become a hot commodity. I spent a lot of money, time and manpower to keep myself out of the national press, and now that whole commotion downstairs is going to completely undo all my hard work.

"She has a hefty inheritance, owns half of the business, and if the press or Felix gets hold of the news, that prick will use her to his advantage in any way he can, publicly. My family's name will be dragged through the mud.

"The calls I have been getting were from my friend in New York. I asked him to keep an eye on her, and when he called me in my office, he told me she was in the hospital. That's why I went there. I told Lorraine to put you and Kate in charge of the shop and took her with me. I thought that together we could try and persuade Lucy to come back here, but she took off before we arrived. We must have searched the whole fucking city for her, but nothing."

I watched him intensely as he continued.

"She finally called that night we were at the bar, your birthday." I cringed at the memory of that awful night. The alcohol I had consumed, mixed with the barrage of information I had just received, made me woozy as I tried to process everything he was saying. Lorraine and his father had an affair, he has a sister who is pregnant by the man my roommate was currently falling in love with and who turns out is an abusive asswipe.

God, why me?

He sat staring at me, waiting with bated breath for me to speak, but I had no words. I was completely speechless.

"I'd just got home when I got her message. She said she was on her way and I couldn't turn my back on her, Layla. She's my sister, and to be honest I was so relieved that she was alive that I didn't care. But I knew whoever this guy was, he wasn't going to just let her walk away and that's why I couldn't tell you. I couldn't tell anyone. I had to keep her safe. If I'd known then that it was Felix, I could have avoided this whole horrible mess, stopped it all months ago. She's really fucked up this time."

I shrugged.

"You can't help who you fall in love with, Jared. She couldn't stop any more than I could have stopped falling in love with you. I'm sure you can make calls, pay people off to keep quiet."

He ran his fingers through his hair and I could see the tension he was holding as his arms and shoulders stiffened as he moved. "Of course I can, and all her problems just go away. But what she cost me…no amount of money in the world can replace what I lost."

Holding my gaze, he spoke clearly with desperation in his voice.

"Layla, I could never be unfaithful to you. I love you completely and entirely. No more lies, secrets, or hiding. I give you my word. Just come back to me, please baby." His hand brushed my cheek, and I jumped as though it caused me physical pain, and for all intent and purposes, it had.

"Jared, I…that's a lot to take in. I believe you. I do. And I'm sorry that you felt you couldn't tell me about something that's been causing you so much distress because I would have understood. It's what you do when you love someone."

Taking my hands, he held them tightly, but I pulled them away, resting them on my lap. "But it's not enough. We don't trust each other. Just look at what happened between us that night at the bar. There are so many reasons for us to be apart. You'll never truly trust Ollie and now that you know about that kiss, you'll never really trust me either." He opened his mouth but I shook my head. "You won't, Jared. Not really. There will always be that piece of you that wonders if I'm hiding something, and I'll always think the same about you too. I guess, sometimes, love just isn't enough."

Sitting beside me on the couch, he rested his elbows on his knees and stared at the floor. "Please don't do this to me, Layla. I can't eat. I can't sleep. I walk around in a daze. I haven't been able to focus at work, and I can't even set foot in that coffee shop anymore because every time I walk in and don't see your gorgeous smile, it cuts like a knife."

Lifting his head with my hands, I gazed at him with tears rolling down my cheeks. "I'm sorry. I just can't go through losing you all over again. It hurts too much."

"Daniel will take the two of you home. I'm sorry for everything I've done to you, Layla. But you should know there will never be anyone else for me. As long as you're walking this earth, the shattered pieces of my wasted heart will love you forever. You're my girl, Layla." Pulling a chain from beneath his collar, he held his pendant in his hand. He still wore it. Holding it tightly he stared at me. "You will always be my only love."

I nodded weakly, understanding exactly how he felt because my broken heart felt just the same. "Goodbye, Jared." A sob escaped my lips as I turned and walked out of the door and out of his life forever.

Chapter 38

Winter Wonderland

Amy had been devastated when I told her about Felix. Crying for days, and becoming withdrawn, there was little Mel and I could do to console her. My own pain was still fresh, but seeing my friend so shattered and hurt because I had chosen to ignore Jared's warning was devastating.

Packing for the holidays, she stared at me. "I don't blame you. You know that, right? He's a slime ball. I can't believe what he did to you at that table, right next to me. Jared should have strangled him. Disgusting, vile, pig!" She was slipping healthily from depression to violent anger. "Urgh, I swear if I ever see him again I'm going to cut off his balls with a blunt knife, slowly, sawing back and forth painfully!"

I winced, and looked at Mel who was laughing hysterically in the corner. "Ouch, Amy."

Shoving a large pile of dresses in her suitcase, she slammed it shut, climbed on top, and began jumping up and down on it, forcing it closed. "Sick, twisted, son of a bitch!" I smiled as I watched her shout obscenities at her poor, crammed, full to the brim case. At least she had a productive outlet for her anger.

The door swung open and Ollie stepped inside, looking rather smartly dressed. "Woo, get a load of you spunk boy."

Mel got to her feet and walked in a circle around him. "Got a court hearing or something?"

Wearing black pants and a deep purple shirt, he looked totally out of place. Grinning at her, he did a little twirl. "Actually I thought if I'm meeting Layla's pops, I should at least look half decent."

Mel smiled at me. "If I know Layla, she'd take indecent over half decent any day."

"Melanie!" I gawked at her.

"I'm kidding, I'm kidding."

I didn't want Ollie to get the wrong impression about us. He'd made his feelings for me perfectly clear, and though I was now technically free and single, I wasn't ready to move on just yet.

"Don't worry, Layla. I'll be the perfect gentleman." He smiled at me, then turned his attention to Amy who was now stomping so hard on her case it could easily have sued her for assault and battery. Giving her a wave, he turned to the door. "That's it, Amy. You tell that son of a bitch suitcase who's boss. Layla, I'll get our bags and meet you outside?"

Nodding, I smiled back at him as he hauled my bag from the floor and heaved it out the door.

Mel regarded me suspiciously with her hand fisted on her hip. "You like him. Oh my god, it's so obvious."

I gave her a confused look.

"Oh come on, Layla. You're blushing!"

Pressing my fingertips to my cheeks, I felt the heat radiating from them. I was blushing, but she was crazy. I wasn't into Ollie; we were friends and I was still nursing a broken heart. It was way too soon for crushes.

"You're nuts. We're just friends."

Landing her ass onto her suitcase, Amy snorted. "Ha! Friends that are totally and completely hot for each other, and have been since they met."

"That's not true. I have not always been hot for Ollie."

Mel interrupted me. "Ah so you admit that you are hot for him then."

I exhaled loudly. "No, I'm saying… I just… oh, shut up!"

Bursting into laughter, the two spoke rapidly at me. Holding up my hand, I demanded silence and set them straight "Ok, ok. So he's hot, and sweet, and kinda great, but I'm not ready to get into anything right now. I still love Jared, and that's not going to change by me getting involved with Ollie."

Walking over to Amy, Mel helped zip up the case before turning to face me, the two of them staring me down. "Look, we're not saying go fall in love all over again. We're not even saying have a relationship, but a little fun wouldn't kill you, Layla. Ollie is a great guy and he likes you. There's nothing standing in your way anymore, and I think you'd be crazy not to at least see where it goes. At least don't completely rule out the possibility, ok?"

Rolling my eyes, I conceded, hoping it would end this tiresome and tedious conversation. "Ok. Never say never."

Making our way outside, we met Ollie and the four of us said our goodbyes. Lugging our bags into the trunk of my car, Ollie grinned. "This is awesome. I've never had a real Christmas before."

Mel gave him a hug and playfully tousled his hair. "Aww, well don't worry little man. If you've been a good boy, I'm sure Santa will bring you something special this year."

Giving me a bashful glance, he smiled. "I hope so."

* * * *

The drive to Pasadena was an experience in itself. Mel had elected to sit in the back seat, leaving Ollie up front with me. Turning up the stereo, he beamed. "Oh, Layla. If I didn't love you, before I do now! I love All Time Low!"

I grinned, blushing as he sat beside me playing air guitar. Mel leaned between the front seats. "Oh that Alex is so fucking hot! I definitely would!"

I laughed as I watched her make lewd gestures with her hands in my rear view mirror. "Hey, behave back there. Don't make me turn this car around." Falling into her seat she cackled hysterically.

The second we pulled into the driveway, Mel was out of the car and taking our bags from the trunk. Ollie climbed out and stared up at the house. "Wow, this is where you grew up?" I nodded as I helped Mel with her enormous case. "Looks nice."

I smiled, and handed him the handle of his case. "It is. Come on, let's go say hi. We'll catch you later, Mel?"

Heading across her lawn, she yelled over her shoulder. "You can bet your ass you will."

Taking Ollie by the hand, I led him to the door and opened it, pulling him in with me. Dropping his case in the hallway, he gazed around in total wonderment. "Wow, it's a proper house. Like a homey house, you know?"

I grinned. "I guess."

Bounding down the stairs, my father yelled, "Baby girl!" Scooping me into his arms, he gave me a tight hug and kissed my cheek. "Oh, I missed you."

Hardly able to breathe, I laughed. "Daddy, this is Ollie." Dropping me, he extended his hand and shook Ollie's. "Of course. I remember, the guitar player at the party, right?"

"Yes, sir."

"Let's not bother with the sir. Andrew is fine."

Nodding, Ollie smiled. "Andrew. Thanks for letting me stay here over the holidays. I really appreciate it."

Wrapping his arm round my waist, Dad pulled me to his side and kissed the top of my head. "Well, my baby said she wasn't leaving you there so that meant either she stayed or you came here. But it's great to have another person to share the cleaning up after she cooks Christmas lunch. I swear, every single pot and pan...none are neglected."

I nudged him playfully.

"Why don't you kids unpack, and we'll get Mel and order a pizza?"

I glanced at Ollie who gave me a warm smile. "Sounds great."

Showing Ollie to the guest room, I smiled at him. "I'm glad you're here. Less time for me to be alone thinking about things when I have all of Pasadena to show you."

He placed his case on the bed. "I'm glad I'm here too. Thanks for this, Layla. I mean that." Leaning in he kissed my cheek. My heart pounded, and my cheek heated instantly at the touch of his lips.

Oh good god, girl. Get a grip!

* * * *

For the first three days, Ollie and I spent most of our time hanging with Mel. Her parents worked all the time, so we were pretty much left to our own devices. We watched dozens of movies and easily ate the local store out of all their junk food. With pizza, Thai and Indian food just a phone call away, we were officially hermits.

Ollie hadn't stopped smiling since we'd arrived, and I was pleased to see him having fun and laughing so much. Sitting on the sofa, he sat on the floor in front of me and I smiled as I saw his eyes dance while we watched one of the comedies Mel had got from the video store.

I was dazzled by his smile.

He had one of those smiles you see on famous movie stars and models on billboards. Dimples appeared on either side of his mouth, and his teeth were perfectly white and straight. His lip ring bounced up and down as he laughed, and I found myself suddenly biting hard on my own bottom lip as I gazed at it.

Mel nudged me gently with her foot. "You are so bad," she mouthed to me silently with a wide grin. I furrowed my brow and shook my head at her as if I had no idea what she was talking about and quickly darted my eyes back to the TV, grateful that Ollie had remained completely oblivious during our exchange.

Friday night, I decided to take Ollie to the local park. Every year some of the people living in the area got together and there would be a huge firework display and loads of food, hot cider and live music. Mel was spending the evening at her grandma's house as she did every Friday.

Dressed in his dark jeans and an "I will rock your world" t-shirt, he looked like the rock star I knew and loved. Pulling on my coat, I grabbed his hand. "Come on, rock star. We'd better get going."

He pointed at my keys on the table as I pulled him out the door. "We're not driving there?"

"Nope, it's not far. Besides, I like the walk." He groaned and stared down at his feet. I couldn't control myself; a fit of giggles started as I looked at his pained expression while staring at his converse trainers.

"These are not walking shoes, Layla. And it's not funny. I'm very fond of these shoes."

I gave him a playful shove. "Well you can always borrow a pair of my shoes if you like."

Laughing with me, he shook his head. "I'll suffer it."

Ollie groaned and moaned as we stepped over grass, mud and dirt, and my giggles continued all the way to the park. Holding his hand, I leaned my head on his shoulder as we walked. "What was it like where you grew up? I mean, I know about home, but didn't you have friends? Go out? Have fun at all?"

Resting his cheek against my hair, he shrugged. "I grew up in a trailer park in Michigan. I didn't have friends, it was better that way. Friends would ask questions or see things. We lived in a bad area, and the nearest park was always full of addicts and needle dick, high school drop outs. It was kinda hard to have fun when you grew up constantly waiting for your next beat down."

I frowned as I thought about the poor dark haired little boy abandoned and beaten. Instinctively, my hand reached for his arm where his tattoo covered a painful scar. His hoodie was covering it, but I knew he understood the gesture. Pressing his lips to my head, he sighed. "It's ok. I'm still here, aren't I? And now I have you guys. I'm having more fun than I've had in all my life." Gazing down at me with his soft brown eyes, he smiled as we walked side by side to the park.

Lanterns hung along wires from the trees, and the smell of cinnamon, apple cider and hot cocoa was intoxicating. It felt like Christmas at last. We walked hand in hand around the different stalls, and every now and then I would see people I knew and make polite conversation. Everyone felt like strangers now and I found myself feeling more and more irritated by their questions.

How is college?

What are you studying?

Is that your boyfriend?

After being asked for the third time, Ollie had taken it upon himself to simply answer yes whenever someone asked about our relationship. Surprisingly, it hadn't bothered me at all.

The band was rocking as we approached the stage and I squeaked with delight. Singing into the mic was a tall, brown haired, gorgeous face who I recognized instantly. Letting go of Ollie's hand, I ran up and waved at the lead singer who grinned down at me, signaling with his finger to give him a minute.

"Who's that?"

Grinning like a lunatic, I turned to Ollie. "That, Oliver Green, is Brad Daily. We were in a band together in high school. It's where I started singing."

Finishing his set, Brad climbed down from the stage and gave me a warm hug. "Layla! You look great! How the hell are you? You here for the holidays?"

I smiled back at him. "I'm good. Yeah I'm here for a couple of weeks then heading to San Francisco to see Mom. This is Ollie. He's Long Beach State's resident rock star."

Shaking hands, the two smiled at each other. "Ah, so you play? Sing too?"

Stuffing one hand in his pocket and the other around my waist, Ollie nodded. "Yeah, but Layla here is way better than I am. She sings with my band at our local bar some nights."

Brad grinned. "Hey, you guys should totally play! You can use my guitar. And the guys will back you up." Lifting the shiny black electric guitar over his head, he handed it to Ollie who gave me a hopeful look.

"I'm game if you are."

Biting my bottom lip, I thought for a moment. To hell with it. I needed a little fun.

"Bring it on, rock star."

Climbing up onto the stage, Ollie held his hand out to me and hauled me up. Turning to the band, he told them what to play and they all seemed delighted with his choice. I gave him a quizzical look, but he shook his head with a grin. Loud and electrifying, the intro to Meatloaf 'Dead Ringer For Love' started playing through the speakers. Grinning back at him, I watched as he belted out the words; strong, powerful and in that husky way he always sang. My breathing quickened as he stood inches from my face, singing into the mic we were forced to share. I could smell the spearmint gum on his breath, and the sweet fragrance of his hair gel. When the song reached the time for me to sing, I looked straight at him and sang every word with all I had. We were a duet after all, and I wanted us to be convincing. He watched me intensely with his gorgeous chestnut eyes, biting and running his tongue over his lip ring. My insides clenched.

Oh my. He was so blisteringly hot.

I didn't remember getting through the song as I'd spent the entire time mentally fucking Ollie. His jeans were perfectly snug and he had one of the finest asses I'd ever seen; perfectly round like a peach. I thought about sinking my teeth into it and biting his delicious flesh.

Jeez Layla. Listen to yourself.

People cheered, and jumping off the stage, Ollie smiled up at me and lifted me down. Handing Brad his guitar, Ollie thanked him and we said our goodbyes. It was getting late and we'd been out for hours. Walking along, I groaned. Ollie eyed me curiously.

"What's up?"

Hobbling, I whined, "My feet are killing me." My warm, but slightly high heeled, boots were punishing me for choosing fashion over comfort, and I felt as though my feet were fit to bleed.

Moving in front of me, he crouched down. "Get on. I'll carry you."

I laughed. "What? You can't be serious?"

Turning to look at me, he gave me a smile. "Do I look like I'm kidding? Get on."

My arms around his neck, Ollie hoisted me onto his back and wrapped my legs around his waist. "Well, I always dreamed that someday I'd have these legs wrapped around me. Though, this wasn't quite what I had in mind."

Swatting him lightly around the head, I rolled my eyes.

Walking home with me on his back, Ollie hummed. Leaning to his ear, my chin on his shoulder, I sighed. I could smell the fruity scent of his hair product, and that mixed with Ollie's natural sweet smell was dangerously intoxicating.

"You ok back there?"

I nodded and smiled. Turning his head he kissed my cheek. "Good. I like to see you smiling more."

Approaching my door, Ollie dropped my legs and I slid off his back to my feet. "Thanks for the ride."

He chuckled. "That's what she said."

I gave him a playful nudge and searched for my keys. Taking my hand, Ollie turned me to face him. "I had a really great time tonight. I got to eat great food, meet new people, and even play on a stage with you. But you wanna know the best part of the whole night? It was when I got to pretend I was your boyfriend."

I stood for a moment, the words on the tip of my tongue, I opened my mouth to speak, but he silenced me. "Don't say anything right now. Look, I know that you're not ready to move on, but I'll wait Layla. I would wait forever for just a shot at making you mine."

In a swift, quick movement, I closed the gap between us and pressed my lips to his.

His hands cupped my face as his cool lip ring pressed against my warm mouth. Parting his lips slightly with my tongue, he opened his mouth and granted me access as his own tongue darted into my mine, softly rolling, caressing and stroking. Pulling me close, he deepened our kiss and my head buzzed with a confusing mixture of emotions. I snaked my hands around his back and we stood, kissing and holding one another.

Our gentle and soft kiss became frantic as the blood in my veins began to simmer. My hands roamed over his back to his behind as he drove me backwards against the door. His palm pressed against it, he pulled me close with the other hand. I nipped and nibbled gently on his lip before rolling my tongue over his piercing. God he was just as delicious as I'd imagined.

His hand slid slowly to my hip. As he lifted it against him, I could feel his erection pressing against my thigh. Fueling my own lustful libido, he pressed his palm against my stomach before slipping it underneath my shirt to my breast. Massaging gently, he moaned into my mouth. Coming up for air, I turned my head as he seized the opportunity to trail kisses over my neck. I gasped as his lips grazed my skin.

I fumbled for the handle of the door and pressed it open, making me stumble backwards, but Ollie grabbed me around the waist and held me tightly to him. Kicking off my shoes, I kissed him deeply and passionately with an aching hunger. Tugging at the hem of his hoodie, I pulled and rolled it up, lifting it over his head. Removing my coat quickly, we stumbled, staggered, and fumbled our way through the hall. I wanted him. I needed to feel his body against mine. Taking his hand, I pulled him to the couch and laid down, pulling him on top of me.

"What about your pops?"

Sinking my teeth into his bottom lip, I smiled before releasing it. "He said he was hanging out with his work buddies. He'll be out for hours."

It was a green light, and Ollie was speeding through it. Ripping my shirt open with his bare hands, the buttons pinged and flew across the room. His face buried in my neck as his tongue stroked my collar bone before heading south to my cleavage. I writhed beneath him. Grinding against his hips, I could feel the bulge in his jeans pressing into me. Sliding my hands between us, I unbuttoned his pants and slid the zipper down. Dissatisfied, I hooked my thumbs into his pockets and pressed hard; forcing them to glide over his hips and rest just beneath his ass. His shorts still in place, I slipped my hand inside and I felt for his cock. Grasping it, I gasped.

He was huge!

"Oh god, Layla, I want you so bad. I've wanted you from the moment I saw you."

Pulling me up, he sat with his hands around my back and unhooked my bra. Begrudgingly letting go of his rock solid piece of equipment, I pulled his t-shirt off of his head and gazed at his perfectly toned body. His rock solid abs were clenching as he breathed hard and fast. His broad muscular chest was delicious and his skin was pale, though now slightly flushed. He was delicious.

Launching myself at him, I pinned him to the sofa as our warm bodies pressed against each other. The comforting feeling of skin on skin was like a fresh breath of air into my deflated and gasping lungs. It had been so long, and my need to feel that warm and wanting touch of a man was something I had ached for since that final evening at the Hyatt. My body was a giant bag of sensation as every breath, touch and lingering kiss drove me wild with arousal. Unzipping my jeans, his fingers brushed against my panties and he let out a moan. The feeling was mutual. I ached to feel him inside me. Sliding his fingers into my panties, my breath hitched in anticipation and I was about to lift up, granting him access when the sound of keys in the door startled me. "Fuck! My father!"

Crawling backwards off of Ollie I scrambled for my bra and shirt as he frantically zipped up his pants and pulled on his t-shirt. My shirt now button less I tied it into a bow trying to make it look like a fashion statement rather than evidence of my almost sexual escapade with Ollie.

The door opened, and the sound of a woman's voice caught my attention. Crawling over Ollie, who was sitting rigidly on the couch, I peered over the back of the sofa. Had he seriously brought a woman back to the house? Surely he wasn't going to have sex in the house where I was sleeping? Well, where he thought I was sleeping. A woman with long blonde hair stood with her back to me, and my father leaned in and kissed her gently. Suddenly, lifting her left hand to his face, I recognized a ring.

"Mom!"

Spinning around, she gawked at me in horror. My father, equally as shocked to see me, stared at her. Hurrying inside towards me, she raised her hands defensively. "Now calm down, honey. I know this must be a shock." I instantly got to my feet, leaving a very uncomfortable Ollie on the couch with a pillow over his bulging crotch.

"A shock? You think I'm shocked? I'm mortified. What the hell is going on?"

Seeing my attire, and Ollie's clearly flustered appearance, she raised an eyebrow at me. "What were you two doing before we came in?"

Blushing, I tried to think of a plausible answer, but shaking my head I got back to the matter at hand. "Don't change the subject. Are you two sleeping together?"

My mother immediately said no but my father, picking up Ollie's discarded hoodie and hurling it at him, gave a very different answer. "For a while now, yes."

My mother glared at him.

"Oh come on, Diane, she's a grown woman. She believes you just as much as I believe these two weren't about to have sex on my couch."

Holding my hands over my face, I hid shamefully from my father's accusing look. Taking a deep breath, I took my hands away and looked at them. "Will one of you please explain what's been happening here because the last time I checked, I was sure the two of you were very happily divorced."

Taking my hand, my mother spoke softly. "So did we. After your party, your father and I came back here and had a few drinks. We talked all night and it was just like old times. We laughed, we talked about you, about the past, the divorce, everything. And we realized something. We divorced because things got hard, Layla. We never divorced because we didn't love each other. I still love your father. I always have. He was my first love, and everything I ever wanted. And I think he feels the same. At least I hope so."

Putting a reassuring hand on her shoulder, he nodded. "I do. We've been spending weekends together here and things have been going really well. We didn't want to tell you until we knew for sure what was happening, but after doing this for a month now, I've asked your mother to move back in."

I stared at them in shock.

"And I've said yes. I'm having my things brought over next week."

I shook my head at them in total disbelief. I couldn't handle this right now, and the need to run from it all overwhelmed me as I stormed past them, grabbed my sneakers, and ran out the door. The cool night air was a refreshing wakeup call, reminding me that what had just happened in the house hadn't been a horrible dream. Walking down the driveway, I hugged myself as the breeze chilled my bare skin, scarcely covered by my shirt.

Ollie yelled as he ran after me. He caught up and wrapped a coat around my shoulders, then pulled me into a warm hug. Safely inside Ollie's arms I cried softly into his chest. "What the fuck are they doing? Why do they have to make everything so damned complicated? I mean, when were they even going to tell me? After a U-Haul truck pulled into the driveway with all my mother's shit in it?"

Rubbing his hands up and down my back, he pressed a kiss in my hair. "I don't know, baby girl. You'd have to ask them. The way I see it, you have a lot of questions and they have the answers. Running away won't make that any better."

Wiping my tears, I gazed up at him. "When did you get so smart?"

He chuckled. "I don't know because whenever you're around, I get all stupid. I guess you're rubbing off on me."

I smiled suggestively. "I'd rather be rubbing against you."

Kissing me deeply, he smiled against my lips. "God, I've waited so long to be able to do that. Layla, I need you to be sure about this. I'm not asking for a relationship, but at least give us a chance."

Cupping his face in my hands, I placed a chaste kiss on his lips. "I want to give this a chance, Ollie. Give us a chance. I can't promise you forever, but I can promise you I'll try."

And I meant it. Ollie was wonderful, sweet, charming, sexy as hell, and most importantly, he was honest. He was everything I knew I should want in a man, and yet not the man my heart truly wanted. I wanted to give him everything, to give him all of me, but as much as I wished I could right now, I couldn't give him my heart.

It still belonged to Jared.

And I hated myself for it.

This magnetic hold Jared had on me was debilitating. It didn't matter where I went, whom I was with, or what I was doing; I couldn't stop thinking about him. I wondered how he was doing, who he was with, even how his sister was coping. I hated her for everything her lies had caused, but seeing a pregnant woman breaking down and sobbing still pulled on the heart strings a little.

I was pissed. Not inhumane.

Maybe he had moved on too; met some long legged bimbo to bang in the back of cars, devour on dining tables, and tie to his bed.

Yeah, Layla, you're not bitter at all.

Besides, how could I be angry about it? I had been ready to fuck Ollie into next week on that couch a moment ago, and without even a second thought to how Jared might feel. Maybe I was getting over him.

Walking back to my door, I glanced back at the sidewalk, and a memory of seeing his car pull up outside swamped my thoughts. My heart sank. He'd been so riled up, but that day was a turning point for us. I'd finally understood his need to control and keep me safe. It was just a shame that the one thing I needed protecting from was him, breaking my heart.

Ok, so maybe I wasn't quite as over him as I had thought.

Chapter 39

Happy Holidays

The tension in the house was so thick, you could cut it with a knife.

My mother had all her things driven across the state, and she soon made herself right at home in the house she had walked away from seven years ago. Sitting on the couch with Ollie, my feet in his lap, I watched her organizing the living room cabinets.

"You know, there was nothing wrong with how Dad and I had it. It worked perfectly well before you came back."

She stood with her hands on her hips, and her head tilted to the side. "Are you referring to the cabinets or me, Layla? Because I'm getting really tired of this shit. I've been back here two days and you've treated me like an intruder the whole time. I know this is hard for you, but could you at least try to be happy for us?"

I glanced at Ollie who was giving me a look that told me he agreed with her. Whose side was he on? Taking my feet off his lap, I stood and headed upstairs.

"Layla, let's at least talk about this. You haven't wanted to talk about it since you found out. Please, sweetheart."

I growled at her, stomping up the stairs as though gravity just made everything ten times heavier. "Leave me alone, mother."

It wasn't that I didn't want my parents to be happy, but did they have to be happy together? The divorce had been a traumatic and life changing event for me. Watching my parent's marriage slowly fall apart at the seams, and eventually tear into two very large pieces, had made me the strong, independent woman I was now. And then there they go, screwing it all up because they're in love. My whole belief system had been thrown into a shredder, and I was frantically scraping up the pieces and trying to make sense of it all.

Slamming my bedroom door behind me, I sprawled out on my bed, flung my arm over my eyes, and sighed deeply. A second later there was a tapping at my door.

"I said leave me alone, Mother!"

"It's me. Can I come in?" Ollie's gentle tones melted my icy mood.

"Of course you can, Ollie. It's not you I'm mad at."

Opening the door, he stepped inside and closed it behind him quietly. He stood with his back against the door, gazing at me. "I really think you should give your parents a break here, Layla. They love each other. That's the bottom line, and no amount of pissing and whining is going to change that so you might as well get used to it. Hell, I don't even understand why you're so upset. At least you have two great parents, and the fact that they're back under the same roof sounds awesome to me."

I gave him a quizzical look. "Why are you whispering?"

"I don't want your folks to catch me in your room."

I rolled my eyes at him. "Ollie last night they caught us pre-coital on the couch. I think the cat's out of the bag."

He ran his fingers through his long black hair. "Oh. Well I still think you should hear your mom out. She was really upset, you know. I think she was crying."

Oh no. If there was one thing my mom did very well it was cry, and it always worked on me.

Feeling instantly guilty, I groaned. "Oh crap. Now I have to go down there and apologize. God, she's so unfair! Why can't she just let me be mad for a while?"

Walking over, Ollie held onto my hands and pulled me up. "You will forgive her, you know. Because you're too nice to hate anyone really, even when you should."

He gave me his trademark, knock your socks off, sexy smile and I couldn't resist him. My hands around his neck, I pulled him to me and kissed him longingly. I loved the feel of his piercing against my lip, and every time it pressed into my flesh, I had the desperate urge to sink my teeth into him. His hands snaked around my back as I pulled him towards the bed. The back of my knees hit the edge, and falling back onto the mattress, I hauled him down with me. I just couldn't help myself. As his tongue and lips caressed my jaw, and his fingertips traced freely over my neck, I groaned. Whenever Ollie's hot body was in the same room as mine, my blood simmered and my insides clenched with desire. He'd always had an effect on me, but it seemed the more time we spent around each other, the more I wanted him.

I wanted him so much it was driving me crazy.

My body and my heart were clearly not on the same page. My heart was still hibernating and rocking in a corner, suffering with post-traumatic stress while my libido did the Lambada whenever the young, smoking hot, wanna be rocker was around me. It was a confusing combination, and at that moment my head seemed to be listening to my body, disregarding the violent warnings my heart was sending as it thudded and drummed loudly inside my ribcage.

Closing my eyes, I surrendered myself to the pleasure of his touch. His tongue grazed my skin, making goosebumps appear all over me. His hands held mine, arrested on either side of my head. "Oh god Layla, I love you so much," he murmured into my mouth, and as if my heart had grabbed for a megaphone it screamed at me to stop this.

My eyes instantly flew open. Springing up, I pushed him off of me. "Wait!"

Falling onto the floor, he stared up at me, panting and completely confused at my outburst. Holding my head in my hands, I shook my head. "I'm sorry, Ollie, I am. And I want to, I really do, you have no idea how much, but I just…can't."

His eyebrows furrowed, and he looked wounded. "But….you kissed me. You pulled me down. I wasn't pressuring you, Layla. You said you wanted this. Us."

Rushing to him, I fell to my knees on the floor beside him. "I do, I really do and we will get there, but right now, I just can't."

Staring straight ahead, his mouth pressed into a hard line "You love him don't you. I'm never going to be enough, am I, Layla?"

"Ollie, no. You're amazing, and I really like you. I do."

"But you love him."

Gazing at him, I nodded. There was no point in trying to deny it. We both knew the truth. Ollie could hold my body for hours, but he wouldn't possess my heart while it still stayed firmly in Jared's grasp.

Getting to his feet, he strode silently to the door and walked out. I followed, yelling after him as we descended the stairs.

"Ollie, wait."

Grabbing his hoodie, he headed for the front door.

"Where are you going?"

"I need a walk."

"But you don't know these streets."

"I'll figure it out."

And without a single glance in my direction, he walked out, slamming the door behind him.

I flinched as the loud bang reverberated through the hall. Sinking onto the bottom step, I hung my head and cried. I'd done the one thing I didn't want to. I'd hurt him. I'd led him on, teased and seduced him, just to end up emotionally kicking him in the crotch and driving him away.

God, I really was a bitch.

Hearing the commotion, my mother had left the sanctuary of the kitchen and was now hurrying to my side. Wrapping her arms around me, she pulled me tight to her chest.

"Oh, baby, what happened?"

Sniffling and whimpering, I looked up at her through teary eyes. "I've made such a mess of everything. I'm a horrible person."

"No, you're not. You, Layla Jennings, don't have a spiteful bone in your body. Now come on, what's this all about?"

Taking a deep breath I tried to explain. "Ollie's in love with me."

"Well, sweetheart, I could have told you that at the party."

"I knew before that, and I knew how deeply he felt, but I tried to pretend it wasn't happening. Then this whole thing with Jared happened, and the other night, after the park, I kissed him. I kissed Ollie, and we started getting carried away. He said he wanted to be with me, and I said that I'd try, but I can't do it, Mom. Every time I'm with him, I want to be with him so much but my heart just can't let go of Jared. And now I've hurt Ollie. Why does my broken heart keep making so many lives miserable?"

Rising to her feet, my mother gazed down at me and lifted my face to her with her perfectly manicured hand. "Now you listen to me, Layla Jennings. Love is easy, falling in love is even easier, but letting that love go is the most difficult thing you'll ever have to do. Some of us never let it go, and sometimes it takes a while to realize what you want, but your heart will always have the right answer in the end. You just have to figure out what it's telling you. You like Ollie?"

I nodded, and she smiled.

"He's a sweet boy, and I think if you're patient with each other, you could be very happy together. But you will always remember your first love. It's powerful. Don't punish yourself for feeling, sweetheart."

I glanced at the door, wishing he'd come back.

"Let him breathe. He'll be back. And very soon, I'll wager. He's crazy about you, Layla, as he should be."

I gave her a half-hearted smile and a deep feeling of regret washed over me. I'd been so unfair to her, and sitting on those stairs I could finally understand. You can't just tell your heart to stop loving someone. It's a force that no man, woman or living being can control, and my parent's hearts had always belonged to each other.

"I'm sorry, Mom. For everything I said, and everything I didn't say. I am happy you and Dad are together, just please don't break his heart again. I couldn't bear it."

Kissing my cheek, she smiled. "Neither could I."

* * * *

Sitting on the couch, I stared at the clock. The room was silent except for the infernal and constant ticking as I watched minutes turn into hours. Ollie had been gone for almost two hours and I was beginning to feel anxious that something had happened to him. Springing from the couch, I grabbed my sneakers and was just about to run out to look for him when the door opened.

I stood abruptly and stared at him speechless. What could I say?

Walking over, he gazed down at me and wiped my tearstained cheek with his thumb. "Oh, god. I swore I'd never make you cry." Wrapping his arms around me, he pressed a kiss to my head and sighed. I buried my head into his chest and breathed deeply. He smelled of laundry detergent mixed with his natural Ollie smell. I found it incredibly comforting, and if I could have bottled it, I would have carried it around wherever I went. Tears were once again sliding down my face and seeping into his hoodie. Lifting my chin, he smiled at me.

"I want you, Layla. And if I have to wait ten years for you to be ready, I will. We can take this as slow as you want and there's no pressure. I just want to be with you." Fisting the hem of his sweater in his hand he lifted it to my face and wiped my tears. "That's better."

I smiled and softly laughed as he stroked his nose along the length of mine. "I'm not saying never, Ollie. I just can't be with anyone else physically right now. But I will get there. You just have to be patient with me."

He placed a chaste kiss on my lips. "I'd wait forever for you, Layla. I love you."

His words swirled around in my head. Hearing those three little words stirred emotions inside me that should have been for the man who had spoken them so sweetly to me. But they didn't. Instead all I felt was a sharp pain as the memory of Jared's own low, sensual voice echoed in my ears. Three words had never meant so much as when he had spoken them to me.

If I was truly honest with myself, I missed him.

* * * *

In the interest of taking it slow, I made it my mission to ensure that Ollie and I were constantly in the company of others. In this instance, that responsibility fell on Mel. Tonight was movie night, and the three of us would be sitting down nice and cozy in a dark theater together for a whole two hours.

"And why do I need to be your third wheel all winter break?"

Pulling on my sweater, I shook my head. "You're not the third wheel. More like a buffer. Look, Ollie and I are just finding our feet right now, and I'm not ready for a relationship. We're taking it slow, and that's where you come in."

"Because you don't trust yourself not to jump his rock god, sex on legs, fuck me till I'm brain dead, bones?"

"Uh, something like...that."

She rolled her eyes at me, and began rifling through my makeup case, testing several different shades of lipstick before deciding none were her desired color. "Well, you'll have to be alone with him eventually, you know. It's been what, four days since you decided to slow things down? What do you do when I go home at night?"

"Take a cold shower and repeat my MC Hammer mantra."

She roared with laughter. "MC Hammer?"

I giggled. "Yeah, you know, can't touch this."

Clutching her stomach she rolled on the floor, laughing at me.

I gave her a playful shove and laughed with her. "Pull yourself together for god sakes, woman. We'd better get downstairs before he thinks we've abandoned him."

Panting, she nodded. "Or deprived him of a girl on girl experience."

Now I was laughing. Ollie's voice echoed up the stairs at us. "Hey, are you two hyenas coming to see this movie or what?" He groaned as Mel yelled out the door at him. "Yeah we'll be right there, hipster dick, don't get your mascara all runny over it."

"Fuck you, ginger pubes."

"You too, Max Factor. Isn't Ollie great, Layla?" I giggled at her sarcasm and dragged her out of the room to join him downstairs.

"'Bout fucking time. Seriously, how long does it take to get dressed for a movie?"

Slipping on her shoes, Mel poked her tongue out at him. "We had to pick the right outfit, and do our makeup which, by the way, Layla didn't get to do because you were screaming up the staircase."

Walking up to me, he kissed me softly on the tip of my nose. "It's dark in there so no one's gonna see you, snaggletooth. Besides, Layla doesn't need it. Baby girl is beautiful all the time."

I smiled and glanced at Mel who was rolling her eyes at him. "Oh god, Ollie. Seriously, dude, get your tongue out of her ass already and let's go."

"Mel!"

"What? I'm kidding, I'm kidding." Walking beside me to the car, she murmured in my ear, "We both know where he'd like to stick his tongue, and it's not that far from your ass."

I climbed into the driver's seat, and smiled with just a twinge of embarrassment at Ollie on the passenger side. "So, what are we going to see?"

"I was thinking a horror flick." Ollie grinned and held his fingers over his eyes mocking me. I playfully batted them away from his face.

"Dick."

Laughing, he kissed my cheek as I backed out of the driveway. "Yeah, but you wouldn't have me any other way."

I beamed back at him. Damn, he was right.

* * * *

Christmas Eve finally landed and the whole house was buzzing with activity. Ollie and Daddy were busy hooking up every Christmas light we owned, and Mom was preparing all the food for Christmas lunch, ready for the refrigerator. Mel and I had taken our usual task of decorating the tree. Hanging ornaments, lights and tinsel, I watched as my father directed Ollie, who was currently hanging some lights over our front door. Climbing up the ladder, his shirt lifted slightly and I caught a glimpse of his rock hard abs. I swallowed hard as I imagined running my hands all over those smooth perfect pieces of male flesh.

"For crying out loud, Layla. Put yourself and that boy out of his misery and fuck him already."

I snapped my head around at Mel who was staring at me with a raised eyebrow.

"I can't. I won't."

"Why the hell not? You want him, and he sure wants you. Why can't you just go for it?"

I exhaled loudly. We'd been over this before, and I'd had this conversation with myself a thousand times already. "Because I can't, Mel. I can't get into a relationship right now.

Things are fine as they are, and once we have sex it will complicate everything."

She chuckled. "Relationship? Honey, I just wanted someone to flick your bean."

I screwed my face up at her "Eww. You're an animal, you know that?"

Giggling, she shrugged. "Why does sex have to complicate it? It's just two good people doing very bad things to each other."

Glaring at her, I pressed my finger to my lip and glanced over at Ollie. Mercifully, he was still completely preoccupied with hanging the lights in a perfectly symmetric design coordinated by my father.

"All I'm saying is that it only has to get complicated if you let it, that's all."

"I'm not risking it, Melanie, so just drop it!"

Using her full name had always been my way of giving my friend her polite warning before I got really pissed. Heeding, she moved her fingers over her lips in a zipping gesture and resumed decorating the tree which at this point looked like a tacky greeting card. Staring up at the disaster Mel and I had created by hanging every decoration in our twenty year old box on it, I sighed contentedly. I loved Christmas, and for the first time in seven years I was spending it with both of my parents.

Wrapping his arms around my waist in a warm embrace, Ollie pressed his lips to my ear. "This is the best Christmas ever. I'm putting up lights, there's an actual tree, I'm surrounded by great people, and best of all, this year I have you."

I smiled as he kissed a spot just behind my ear. Placing my hands over his, I turned my head and kissed him softly. The year was almost over, but as I thought back on everything that had happened, my chest tightened. I wondered how Jared would be spending the holidays. Would he be with Lucy and

Lorraine? Would he be alone? The most important question I had was if he would be thinking about me.

Because I was definitely thinking about him.

* * * *

"Layla, wake up. Come on, sleepy head, get up. I need to give you your gift."

Slowly opening my eyes, I stared at him. "Ollie, it's like six in the morning." Pulling my pillow from beneath my head, I turned over and shoved it over my skull.

"Come on, baby girl. I can't wait for this. You have to get up."

Groaning, I swung my legs out of my bed and stood up, stumbling to the bathroom. Ollie sat on my bed with a big grin on his face. Brushing my teeth, I questioned his early riser routine.

"Why exactly do I have to get up at six in the morning to open my gift?"

"Will you stop asking questions and just hurry your ass up and get dressed. I'll wait for you downstairs, but be quiet. Your folks are still asleep."

I heard the bedroom door close and glanced at my bed, half tempted to crawl back into it and cocoon myself in my quilt. But since he'd gone to so much trouble to get me up, I decided I might as well humor him. Pulling on some sweat pants and a hoodie, I walked out of my room, creeping past my parent's door on the way.

Beaming at me from the bottom of the stairs, Ollie held out his hand for me. Taking it, I eyed him suspiciously.

"How are you so chirpy for this time of day? You could at least have the common decency to look a little rough."

His perfect straight black hair and typical rock boy clothes were pristine. He had to have been up for at least an hour already. Shaking his head with clear amusement, he grabbed my sneakers and slid them onto my feet as I stood gripping the banisters and yawning. "Ready?"

"For what?"

"Your gift."

He led me to the front door and pulled it open.

"I have to go outside for this?"

He chuckled and yanked my arm, pulling me through the door. "Come on. Trust me, you'll love this."

I rolled my eyes and followed him out into the cool morning air. The sun wasn't up yet, and the sky blue of the early morning light instantly reminded me of Jared's piercing eyes. I could have kicked myself for thinking of him, especially as I was currently walking hand in hand with Ollie on Christmas morning. Looking up at his bright, fresh face, I smiled. "Where are we going?"

He pressed a kiss to my forehead as we walked and grinned at me. "It's a surprise."

As we walked further, I glanced around sleepily at my surroundings and became aware of where I was headed. "Why are we going to the park?"

"God, you ask so many questions."

"But you won't answer them?"

He shook his head. "Nope."

Slipping behind me, he held his hands over my eyes. "Ok, no peeking."

I giggled at him as we walked unsteadily forward. "Ok, open."

Taking his hands from my face, I gazed in awe at the scene he'd set up. A tartan blanket was lying on the ground with a bottle of champagne, two glasses, and a picnic basket. I pressed my fingertips to my lips, and grinned as I turned to face him. "What is all this?"

Wrapping his arms around my waist, he smiled. "It's breakfast by sunrise. I wanted to start today off the very best way possible, with you."

I gazed up at him and shook my head in amazement. "Ollie, I…I don't know what to say. It's incredible."

Taking my hand, he led me over to a tree opposite our picnic, and I stood with my mouth gaping open as I saw our names carved into the bark.

'Ollie & Layla 4Ever'

It was the most beautiful engraving I'd ever seen. Flinging my arms around his neck, I kissed him deeply. "It's the most romantic thing anyone has ever done for me."

He grinned back down at me and brushed the tip of his nose over mine. "Well, hold that thought because I'm not done yet." Leading me over to our cozy spot, and taking a seat, he pulled me down to sit in front of him. His legs apart, I sat snuggly with my back to his chest, aware that my ass was pressed against his crotch. Leaning over me, he opened the basket and kissed my cheek. "Take a look."

I beamed as I discovered two delicious, lightly toasted bagels with salmon, cream cheese and poppy seeds. It was my favorite breakfast and Ollie knew it. I turned my head and kissed his soft lips gently. I grabbed the cool bottle of champagne and poured us each a glass. Holding his in the air, he beamed at me.

"Merry Christmas, Layla."

Clinking his glass with my own, I gave him a quick peck on the cheek. "Merry Christmas, Ollie."

His lip ring clanked against the glass as he sipped the champagne. Holding it away from himself, he screwed up his nose, making me snort my laughter so hard that bubbles ran up my nose. "Wow, I thought champagne was supposed to be real good? This sucks. You like it?"

I nodded and took another sip. He shrugged, grabbed a bagel and held it to my mouth. I immediately took a bite and moaned with pleasure at the delicious taste of fresh salmon. I was starving, and the early morning wakeup call had left me no time to think about food but I was certainly in the mood for it.

The bagels devoured and the champagne discarded, I leaned back against him with my knees to my chest. His arms wrapped around me as we watched the sun come up. The beautiful shades of yellow, orange and red were intensely romantic, and as the warmth of the first sunlight hit my face, I sighed.

Resting my head against his shoulder, I thought about how Ollie must have spent every Christmas previously. Alone, hungry, frightened, and unloved. There was nothing worse than the thought of someone I loved being abandoned at the holidays, and I was once again flooded with thoughts of Jared. My heart gave an almighty thud as I thought about what he would be doing today. Working, watching TV in his sweats, or maybe spending time with his new family. The family he felt he couldn't tell me about; that he couldn't trust me to keep a secret. It was still as painful as it had been those few weeks ago, and I mentally chastised myself for letting my mind wander. I wasn't willing to allow thoughts of Jared to ruin my holiday or Ollie's beautiful gift.

Leaning to my ear, Ollie whispered gently, "I have another gift for you. Wait here."

I watched him curiously as he disappeared behind a tree, and when he re-emerged I grinned. In his hand he held an acoustic guitar. He strummed as he walked back to me and sat, cross-legged on the blanket. I sat staring as he began to sing, low, husky and deliciously, the way he always did.

> Every time I look at you
> There's something that I have to do
> And I don't know what I should say
> Baby, I get speechless
> I'm just a complete mess
> You take my breath clean away
> I've never loved anyone like this before
> Never felt so sure
> I can't understand it
> But you're all I need
> You're everything I've ever dreamed about

I could never work it out
You just make me breathless
You're beautiful and I want you to know
There's nowhere I won't go
If it means I am with you
No matter where you are or what you do
Layla, I'm in love with you

Tears pooled in my eyes as the beautiful melody and emotionally charged lyrics fluttered around me like feathers being carried on the breeze. I'd never experienced anything so powerfully romantic. Not even with Jared.

Damn. Jared again.

The setting, the picnic, the song...it was overwhelming and my heart was so crazy confused that it had stopped it's rocking and was now running around in circles stark naked while my mind danced around happily like a free spirited hippie at a love-in. My emotions were all over the place, changing so rapidly that it gave me whiplash.

Placing his guitar beside him, he gazed at me anxiously. Shaking my head and finally regaining consciousness from my reverie, I leaned in and kissed him passionately and meaningfully, trying to express how I felt through my act of affection. If only I could figure out what that was exactly. Ollie's wonderfully sweet gift was entirely amorous, and very thoughtful, yet hearing those three little words didn't have the effect on me that I desired. My heart hadn't raced, my pulse hadn't leaped and my own deep emotions remained buried inside me, suppressed by the ever present dull ache of my heart.

He still had a hold over me, and no matter how hard I tried to shake him off, Jared was the one my heart desired and it wasn't willing to let him go yet.

Resting his forehead against mine, he brushed the tip of his nose back and forth over mine. "What are you thinking?"

I gave him a smile. "How wonderful you are, and how lucky I am to have you."

I lied.

I wasn't about to tell him that I was thinking of Jared. That would have gone down like a lead balloon. Thanks for the song Ollie, but I'm just going to sit here and think over how much I still pine for Jared.

He smiled back at me, and pressed a chaste kiss to my lips. "We'd better get back before your parents wake up and worry where you are." Clambering to his feet, he held out his hand for mine and hauled me off of the ground. We packed away our breakfast picnic, and with his arm around my waist we walked back to the house, to my parents, to Christmas morning and to the secure company of others. Time alone with Ollie was not just giving me ideas; it was playing horrible games with my frail emotions.

Creeping in, we tried to be as quiet as possible. As a floorboard creaked below my feet, I winced looking at Ollie who had to stifle a laugh. Setting down the picnic basket on the kitchen counter, he fired up the coffee machine and gave me a warm hug.

"Ahem."

I turned around to see my father standing at the entrance. His arms folded, and with an arched brow, he scanned us both from head to toe. "Up awfully early, aren't we? And dressed. What's the basket for?"

Walking up to him, I kissed his cheek and grinned. "Breakfast, Daddy, what else?"

He eyed Ollie suspiciously. "A picnic for breakfast, in the house?"

I skirted around him and collapsed onto the sofa, slightly amused at where this was going. My father, although perfectly aware that as a grown woman I was entitled to a sex life, was not one to sit idly by while someone defiled his daughter under his own roof.

I decided to play. "Actually, Daddy, we took it to the park. We had champagne, watched the sunrise, and made wild passionate love right there in the open. Disturbed only by locals walking their dogs."

My father's eyes darted to Ollie, who sputtered his coffee all over the counter. Shaking his head quickly, he raised his hands defensively. My father grinned at me, and clutched his hand to his heart in jest. "Oh, how will I face the neighbors? A shot gun wedding it is."

Ollie breathed a sigh of relief. "Oh god, I think I nearly had a heart attack." Bending over, he held his hands over his knees and breathed deeply. I chuckled and shook my head in amusement.

Once Mom had spent the best part of the morning getting ready, we finally did our gift exchange. Mel had come over once she'd done the same with her family as she had done every year since we'd met. Her parents always bought me gifts, and my parents had done the same with Mel. Sitting cross-legged on the floor, she began handing them out to everyone. There was even a small token gift for Ollie. Mel had told her parents he was coming, and her mother had insisted he not be left out. She had given him a small replica of his Ducati. It even had the hot red paint job and sparkling chrome.

Running his thumb over it, he pouted playfully. "I miss my baby. Sitting back in that parking lot all alone. All because her aunt Layla wouldn't let me ride her here."

Snatching the toy from his hand, I poked my tongue out at him. "You don't know your way. Besides, there was plenty of space in my warm, secure car."

Kissing my cheek, he whispered in my ear. "I knew you cared about me really."

Of course I did. He was my friend. Boyfriend? Oh hell.

I gave him a half smile and diverted the attention to Mel. "So, shall we do gifts?" I'd bought her a set of small diamond earrings back when Jared and I were together. I'd got them at his store, and although he'd insisted I not pay for them, I told him they simply wouldn't be a gift if I didn't. After being forced to quit my job, I was relieved that once again my organization skills had paid off. Aside from Ollie, I had gotten everyone's gift fairly early.

Shooting up the stairs, I reached under my bed and pulled out a bag that I'd kept all the pre-wrapped gifts in. Ollie's I had in my closet, but Mel's and my parents were all there. Returning to the living room, I rummaged through them. Handing them out to each recipient, I stopped as I came across a small blue gift. Reading the tag, I could feel a lump in my throat. It was the cufflinks I'd bought for Jared. I'd had them engraved with his initials and a small diamond was in each, much like our pendants. Grabbing it from my hand, Ollie stood and walked to the trash can before dropping it inside and casually walking back to me.

"There, now it's exactly where he belongs. Dumped." Although I understood his reasons for that, I still felt it extremely harsh and found myself almost wanting to leap to Jared's defense. Why? He had lied, hurt me, and broken my heart; why should I have given him even an ounce of loyalty? I knew the answer, and Ollie did too.

Seeing my irritated expression, he scowled at me. "No, Layla. He doesn't deserve it."

Mel gave me a knowing look, and shaking my head softly, I continued to open my gifts. Mel had given me a beautiful new purse which was white and encrusted with crystals around the edge. My parents had bought me everything from makeup, perfume and stunning dresses, to chocolate and car accessories. I was surrounded by a pile of gifts and people I loved. Missing the one person to make my circle complete, I grabbed my cell and dialed Amy, putting her on speaker phone.

"Merry Christmas, Layla!"

The sound of her voice made me grin as Mel and Ollie shouted down the phone at her.

"Merry Christmas, Amy!"

She giggled. "Oh, Merry Christmas, guys. So how's everybody doing?"

We all talked about our gifts, how we would be spending the day and how we couldn't wait to all be together again.

"Layla, could you take me off speaker please? I need to talk to you."

I was curious, so I complied and walked out of the living room to the hall. My parents were in the kitchen drinking coffee, and Mom was beginning to make preparations for lunch.

"What's up?"

Amy sighed. "Have you seen a newspaper this week?"

"No, why?"

"Felix's restaurant chain has been completely destroyed. Apparently one of his biggest investors pulled all funding, and now the whole thing has collapsed like a house of cards. Layla, was Jared at all involved with Felix's business? It would make an awful lot of sense."

I thought for a moment back to that evening at the ballroom. Jared had told me he was invested in a restaurant, and Felix had asked if he was seeing that his money was well cared for. "I think you're right, Amy. Jared did say he had stakes in a restaurant. But if he hated Felix so much, why would he invest?"

"I don't know. He is fucking livid, Layla. Felix went all crazy at a journalist who asked if the sudden collapse had anything to do with the young woman he had recently been involved with. You were pictured as his date, remember?"

Shit. Things just got messier.

Exhaling loudly, I massaged my temple as a tension headache began to throb. "Great. No doubt I'll now have a whole heap of trouble heading my way. Thanks for the heads up, Amy."

"Sorry, Layla. Just thought you outta know. I gotta go, but I miss you all like crazy and I can't wait to see you."

Hanging up, I stared at my cell. My fingers hovered over the key pad as I fought with myself. Typing out a quick text, I hit send. Too late now. It buzzed in my hand a second later. Glancing into the sitting room, I saw Ollie and Mel looking through the pile of classic rock CD's I'd gotten him for Christmas. I bolted up the stairs to my bedroom, took a deep breath and answered.

"Layla."

Oh good lord. My legs turned to jelly as his voice purred down the phone at me, causing me to quickly take a seat on my bed.

"Hello, Jared. I just heard that Felix's company has gone under, and that the press seem to be looking at me as a possible cause. I just need to know if this is something I should be worried about."

"It's true his company has now come into difficulty but you should be fine, Layla. He has yet to disclose details of your association with him, and after the warning I gave him, he won't be. Was that all?"

His tone was clipped, and his patience short. I felt as though we had just discussed a business deal, and deep down that hurt.

"Um, yes, I guess so. I just needed to be sure. Thank you for your time. I realize you probably have a lot going on today. Merry Christmas, Jared."

The line went dead. Inhaling sharply, I fought back the urge to cry. No, I wouldn't do this to myself anymore. I had to move on. He'd clearly left his feelings for me in a dumpster, so why shouldn't I do the same.

Straightening up, I left the cell on my bed, and headed back down to my family and friends. A distinct sparkle in his eye, Ollie smiled at me and my bad mood melted away. Jared who?

Chapter 40

Steady As She Goes

    January and February seemed to flash right before my eyes. After Christmas break was over, we'd all come back to reality and seemed to settle right back into our old routine. Classes were getting more intense, and my stack of books seemed to increase a foot every week, so whenever Friday night arrived, our weekly trip to the bar was a welcome reprieve from reading.

    I hadn't spoken to or heard from Jared since Christmas morning, and to be honest, I was glad. Without him constantly invading my thoughts, I could finally try and move on with Ollie. Forming our own two person study group for Dr. Harman's psych class, we'd been dating for well over two months. We went to movies, out for dinner, and sometimes I'd hang out with him and the band while they rehearsed.

    Ollie kept persistently messing up during rehearsals, so Nick had tried to ban me by saying that I was a distraction. Kissing me and giving me that sexy smile of his, he would often miss a note, key change, or in one case an entire song completely because he was too busy making out with me on Eric's couch. Things were intensely hot and heavy between us, and whenever we were alone for more than five minutes I ran the dangerous risk of getting totally carried away. We still hadn't had sex, and I was getting the feeling Ollie's patience, and his junk, were becoming very tired of waiting.

On Valentine's Day, he'd taken me for a ride on his motorcycle up to the hills where he'd prepared a candle lit picnic dinner for just the two of us. Sitting astride his Ducati, he was more than hot; he was off the thermometer scorching! His black leather pants and matching jacket made him look every bit the rock star. Holding out his hand to me, he grinned.

"Wanna take a ride on my monster? It's big, powerful, and can go from zero to 'oh good fucking god' in sixty seconds."

I rolled my eyes and smiled as I climbed onto the beast. Sitting behind him, my arms wrapped tightly around his waist and my thighs pressed against him, I could feel the heat radiating between my legs. I really wasn't sure how long I could go on waiting. With the best intentions, we'd continued to hold off giving into our sexual urges, but that night he'd successfully rounded second base and was sliding his way quite literally into third.

We'd finished our picnic and we're gazing up at the stars as I snuggled into the crook of his arm. Turning his head to face me, he gave me one of his trademark heart stopping Oliver Green smiles and I swear the elastic on my panties snapped. His flushed pink lips begged to be kissed, and my own were only too happy to oblige whenever the demand was made. His cool metallic lip ring against my warm lips always made me smile, and I couldn't help but flick my tongue over it every chance I got. He was delicious, sexy as hell.

And hot, hot, hot.

My insides were practically begging for him to give me ecstasy, but whenever we came close, my heart would pull out that megaphone and give me that 'Are you sure you want to do this?' warning. Once we had sex, things would be different between us and we would never be able to go back to how it was.

Pressing his lips to mine, he groaned. I could feel how much he was struggling to contain himself as his hand slid over my hip, lifting my shirt and skimming over my waist.

"Oh god, Layla. I want you so badly."

I moaned into his mouth, taking his hand in mine and guiding it slowly across my stomach and down to the waist of my jeans. He hesitated. Pressing his forehead against mine, he breathed hard.

"Are you sure?"

Undoing my button and pulling down the zipper, I placed my hand on his and slid it gently down underneath my panties. Gazing into my eyes, his breathing hitched, and he took in a sudden sharp breath as his fingers grazed the fleshy folds of my sex. I felt like a virgin again, and Ollie seemed so nervous that I actually began to wonder if he'd ever done this before. But as he teased his fingertip up and down my moist slit, I knew he was an expert at this game. I wriggled underneath his gentle fingers, and I closed my eyes. I licked my lips as a shiver of anticipation ran down my spine. I could hear his breathing becoming harsher, and the warm sensations on my skin were putting me firmly under his spell. His eyes glistened and sparkled as he clenched his jaw and groaned gently. His long finger slid slowly between the lips of my sex and grazed my clit ever so slightly, making me gasp. I brought my knees up, pressing his hand firmly between my thighs.

His teeth nipped gently on my earlobe before his tongue slid sweetly into my ear, causing my body to tremble and quiver at the tickling sensation. I let out a tiny giggle, but was silenced by his mouth closing over mine. His fingers moved gradually further and further down, and as I felt him touch the opening to my sex, I thrust my hips upwards and held his wrist firmly with my hand, forcing him to push inside me. He chuckled, but obliged, swirling and sliding two of his perfect fingers in and out of me. It had been months since I'd had sex, and my body was practically convulsing as he touched, stroked and fingered my g-spot.

"Oh my god, Ollie."

His erection was pressing into my hip and his pelvis rocked back and forth against me, giving him a little of that friction he clearly desired. I reached out for his zipper, but using his free hand he seized mine and threaded our fingers together. His thumb found my clit and began unhurriedly and tenderly caressing the throbbing ache between my thighs. I arched my back, bowing and bending as the blissful pre-orgasmic pulsations began to surge through my body. The desperate need to climax becoming my one and only goal, I held his wrist tightly in my hand and squeezed my thighs together urging him to grant me the pleasure I so desperately desired. He didn't disappoint. Thrusting his fingers deeper, he massaged the sweet spot inside and I instantly felt my orgasm draw nearer. His thumb pressed and rubbed determinedly on my clit as I panted, writhed, and grinded against his hand.

Kissing me deeply, he groaned a primal and hungry sound from deep in his throat. He bit down gently on my bottom lip, and it sent me hurtling over the edge. Fierce, body shaking clenches inside me throbbed against his fingers. The sweet, gratifying surge of orgasmic electricity shot through my veins, causing me to cry out in pure ecstasy. Burying my head in his chest, I bit down hard on his hoodie, muffling my loud and grateful moaning. His eyes were tightly closed and I could feel his chest rising and falling rapidly beneath my head. His heart thundered loudly against my ear, and I felt him shudder as though trying desperately to contain himself. His erection was pressing so hard into my hip; I could only assume how painful he was finding it being restrained so tightly in his pants. I wanted to grant him the same sweet release but as I tried once again to reach for him he halted me, gripping my hand firmly in his palm.

Through his ragged breathing he spoke softly and warmly into my ear. "No, I wanted to do this for you. I'll wait, Layla."

My heart surged with a rush of emotion for him. Pulling him to me, I wrapped him in my arms and kissed him, allowing my breath to leave my body and becoming totally absorbed in his arms. He was wonderful, so sweet, attentive, caring and he loved me. I wanted so much to give him all of me right there on that blanket. To be everything he wanted and needed was all I desired to give to him but something kept on holding me back like a harness around my heart and I got the impression that Ollie knew this.

After that night, our physical contact seemed to become less frequent and he seemed reluctant to go anywhere past making out. I'd tried to talk about it but he just kept telling me he wasn't willing to rush and that he would wait. I wasn't ready to have sex, for sure, but I felt I could happily slide into third base with him at least. During one of our study sessions I'd tried desperately to seduce him into the idea, but he was not going to be swayed by my attempts to unzip his pants and fondle his crotch.

I had never felt so guilty.

There he was, giving me all of him, and I was still only giving him ninety percent. He told me every day how much he adored me, and every time he said he loved me, he would hold his breath for a moment, and I knew he was holding onto a hope that I would reciprocate. When my words wouldn't come, he would just smile, kiss me and say it was alright; that we'd get there. I did wonder if that's the reason he wasn't willing to go too far sexually. Maybe he didn't feel I really wanted it; that I was just going through the motions.

And, well, wasn't I?

As hard as I tried, I couldn't fall in love with Ollie. I loved him, but I loved him the way you can love someone that you care about. I loved his sense of humor, the way he took care of me, the way he looked at me with such wonderment, and most of all I loved that he loved me.

But I couldn't love him the way he wanted me to.

I cried myself to sleep many nights, wondering how long the whole charade could possibly continue before one of us would break.

* * * *

Sitting in the spring sunshine, I had my nose buried in my book. Dr. Harman had assigned us a new reading list ready for the semester after spring break, and I wanted to get a head start before the holidays. The sun was warm and the temperature was mild, so it was a perfect day for reading.

A shadow cast over my book, and rolling over onto my side, I gazed up to find Ollie holding his motorcycle helmet. Crouching down beside me, he brushed a hair from my eyes and kissed me. I smiled, but it immediately dropped when I saw the look on his face. His eyes were sad, and his expression was one of regret; it worried me. Glancing behind him, I noticed a large overnight bag.

"You're going somewhere?"

He nodded, and my heart sank.

"I have to go to Utah. I got a letter from my mother this morning. I need to see her."

I sat upright, and held his hand as he hung his head and sighed deeply.

"What happened? Why the sudden change of heart?"

The last time we'd spoken about his mother, Ollie had gone crazy and said he never wanted to hear about her, or speak to her, ever again. And now he was driving across the country to see her?

"She says she needs to see me. Says that she has a lot to tell me and that she wants me to just hear her out. So I called her and told her to leave me the hell alone. She got all upset, crying and shit, so I said I'd agree to meet her just once, but that's it. Then she disappears and leaves me the fuck alone for good. I have to leave now to get there by sundown. I'll stay overnight in a hotel, then come back tomorrow night. I won't be gone long, and I should be home by sun up. I promise you. I'd ask you to come with me, but I really don't think I could handle you and that bitch in the same room together. She doesn't deserve to even breathe the same air as you do."

He was getting worked up and he had a long drive ahead of him. I didn't want him going on the road upset. Rolling onto my knees, I pressed my lips to his. "Shhh, it's fine. If you're sure that it's really what you want, then I am behind you all the way. I think you should hear her out. At least then you won't spend your life wondering why she got in touch."

He nodded and brushed his nose the length of mine. "Come see me off?"

Smiling, I took his hand and got to my feet. His Ducati was parked just across from the lawn. Its hot red paintwork gleamed in the sun, and the chrome was sparkling. His black leather jacket hung over the seat, and placing his helmet on top, he turned to me. Cupping my face in his hands, he rested his forehead against mine. "I'm going to miss you so much. It'll be the longest twenty four hours of my life. I'll call you as soon as I get to the hotel, and again after I've seen her tomorrow, ok?"

I nodded, then grabbed his helmet from behind him. "Drive safe, ok? I want you back here in one piece. Don't take risks, always look twice at the junctions, and please, please, watch your speed. These things are a death trap." God, I sounded just like Jared now!

Ollie laughed, but nodded his head, understanding my anxiety for his safety. Wrapping his arms around me he inhaled deeply into my hair. "I'll be careful, I swear. What are you going to do all weekend while I'm gone?"

Weekends were usually date night Saturday and lounging around Sunday. "I don't know, read and catch up on my assignments. Maybe go out with the girls. I'll keep busy."

Taking the helmet from my hand, he gave me one last long and lingering kiss before sliding it over his head. Grabbing his jacket, he slipped it on and straddled the huge piece of machinery. Ollie always looked so hot on his bike; it gave him that extra oomph of sex appeal. If it were at all possible for him to get any sheet clenching sexier, that bike certainly helped.

Hooking his fingers under my chin, he pulled me towards him. "I'll be back before you know it." His words were muffled through the helmet, and I had to stop myself from giggling a little. Holding my hands on either side of his helmet, I placed a soft kiss on the tip of his nose. I couldn't see his mouth, but the way his eyes danced I could see he was smiling at me.

The bike revved and growled as Ollie started her up. His hands gripped the handlebars, and he kicked the stand away, giving me a nod before zooming off and out of the parking lot. For reasons I didn't want to explore, I stood and stared at the tire marks he had left.

Why didn't I feel upset?

I wasn't sad, longing for him to come back, nor was I absolutely devastated to be without him for a couple of days. When Jared had gone for four days, I was completely beside myself with grief. I was worried about Ollie, but I wasn't aching for his return. I should have realized then that my heart was trying to speak to me, but pushing the thoughts away once more, I ignored its warning.

* * * *

On Friday night, Amy and Mel decided that we were absolutely going to the bar, even in Ollie's absence. "If he were here we'd be going, so we should go even when he's not. Come on, Layla. You're not going to pine for two days, are you? Like you did when that other one went away."

Mel had refused to even utter Jared's name since we'd broken up. She hated him with a passion for hurting me, and every time I'd mention his name she'd wince, or make a hissing sound as though it caused her physical pain to hear it. The truth was I wasn't pining. I wasn't anything. I was worried as I waited for his call, but other than a general anxiety for his safety and emotional wellbeing, I didn't feel a thing. Seeing his mother was going to be tough for Ollie, but I understood his need for closure. I wished I could have been there to support him, but Ollie was my friend.

Boyfriend.

Damn it!

Sliding into our booth, I gazed at the empty stage and my heart gave an almighty thud. Ok, so I did miss him, at least a little.

Amy's tactic of flashing the bartender was once again a raging success. I sat sipping on my gin and lime, and I smiled to myself as I watched her and Mel flirting at the bar. A vibrating in my pocket distracted me, and knowing Ollie would be calling when he arrived, I pulled it out quickly and answered without checking.

"Hi, honey!"

"Honey? Well that's a greeting I didn't expect."

Oh shit. The low purr of Jared's voice echoed through the receiver and into my ear.

"Jared, I thought you were Oliver."

"I see. Sorry to disappoint you." His tone became slightly irritated and clipped. He clearly wasn't thrilled at the news that I was waiting for Ollie to call.

"What do you want, Jared?"

"Arthur Kent would like to arrange that dinner. He's looking to move forward with his project, but feels it necessary to gain the view of a potential consumer. When are you available?"

I'd completely forgotten my promise to Arthur, and though I liked him a lot and wanted to help with his project, I felt there was a six foot, golden haired reason for me to decline.

"Will you be attending?"

"I will. I have a vested interest in this project, and as a potential investor I'd like to have all the information available so that I may make an educated decision. It's strictly business, Layla. Nothing more."

It was what I needed to hear, but clearly not what I wanted to hear as my heart sank once again to the bottom of my ribcage. He'd moved on. His tone reminded me of the way we'd spoken on Christmas morning. I'd felt then that he was indifferent to me, but now that was even clearer. Well if he could do this, so could I.

"How about tomorrow evening?"

I heard him flick through some papers and assumed that he was checking his schedule. "It appears Arthur has that date free as do I. I'll have Daniel pick you up at seven. Please be prompt."

I sat back in my seat, and my jaw clenched. How could he be so indifferent? Had we really meant so little to him? Now I was irritated.

"Absolutely, Mr. Garrett. Seven sharp it is, sir."

"Don't take that tone with me, Layla. It's childish and uncalled for. It insults your intelligence. I'll see you at seven. Goodbye."

I slammed my phone onto the table, and growled just as Mel and Amy were sliding in to their seats.

"What did it ever do to you?"

Handing me another drink, Mel looked at me curiously. Exhaling loudly, I glanced up at them both. "Jared called. I'm having dinner tomorrow night."

As predicted, they both immediately began to protest, giving me dozens of reasons not to go, Ollie being the most significant. Holding my hands up to silence them, I shook my head.

"We won't be alone. It's a business dinner. I met a man at the dinner dance, and he's looking to get a building project for students in the area started. He wants my input as a potential consumer, and Jared's company is looking at investing. It's strictly business. He said so himself."

They stared at me with suspicious looks.

"It will be fine. It's just dinner and shop talk. He's picking me up, we'll eat, talk business, and then I'll be home. Ollie will be back Sunday morning, remember? Don't look at me like that."

Mel shook her head as she exchanged a knowing look with Amy

. "You're playing with fire Layla, and eventually you're going to get burned. You just can't seem to stay away from each other. Christ, when I saw him parked outside on Christmas I nearly killed him."

Almost choking on my drink, I gawked at her. "What did you just say?"

Rolling her eyes, and taking a deep breath, she leaned into the table and took my hand. "I should have told you, I know, but things were going so well with Ollie. I came out of my house to come over to you guys and his Jag was parked out front. He was just sitting there, staring at your door. I marched over and told him to get lost. That you'd moved on and were with Ollie now. He slammed the car door in my face and drove away."

I stared at her in disbelief. "He was at my house and you didn't tell me? Was that all that happened? What did he say?"

Letting go of my hand, she sat back in her seat and sighed. "No, he gave me something to give to you. A Christmas gift. But I didn't think it was a good idea, so I tossed it in the trash. He said he just wanted to give it to you and then leave, so I said I would do it and that he could leave right now."

I shook my head and ran my hands over my face. How could she not tell me this? I'd called him that very morning. No wonder he was so pissed. "Mel, I cannot believe you didn't tell me this! You have no idea what you've done!"

She looked confused, and a little hurt, but I was pissed at her and she needed to know why. "I called him that morning. Amy told me Felix's restaurant went bust and I knew it had something to do with Jared. I called to see if I had anything to worry about and he was totally impersonal. Now I know why! He probably wondered why I didn't thank him for my gift, and he definitely wouldn't have liked finding out I was seeing Ollie! Just when I think this whole thing couldn't get any messier, you go and put everything into the mixing pot and stir it all up. I need to go home."

Grabbing my cell and my purse, I slid out of my seat. "Layla, you're overreacting. I was protecting you. If you had seen him that morning, you would have ruined every chance you and Ollie had. I was doing what was best for you."

"No, Mel. You did what you thought was best for me. You made a decision that wasn't yours to make, and now I'm left picking up the pieces, again. How am I going to face him at dinner now? And before you even suggest it, no, I will not cancel. I'm going home. Do me a favor and don't follow me. God, Mel, why didn't you just butt out?"

She got to her feet and tried to apologize, but I was already on my way to the door. My words may have been harsh, but I'd spent days brooding over the fact that Jared was so distant with me; that he simply didn't care and had clearly moved on. It meant I could move on and try to get over him. The comfortable little security blanket I'd woven around myself with Ollie was being picked apart thread by thread.

I'd just made it back to my room, when my cell buzzed again. I expected it to be Mel trying to make amends, but seeing Ollie's name flash across the screen, I smiled with relief.

"Hey, rock star. You made it then."

He chuckled, and I could hear his lip ring clunk against the phone. "Yeah, I'm here. So what are you guys all doing without me?"

I wondered for a moment whether I should tell Ollie what happened, but with him so far away and still having to drive back, I decided not to. "The girls went to the bar. I'm not feeling it, so I'm just reading in my room. You know how it is."

"Missing me too, huh?"

"Of course."

"I won't be gone long. I'm meeting her tomorrow, and then heading straight back. Leave the door unlocked for me?"

I smiled, knowing that he'd want to see me the moment he got in. "Sure thing, stud. I gotta go, battery's a little low. Call me tomorrow?"

"Naturally. I love you, Layla."

I paused, and bit my lip. God, how I wished I could say it back to him.

"I know. I miss you too."

Damn it. I was sure I heard him sigh, and it filled me with guilt. His endless patience with me was endearing, but I couldn't help but feel I was wrong in all this. I'd been stringing him along for four months now, and it was bordering on cruelty. I needed to get a grip on things, and figure everything out soon because what I was doing to Ollie wasn't fair. It was damaging for everyone, and the longer it went on, the more hurt and pain it would cause.

Chapter 41

Playing Games

I hardly spoke to Mel all day on Saturday, and as I sat at the doctor's office waiting for my shot, I still simmered with anger. I was still mad at her, and although I understood her reasons, I couldn't get past the fact that she'd kept it from me. The one person in my life who I always counted on for honesty was Mel, and she had just let me down.

Deciding not to get too dressed up for the dinner, Amy had lent me the little black dress I'd worn on the first date Jared and I had been on. Part of me was doing it to spite him, but other than the fancy designer dresses he had bought me, I really didn't have anything nice to wear. I searched through my jewellery box for a suitable accessory and found the bracelets, earrings and ring Jared had given me. I decided to up the ante. I could prove I was over him, us, and that I too was moving on. Slipping the white gold and diamond bracelet over my wrist, I smiled. See, just a piece of jewellery. Nothing more.

The light hit the stones and it glistened and shimmered on my wrist. Jared's words echoed in my mind 'a bracelet fit for a princess'. It was painful. I stared at it as it hung heavily around my wrist. How could things have gone so horribly wrong when it started out so right? Of course. I knew the answers. But I needed to stay strong tonight. If I could get through this dinner with him, then I could finally leave our history where it should be; behind me.

At seven sharp, Daniel pulled up to the sidewalk, and hurried to open the passenger door for me. Sliding into my seat, I stiffened. Sitting over at the far side of the bench was Jared. Dressed in a stunning gray suit and black tie, he stared out of the window. His hand was covering his mouth, and his elbow rested on the door handle. Turning my attention to Daniel, I thanked him and got comfortable; well, as comfortable as you can be sitting mere feet away from your ex-lover. We drove in silence for a while, and the tension between us was so thick it could have been sliced with a blade.

"Where are we dining?"

Without looking at me, he answered in his very business-like tone again. "The Arlington. It's not far, and it's Arthur's favorite restaurant."

I slumped in my seat. Why did everything have to feel so strained between us? Could we not even be civil? "If we're to spend an entire evening at the same table, I would think we can at least be civil to one another. There's no reason for you to hate me, or to treat me like a stranger, Jared. I've done nothing wrong. You broke my heart, remember?"

His head snapped around and his eyes bore into me. "Hate you? You think I hate you? You really have no fucking idea, do you Layla? I couldn't hate you if I tried, and believe me, I've tried. Especially after what happened Christmas morning. And for the record, if you care to remember, Layla, you broke mine first when you kissed that prick."

Now I was infuriated.

"How dare you put this on me, you jackass! You lied, snuck around, and kept things from me from the first moment we met. Yes, I kissed Ollie, and you know what? I liked it. I never asked, or wanted him to kiss me, but I wanted to know how it felt. I wanted to feel his lips on mine, and I love feeling them on mine every time he does it now! And as for Christmas, I didn't even know you were there. I only found out last night, and I certainly never received your gift. If you'd had the guts to face me, maybe I would have, but I still would have handed it right back."

My words were harsh, and in retrospect I didn't mean half of them, but I wanted to hurt him; make him feel an ounce of how I felt every time he was near me.

Leaning forward, he knocked on the dark glass separating us from Daniel. "Pull over and call Mr. Kent, please. Inform him we're going to be a little late."

What the hell was he doing? There was no way we were spending any more time together than was absolutely necessary. Grabbing the door handle, I tugged hard but hitting the central locking on the panel next to him, Jared thwarted my attempt at escape.

Fuck.

"Sit down, Layla. You and I need to have a conversation before dinner."

I glared at him as he shifted closer to me. My heart raced with every inch he drew closer. "I sat in that car for an hour trying to find the courage, the words, the strength to walk up to your door. But your friend made damn sure I stayed away. Finding out you had already moved on with someone else nearly tore me apart. It took every bit of my willpower not to break your door down and beat the shit out of him. Then just when I think I could maybe try and move on, you come out tonight wearing that. Don't think I haven't noticed that's the dress you wore on our first date and this…"

He grabbed my hand and lifted the bracelet into the light.

"This is by far the lowest blow you've ever dealt me. You tell me you've moved on with him, yet your body, dress and choice of jewellery tells me something totally different. Stop playing games! Maybe, for the first time since we've known each other, we could try a little honesty for once!"

Snatching my hand from his grasp, I got in his face, practically spitting feathers.

"Honesty! You wouldn't know what honesty was if it kicked you in your uptight, tattooed ass! Don't lecture me on playing games when we both know you're an expert at them. And you always seem to win."

He snorted. "Win? You think I win? I don't think so, Layla. The most important game I ever played, I lost! I lost everything!"

His eyes were dark, and the vein in his neck was protruding as I watched him get angrier and angrier. It both thrilled and frightened me that I could still provoke such emotion in him. And the realization that he could do the same was a reminder that I clearly wasn't over him. I was still entwined in the web our relationship had spun, and there was no clear way to get out.

"You only have yourself to blame for this, Jared. Your secrets were so important, so big, that I wasn't trustworthy enough to keep them. And that's the bottom line. You didn't trust me."

He backed away. I'd just driven home the very core of our problems. He sat back in his seat and regarded me coolly.

"You don't think I wanted to tell you, Layla? Of course I did, but I thought I was protecting Lucy, and protecting you. But you kept things from me too. You questioned everything I did, everything I said, and everything I gave you. You always second guessed my reactions and motives. I'm not a monster, Layla. I would have understood. I may not have liked some of those things, but I would have respected you for telling me the truth."

He let out a long sigh as I sat there speechless. It was a conversation that was long overdue, but I never thought I'd be left feeling so confused.

"Let's just get through this dinner. Then you can go back to your life with him, and I can go back to my personal hell without you."

Staring at the floor, I nodded. Tapping on the glass, he instructed Daniel to drive us to the restaurant. There was nothing left to say.

* * * *

The restaurant was beautiful. Large crystal chandeliers hung from the ceiling, and paintings of food and wine were scattered across the vast walls. The tables and chairs were draped in ivory covers, and the silverware was gleaming beneath the bright lights and crystal.

Rising to his feet, Arthur took my hand and placed a kiss on my knuckles. "Miss Jennings, delightful to see you again. How are you, my dear?"

I smiled politely. "I'm well, thank you."

Jared pulled out my chair as the true gentleman in him always did. I sat as the two men began to discuss the building plans for the new forum. Studying the menu, I furrowed my brow, unable to understand what any of it was. Written entirely in French, the most I recognized was the word 'vin' which I immediately knew to be wine. That seemed to be the most appealing thing on the menu, considering the gut wrenching anguish I was feeling after our car ride.

Leaning over, Jared whispered into my ear. "I already ordered you the chicken roulade. You'll like it. By the way, I can't stand seafood."

What?

"Makes me violently sick. But if I'm at a seafood restaurant and entertaining clients, I eat it, make my excuses to go to the bathroom, then throw it all up. True story."

I stared at him completely perplexed.

"You wanted to know my secrets. I have a fair few more too."

He returned to his conversation with Arthur as I sat there in bewilderment. So he hates seafood. Big deal.

"So, Miss Jennings, how do you feel my new assortment of stores could appeal to you and your friends?"

Straightening up, I gave him a smile, "Well, we're terribly poor. Awful I know, but true. The main issue for students is not only the ability to afford luxuries. It's now become a daily struggle to be able to simply buy our basic items such as food and books. Your stores need to offer something that others do not. Discounts, good values, multiple purchase rewards...but also somewhere to simply hang out with friends that doesn't cost the earth. I love the idea of your development, Mr. Kent, and I am very much in favor of the jobs it will create for students like me."

I glanced at Jared as an expression of regret swept over his face. I'd left the job I loved after we'd broken up, and he was only too aware that I would now be struggling for cash. "Long Beach is an expensive place to be a student and many of us come from humble beginnings. If you can give them good quality products with low prices, they will come, Mr. Kent."

Jared's hand immediately covered mine on the table as he leaned into my ear. "I'm sorry you felt you had to leave, Layla. I know what it feels like to be struggling, and if there's anything I can do, please tell me. But there is always a job for you at Lorraine's. Always."

My hand was on fire; the feel of his skin on mine was like an explosion of heat on my flesh. I pulled it away gently, and nodded in thanks at his gesture. My heart was pounding every time he spoke, and now it was practically thrashing inside my chest. Megaphone in hand, it was screaming at me to get out before we got hurt again, but my ass stayed firmly in my seat. I could get through this.

As the evening went on, I began to relax a little. Jared was strictly hands off after that hand holding, and aside from his little disclosure about seafood, nothing out of the ordinary happened at all. Mr. Kent was delightfully funny, and I would often find myself grinning at his jokes. He and Jared clearly had a good business relationship and they appeared to be almost friends. My phone buzzed in my purse, and I slipped it out beneath the table. There was a single text from Jared. I glanced up at him and catching my eye, he smiled at me.

> I haven't swam in the sea since I was twelve and saw the movie Jaws for the first time. That shit was scary.
> **Received: 19.57**
> **From: Jared**

I had to stifle a laugh. Putting it away, I gave him a mock sympathetic look. The corners of his mouth curled up, and he nodded. I was almost having fun.

Sipping a little more of the delicious white wine Jared had selected for us, I was beginning to feel a little tipsy. Jared's hand reached out, and gently taking the stem between his finger and thumb, he moved it out of my reach and replaced it with a glass of water. I stared at him, irritated for spoiling my fun.

"Don't pout, Layla. You're a glass away from landing on your ass the moment you stand up."

I rolled my eyes at him, but truthfully I was fully aware that I was reaching my limit as far as my bodily coordination went when drinking wine. Arthur excused himself and headed for the bathroom, leaving the two of us alone, and me slightly inebriated.

"I once got so drunk in college I stole a rival college's mascot. I was on the soccer team, and we had a game against the other team on the Friday. So, at the pre-game party, a few of us got into several bottles of tequila and stole their sheep. I woke up the next morning to find a two hundred pound ball of fluff in my room, I hadn't considered where exactly we were going to hide it. Not just that, those things make a god awful mess, and they fucking stink."

Spraying my water across the table, I laughed.

"It was bad. I ended up hauling it to the dean's office and leaving it there. I figured he'd find it, give it back, and no one would know it was me. Wrong. Apparently, in my drunken state I'd written the words 'you just got Garrett'd' on the side of their team bus with a can of spray paint. Needless to say, I got caught and punished. I had to clean the damn team's bus, then go there every weekend for a month and apologize to the sheep!"

Tears were filling in my eyes as I pictured him speaking sweet nothings to a sheep. I'd learned more about him in one evening than I had our entire relationship. The thought suddenly made me a little sad, and my laughter dissipated. Why couldn't we have had this conversation before? Why did it take us falling apart for him to finally open up and confide in me? He sat gazing at me across the table, and I felt my cheeks warm.

"You seem a little flushed, Layla. Perhaps we should call it a night, and I'll take you home. I think that wine has gone to your head. I've never seen you laugh so much."

I gave him a rueful smile. "I haven't had much to laugh about recently."

Hanging his head, he looked at the table and I was sure he was thinking the same as I was. This was hard; so hard I wanted to scream. My heart was so confused, and my mind was swimming with the complexity of the emotions I was feeling. I was hurting from our harsh words in the car, happy to have discovered new things about him, sad that it had taken so damn long to get there and now guilty that I was actually enjoying his company.

Rising to my feet, I stumbled slightly, but Jared's hand caught my arm as he jumped from his seat to stop me from falling over on my heels. "I think you should go home. You look a little pale."

"I'm fine, just a little woozy."

"It wasn't a request, Layla. We're leaving. Now."

Arthur was just returning to the table when Jared informed him we were leaving. Giving me a warm hug and a peck on the cheek, he thanked me for my company and I wished him well on his project. Jared's hand never left my arm as he escorted me to the car which was waiting for us curbside. The cool air made me feel giddy as the wine went straight to my head. I swayed a little, but with his arms wrapped around my waist, Jared lifted me into the car and off of my unsteady feet. Sliding in beside me, he watched me like a hawk.

"Layla? Are you alright? You're white as a sheet right now."

I felt incredibly tired. "I'm fine, I just feel a little sleepy."

Without thinking, I shifted and rested my head against his shoulder. Drifting into an alcohol induced sleep, I felt his lips press against the top of my head as he inhaled my scent.

The sound of a door slamming woke me. My head was pounding, and as I began to try and sit up, I scanned my surroundings with blurred vision. The blue and green marble coffee table in front of me immediately told me exactly where I was. Scrambling to my feet, I felt woozy and found myself falling back down onto the plush cushion of his couch.

"Whoa, don't get up so fast. Here, drink this." Sitting beside me, Jared handed me a glass of water.

"Why am I here?"

"You passed out in the car, and I didn't want to leave you in that state alone. You've been out for a couple of hours."

I rubbed my hand over my eyes, then drank the cool and sobering water.

"I should get home."

"It's almost midnight. Daniel's off for the night. I've been drinking, so I can't drive, and I don't like the idea of you taking a cab alone. You're staying here. It's not up for debate. The guest room is just how you left it, so there are things for you to get washed up. I'll take you home in the morning."

I shook my head. "I can't. Ollie will be back in a few hours, and I want to be there when he gets home."

"I said no, Layla. Stay here and I will drive you home in the morning. If you're that concerned, then call and tell him you're staying here. He does know we had dinner, doesn't he?"

It was a loaded question, and one I didn't want to answer, but the words were flying from my mouth. "No, I didn't feel the need to bring it up when he has a long drive back on his motorcycle. I need him level headed and concentrating."

He raised an eyebrow at me.

"Don't give me that look. I'm keeping him safe. The moment he's back and safe with me, I'll tell him."

"Have you slept with him?"

What? Where did that come from? "Jared that really is none of your-"

"It's a straight question. Have you had sex with him?"

"I care about Ollie, very deeply, and I'm not willing to make the same mistakes we did, Jared. There's a lot to be said for taking things slowly, so not that it's any of your damn business, but no, we haven't had sex."

The corners of his mouth curled up, and it irritated me. "Yet."

That wiped his smile clean off as his head snapped up and he glared at me. Rising to my feet, I skirted around him and headed to the kitchen. I needed something to eat to calm my churning stomach.

Jared followed me, keeping his eyes on me as I moved about the kitchen. Standing in the doorway, arms folded across his chest, he leaned into the frame. He had a slight smirk on his face, and seeing it, I rolled my eyes.

"I noticed you didn't say you loved him."

I tried to think of a plausible excuse to give him. There was no way I was getting in to this with him. He had no right to question my feelings for Ollie. It was none of his damn business. "I don't have to profess it all the time to know exactly how I feel about him. Ollie knows how much I care, and that's all that matters."

He chuckled. "So let me get this straight. You've been dating for four months now, you haven't had sex, and you don't confess that you love him. You sure it's an actual relationship you're having, Layla? Because it sounds like the same relationship you had with him when you were just friends."

He walked up to me, and his lips were mere inches from mine. His breath warmed my lips, causing me to lick them involuntarily. "Admit it, Layla. You're still completely, uncontrollably and entirely, in love with me."

I stood, silently staring at his lips as he spoke.

"Say it." It was a command, and I couldn't help but respond.

"Fine. I still love you. Happy now?"

"No, but I will be."

Wrapping his arms around me, he kissed me fervently. My mouth opened obediently, and my tongue darted into his mouth, seeking his own delicious tongue. Rolling, thrashing and stroking together...it was a sweet and familiar sensation, one I thought I'd long forgotten. But there, in his arms, I fell apart at the seams.

Gripping the countertop behind me, he caged me in, breathing heavily into my ear. "I won't give you up without a fight, Layla. I hope he's ready for one. You belong with me. I love you, and I always will."

Reaching beneath his slightly unbuttoned shirt, he pulled out his pendant. "You're still the only love of my life, Layla. Your heart belongs to me, and I won't let him steal it away."

I stared at him as his words ate away at my emotions. I was so confused. The feelings I had swarming inside me, and the pure unbridled lust I experienced whenever he was around, was driving me crazy.

"You love me, Layla, and you know we belong together. I'll do whatever it takes to get you back. I won't let you slip through my fingers again."

Ducking beneath his arm, I panted as I hurriedly walked away, my heart pounding like a bass drum in my ears. I needed to get some distance between us, and the guest room would ensure at least four inches of wall would do just that.

"Where are you going?"

"To bed. I need to sleep on this."

He didn't follow me.

Stepping into the room I had frequented only a few months ago, I slammed the door behind me and leaned against the cool wood, trying to catch my breath.

This was insanity!

Locking the door, I stripped down to my underwear and climbed into bed. I lay there staring at the ceiling as images of Ollie, Jared and that kiss ran through my mind at warp speed. My heart was thundering in my chest, and I felt that at any moment it might tear its way out and scream at me for being so stupid. The sound of movement in the next room, and the crash of a door slamming caught my attention.

His voice bellowed through the wall. "Fuck!"

I groaned, and slammed my fist against the mattress beneath me.

"I really don't know what you expect me to do, Layla. God, you make me nuts!"

Turning over, I yelled back at him. "I expect you to leave me alone and go to bed before you drive us both crazy!"

Silence fell in the room and I was sure I heard him cursing under his breath. I needed to forget him; to sleep it all off and make my escape in the morning, but my mind wandered to the steaming hot mess of a man who was separated by only a few inches of wall from me. He was probably taking off his shirt right about now. Undoing the buttons and sliding it off of his muscular, broad frame. His slacks would be hugging his perfect hips, and that hot V would be dipping and leading to the most delicious part of his body. My insides clenched as I mentally undressed the smoldering delicious man in the next room. I was hot, scorching even. A gentle throbbing had settled between my thighs, and I wondered if he might hear me…

No, I couldn't do that. Not here, not now…could I?

My fingernails traced gently over my cleavage, teasing myself with the gentle touch on my skin. Closing my eyes, I slid my hand further and further, swirling my fingertips over my stomach. I pressed my palm flat over my navel, hesitating to go those last few inches. A low groan brought me out of my reverie. It was coming from next door.

Pressing my ear to the wall, I listened to the heavy breaths and soft moaning vibrating through the wall.

Oh, my god.

Clearly, Jared had the same idea. Adrenaline was still pumping through my veins, and the wine I had consumed gave me the courage to explore a little further. I heard him inhale sharply, and my insides clenched again, hard. Lying back down, I didn't hesitate. Plunging my hand inside my panties, I pushed my fingertips against my clit. Biting down on my bottom lip to keep me from moaning, I began to rub the ache away. My free hand pressed against the wall as I imagined what he was doing only inches away from me. His hand sliding up and down his long, solid cock.

My tongue grazed my lips as I thought about the pulsating, throbbing veins protruding up his shaft. I let out a whimper, and suddenly his moaning, groaning and panting stopped. Had he finished already? Surely not.

I was panting, still aching for release and listening intently for any movement in the room next to me. The sound of a door closing echoed through the room, and I jumped out of the bed and bolted to the door. Clutching the handle, I unlocked it and stared at the blank wood for a moment, knowing what was no doubt awaiting me on the other side. It was wrong, deceitful and unbelievably unfaithful, but I found myself pressing down on the golden handle and opening the door. Standing in front of me in a pair of tight black shorts was Jared. His chest was rising and falling rapidly, matching my own ragged breathing.

"You are fucking infuriating, you know that?"

Growling at him I panted. "I'm infuriating? You're the one that keeps walking himself right back into my life! You're back and forth so much that you're making me dizzy. It's cruel, unfair, and I hate the way you make me feel whenever you're around me. It's making me crazy."

"You want to talk about crazy? Telling me you're with some other guy, wearing that dress tonight, and then falling asleep in my arms didn't just drive me crazy, Layla. I'm bordering on psychotic! I'm so fucking hot for you."

Squaring up to him, I snarled. "You can't just waltz in here and expect me to bend over begging for you. I was done with that a long time ago."

His lips parted, and I could see the ghost of a grin. "Really? Because from what I heard, it sounded like you were just getting started."

He *had* heard me.

I stood close enough so that I could feel his hard breath on my lips. "Fuck you!"

Gripping his hand on my behind, he held me flush against him and I gasped. "No, but I am going to fuck *you*."

Sliding his hand around my neck, he pulled me to him, closing his mouth over mine. Wrapping my arms around his neck, I dragged him into the bedroom, kicking the door closed with my foot. His hands slid over my shoulders, slipping the straps of my bra down my arms in the process. Kissing me deeply, he murmured into my mouth. "God, you make me so fucking mad."

The feeling was mutual as the ever familiar fire in my belly roared into an inferno. The well-known feeling of his hands on my body, and the pleasurable sensations of his kiss, provoked emotions inside me that I thought were buried.

His hands reached behind my back and unhooked my bra as he guided me towards the bed. The back of my knees hit the edge and I fell back, landing with a bounce on the firm mattress. Peeling my bra over my arms, he tossed it across the room and placed his hands firmly around my back, lifting me up the bed so that my head was resting comfortably on a pillow.

His lips pressed against mine, and the scent of vanilla, sweet cologne and sex filled my senses with the powerful and pungent aphrodisiac that was Jared's natural aroma. Hooking my thumbs into the waist of his shorts, I gave them a sharp push downwards. Obliging me, he slid them down over his behind, releasing his impressive erection. Grasping it in my hand, I ran my fingers up and down the full length of him. He groaned into my mouth, and my insides clenched deliciously. His fingers threaded through my hair as his tongue rolled and stroked inside my mouth.

Coming up for air, I stared at the ceiling as his lips trailed soft kisses over my jaw to my neck. His tongue flicked and licked across my collar bone and a moan escaped my lips. Gradually, and oh so achingly slowly, he kissed his way down to my breasts. Arching my back, I thrust my ample breasts to his lips as his mouth closed over my nipple, sucking, nipping and licking the pert and puckered tip. Gripping a fistful of his hair in my hand, I grasped the sheet with the other as his mouth on my breast sent a direct message to my sex. I was practically begging for his hard long cock to slip inside me.

Grazing his splayed fingers over my stomach, his mouth followed the trail of his soft fingertips down my wanting skin. Gripping my thighs, his tongue dipped into my navel and I gasped, bowing and writhing in his hands. "Oh, Jared."

I could feel him smile against my skin. "I know, baby. I'm going to take care of you. I'll make it all good again."

I could barely hear his words as my heart thundered. His thumbs slid inside the delicate lace of my panties, then tugged them down and over my behind. Running his nose up my slit, his tongue grazed the fleshy lips. I groaned, desperate for him to give me what I needed, what I'd ached for since the moment I'd see him in that suit.

He must have heard my mental plea because the next thing I knew, my panties were in shreds beside me and his long hard cock thrust inside me, making me cry out with pure unadulterated gratification. His hips rocked back and forth as I grinded and writhed beneath him, matching him thrust for thrust. I was brimming with lust, and my body was almost levitating off of the bed as his arms wrapped tightly around me, lifting me close to his chest. His mouth closed over mine, and I pressed my palms firmly around the back of his neck, pulling him close and deepening our kiss.

The muscles inside me pulsated and convulsed as his tip brushed against my g-spot. Running my hands down his broad back, I gripped my fingernails tightly into his behind. My thumb rubbed gently over the raised letters of my name tattooed into his luscious caramel skin. A deep and carnal moan came from my throat as the pre-orgasmic waves began to crash and roll through my body.

"Don't stop, Jared, I'm so close."

His face buried in my neck, he bit down on my shoulder as he slammed into me over and over, making me jolt and bounce back and forth beneath him.

"I've missed you so much, Layla. Your eyes, your hot, sexy little body beneath mine and this wet, delicious cunt. I need you to come with me, Layla. I want to feel how much you've missed my cock right here."

He thrust hard into me twice as the words left his lips. Clutching his flesh in my hands, I cried out his name as my orgasm flushed through me like a tidal wave of erotic bliss. Thrashing into me a few more times, he stilled and held me in a tight embrace against his chest. Lying beneath him with my eyes closed, I listened to the frantic beat of my heart and the rapid panting of our breaths. His forehead pressed against my shoulder where his teeth had left a slight imprint. Resting my cheek against his sweat soaked hair, I could feel the tears pooling in my eyes. They slid warmly and silently down my cheeks and onto his face.

Lifting himself onto his elbows, he gazed down at me and wiped my tears with his thumbs. "What's wrong?"

Rolling over and out from under him, I curled into the foetal position, buried my face in my hands, and sobbed uncontrollably. His arms snaked around my waist as he pulled me against him so that our bodies lay spooning against one another. Brushing the hair from my face, he kissed my cheek and hushed me.

"Shhh, baby. Come on, it's alright. Layla, stop. Please, I can't stand to see you cry like this."

Turning to face him, I looked into his piercing blue eyes and sniffled, swiping the tears from my cheeks. "I'm a whore, Jared. A cheating, lying whore."

Holding my head to his chest, he shook his head. "No, Layla. I won't tolerate you talking about yourself that way. Why would you even think that?"

"Jared, I'm dating Oliver and I just had sex with you! Tell me there's not something completely sick about everything I did tonight."

"Layla, I love you. I love you with every fiber of my being, and what we just did, making love, was nothing but an act of that deep passionate emotion. I know you love me too, so what we just did wasn't wrong. It's the only right thing I've done in months."

Turning away from him, I snuggled down into my pillow and continued to cry. My mess had just turned into a bomb site. "Please, leave me alone, Jared. I need to be by myself."

Taking his arms from around my waist, he begrudgingly left the bed. Standing at the door, he glanced back at me and raked his fingers through his hair, shaking his head. "I love you, Layla. I can't be sorry for making love to you. I just wish you weren't sorry for wanting it."

Closing my eyes, I sobbed into my pillow, and as the door closed behind him, I felt the breaking of my heart as fresh as it had been all those months ago. I should have listened to the warnings, should have stayed away and protected myself, but most of all I should have chosen Ollie that night.

Chapter 42

Unfaithful

I woke feeling numb. I must have laid there for over an hour just staring at the ceiling. I could hear Jared moving about downstairs, and I knew he'd had as little sleep as I had. Thinking over the events of our night together sent a shiver up my spine, and as I looked at the clock, I knew I didn't have much time. I needed to get home, back to the dorms, and wait for Ollie. My stomach churned as I thought over what might happen when I saw him. Getting out of bed, I headed to the bathroom and quickly showered before scooping up my clothes. My torn panties on the floor were a bitter reminder of my betrayal. Snatching them up, I dumped them in the trash where they, and I, belonged. That's all I was; cheap trash.

Jared had brought me a pair of his shorts to wear in their place, and slipping them on I couldn't help but feel dirty. Once I was dressed, I made my way to the kitchen. Standing with his palms on the countertop, dressed in his black pants and white t-shirt, was Jared. He was staring out of the window, and the hard hitting and soulful voice of Amy Winehouse echoed over the sound system. The words hit me like arrows in the heart. Singing about still loving someone in the morning after a night of passion, her words could have been written about the two of us, and I understood his song choice immediately.

I'd wanted him, ached and needed him that night, and yet now I was detached and closed off. My heart was too afraid to feel for fear of shattering into millions of tiny shards, and my own sadness and hatred of myself consumed me as I stood in the door way.

"I need to go home. Ollie will be back soon."

Hanging his head he nodded, but continued to face away from me. "Will you tell him?"

His body was tense and his voice was filled with pain.

A lump formed in my throat as I stared at him. "Yes. I have to. I can't lie to him. It'll hurt, but it'll hurt more if I keep it from him."

"Do you love him?"

Tears welled in my eyes as I swallowed hard. "Jared."

Clenching his fist he slammed it on the counter. "Just answer the question, Layla. I need to hear it." He turned to face me, his eyes full of pain and darkness.

"I can't love him." I stared down at my hands as I mindlessly rubbed and stroked my right hand where his ring had once been. "Because I could never stop loving you."

He winced and I knew my words were bitter sweet. There was a 'but' hanging in the air and we both knew it only too well.

"But it doesn't change anything. I can't be with you, Jared. My heart aches from what we did last night. Us, our history, it still hurts too much." Walking over to him I placed my hand over his chest. Taking his pendant from his neck, I lifted it over his head. Holding it in my palm, I pressed my forehead against his and let out a long breath. The diamond sparkled in the light and the inscription gleamed.

"You have to let me go. We have to let this go, or we'll tear each other apart." Tears rolled down his cheek and cupping his face in my hands, I brushed them away with my thumbs before placing a chaste kiss on his lips. Releasing him, I dropped the pendant on the countertop and walked away.

The Mercedes was parked on the driveway, and seeing me approaching through the foyer, Daniel opened the passenger door. A loud smash reverberated through the hall, and I glanced back toward the kitchen, holding my breath. But he wasn't coming after me this time.

It was over.

Closing the door behind me, I walked out to the car and slid in. The moment the door was closed, I fell apart. Respecting my need for privacy, Daniel slid the screen between us, allowing me to sob and cry my heart out alone in the back seat.

The drive back to the dorm was the longest journey of my life, and as we pulled into the parking lot my heart plummeted. A hot red, gleaming Ducati caught my eye, and my insides twisted as grief swept through me.

Opening the door, Daniel gave me a sympathetic look. "Take care, Miss Jennings."

I nodded. "Thank you, Daniel. Take care of him for me. He needs someone to care about him." Tipping his hat he got in and drove away, leaving me alone on the sidewalk.

The whole place was deserted as it always was on a Sunday morning. Staring at the ground, I walked slowly to the entrance of the building. I froze, glued to the spot as I came face to face with Ollie. Sitting on the ground, with his arms wrapped around his knees, he stared at me with the saddest brown eyes I'd ever seen. Tears threatened again as I swallowed hard, gulping my sorrow down into my chest where it constricted and left me breathless. Tears were in his eyes and from the red and blotchy patches on his cheeks, I knew he'd been crying. Sniffling and shuddering through my tears, I sobbed.

"I missed you, so I came back early. I went upstairs, and when you weren't there, I made Amy tell me where you were. She told me about your dinner. And then you pulled up in his car...well, I guess I don't have to ask. That, paired with the distraught look on your face right now, tells me all I need to know." Swiping his own tears away with his hands, he stared at me, shaking his head.

"I'm sorry, Ollie. I'm so sorry. I never planned for it to happen. I swear."

Looking away, he let out a snort of laughter. "I never stood a chance, did I Layla? It was always going to be him. You were never going to be mine. I was kidding myself."

"No, Ollie. I care about you so much. All I've ever wanted was to give you everything, and to be everything you want me to, but…"

"But you can't stop loving him. And as long as you love him, you can't love me." His expression instantly turned from sadness to determination as he breezed past me towards his motorcycle.

Sprinting after him, I yelled and pleaded for him to stop and think about what he was doing. "Ollie, please. Just wait. Let's talk about this. Please don't go. Not like this. Not when you're angry."

Grabbing his helmet, he turned to face me. "Was it worth it?"

I stood speechless for a moment. "What?"

"You heard me. Was it worth it? How was it? Good?" He was furious, and his words cut through me.

"No. It was…I don't know, Ollie. It just happened. I can't explain it, but it won't ever happen again, I swear. I ended it. Please, just hear me out."

He shook his head. "There's nothing to say. You fucked your ex-boyfriend. You don't, and can't, love me. I don't see much point in talking that out, Layla." Slipping his helmet on, he revved up the Ducati and gazed at me with a pained expression before flipping his visor down and speeding out of the parking lot.

I fell to the ground, heaving and gasping for air. I felt as though the oxygen had been ripped from my lungs as my heart screamed 'I told you so' in my ears.

"I thought it was you I heard screaming out here." Appearing at my side as if by magic, Mel hauled me off the ground and pulled me inside the building. Safely inside my room, I broke down.

"Oh my god, what have I done? I've destroyed everything. I'm a whore, a slut a god awful human being."

Sitting me down on the bed, Mel sat beside me as Amy emerged from the bathroom. She gave me a stern look, and I could see she was pissed at what I'd done. "Amy, please don't hate me. No one can possibly hate me more than I do right now."

Rolling her eyes, she sat the other side of me and wrapped her arms around my shoulders. "Oh, Layla. You really have made the most awful mess. What were you thinking?"

"I wasn't thinking. I was all caught up in the sexual attraction of it all. The dinner was...I don't know. He made me laugh, and he took care of me. I couldn't help it. My emotions took me over, and before I knew it we were in bed together."

Mel let out a long sigh. "I don't think you can get past this, Layla. Ollie was really upset when he realized where you were. I've never seen someone look so completely devastated. Please tell me you ended it with Jared. That he's not expecting some great reunion between the two of you."

I shook my head.

"No, it's over. I told him we have to move on and forget about each other. He must have understood because he didn't come after me this time. But the worst part, the part that is tearing me to shreds, is that no matter how much I know what I did was wrong, I love him. I wanted him, and I let it happen. We made love and I felt complete. Like I was whole again, lying there wrapped in his arms. Now I feel like there's a horrible hole in my stomach. I hate myself for what I've done to Ollie, and I hate that I can't stop loving Jared!" Climbing into bed, I continued to sob. I cried until I couldn't anymore, and just when I thought I had nothing left, I cried again.

At my request, Amy and Mel had left me alone to go and hang out in Mel's dorm room. She'd been lucky enough to get a private single room, so they would be able to be in there as long as they wanted. I was grateful for the peace as my body, mind and emotions were exhausted. Curling up on my bed, I fell into a deep and grief stricken sleep.

"Layla, wake up."

I turned over and slowly opened my eyes, unsure if I was hallucinating or dreaming.

Crouching beside my bed was Ollie. Quickly, I wrapped my arms around his neck and held him tightly as relief swept through me. He'd been so mad when he left that I was terrified he'd be in an accident, or that he'd decide to never return.

"I'm so glad you're safe. I was worried sick."

Placing his hands on my back, he held me to him and buried his face in my neck. Pulling away, I sat motionless and silent, waiting for him to say something, anything, but when he didn't, I knew I had to say something.

"Ollie, I'm so sorry. I hate myself for what I did, and I understand if you never want to see me again, but-"

He stopped me, pressing his fingers to my lips. "Stop. Just this once, don't say anything and listen instead." He gazed into my eyes, and took a deep breath. "I don't care."

I stared at him, confused.

"You slept with Jared. And I don't care. Well, I care, of course I care. It's ripping me apart, but I won't let it destroy us. I waited too long for my chance with you to let him obliterate our relationship with one night. I know what it's like to be completely in love with someone, Layla. It drives you crazy, and you do things you never intended. Like kissing someone in a dorm room when their boyfriend is out of town."

I couldn't believe what he was saying. Not only had he come back, he was coming back to me.

"How many times did it happen?"

"Once, I swear, and I felt awful right after. I cried myself to sleep over what I'd done to you."

He held up his hand, indicating for me to be quiet. "Is it over?"

I nodded, and stared at the floor.

"Ok."

Placing his helmet beside my bed, he took off his t-shirt and wearing only his black chinos, climbed on to the bed behind me. Wrapping his warm arms around my waist, he pulled me close and nuzzled into my hair. Tears were rolling down my face.

He'd forgiven me, just like that. He'd accepted my mistake for what it was, a mistake, and he'd come back. How could he just accept it all like that and climb into bed with me? I'd hurt him, moaned, touched and laid with another man, and yet here he was beside me, holding me close. Ollie was a good man. I didn't deserve him, or his forgiveness, but deep down I understood why and how he was able to be anywhere near me. He loved me.

Turning to face him, I rested my forehead against his. "Ollie, I'm so sorry."

"I came back because I wanted to, Layla. I'm not ready to quit on us yet. Go to sleep. I don't want to think about it anymore tonight. We'll talk about it in the morning."

I nodded weakly and pressed my lips to his. He responded, but only briefly before turning his head and going to sleep. I'd had every intention of breaking things off with Ollie when I left Jared that morning, but as he lay next to me I knew I couldn't. I owed it to him to try and make things work. I had to leave Jared in my past. Ollie was my priority now, and he deserved the chance at making a future with me.

* * * *

"Ollie! Ollie!"

Opening his eyes, he stared at me and groaned. "What? Layla, it's like seven in the morning, and its Saturday."

I stifled a laugh. "I know but I have to show you something. Come on!" Pulling on his hand, I hauled him out of bed and out the door. Covering his eyes with my hands, I led him down the hall to Mel's room.

"Ready?"

He smiled. "That depends. You naked?"

I laughed, and lifted my knee to his ass as my hands were currently covering his eyes.

"You wish, stud. Ok, open."

A picnic basket sat on the bed, and candles were laid out across the room.

"What is all this?"

I grinned, taking his hands and leading him into the bedroom. "Well, it is Saturday, and that means its date day, so I thought we'd start with breakfast."

Pressing his lips to mine, he smiled against my mouth. It had been four weeks since my night of betrayal with Jared. Ollie had been so incredibly understanding, and as the days went on we slowly tried to glue the pieces of our broken relationship back together. We still weren't sleeping together, and I felt that was more Ollie's choice now than mine. Taking my hands, he sat down on the floor and pulled me down with him.

"Ollie, we need to talk."

He gave me a curious look, and began unpacking the picnic basket. Gripping his hands in mine, I stopped him. We needed to have this conversation whether he liked it or not. "Ollie."

He let out a long sigh. "I know, I know. You want to talk about what happened between you and *him*."

"We have to, Ollie. Ever since it happened, you hardly come near me. It's like you don't want to touch me or something. We barely make it past first base these days. If you can't get past what I did, you have to tell me because I can't keep carrying this gut wrenching guilt anymore, Ollie. I made a mistake, and I will hate myself forever, but you can't keep punishing me. Please, either hate me and let me go, or tell me how I can make it right."

Raking his hand through his hair, he let out a long breath. I couldn't look him in the eye. My frail emotions made me afraid of what he may say, and my fragile heart was unsure it could take anymore guilt.

"Shit. You thought I was avoiding touching you?"

I nodded weakly. "Weren't you?"

"No, of course not. And I don't hate you, Layla. We weren't exclusive, we weren't sleeping together, and you made a mistake. You know it and you have to live with it. We could talk about it till we're blue in the face, but I don't think that there is anything more I can possibly say.

"You know how I feel about what you did with him that night. I can forgive your fuck up, Layla, but I won't forget it. It was your decision, and you made it. You have to forgive yourself, not me. We all do things we're not proud of. Hell, I've done things in my life I'd rather forget, but they make us who we are. I can't hate you, but I can't get close to you while you're still torturing yourself over this. I don't want you to sleep with me out of guilt, or because you think you should. I told you before, I'll wait as long as it takes. Hell, it's been five months, what's another five?"

Leaning across the basket, he pressed his lips to mine and relief washed over me. Finally we'd got it all out there in the open, and for the first time in a month I could breathe again.

"So, now that's all cleared up, can I eat my breakfast? I'm starving. Someone dragged me out of bed, and I didn't even get time to readjust, so I'm pretty sure the guy coming out of room twenty four got a great eyeful of my morning wood."

Glancing down, I saw Ollie's sweat pants pitching a tent and stifled a laugh.

"Not quite the reaction I'd like to get from you when faced with my hard-on, but I'll take it."

Giving him a playful nudge, I handed him a bagel.

"I'm sorry, did you want to play ring toss? I was thinking of a better hole I'd rather be aiming it at."

He was giving me his knock your socks off Ollie smile and it was contagious. Grinning back at him, I leaned forward and grazed my tongue over his lip ring. "You know, I could fix that for you, if you'd like." Taking his lip between my teeth, I nipped gently before releasing him.

"As tempting as that is, Layla, I'd rather the first time you make me moan it not be in Mel's bedroom. Besides, the coffee will get cold." Slightly disappointed, I sat back on my heels as Ollie handed me one of the coffees to go that I'd gotten from Lorraine's. I'd gone down there to see Kate also. I missed her and our girl talk. We made plans to get together in the week, and I agreed to meet her at the shop after she assured me Jared was out of town on business.

I hadn't spoken to, heard from, or thought much about him since we said goodbye in his kitchen. It wasn't that I was moving on, so much as it was just too painful to think about. The very next day I'd gathered all my jewellery, dresses, and the New York mug and placed them in large box beneath my bed. I didn't have the strength, or the heart, to throw them out or return them, but I knew that I would, eventually.

Finishing our bagels and coffee, we talked about everything from classes to what movie we should watch that night. As per our deal, it was Ollie's choice, and I was going to have to suffer his selection as he had suffered two hours of 'My Sister's Keeper'. I had a feeling I was in for another horror flick; as if my life didn't contain enough scenes of gruesome devastation. Pulling me across the floor to him, Ollie wrapped his arms around me and closed his mouth over mine. His kiss was deep, and I could feel his erection pressing against my stomach as our chests compressed from the embrace he was holding me in.

Smiling down at me, he brushed his nose the length of mine. "God, you're beautiful. Hey, why don't we go out for dinner tonight before the movie? I want to show you off a little."

I chuckled. "Show me off?"

"Yeah, like the gorgeous, sparkling diamond you are."

That Oliver Green charm was gradually loosening my panties again and I was more than happy to lose them to him.

"Alright. Should I get dressed up?"

"No need to on my account. I think you look hot in whatever you wear, but it is kind of fancy."

I placed a chaste kiss on his lips. "Sounds awesome."

* * * *

"So where's he taking you?"

Amy and Mel were sitting back to back on the bed while on their laptops, and the position they were in reminded me of bookends. Smiling to myself, I turned to the mirror and put in the earrings my parents had bought me. With Mom now back in Pasadena, our trip to the spa was cancelled, and she felt so awful she went right out and got me a dazzling pair of white gold and diamond earrings.

"I don't know, he wouldn't tell me. But he did say it was fancy."

Amy's eye lit up as she dropped her computer on her bed and hurried over to mine. "Wow. You look amazing. That dress is perfect."

In preparation for our dinner, I'd taken the small amount of money I had saved from working at Lorraine's and headed to the mall. I'd managed to make it all the way to the store and back to my car while only thinking of Jared eight times. It was definitely an improvement on my previous record of constant.

My knee length purple dress was an elegant, yet cheap selection. Slim line and straight, it accentuated my hourglass figure perfectly. A knock on the door indicated Ollie was ready for me, and as I hurried to get it, I had to take a deep breath to calm my nerves. Standing in the doorway, he looked stunning. His hair was perfectly straight, and dressed in slacks and a black shirt that he'd left slightly unbuttoned, he looked like a hot rock star ready to party.

His eyes scanned my body, and he whistled loudly. "Wow. You look incredible."

I smiled, and gestured for him to come in. "I just need to grab my shoes and we can go."

"Ok. Hey, Mel, Amy. How's it hanging?"

They eyed him curiously, and Mel stifled a laugh. "Ollie, you couldn't look more uncomfortable if you tried. Fess up, you've never taken a date to a fancy dinner before, have you?"

I glared at her. "Mel!" She was stirring again.

"Honestly? No, I haven't, but I'm glad that the first time I do it's with a girl as amazing as Layla. No other girl has ever deserved it, in my opinion."

Pressing a kiss on his cheek, I smiled before turning to Mel and sticking my tongue out at her. Shrugging, she and Amy resumed toying with their computers, merely giving us a raise of their hands as we left.

The restaurant was small, yet exquisite. The lighting was dim, yet bearable, and candles sat in the center of every table. Seated near a window, I beamed at Ollie across the table.

"Nice place, right?"

He slid his hands across the table and nodding, I placed mine on top of his. "It's lovely, Ollie. Thank you for bringing me here." He grinned, and bit his bottom lip.

Picking up a menu, I began scouring it for a dish that seemed appropriate, but also sounded somewhat appetizing. Selecting the braised beef, I placed my menu on the rack, then focused on the hot rock god sitting across the table.

"I spoke to my mom today."

Ollie and his mother had been on speaking terms since he went to see her a month before, but other than the usual pleasantries they hadn't gotten very far toward reconciliation.

"Oh? How…was it?"

He clutched my hand. "She wants to get to know me better. She gave up the drugs over ten years ago and I know she's changed, I can see it, but there's still that part of me that hates her so much, Layla."

I brushed my thumb back and forth across his knuckles. "What do you want?"

He sighed deeply. "I want a family. I want to belong to somebody."

I smiled. Any family would be lucky to have Ollie, and his mother was finally trying to make up for lost time. "That's good, Ollie. Maybe you could go visit during spring break, or she could come here."

Sitting opposite me, his smile faded as he gazed into my eyes. Reaching his hand to my face, he brushed a strand of hair from my eyes. A long sigh left his lungs, and he pressed his eyes closed tightly.

My insides twisted as anxiety and worry flooded my body. "Ollie? What is it?" Opening his eyes, he stared down at our joined hands.

"I'm going to Utah."

I stared at him, not completely understanding his sudden sorrowful expression. "How long will you be gone?"

He shook his head, and I knew the answer without him saying a word. "You're not coming back, are you?"

Looking into my eyes, he shook his head again. A lump formed in my throat. I'd had him all this time, and now he was slipping through my fingers just when we were finally moving forward together, and I was powerless to stop it.

"My mother wants us to give our relationship a chance. I've spent the past four days thinking it over and I have to try, Layla. She's got a little boy. He's my half-brother. He's real funny and he loves music. He wants me to teach him guitar. This is my chance at having a family, a real family. She's changed. She's been clean for over ten years now and we've talked. A lot."

He was gushing, but I couldn't focus; his words were hitting me like bullets. "But, what about us? What we have?"

He tilted his head to the side, and held his palm to my cheek. "You know how I feel about you. I love you. That's why I had to tell you. I wanted to give you time."

Give me time? Time for what?

I gave him a bewildered look, completely confused.

"Layla, I want you to come with me. Let's get out of here. Start a new life in Utah. Leave all the hurt and pain behind us here, and start our new life there."

Was he serious?

Snatching my hands from his, I sat back in my chair and stared at him. I couldn't get my head around everything he'd just said. "I can't leave. My life is here. Amy, Mel, my parents. What about college?"

Leaning across the table, he rested his hands on my forearms. "We'd be a ten hour drive away, less if you go by plane. Your folks can come visit us, we can visit them, and you could transfer to college there. My mom has an apartment above the garage, and she said we can live there completely rent free. She's actually a successful realtor now. I can't believe how different she is. I'm going in summer break once the year is over, and I'll transfer to college there. Look, this is a big decision and I need you to think it through. Be completely sure. Don't answer right now. Think about it."

I nodded. There was nothing I could say. I was in shock. Rounding the table, he crouched in front of me and pulled me into his arms, holding me tightly. I swallowed hard and found the strength to speak, "What do we do now?"

His lip ring pressed against my cheek, and I closed my eyes tightly, savouring the sensation. "We carry on. Like right now, we have dinner, and tomorrow we hang out with Amy and Mel. Friday nights we go to Benny's, and we continue to do everything we always have. Nothing has to change right now, ok?"

Lifting my face with his hand, he kissed me. He was wrong. Everything was about to change.

Chapter 43

Time

Days turned into weeks, and before I knew it, spring break was upon us.

Carrying a bag of essentials in his hand, Ollie entwined our fingers. We were heading for the beach, and since the weather was so fine, I'd elected to walk there rather than drive. In my denim white hot pants and bathing suit, it finally felt like summer was coming to Long Beach. Ollie looked like an underwear model with his white cotton shorts and slim, muscular body. He was utterly scrumptious to look at.

Holding his hand tightly, I couldn't help but smile. We'd grown so close over the past few weeks, and I was really beginning to let him in a little. We spent every day together in class, in his room hanging out, and in the evenings we'd take his Ducati up to the hills for some privacy.

He and his mom had been in constant contact, and she was planning on coming down to visit him on Saturday. "I can't wait for you to meet her, Layla. She's only staying one night, so I figured we could go for dinner and then I'd hang with her a while at the hotel. That ok with you?"

I nodded. "Sure, can't wait."

Meeting Ollie's mother was not an experience I was looking forward to. He may have forgiven her for walking out on him, but I was not so easily persuaded. What kind of woman walks away from her child and leaves him with his abusive father?

Deciding I would keep my mouth shut for Ollie's sake, I listened as he gushed about the apartment she was readying, and although I'd yet to give him my answer, he still insisted on saying we. "It'll be amazing. There's already a couch and a bed, and we can get everything else we need once I sell the bike."

Halting my steps, I gawked at him. "What do you mean sell the bike? You love that Ducati."

Pressing his lips to mine, he smiled. "I know. But I love you more, and I want to make a nice home for us."

My stomach churned. Oh god, he was giving up his pride and joy for me, and I wasn't even sure I was going with him. "Ollie, don't make any big decisions yet. I still haven't decided if I can do this with you. Just hold fire, ok?"

Staring at the ground, he nodded, and I knew my words had hurt him.

"I'm not saying no, Ollie. I'm saying I'm not sure yet. You said I should think it through and that's what I'm doing. Can we please not talk about it and just have a nice day at the beach? Wanna rub lotion on my back for me?" I gave him a suggestive smile and it worked.

"I'd happily rub anything you want, Layla. All day and night if you'd let me." I grinned and placed a soft kiss on his lips. "Let's just start with sun lotion for now. We can discuss the rest later."

* * * *

The sun was gloriously hot. I lay on the warm golden sands, my head in a book, and tried to catch up on my reading for our psych class. But as he lay beside me, skin glistening in the sunlight, Ollie became a big distraction. Closing my book, I put it aside and leaned on my elbow. He was so still he could have been sleeping, and with his dark shades over his eyes, I'd be none the wiser.

His hands behind his head, he let out a satisfied moan and it called to me like a siren to unfortunate sailors. Placing my hand on his chest, I traced my fingertips over his perfectly formed pecs. A trail of hair led from his chest to his happy zone, and with a smile on my face I twirled and dragged my fingers down to the waist of his shorts. The corners of his mouth curled up, and I knew he was watching me from beneath those specs.

So we were going to play, huh?

Brushing my fingertips across his torso, I grazed it gently, swirling my fingers back and forth before sliding my hand beneath his shorts.

Gripping my wrist, he caught me and grinned, tut-tutting. Flipping me onto my back, he laid on top of me. My toes pressed against his feet as he pinned me to the sand. My heart pounded, and my insides clenched as his mouth closed over mine. His kiss was sweet, loving, and passionate.

"That's a risky game you're playing. We're in public, for a start."

Pressing my palm against his chest, I could feel his own thundering heartbeat beneath it. I could tell that he was clearly as turned on as I was as his erection pressed against my sex. If I could have willed the world to disappear, and our clothes to disintegrate, I would have been in the throes of ecstasy right there on that beach.

"Layla, stop. We can't do this here."

I shifted under him, and slid my hand between us to his crotch. Grasping him in my hand, I breathed heavily against his mouth. "When, Ollie? I don't think I can wait much longer."

I was giving him the green light, and I expected him to dart right through like a bullet. Rolling off of me, he laid on his front and shrugged. "Not yet. Soon."

We'd been holding off so long I was fit to burst, and I feared soon wouldn't be soon enough to save me.

* * * *

"What do you think, Layla? Layla?"

I shook my head, not hearing what Amy had said to me. "What?"

Rolling her eyes, she sighed. "I said, what do you think about throwing Ollie a going away party?"

"Oh. Yeah, sure. Whatever."

As the week had gone on, I'd found myself becoming more and more despondent. Talk of Ollie leaving was a subject I didn't want to discuss. After he'd asked me to go with him to Utah, he hadn't brought the subject up once, and I knew he was avoiding it because he was afraid of my answer, but I didn't have one yet. I'd tried desperately to figure it out, and even spent three hours with Amy and Mel drawing up a list of pros and cons, but even that didn't get me very far. For every pro there was a con, and it ended in a tie breaker with me tearing it up and groaning into my pillow. How could I make such a huge decision just like that? I wasn't just leaving college; I was leaving my friends, family, and everything I'd built over the past year.

I didn't want us to break up, but could I seriously leave and follow him across the country? My heart was torn between my family, friends, and the man I'd grown desperately close to. Sitting down next to me on the bed, Mel nudged me with her shoulder.

"Still can't figure out what you're gonna do, huh?"

I shook my head. "I can't just drop everything and go, Mel. I care about Ollie, I do, and I don't want to end what we have but..."

The words were stuck in my throat like a thorn. Amy and Mel were only too aware of the reason I was holding back.

"You don't love him, do you, Layla?"

Holding my hands over my face, I shook my head. "I want to. I want to so much, but I just can't. He's amazing, wonderful, and everything I could ever want in a man, but my stupid broken heart can't seem to let go of Jared. It's killing me!"

Draping her arm around my shoulder, Mel let out a long breath. "You know what you have to do, Layla, don't you."

I nodded weakly.

"When will you tell him?"

Gazing at them both, I sighed. "Not yet. I don't want to ruin these last few weeks with him. I will tell him, but I need to give him this. I owe him that much."

Sitting on the floor in front of me, I could see tears in Amy's eyes. "Oh, Layla. I can't believe he's leaving, and that he's got to go with a broken heart. Maybe you'll change your mind. Maybe, if you really try and spend more time together, you'll see how amazing he is and you'll just forget about Jared. Ollie loves you, Layla. He can make you so happy, I know it. You'd have an incredible life. You'd be his queen. What's not to love about him?"

Poor Amy. She really was a hopeless romantic. Just because someone is the good choice, it doesn't make it the right choice. "Amy, if I went with him it would be out of guilt, or because I feel I should. He wouldn't want that. He said he wants me to *want* to go with him."

"Don't you?"

I sighed.

"Of course I do, Amy, but for all the wrong reasons. I should go because I love him. Because I can't bear to be away from him. Not because I don't want to break his heart, or because I'll miss him when he's gone. This is his chance at a new life. A start over. He deserves it. If I went with him, we'd just be living one huge lie. I won't put him through it. It wouldn't be fair on either of us. Look, how about this. I won't say anything to Ollie until I'm one hundred percent sure of what I want. I'll just…take it slow. Never say never, right?"

She knew I was right, and though I could see it pained her to accept it, she respected my choice. "Ok. But just give him a chance. Please?"

That's exactly what I had been doing since Christmas and I was no closer to knowing what I wanted now than I had been then.

* * * *

Staring at myself in the mirror, I sighed. In less than an hour I would be face to face with the woman who abandoned Ollie. I could already feel the anger building inside me. I didn't care what he said; there was no excuse close to acceptable for what she'd done.

Deciding on the purple dress I'd worn for our dinner date, I twirled, patting down the garment for any dust or lint.

"You look incredible." A pair of warm arms snaked around my waist as his lip ring pressed against my cheek.

"Thanks. Hope she approves."

"I don't care what she thinks. I approve."

Turning to face him, I pressed my palms against his chest. He was wearing his black pants and a deep blue shirt, slightly unbuttoned.

"You don't look so bad yourself."

Pressing his lips to mine, the spark of electricity between us made me smile. Ollie really was amazing, and whenever I was around him I felt so comfortable and happy. Ollie's natural charisma and gentle charm was completely disarming and totally swoon worthy. I wasn't just with a great guy; he also happened to be one of my best friends.

"Well, let's get this show on the road."

Holding my hand tightly in his, we walked outside where a cab was waiting for us. My mind suddenly drifted to Daniel, the Mercedes and Jared. Angry at myself for letting my mind wander, I glanced at Ollie and tightened my grip on his hand.

Entering the restaurant I could feel the nerves swarming in my stomach. Still holding my hand firmly, Ollie led us through to a table in the far corner where a slim woman with long dark hair was sipping a glass of water. Seeing us approach she stood and immediately wrapped her arms around Ollie who, albeit rigidly, hugged her back.

"Mom, this is Layla."

Leaning in to me, she gave me a peck on the cheek and smiled widely. "It's lovely to finally meet you, Layla. I've heard a lot about you."

I eyed her with skepticism. "I've heard a lot about you too."

Looking at Ollie and then at the floor, she sighed. "Yes, I imagine you have."

Noticing the tension building between us, Ollie gestured for us to sit. Taking the seat next to me, he held my hand on top of the table and brushed his thumb back and forth over my knuckles. "So, Layla. Ollie tells me the two of you have been dating for several months now. How did you meet?"

I shifted uncomfortably in my seat. "Well, I actually bumped into him on my first day at college, literally. We became good friends and started dating around Christmas time." Ollie held my hand firmly and smiled at me.

"That's sweet. So why the long wait between meeting and dating?"

I gave Ollie a discomfited look. I didn't like the direction the conversation was going.

"She was in a relationship. He treated her badly. They broke up. That's it."

Ollie to my rescue.

Sitting back in her chair, his mother gave me a smile, but I got the district feeling she was sizing me up. What gave her the right? She'd only just crawled her way back into his life, yet here she was questioning me? I gave her an icy glare. I was not going to be intimidated by the likes of her.

Taking my menu, I gave the waiter my order and sipped on my water, all the time keeping my eyes fixed on the woman sitting opposite me. Her hand brushed Ollie's as they spoke about his move to Utah this summer and my stomach twisted into knots every time they made plans, spoke about the apartment, or even said the word move.

"Oliver tells me he's asked you to come with him, Layla. Well, we'll be very happy to have you join our little family. My younger son Patrick has always wanted a sister."

I almost choked on my water.

"Mom, I told you to drop it. I won't pressure Layla into a decision." He placed his hand on the small of my back, and I couldn't have felt more awful.

"What's to think about? You love each other, you want to be together, and Utah is only a different state, not another country."

"Mom! That's enough. Just drop it."

Raising her hands defensively, she shot me a questioning look and it instantly got my back up. I was glad when our food arrived as it gave me a reason to remain silent while the two of them continued to talk about Ollie's new life that waited for him.

"Well, if you'll excuse me I need to use the bathroom," Ollie said. Resting his hand on my shoulder, he leaned in to my ear. "You'll be ok?"

I nodded, and giving me a quick peck, he left the table and the two of us alone. Watching him leave, Ollie's mother turned her attention to me.

"Layla, I'm going to be frank and say what I have noticed this evening. You don't want to come to Utah, and you certainly do not feel about Ollie the same way he does about you. Now, why don't we stop pretending and lay the cards on the table. You don't like me for what I did to Ollie in his past. And I certainly won't like you if you jeopardize his future happiness. If you don't want him, let him go."

I stared at her in total shock. "How dare you? I am crazy about your son, and I would never jeopardize his future."

"Oh come on, dear. Be honest with yourself. You don't love my son, and the way you have responded to his enthusiasm about moving has left a lot to be desired. I appreciate you care about him, and maybe on some level you do love him, but I've been the woman you are now. You stay because you feel you should, and if you came to Utah it would be for him, not you. Be kind, let him go."

Now I was irate.

"I don't know who you think you are, but the only one hurting Ollie around here is you. You come wandering back into his life and offer him this perfect little family, and just like that he's leaving his whole life to come to Utah. His college, his friends, everything."

She gave me a satisfied grin. "I notice you never mentioned yourself in that list. You are hurting him more and more the longer you give him hope. Cut the strings and let him go. I made the biggest mistake of my life when I left Oliver and his brother, but I had my reasons, reasons I do not have to justify to you. Oliver has found it in his beautiful heart to give me a chance to make it up to him, and I will not stand idly by while you tear his heart out."

Standing, I slammed my napkin on the table, grabbed my purse and walked away. Her words, though harsh, were right on the money. She'd seen through me and called me on it. As I reached the door, I saw Ollie coming out of the bathroom and putting my head down, I quickened my pace out into the street and across the road to hail a cab.

Sprinting out of the doors he yelled after me. "Layla! Wait, where are you going? What's going on?" I stood staring ahead, looking for a cab to pass for me to take. Reaching me, he held his hand on my arm and lifted my chin to face him. "Layla, what's happened? Why did you take off?"

I shook my head, unable to look him in the eye. "I have to go home, Ollie. I can't stay here."

"I don't understand. When I went to the bathroom everything was fine, then I come back and you're taking off. What did she say to you?"

Pulling away from him, I exhaled loudly. "Nothing that I didn't already know. Ollie, I-"

He cut me off, closing the space between us and pressing his lips to mine. "You're not coming with me to Utah, are you Layla?" His forehead rested against mine, and weakly I shook my head. He sighed. "I know. I always knew. I understand. It's a lot to ask of you, and I shouldn't have expected you to leave everything for a man you don't even love."

Tears pooled in my eyes. "Ollie…I'm so…"

"It's ok. We gave it our best shot, didn't we? Sometimes the story doesn't end the way we want it to. Can you do something for me?"

I gazed into his eyes "Anything."

"Let me pretend, just a while longer. I need it."

Warm salty tears rolled heavily down my cheeks. "Ok."

We didn't stay for dinner. Leaving me on the sidewalk, Ollie ran back to the restaurant to say goodbye to his mom. Sliding into the cab beside me, he held my hand, threading our fingers together. My heart gave an almighty thud as I gazed into his deep brown eyes. He smiled, but I knew he was hurting as deeply as I was.

The walk down our hall was a long and silent one. Standing outside my room, we stared at each other. Taking my hand, Ollie pressed my palm to his lips and kissed me softly before holding it against his cheek. My heart swelled and my eyes blurred with unshed tears. "I love you, Layla. Thank you."

I couldn't believe what he was saying. Everything I'd put him through and he was thanking me. "What for? Breaking your heart?" Tears fell silently from my eyes.

"No. For letting me know I have one."

A sob escaped my lips. Pulling me to him, he held me in a warm embrace and stroked his hand up and down my spine. "Shhh. It's ok. It'll be ok. I promise."

I nodded weakly, unable to believe his words and I was sure he didn't believe them either. Releasing my hand, he smiled and reached for his door handle.

Taking his other hand, I stopped him. "Don't."

He looked at me, confused.

"Stay with me. Even if it's just for tonight. Be with me, Ollie."

Cupping his face in my hands, I kissed him passionately. I kissed him like it was my last, and the way things had played out that night, I feared it could be.

"Are you sure about this?"

Catching my breath, I gazed at him and nodded. "I want to be with you tonight, Ollie. I want to do this with you."

Taking his hand, I led him into my room. Amy had gone home for the weekend, so I knew we had the whole night alone. He looked nervous. Closing the door behind us, I lit a few candles around the room. His eyes glistened and sparkled in the dim light beneath his long black hair. My palms pressed against his chest, I gently and slowly unbuttoned his shirt. I felt him tense beneath my fingers, and momentarily I pulled away. Catching my wrist in his grasp, he placed it back over his heart. Gazing down at me, he kissed me softly and slid his hands over my shoulders, making the straps of my dress loosen and rest on my arms.

Turning around, I held my hair up as his fingers traced across my neck before gently unzipping my dress. Turning back to face him, I shrugged it over my body and it fell lightly to the floor. Stepping out gracefully, I ran my hands over his bare chest, beneath his open shirt. My mouth closed over his as I pulled and tugged it from his torso. Tracing my fingertips over his chest, I followed every line, curve and contour of his body. I drew in a sharp breath as I slid my hands downwards to his pelvis.

Snaking my hands over his hips and around his waist, I pressed my hands firmly to his back, forcing him close to me. His own hands glided up and down my spine gently before resting on my hips. His forehead rested against mine, and I could hear how breathless he was and my own chest rose and fell heavily.

"Make love to me, Ollie." His lips sealed over mine as he scooped me into his arms and carried me to the bed.

Gently placing me on the bed, he kicked off his shoes and took off his socks. I stifled a giggle, and sat up to face him.

Looking up into his eyes, I began to unbuckle his belt and unzip his pants. Tugging them down, I ran my fingers gently over the bulge in his shorts. I'd learned firsthand that night on my couch that he was big. Very big.

Licking my lips, I hooked my thumbs into the waist line of his shorts and gently slid them over his thick, muscular thighs. His long, thick erection sprang free, and I grinned. It was beautiful. Solid as stone, I took it in my mouth. Rolling my tongue gently around the tip, I heard Ollie let out a deep moan. His fingers threaded through my hair as he stood in front of me, rocking his hips back and forth with the movements of my mouth. Sliding my lips up and down his shaft, I gripped my hands around him, creating a mixture of sucking, licking and rubbing. His jaw clenched, and I felt him tense. His hand hooked under my chin and he pulled me away. He gazed down at me, rubbing his thumb over my cheek as he slid his hand behind my head and gently laid me down on the bed.

Sliding on top of me, he kissed me deeply with a sense of longing. His hands glided down and slid behind my back, releasing the clasp of my bra. Peeling the straps over my shoulders, he trailed kisses over my skin as the cotton grazed my arms. Tossing it to the floor, he took my breast in his mouth and rolled his tongue over my nipple. I moaned and arched my back as his hand massaged, caressed and stroked my swollen breasts. Kissing, licking and grazing his way down my body, I writhed beneath him. Reaching my panties, he placed a soft kiss onto the cotton at the opening of my sex. I could feel his warm breath on the fleshy lips beneath. It was hugely erotic, yet completely romantic all at once.

"I've wanted this for so long that I can hardly stand it. You're so beautiful. Every last curve, line, and inch of your delicate skin is perfect. You're perfect."

His fingers gripped the elastic at my hips, and I automatically lifted to allow him to slide them off of me. Once he had disposed of them, he continued his attention to my swollen, aching clit. I gasped as the cool metal of his lip ring brushed against my warm skin, the tip of his tongue gliding slowly and gently from the opening of my sex to my clit over and over. He was teasing me, and I was going crazy with anticipation.

His tongue swirled, flicked, and pressed against my clit. I cried out as my orgasm quickly built inside me. I'd wanted Ollie for so long, thought about this moment for so long, and now that it was finally here I could hardly control myself. The build-up of months of sexual chemistry and tension was coming to a climactic end at last. I gripped the sheets beside me as my legs and arms grew stiff, preparing for the convulsions of the muscles inside me. I panted harder as his tongue drove me rapidly to the edge.

"It's okay, baby. Let go. I want to give this to you."

His sweet words echoed in my ears as I rocked and ground my hips against his mouth, desperate for my release. My fingers holding on so tightly to the sheet below, I feared I would tear it. Bringing it to my mouth, I bit down hard, muffling my loud and pleading groans. His hands caressed and stroked my thighs, heightening the pleasure I was feeling between my legs. Closing my eyes, I stilled as the crashing and thrashing waves of my orgasm rolled through my body. Pulsating, surging and tightening inside me, I cried out his name as tears streamed down my face.

His lips trailed kisses from my sex all the way up to my neck where he nuzzled and breathed me in deeply. His hand beneath my head, he kissed me. Never speaking a word, we gazed at each other as he gently slid inside me. Closing my eyes, my head fell back and he took in a sharp breath, almost hissing. Pressing my palms to his back, I ran my hands all over his body. His chest, his broad shoulders, the length of his spine, and finally resting on his tight, firm behind. He gasped as I squeezed and palmed his flesh in my hands. His hips rocked back and forth unhurriedly, withdrawing before gradually sliding back inside me. His eyes glistened in the light, and as I lay there beneath him, I could feel the thundering of his heartbeat.

Pressing his lips to mine firmly, he closed his eyes and his body tensed. He was close, and I wanted to go to paradise with him. Pushing my hands into his behind, I urged him deeper. Withdrawing slowly before gently pushing back inside me, his tip brushed against my g-spot and I gasped. It was heavenly. Our eyes fixated on one another, we held each other tightly, lovingly; as though we were dependent on the other for our next breath.

His eyebrows furrowed, and I could feel him pulsing and throbbing inside me. "Oh god, Layla. I love you so much." He was breathless and his words hit me hard. As my muscles tightened around him, I was swimming in a pool of lust, need and hurt. His tongue ran over my bottom lip, and I moaned as another mind blowing orgasm ripped through me. I bowed and practically levitated off the bed. I cried out his name as he held me close, finding his own release. We were so painfully close that I couldn't tell where his body ended and mine began. We'd become one sensual, post-coital mess.

Panting, and trying to control my rapid breathing, I lay there gazing deep into his eyes. Brushing a lock of hair from his face, I pulled him to me for another heart stopping kiss. Rolling onto his side, he wrapped his arms around my waist and spooned me. I could feel his breath on my neck and its comforting warmth allowed me to doze in and out of consciousness. Neither of us spoke. It was too painful, and there was nothing left to say. It was over and though we both knew the implications of our night together, I knew he'd needed it just as much as I did.

With his head pressed against my back, I silently cried, shuddering as the tears fell down my cheeks. Turning me to face him, Ollie stroked and wiped away each tear as it fell without a single word. He held me for hours as we gazed into each other's eyes, until we could no longer keep them open and fell into a deep and sorrowful sleep.

****

Reaching out my hand, I opened my eyes as it fell on an empty space. I leaned up on my elbows, scanning the room, but he wasn't there. Getting out of bed, I headed for the bathroom, but he wasn't there either. In a panic, I grabbed my robe and flew out the door to his room. Hammering my fist hard on the wood, I waited for an answer, but none came.

Taking a chance, I opened the door to find it unlocked. My heart shredded into a thousand pieces as I stared at the empty side of Ollie's room. His posters, guitar, everything was gone. I held my hand to my mouth as tears began streaming down my face. I walked to his bedside cabinet where I found an empty frame. My picture had been replaced by a note with my name on it. Clutching it in my hand, I ran back to the solace of my bedroom. Slumping onto the bed, I read it as my body racked and convulsed with sobs.

Layla

I couldn't bear to wake you. You looked so peaceful laying there that it seemed the greatest sin to disturb an angel as she slept. I've never been good at goodbyes and honestly I don't think it's a word I could ever use with you. I can never say goodbye to you, Layla. It feels so final and the thought that I will never see you again would kill me. What you gave me last night, I will never, ever forget that and you have no idea how much it meant to me. I hope you don't mind but I kept the picture. I wanted a reminder of our time together and of you. I can't tell you how much I'm going to miss you but I couldn't stay, not now. Spending seven more weeks with you and not being able to touch you, kiss you or hold you in my arms would be agony. I won't put you or myself through the pain. I always knew you couldn't come with me but the fact that you even considered it and maybe even thought you could do it, tells me all I need to know. I will love you forever and you will always be my first and true love. I was your friend before I was your lover and I will always be here for you whenever you need me.

There's just one last thing you have to do for me Layla and it's the most important. Don't feel guilty. We gave it our best shot and that's all I could ask for. I don't regret one moment and you shouldn't either. So smile, laugh and sing at that god awful bar every Friday. Eric may not look as good as me doing it but he's a hell of a guitar player. Take care of Amy for me and don't let her and Mel get into too much trouble. One fuck up in our group is enough and in my absence I'd rather they not take my title. Loving you with every beat of my heart. I'll see you soon.

Ollie xxxxxxxxx

P.S I left you a gift in your closet I got it for you as a kind of going away present. It's yours whenever you need it.

Droplets of my tears fell onto the paper, smearing and smudging his words.

He was gone.

Placing it on my bed, I walked to my closet and found a single red envelope containing a plane ticket a note and a CD. Turning on my laptop, I sat and read the note.

"This is an open ticket. If you ever change your mind my address is on the back of this note. Ollie. Xxx"

He'd given me the choice. It wasn't too late, but deep down I knew we were done. I didn't love him, and though my heart was breaking because he was gone, I knew it was for the best. The CD fired up and I gazed at it as Ollie's face, body, guitar and smile filled the screen. He didn't speak, he sang. I recognized the song. It was one of my favorites.

Ollie really had known all along; the video had been recorded only a week after he'd asked me to go with him. I stared at him as he sang the song 'In My Life' by the Beatles. His face expressed every word, each heartfelt emotion; and the words enveloped me as each one left his beautiful lips.

Hitting repeat, I laid there for hours just watching him. I hadn't even noticed when the sun had gone down. I'd been lying there, watching him all day. Crying, sobbing, and just staring at him on the screen. The door flew open, and Amy stormed over to me with tears streaming down her face.

"How could you, Layla? He's gone. Just like that, and he never even said goodbye before he left. I knew you were going to break his heart. God, you really are a heartless bitch."

Leaping to my feet, I squared up to her. "I am not a heartless bitch, Amy. It's because I care about him so much that I had to let him go. You think that was easy for me? Of course not, but I couldn't keep stringing him along, believing that we had a future together. He's my friend, Amy, and I love him the way I love you and Mel. I can't even begin to tell you how much it hurt me to let him go, but I had to. He's better off this way before we got in too deep."

She snorted a laugh in disbelief. "Too deep? Layla, he was jumping in feet first the moment you met! He's been in love with you from the very start, and you think it's all just going to go away for him? That he'll just forget and get over you? Well he won't. You never forget your first love. It's the most awful feeling in the world to love someone who can't love you back. I should know!"

I stared at her waiting for an explanation. "What do you mean? Amy do you love Ollie?"

She flushed. "No, not Ollie. Someone else."

I gazed at her, but she remained silent. She seemed completely embarrassed, and a little mortified, that the words had escaped her mouth.

"Amy, talk to me. What's going on?"

Holding her hands over her face, she sighed. "I'm in love, Layla. Completely, totally, and unbelievably in love. And my poor heart will never experience that love returned."

Pressing my hands on her arms, I looked into her tearful eyes. "Amy, tell me. Who is it?"

Biting her lip, she gulped a sob. "It's Melanie."

I gawked at her, unsure if I had heard what I thought I had. "Wait, what?"

Slumping onto her bed, she held her head in her hands. "I'm in love with Mel. Oh god. I have no idea what's going on with me, Layla. I've always been with men, and I like men. I'm totally sexually attracted to them, but when she's around me I feel, I don't know. I can't stop thinking about her. She's smart, funny, exciting, and sexy as hell. Her eyes are gorgeous, and her body...oh my god. I think about doing things with her I've only seen in porn. She makes my skin warm and my heart pound in my ears. Her smile could knock me out. I've always been a little tri-sexual. I'll 'try' anything once. But it's more than just sexual desire I feel for her. I really like her, Layla. I'm so confused."

My eyebrows shot up, and I stared at her in pure and utter surprise. Mel had never had a boyfriend, but she'd had her fair share of one night stands and flings, so I was pretty sure poor Amy was barking up a heterosexual tree. "Amy, I don't know what to say, but you know Mel's not-"

"I know, she's into guys. But I can't stop loving her, Layla. It's like a force of nature. I just want to be around her all the time. Last night, when we were hanging out in her room, I thought about telling her a thousand times. But if she knew, she'd never go near me again, and I couldn't stand not having her around. Do you know what it's like to just completely be cut off from someone you have such strong feelings for?"

I gave her an understanding look. Of course I knew. "You know I do, Amy. I want to tell you it will all be ok, but unrequited love is a killer. But I do think you need to think long and hard about this. Telling her could end your friendship, and I love you both too much to watch that happen. Not to mention if it leaves you with a broken heart."

She nodded weakly, and I knew the pain only too well. Loving someone so much, and knowing you can't be with them, was cripplingly painful.

Falling backwards on her bed, she flung her arm over her eyes. "I'm sorry I screamed at you. I don't blame you. Ollie knew he was taking a chance. I warned him about rebounding, but he wouldn't listen. I miss him already though. Feels kinda black and white without him. He brought a lot of color around here."

I smiled, knowing exactly what he would have thought about his colorfulness. "How did you know he was gone?"

Removing her arm, she sighed deeply. "He called me. Told me he was in Utah safe and sound. We talked for a while about everything, but he didn't feel much like discussing it. I asked him if I should give you a message."

I held my breath, hoping there was the possibility of some form of communication from him. Anything would do. Something to let me know we would be alright.

"He said no. He actually said I shouldn't mention he called. Said the two of you need distance right now."

My heart plummeted to my stomach. Ollie was grieving, and I had been the cause of his bereavement.

Sitting up, she draped her arm around my shoulder and wiped a tear from her eye. "Well, I would say we make a great pair. With Jared breaking your heart, you breaking Ollie's, and Mel breaking mine, we have three beautifully broken hearts between us. Two belong to us, and the others we can do nothing about. So, my suggestion? We gotta pick up those pieces and start to rebuild. Because I swear, I can't stand the pain anymore, Layla. From now on it's just us girls having fun. No men, no fuss, no mess. Just good clean fun. Well, maybe we could get a little dirty." She winked at me, and together we laughed lightly.

She was right. I'd had enough heartache to last me a lifetime. Fiery, independent and obstinate Layla was buried beneath the rubble of two broken relationships, but she was in there somewhere.

And I was determined to dig her up!

Chapter 44

Fired Up

Staring at myself in the mirror, I grinned. My new look wasn't just totally hot, it was life changing. My long blonde hair was no more. My new chocolate brown locks had been chopped, hacked, and feathered into stylish shoulder length curls. My eyes had that smoky effect, and my bright red lipstick really completed the look. Per our shopping trip that day, Mel and Amy had helped me find the perfect outfit for our evening out. We were heading to a great new swanky bar in town called Delicia. Amy had met a guy at Benny's and had scored an invitation to their opening. Naturally, she'd neglected to mention that we were only twenty years old and as it was a free bar; she figured it was a moot point.

My dress was black, indecently short, and with a sweetheart neckline it pushed and plumped my breasts, giving me knockout cleavage. We weren't looking to score, but I still didn't mind a little attention. Running my hands over my curves, I smiled to myself. It was the first time I'd been out since Ollie had left and that was almost three weeks ago. He called Amy from time to time, but was eager to divert my calls. I must have left him a hundred messages, begging for him to talk to me, but he never called back. My emails, texts, and letters went unanswered, and whenever he called Amy he would tell her not to mention he had done so.

It was painful, and I was beginning to resent him. He'd said in his letter how we were friends, that he would always be there, and yet here he was, shutting me out. It was a punishment, and part of me believed I deserved it. After all, I had hurt him and those scars were going to take a long time to heal.

Coming out of the bathroom, Amy whistled at me. "Well look at you, hot stuff. You are smoking! That hair is awesome, if I do say so myself."

I smiled at her. "That's because you did it. You don't look so bad yourself."

With her hair in a sexy up do, and her hot new pink dress with the plunging neck line, she looked stunning. Slipping on my heels, I dropped my cell into my purse, checking for any messages before I hid it away.

"Amy, did Ollie call?"

She gave me sympathetic look. "He called this morning. He's doing ok. He's got a part time job, actually. He's fixing up motorcycles, so he loves it, of course."

I nodded, wishing he could've told me himself. "Anything else?"

Walking over to me, she rested her hand on my arm. "He's in pain, Layla. He misses you, but he's just protecting you both right now. Give him some time. He'll come around."

I hoped she was right because I was missing him too. Badly.

Swinging the door open, Mel swanned in. Dressed to the nines in an electric blue dress, she gave us a twirl. Amy smiled as she stared at her. "Wow, Mel, you look amazing. Totally hot." Grinning, Mel hugged her.

"Thank you. You both look great as always. I swear, if this little baby doesn't snag me a man tonight, I'm switching teams."

I glanced at Amy, who cleared her throat and busied herself with putting her shoes on. "Mel, our goal tonight is to have a girl's night out. Fun, drinking, and dancing, remember? No guys. Well, not all night anyway."

She laughed and gave me a salute. "Yes, sergeant."

Nudging her, I rolled my eyes before grabbing my purse and heading out the door. Waiting curbside was our cab, and as I walked up I couldn't help but stare at the empty spot where Ollie's Ducati used to sit. My heart gave a thud and I knew it was warning me to get into the cab and forget about it. Tonight I was Layla again. The fiery, sarcastic, independent and kiss my ass girl that I had been the first time I set foot in Long Beach State. I had missed her most of all.

The bar was amazing. Florescent blue lights were mounted onto the wall and integrated into the floor around the whole place. The bar was crystal clear glass, and the blue lights around it made it look as though it were made of ice. Long slim black bar stools were surrounding it, and several tables and chairs were scattered around the floor. A staircase led upstairs to a sectioned off V.I.P area with a balcony overlooking the bar. Downstairs was another large bar and an area for dancing. The music was pulsing, and there were dozens of people crowding around trying to order drinks.

Giving me a wink, Amy nodded at the bartender.

"Oh my god. Is that Greg? From Benny's?"

"Sure is. I bet I can score us some drinks."

Pushing her way chest first through a crowd of now drooling men, Amy leaned on the bar. Giving Greg her prize winning smile, and a flash of her cleavage, she got us a round of drinks and three shots of Sambuca.

"This ought to get us started."

I cringed as the memory of Amy's vomit and tequila breath wafted up my nose. Taking a shot, Mel held it in the air.

"To being a proud, independent woman."

I was more than happy to drink to that.

After two hours, four rum and cokes, and three shots of Sambuca, I was really starting to let loose. Sitting at the bar, Amy and Mel were in fits of laughter, but I had yet to discover what was so funny. The alcohol clearly had gone to their heads. Ordering another round of shots, Mel decided we should play a game. A group of three young guys were sitting just a few feet away. Sliding out of her stool, Mel sashayed over and worked her magic.

Following her over to us, they grinned. "So Melanie here says you girls are up for a little drinking game? Personally I prefer strip poker, but have you ever played 'I have never'?"

I shook my head. "Nope, you're going to have to explain the rules."

His gray eyes glistened beneath his deep black hair as he spoke and I found them a little distracting. "Well, each person says something they have never done, and if you've done it, you take a drink. Sound fair?"

I raised an eyebrow at Mel, but giving me a wink she nodded. "Ok, bring it on boys."

* * * *

Slamming my shot glass on the table, I sucked the lime hard and winced at my opponent as he spluttered. "Urgh. Damn, that shit is nasty."

I gave him a triumphant smile. "Give up yet, Henry?"

He leaned in and whispered in my ear. "I never quit."

Picking up another shot, he gave me a wicked grin. "I have never had sex in a public place."

Rolling my eyes, I picked up another drink and downed it along with Mel, Amy, and one of the other guys at our table. "Wow, how many you had so far now, Layla? I'm beginning to think you play a little fast and loose with your morals."

"Nope, just like to have fun."

Beaming at me, he sipped his beer.

A buzzing caught my attention as my purse began to move across the table. Giggling, I grabbed it and slipped my cell out. Oh for heaven's sake. What the hell does he want? Irritated at the intrusion, I opened Jared's message.

> What are you doing?
> **Received: 22.35**
> **From: Jared**

> What business is it of yours?
> **Sent: 22.38**
> **To: Jared**

> Answer the question.
> **Received: 22.42**
> **From: Jared**

I rolled my eyes and sighed heavily. Why the hell did he care what I was doing? What's more, why did he have an urgent need to know?

Henry placed his hand on my arm. "You ok?"

I nodded. "Just have to deal with a little pest problem." It buzzed in my hand, and I glared at the screen.

> Don't be fucking difficult, Layla. And get his hand off of your arm. Now. It's not a request
> **Received: 22.44**
> **From: Jared**

He was here. Shit.

Scanning the bar, I searched for him before finally it dawned on me where he would naturally be. Lifting my head, I glared up at the balcony. Standing there, drink in one hand and cell phone in the other, Jared stared down at me. His jeans and slightly unbuttoned black shirt made him look every bit the playboy once more. I could see his piercing blue eyes glowering at the back of Henry's head. I was not taking orders from him anymore, and he had no right to tell me what to do. Smiling at Henry, I placed my own hand over his.

"I think I've made my point."

Handing me a piece of lime and another shot glass, he clinked his to mine. Tossing my head back, I drank it down and sucked hard on my lime before taking it from my mouth and pressing it to Henry's lips. Raising an eyebrow, clearly amused, he took it from my fingers with his tongue and sucked.

I chanced a glance up at the balcony. As predicted he wasn't just staring anymore, he was on fire. Gripping the rail tightly, I could see his fist clenched around his glass. I gave him a sarcastic smile. Take that, Mr. Garrett!

My phone buzzed, and nervously I opened the message.

> If he touches you again, I'm going to leap off of this balcony and strangle him with my bare hands. I'm not kidding, Layla. Do not push me.
> **Received: 22.57**
> **From: Jared**

Now I was pissed. I'd had enough of his patronizing, do as you're told, my way no highway option, attitude. Snapping my head up, I gave him the filthiest look I could manage, and flipped him the bird. I could see the rage on his face, and it filled me with lust and fear.

Game on Jared.

Leaning into Henry's ear, I had to speak up to be heard over the pumping bass of the music. "I feel like dancing. You wouldn't make me go alone, would you?"

Immediately getting to his feet, he held out his hand for me which I took instantly. Passing beneath the balcony, I made the conscious effort not to look up at Jared, though I knew he'd be watching my every move.

Amy and Mel had decided to ambush the two guys left at our table and were now following us downstairs to the dance floor. The booming bass lines, and electronic trance music, filled my ears as smoke machines bellowed white misty clouds onto the dance floor. Holding onto Henry's hand, I followed him out into the center of the floor and began swaying my hips to the music. His hands on my waist, he pressed close against me as we danced. It was perfectly innocent, and I was having a good time just drinking, dancing, and irritating the life out of my ex-boyfriend.

I was beginning to get into the swing of things when a familiar dark haired woman breezed past me onto the floor. Her hair flowing to her shoulders, Alicia began to move to the music and extended her hand out to someone across the floor. Closing my eyes tightly, I prayed, pleaded, and begged for it not to be him, but as I opened them I saw her grab onto his hand and pull him flush against her chest. My insides twisted as anger and intense rage built inside me. If he wanted to play this game, then I was definitely willing to participate.

Amy and Mel hadn't spotted the enemy in our midst, and I was glad. The last thing I needed was the two of them starting a fight. The last time I had gone a round with Alicia, I ended up in handcuffs, I wasn't willing to do that again. Besides, there were better ways to ruin his fun.

Turning around, I placed my hands against Henry's chest. He had one of those fit, athletic figures, and his black hair made his eyes look even more striking. Wrapping his arms around my waist, he held me tightly pressed against him as we moved. My hips grinding to the music, I chanced a glance at Jared. Alicia's hands roamed all over his body, sliding over his shoulders and down his back before grazing her palm over his behind. I thought about his tattoo and smirked.

You can feel him up all you like, slut bag, but it's still my name carved into his skin.

With his hands on her hips, she leaned in and I nearly choked on my breath as her tongue slid into his ear. Furious, I grabbed Henry's hand and stormed past them to a table at the edge of the floor. Pushing him back against it, I hooked a finger into the open button of his shirt and leaned in, licking my lips. His eyes sparkled with excitement. Closing the gap, I pressed my mouth against his. His tongue grazed my lips, and with a quick sideways glance at my ex and his slut, I granted him access.

I was playing games, and I knew it.

As Henry gently kissed me, my eyes fixed onto Jared. His hand slid down Alicia's back, and gripping her ass in his palm, he pressed his cheek against hers, whispering something in her ear. She grinned at him, and bit her lip before sealing her mouth over his. Her eyes closed, she kissed him, and he reciprocated.

My rage was reaching boiling point. I couldn't take my eyes off of them. It was like watching a car crash. It's horrific and ugly, yet you can't help but stare at the damage. There we were, two ex-lovers, kissing someone else and completely unable to tear our eyes away from each other. It was so twisted that it was almost sickening. Her hand slid into his shirt, and I saw a glimmer of something sparkling in her fingers. Thumbing the shiny black pendant in her hand, she grinned at him.

My pendant. *Our* pendant. He let her touch it.

My stomach lurched, and I instantly pulled away from Henry, breathless, tearful and completely devastated. I knew I had no right, it was his pendant and she had every right to touch it all she wanted, but that was more than just a piece of jewellery; it meant something to me. It was my heart, his heart, our time together. All the horrifically bad, and the heart stopping good too.

I stared at him in horror for a moment, before coming to my senses and storming past them, leaving poor Henry dazed and confused. I made a dash for the exit, desperate for some air after the oxygen in my lungs had just been ripped right out of me. Anger, grief, and pure unbridled fury surged through my body as I pushed my way through the crowded bar to the exit. Stumbling out into the cool evening air, I panted and gasped for breath. How could he let her man handle something so important to him? Well, what I thought was important to him.

My insides were churning, and the alcohol was going to my head. Leaning my back against the wall, I slammed my palms against it. He still had the innate ability to totally disarm me and tip my world on its head. I hated him for it. Closing my eyes, I took a deep breath.

"Are you ok?"

My eyes flew open to find Henry standing in front of me. With a furrowed brow, I shook my head. "I'm sorry, Henry. What I did in there, was wrong. I saw my, well, someone I used to be with, and I wanted to make him jealous. I used you, and I'm really sorry."

He shrugged. "We've all been there. He shook you pretty bad then, if you had to come out here."

"He's with a woman. I couldn't watch anymore."

Taking my hand, he smiled. "Well, if you stay out here, he wins. I say you get back in there, have a stiff drink, and shake your ass like it's on fire. No man in there could take their eyes off you when you danced, and I'm pretty sure your ex was probably one of them."

I gave him a grateful smile, and followed him back in. Layla Jennings, the strong independent woman, was not going to let him win this time.

Spotting me by the bar, Amy and Mel rushed over. "I cannot believe that dick chin is here! Did he speak to you? Did he upset you? I swear I will kill him."

Mel was beyond angry; she was practically foaming at the mouth.

"It's ok, I'm fine. He's just trying to screw with me. Did you see who he's with?"

Fisting her hands, Amy glared up at the balcony. "Don't even get me started on that bitch. If she comes within ten feet of you, I'm going to rip her fake, tacky extensions off of her skull."

I chuckled, and shrugged at them. "Who cares? They're welcome to each other. She's a bitch, and he's a dog. They go together well, if you ask me."

Amy growled. "Has he no respect or care for your feelings at all? He should have left the moment he knew you were here. Especially if he's dragging that 'ho' around with him."

"Well, he didn't care when he was feeling her up and making out on the dance floor. Whatever. It's none of my business, I turned my back on him, remember?"

I gave Henry an awkward smile. "Come on, forget about him. Tonight is about fun, and Jared Garrett is not going to spoil it for me." Grabbing Henry's hand, I pulled him to a table where his friends had a round of drinks and shots waiting.

Picking up a shot glass full of something that smelled very strong and bitterly pungent, I was just about to take a seat when my cell buzzed. Glowering at it I read the message.

> Are you determined to hit that fucking self-destruct button? I thought you had more respect for yourself than that. You look ridiculous, and you are not fooling anyone. Last chance, Layla. Put the drink down!
> **Received: 23.28**
> **From: Jared**

That's it. Enough is enough.

Standing up, I held the shot glass in my hand, faced the balcony, and meeting his icy glare, raised my glass to him and downed it before slamming it onto the table. His eyes fixed on me, I took another glass from the table and again raised it to him. He shook his head in warning but I was having none of it. Tossing it back, the bitter liquid burned my throat and I had to struggle to hold my composure, pressing the back of my hand to my mouth.

Pounding his fist on the rail, he turned away and I grinned to myself with satisfied triumph. He'd played, he'd lost, and I had proved my point.

Sitting myself at the table, I smiled at Amy and Mel who applauded loudly at my winning performance. My cell buzzed on the table, and with a smug smirk on my face, I scrolled down to read his message. This ought to be good.

> I warned you. You brought this on yourself.
> **Received: 23.35**
> **From: Jared**

I stared at it, then frantically scanned the area, but I couldn't spot him anywhere. What the hell was he planning to do? I got my answer. A loud, ear splitting ringing sounded throughout the entire building, and one by one the sprinklers began to shower everyone with cold water.

He didn't?

Grabbing my purse, I followed as Amy and Mel darted for the exit, covering their heads with their jackets. I had neglected to wear one, so I found myself getting predictably wetter and colder by the second. Entering the crowd of party goers outside, I tried to find my friends, but in the struggle to get out we'd gotten separated.

I was just about to call them from my cell when I found myself lifted from the ground and thrown carelessly over the shoulder of a tall man. Initially horrified, I kicked and screamed until I caught a glimpse of myself in a passing window.

"Jared! Put me down. Put me down right now, or I swear I'll scream so loud they'll hear me across the state!" He ignored me and continued to walk down the street. Kicking even harder and pounding my fists on his back, I roared at him. "You are such a cock! Did you seriously just pull a fire alarm? Put me down!"

We turned the corner and he set me onto my feet. Slamming my palm against his cheek, I slapped him, hard. "Who the fuck do you think you are?" I raised my hand to strike him again, but he caught my wrist tightly in his hand.

"Don't do that ever again. Understand?" His tone was clipped and serious.

"Don't do what Jared? Hit you?"

Still gripping my wrist, he pulled me towards him, so close that I could smell the liquor on his breath. "You know what you did. Can't imagine your boyfriend would be happy about what I just saw either."

"I don't have one! I can do whatever I want. You don't get to tell me what to do, or who to do it with anymore. You gave up that right!"

"I never gave it up and I never will! See this?" He pulled his pendant from his shirt and clasped it in his free hand. "This still means something to me, and I will never stop caring about you! You were fucking embarrassing yourself in there, and you were not kidding anyone but yourself. You're drunk out of your fucking skull, grinding up against some stranger, and then making out with him in some bar. It's pathetic. It's a desperate cry for help, just like your hair, over the top make up, and this fucking dress. I swear, when I saw it I could have spanked the shit out of you. You look ridiculous! This isn't you. What the hell happened to that fiery, sarcastic, take no prisoners woman I fell for in the coffee shop?"

Twisting my wrist from his vice like grip, I glared at him. "She got torn apart by the man she thought loved, trusted and respected her! That's what happened. And you want to talk about humiliation? You are the only thing I was embarrassed about in there! Feeling up the woman who scratched my face, split my lip, and got me arrested. That was by far the greatest moment of my year so far! Congratulations, Jared, you've hit rock bottom and are officially scraping the bottom of the barrel if you're screwing her. Which, by the way, brings me to my next point.

"If this," I swatted at his pendant which was hanging from his hand, "meant so much to you, then why the fuck would you let her put her disgusting, dirty whore hands all over it? You may let her touch you, stick her tongue in your ear, mouth and god knows where else, but don't try and tell me you care when you had the nerve to stand there while I watched her manhandle the one thing I thought was precious to you! She was right about you, and I should have listened. Chew them up and spit them out, right, Jared? Now I'm just another notch on your bed post. Now serving number sixty one."

I could hear Amy and Mel yelling my name, and I turned to walk away, but grabbing my waist he halted my feet. "Urgh! Let me go!"

"What's the matter, Layla? Jealous?"

Glaring at him, I smiled sarcastically. "You're right, Jared. When I saw her hands all over you, her tongue in your ear and rammed down your throat, I did feel something."

Raising an eyebrow he gave me a satisfied smirk.

"I felt nauseous."

My comment wiped the smirk from his lips, and his icy glare returned as his hold on my waist strengthened, making my attempts to escape him by fighting back completely futile. "I did not willingly let her do anything, Layla! I was so busy watching you sticking your tongue down some guys throat, I never even noticed her take out my pendant. The moment I did, I gave her marching orders. And I am going to make one thing very clear right now. You were not, are not, and never will be a notch on my bed post. I loved you, I still do, and I will not just stand there while you destroy yourself. You have no idea who that guy is. He could be a rapist or murderer, for Christ sakes. Stop acting like a child and grow up! You think I wanted to be with her? I didn't bring her here. She came by herself and happened to see me at the bar. I only decided to allow her my company after you decided to let him touch you, dance with you, and stick his tongue in your mouth!"

Standing in front of him I got in his face. "I will kiss, touch, and sleep with anyone I like. You don't own me, Jared, I will do whatever I want. Understand?"

Leaning close, I felt his warm breath on my lips. "No, you are mine. And I will protect what's mine with every breath in my body, and every beat of my heart. Go home, sleep it off and get your shit together, Layla, because you're falling apart and I can't stand watching you do it. It's like you want to get yourself hurt, punish yourself, and I won't let you do it."

Holding my hands over my face, I growled with frustration. "Jared, I'm not yours anymore. We're over, done! Our relationship has ceased to be. Just, for the love of god, let me go. Every time I think I'm moving on, getting over you, you claw your way back into my life and I can't deal with it. I'm still getting over the last time you tore my heart to shreds, and I can't grieve for two failed relationships anymore."

He gave me a puzzled look.

"Ollie left. He's in Utah."

I stared at my feet as Ollie rolled off my tongue and into my thoughts. Placing his hand under my chin, Jared lifted my head to look at him.

"I'm sorry."

I snorted a laugh, and yanked my face away from him. "No you're not."

His lip curled up slightly. "You're right, I'm not. I'm glad he's gone because I will never be done with you, Layla, and we will never be over. I love you. And you hate to admit it, you still love me too. That's why you and Oliver could never have made it work. Your heart still belongs to me, and you know it."

I swallowed hard. "No, Jared. Ollie and I couldn't make it work because my heart is still recovering from the trauma you caused. I'm still healing my battle scars. I'm going to ask you one last time, and then I'm going to scream. Let. Me. Go. And leave me alone. For good."

He took a step back, all the while gazing at me with his hypnotic piercing blue eyes. Without a word, he turned and walked away down the side walk. I could feel my heart thundering in my chest as I made my way back towards the bar.

"Layla! Oh my god, we were worried sick. Where were you?" Wrapping her arms around me, Mel held me tightly. Feeling a little fragile from my encounter with Jared, I squeezed her back just as hard.

"I'm fine. I just got separated, that's all. I don't feel much like partying anymore. Could we just go home? I'm really tired, and I'm all damp."

Brushing my wet frizzy hair from my face, Amy tilted her head at me. "Are you ok?"

I thought of telling them about Jared, about our fight and about what happened in the bar, but I didn't want to relive it all. "I'm fine. Just had too much to drink, I think."

Chuckling, Mel nodded. "Yeah, I'll say. You hit a home run tonight though girl and I'm proud of you. He tried to knock you off your game, and you bounced right back. Way to go."

I smiled at her, knowing deep down that my victory had been bittersweet at best. Hailing a cab, we climbed in and with her head on Mel's shoulder, Amy fell into an alcohol induced sleep.

I sat watching her for a while, thinking how tough she must have been finding it that night. She was in love, and all night Mel had been throwing herself at some guy. My heart ached for my poor friend and her wasted feelings for my best friend. It was going to be a long road to recovery, but we had each other and that was all that really mattered. I would do whatever I could to mend Amy's broken heart, and as for my own, I'd taken the first step that night and now all I had to do was keep walking.

Chapter 45

Moving On

Laying on my front, my bikini top cast aside, I basked in the warm sunshine. Sunglasses on, and sun lotion applied, the girls were having a day at the beach. The end of the college year was only two weeks away, so we were taking every opportunity to relax, unwind and hang out together. I hadn't had any contact with Jared at all since the bar, and I was relieved beyond belief when I heard from Kate that he was back in New York again for a while. Having him absent from Long Beach meant I wouldn't run the risk of bumping into him again anytime soon. I did wonder if maybe my warning to stay away had finally sunk in. Either way, I finally felt that without him constantly appearing in my life, I was moving on.

I was top of my class, and every day I spent with my girls having fun. Nick and Eric were still regulars at the bar, and sometimes Amy and Mel would go down there, but since Ollie had left, I couldn't face it. I'd tried, but looking at his empty seat at our booth and the empty stage, were painful reminders of the broken relationship that slipped through my fingers.

Removing her earphones, Amy smiled at me. That smile usually only meant one thing; Amy wanted something. Remaining in my relaxed position, I questioned her. "What do you want this time, Amy?"

"Well, I was just thinking."

Mel snorted beside her. "That's dangerous."

Amy screwed up her towel and hurled it at her.

"I was thinking that with the end of the year only two weeks away, we should totally throw a party!"

I groaned at the idea. "A party? Really? Haven't we partied enough these past few weeks? I don't think my liver could take any more."

"You can never party enough, Layla. Besides, I spoke to Eric and Nick and they are totally up for playing at Benny's. We can do vocals."

My heart plummeted as I thought about Ollie's absence in that line up. It had been almost five weeks since he'd left and he was still avoiding me. I'd sent countless emails, I'd sent letters, and I'd called so much that my cell phone bill was sky high. But he kept dodging me. I knew I hurt him, but I at least wanted us to stay friends, and I thought he'd wanted that too. Clearly, we weren't on the same page and had slightly different ideas of what being friends entailed; conversation or acknowledgment being the key aspects.

"I don't know, Amy, it just doesn't feel right."

She tilted her head and gave me a sympathetic look. I hated that look and the pity it always portrayed.

"You mean it won't be right because Ollie isn't going to be there. Layla, he so would not want you to keep pining over him. I don't know why you still are. It's not like you were in love with him."

I sighed. "I still cared! I can't just forget him, Amy. He's my friend, and I hate that we're not even speaking anymore. It's killing me. I'm not in the partying mood." Grabbing my bikini top, I slipped it on, grabbed my things, and stood up.

"Layla, don't be so over dramatic. I think it's a great idea, and it's about time you got it into your head that Ollie is gone. He's obviously decided you two can't be just friends and has moved on. Maybe you should do the same."

Mel had always been a very straight shooter, but I really needed her on my side this time. "Mel, I can't just move on. I hate myself for what I did to him. I led him on, went out with him, cheated on him, and then broke his heart. How do you get over that? I can't, and I won't. I deserve to be unhappy for the rest of my life for what I did, and I am not going to a party that celebrates the most horrible year of my entire life. Ok?"

She shook her head at me and it was the last straw.

"You wouldn't understand. I'm going home."

Amy tried to get me to stop, but I just kept walking. I wanted to be alone, and lately I had very little tolerance for Mel and her suck it up and move on attitude. I did feel something for Ollie, and though it may not have been the deep and consuming love I had for Jared, it was still real and I couldn't just forget it. I slipped my cell from my pocket and scrolled down looking for his number. Hitting call, I held on and on praying he might pick up. But again, I was left hanging.

Turning the corner to the campus parking lot, I stopped as I spotted a very familiar face striding towards me. Continuing on my way, I breezed past him, but his hand caught my arm.

"Now, now Layla. Is that really necessary?"

Gripping his hand, I shoved it away from me. "With you Felix, I'd say it was polite. I'd rather swallow razor blades than talk to you."

"Ooh, ouch."

"What do you want, Felix? Amy isn't here, and after that very eye opening dinner, I don't think you're high up on her list of would be suitors anymore."

He grinned, and it made my skin crawl. "Actually, I'm here to see you. I wondered if you could give a little message to your ex for me."

I glared at him. "I have no intention of speaking to him ever again, so whatever it is you want him to know, you'll have to tell him your damn self. I'm out of it."

He squared up to me, and a shiver ran down my spine. He made me feel uncomfortable and sick in a way I couldn't explain. His general presence made me feel in danger, and yet I wasn't afraid of him.

"Well, I'll have to think of something that will give him a message that will sink in."

Raising his hand, he traced the back of his fingertips over my face. "Nobody fucks with my business or my women. Take care, Layla. It was good to see you."

I watched him walk away, and once he was safely around the corner, I let out the breath I was holding and bolted for the dorm.

My heart raced and my pulse was rapid as I slammed my door closed. Grabbing my cell from my pocket, I scrolled for Jared's number and hit dial. "Come on, come on, pick up."

It went to voicemail. Dropping it on the bed, I pulled out my laptop and frantically searched for any recent news regarding the creep I'd just had an encounter with in the parking lot. Scanning through the results, I found something that made my blood run cold as I read it.

"James Felix is said to be furious that his long term friend and business associate Jared Garrett is not only withdrawing funding in his restaurant chain but is now dating Felix's ex-wife Alicia Paige. The two were snapped at the popular new bar Delicia a few weeks ago and have been seen in each other's company at many social occasions since. A source close to the couple has confirmed the rumors and said that they have spent very little time apart. Miss Paige refused to comment when she was spotted leaving the Garrett property only yesterday and as ever, Mr. Garrett is keeping a quiet and dignified silence over the matter." I stared at the screen in horror. No wonder Felix hated Jared. It all made sense. Jared had been sleeping with her a long time before I came along, and his comments at the police station to her made sense now too, but it couldn't be true. It just couldn't. His words from that night at Delicia swirled in my head. I'd pushed him away and straight into her waiting arms. Tears began to pool in my eyes as the realization that we truly were finished; that he'd moved on and that he didn't care anymore. It hit me like a ton of bricks, and swiping at my eyes, I slammed the laptop shut. I wouldn't do this to myself anymore. Enough was enough. I'd shed enough tears to last me a lifetime, and my heart was entitled to a break.

My cell rang and seeing the name on the screen I answered immediately. "Layla, you called? Something I can do for you?" Jared's voice purred at me down the phone, but I was wild with anger, jealousy and hurt.

"Actually, Jared, yes. There is something you can do for me. You can drop dead, asswipe. I hope you and your new pastime Alicia are very happy together." I hung up before he could protest. I wasn't interested in his reasons. He'd broken my heart for the last time, and the way I was feeling bordered on hatred.

Kneeling on the floor, I pulled out the box of mementos from our time together and piled them into a bag. The jewellery was the first to go. Driving to the mall, I smiled to myself. I wasn't willing to take money for the gifts and I certainly didn't want them anymore. I walked into the store and placed the boxes on the counter.

"Good afternoon, madam. What can I do for you?"

The assistant was young, sweet faced, and far too cheery for the mood I was in. "I'd like to return these items, please. I no longer need, want, or care about them."

She stared at me as I opened each box. "But, this is a black star sapphire."

I rolled my eyes. "I know what it is, and I don't want it. Scratch off the inscription, melt it down, and give it all to charity. I don't care, just please get rid of it."

She gave me a sympathetic and knowing look. "He must have really hurt you if you can't even keep items as stunning as these."

I nodded. "They don't mean anything to me. They were an ideal. A perfect picture that never existed."

Taking the boxes, she placed them under the desk. They were gone. All that was left was to dispose of the rest of the box's contents.

I drove around for an hour, not knowing where to go or what to do with the remaining items; designer dresses, the laptop, and the mug he had left silently in my room that night of our fight. My heart gave a thud as I thought about it, but I ignored it, reminding myself that it meant nothing. He simply didn't like to lose and it was a game tactic.

I pulled up to the enormous black iron gates and typed in the security code before driving down the long driveway to the house. I hadn't been back to his house since we had spent the night together and the memory was nauseating. I parked and quickly hauled the box from the back seat. I had every intention of just dumping it on his doorstep and leaving, but as I placed it on the porch I was spotted by a heavily pregnant Lucy through the glass doors. Turning on my heel, I headed for the car, but she yelled after me, waddling down the path to catch up. I felt bad for her, and decided I could at least hear what she had to say.

"What do you want, Lucy?" She huffed and puffed for breath in front of me and it made me feel slightly bad for her. "Jared said you called him. You don't know the whole story. He's not doing this to hurt you, Layla. Felix is really bad news. He's just trying to even out the playing field. I know how bad it must look, but you have to believe me that he isn't dating Alicia."

I snorted. "Oh really? So it wasn't her I saw him dry humping at Delicia? And all those pictures of them together at these so called social events are total fiction right?"

She stared at me speechless.

"That's what I thought. You know what, Lucy? Jared Garrett isn't my problem anymore. He can screw whoever he wants because it sure as hell won't ever be me again. I am so done with your brother. Can you make sure he gets his box of lies, cheap sentiment, and painful reminders of his betrayals back please? Thanks."

Opening my car door, I glanced back her as she made her way back to the house. I'd done it. It was finally over. I was supposed to feel liberated, free and weightless, but that feeling never came. All I had was an empty hole where I'd held him so tightly for an entire year, and I feared I would never fill it again.

The moment I got back, Amy sprung on me. "I'm really sorry, Layla. I wasn't thinking. If you don't want to go party, we'll stay here. Just us girls and have fun. It's no big deal."

I smiled at her and shook my head. "No. You were right. We should celebrate. I spent a whole year nursing a broken heart, and I'm done with it. I want to go out, get hammered, and dance my ass off. Let's do it next week. What do you say?"

Draping her arm around me, she pecked me on the cheek. "I say, hell yes!"

Giving her a hug, I sighed. "Hey, Amy, how's things going with you? I mean, since you told me about Mel I know you haven't really talked much about it."

Pulling away from me, she sat on the edge of her bed and shrugged. "Nothing to say. She likes guys, and I'm hopelessly in love with her. What can I do? I can't tell her. It's too risky. I have to just get over it."

I gave her a half smile. I knew only too well how much it hurts to love someone who simply can't give you what you need. "And how's that working out for you so far?"

"Awful. I can't get her off my mind, and whenever I'm around her I hate the way I feel. I feel like I'm not being me, not really. She knows I'm hiding something. She keeps asking me why I'm so quiet lately, and when I refused to go out with one of the guys at Delicia she said I was acting weird. I had to tell her he just wasn't my type, and I guess that's kind of true. He's not. I want her and I hate it. I'm so confused. I like guys, and I like sleeping with them, but I love her. How could I not know I was bisexual all this time?"

Taking a seat next to her, I draped my arm around her shoulder and pulled her to me. Her head rested against my shoulder as I stroked her hair. She was going through such a tough time. Not only was she questioning her sexuality, but she was also in love with my best friend who was certainly into men.

"Sometimes it takes finding that one special person, I guess. You can't help who you fall in love with, and for you it's Mel. There is nothing wrong or unnatural about how you feel, Amy. Lots of people these days discover they're bisexual or gay in college. Don't hate yourself, ok? You're in love, and it's an amazing feeling. Always be glad you have felt it, even if it is unreturned."

Hearing my own words, I couldn't help but think of my time with Jared and Ollie. I loved Jared, and although he'd hurt me time and time again, at least I knew I was capable of love and that I had experienced being loved in return. Well, I thought he loved me.

Ollie had given me so much, and I had given him very little in return, yet he thanked me for letting him know he could feel love and what it felt like to love someone. I missed him.

Giving Amy a peck on the cheek, I told her I needed to run to the store, but truthfully I just needed some time to myself. I headed for the car and shut myself inside, reaching for my cell phone. I scrolled to Ollie's number, and as it rang I held my breath, hoping and praying he would answer. But he didn't. Listening to his voice on his voice mail made my insides twist and a chill run through my veins. Surely he couldn't punish me like this forever? I needed him to come back to me.

Soon.

* * * *

Amy's meticulous planning had paid off enormously, and as Benny's began to fill to the point of bursting, I was pleased that her efforts were being appreciated. The senior class was so hyped up about graduating that they had been buying everyone drinks all night, and as hostess, Amy was never without one in her hand. Handing me a pink cosmopolitan, she grinned.

"What are you so happy about?"

She shook her head, and it made me suspicious. "Nothing. Just having a great time. I have a delicious drink, great friends, and a party that people will be talking about all year. What's not to like?"

I gave her a half smile, and she instantly knew where my mind was at. "You're thinking about Ollie, aren't you? You know, for someone who claims not to have been in love with him, you sure are pining like a love sick puppy."

Staring at my drink, I sighed heavily. "I miss him, Amy. He won't even acknowledge my existence. I thought we could still be friends, but he's totally cut me off and out of his life. I just want to see him, touch him, and be around him again."

Placing her hand on my arm reassuringly, she smiled. "He'll come around, you'll see."

I wanted to believe her blind optimism, but I couldn't. It had been seven weeks and if he hadn't talked to me by now, I imagined he never would.

Sliding into our booth, we joined Mel, Nick and Eric who were busy arguing over the set list for the party.

"I am telling you that no one wants to listen to your grunge shit, Eric. I thought we already agreed on modern and classic rock? You know, Bon Jovi, Greenday, that kind of stuff."

He rolled his eyes at her. "I told you, Ollie always sang that shit. I can't hit the notes he can, and the songs wouldn't sound right if you guys sang them. We'll have to come up with something else."

I groaned loudly in frustration. "Ok, shut up, both of you. Eric, you can sing a lot of classic rock absolutely fine, so stop bullshitting us. Mel, pick some chick rock and we'll do that. We'll mix it up, and then toward the end we'll slow it down, ok?"

Giving each other the evil eye, they nodded in agreement. It was like refereeing children some times. Nick whispered something into Amy's ear, and she visibly stiffened. Giving her a nudge, I mouthed "What was that about?"

She shook her head and nodded in the direction of the bathroom. Sliding out of the booth, we made our excuses and I had to practically run to keep up with her as she stormed to the toilets. Slamming the door closed, she ran her fingers through her hair repeatedly. "I can't do it anymore. I can't, I honestly just cannot do this."

Grabbing her hands, I forced her to face me. "Can't what? Amy, calm down and talk to me. What's wrong?"

Tears were in her eyes, and I knew. "Mel and Eric are banging each other, aren't they?"

She nodded as the warm droplets fell from her eyes and over her flushed cheeks. "Nick says they went out a couple of times, and last night they spent the night together at Eric's place."

Wrapping my arms around her, I held her tightly as she sobbed. "It hurts so fucking much, and it shouldn't. She's not mine, never has been and never will be, but watching them together, knowing what I do now, makes my stomach churn and my heart ache. I don't think I can be around her anymore. Not until I can get over this thing I have for her."

Taking some tissue from the stall, I wiped her face, trying to clear up her smeared make up. "Amy, I can't possibly try to begin to understand what you're going through with your sexuality, but I do know how much it hurts when the person you love is with someone else. I found out last week that Jared and Alicia are a couple now."

She gawked at me.

"I saw Felix on campus. He asked me to give a message to Jared, and I told him that we weren't together anymore so he could deliver the message himself. He gives me the creeps. Anyway, I was curious as to why they hated each other so much. Alicia is Felix's ex-wife. According to the article I read, she and Felix divorced after Jared had been sleeping with her. The time frames are so close they had to have been having an affair. Now the two of them have been photographed at bars, social events and one reporter even saw her at his house."

She stared at me with her jaw almost to the floor. "Alicia is Felix's ex-wife? Oh my god. No wonder he hates him. I mean, ok, he's a little hypocritical because he screwed his best friend's girlfriend, but still, she was his wife. Are they really a couple now? I know they were at Delicia, but I thought that was just a date. That sucks ass. Are you ok?"

I shrugged and continued to clean her face. "I'm done with it all, Amy. I can't keep killing myself over him. He's single and free to be with whoever he wants, and now that I have rid myself of all that stuff he gave me, maybe now I can move on too. Why should he be able to get over me so easily, but I carry on aching over the loss? I won't do it to myself anymore. Jared who? That's what I say."

She smiled at me, but I knew she wasn't buying it. Truthfully, neither was I. It hurt, deeply, and as much as I hated him, I loved him in equal measure. Tossing the tissue in the trash I smiled at her, trying to seem unfazed by our conversation. "There, all better. You ready to go out there?"

She nodded and hugged me. "I know everything seems bad right now, Layla, but I promise it will be ok. We'll both be ok. Ollie will come round, and I'll get over Mel. Eventually. We just need a little patience."

The sound of a guitar caught our attention, and I smiled. "Sounds like Eric's firing up the band. We should probably get out there before Mel throws her weight around at him."

Taking my hand, Amy led me out into the heaving bar. The crowd was completely blocking the stage and I couldn't see Mel up there at all. Maybe she was having as much trouble as I was getting to the stage. I turned around, but Amy had disappeared. Feeling rather abandoned, I tried to push my way through the hoard of bodies, but the sound of a husky, deep and low voice booming through the speakers halted me in my tracks. My heart raced, and my breathing quickened as a familiar song began to play. I shoved hard at the people around me, desperate to reach the stage. I had to see. I had to know it was real. The words hit me like darts as each left his lips. Reaching the stage, I stared up at him.

Standing there, caressing his guitar and singing into the mic, was Ollie. Wearing his ripped black jeans and an unbuttoned white shirt, he looked blisteringly hot. Every girl gazed at him dreamily as his perfectly sculpted chest gleamed in the spotlight. He was singing my song; the song he'd written for me at Christmas. He'd changed the music from slow and light to heavy and rocking, but the words still held the same emotional message they had that morning.

Gripping the edge of the stage, I hoped he'd look down and see me, but as he continued to stare into the crowd I suddenly felt nervous, anxious, guilty and sick. Pushing my way back through the crowd towards the door, I had to gulp hard to stop myself from bursting into tears.

He was here. In the bar. Singing my song.

I felt like he was a million miles from me. He was out of reach to me now, and I'd pushed him away. Pressing my hand against the wall outside, I tried to catch my breath. The music ended and the cheers, whistling and screams from the crowd inside made me smile. I loved it when people enjoyed Ollie's music. He deserved the success, he received, and I deserved his ignorance of me being there. Holding my hand to my chest, I could feel my heart beating fast, hard and heavily inside my ribcage.

"Little dangerous for you to be all alone out here, don't you think?"

My breath caught in my throat. Turning around slowly, I closed my eyes, praying that when I opened them again it wouldn't be a horrible hallucination.

But there he was. Tears threatened as I gazed at his gorgeous face. His warm brown eyes gazed back at me, and his lip ring pinched as he smiled. "Aren't you happy to see me?"

I couldn't speak. I couldn't find the words. Leaping at him, I enveloped him in my arms and held him tightly as tears began to drip from my eyes onto his shirt. His hands pressed against my back as he held on to me.

"I missed you so much. I woke up, and you were gone. I found your letter, but you wouldn't answer my calls. I thought I'd never see or talk to you again."

His lips pressed against my hair. "I'm sorry. I just couldn't face a last goodbye with you, Layla. I wanted to answer your calls. Every text, every email and every letter was like an arrow through my heart, knowing how much you needed me to tell you it was all ok, but I couldn't give you that. I thought if I stayed away, distanced myself from you, that we could move forward and get past everything between us, but it didn't work. Through my entire journey here I was thinking about this moment. Holding you, being around you, and seeing you again. I missed you like crazy."

Burying my head in his neck, I sniffled. "You cut me off, Ollie. I thought you hated me, that our whole friendship was over."

He shook his head, and lifted my face to look at him. "No, I could never hate you, Layla. I can't hate you because I'm still completely and totally in love with you."

Releasing him, I continued to gaze into his eyes. Threading our fingers together he took me by the hand and smiled. "I think we should talk. Since I took off after that night we had, I think there's a lot that needs to be said. Will you come with me?"

I was so happy to see him that I would have gone with him into a circle of hell and not thought twice. "I should tell Amy where I'm going."

"She knows. I told her I was stealing you away. So, will you come?"

I nodded, and followed him across the parking lot where his beautiful Ducati was sitting, gleaming in the moonlight. I was suddenly aware why Amy had told me to wear jeans for the party. She must have known all along that he was coming and the two of them had planned the whole thing.

Slipping the helmet over my head, he lowered the visor and placed a kiss against it. My heart stopped at the sweetness of his gesture, and yet I was severely disappointed that he had preferred to kiss the plastic rather than me. Once he was all leathered up with his helmet securely in place, he started the awesome machine that was straddled between his legs. It always did something to me when we rode on Ollie's motorcycle. It was a huge turn on, and as I sidled up to him, wrapping my arms around his waist, I grinned into his back.

The song 'Cool Rider' played in my mind as we sped through the streets. Ollie was the hottest thing on two wheels right now, and there was nowhere else I'd rather have been. Since I'd met him, I had a new soundtrack to my life and it was full of heavy guitar and electrifying bass tones. I knew exactly where he was taking me, and the delicious memories made me smile even more. Euphoria was coursing through my veins.

Letting go of his waist, I leaned back a little, my head fell back, and I held my arms out as though they were wings. I felt like I was flying and it was exhilarating. I could feel the air against my hands, flowing through my fingers, and the heat from Ollie's body between my legs. It was hugely arousing and completely intoxicating as adrenaline surged through my body. Letting go of one of the handles, he caught my thigh and gave it a squeeze, bringing me back to earth and down from my awesome high. I got his message loud and clear. Slumping forward into his back, I snaked my hands around his waist again, tightly. Turning his head to the side, I saw his eyes and I was sure he was smiling as he shook his head at me.

Slowing, we pulled up to the sidewalk and Ollie killed the roar of the engine. He held out his hand for me which I accepted without hesitation, thrilled at the physical contact with him as I hauled myself off the bike. Taking off my helmet, I stared at him as he slid his own over his head and his long black locks fell around his gorgeous face. There was no denying that the sexual chemistry between us was not dead, and my desire for him was alive and kicking. My heart gave a thud and placing my hand over it, I took a long, deep breath. It was warning me, and this time I was going to heed its plea. This was a delicate situation, and our entire friendship hung in the balance. I needed to be very, very careful.

Chapter 46

Heart To Heart

Sitting on the grass next to him, I couldn't help but feel a rush of emotion for Ollie. Sliding my hand over his, I smiled. "I missed you, Ollie. Why couldn't you have just talked to me about things? I thought I was never going to see you again. Devastated is not a strong enough word for what I felt that morning and every time you rejected my calls."

He frowned and looked at the ground. "I couldn't say goodbye, Layla. I laid there for two hours, just watching you sleep. For a moment I thought maybe we could have made it, maybe you would choose me, but as you lay there, blissfully unaware of my thoughts, you said his name. And I knew. You weren't ready, and what I was asking of you wasn't fair. I couldn't do it to you, and I couldn't do it to myself either, so I left before you woke up. I know it was selfish, and I hate myself for what it did to you, but it was self-preservation. The pure and selfish protection of my own broken heart. But I am sorry."

He looked up and met my gaze, and I could see he was genuinely pained by what had happened between us. "I understand, Ollie, but please don't cut me from your life. I need you in my world. I must have called every day and sent dozens of emails. We'd slept together, and I woke alone and abandoned. It isn't really up there on my list of wonderful moments this year."

He nodded weakly. "I know it was mean, cruel, and totally unfair of me, but you have to understand, I didn't have a choice, Layla. I had to get some distance between us. You needed to heal, and I needed to try and get over how I felt about you. But I couldn't. I thought about you every damn minute of every day. Do not, for one second, think I didn't care. Because I did. I do."

Unable to form a coherent sentence, I sat in silence staring at the night sky. Ollie didn't say a word either, and I felt that everything was not yet said. I had missed him so much, pined and longed for him to come back, and here he was. My world was back on its axis and spinning at the speed of light.

He let out a long sigh and rubbed his hand over his eyes. "Layla, I still love you. I can't shut it off. Being around you is like all my dreams come true, but I know that this, right now, is just a single moment and once we get back on that bike it's over. You go back to your life, and I go back to Utah, without you. Back to broken hearts, painful memories, and wishes that won't come true."

I couldn't bear the thought of being without him again. "Then don't go. Stay. Come back to Long Beach. We miss you, Ollie. I miss you."

He shook his head. "There's nothing left for me here now. My family is in Utah. My mom and I have finally got some kind of functional relationship, and I can't turn my back on my brother. He's just a kid."

I knew a thousand reasons why he should leave, but one reason for sure why I needed him to stay. "I need you in my life, Ollie. Always. I think I love you."

His head snapped up and he stared at me. My words hung in the air, and I couldn't quite believe I had said them myself. Blinking rapidly, I felt the thunder of my heart beneath my chest as it smugly hugged itself with megaphone in hand shouting a massive I told you so at me.

Well, thanks for the warning!

But I did love him, and it had taken me believing I had lost him to make me realize it. I was in love with Ollie, and here he was loving me back. Pressing his hands behind my neck, he pulled me to him as he closed the space between us and kissed me deeply. I couldn't think, couldn't breath as his mouth sealed over mine. His lip ring pressed against my bottom lip, and I could feel my heart pounding like a jackhammer. His hands slid around my waist as we lowered ourselves to the ground, laying there all tongues, lips and roaming hands. My fingertips brushed against his waist band before skimming upwards beneath his barely buttoned shirt. His perfectly sculpted abs flexed and tightened beneath my palm, and a thrill of excitement shot through me. His own hand slid around my back, and my vest lifted slightly, exposing my bare skin as his palm pressed against it. The sensation of his warm hands on my body ignited the electricity that was running through my veins.

Rolling onto his back, he pulled away from me panting and breathless. I felt exactly the same as I lay there gasping for air beside him. Leaning on his elbow, he smiled down at me and my pulse quickened at the sight of his trade mark, smoldering, sexy, make your toes curl in ecstasy, Ollie smile.

"Wow. I'd almost forgotten how amazing that feels. I mean, I know it's incredible, but being able to touch you, hold you and kiss you like that, Layla...oh baby, it's a force of nature, and I'm powerless to control it. You have no idea how much I want to take that further."

I grinned, and trailed my fingers over his chest. "Why don't you?"

Seizing my wrist, he kissed my palm and grazed his lips across my fingertips. "Because we need to take a breath. You just told me you love me, Layla. I've waited almost a year to hear you say that and you have no idea how happy it makes me feel."

There was a 'but' there, and I knew it. Holding my breath, I stared at him, waiting for the dagger to plunge into my chest.

"But you still love him."

I opened my mouth to try and reassure him, but he pressed his lips against mine to silence me.

Smiling, he gazed into my eyes. "It's ok. I get it. You can't just turn off your emotions, Layla, I know, I tried. But I can't fight for you and compete with someone who isn't even there. I know when you're thinking about him. You get distant and closed off because you feel guilty for loving him. I get it. I don't expect you to leap into my arms and come away with me, even if I desperately wish you would."

My insides twisted at his words. I wished it wasn't true, and that I could tell him there was only him, that he was the only one to ever hold my heart, but I couldn't. It would have been a cruel lie.

"Ollie, I don't know what to tell you. I don't have an answer right now. I didn't even know how I truly felt about us till about five minutes ago. I don't know what to do, how to deal with this."

Brushing my cheek with his thumb, he hushed me. "Nothing. You do nothing. You go back to Pasadena for the summer, and I head back to Utah. You need time to figure out what you want, Layla, and you can't do that with me around too. Take time out. Think, and when you're ready, my offer still stands. Come to Utah, live with me and you'll make me the happiest man in the world. But I want you to be happy too. I want you to be sure that this, us, is what you really want because I cannot face the heartache of losing you all over again."

I closed my eyes tightly as a tension headache began to strike. Once again, I was faced with the same dilemma. Stay, or move to a new state and be with Ollie. I suddenly felt shaky as the headache paired with the churning in my stomach overwhelmed me. I must have swooned because Ollie immediately gripped hold of me and held me to him.

"Hey, you ok?"

Shaking my head, I regained my equilibrium and clambered to my feet.

Brushing myself off, I stared out at the night sky overlooking the brightly lit streets of Long Beach. This was my home, and I had so much here that was worth staying for. Taking my hand, Ollie pressed it to his lips. "Come on, enough love dilemmas for one night, I think. You have a party to get back to, and I have a set to play. It was part of my deal, after all."

I gave him a puzzled look.

"I told Amy I was coming, that I needed to see you, and naturally I got a strict warning not to upset you. She promised me some alone time with you as long as I promised to play at her party. I had to tell Nick and Eric, and I think they must have told Mel because she didn't seem surprised to see me at all. She and Eric seemed very cozy though."

I let out a long sigh as we walked back to the bike. "Yeah, they're sleeping together. It's awful." His eyebrows furrowed, and I knew I was going to have to come clean. Ollie could be trusted after all. "The thing is, there's someone else that's completely besotted with my best friend. In fact, totally head over feet in love with her."

He chuckled. "Who?"

Swallowing the lump in my throat, I stopped walking and faced him. "Amy."

He almost choked on a breath as he stood there, coughing and spluttering. "What? You're kidding, right? I mean, seriously. Layla, who is it?"

I shook my head at him. "I'm as serious as a heart attack. She told me a few weeks back. She's bisexual, and her heart wants Mel. It's been awful for her. She's so tormented, and she has to deal with it every single day."

His mouth pressed into a hard line, and he gave me a rueful smile. "I know how she feels. Loving someone that doesn't love you back sucks ass. Maybe I should talk to her."

"No, you can't let her know that I told you. She'd never forgive me for it. Please don't say anything, Ollie."

Pressing his lips to mine, he smiled. "Ok, I promise. You're a great friend, you know that? Me, Amy and Mel...we're lucky to have you looking out for us." Pulling me into a warm hug, he pressed his lips to my forehead.

"I don't know what to do next, Ollie. How do we go back to that party after everything that just happened?"

"It'll be alright. We'll drink, laugh, play on stage and have a great time. And if it's the last time we're together, then at least we'll go out with a bang."

A sharp pain stabbed through my heart as his words left his lips. The last time we're together. It was a truly depressing thought, and one I didn't wish to dwell over. Taking his hand in mine, we walked back to the Ducati, hopped on and headed back to the party. My arms wrapped snuggly around him, I didn't want the ride back to end. I wanted to be trapped in that moment forever without the burden of the decision I was going to have to make. It weighed on me like a ton of bricks, and I was exhausted from hauling it around on my shoulders.

Pulling up in front of the bar, Ollie held out his hand once more and helped me off the bike. Taking off my helmet, I stared at him as he removed his. Reaching for my hand he smiled.

"Hey, stop it, ok. This sad face you keep making is killing me. We still have nine hours until I have to head back. Let's have some fun, alright?" I nodded weakly, but the way I was feeling, fun was definitely not on my list of priorities. Leading me through the doors, he entwined our fingers together tightly.

Eric spotted us from on stage and waved us over. Glancing back at me, Ollie dragged me towards the stage and stopped as we got to the bottom of the steps. "Do a song with me?"

The last time we had performed together was at the park during winter break. It was the moment I knew I had to have him, and that giving us a chance was everything I wanted. Maybe I even loved him back then. Giving him a quick peck on the cheek, I agreed and scanned the bar for my girls to come join us.

I spotted them at the bar, and from the look on Amy's face they were exchanging harsh words. Letting go of Ollie's hand, I nodded in their direction. "I better go see what's going on. Give me five minutes?"

Keeping his eyes fixed on our friends, he nodded and I made my way through the crowd to the bar. I could hear Amy's voice before I even got within three feet of them and that was over the bustling crowd. "You have no idea do you. You just run around, sleeping with anything in a pair of pants with a pulse. I can't believe you after everything he did to me. You are such a slut!"

Mel's face turned thunderous as she prodded Amy in the chest. "I'm a slut? You want a list of the guys you've banged since you got here? Here's just a few. Nick, Felix, Mike, Adrian, Greg behind the bar. Should I go on?"

Pushing myself between them, I held up my hands to each of them. "Whoa! Time out! What the hell is going on?"

The two of them began screeching abuse and accusations at each other and right into my ears. "Stop! Both of you, just shut up. Amy why the hell are you calling her a slut? She's your friend."

"She's sleeping with Eric and Nick!"

My mouth hit the ground, and I immediately stared at Mel. "Oh come on, Layla, don't look so surprised. Besides, you can't exactly take the moral high ground here. You screwed Jared when you were supposed to be with Ollie, remember?"

I glared at her. "I can't believe you're bringing that up. I'm not judging you, Mel. I just think it's a little insensitive to sleep with your friend's ex-lover, that's all. Don't compare me, and what I did, to what you're doing to both of them. I assume Nick knows, but does Eric know you're screwing his band mate?"

She diverted her eyes rapidly around the bar, giving me my answer.

"Didn't think so. God what is wrong with us? We're supposed to look out for each other, not rip each other to shreds. We have one more week before the year is over, and I am not spending it fighting and refereeing between you two. Got it?"

They nodded, but continued to exchange filthy looks.

"Hey! I mean it. We have enough trouble handling the men in our lives, we don't need to be at each other's throats too. Amy, Mel is free to sleep with and date whoever she wants, and I know what she did is hurting you, but you have to let it go."

I stared at her as an understanding passed between us. She didn't care who it was Mel was sleeping with, she was upset that she was sleeping with anyone at all. Hanging her head, she shrugged and I knew she got the message. Turning my attention to Mel, I gave her a stern look.

"First of all, I didn't intentionally set out to sleep with Jared. And for your information, when I did sleep with him, Ollie and I hadn't had sex yet. You're supposed to be my best friend. Don't throw that shit in my face ever again. Now, both of you hug and get on that stage. I need to party my ass off after the conversation I just had with Ollie."

The two of them gawked at me, waiting for me to elaborate, immediately forgetting their heated exchange.

"What happened? What did he say?" I was bombarded with questions from each of them, and raising my hand, I requested silence.

"He took me to the hills, we talked, and I told him I loved him."

Amy squeaked as Mel grinned at me, before wrapping her arms around my neck. "I knew it! I knew with a little time you would get over that assfuck and fall for our resident heart throb rock star!"

I shook my head at her, and pushed her away gently. "It's not that simple, Mel. I do love Ollie, a lot, but I still love Jared too. And Ollie knows that. He's asked me to reconsider going to Utah with him, but he wants me to think about it first and be positive it's what I want."

Sliding me a glass of something that smelled like rum and coke, Amy smiled at me. "And what do you want?"

Picking up the glass, I shrugged, then swallowed it in one go.

"I don't know. I wish I did. Knowing how I feel about him doesn't change the fact that I'm in love with another man. Besides, my life is here now with you guys. I don't think I can just give it all up for a life in Utah with Ollie and his family. I have no idea what I'm doing, but I am damn sure that I need time to get my shit together and figure it out."

Placing a reassuring hand on my shoulder, Mel smiled. "Well, we're here for you, and we'll support you in whatever you choose. Ok?"

Sliding an arm around each of them, I pulled them to me. "I love you guys. I don't know what I'd do without you."

The screech of the microphone caught our attention as Ollie stood scanning the crowd. "Uh, could the girls in Room 21 please get their asses on stage? Oh, you too, butt munch."

Mel raised her hand and flipped him the bird, making him grin widely at her as he slipped his sexy, sleek white guitar over his head. Ollie the rock star. My Ollie the rock star was smoking hot as he hooked up the amp to his instrument. Licking his bottom lip, he winked at me as I climbed the steps to the stage. My heart skipped a beat, and my blood heated as he leaned to my ear. His warm breath on my neck reminded me of our night together, and thoughts of his lips caressing my body flowed through my mind. I felt my insides clench at the sensual, sexy memory.

"So, I figured we'd start with 'Need You Now' and just wing it? Maybe revisit that song we did at the park too? You game?"

Pressing my lips to his ear, I nipped on his earlobe playfully. "For anything you want to throw at me, stud."

Cupping my face in his hands, he kissed me deeply, thrusting his tongue into my obliging mouth. Wrapping his arms around me, he dipped me low and placed another chaste kiss on my lips. "I'll see what I can do." A shiver ran up my spine as he released me, gesturing to the mic that we would be sharing.

God he was so smoldering hot!

* * * *

Three hours later, I was exhausted. Ollie and the guys had played nonstop and had performed tracks by all my favorite classic, modern, indie, and alternative bands. They were on fire, and our duets had blown me away.

Singing every note with such passion, Ollie never took his eyes off me. Sliding his hand up and down the mic stand, caressing his guitar, I could have jumped his bones right there on stage. His crisp white unbuttoned shirt was revealing his delicious body beneath and was a distracting view. I believe the sound that escaped my lips when he thrust his hips at the mic stand was 'Uragha'.

After one of our songs, he'd been so worked up that he'd poured half a bottle of water over himself and the droplets were now glistening on his pale skin. Sitting at our booth with a drink in hand, I licked my lips as I wished I could do the same to every inch of his wet body. Finishing their set, the three guys headed to our table. I stared at Ollie hungrily as he laughed with them. Sliding in next to me, he draped an arm around my shoulders and pressed a kiss against my cheek. Amy and Mel had forgotten their row, and were now talking to Nick and Eric about what they were doing for the summer. Glancing at Ollie, I held his hand under the table. He smiled at me and ran his nose the length of mine.

It was the push I needed. Getting to my feet, I pulled on his hand and nodded in the direction of the bathroom. He gave me an amused look, but knocking back his shot of bourbon, he slid out of the booth to join me. Amy and Mel gave us a raised eyebrow, but I didn't care. Winking at them, I yanked Ollie beside me to the bathroom, desperate to get him alone in a locked room. Backing my way through the door, I gripped his shirt in my hands and pulled him flush against me. My lips sealed over his as his hands slipped around my midriff rolling my vest up in the process. His lip ring grazed my collar bone as his kisses trailed down my neck.

Breathing heavily, he murmured against my skin. "You sure you want this?"

Closing my eyes, I nodded. "More than oxygen."

He smiled, locked the door, and drove me backwards to the wall. "Well, then hold your breath, baby."

Gripping his hand behind my thigh, he lifted it against his hip as he pressed my body against the wall. Fumbling for his belt, I frantically ripped it loose from his jeans and slid his zipper down. Biting my bottom lip gently, he ran his tongue over it making me moan into his mouth. With his belt gripped firmly in one hand, my fingertips traced the outline of his abs as they hardened beneath my touch. Skimming them downwards, I slid my palms around and into the back, forcing the waist down with my thumbs. Releasing my thigh, he pushed away from me and silently unbuttoned my pants, revealing a glimpse of the white cotton panties beneath. Biting his lip ring, he groaned before holding them tightly and slipping them down over my ass.

Pulling down his own shorts, he resumed his position against me and gripped both of my thighs, hoisting me from the ground. I wrapped my legs tightly around his waist as his hand reached between my legs, stroking and rubbing my clit. I was slippery with arousal, and his hand gripping my behind, urging me closer to him. Sliding inside me in one quick movement, his mouth fell open and his eyes shut tightly. I wrapped my arms around his shoulders as he filled me, making me gasp at the sensation. Ollie was not a small man and his length inside me, in the current position, was overwhelming. His tip glided back and forth over my g-spot repeatedly. I was one big mess of sexual frustration, desire, and starving hunger for him.

His forceful pushes inside me thrust me upwards and my back slammed against the hard wall behind me. His lips roamed freely over my face, neck and cleavage, driving me crazy. Arching my back, I surrendered to him completely as his hand snaked behind me. He panted into my ear and purred my name. "Oh, Layla. I love you so much."

My head swam with the emotion in his words, the pleasure between my legs, and the intimacy of his body against mine. "I love you too, Ollie."

Holding his belt in my hand, I caught the other end in my free hand and slid it down lower before pulling it tight around the bottom of his perfect ass. Hooking my feet onto his behind and pulling hard on the belt, I urged him deeper, harder and further into me. A carnal noise growled in his throat, and my muscles tensed in my legs as my insides clenched, convulsed and a sweet ripple of pleasure ran through me. My orgasm imminent, I gripped the thick leather in my palms tightly burying my face in his neck moaning, groaning and panting shamelessly.

"I'm coming. Oh god, Ollie, don't stop."

He grinned. "Never."

Surging inside me, he slammed his hips against mine, driving me to the brink rapidly. His teeth grazed my ear as he thrust into me, and the combination of pleasure and pain sent me hurtling over the edge. Inhaling sharply, I cried out as the blissful pulsations of my orgasm consumed me. The room disappeared as my senses became filled with nothing but the euphoric pleasure running through my body like an electric current. It was mind blowing, pillow biting, and toe curling heaven. Grunting, he continued to thrust inside me, prolonging the spasmodic pleasure. Dropping the belt, I ran my hands over his damp skin. His body tensed beneath my hands as his own release surged through him. Slamming into me a few more times, he suddenly stilled and collapsed against me.

Gasping for air, I held him tightly as his head rested on my chest. I could feel his ragged breathing against my skin, and his sweat dripping from his forehead. My heart was racing, and my mind was in the clouds as we stayed in our post-orgasmic embrace.

Able to form words again, I smiled against his hair. "Well, I wasn't expecting that when I came out tonight."

Raising his head, he pressed his lips against mine. "Regret it?"

I shook my head as he released my legs, placing my feet back on solid ground once again. Pulling on my jeans and panties, I stole a glimpse of him doing the same and chuckled. Taking my hand, he pulled me to him and kissed me deeply. "What's so funny?"

"Nothing. Just you being you. We should probably get back out there."

Walking back into the bar, hand in hand, the two of us grinned like teenagers. I slid into the booth, and stared at the table as all eyes fell on the two of us. Leaning across the table, Mel pressed her thumb to the corner of Ollie's mouth and laughed.

"You got a little lipstick there, lover boy."

Wiping his mouth, he shrugged. "Damn groupies can't keep their hands off me. I was assaulted in the bathroom. Tragic." Nudging him in the ribs, I smiled embarrassedly at him.

The drinks kept coming all night courtesy of Nick and the guys, and the five of us laughed so hard throughout that my sides were splitting. Checking his watch, Ollie sighed deeply. "I gotta go. I'm heading back to Utah pretty early tomorrow for my brother's soccer game." I gazed at him as his fingertips stroked my cheek affectionately. "If you're ready to go, I'll give you a ride back."

"Where are you staying tonight?"

He shrugged. "I figured I'd find a motel since Nick already got a new roommate."

I gave him a quick peck, and took his hand as we slid out of the booth. "Why don't you stay with me and Amy? We've managed to share my bed before."

"You sure?"

"Of course. No sense in spending cash on a motel when there's a perfectly good bed waiting for you, Oliver."

He chuckled, and it was the sweetest sound I'd ever heard. "I'm Oliver now, huh?"

"You are when you question me and my generous nature. Come on, before I change my mind. You guys gonna be ok?" I glanced back at Amy and Mel who assured me that they would be getting a ride in Eric's van.

* * * *

Walking down the hallway to my room, Ollie laughed. "Feels kind of weird being here now."

Searching for my key, I smiled at him. "Why? It wasn't that long ago you lived here."

"I know, but it's not home anymore, you know?"

I nodded. "I guess so. You decided which college you're going to in the fall?"

"Not yet. I have options, but I'm not setting anything in stone right now. Besides, I've got pretty great job back home."

"Yeah, I heard you get to play with motorcycles all day now."

He rolled his eyes. "Not play. I work on them. Fix them up so that they can grace the roads of Utah with their gorgeous, powerful roar once again."

I laughed at him as I unlocked my door. "Whatever you say, grease monkey."

Slinging my purse on the bed, I slid off my jacket and pulled the band from my hair, letting the curls fall onto my shoulders. Wrapping his arms around my waist, Ollie breathed into my ear behind me. "Did I mention I love the new look? Not that I hated the old one. You're beautiful all the time, but you look really hot as a brunette. What made you change it?"

Turning to face him, I shrugged. "I needed a change."

Pressing his lips to mine, he smiled. "Well you look great." Releasing his grip on me, he flung himself onto my bed, resting his hands behind his head and grinned at me. "So, you gonna give me a little strip tease goodnight gift?"

Grabbing Amy's pillow, I hurled it at his head.

"Is that a no?"

Sliding my hands into my jeans, I slid them slowly down my thighs, letting them crumple at my feet before gracefully stepping out of them. His eyes widened, and he licked his lips as he stared at me. Turning my back to him, I headed for the bathroom. Glancing over my shoulder, I winked. "I think you've seen and sampled enough of my goodies tonight."

Closing the bathroom door behind me, I heard him yell. "Tease!" Smiling to myself, I slipped into a pair of shorts, brushed my teeth, and made my way back to the bedroom.

I'd only been in there a short while, but Ollie had fallen asleep already. Smiling, I shook my head and made my way over, switching off the light on route. Climbing into bed, I snuggled closely to him. He opened his eyes a little and reached his arm out, allowing me to rest my head in the crook of his arm against his chest. Nuzzling into his chest, I inhaled deeply, taking in the sweet scent of his naturally delicious, Ollie smell. I sighed as I lay there just gazing up at him. He let out a soft groan, and it made me smile just hearing the sound and feeling his chest rise and fall beneath me.

I'd missed him so much, and the reality of him being there next to me was a relief I felt would never come. I'd spent so long wishing he would get in touch, hoping he could forgive me, and now he was in my bed while I curled up in his arms. Reaching up, I brushed a lock of his dark hair from his eyes and ran my fingers through his long hair.

He smiled sleepily. "Leave me alone, fiend. Unless you're about to give me a very sexy wake up call."

Leaning up, I pressed my lips to his and sighed. "Not tonight. You should sleep. You have a long ride tomorrow."

Turning to face me, his eyes opened and he pressed his forehead against mine. "Don't talk about tomorrow just yet. The thought of leaving you here makes me want to stay up all night, savoring every minute, and I have a ten hour drive ahead of me in the morning. Let's just live in the moment right now, ok?"

I nodded in agreement, and he quickly responded, giving me a passionate and lingering kiss. I didn't want to sleep, or even close my eyes, for fear I'd wake to find him gone again, but I was so tired and comfortable in his embrace that I simply couldn't force my eyes to stay open any longer.

Pressing my head onto his chest, I ran my fingers over his stomach gently. "I love you, Ollie."

<u>Placing a kiss on my forehead, I felt him smile against my skin. "I love you too, Layla. So frickin' much."</u>

Chapter 47

Dangerous Territory

The light streaming through the windows woke me, and I could hardly see through my blurry eyes and the blinding sunlight that was hitting my face. Reaching out my hand, I searched for my bed buddy, but all I felt was an empty space. My heart in my throat, I sat bolt upright and stared in horror at the bed.

No. No, not again.

Jumping out of bed, I searched for my clothes and cell phone, desperate to reach him, needing to know why. Frantically, I paced around the room, raking my fingers through my hair. Amy was sound asleep in the bed beside me, completely oblivious to the drama that was unfolding. Scrolling through my contact list, I hit call but he never answered. Hurling my cell across the room at my bed, I sank to the floor. Pulling my knees to my chest, I wrapped my arms around them tightly. My head rested against my forearms as tears slid down my face. How could he just leave like that again? After everything that happened. My heart plummeted to the depths of my chest.

The door opened slowly, and my head snapped up. My heart momentarily stopped as I saw Ollie, backing his way in with a tray of coffee in one hand and a brown paper bag in the other. Turning around, he saw me and his face contorted into an expression of utter horror, concern, and panic all at once. Dropping the bag, he placed the tray on the floor and practically skidded across the wooden floor to me. His hands moving quickly over my body, and lifting my face to look at him, he scanned my features.

"Layla, what is it? Baby, talk to me. What happened?"

Trying to speak through my heavy sobs, I took a deep breath. "I woke up, and you were gone. I thought you'd left me again, like before."

Wrapping his arms around me, he held me tightly to him and pressed his lips against my forehead. "Shhh. No, baby. I wouldn't do that to you again. I just went to get breakfast, and I didn't want to wake you. Calm down. I'm here. I would never have left without saying goodbye. Not this time."

Gripping his shirt, I tried to calm my rapid breathing. Amy stirred in her bed, and seeing me in my state she glared at Ollie who shook his head at her. She got the message because she quickly got out of bed, and shut herself in the bathroom, leaving us alone.

Cupping my face in his hands, he wiped my tears with his thumbs. "Please stop crying. I'm here. Don't do this to yourself. We have a few hours left before I have to go, and I don't want to spend them wiping your tears away. Come, have breakfast with me. You'll feel better."

Taking my hand, he pulled me to my feet and pressed his lips to mine. I let out a long breath and followed him to the bed. Once I was sitting comfortably, he strode over to the door and closed it, grabbing the coffee and bag on the way. He dangled the bag from his finger, and smiled. "I got your favorite. A toasted poppy seed and salmon bagel." Handing me a cup he kissed my cheek. "Coffee. Hot, strong, and delicious. Just like me."

He winked at me as I took the bag from him, sniffled, and smiled back, mouthing a thank you. He shrugged as though it was no big deal, but it meant a lot to me. Not only had he stayed, but he'd brought me breakfast in bed too. It was certainly on my list of romantic gestures he'd made. It was up there with Christmas morning, carving our names in a tree, and my song.

"Thank you, Ollie. I mean it. For still being here, for breakfast, for last night. Everything."

Leaning over, I kissed his cheek and he blushed. Ollie was adorable when he did that, and his pink flushed skin made me melt inside. "You don't have to thank me. I love you, remember? It's how this works. You need me, I'm there for you. Always. It's easy like that."

Grinning, I gave him a quick kiss.

* * * *

Finishing my bagel, I sipped my coffee and glanced at Ollie who was busy devouring his own while browsing his social network page on his cell phone. Opening the bathroom door, Amy arched her eyebrow at me, clearly wondering if it was safe to come back in yet. Nodding at her, I smiled. Without looking up from his phone, Ollie held out the paper bag for her.

"Got you something to eat as well. There's a bottle of O.J in there too, Miss 'I don't pollute my body with caffeine, but I'll guzzle Cosmos till I puke'."

Poking her tongue out at him, she snatched the bag and dug out her bagel. Dropping his cell on the bed, Ollie gave me a rueful smile and sighed loudly. "I have to get going."

Nodding weakly, I stared at the floor, knowing that tears weren't too far away. I didn't want to cry in front of him as it would only make him feel guilty for leaving me. Threading his fingers in mine, he held my chin in his free hand and turned my face to look at him. His big chestnut brown eyes glistened in the light, and I couldn't help but gaze dreamily into them.

"Come see me off?"

"Of course I will."

Releasing my hand, he walked over to Amy and wrapped his arms around her. "I'll catch up with you soon, ok? And

Aims, it will work out, I promise. You know where I am if you need to talk though, alright?"

Hugging him tightly, she nodded. "I know. Thanks Ollie. I'll miss you. Don't stay away so long next time, ok?"

I gave them both a puzzled look. I'd made Ollie promise not to breathe a word about Amy's feeling for Mel. Catching my confused expression, Amy smiled. "I told him. Tequila and a shoulder to cry on. Ollie, you are perfect."

Grinning, he spoke into her ear and I could just about make out what he said. "Take care of my girl for me. She's gonna need you guys, she's got a lot to think about."

Winking at her, he turned his attention back to me and held out his hand.

Immediately taking it in my own, I followed him out and down to Mel's room where he began knocking loudly. "Get out of bed, lazy ass."

I heard a groan from inside the room. "Screw you, punk dick."

Chuckling, he hammered on the door again and this time she answered. "Come to tell me you're kidnapping my best friend? Because if you are, just remember to feed her three times a day and screw her at least once nightly."

I gawked at her, completely speechless. She always did know how to make a situation just a little more difficult. Grinning, Ollie nudged me. "I'll keep it in mind, but no, I'm not stealing her away. I'm leaving. Heading home. Just wanted to say see ya."

Smiling, she hugged him. "See ya soon, rock star. Drive safe, and try not to miss me too much."

Rolling his eyes, Ollie gave a salute. "Absolutely, sergeant. Anything else?"

Pulling away, she glanced at me. "Yeah, just one more thing. Don't be a stranger. It gets pretty depressing around here without you."

He nodded, and looked at me as his lips curled ever so slightly upwards. "I know."

There was only one more goodbye left, and I dreaded the moment as we approached his Ducati. My insides twisted, and I felt my blood run cold. Facing me, he took my hands in his. "God, this is hard. I wish I didn't have to go."

Pressing my hands to his chest, I gazed up at him. "Then stay."

"You know I can't, Layla, and you know why. That ticket I gave you is yours whenever you need it. There is always a place for you in Utah. You just have to take the chance and make the choice. I'll be right there waiting for you, but it has to be what you really want." Closing the gap between us he snaked his hands around my waist.

"I don't know how to say goodbye to you, Ollie. I never thought I'd have to."

"Well, you could start by letting me kiss you."

Without hesitation, I pulled him against my chest and sealed my mouth over his as his tongue darted inside, rolling and gently stroking mine. It was a deep, loving, and sensual kiss. It was as though all our emotions, were being expressed with just that one act of affection.

Breathless, I gazed into his eyes. "I love you, Ollie. No matter what happens, never forget that. I will always love you. You have a piece of my heart forever."

Beaming at me, the tip of his nose touched mine as his forehead rested against my own. "I love you too, Layla. You've had my heart since the moment you looked up at me from the hallway floor. You always will."

Placing a last chaste kiss on my lips, he released me and grabbed his jacket and helmet from his bike, sliding it over his thick black hair. Standing in front of him, I stood on my tiptoes and placed a kiss on his visor. Mouthing the words I love you, I crossed my heart with my finger and I could see he was smiling as his eyes glistened and danced. Nodding, he pointed at himself and held up two fingers, signalling he loved me too before mounting the bike. The roar of the engine made my heart leap. Taking my hand once more, he ran his gloved thumb over my knuckles before letting go and speeding out of the parking lot.

I watched him go with a lump in my throat and tears in my eyes. Appearing at my side, Amy and Mel draped a comforting arm around me and rested their heads on my shoulders.

"It'll be ok, right?"

Neither answered. They simply hugged me and turned me around, walking me back to the dorm. Walking into my room, my heart felt heavy as I looked at the empty coffee cups and discarded bagel wrappers. Seeing my line of sight, Mel dashed over and began clearing up.

"Mel, its fine. I'm alright. Honest. Can we just veg out in here today? I could use a day with my girls eating junk food."

Grabbing her purse, Amy hugged me. "Of course we can. I'll go to the store and pick up so much junk they'll have to get us out of here with a crane."

Shaking my head, I watched as she breezed out of the room closing the door behind her. Pulling me to the bed, Mel pushed me down and sat next to me holding my hand. "How are you really?"

I shrugged. "Sad that he's gone, confused over how I feel about him, and totally terrified of this decision I still have to make."

Shaking her head, she stared at me. "Layla, Jared is with Alicia now. You said so yourself that he's moved on. Ollie is your fresh start. Look, if you choose Utah, choose Ollie, I will back you a hundred percent. So will Amy. Your parents will have a hissy fit, no doubt, but they love you and they'll understand. But no one can make this choice for you. I just don't think Jared Garrett should be a factor in it anymore."

I knew she was right, and hearing it out loud made it even more clear to me that we really were through. Why was I still pining for a man that had cast me aside so easily and ripped my heart to shreds, leaving it scarred, tattered and torn?

"You're right, but I still need time to think about this. It's not just what I'd be giving up, Mel. Its everything I'd be taking on too."

Nodding, she bit her bottom lip, and I knew there was something she needed to say.

"What is it, Melanie?"

Reaching into her pocket, she pulled out a small gift wrapped box. I stared at her blankly. Sighing deeply, she winced. "I've been keeping this in my things for months, and I think I should give it to you now. Remember how I took that gift from Jared at Christmas?"

I gawked at her, and then the tiny box in her hand.

"Well, I didn't quite put it in the trash. I kept it. I was going to give it to you sometime, but I thought you and Ollie were meant to be, but now I think you should have all the information, all the facts before you make a decision. So, here."

Handing it to me, she got up and walked over to Amy's bed where she sat with her head down. Carefully opening the paper, I held the box in my palm, contemplating whether I should open it or not. In the end, my morbid curiosity got the better of me and I flipped open the lid. Inhaling sharply, I pressed my hand to my mouth.

"Oh my god."

Sitting on a plush velvet cushion was my pendant. The single diamond and engraving was now accompanied by a new engraving into the black stone. "Ever thine, Ever mine, Ever ours." The words were those that he had used in his letter, borrowed from Ludwig Van Beethoven, but from the heart of Jared Garrett.

Raising my head, I held it in my palm and gaped at Mel. "He had it engraved, Mel. He still loved me, and he wanted me to have this on Christmas. And you shunned him. Turned him away."

"I'm so sorry, Layla. There's more." My heart raced as she walked over and handed me an envelope. His handwriting on the front brought back memories of his trip to New York, and gingerly I opened it.

Layla

This gift comes with no agenda, no game or malice. Simply a hope that you will see it and remember everything we shared. Since the moment I met you I've been consumed with one thing and one thing only. Making you mine. I love you eternally our love, protection and safety are my priority and I only wish I had done more to keep you. You were right I didn't trust you and I should have. I thought I was doing what was best for everyone by not telling you about Lucy. The less you knew, the less danger you were in and I had to keep you safe. I didn't know what that man could be capable of. I feared he'd come after Lucy and that meant coming up against me. I couldn't let you be a target too Layla. If I'd known then that it was Felix I still would have done the same because that man is a monster of the worst kind. I don't ask for you to forgive me. God knows I don't deserve it. I just need you to understand why.

Merry Christmas My Lady

Jared xxx

I gazed at the piece of paper in my hand before turning my eyes to Mel. "I can't believe this. All this time I had the explanation right there in black and white, but I never knew. He was scared I'd get hurt. Why couldn't he tell me this?"

Draping her arm over my shoulder, Mel sniffled and it was only then I noticed she was crying. "I'm so sorry, Layla. I should have given it to you, but I thought I was protecting you. I didn't want you to get hurt again."

Wrapping my arms around her, I gave her a hug. "It's ok. I understand why you did it. I just wish I understood why he couldn't tell me all of this."

"Maybe he thought it made him weak. You know, being afraid of something. He's a big deal businessman and it's not in their nature to be scared of anything. Everything is supposed to be a challenge, rather than a threat to people like that."

Holding the paper in my hand, I shook my head in bewilderment. "I don't really know what to do with this information. It seems rather pointless now. He's moved on and found someone else. This was written months ago. When he still had hope for reconciliation."

Crumpling it in my hand, I tossed it in the trash and placed the box on my bedside table. "I just had to give you all the facts before you made your decision. Now you know everything. It's up to you to decide where you go from here."

There was nothing to decide where Jared was concerned. We were over, and I was in love with Ollie. Granted, I loved Jared too, but Ollie was the one waiting for me in Utah, and Jared was probably doing all kinds of deviant acts with Alicia.

Taking her hands, I stared at Mel. "We don't mention this again, ok? Not to Amy, or even talk about it to each other. Understood? It's done. Over and finished."

Nodding, she kissed my cheek. "Understood."

* * * *

Sitting amongst the pile of junk food wrappers, I grinned as the three of us swapped stories about our teenage years. Amy laughed hysterically when I told her how Mel got suspended for breaking a girls tooth in high school. Shrugging her shoulders, Mel gave me a satisfied grin, extremely proud of the time she had served for her assault on my tormentor. Looking at the clock, I thought about Ollie. He was sure to be back in Utah by then, and I had a feeling the buzzing of my cell phone was a message telling me just that.

Clambering to my feet I grabbed my phone and smiled as I read his text.

> Finally home. Missing you all, but mostly you. Be in touch soon. I love you. Ollie. Xx
> **Received: 19.27**
> **From: Ollie**

Dropping it back onto my bed, I re-joined the girls on the floor. "Ollie says hi."

Gathering up the trash pile, Mel glanced at Amy. "So, what do say we get out of here and go hang out with the guys at Benny's? Don't want to stay here all night wallowing."

Amy beamed at me. "Definitely. You're coming, Layla?"

"Do I have a choice?"

They answered simultaneously, something they were getting very good at. "Not really."

I grinned at them and rolled my eyes. "Then I guess I'm coming." Heading to my closet, I grabbed a denim skirt and a simple white vest. I wasn't dressing up just for a night with Nick and Eric at the bar. Amy and Mel donned their shortest dresses, of course, and piled on the makeup as they always did when we went out.

Calling a cab, I waited in the hallway for them, adjusting my boots as I did so. Nick emerged from his room, and scanned me from head to toe. "You guys heading to Benny's then?"

I nodded.

"Great, means I don't have to listen to that asshole go on about Mel all night. She realizes Amy is into her, right?"

I gawked at him in horror.

"She didn't tell me, but it's freaking obvious. I've seen that look on a guy's face loads of times. Hell, Ollie used to stare at you that way whenever you were in the same room as him."

Pressing my finger to his lips, I looked back at my door. "Shhh. Don't say a word to anyone, Nick. I mean it. If you even breathe a syllable, I will end you. Got it?"

He nodded, and his eyebrows pinched together. "Ok, I got it. God, chill out will you? I'm going to catch a ride with Eric. See you there."

Letting out a long breath, my head fell back as worry for Amy and her secret flooded me. Opening the door, she spotted me and gave me a puzzled look. "What's up with you?"

Shaking my head, I smiled. "Nothing. Just tired. You look great. Ready to go?" I heard Mel shout over her shoulder that she was almost ready, and once she was happily suited and dressed to the nines, we headed out.

Pushing our way through the glass entrance doors, I spotted a silver Mercedes parked outside the dorm building and groaned. Amy recognized it immediately, and when Mel saw it she practically foamed at the mouth. "What the fuck does he want?" Amy grabbed her arm, and shook her head in warning.

I had no desire to see my ex, or discuss his new lover anytime soon. Storming to the car, I hammered on the back window. It rolled down slowly, and I came face to face with someone I didn't expect to see.

"Hello, Layla."

Sitting there, looking pale, withdrawn end extremely self-conscious, was Lucy. I fisted my hands on my hips, and glared at her as she climbed out of the car.

"You have some nerve coming here, Lucy."

Resting her hand on her considerably sized bump, she lowered her head. "I know. I'm so sorry for everything my stupid mess caused between you two, and I know there is no way I should be asking you this, but I don't have anyone else. I don't have any friends, Jared hardly speaks to me, and my mother is smothering me so much I could suffocate. Please, just hear me out. I really need your help."

She looked absolutely awful. Her hair was a mess, her eyes looked as though she hadn't slept in a year, and her frame was so slight, I was amazed she could still stand, let alone support the weight of her growing child.

I glanced at Amy and Mel who were watching me with avid curiosity. I told Lucy to give me a moment, then made my way to them. "I'll meet you at the bar. I need to hear what she has to say. I promise, I'll be ok. He's not with her. I don't think he has any idea she's even here."

Begrudgingly, they agreed and walked away, leaving me and my new friend alone. Sliding in next to her, I caught Daniel's eye in the rear view.

"Not a word to him, Daniel. I don't want him interfering with this." Lucy's tone was serious, and he immediately pressed the button for the screen to separate us.

Turning to me, she sighed, and I could see she was close to tears. "Layla, let me first just tell you how completely, totally, and unbelievably sorry I am about everything I put you through. I made him keep me a secret. I knew that if Felix found out I was Jared's sister, he'd leave me and this baby faster than a bullet from a gun. When Bastian found out I'd been unfaithful, he left me totally alone and I didn't have anyone to turn to. Sure, Jared protects and takes care of me, but I just wanted to feel loved and special. Felix made me feel like a princess. He has a way of making you think you're the most exquisite creature on the planet, and I honestly thought he loved me. Evidently he didn't, and you'd think after he put me in hospital I could stop loving the sick bastard."

I sat rigid, and listened as she continued to tell her woeful yet completely self-inflicted story.

"When he first hit me, I told myself it was my fault. I'd made him angry. He got jealous that I was with Bastian, and even though he didn't want me, he didn't want me to be with anyone else either. When I found out I was pregnant, I thought maybe it would make us stronger and he'd calm down a little, but he didn't. He got so mad that he beat me repeatedly for an hour straight. I got a fractured arm and a broken jaw just for carrying his child. He dumped me at the hospital, and I knew Jared would be there, he always knew what was happening with me. He has spies everywhere, I swear. So I ran. I couldn't face him and tell him it was Felix. They hate each other. If Felix knew I was Jared's sister, it would make his year. He'd completely destroy everything that Jared has worked for and drag him down. There a lot of wealthy men out there just waiting for him to fail so that they can scoop up the pieces of my father's company."

"Lucy, your brother was screwing Felix's wife. I'd say that might make someone a little unhinged for a while." Scooting towards me, she was wringing her hands and I could see she was nervous.

"Layla, I need help. Felix has something of mine, and I want it back. It's something very important, and with it he could destroy Jared. That's why I can't tell him or ask for his help. Felix won't be there. He's in New York, but I have the code for his apartment. Please, I can't go alone. I just need a look out. Please, I'm begging you. I'm desperate."

I stared at her, wide eyed. She was kidding, right? After everything, she actually expected me to help her? I shook my head in bewilderment, before finally focusing on her. Staring her down, I answered. "Fine, I'll help. But I'm not doing this for you. I'm doing it because as much as I hate him for what he's put me through, I don't want to see Jared torn to pieces by money hungry dogs. Understand?"

Taking my hand, she thanked me profusely and instructed Daniel to head for Felix's apartment. Taking out my cell, I sent Mel a message, telling her I was going to be a little while and would call later before slipping it into my back pocket.

Lucy was looking right at me as I stared blankly at the screen between us and Daniel. "He's still in love with you, you know. He's been like a shadow of himself these past months. He won't talk or eat. He hardly sleeps. He works long hours, and when he's not working he's just functioning, walking around like a zombie. I've never seen him so broken, Layla. I know you love him too. It's in your eyes when you say or hear his name. Isn't there some way you can work it out?"

Without turning to face her, I snorted. "No, Lucy. This is the real world. Jared lied to me over and over again, and he never trusted me enough to tell me the truth, or trust that I was capable of taking care of myself. I would never have told anyone about your existence, Lucy. I would have respected his need to keep you safe, and guarded that knowledge with my life. But no matter how much he said he loved me, how much he wanted to be with me forever, he just couldn't be honest with me. From day one he was lying.

"Did he tell you that I worked at the coffee shop? That he'd asked me out, wined and dined me before I found out he was my boss? He wouldn't know honesty if it came up and slapped him clean across the face. So, no offence, Lucy, but butt out. I'll help you do this, and then I want him and you out of my life for good. Besides, he has Alicia now."

I gulped the lump in my throat as the words left my lips. They just weren't true. The thought of him forever being out of my life was painful. Necessary, but still so painful.

"He's not with Alicia. I can't explain it, only he can, but you have to believe me. He's not with her. She's a psycho."

Rolling my eyes, I stared out of the window. "It doesn't matter anymore, Lucy. Jared and I are done."

Slumping back in her seat, she shook her head and resumed her mindless, anxious fidgeting.

Chapter 48

Risky Business

The drive to Felix's place took less than ten minutes from the campus, and as we pulled up outside the enormous classy building, I suddenly felt nervous. Lucy was practically shaking as she sat huddled in the corner, staring up at the building we would soon be trespassing in.

"You sure you want to do this?"

She looked at me, and with panic in her eyes she nodded. "I *have* to."

Exiting the car, she stood on the sidewalk trembling. I knocked on Daniel's window, and he scowled at me. "Mr. Garret is going to hit the damn ceiling, Miss Jennings, I strongly urge you to reconsider your actions."

"Daniel, I'm perfectly capable of making my own decisions. The fact is, he's the only reason I am doing this. Park around the corner, it's not good for you to be seen here. I'll call you when were done. And Daniel, not one word to Jared. I mean it."

He leaned forward and rested his head on the steering wheel, and I sympathized with the difficult situation we'd put him in. He was clearly torn between our safety and our need for him to keep quiet. Lifting his head, he nodded and drove around the corner.

Taking Lucy's hand, I held it tightly. She looked like a frightened child, and it suddenly occurred to me that she couldn't be more than nineteen after all. Taking a deep breath, she walked to the doors and entered the building. We waited for the elevator, and the nerves in my stomach began to swarm as I continuously checked the doors for any sign of Felix. The bell of the elevator arriving startled me, and a small squeak of fright escaped me. Breathing hard, I looked at Lucy who was clearly just as scared as I was.

The ride up to the seventh floor was tense as we both struggled to hold our nerve. Punching in the security code next to the door, Lucy pushed the door open silently. The entire apartment was coated in darkness, and Lucy's prediction of Felix being out of town was clearly right on the money. Switching on the lights, I scanned the room. Everything was pristine. His white wash walls and minimalistic décor were a fitting choice for the controlling social playboy. The black leather sofa and matching chairs were very square, and their straight lines reminded me of his unfeeling and callous smile. A shiver ran up my spine as I closed the door behind me and searched for Lucy.

Wildly searching through Felix's office, she emptied boxes, files and drawers full of paper work. She was positively frantic.

"Lucy, what exactly are we looking for?"

She ran her hands repeatedly through her hair, and stuttered as she became more and more panicked. "He has photos of me, Layla. Bad, really bad ones. In some of them, I'm not alone. You have to help me find them. If anyone got their hands on them, it would be the biggest disaster of my life!"

I stared at her. No wonder she couldn't tell her older brother. If those photos went public, Jared's whole image and private life would be turned on its head. "Ok, I'll help you look. Where would he keep them?"

"I don't know. Maybe the bedroom?"

Leaving the office, we scrambled to his bedroom. It was like a chamber of horrors. Lucy froze, and held her hand to her mouth as she gagged and heaved. On the walls, covering every possible space, were photos. Endless pictures of women bound, gagged, blindfolded, and suspended from chains papered the room.

"Sick son of a bitch."

I walked around the room until I spotted something that made my stomach turn. Pinned above his dresser was a picture of my roommate. She was topless, wearing only her lace panties and blindfolded. The sick son of a bitch had snapped her without her even knowing, and was now keeping it as a memento in his den of seedy sinful shame. Grabbing it from the wall, I tore it up into tiny pieces.

Lucy was standing in the doorway, clearly in shock. "Lucy, wake up. Snap out of it, and help me get all these photos down."

Shaking her head, she finally came back to earth and began tearing each twisted photograph from the walls. In some of the photos the women were clearly in tears, forced to do horrible things to avoid a beating, no doubt.

"We're taking all of these and burning them. Every last one." But none were of Lucy. We scanned every face, every body, and none belonged to her.

"Where the fuck are they?" She was getting hysterical. Tipping out drawers, pulling out closets. If there was any chance we could have done this without him knowing, it was officially out of the window now. We searched every inch of the bedroom, but still came up empty handed. Lucy made her way back to the office while I headed for the living room.

A blood curdling scream echoed through the apartment, and I sprinted as fast as I could to the office. As I rounded the corner, I stopped dead in my tracks. My eyes fell on Felix's. Lucy was lying flat on the desk, and his hand was tightly gripped around her throat. She was sobbing and shaking with fear, pleading with him to let her go as he stared at me.

"Well, well, well. What do we have here? Just when I think my day can't get any better, I end up with two delicious little beauties just waiting for me in my apartment."

Fisting my hands, I stared him down. "Let her go, Felix, or I swear to god you'll be sorry."

He laughed loudly and smirking at me he released her. Rolling off of the desk to the floor, Lucy crawled over to the corner of the room and huddled up tightly, guarding her bump. His eyes were dark, and I could see the excitement this entire situation was provoking in him. He stalked slowly towards me, and I felt my insides churn as fear flooded my veins. But I would not run. If I ran, it would just increase his fun, and I was not going to put myself and Lucy in that danger.

His face close to mine, he sniffed and inhaled into my hair. He made my skin crawl. The back of his hand grazed gently up and down my arm, and I swallowed hard, trying to stay calm as the instinct to run overwhelmed me. I glanced over at Lucy, who was sobbing and staring at me with terror in her eyes.

"You smell good enough to eat, Layla. Oh, you and I are going to have a lot of fun. Being one of Jared's girls, I'm sure you're familiar with a little slap and tickle, right?"

I remained silent. "Oh, come now, sweetheart. Don't be shy."

His hand moved slowly down my arm to my hip before gripping onto my thigh. I could feel tears begging to release, but I had to stay strong. If he saw my weak resolve, he would pounce on me like a lion, and I was no match for his broad muscular body. His hand slipped beneath my skirt, and he began pushing it upwards with his fingers. Turning my face to him, I snarled. "Get your disgusting hands off of me, or it will be the very last thing you do."

Staring into my eyes, he grinned. "I do love the fiery ones. They make it so much more fun."

Gripping my waist forcefully, he lifted my feet from the floor, hauled me over his shoulder, and carried me kicking and screaming for help to his bedroom as Lucy watched powerless from the corner.

Pushing me onto the bed, he pinned me down by my wrists with one hand and unzipped his pants. I tried to kick him off of me, but his large frame weighed me down. Tears began to stream down my face as I struggled to free myself from his grasp. The realization that I was about to be attacked was horrific, and closing my eyes, I tried to escape the hell. I wanted to remove myself from this moment, to free my soul from my terrified and helpless body as he did this to me. His lips grazed my ear as his hand reached up my skirt to my cotton panties.

"You're a very bad girl, Layla, and now I'm going to teach you a lesson. No one, comes into my home and steals my possessions."

A sob escaped my lips as I screamed and cried for someone to help me. Closing my eyes, I laid there waiting for my hell to begin, praying it would be over quickly.

Without warning, his entire weight lifted from my body, and opening my eyes I watched as he flew clean across the room into the far wall. Standing over him with his fists clenched was Jared. Striking blow after devastating blow into Felix's face, ribs, stomach and head, he attacked him with a wild and uncontrollable fury. Gripping him by the collar, Jared hauled him to his feet and round house kicked him in the gut, making Felix propel through the air and out of the bedroom. Jared followed him out, and shakily, I got off the bed and chased after them.

Felix stood in the living room, blood leaking from his nose and mouth. His face was covered in cuts and bruises from Jared's harried attack. Walking around the glass coffee table, he smirked at Jared who was stalking him like a wolf and its prey. His eyes were dark and hooded. I could see the anger and absolute rage as he watched Felix's every move.

"Nice of you to join me, old boy. You, me, and two little whores. Feels just like old times. Remember what fun we had at those parties? It's not been the same without you."

My stomach lurched. Jared didn't respond, but continued his evil and hateful glare at Felix.

"Come on, Jared. They're just women."

Jared flew at him clearing the table in one swift leap. The two of them crashed to the floor, and Jared straddled Felix, immobilizing him on his back against the marble floor. Lucy was pinned like a statue to the door. I'd never seen anyone so terrified.

Gripping Felix's shirt in his grazed hands, Jared spat and roared at him. "The woman you had pinned to your bed, trying to rape, is the love of my life! And the one you were beating the shit out of in New York is-"

No! He couldn't. I wouldn't let him. "My friend!"

His head snapped up, and he gave me a confused look. Staring at him, I nodded and an understanding passed between us.

"Did you think no one would find out? That your dirty, disgusting little secret would just go on and on? Thought you could continue to abuse, rape and beat women, didn't you? You had this fucking coming, you sick, twisted, fuck. I'm going to destroy you."

Felix grinned at me, "I wish I'd known she was your friend. It would have made her a lot more interesting."

Jared's hand slid around Felix's throat, and I could see his bicep flex as he gripped tighter and tighter around it. He was going to kill him! Rushing to his side, I wrapped my arms around Jared's bulging biceps and pulled hard. "Please, Jared, don't! You'll kill him! Jared!"

I screamed, and he immediately released him. Felix gasped and panted for air. Slamming Felix's head back down onto the floor with an almighty thud, Jared knocked him completely unconscious. Standing over his still body, he wiped his mouth with the back of his hand.

It was over.

Suddenly, the realization of what had almost happened to me sank in, and I lost control of my legs. The room began to disappear as darkness consumed me. Collapsing into a heap on the cold floor, I could hear their voices calling out to me, but I couldn't respond.

I was broken.

* * * *

My arms and legs felt heavy, aching as I turned over. Opening my eyes slowly, I scanned my surroundings. Where the hell was I? Lifting myself onto my elbows, I rubbed my blurry eyes and squinted as light poured through the tall arched windows. Magnolia walls and the familiar sound of Elvis in the hallway reminded me of where I was, and also of what had happened last night. Holding my face in my hands, I winced as the whole horrible event flashed before my eyes. Breaking in, the photos, Amy, Felix, the bed, the fight, everything.

My stomach turned, and I scurried out of bed and sprinted for the bathroom, emptying my stomach contents into the toilet. I brought my knees to my chest, and rocked gently as I tried desperately to calm down. My clothes were gone, but I still had my underwear on. My forehead against my knees, I cried softly.

A warm pair of arms slid around me as Jared held me tight against his broad chest. "It's ok, baby, it's alright. I got you. You're safe." Jared's soft and reassuring voice enveloped me as I clutched his t-shirt in my hand. My tears flowed freely down my face as the horror of my ordeal replayed in my mind like a terrifying movie. "It's alright, baby. I've got you. That sick son of a bitch is never going to lay a finger on you as long as I'm living. I will never let anyone hurt you, Layla. Oh god, baby. Why didn't you listen to me? I told you to stay away from him. Why did you go there?"

Lifting my head, I looked up at him through my tears. "Lucy needed help, and I couldn't let her go alone. I did it for you. He had something that could have destroyed everything you've worked for. I couldn't let him do that."

He wiped my tears away with his thumbs, and shook his head at me. "Layla, nothing on this earth is worth risking your safety over. God, when Daniel called to tell me, I couldn't breathe. I died right there on the spot, thinking about what Felix could be doing to you both."

So it was Daniel who'd called him. I nuzzled my face into his chest, and took a deep breath. The familiar scent of vanilla, soap and Jared warmed my blood, and like a sedative it calmed my frayed nerves.

Realizing what a dangerous situation I was currently in, I pulled away and clambered to my feet. He gazed down at me, but I couldn't look him in the eye. "I need to go home. Amy and Mel must be worried sick."

"I called them when we got back here. I told them everything, and that you and Lucy were staying the night here for your own protection. I told Amy and Mel to deadbolt the door, and not to answer to anyone. He could still come after you, Layla. You need to stay here until I know it's safe for you to go back there."

I shook my head in a definitive no. "That's not going to happen, Jared."

Pushing past him, I searched for my clothes, finally locating them hanging over the small cream couch in the corner of the room. Turning to face him, I pulled the sheet from the bed and covered myself up. "I want to get dressed. I'd like some privacy, please."

"Layla, I've had you naked and panting on this very bed. I think I've seen everything you have."

"That was different. We were together then. Please go."

Rolling his eyes he walked out and closed the door behind him. Locking it, I pulled on my clothes and gazed at myself fin the mirror. My hair was a mess, and my eyes were red and puffy from crying. I opened the door, and checked to see if he was there. Discovering he was still absent, I sat on the bed and put on my shoes. There was no way I was staying there.

Creeping down the stairs, I almost reached the door when Lucy spotted me from the living room. "Layla. Thank goodness." Hurrying over to me, she flung her arms around my neck. "I know you must be in a terrible rush to get away from us, but please just spare me a minute?"

Nodding, I followed her to the plush sofa and sat beside her. "I wanted to thank you. You saved my life last night, and put yourself in danger to do it. I can never repay you for what you did."

Staring at the door, I closed my eyes as the memory of Felix pinning me to his bed flashed in front of me. "I couldn't let him strangle you, Lucy. It wasn't just you I was protecting." I glanced at her bump, and she immediately rested a protective hand over it.

"Thank you."

Rising to my feet, I headed for the door.

"He loves you, Layla. Give him a chance to say goodbye."

I turned around and stared at her. "What do you mean?"

"He's leaving. He has to fly to New York in a couple of days. He'll be in Europe for a year."

Walking back towards her, I shook my head as the words didn't quite sink in. "A year? What about you, the baby, and Alicia?"

She shook her head. "I told you. Layla, he isn't with her. He's in his office right now. Go, talk to him, hear him out, and then you can walk away, go back to your life. But please, just give him that chance to put things right before he goes. You owe it to yourselves."

Staring into her bright blue eyes, I felt my heart thud as I thought of everything Jared and I had been through. Maybe we did owe it to ourselves to get that closure. That final goodbye. Walking to his office, I gently pushed the door open. Sitting at his desk with his head in his hands, he glanced up at me. "You need something?"

I shook my head. "I thought maybe we should talk. There are things we need to say."

Nodding, he rose from his desk and gestured to the black leather couch in the corner of the room. Taking a seat, I took a deep breath as he sat down beside me. "First, I want to thank you for rescuing me last night. If you hadn't showed up..." I swallowed hard. "Well, we both know what would have happened."

Taking my hand, he stroked my knuckles with his thumb. "Don't think about it. You're within your rights to call the cops and report his assault, Layla, but I urge you not to. He's got friends in high places, and I need to deal with him myself."

I sighed, and stared at my feet. "I'm not reporting him. It's too risky for Lucy, and you'll be arrested for assault."

He nodded and stared at the floor.

"Jared, I've been meaning to apologize for your car."

A ghost of a smile appeared on his lips. "Forget it. It's glass and steel, Layla, and compared to what I really lost that day, it's meaningless. Don't give it a second thought. You were pretty kick ass, though. Where did you learn to swing like that?"

I laughed lightly. "My father used to coach little league. I was his star player."

Smiling, Jared nodded.

"Lucy tells me you're going to New York, then Europe."

His expression immediately changed to the hard business man again. "New York until the baby is born, then London, Paris, Rome, and wherever else I have to go to get this development off the ground."

The thought of him leaving pained me, and knowing that this really was the end, the final time we'd be together brought tears to my eyes, but I was determined not to cry. "How does Alicia feel about it?"

He gave me a puzzled look.

"I heard the two of you are quite the social couple right now."

Closing his eyes, he shook his head. "Is that what that call was about the other week? Layla, I'm not now, nor have I ever been dating Alicia. She's been attending functions, desperate to be photographed with me to get at Felix. She heard from Sebastian about the affair, and she's pissed at him for screwing her over in the divorce. If she'd had evidence then of his infidelity, she would have got millions more in her settlement. I had to invite her here and have a lawyer hand her a restraining order, keeping her away from me. You really thought I could be with anyone else when I'm so completely and devotedly in love with you?"

I stared at him, lost for words.

Cupping my face, he gazed into my eyes. "Didn't you hear a word I said to you the entire time we were together? You're my whole world, Layla. You hold my universe in your hand, and no matter where I go, who I'm with, or what I'm doing, you are right there with me. Here." Taking my hand he held it against his thundering heart. "Our lives are entwined, and we're bound together by everything that we've been through, what we feel, and the love I have for you. I know you love me too, Layla, and I wish I could make it all right again, but I can't."

Taking his other hand in mine, I gazed deep into his deep pools of piercing blue. "I do love you, Jared. I love you so much that it hurts me. When Mel gave me that letter and my pendant yesterday, I couldn't breathe. Why couldn't you just tell me? That letter was too little too late. The damage was done."

Standing, he raked his hands through his hair. "I couldn't put you at risk. Look at what happened last night, Layla. He was going to strangle Lucy, and he would have raped you if I hadn't been there. He's dangerous, and I was protecting you from that. I didn't know it was Felix back then, but I knew based on every cut, bruise, fracture and broken bone Lucy had been given, that whoever he was, he was dangerous. You would have been a walking target to get to me. I love you, and

I will not let anyone use you as a pawn in their sick twisted game. He came to your dorm, for Christ sakes, Layla."

Getting to my feet, I strode over to him. "How did you know that?"

"I've been having him followed ever since he made a pass at you at that dinner. Once he knew you were my weakness, he was going to come after you. I needed to know every move he made. He followed you to Benny's, to the coffee shop to see Kate, and even to Delicia that night. Why do you think I went so fucking crazy when I saw you with that guy? It's the same reason I used Alicia. I figured he'd be more distracted with what I was doing with his ex-wife, than watching you all night. You were getting drunk, and it made you a very easy mark."

I stared at him, blown away by his confession. "You weren't trying to make me jealous or control me? You were protecting me from Felix?"

He nodded, and placed his hands on his hips exasperated. "I had to do something. Even if it meant you hating me for it. You being safe meant a lot more." These new revelations were making my head spin. Everything I had thought about him and us was wrong.

Taking my hands in his, he gazed down at me. "I love you, Layla. I can't just stop taking care of you. If anything happened to you, I'd never survive it."

Closing my eyes, I watched as my mind replayed our entire relationship in front of my eyes at warp speed. Opening them again, I raised my hand to his face and pulled him to me. Pressing my lips against his, I slid my other hand behind his back as his hands pulled me tight to him, wrapping me in his arms.

"Come back to me, Layla. I miss you so much. From now on, I swear I'll never keep anything from you. Just please come back. I need you." My heart swelled as he murmured into my mouth.

Pulling away, I gazed at him, breathless and confused. "I want to Jared, but I can't. It's more complicated now than it was before."

His hands rubbed up and down my arms as he tried desperately to change my mind. "What's complicated? I love you. You love me. It's the simplest thing in the world."

Turning away, I took a deep breath, forcing myself to hold back the tears that threatened to spill over any moment. "I'm in love with Ollie."

I couldn't look at him, but grabbing my arm he spun me around to face him. I could see the deep hurt in his eyes as he stuttered and struggled to get the words from his mouth. "You love him?"

I nodded. "But I love you too. It's so confusing, and my head is a mess right now. Ollie wants me to go to Utah and be with him, and now you tell me all of this. Put all that together with what happened last night, and it's just too much. I can't deal with it all right now." I was getting worked up, and my cheeks reddened as I became more and more flustered.

"You're leaving? You're leaving Long Beach and moving in with him? I can't believe this is happening to me." Panic was painted all over his face as he paced the room frantically. "You can't go, Layla. You just can't. I won't let you go like this."

"I haven't decided anything yet. He told me to think on it."

"But you're considering it?"

"I don't know what I'm doing, Jared! I can't think. It hurts too much knowing that either way I have to give one of you up. That I lose one of you from my life. I can't do that."

Striding over fast, he held my arms tightly. "Come with me."

I stared at him in shock. "What?"

Gazing into my eyes, he repeated himself. "Come with me to New York, to Europe."

I shook my head in a complete daze. "You can't be serious, Jared. You're not thinking straight. Have you heard yourself?"

"I am thinking clearly, and for the first time in my life everything is totally transparent. I want to be with you, Layla. I love you." Wide eyed I stared at him, unable to form words or even breathe. "Say something."

I couldn't. There was nothing there. As I opened my mouth, I tried to find the words or even a simple syllable, but nothing came. Walking over to the sofa, I dropped onto it and held my head in my hands. "This is such a mess. My life is one huge bomb site. I need to go home."

Grabbing my purse, I made for the door, but Jared reached it before I could and blocked my way. "I'll wait for you, Layla. Forever if I have to because there will never be anyone else for me. You are my only love, and I won't give up fighting for you." Standing aside, he let me pass.

I couldn't get my feet to move fast enough as I hurried through the grand foyer to the door. Seeing me approach, Daniel dutifully opened the car door and giving him a grateful look, I slid inside, thankful for the silence and seclusion as everything whirled around in my head. Daniel sat rigid and awkward as he drove.

"Miss Jennings, I need to apologize about last night, but I was only thinking of your safety."

"It's alright, Daniel, really. I'm forever in your debt. If Jared hadn't been there…"

I couldn't finish my sentence, and my silence portrayed more than my words could as Daniel's eyes fell on me in the rear view.

"Oh, Miss Jennings. Please tell me that sick bastard didn't hurt you?"

I shook my head. "He didn't get the chance, thanks to you and Jared. Thank you, Daniel. I mean that."

Chapter 49

Listen To Your Heart

Pulling up outside my dorm, I waited in the car while Daniel checked whether the area was safe. Jared had instructed him to ensure Felix was not in the vicinity before allowing me to exit. Opening the car door, he nodded that it was clear and insisted that he would walk me to my room. He'd been there for me, looking out for me and even protecting me so many times recently that I felt we were more like friends than acquaintances. Yet I knew very little about him.

"Thanks, Daniel. I didn't realize bodyguard was part of your job description."

He smiled. "It's not. Jared- Mr. Garrett is an old friend and I owe him a lot. He gave me this job when I was down and out. He really took a chance on me. I was in a mess and he bailed me out."

I gave him a curious look.

"I met him in high school. One day he got in a fight with these two guys, and I jumped in to help out. We lost touch until about four years later, just after his parents died. I was heavily into coke and heroin. I was dealing and things went bad. I ended up getting stabbed in the gut."

I stared at him in horror. I had no idea he'd had that kind of life. I knew he was young, but I hadn't realized he and Jared were the same age.

"Anyway, Jared was at the hospital visiting Lorraine, she'd just had some minor surgery, and he saw me. We talked, and he said he wanted to help me. Said he owed me for what I did for him in school. He got me into rehab, paid for all my treatment, and gave me this job. I even have one of his apartments rent free while I work for him."

Reaching my room, I wrapped my arms around him, and he stood stiffly as I hugged him. Pecking him on the cheek, I smiled as he blushed. "Thank you, Daniel. For everything."

"Anytime. You're a good person, you know? People like you are rare these days, and I'm sorry we've had to part in such sad circumstances." He frowned, and I felt a little upset myself. Daniel was a good man, and he genuinely cared about Jared, about Lucy, and even about me. "Take care of yourself, Miss Jennings." I gave him a weak smile before watching him as he walked down the hallway and out of sight.

Opening my door, I froze, screamed, and turned to face the door as I saw Amy in bed, naked with my best friend.

"Oh my god! I'm so sorry. I'll go." Closing the door, I heard them giggling as I stood in the hallway.

Mel yelled through the door, "Layla, come back in here. It's fine."

Squeezing my eyes closed, I re-entered. "Is it safe? Are you both decent?"

Mel laughed. "Depends what you consider decent, I guess."

"Are you clothed?"

Simultaneously, they answered with a resounding yes. Opening my eyes, I stared at the two of them as they sat snickering in Amy's bed.

"Someone want to explain this to me?" Glancing at Mel, Amy grinned.

"Well, we got a little tipsy last night, and when Jared called to tell us to stay put and bolt the door, Mel said we should stay together for safety. She was about ready to murder Felix when Jared told us, but once we knew you were safe and that he hadn't...you know, we got to talking. We drank some more, and I kind of blurted out how I feel about her."

Leaning in, Mel kissed her cheek. "And I told her that she should have said something sooner."

Getting out of the bed, I was relieved to see that Mel was wearing shorts with her tank top. Approaching me, she looked nervous; the most anxious I had ever seen her in our entire time as friends.

"I'm bisexual, Layla. I've known since we were fourteen. I figured it out when I developed a crush on Samantha Bowman in our gym class. I couldn't tell you because I didn't want you to think I was different from the Mel you'd always known. The play fights, and the way we've always been so close and intimate, that's always been us and I didn't want you to think it was sexual and pull away from me."

I was sure she expected me to be shocked, amazed, or even disgusted, but very little shocked me anymore. It seemed to make perfect sense that my commitment phobic friend swung both ways.

Tilting my head, I gave her a sympathetic smile. "Oh, Melanie. I would never think that. I love you like a sister, and as long as you're happy, I'm happy. I don't care if your preference is a table. I would still love you. I might have you committed, but I'd still love you." Turning my attention to Amy, I smiled at her. "So I assume the two of you had an interesting discussion last night."

Glancing back at Amy, Mel winked at me. "We're taking it slow, but we do like each other a lot. I always thought she was hot, and now that I know how she feels, I don't see any reason in hiding it. You know, we know, Ollie knows we're into each other. He figured it out at the bar. And as for our parents, well we said we'll tell them when the time comes."

Bouncing out of bed, Amy wrapped her arms around Mel's waist and kissed her cheek. My heart swelled with happiness as I watched my two best friends hug, kiss, and make goo-goo eyes at each other. It was that perfect honeymoon moment every new couple shared, and it immediately made me think of my own romantic predicament. Noticing my expression, Mel gave me a quizzical look.

"What is it? What's wrong?"

Walking to my bed, I crashed down onto it and let out a long breath. "You mean aside from almost being raped by Felix last night? Jared. What else?"

Sitting on either side of me, they waited for me to elaborate. "He told me everything. The reasons he's been acting the way he has lately. He told me about Alicia, who he is not dating by the way, and that everything he did was to protect me. All of it. The dishonesty, what he did, with Alicia in the bar, everything. He said he still loves me, and he begged me to go back to him."

Mouths open, they gawked at me.

"That's not all. He's going to Europe for a year, and he asked me to go with him."

Shaking her head, Mel stared at me. "God, Layla, you don't do simple, do you? First Ollie and Utah, now Jared and Europe. What did you say?"

"What could I say? I told him I love Ollie too, and he said he wouldn't give up fighting for me. Said he'll wait forever. Either way, no matter what I decide, I lose one or both of them. I can't do that."

Leaning my head on Mel's shoulder, I could feel tears stinging my eyes. Amy placed a reassuring hand on my shoulder. "It's not the choice between Utah or Europe you have to make though, is it, Layla? It's Jared or Ollie."

Nodding, I flopped my face into my hands. "What am I going to do? I love them both, and I want them both, but I know I can't have that. It's one of them, or neither, and it sucks. It's not fair for them to put me in this position."

Mel snorted. "I'd say you put yourself there, sweetie, and now you have to find your way out. You'll figure it out. You just need time."

I stared at the window. My gut told me exactly what I needed to do, and grabbing my keys and an overnight bag, I packed a few essentials.

"Where are you going?"

Stuffing some clothes into the large duffle bag, I glanced back at my friends who were watching me with curiosity. "I need some space. I'm going home to Pasadena for a few days. I need to talk to my mom. I'll call in a few days, alright? We have all week to get our stuff before summer break, so I'll be back before Friday, ok?"

Handing me my cell and purse, they gripped me tightly in a group hug. Placing a quick peck on both their cheeks, I smiled and gave them a wink. "Behave yourselves while I'm away."

Grinning, they nodded, and with a final glance at them, I headed out to my car. Tossing my bag and purse into the passenger seat, I started her up and the sound of 'All Time Low' echoed through the speakers. It reminded me of Ollie. Switching it off, I decided silence was my best option. I needed a clear head and the distracting memories of winter break were not making it easier at all.

* * * *

Parking in the driveway, a wave of relief flooded me as I saw Dad's car missing. I needed a little mother daughter time, and with him at work we had at least six hours to ourselves. Grabbing my bag, I jogged up the driveway to the door. I could hear the sound of 'Duran Duran' as I stepped inside. Mom was definitely home alone. Dad was strictly a classic rock and Clapton man. Dropping my keys on the table in the hallway, I dumped my bag by the door and went in search of her.

Turning the corner into the living room, I smiled to myself as I watched her dance around with a duster in one hand, and her spring cleaning bright yellow bandana over her hair. It was as though she'd never left. It was so normal, so routine, and it was exactly what I needed.

Shimmying and shaking my ass, I joined her. Spotting me, her mouth flew open and her face lit up as she sang loudly to the music and continued to dance around the room. Opening my lungs, I belted out the words with her, letting go of the tension I had been holding for the past hour as I drove home. It was freeing, and my favorite type of therapy. Taking my hand, she pulled me around the coffee table, shaking her ass and holding her duster in the other hand like a mic.

The music ending, we landed on the sofa, panting and laughing breathlessly. Turning to face me, Mom curled her leg beneath her and leaned her head on her hand. "So, what brings my baby home a week early?"

Scooting over to her, I laid my head against her chest and exhaled loudly. "I'm in such a mess, Mom."

Stroking my hair, she held me to her "What's happened?"

"I'm in love with two men."

I felt her smile against my forehead, and she pressed a kiss on skin. "Well I'd say that's quite a situation."

"That's not all. Ollie moved to Utah, and he wants me to follow him there."

Her head snapped up, and she lifted my chin to look at her. "Utah? Are you here to tell me my little girl is leaving California for good?"

I shook my head. "No, I don't know what I'm going to do, but there's more. Jared's leaving in two days to go to Europe for a year, Mom, and the thought of being without him is tearing me apart. I learned some things recently that change everything I knew, or thought I knew, about us. And to top it off, I still love him. He wants me to go with him, but I have a life here. I'm so confused and it's making me sick."

Shaking her head, she gazed at me wide eyed. "I'm lost for words and that never happens. Well, first things first. We need ice-cream, lots of it, and at least one bottle of wine."

"You know Daddy won't like me drinking, Mom."

Getting up from the sofa, she headed for the kitchen and yelled over her shoulder, "It's not for you, baby. I'm going to need a drink if were honestly going to talk about you leaving me for either another state or country."

Two tubs of ice-cream later, I leaned back into the plump cushion of the couch and pulled my knees to my chest. My mother, who was now on her second bottle of chardonnay, was beginning to get very affectionate. As she pulled me to her, spilling some of her wine in the process, I rolled my eyes.

"Baby, I don't know what to say. We could sit here all day and weigh up the pros and cons for each option, but in the end you're going to have to let one of them go. Yes, it will hurt, and it will most certainly be a horrible thing to go through, but you know it's right. You can't keep them both holding on, praying you'll choose them."

Tears rolled down my cheeks as I thought about my life without them in it. "But how do I possibly decide who it is. I love them both, and I don't want to lose either of them."

Hushing me, she stroked her fingertips up and down my arm. "I know, baby, and it hurts me seeing you so tormented, but you have to do this by yourself. No one can make this choice for you. You remember what I said to you that day on the stairs? Falling in love is easy, letting that love go is hard. But your heart will always have the right answer. You just have to listen to it and figure out what it's telling you."

Wiping my eyes, I gazed up at her. "Either one I choose means I'd be leaving you, Daddy, Mel and Amy behind."

Smiling, she pecked me on the forehead. "And we would miss you more than the desert misses the rain. But this is your life. College will be waiting for you when you're ready to go back, and Amy and Mel will understand. There are always cell phones, email, and that social networking thing you use, the one with the bird. I'm sure you girls can keep in touch. You can come home whenever you want, and you just try and stop me from visiting."

Opening the front door, my father yelled out my name, obviously seeing my car in the driveway. Mom called out to him that we were in the living room, and within seconds he was crouching in front of me stroking my face with his black, greasy thumbs. "Hey, baby, what's going on?"

I really didn't want to go over it all again, and especially with my father. I gave Mom a pleading look. She nodded, and signalled for my dad to follow her to the kitchen.

Turning on the TV, I tried to drown out the sound of my parents talking about my situation. My father was clearly not thrilled at the idea of me not only dropping out of college, but also leaving California. Leaving him. "This is her life, Andrew. You always tell me I should let her live it, so I am. She's twenty years old. We have to let her go sometime. She has to make her own choices, and if they turn out to be the wrong ones it's our job to be here waiting for her when she needs us to pick up the pieces. Now, get in there and give your little girl a hug. I think right now she could use the one man in her life that's always been her rock to give her a little support."

I smiled a little hearing her words. My mother was a force of nature, and hearing her finally accept my right to lead my own life was liberating.

Slumping down next to me on the couch, my dad sighed deeply. "Layla, for the past seven years you and me, we've been a team, right?"

I nodded, and stared at him as he ran his hands over his face. "Well, I'm cutting you from it. It's time you did a little exploring and searching on your own. But always remember that this house is your home. Always. You will always have a place to come back to when you need it. I love you, baby girl, and I want you to be happy. Even if it means being away from me."

Pulling me into a tight hug, he pressed a kiss to my forehead and sighed. I smiled up at him reassuringly. "Thank you, Daddy. No matter what, you're always going to be the first man I ever loved."

He chuckled in my ear. "I know, baby. Hey, why don't you stay here a few days and take some time out? It'll be just like old times."

Nodding, I kissed his cheek. "Sounds great."

* * * *

Waking up the next morning was not a welcome experience as everything came flooding back to me, and the enormous weight once again landed on my shoulders. Grabbing my cell, I dialled my girls.

"Hey, sweetie pie. One sec." Mel's cheery voice on the other end of the line was far too perky for the mood I was currently in, and it kind of irked me.

"Ok, you're on speaker with Mel and Amy. How are you today?" She sounded like a radio show host.

"Could you try and be a little less upbeat? I'm wallowing in self-pity here, remember?"

"Still feeling like the world has been tipped on its head, huh?" Amy's voice echoed from the background.

"Dropped on my ass feels more like it. I talked to my mom and dad last night. Basically they'll support me whatever I decide which is great, but it doesn't solve my problem."

"Have you spoken to either of them?"

Was she kidding? Of course I hadn't. "The idea is to get away from them and think about what I'm going to do, not cloud my judgment with their presence."

I heard Amy say something, and muffling the cell receiver Mel answered her.

"Hey, I'm right here, so if you have something to say, just say it."

Mel sighed loudly. "We were just saying you can't drag it out forever, wishing it will work out somehow. You have to choose, Layla. Otherwise you're just stringing them along. Pick one, and put the other out of his misery, for heaven's sake."

Her attitude was beginning to irritate me. "I'm not doing this for my own sick entertainment, guys. If you were me, tell me, what would you do? I love them both, and there are so many reasons why I should pick each of them. So tell me, how do I choose? Because I don't have the first fucking idea."

"But if you don't figure it out soon, you're going to lose them both, Layla."

She was right. She was always right, but she wasn't the one about to lose someone important from her life. It was one thing dishing out advice, but it really wasn't as useful as she thought. "Don't you think I know that? It's killing me. But I don't have the answer right now. I gotta go. I'll call you tomorrow."

I needed some peace, silence, and breathing space. Glancing at my clock, I groaned. I'd been asleep for almost twelve hours, and it was now closer to lunch than breakfast. Kicking off my covers, I hauled myself out of bed and into my bathroom. I stared at myself in the mirror. My red hair was matted and had seen better days by far. My poor tired eyes were bloodshot, almost matching the shade of my hair, and my pale skin completed the Raggedy Ann look perfectly. Rolling my eyes, I began the tedious task of getting washed, dressed and presentable, when all I really wanted to do was crawl back into my bed and pretend my life wasn't one huge disaster.

The delicious smell of coffee pulled me from my mood and down the stairs to the kitchen. Raising her head from her magazine, Mom smiled at me. "Morning, sunshine. How you feeling?"

I shrugged. "Same old. Nothing changed in the past twelve hours, so I'm still caught between a rock star and a hard bodied sex god."

She winced. "Layla, please, I'm your mother, for crying out loud."

Pouring myself a cup of very strong coffee, I sighed. My mind instantly traveled back to the coffee shop, Jared, breakfast coffee with Ollie, and the safe word. Jared had introduced me to a whole new world of carnal pleasures, sex and erotica. I'd never tried bondage before, and I think if it had been anyone else, I would never have agreed to it. But Jared was so caring, open and straight about it, that it didn't seem so scary. The payoff was immense. Pleasure, pain and sheet clenching orgasms were just naming a few. He'd even allowed me to indulge in my biting fetish. But that wasn't all he'd shown me. The all-consuming love I felt for him was addictive. My heart ached without him, and a love that intense and powerful doesn't just disappear. It grips you and sets your soul on fire. That's how I always felt around Jared. Hot, burning and incendiary. He had the ability to boil my blood with anger, and simmer it with desire. It was confusing, and completely exhausting.

Slumping into the chair opposite Mom, I leaned my elbows on the table and stared into space.

"You can't avoid it forever, sweetheart. Why don't you go out today? Get some air, clear your head a little."

I snorted "It will take a lot more than some air to clear my mind, Mom. I'd need a lobotomy to clear all the stuff I have crammed in there right now."

She chuckled, and took a long gulp of her coffee. "Well, I just think a change of scenery may help."

Rolling my eyes, I finished my coffee and shrugged. "Fine, I'll go for a walk, not that I think it will do much good." Leaving her shaking her head and sipping her coffee, I grabbed my shoes and headed out.

The weather was gloriously warm, and the heat on my body instantly relaxed my tense muscles. I wasn't headed anywhere specific, but almost instinctively, my feet seemed to lead me right to the park. Shaking my head, I smiled to myself.

Ah, sneaky move feet, sneaky move.

My heart and mind were trying to sway my decision just as they had in Jared's office. The park held so many sweet memories of Ollie, and being there was certainly going to provoke some deep emotional responses. However, I wasn't holding my breath for it to be a response that would give me any guidance one way or the other whatsoever.

Walking through the luscious green and very picturesque scenery, I found myself only a few feet away from a tree that, when catching my eye, made my heart skip a beat. It was the spot where Ollie had brought me on Christmas morning. The place where he had sung me the most beautiful song I had ever heard, and carved our names into the very tree that loomed over the grassy area of which I was now heading. Trying desperately to calm my breathing which was now become a little ragged, I walked over to examine the engraving more closely.

The weather hadn't changed it at all, and our names were as vivid now as they had been the morning he'd carved them. Running my fingertips over Ollie's name, I felt my heart plummet into my stomach. God, I missed him so much. Turning around, I leaned my back against the bark and slid all the way down the ground with a thud.

Well doesn't this just suck?

My cell buzzed in my pocket, and checking the caller I.D, I rolled my eyes as I answered. "Mother, I thought the idea was for me to get some time alone and clear my head?"

"I know, sweetheart, but I think you should come home. A big package just arrived for you."

My stomach did a back flip, and my mind boggled as to what it could possibly be, and who could have sent it. I had two possible culprits in mind. Getting to my feet, I brushed myself off, took one last glance at the tree, and headed home.

Walking through the front door, I scanned the hallway for the mysterious package. Sitting in the kitchen, my mother gave me a smile. "It came just after you left. I put it in the living room."

She walked in front of me, and promptly took a seat on the sofa where a large black box occupied half of the couch. I approached it cautiously, biting my lip as anxiety flooded my veins. My mother was acting like a child on their birthday as she eyed the mysterious package.

"I don't know who it's from. The doorbell rang, and I ran down to get it, but all that was there was this box and a Post-it note with your name on it."

Lifting the box from the sofa, I placed it onto the floor and sat in front of it. It wasn't heavy as such but certainly required a little strength to move. Holding my breath, I lifted the lid and peeled back the layers of crate paper inside. The breath I was holding got caught in my throat and I coughed, spluttered and gasped as my eyes fell on the contents of the box. My mother was leaning so far off the couch I thought she may fall off as she tried to see what was inside my mystery gift.

"It's from Jared."

Tilting her head at me, she gave me a puzzled look. "How do you know?"

Reaching into the box, I grabbed the 'I heart New York' mug and held it up to her. "Because he gave me this. He gave me all of this. This is the box I sent back to him after we broke up. He even got all that jewellery back from the shop."

Taking each item carefully from the package, I sighed as each provoked a warm and wonderful memory. The blue dress I'd worn to dinner at the Hyatt Regency was folded neatly, and pulling it out I grinned as sweet, sensual memories of our sexual escapades beneath the table came flooding back to me. My insides clenched with remembered pleasure.

A small black velvet box was hiding in the corner of the package, and pulling it out I opened it, knowing what rested inside. The stunning black star sapphire and diamonds glistened and gleamed in the light, and a note had been folded up tightly and placed in the lid. Taking it out, I read it as tears began to fill my eyes.

I still promise. Every day for the rest of my life. I'll hold your dreams, wishes, hopes and fears forever. I Promise to never give up on us and to love you with every beat of my heart till the end of time.

I miss you.

Jared xxx

Dropping it to the floor, I held my head in my hands. *Crap.*

Just when I'd thought things couldn't get any harder, he'd sent me all of these sentimental memories. It wasn't fair. How could I possibly try to figure out what I wanted when everywhere I turned I found reasons to choose them both? The tree, the park, the box, the ring. It was all too much, and I felt instantly exhausted and emotionally drained. Falling back onto the floor, I flung my arm over my eyes.

The ring was still firmly grasped in my hand, but prying it from my fingers, my mother seized it, whistling. "Oh my. This is stunning. It must have cost a fortune."

I let out an exasperated sigh. "The diamond and white gold bracelet was $11,050. The diamond emerald and crystal ring was at least another twelve thousand. Then there are the earrings, headband, ruby bracelet, and the ring you currently hold in your hand. He also gave me a pendant and he has one that matches. That, and the ring are engraved."

Lifting the ring from its box, my mother examined the message etched into the metal.

Looking across the floor to the box, I spotted the mug sitting on the carpet, begging for me to pick it up and examine it. My plan to avoid a painful and confusing trip down memory lane was officially out of the window, and my willpower had completely deserted me. Picking up the cup, I turned it around and ran my fingertip over the words that were permanently scribbled on the back.

"Don't give up on me? Sounds like he was scared." My mother, ever the nosey and overprotective person she was, was reading it over my shoulder. Covering it with my hand, and quickly returning it to the box, I shook my head

"We'd had a fight. I'd rather not talk about it. In fact I'd rather not talk about, look at, or think about any of this stuff." Getting to my feet, I skirted around the box and ran for the solace of my bedroom.

Slamming myself onto my bed, I buried my head in my pillow. Just as I had when I was a child, I threw the biggest tantrum of my life. Hurling my pillow across the room, I kicked, growled and thrashed about on my bed. I was angry, frustrated, and so worked up that I could have exploded from the tension building inside me. What they were making me do, and what they were putting me through, was beyond unfair; it was downright cruel. Jared would be leaving the next day, and I was still no closer to having an answer for him or Ollie.

Lying on my bed, I stared at the ceiling. Images of the two men I was hopelessly in love with swarmed around in my thoughts and made me dizzy. Closing my eyes, I took a deep breath and begged my heart to speak to me, to help me figure out what was happening to us. But it wasn't willing to play ball this time. Placing my palm over it, I pleaded that something, anything might happen; that maybe thinking of one of them I might feel a thud or a beat skipping, but it continued to thunder and hammer inside of my chest as Ollie and Jared both simultaneously ran through my mind.

Turning over, I could feel tears in my eyes, pushing hard for release. I'd cried so much that I couldn't believe there could possibly be any more tears left for me to shed. But as the salty warm droplets fell onto my sheets, I curled up and gave in to the sobs that racked and shook my body. If I couldn't choose one, I was going to have to let them both go.

It hurt deeply, and the pain left me breathless as I cried myself slowly to sleep.

Chapter 50

Making The Leap

Sitting on the couch, I held a cushion close to my chest and stared at the blank TV screen. Slumping down next to me, Dad draped an arm over my shoulders and pulled me to him for a warm hug. "Baby girl, I hate seeing you so hurt. What can I do to make it better?"

I shook my head, and snuggled into his chest. "Go back a year and stop me from ever going to college." I didn't mean it. If I hadn't gone I would never have met Amy, Ollie or Jared. And though I was hurting, I wouldn't have changed a single moment. All the good, bad, and awful things had changed my life forever, and changed me for the better. Amy's fun and wonderfully upbeat personality had encouraged me to be free, take chances, and have more fun than I ever had in my life. Ollie's loyal and sweet friendship was like a drug, and I was addicted to the sound of his beautiful voice in my ear. Bringing me comfort, and making me feel like the most important person in the world, Ollie was everything a girl could ever dream of.

And then there was Jared. He'd shown me a world I never knew existed. A world full of hot, sheet clenching bondage play, spanking, and euphoric sexual pleasure. The intense and all-consuming love between us had been a thing of fairy tales and movies. And I was about to lose it all. Ollie and Jared were soon going to be leaving my life for good, and the thought made my chest feel tight as the nausea began creeping inside my stomach.

Checking the clock on the far wall, I wondered what they were doing. Jared would probably be on his way to LAX by now, and Ollie, no doubt, had his skilful hands on someone's motorcycle. Hugging the cushion in my arms tightly, I took a deep breath, forcing myself not to cry.

My cell was sitting on the table and startled me as it rang loudly. Releasing me, my father grabbed it and handed it to me with a slight smile. Seeing the caller I.D, I smiled as well.

"Hi, Amy."

I could hear Mel in the background, and realized I was on speaker phone. "Hi, Mel."

They whispered something to each other as I waited patiently on the line. "Hi, sweetie. How you feeling?"

"Lousy."

"Sorry. Well, Mel and I just wondered if you wanted us to get your stuff ready for summer break for you since you're still at your folks."

Shit. I'd completely forgotten that I needed to clear my things before the end of the week. "No, it's ok. I'm going to head back today."

"You've made up your mind then?"

I exhaled loudly. "No, and yes. I can't decide between them, Amy, so I know what I have to do. I have to let them both go."

"Oh, Layla, hurry home because I need to hug you right now. We'll be right here when you get back, ok?"

"Ok. I'll be there soon. I love you guys." They answered simultaneously with a chorus of "we love you too" and hung up.

Pressing a kiss to my forehead, my dad smiled. "You're doing the right thing, baby. It's going to hurt, but you're doing the kindest thing for all of you."

Gazing up at him, I wondered if he was right. "Am I? It sure doesn't feel that way. I feel like the most awful person in the world right now, breaking two hearts and my own. Doesn't feel too right from where I'm sitting. I feel like someone ran a truck over my heart."

"You are not awful. You're doing what's right. You should have faith in yourself, Layla. I knew your head would figure this all out, and that you'd make the right choice in the end."

Staring at him, I heard my mother's words replay in my ears. Your heart will always have the right answer. But my heart didn't have an answer at all which meant I had no option but to do what my head told me was right. Getting to my feet, I shuffled upstairs to pack my overnight bag, ready to head back to campus.

Knocking lightly on my door, my mom peered through the gap. "Is it okay to come in?"

I nodded and continued to gather my things from my dresser as she sat on my neatly made bed.

"I heard you and your father. I just need to say something before you go."

Sighing, I turned around to face her and shook my head. "There's nothing to say, Mom. I know what I have to do. It's for the best."

"The best for whom?"

"For everyone, Ollie and Jared deserve to move on, and they can't do that while they're hanging on, hoping I'll pick them over the other."

"And what about you? What's right for you?"

I growled in frustration. "I don't know, Mom! I don't know what I want, or who I want, which means I lose both!"

Standing up, she cupped my face in her hands and smiled. "You do know, baby. You're just scared, and that's okay. But don't throw away your chance for happiness because you're afraid to take the leap, or because you know someone ends up hurt. No matter who you choose, someone is always going to end up heartbroken. But if there's a chance two hearts can be blissfully happy together in love, then that's worth the broken heart of one. They will mend. They will find love again and be happy. But if you do this, let them both walk away, the only heart that will break and stay broken is yours, baby."

I stared at her as her words hit me hard. Rubbing her thumb over my cheek, she leaned in and placed a kiss on my forehead. "Think about it. You're heart knows, Layla. Listen to it. Really listen. It will tell you what to do." Winking at me, she smiled and left me alone with my thoughts.

Holding my palm firmly to my chest, I took a deep breath as tears ran over my cheeks slowly. "Please, tell me what I'm supposed to do because this is killing me. Just tell me, please." As if hearing my plea, it gave an almighty thud, making me jump slightly. I sat with my hand still clutched over my heart and I waited. I waited for a sign, for a feeling, anything to give me some kind of clue as to what I needed to do. But it never came.

Cursing myself for ever believing that my heart would speak to me somehow, I grabbed my overnight bag and headed downstairs to say goodbye to my parents. Not wanting to drag it out, my father took the box of memories Jared had sent me and my bag out to the car, and hurled them into the passenger seat as my mother held me in a tight embrace.

"Goodbye, baby. I love you."

It felt as though we were saying goodbye forever, and I got the feeling she maybe thought it could be. Shaking my head, I kissed her cheek.

"I'll be home on Saturday, okay?"

She nodded, holding my hand as I turned to my father for a heart stopping hug. Lifting me from the ground, he clutched me to his chest. "Bye, baby girl. Safe drive back, okay?"

Smiling, I gave him a salute and slid into the driver's seat.

* * * *

The drive back had taken no time at all, and as I pulled into the parking lot of the dorm building, I breathed a sigh of relief. I needed my girls, and lots and lots of junk food.

Parking, I glanced over at the building and saw Amy bounding over with a grin on her face.

"Layla, I'm so glad you're back! Hurry up, there's something inside for you that you have to see. I know you're going to want to see this."

My heart skipped, and my pulse raced as the thought crossed my mind that one of them could be waiting for me in the room. Leaping to my feet, I sprinted as fast as my legs could carry me, leaving Amy trailing behind through the halls as I burst into the dorm room, panting and breathless.

No one was there, and disappointment plagued me. Seeing my reaction from her seat on the bed, Mel smiled.

"Which one were you hoping it would be?"

I stared at her stunned.

"What?"

Walking over, she grabbed my hands. "Which one did you hope it would be? Jared or Ollie?"

I shook my head at her "Did you do that to try and force my decision?"

Clearly becoming a little irritated, she repeated her question. "Which one, Layla?"

I gazed at her speechless. Amy stood in the doorway as I turned around and gave her a confused look. "You both set me up. I can't believe this. How could you do that? It's sneaky, underhanded and-"

"Which one, Layla!?"

They both simultaneously shouted it at me, and all of a sudden my heart decided to scream back at them and me. My mouth falling open, I gawked at them and clutched my hand to my chest. Hammering like drum it pounded in my ears, my whole body rocked with every thunderous thump. I could hardly speak. My voice barely a whisper, I swallowed hard before pulling them to me and holding them tightly in my arms.

"I know what I have to do. I love you guys, and I'm so glad you're here."

Leaving them gawking at me I hurried to the closet and hauled out my suitcase, slinging it onto the bed.

"What are you doing?" Standing beside me, they watched as I frantically pulled clothes, shoes, and everything I could lay my hands on out of my closet and into my case.

"I'm packing. Are you two going to stand there, or help me?" Giving each other a grin, they headed in different directions and grabbed my things. Amy had everything from the bathroom and Mel was stuffing my underwear, laptop and beauty products into the crammed full case. Zipping it up, I turned to face them.

Flinging their arms around me, they laughed. "So, where to?"

Grinning, I bit my lip. "The airport. I have a flight to catch." They gave me a knowing look, and as an understanding passed between us. I knew they had already figured out where my heart was a long time ago.

"Well, we'd better hurry up then."

Mel called a cab, and as we waited I could hardly stand still. I was full of nerves and I jittered, fumbled and paced up and down as I thought about what I was doing. Pulling my cell from my pocket, I dialed my mom.

"Baby girl, everything okay?"

Stopping a moment, I breathed deeply. "I've made a decision, Mom, and I'm going to the airport right now. I love you both, and I promise I'll call as soon as I get there. I have to do this. Please understand."

"Oh, baby. We love you too. Good luck, princess. Give him a big hug for me, sweetheart, and Layla…I knew your heart wouldn't let you down. It's too big and too wonderful not to give you everything you have ever wanted."

Tears in my eyes, I spotted the cab heading down the street, and said my goodbyes before shoving the phone into my pocket. Heaving my case in the trunk, Amy and Mel climbed in and I gave them a puzzled look.

"You really think we're going to miss seeing you off? You're kidding right? Get in!"

The entire ride to LAX, we sat in the back of the cab holding each other's hands tightly. My feet were unable to keep still, and the butterflies swarmed in my stomach. I felt scared, nauseous, excited, and apprehensive all at once. Placing her hand on my knee, stilling my mindless jerking, Mel smiled reassuringly.

"It'll be alright. I promise."

Nodding, I stared out of the window, watching the world pass by as we sped to the airport.

The second we pulled up, Amy insisted on paying the driver as Mel ran around to get my case. Pulling it through the entrance, I headed for the desk to buy a ticket, but Mel halted me and ran over, leaving me and Amy wondering what she was doing. Returning a few minutes later with an envelope, she grinned at me.

"You're traveling first class and your plane leaves in an hour, so we have to run if you're going to make it."

Pulling her into a tight embrace, I kissed her cheek. Pushing me away, she smiled. "Come on, no time for this. Let's go!"

Sprinting through the terminal, I could hardly breathe as I tried to haul my ass to the gate as fast as I could. Catching my arm, Amy pointed to the gate I needed and stopped.

"This is where we say goodbye."

I gazed at them both as tears streamed down my face. "I don't want to say goodbye to you guys. It's so final."

Smiling, Mel hugged me tightly. "Then try this. See ya soon, Layla. I'll miss you."

Smiling back at her, I nodded. "See you soon, Mel. Amy."

Tears running over her flushed cheeks, Amy nodded as she wrapped her arms around me. "Thank you so much for coming into my life, Layla. I love you, don't ever forget that. We're right here. Call, text, email, I don't care. Just don't ever forget we're here, okay?"

Pulling away, I brushed her cheeks with my thumbs. "I couldn't get away from you guys if I tried. I'll call as soon as I land. I love you guys so much."

Pulling them both in for one last group hug, I sniffled through my tears and closed my eyes, savoring the memory of my best friends in my arms one last time before leaving them for my new life.

Holding hands, the two of them smiled at me as I took my case and walked towards the gate. Glancing back, I grinned at them then turned and strode quickly through the long corridor to the check in desk. A beautiful young blonde greeted me and checked my ticket, boarding pass and passport. In my hurry to leave I'd almost forgotten it, but Mel had grabbed it for me, giving it to me in the cab. "Okay, Miss Jennings, you're in first class. Follow the signs and someone will show you to your seat at the end. Have a great flight."

My bag checked in and shown to my seat, I gazed at the luxury. With fully reclining seats, free beverages and small TV screens mounted onto the seat in front of me, I smiled to myself. Mel was amazing.

Waiting for the engines to start, I knew there was something I still had to do, and as I slid my cell from my pocket I swallowed hard trying not to cry. Typing out the text, I knew it was a cowardly and completely selfish thing to do, but I couldn't face the conversation over the phone. It would be too painful and I couldn't bear it. I had to let him know; tell him that I had made my choice. I had to let him go.

> I'm sorry. I can't do it. I will always love you, and you will always hold a piece of my heart forever. Forgive me.
> **Layla xxx**
> **Sent: 16.43**

Taking a deep breath, I swiped my face as a few tears escaped my eyes. And as I thought about what he must have been going through at that moment, I could hardly contain my grief. Pulling a Kleenex from my purse, I dabbed and wiped my eyes as a barrage of tears fell freely. Flagging down the flight attendant, I asked for some water. I needed to calm down, to gather myself and prepare for my journey. It was going to be a long flight, and I knew that meant lots of time to wallow in my self-loathing over the heart I'd just crushed.

Realizing I would still need someone to pick me up from the airport at the other end, I gripped my cell in my hand, knowing the next text I was setting my future in stone. There was no turning back now, and I could imagine the smile on his face as I hit send. Sending my flight details, I switched it off and slipped my cell back into my pocket, ready for take-off. I stared out of the window, and bit my lip. This was it. The first day of the rest of my life; of our lives and our future together. The roar of the engines made me jump, and as the captain's voice came over the speakers, I smiled to myself while sniffling back my tears.

No turning back now, Layla. Here we go.

* * * *

Waiting at the baggage collection, I reached for my cell and turned it on. There was only one message. Opening it instantly, I smiled as I read his text. He was waiting for me at arrivals, and as my bag rounded the corner, I couldn't have gripped it and swiped it off the collection belt any faster.

Hauling it from the counter, I pulled it behind me as I headed out to the arrivals lounge. I scanned every face in the room before my eyes fell on one that made me squeak with delight. Standing a little way across the vast lounge, he grinned at me as he pushed through the crowd of people in his path.

Grinning myself, I practically sprinted towards him, and as he approached I was so relieved and happy to see him that I threw my arms around his neck and held him in a tight hug. He laughed, lifting my feet from the floor as he hugged me back.

"I can't believe you're here. I've got the car parked right out front. God, it's great to see you."

Releasing me, he reached for my case, and I smiled back at him, unable to contain my own happiness. Grabbing his cap and pulling it playfully to the side, I beamed at him.

"It's good to see you too, Daniel."

flight attendant, I asked for some water. I needed to calm down, to gather myself and prepare for my journey. It was going to be a long flight, and I knew that meant lots of time to wallow in my self-loathing over the heart I'd just crushed.

Realizing I would still need someone to pick me up from the airport at the other end, I gripped my cell in my hand, knowing the next text I was setting my future in stone. There was no turning back now, and I could imagine the smile on his face as I hit send. Sending my flight details, I switched it off and slipped my cell back into my pocket, ready for take-off. I stared out of the window, and bit my lip. This was it. The first day of the rest of my life; of our lives and our future together. The roar of the engines made me jump, and as the captain's voice came over the speakers, I smiled to myself while sniffling back my tears.

No turning back now, Layla. Here we go.

* * * *

Waiting at the baggage collection, I reached for my cell and turned it on. There was only one message. Opening it instantly, I smiled as I read his text. He was waiting for me at arrivals, and as my bag rounded the corner, I couldn't have gripped it and swiped it off the collection belt any faster.

Hauling it from the counter, I pulled it behind me as I headed out to the arrivals lounge. I scanned every face in the room before my eyes fell on one that made me squeak with delight. Standing a little way across the vast lounge, he grinned at me as he pushed through the crowd of people in his path.

Grinning myself, I practically sprinted towards him, and as he approached I was so relieved and happy to see him that I threw my arms around his neck and held him in a tight hug. He laughed, lifting my feet from the floor as he hugged me back.

"I can't believe you're here. I've got the car parked right out front. God, it's great to see you."

Releasing me, he reached for my case, and I smiled back at him, unable to contain my own happiness. Grabbing his cap and pulling it playfully to the side, I beamed at him.

"It's good to see you too, Daniel."

Acknowledgements

I am incredibly thankful to so many people who made this book possible. To my wonderful family for believing in me and for your infinite patience while I gushed, cried and sulked through the process. To my lover, friend and soul mate for being so understanding when I neglected you for the company of fictitious males. I know it was difficult.

To Giselle who fell in love with Ollie before anyone else and encouraged me to continue his story when I needed that extra push. Roxanne & Polina, my rocks who kept me going even when it all seemed lost and pointless. I am forever in your debt. Emma, Angela, Tina and Christine and Charmaine. Thank you for reading, loving and believing it was good when I couldn't believe it myself.

To my editors Annatassia Parchment and Jennifer Roberts-Hall. Your understanding, patience and professionalism were indispensable; even when we are emailing at three in the morning. I heart you!

Sarah Hanson at Okay Creations for designing me a kick-ass cover that I simply adore. You rock!

To Amanda Heath who formatted Bound Together so that it was ready for the masses! I cannot thank you enough.

My Flirty and Dirty Book Blog ladies, I loves ya both billions!! To all my Bookaholic babes and, of course, Fred and Charles. Where would I be without you all? I love each and every one of you to the stars and back. I consider you all as much a part of this book as the characters themselves. You kept me sane, talked me off that ledge and made me laugh even when I felt I was going crazy. I love you all! My book pimps Jamie and Vanessa, I heart you!

My beta readers: Nina, Karen, Madison, Lisa, Shaina, Wendy and Deana. For your time and extremely invaluable help in making my baby as perfect as could be.

To all the awesome bloggers that have spread the word and book love for Bound Together- I couldn't possibly name you all, but I thank you from the bottom of my heart.

Look out for the scintillating sequel to Bound Together

Burning Up

Coming 2013

Layla's Story Continues…….

Bound Together

Copyright © 2012 by Marie Coulson

Find me on Facebook
http://www.facebook.com/authormariecoulson
On Twitter
https://twitter.com/marie_coulson

By Email
authormariecoulson@hotmail.co.uk

Made in the USA
Charleston, SC
03 April 2015